GLOBAL CULTURES

World Map: Peters Projection. © Akademische Verlagsanstalt. Distributed in North America by
Friendship Press, New York. Used by permission.

Wesleyan University Press
Middletown, Connecticut

GLOBAL CULTURES

A Transnational Short Fiction Reader

*Edited and
with an introduction by*

Elisabeth Young-Bruehl

Published by Wesleyan University Press, Middletown, CT 06459
www.wesleyan.edu/wespress

Printed in the United States of America   5   4   3
CIP data appear at the end of the book

ISBNs for the paperback edition:
    ISBN-13: 978-0-8195-6282-1
    ISBN-10: 0-8195-6282-3

The following pieces are reprinted with permission:

Permissions continue on page 503.

CONTENTS

PART II

NEW NATIONS *National Liberations, Civil Wars, Apartheid*

PART III

CULTURE CLASH *Modernization, Urbanization, Westernization*

PART IV

CULTURE CREATION *Women Writing*

Do You Understand?   483

PREFACE

ANYONE WHO reads literature, who loves browsing in bookstores and through book reviews, anyone who has an ear to current literary debates about "multiculturalism," knows that we live in the middle of a publishing revolution. When I was a college student some thirty years ago, good bookstores had "World Literature" sections. But in these there were only a few books that were not European. Europe was, in the geography of our then prevailing American culture, the world. The whole of the African continent was usually represented by *Cry, the Beloved Country*; only English-speaking, neither Arabic nor Hebrew, voices came from the Middle East; the Cultural Revolution was in crescendo in China, but no Chinese writer after Confucius, the chief object of cultural revolutionary scorn, was in "World Literature"; a slender volume of Ho Chi Minh's poems was the single signal from Southeast Asia, where the United States was locked in a dreadful war with that poet's army. By contrast, the students I now teach can find in their college bookstore, and in the better bookshops in all our towns and cities, a crowd of volumes from Africa, from the Middle East, from China, from Southeast Asia, as well as from the Indian subcontinent, from the Caribbean, from the Pacific Rim, and, in enormous numbers, from Central and South America.

While the traffic in books and translations used to flow overwhelmingly from the so-called First World outward, an unprecedented surge of books from around the world is now diffusing into American and European bookstores and publishing houses. Some of these books, then, make their way into our American high school and college literature courses. A few become representatives—some would say tokens—of the "Third World" in humanities courses that were once entirely American and European.

But most of the publishing revolution is assimilated in our universities by a simplistic arrangement: the Central and South American books go to Latin American studies, the Chinese ones to East Asian studies, the African ones to African studies, and so forth. Recently, however, this regionalizing of "World Literature" has begun to give way a little, and courses with titles like "Postcolonial Literature" have appeared. The reading lists feature texts from different parts of the world, and the instructors are not area specialists.

Several years ago, as this climate of curricular controversy and experimentation was moving in, I decided to design a course that would allow me and a group of students to read as widely as a semester allows. We traveled with only our cultural preconceptions, neither burdened by nor enlightened by any expertise (in my case, not even by an appropriate Ph.D., since mine is in philosophy and I write mainly as a biographer and intellectual historian, not as a literary critic). This anthology is the product of our adventure. It contains short fictions from all regions of the globe except North America, Europe, and the former Soviet Union, the regions that have been richly represented in American bookstores and published for a long time. But this anthology is not, on the other hand, just "postcolonial," as that term is currently being used to refer to former colonies of European nations and America. China and Japan, for example, are represented here, but so is Korea, Japan's former colony. The title of this anthology, *Global Cultures*, is meant to invoke not a political development like postcolonialism but rather the current worldwide publishing—or, more generally, culture distributing—revolution.

There are many cultures in our one world, and they exist both in their sites of origin—their tribal, provincial, or national sites—and in the phenomenon that I will call Global Cultures; that is, they flow out from their sites of origin into a globalized publishing, distributing, and reading network, and the effects of this outflow also flow back into particular cultures. The Heinemann and Longman and Penguin publishing groups, with offices on every continent, each produce an Africa series—for Africans, for Africans abroad and going home again, for English readers anywhere. And it is not only the texts that move out and back, here and there, and everywhere; the authors move, the readers move. Cultural institutions foster—broker, one might say—the traffic, just as a character named "Mr. Penman" does in a Japanese short story in this anthology. In real life, the brokering may bring a young Indian from Bombay to work as a bank teller in Toronto, supporting him culturally while he emerges out of his journey as a writer. A professor from Uruguay goes into exile in Spain and sees her brilliant fictions translated into English, into German, and registers that she is having an influence on feminists—in South America. Writers from Malawi, from Sri Lanka, attend the International Writing Program in Iowa City and go home with new friends, connections, fellow writers to visit in Singapore, in Australia. Out of the immigrant barrios of Texas and California come young Salvadorans who want to go home to a place they have never seen and to publish there, to translate there the American works they admire. Out of London's Caribbean communities or Pakistani communities writers come and go, writing in English, but perhaps also in Creole or in Urdu, for London readers, for readers at home, for readers in Global Cultures.

Global Cultures is not an English language phenomenon; it is much broader, and it is in many media, not just words. But in this anthology, because it is literary and for an American audience and for English speakers, the facets of the Global Cultures phenomenon that will stand out relate to English. There is a bias toward representing cultures in Africa and in Asia that have a British (or, in the case of the Philippines, American) colonial heritage. Mostly, the rationale for this bias is to avoid as much as possible using translations. The difficulties of reading cross-culturally are quite formidable even without the specific problems of translation. Now, given Global Cultures, the general problem of translation has become such a huge enterprise, no longer a guild or craft enterprise, that many translations sound vaguely alike, denatured, decultured rather than transcultured. Francophone writers, for example, are not represented here; texts originally in local, tribal languages are not well represented—although advocates of national cultural plurality and multiculturalism who can write in local languages as well as in English are well represented.

The texts from different cultures that circulate in Global Cultures often have features in common. Some have European and American literary influences in common, others have rejection or subversion of European and American literary influences in common. Some have in common literary techniques like stories within stories, narrators within narrations, or like allegorical references—but these may derive either from literary models, local or transnational, or from oral literary examples. Aesthetic matters aside, however, what struck me most forcefully as I gathered up the texts that my students and I read together and that are now in this anthology was how certain broad themes are common in stories from everywhere. The anthology is organized to reflect these general themes that come from very diverse cultural sites into Global Cultures. Learning to read cross-culturally is learning of a very high order of complexity—or, more accurately, it requires a very high degree of self-awareness in combination with wide cultural experience. Becoming able to see similarities along with differences, differences along with similarities, is certainly central to such learning. By offering you, for example, two stories by two women of two different cultures and two different literary generations about two women who rebel against the men and social arrangements that have virtually en-slaved them, this anthology registers upon your aesthetic and moral senses the rebellious motives and actions that are, simply, human, but that occur in and from contexts that are particular, culturally specific.

In the Introduction that follows, I have written in more detail both about the phenomenon of Global Cultures and about the problems of reading cross-culturally. This Introduction is for those readers who want a tour in these matters, and it can certainly be skipped by those who want to get right to the stories. Along with the stories, you will find brief commentaries on the authors and information that will make contextual references in the stories clearer.

ACKNOWLEDGMENTS

MANY THANKS to William Chace, president of Wesleyan University, who made it possible for me to prepare and teach "Contemporary World Literature" to a group of seventy-five Wesleyan first-year students. The project of acquiring dozens upon dozens of books and reading through the stories they contained was made feasible by my friend Sukey Howard's help and encouragement. Her knowledge of American publishing, experience on the bookstore beat, and excellent literary taste are everywhere reflected in this anthology. Janine Mileaf also joined in as a reader. Various colleagues offered guidance through the national and regional literatures that are their specialties. Thanks particularly to Ellen Widmer of Wesleyan's East Asian Studies Department, who put a box of wonderful Chinese books on my desk. Some of the stories in this anthology were located by my students, and the introduction and commentaries owe a good deal to conversations I had with my teaching associate for the course, JoAn Johnstone. Terry Cochran and Suzanna Tamminen of Wesleyan University Press have been supportive of this project since its inception, and Suzanna undertook all of the often frustrating task of seeking permissions to reprint the stories in this anthology, thereby learning many lessons in how complex Global Cultures is as an economic phenomenon.

INTRODUCTION

IN THE St. Marks Bookstore on the Lower East Side, New York City, there is a section devoted to literature anthologies: eight shelves, about three hundred and fifty titles. The array provides a brief tour of the way literature—at least in forms shorter than the novel—is categorized now. There are national anthologies—stories from Japan, stories from Argentina. There are regional and continental anthologies—stories from Southeast Asia, from Eastern Africa, or from Asia and Africa. Then there are anthologies that use these geographical and political categories in combination with another axis: stories by Japanese women, stories by Argentine women. A third axis is represented in other collections: stories by lesbian writers from Latin America, writings by Latin American women in exile. Usually, the more specific the writers' identity category, the broader the geographical and cultural range represented. There are several anthologies of women's writing that are worldwide in scope, like the *Longman Anthology of World Literature by Women, 1875–1975* or the stunning anthology called *Daughters of Africa*, which includes writings by African women, by African-born women living elsewhere, and by women of African descent throughout the worldwide African diaspora, all arranged chronologically by the authors' birthdates rather than by their residences so that the volume constitutes a history as well. From shelf to shelf in the anthology section, evidence abounds that women's writings are being gathered under every kind of rubric—the range is astounding, wonderful.

Some of the stories in this anthology have come from the volumes that are on those shelves in New York, consequently they have already been through one filtering process before they came into my screen. The stories have fit into one of the geographical categories; the writers have usually fit some criterion of reputation and publishing record; and the language they write in has qualified the story for inclusion. National and regional anthologies, and sometimes books of wider scope, often have a language limit—they are made up of pieces originally in one language, seldom more, and usually in a hegemonic or dominative language. By hegemonic or dominative language I mean that, if a given country has a national language but also uses others—sometimes dozens or hundreds of others—the others will not usually be represented in anthologies representing the country. If a region has a plurality of languages, as the Caribbean does, anthologies may favor one; for example, *Caribbean New Wave* (1990) is a collection of English stories, not in Spanish, French, Creole, or any Indian language. Excellent recent exceptions to this generalization exist; however, most exceptions only make use of two languages, like *A Land Apart: A Contemporary South African Reader* (1987), which includes English and Afrikaans pieces but nothing translated from Xhosa, Zulu, or Sotho. Similarly, stories that do not come from the "high" culture of the area usually do not qualify, although this tendency has been challenged so effectively in recent years that many anthologies now include legends and folktales as well as transcriptions of oral literature. The Nigerian writer Chinweizu created *Voices from Twentieth-Century Africa* (1988) explicitly and polemically to insist that most of what is known of African literature outside of Africa is "Euro-assimilationist junk," not literature rooted in African traditions and "orature."

As this judgment of Chinweizu's certainly shows, anthologists often have cultural or political axes to grind. They also, of course, have specificities of personal taste, linguistic range, educational formation, and connections to literary communities and individual writers. The same should be said of series editors, those agents of publishing houses who filter collections of stories by individuals into national and Global Cultures. The multinational publishing houses of Great Britain or Great Britain and the United States—Longmans, Heinemann, Faber and Faber, Viking-Penguin—each have series of volumes by single authors from all the areas of the former British Commonwealth, where English, of course, is the predominate postcolonial language. Until recently, certain countries and regions loomed large in the lists of single author collections—Nigeria, for example, was the most represented West African country, a role Kenya played for East Africa, while a Cameroonian or Ugandan writer was hard to find—but now there is more diversity. Australian fiction (of a rather English sort) was readily available, but now you can read *Three Novels from Papua New Guinea*.

Both anthologies and single author story collections, national and regional, are also being produced by small presses. Three Continents in

Washington, D.C., established in 1973, has a sub-Saharan Africa series, a Middle East series, one for the Pacific Rim, one for the Caribbean. China Books both produces books and imports other publishers' books in English from China. Kodansha does books in English from and about Japan. Africa World Press ranges over that continent, while Curbstone does Latin American fiction. Because of their geographical locations, certain American university presses have special interests in one region, as the University of Hawaii has in Asia, the University of Houston (via the imprint Arte Publico) has in Spanish-language literatures of North and South America, or the University of New Mexico has in Chicano texts. Multifaceted institutions specializing in one region have evolved, too, such as a combination publisher, importer, and bookseller located in Detroit, Cellar Books, that has a huge inventory from many publishers in Southeast Asia and particularly from the Philippines. Reader's International, based in Louisiana, is unusual in providing English translations from Europe, particularly from Eastern Europe, as well as from Latin America and Africa, and also takes a special interest in writers who have been censored in their own countries. Among the most exciting publishing projects in this complex scene are those undertaken by small outfits with special interests in women's writing. Wonderful books have been issued by Cleis in Pittsburgh, White Pine in Buffalo, Seal Press in Seattle (with its spin-off series, Women in Translation), Kitchen Table: Women of Color Press in New York City, Spinsters/Aunt Lute in San Francisco, as well as by the wide-ranging, scholarly Feminist Press. London houses like Zed Books and Women's Press also contribute to this stream.

All of these publishing and distributing ventures are part of Global Cultures, a fact that makes them quite different from small houses in particular locations that provide books to an immediate audience. An example is the cooperative Savacou Press in Kingston, Jamaica, with which one of the writers in this anthology, Hazel Campbell, is associated. Books from such houses are not available in even the richest of American bookstores, like City Lights in San Francisco, which has a treasury of books from Third World presses like Zimbabwe Publishing, East Africa Publishing, Panda Books, or Latin American Literary Review Press that all have distribution means in America and Europe. Still, stories from houses like Savacou do make their way into anthologies and thus into Global Cultures, and, as the demand in other parts of the world for literature from the Caribbean increases, larger houses will take up complete volumes and reissue them in Global Cultures. As always, both market factors and cultural needs are involved in the gathering process.

Without being a specialist, it is certainly no easy matter—indeed, to some extent impossible—to determine what kind of filtering has gone on when you read an anthology like, say, *The Penguin Book of South African Stories*. But the best contemporary anthologies make their selection principles quite clear, and some, like *Bamboo Shoots After the Rain: Contemporary Stories by Women Writers of Taiwan* (Feminist Press, 1990), are a wonderful education. Reflecting the best of feminist publishing sophistication, that volume contains both a historical essay on Taiwan's women writers by one of its editors, Sung-Sheng Yvonne Chang, and an essay entitled "Can One Read Cross-Culturally?" by the other editor, Ann C. Carver. When such helpfulness is not available, readers must either take the initiative to find out what they are experiencing or read on a strictly aesthetic level. Of course, what is deemed "good" aesthetically is both a subjective and a culture-bound matter for readers and for editors. A very particular kind of result will be achieved if an aesthetic criterion alone has been used in selecting works for an anthology.

This point becomes very obvious if you look at the anthologies of short fictions in English or in translation into English that advertize themselves as "international." The heftiest candidate is the eight hundred-page *The Art of the Tale: An International Anthology of Short Stories* (Viking-Penguin, 1986). This collection is aesthetically superb, but it also has a very familiar feel; that is, the word "International" in the subtitle turns out to mean predominantly European and particularly American (sixty of the eighty-two authors) and also of internationally established reputation. The two Japanese included, for example, are the Nobel Prize winner Kawabata, who died in 1972, and Mishima, who died in 1970, probably the two modern Japanese writers best known in Europe and America. "The art of the tale" turns out to mean the art descending from the list of European and American "masters of the form" offered in the editor's introduction: Pushkin, Balzac, Hawthorne, Poe, Gogol, Turgenev, Flaubert, and so on into the twentieth century. In other words, this anthology is cued to the literary history of the short story as a genre developed by European (including Russian) and American masters. Tales indebted primarily to, say, oral traditions or non-Western religious traditions or to specific historical experiences of national liberation and anti-imperialism would have no place here, and neither would stories not of the "high" cultural or "pure" literature provenances valued as "great." Similar limitations govern the high quality (in similar aesthetic terms) of *Sudden Fiction International: 60 Short Short Stories* (Norton, 1989), although this collection is more international in the geographical sense.

An aesthetic or "literary quality" criterion also shaped the much more interesting and experimental sixth Graywolf Annual called *Stories from the Rest of the World* (Graywolf Press, 1989), which offers thirteen fine stories from two Japanese, a Chinese, a Bengali, an Estonian, two Iraqis, a Palestinian, a Libyan, a Syrian, an Egyptian, a Congolese, and a Kenyan. But the editor, Scott Walker, also realized that, when he read beyond the European, American, and Russian masters and into "the rest of the world" (as his Americo-centric title has it), challenges were being posed to his notions of literary quality. He noted that his "strongest impression received from a reading of dozens of books of contemporary short stories in translation" was "how politically alert are the writers, the characters, and the cultures in which the action takes place." Elaborating, he concluded that "most characters are keenly aware of their social station and sensitive to the political implications of their actions: the writers seem to have a political purpose in the writing of the story; and many of the stories seem to be written against a background, hidden to those of us who are travelers, of social, historical and cultural struggle."

This earnest, wide-eyed remark would be immediately recognized as coming from an insular, protected social position and lack of political experience—its peculiarly "innocents abroad" American quality—by any of the editors from "the rest of the world" who produce anthologies and series. "Literary quality" as an isolated virtue—like the notion of "art for art's sake"—only exists in cultures that can afford to produce intellectuals who are not politically alert. It is unknown in cultures—"the rest of the world"—where there are no predetermined divisions of labor between critics and politicians, university professors and labor activists, medical doctors and fiction writers. Actually, within our own American cultural scene, no one unalert to politics could come from what are known as "non-dominative cultures" inside or nearby the dominating commercial ones. On the contrary, people from such non-dominative cultures produce anthologies like *Cuentos: Stories by Latinas* (Kitchen Table Press, 1983) and *Reclaiming Medusa: Short Stories by Contemporary Puerto Rican Women* (Spinsters/Aunt Lute, 1988) that contain stories, some in English, some in Spanish, some that alternate between both languages, "from elsewhere" even when they are written in Brooklyn or in Iowa City. Out of such cultures come works such as Gloria Anzaldua's brilliant genre-traversing *Borderlands/La Frontera: The New Mestiza* (Spinsters/Aunt Lute, 1987). These are works about intra-American culture clash, political and cultural domination, and liberation struggle, stories in which political alertness is a matter of identity and survival.

In universities, the categorization of literature that is apparent in bookstores and publishing is institutionalized in programs and departments. Area programs from national to regional to continental to transcontinental (like "Third World Studies," although there are no First World Studies or Second World Studies) include the study of literary works along with history, politics, and sociology, although literary works may also be studied through particular language and literature programs. When courses with titles like "Postcolonial Literature" are offered, the geographical categories are transcended, although broader courses often reflect a bias toward one of the major colonial languages—especially English, French, Spanish— and sometimes toward a particular area.

These postcolonial courses are part of a trend toward doing comparative literary studies on a global scale. The type of inquiry that used to be called comparative literature is opening up, after a complicated decade from 1975 to 1985 or so that was characterized by arcane theoretical jargons, quite laughable to all but their speakers. Comparative literary studies, now evolved into the broader "Cultural Studies," were infused during that decade with literary theories of various sorts. The concentration on theory was of dubious benefit in helping students learn to read carefully, but it did have the consequence of rattling every staid notion about "the canon" of texts taught, about who is reading, how they read, and why they read. In other words, questions that were never asked before are now being asked. Comparisons of French and German short stories of the late nineteenth century are still being written, of course, but the emphasis has shifted to, for example, comparisons among literatures written on the margins of dominative national or continental cultures, literatures written by peoples who are multilingual and multicultural, literatures by peoples newly literate but with ancient oral traditions, literatures complexly coded to reach more than one audience with only one text, and so forth. Issues of gender, race, and ethnicity in, around, and about texts are circulating. The idea has gone abroad that Puerto Rican, Irish, and southern Italian writers might share a cultural position, or that Malaysian writers, growing up multilingual and bombarded by languages, might have something important to show to city dwellers just now beginning to live in multicultural chaos. All of these inquiries welcome into their purviews cultures once of more interest to anthropologists than to practitioners of comparative literature.

But, even though the meaning of comparative literature is changing, history and social science are further along in comparing the "Third World" or the "World" than are literary scholars and editors. Comparative studies of revolutions, like comparative studies of socioeconomic development involving many nations or different regions, for example, are fairly common now, even though they are often distorted by either Eurocentric bias or specific political purposes. But established methods to study together, in classrooms or in books, a short story from China and one from Ecuador, one from Syria and one from Kenya are few and far between. Even less often are the distinctions among the First, Second, and Third Worlds, which are taken for granted—very unfortunately, I think—in socioeconomics and among social scientists, open to question. In literary studies, "multiculturalism," when used to refer to the contemporary global cultural scene and not in reference to the many cultures making up our own American culture, is a term almost empty of content. It reminds one of the trendy imperative popular in the simpler 1960s that Americans overcome their provincialism by glancing at Europe and Europeanized "elsewhere." As such, it invites tokenism.

The complex publishing and academic scene that I have tried to sketch here illuminates the main challenge Global Cultures poses now to those who would like to experience it, learn from it, understand it: The territory is unmapped. It needs maps and guidebooks of a peculiar sort, however, both because the territories of the publishing revolution and of literary studies are in great flux and because it is so easy to get caught in particular cultural prejudices while seeking familiarity·with a global phenomenon. In its preliminary stage, the mapping task will be like the one undertaken by the German historian Arno Peters. Peters made a map of the world (you will find it reproduced as the frontispiece and on the cover of this anthology) based on mathematical projections and designed to show clearly and fairly the proportions, sizes, and locations of the world's land masses and oceans. The map, which was perspectiveless, showed, for example, that South America is nearly twice the size of Europe, not equal to it as traditional maps imply, and that Africa is larger by some 6 million square miles than the Soviet Union, which is usually shown as the larger area. The colonializing North is not presented in the Peters Projection as larger than the colonialized South, a distortion that has many equivalents in the intellectual view of the world that is now polemically labeled "Eurocentric" or, more narrowly, "Americo-centric." The latter view is very subtly exposed in a story by Clarice Lispector collected here, "The Smallest Woman in the World," which shows a "big" European explorer's incomprehension of a "small" African. But more than measurability in square miles and mathematical projections are needed to overcome the habit of knowing nothing about cultures in "the rest of the world," except for what is permitted and presented in inherited intellectual maps.

If every anthology or series has a selection process and if the types of processes available in Global Cultures determine the selection's shape, its range, its hierarchies, its representativeness, and if, similarly, every academic or curricular agenda has its own way of drawing upon and, in turn, reinforcing the publishing production, then these modalities and institutions need to be a part of every alert reader's knowledge. If you want to push against the boundaries of Global Cultures as now constituted, you must understand what kinds of selection processes are *not* contributing to

Global Cultures and what kind of educational experiments are *not* being undertaken. This anthology is largely a result of such *negative* reasoning.

The "nots" that governed my selection are these. First, this anthology is not "international" in the old sense, that is, it does not concentrate on the European, American, and Russian. It is "international" with respect to all the world that is not those areas. The anthology is, thus, not geographically organized—it is neither national, regional, nor continental. Second, the writers collected here are not all well known; they are a mix of well known (at regional and international levels) and little known. They range in age from the oldest born in 1888 to the youngest born in 1957, but the majority are children of the 1930s. The fact that this anthology presents a large population of writers born between 1930 and 1940 was not the result of any plan of mine. Interestingly, the age cluster developed of its own accord, out of a reality. This reality, I think, has to do with the global experience of World War II and the immediate aftermath of independence movements throughout the colonialized territories. This cohort of writers is the same cohort that reached adolescence—reached literary consciousness—during a wave of immigrations, of quick socioeconomic changes, of developing new nations, and of new visions and new hopes—often hopes quite horribly unfulfilled—that rose after the global war.

Third, the anthology makes no distinction between writers who have never left their homes and those who have. Some of the authors represented here are cosmopolitans, by choice or by circumstances, having moved physically in Global Cultures—traveling, studying, or, all too often, fleeing impossible conditions. Others are very much of their home places and cultures. I have, for example, included works by two writers from the Philippines (partly on the assumption that most Americans are unfamiliar with our former colony's cultures). One, Paulino Lim, Jr., is a university professor living in the United States; the other is from the rural southern Philippines and still makes his home there, writing about the cultural mix and clash of north and south in the Philippines. There are stories by two Indians, one, Rohinton Mistry, living in Toronto, and the other, Saloni Narang, widely traveled but living in Bombay, still writing about the people of the Punjab with whom she grew up. It is not surprising that many of the writers, both those living abroad and those at home, were children of immigrants or migrants, and it is perhaps equally predictable that so many belong to the tribe of the archetypical wanderers, the Jews. For example, one writer is the daughter of an American Jew living in Puerto Rico (Aurora Levins Morales), two are Brazilians whose parents were Russian Jews (Moacyr Scliar and Clarice Lispector), two are children of Jews who sought refuge in South Africa. "It is not unusual for writers to be the children of foreigners," the American short story writer Grace

Paley has observed. "There's something about the two languages engaging one another in the child's ears that makes her want to write things down. She will want to say sentences over and over again, probably in the host or dominant tongue. There will also be a certain amount of syntactical confusion which, if not driven out of her head by heavy schooling, will free the writer to stand a sentence on its chauvinistic national head when necessary. She will then smile." [1]

Fourth, the authors in this anthology are not predominantly male, as is the case in every anthology I consulted that is not specifically dedicated to women's writings. There are fifty-six authors, twenty-seven women and twenty-three men. One section of the anthology is specifically devoted to women's writings and to the condition of women, but throughout the anthology there is a thematic emphasis on women and children—on being female and on growing up in conditions of immigration, modernization, war, prejudice. Again, I did not set out looking for this emphasis; I found it—even to the extent, very unusual in earlier literature from any culture, of finding many stories written by men from the narrative point of view of a woman (a fine example is the South African Najabulo Ndebele's "Death of a Son"). The world is full of processes for which the word "feminization" is rightly used, most of them, like "the feminization of poverty," signaling prejudice at work; but the global feminization of culture, the feminization of Global Cultures, that is so obvious to any wide reader is certainly something to celebrate—and such institutions as the Nobel Prize might catch up with it one day.

Finally, though this anthology is not arranged either geographically or historically, it is also not just one story after another. The anthology is thematically divided, the main and subsidiary themes representing my reading experience—that is, they came to mind as I read, they register a feeling of familiarity. The diversity of the world's cultures, as you can encounter them in Global Cultures, is amazing; it induces a kind of wonder. But so, too, is the similarity in the concerns that come out of this diversity.

For example, what struck me immediately and forcefully as I read is that the publishing revolution I have described is intimately and often heartbreakingly connected to a startling reality: In the years since World War II, more people have left their homes and moved elsewhere—or sometimes kept on moving, place to place—than in the preceding history of humankind altogether.[2] The stories of revolutions and wars, of economic

---

1. Grace Paley, "Introduction" to Clarice Lispector's *Soulstorm* (N.Y.: New Directions, 1974).

2. The world in mid-1992 had some 17 million refugees living in it, but this statistic is only part of the picture formed by the postwar phenomenon, which also resulted in migrations within countries and changing national boundaries.

collapses and famines, of natural disasters and manmade interferences with nature, of generation gaps and reorganizations of basic social ties—all the stories that lie behind this reality—are everywhere in contemporary literary production.

That is, the thematic content of Global Cultures is woven from the events that have produced the largest migration of people and peoples—whole groups—in the history of the world. Very specifically, as I noted before, a great portion of literature is being produced now by people who are perpetual travelers, migrants, emigres, refugees, stateless persons. They carry their work with them, they write with their eyes on a lost home, or they chronicle the differences—only rarely the similarities—between the culture in which they grew up and the one or ones they came to later. The changed direction of world literature, the flow of it predominately to and not from America and Europe, is in part a reflection of where younger writers have migrated and of where younger translators live, that is, often in the emigre communities of North America and Europe. There they grow up bilingual and bicultural, infused with a mission to bring into the new land the language of the old.

In American literary history, we are very familiar with the importance of being an expatriate for fiction writers. Greenwich Village bohemianism had its annexes on the Rive Gauche, as did the Harlem Renaissance. In the literary histories of the colonialized regions of Africa and Asia, trips to Europe—to London and Paris particularly—for higher education and for a cultural forum also figure very prominently. To consider just one regional example: The most famous (among Americans and Europeans) contributor to the post–World War II African literary renaissance, Leopold Senghor, was a model of cosmopolitanism for his generation. Educated in francophone Senegalese schools, he went to Paris, was hailed as a young genius, and began publishing there; later, after a period in French politics, he returned to lead his country and to bring home a literary style accessible only to those of his countrymen who shared his complex cultural formation. Now, among sub-Saharan Africans born after World War II, the more familiar patterns are leaving home for permanent residence abroad—as often, now, in America or Canada as in Europe—or staying home or in a neighboring country to cultivate an accessible literature, closer to nativist traditions, sometimes in tribal languages rather than those of French or English colonialism. The writers who stay home are not untraveled, but they have sojourned rather than resided elsewhere. Their culture is the culture of postindependence, not of fighting for independence.

There is a difference between the prose and poetry of the postwar, postindependence *negritude* developed by Senghor in his *Anthology of the New Black and Malagasy Poetry in the French Language* (1948)—

which was a key development in the history of the anthology as a medium of cultural influence—and the anthology *African Short Stories* (Heinemann, 1985) assembled by the Nigerian novelist Chinua Achebe, now a resident of New York. Achebe's anthology is broad—it is African, not sub-Saharan, it is not predominantly French, it does not stress "black"— and at the same time local—clued to stories of village life and tribal backgrounds. It is both for Africans and for the rest of the world (not just for the colonial power, like an arrow of revenge). All the cultures it represents are globalized in the representation, linked to a continent, a world.

In other parts of the world, too, there are palpable tensions between impulses to conserve and employ particular cultural traditions and impulses to reach out, to connect to other cultures, to participate in Global Cultures. These tensions are often the thematic focus of fictions, as they are of literary critical reflections and manifestos, whether penned by those who have stayed home or by those who have emigrated or been exiled. There is hardly a literary community in the world without its diaspora, and influences flow back and forth between home and abroad. Many of those younger writers who have left their countries to reside elsewhere are producing a literature that is also global, for it presents the individual's Before and Now cultures as refracted through one experiencing sensibility, a crucible in which literary traditions mix. The "art of the tale" is not learned from American and European "masters of the form" during residence in these cultures; rather, an art for the tales that clamor to be told is hammered out in a clash of cultures, it is an unstable alloy. Sometimes this crafting process is shown explicitly in the stories—as it is, for example, in one by Aurora Levins Morales included here that is in English except when it must be, when it cannot avoid being, in her native Puerto Rican Spanish. Sometimes the crafting process is more noticeable through the obvious subverting of the ingredients that the "masters of the form" would say make a short story a short story, like consistency of narrating voice. (To call any of these techniques "postmodern," as literary critics often do, is to assume that they are part of the aftermath of European and American modernism—a judgment that obscures the extraordinary diversity of literary and political histories that make Global Cultures so scintillating.)

I have opened this anthology with a section called Between Cultures, which includes stories by writers who have left their native lands, stories in which cultural plurality is everywhere and the pain of cultural loss is palpable, stories in which there is a great deal of meditation on what makes cultural confusion endurable and sometimes even invigorating. The theme of cultures—in the plural—mixing, clashing, and, sometimes and in some ways, amalgamating, is a global theme. It is common to a West Indian living in Canada and an Urdu-speaking Indian living in New York, a Puerto Rican in San Francisco and a Filipino in Los Angeles, a Japanese in Paris and a Palestinian in Kuwait—although the variations on the theme are as great as this list would lead you to expect.

In the second and third parts of this anthology, New Nations and Culture Clash, we turn to stories that explicitly present the kinds of changes, upheavals, and dislocations that have produced the great contemporary migration; but we meet these events at home, in the homelands of writers, not in their memories or their reflections. Most of the authors in this section are people who stayed home. In New Nations, the stories focus on political events, and, given the history of the world since World War II, which, mapped, would look like a fully lit switchboard of intra- and international violence, there is war everywhere—war for independence or national liberation, civil war, and on-going civil strife and guerrilla war. In Culture Clash, the focus is on development and modernization or Westernization, and on all of the human complexities that such abstractions of Western social science do so little to convey. These stories present very clearly the great ambivalence that development has produced and the great struggle for modes of development that do not alter beyond recognition or even destroy the lands and cultures being developed.

Culture Creation, the fourth part of this anthology, contains the collection of writings by women that I mentioned before. Most of these pieces were written during the decade separating the two international gatherings of women that have taken place under United Nations aegis—the first in Mexico City in 1975 and the second in Nairobi in 1985. This decade was, most commentators would agree, one of growing appreciation among women for both the differences and the similarities among their experiences. Meditations on diversity and similarity have replaced to a large degree the tendency of Western women to prescribe liberation formulas to their sisters elsewhere, or to protest without first trying to understand institutions like polygamy or concubinage. The ubiquity of sexism and oppressive practices against women is indisputable, the women attending these two meetings agreed, but the universal is only comprehensible in and through all the variations, the particulars. I have tried to select for this section of the anthology a range of stories that presents both oppression and images of liberation, which, I found, tend much more often to be images of exemplary individuals—often, not surprisingly, maternal figures—than of the social or political liberation movements that are, only now, building.

The final section of this anthology contains stories that, for lack of a better way to express what they have in common thematically, I call Complex Communications. These stories deal with spiritual dimensions or matters of the human spirit. Some of the stories present religious understandings and visions and particularly address clashes among those visions. They are just a tiny fraction of a vast library of stories with religious intention being produced worldwide by Buddhists, Muslims, Christians, and members of smaller tribal faiths in which various types of materialism are criticized. Some of the stories, on the other hand, deal with what, in the West, is known as mental health, with questions about who is sane and who is mad and by what criteria such judgments are made. Some of the stories deal with how difficult it seems to be for people to understand each other across differences of culture, of skin color, of religious background, of generation, and with how debilitating to the spirit are these failures of communication. All of these stories, from their various angles, in their various contexts, center on problems of understanding and communicating with people who are "other."

In a sense, this last section of the anthology returns us to the complexities of communication presented in the first section, but these final stories were not written by emigres or refugees or travelers. They arose from deep in the heart of homes, where there are, often enough, cultural conflicts aplenty. The common ground shared among the final stories has not been laid by the vast migration of peoples or the "shrinking" of the globe given transport and communication technologies, although it is not detached from these developments. It is the common ground of what old Marxists used to call our "species-being," the human sharing of the world and its resources and problems.

In this last section of the anthology, as well as in the anthology as a whole, I want to reflect an attitude that I find widespread among contemporary writers and that the title *Global Cultures*—with its singular adjective and its plural noun—is meant to summarize. Learning to think and to enjoy literature globally, to think of human culture as a single vast field, requires an attitude that opposes the many ways in which cultures have been viewed hierarchically or, more subtly, separately but not equally; a view that resists the will to dominate while respecting, yet not serving, the righteous resentments accompanying the will to overcome domination. It requires simultaneous appreciation for what is one in our world—or the modes in which our world is one—and for the necessary, important, and irreducible pluralities of our cultures and our existences. This anthology tries to provide an introductory map to the great wealth of literary works now being produced in the particular settings of the writers' experiences and, at the same time, in the global setting.

Part One

BETWEEN CULTURES
Emigres, Refugees, Exiles

CROSSED CULTURES,
CREATED IDENTITIES

LEANNE HOWE, born in 1951, is a Native American of the Choctaw tribe, which was located in the Southeast, particularly Mississippi, before being forced to cede it lands and move to the Indian Territory in Oklahoma in 1832. She has written as a journalist for newspapers in Texas, her current residence, and published *A Stand Up Reader* (Into View Press, 1987), where "An American in New York" appeared before it was more widely circulated in a superb anthology edited by Paula Gunn Allen, *Spider Woman's Granddaughters: Traditional Tales and Contemporary Writing by Native American Women* (Fawcett Colombine, 1989). The story, its title presumably a parody upon "An American in Paris" and upon the great American literary theme of innocents abroad, is a study in preconceptions of identity. The story's narrator has spent her life being identified—she is an Indian, and she ought to look like one for the tourists who have come to her hometown in Oklahoma with their cameras in hand. But now she is a tourist, off to the island, Manhattan, which her people, *the* Americans, the Native Americans, once sold for "twenty-six bucks and some beads." And what she finds there is all the newer immigrants, the recent ones, trying to buy *their* little pieces of Manhattan. She hates them and loves them, resents them and identifies with them—adding a layer to her own identity. In her hilarious "half-breed" way, she is "some kind of native sojourner on a vision quest"—and she finds: the New World.

MASAHIKO SHIMADA, born in 1961, is a graduate of the Tokyo University of Foreign Studies. His novels, which he began to publish when he was still a student, have been rewarded in Japan with literary prizes but have not yet been translated into English. "A Callow Fellow of Jewish Descent," which appeared in *New Japanese Voices: The Best Contemporary Fiction from Japan* (Atlantic Monthly Press, 1991), is itself a fine example of foreign studies. It shows the influence of the foreign fiction masters Shimada has claimed as his favorites—the Pole Witold Gombrovich and the Czech Milan Kundera—rather than of the modernists who so attracted the postwar Japanese writers like Kawabata, Tanazaki,

Abe, Oe, and Mishima. And the story is, literally, a report on foreignness, on cultural alienness. The central character is in Paris because he needs psychiatric help, or at least he thinks that psychiatry might help him construct an identity. But he gets something else from the allegorical Mr. Penman, "a jack-of-all-trades in matters related to national borders," a trafficker in refugees, who, it turns out, is also a master of identity construction. Mr. Penman offers no cure, but he does at least show that there is nothing specifically Japanese about cultural imposture— he, a Pole, turned himself into a Jew by assiduous study. One does not have to be from an island with anciently imperious traditions to realize that, for some people, living humanly in the Global Cultures may require renouncing "a traditional view of human beings."

An American in New York

LeAnne Howe

THE FIRST thing I realized when I went to New York City was that everyone is something different from what they seem: JAPs are Jewish American Princesses; Arabs are Towel Heads, and Haitians are cab drivers.

I was sent to New York on financial business. The high-stakes bond business. There's something hypocritical about an Indian selling and trading U.S. Treasury Bonds. Even the word *bond* connotes servitude. To bond, to bind, to restrain, to obligate, to indebt, to enslave.

Bonds also help prop up, and perpetuate, the country's economy. They're printed on one-hundred-percent white bonded paper by the government, so the government will be able to pay interest on the other bonded pieces of paper they printed last year. The government's bonds are its words to its people. This is what we're worth. Our word is our bond.

"We're all bonded," said the head of government operations at Saloman Brothers. "When you're responsible for receiving and delivering four billion dollars a day worth of government bonds you have to be bonded."

I was sent to New York with a wad of expense money to entertain, beguile, and prepare the hogs (our operations people) for the slaughter. My boss gave me a pep talk before I left for the Big Apple.

"Show 'em a good time, take 'em out to eat, get 'em drunk, take 'em to a show. Do whatever you have to do to get 'em to handle our bond trades more efficiently."

Yes, Kimosabe. Me go to New York. Me make 'em like Indian.

I saw this assignment as a kind of reversal of historic roles. This time an Indian was going to buy immigrants. And I thought it a perfect opportunity to trot out my Tonto-with-tits garb. I'd learned a long time ago that even in Texas people don't recognize you as an Indian unless you're wearing a costume. They've seen too many Hollywood movies. So I packed my leather and feathers and flew back East.

For most of the three days I was in Manhattan, I wore my hawk feathers for protection from the enemy and as a way of advertisement. An American in New York. No one caught the irony.

Now that I put the whole episode in perspective, I think I saw myself as some kind of native sojourner on a vision quest, in search of that magical ambience Frank Sinatra sings about in *New York, New York*.

I wanted to see the Empire State Building, Fifth Avenue, the Garment District, Central Park, Broadway, Rockefeller Center, the World Trade Center, Radio City, the Statue of Liberty, and Hell's Kitchen.

No wonder we sold the whole place for twenty-six bucks and some beads. I wouldn't give you twenty-six cents for the entire island right now. It stinks. There's trash piled higher than your head on every corner. Old men and women are puking and peeing all over the place. You can't see the sky. Everywhere you look there's black grunge growing up the walls on the buildings, and there are rats the size of small coyotes climing trees in Central Park. It's horrible.

Outside my hotel at the World Trade Center there was a young man who thought he was a bird. He ran day and night, up and down the concrete median between the streets, flapping his arms trying to fly away.

I asked the hotel doorman what was going to happen to the Bird Man. He told me when the Bird Man dies the city health department will pick up his body and bury it.

Sonofabitch. Those scenes from Woody Allen's film *Manhattan*, where he and Mariel Hemingway are taking a romantic carriage ride around Central Park, are as fabricated as those where Ward Bond is looking for smoke signals in *Wagon Train*.

I was as surprised by what I saw as the New Yorker who landed at Oklahoma City's airport and asked me where all the Indians and tepees were. I was working as a waitress at the airport coffee shop.

I stood there proudly pouring him a cup of coffee and said, "Right here, sir. I'm an Indian."

As I stood there in my stiffly starched yellow and white SkyChef's uniform, the New Yorker looked me up and down and asked, "You're it? I've come all this way to see Indians and you're telling me you're it? My God, darling, you mean you live in houses just like the rest of us?"

I said, "Well . . . I live in an apartment."

While I was working with the people in government operations during the day, my friend Sheree Turner, who'd flown to New York with me, was learning a lot about the city and its residents.

She told me that more than two million of the city's seven million residents are from overseas. There are more Dominicans in New York City, some 350,000, than in any city but Santo Domingo, more Greeks than anywhere but Athens, more Haitians than anywhere but Port au Prince. She told me most immigrants come to New York City because they know they can find fellow countrymen in this city, where everyone is an alien and no one is an alien.

On our last night in Manhattan, Sheree and I decided to see a show and do some exploring on our own.

We dressed up like some kind of tourists in semi-evening clothes. Again, the victims of commercialism. We thought you dressed for the theater. Sheree wore a backless dress with feathers and I wore a shirt that was slit down to my navel (sans feathers).

Most everyone else attending that evening's performance of A Chorus Line looked like they were going to a Texas Ranger baseball game, except two little old ladies from Kansas City who were wearing synthetic velvet.

After the show, I flagged down a horse-drawn taxi. A man steered his carriage toward us and stopped. Sheree jumped in back and the driver asked me if I'd like to ride up front with him. I was ecstatic.

As I was climbing into the coach, I realized why he asked me to ride up front. Both my tits were hanging out of my shirt as I'd flagged him down.

"Where you be wantin' to go, Miss?"

God! A real Irishman with a thick Irish brogue, complete with auburn hair and freckles. I imagined him a cross between Barry Fitzgerald and John Kennedy. (My faith in Woody Allen was restored.)

"We want to see everything, go everywhere, and spend some of my company's money."

He gave me a delicious grin and said to my tits, "Okay, Miss, we're off."

Seamus MacDonald was a wonderful guide. I loved the way he talked. He dutifully drove us around the Rockefeller Center and seemed to genuinely enjoy pointing out the sights. He told us where we could catch the Staten Island Ferry to see the Statue of Liberty after he dropped us off. He pointed out some hot night spots, and asked me where I was from.

We got on very well. I played the part of an investigative reporter, asking him everything from how long he had been in this country to what kind of girls he dated.

He was Catholic. His three older brothers were in this country going to law school. There were ten children in his family and his mother was still in Ireland raising the other six. His father worked in America and sent money to Ireland. Seamus said he was a boxer and eventually wanted to go professional. He planned to win the New York City Golden Glove Heavyweight Championship coming up in the fall. He said he loved to fight. (I knew we'd get along.) He dated girls who weren't Catholic. He was open-minded, but knew he would never marry outside the church.

I said I didn't believe he was big enough to be a heavyweight boxer.

"How tall are you? You don't look like you weigh enough to be a heavyweight."

I was baiting him. I like to symbolically challenge men. Whether it's a question of their manhood, their physical stature, strength, or just a game of trivia questions, they can never resist a challenge. Then, once they've proven they're stronger, taller, bigger, faster, or smarter, you have them hooked.

Women are no fun at this little ritual. They'll never meet a challenge head-on with another woman; they'll just go in another room and talk bad about you behind your back.

Anyway, Seamus fell for it. Putty in my hands. He laughed at me, gave me the reins, and stood up as we were going around 42nd Street.

He was big. (I'm attracted to big men.) Standing up in the carriage seat, his crotch was at eye level. He was also thick and very tall. He had a good size butt on him, too.

I bit my lip. My eyes glazed over and I swallowed hard. I began to struggle with my conscience. I was married. I was also averse to fucking someone only five years older than my son. (I wondered if my deodorant was still working? Was I wearing clean panty hose?) He probably had AIDS, or herpes. Besides, I hadn't lost that twenty pounds or so I was going to lose before coming to New York.

I looked around at Sheree sitting in the back seat of the carriage. I'd been ignoring her ever since I'd climbed in the driver's seat. She'd passed out with a grin on her face.

Just as I looked up at Seamus, our eyes met. He was still standing up in the carriage. His eyes were green and heavy-lidded. He smiled wide, revealing deep dimples and brilliant white teeth. I let my gaze match his and he said softly, "Your time's up. This is where you get off."

Oh shit. How humiliating. He'd just been playing the game, too. I wanted to kick myself. What am I going to be like in twenty years, a heavy-breathing old broad lusting after young boys with supple bodies?

"Wait a minute. I have more money and you didn't take us anywhere except around Central Park. I want to see things other tourists don't get to see. This is my last night in New York, and goddammit, I wanna see everything."

"Okay. For another twenty dollars I'll drive you places I don't take out-of-towners, then I'll drop you near a cab stand so you can get back to your hotel."

He headed toward streets partially lit by dim street lamps. We passed small, all-night coffee shops with outdated 10, 2 & 4 Dr. Pepper signs in the windows. Our carriage stopped behind a delivery truck and I watched a man with no shirt, and what looked like a dirty, wet towel on his head, rummage through piles of garbage. He picked up a crate covered with wilted lettuce leaves, shook them off, and carried it somewhere toward the dark end of the street.

"They are everywhere," said Seamus. "New York nobility used to be-wail each succeeding wave of Irish immigrants. Now there's a lot of concern around here that the new immigrants, these Middle Easterners, these Haitian boat people, these wandering Hispanics, can't be assimilated into our society."

"Our society?"

"Yes, our society. I'm going to get my American citizenship one day soon. Most everyone wants the same things. We wanna eat hamburgers, and pizza, buy designer clothes, and Swiss-made watches. Maybe that's materialistic but that is why everyone comes here."

"But there's more to life, and more to America than just things."

"More to life than expensive carriage rides and Broadway theatre, you mean."

I shut up.

We continued our trip around a curve and slowed behind several cars that were in some kind of a line.

Standing on both sides of the street were women with strangely exaggerated facial expressions. Painted women. Women with day-glo faces.

"Whores," he said softly. "You wanted to see unusual sights. Here they are."

"Where are we?"

"We're close to what used to be Hell's Kitchen."

The whole scene became surrealistic. The women, some wearing bras and panties, some completely naked, reminded me of South African baboons I'd seen in film clips on Channel 13. Like wild animals running down from the hills to beg tourists for sweets, the women ran from behind massive iron trash dumpsters and empty warehouses to beat on the sides of the cars and throw themselves on the car hoods.

It was another kind of feeding frenzy. There were thin-lipped, gaunt, white girls; pregnant older women; kinky-haired Asians; flat-chested black/white girls with gray, anemic skin and bleached hair. They were pandering, competing, cajoling, and hustling up their dinner money from the car men in line.

When the Ford Pinto in front of us finally came to a dead stop, I grabbed Seamus's arm.

"Don't worry. They won't come over here, we're not customers."

The white man rolled down his window and the tall, black/white girl in a red garter belt, red hose, and heels with waist-length, mica-white hair leaned through the driver's window. I was drawn to her and the moment in a way I'd never felt before. My breathing quickened and my palms felt sweaty. I reckoned this was what it felt like to be a voyeur peeking into someone's night room.

All we could see were the buttocks and legs of the girl leaning through the car window. The engine sputtered for lack of gas. The whole car body shook for a brief instant, then went dead.

My eyes watered from staring at the girl's legs and then she raised up out of the car and looked in our direction.

Her mouth was open and she spit on the sidewalk.

I stood up. I was amazed. "God, she's spitting cum on the sidewalk."

Seamus pulled me down in the seat.

"Shut up."

The woman-whore met my gaze.

"You want some of this?"

She rubbed her stomach and then rubbed the wadded bills between her fingers. Her gaze pulled me into her circle. The Pinto engine started up and from the distance we heard an ambulance turn the corner. I looked toward the sound and then looked back toward the black/white girl. She was gone. They were all gone. There were only the cars in front of us pulling out one by one.

"Where'd they go?"

"They're like rats. They run and hide when a city car comes. If they get picked up by the police, their pimps pay their bond."

We spent the rest of the ride in silence. Seamus gave me his address and promised to call me when he won the Golden Glove Championship, so I could write a story on him. I've never heard from him.

He dropped Sheree and me off at a taxi station and we waited for someone to pick us up. It was two in the morning.

I put on my hawk feathers for protection while we were waiting for a cab to come along. About twenty-five minutes later, one stopped and we asked the cabby to drive us around Greenwich Village. He was very black and slight. He must have thought we were lesbians because on the way to Greenwich Village he pointed out every lesbian bar we passed. He stopped in front of a building with a giant plaster head of the Statue of Liberty and said, "Largest lesbian club in New York. Men not allowed there. You like?"

When we told him we didn't want to stop, he gave up. I asked him where he was from and he said Nigeria.

"I been in America seese months."

He looked at me with my feathers and asked where I was from. I told him I was born here, that I was an American Indian. He pulled the cab over to the corner and stopped.

"Oh, how much would I like to talk to you. You are the real Americans. This was all your home before we started coming here. I am learning about you in my classes. Right now, you are having a lot of problems with the government discriminating against you. To me, it's so sad. I want to do something."

I was stunned and a little ashamed. For a moment I couldn't decide whether to say something flippant or believe his sincerity. I believed he meant what he was saying, even if it was just a temporary state of naiveté. I answered lamely that there was always hope or something stupid like that. Here was this black Nigerian who barely spoke English, guiding us around New York City in the early morning hours, trying to comfort me about the problems of the American Indian.

He again said he wished he could talk to us but he must go home to his family. We were his last fare. We asked him to drop us off at the Staten Island Ferry. As he drove away, I thought about my ambivalence toward newcomers. Ambivalence at best; racism at worst.

After all, the flood of white people is responsible for my being alive. (I am part white.) And yet, according to the melting-pot theorists, turning "us" into "them" has not been easy. Even after two hundred and ten years of world-wide immigration into the United States, Indians still exist, numbering two million people in some eight hundred and forty-six tribes. About the same number of new immigrants living in New York City.

We took the ferry to see the Statue of Liberty. The Nigerian had made my feelings toward immigrants soften. Maybe more newcomers was a good thing. In a way, newcomers have forced us, at least some of us, to be stronger.

I've always believed that mixing white and Indian blood makes first-generation half-breeds unpredictably mean, and often confused. Confused by their misdirected anger, confused by their choices, confused by their inherited instincts which the scientists say don't exist.

Man is a thinking animal therefore he suppresses any instincts and he learns from his environment. Take an Indian child from a reservation and put him with a white family in Boston and chances are that he'll become a Bostonian and a working member of society. Eventually the Indian child will forget about his home and ancestry.

That's the theory I learned from a behavioral psychologist at the University of Oklahoma. But that was ten years ago. Now a recent university study, completed in 1986, says that your genes determine whether or not you can do mathematics. I believe if your genes can help you find the answer to a trigonometry problem, then they can likewise make you crazy.

John Stuart says it more directly: "You never know what you're gonna get when you breed two different kinds of dogs. Most of the time, the dog is smarter than its parents, but then there are those times when the dog is born a complete idiot. You just never know when it comes to breeding."

Half-breeds live on the edge of both races. You feel like you're split down the middle. Your right arm wants to unbutton your shirt while your left arm is trying to keep your shirt on. You're torn between wanting to kill everyone in the room, or buying 'em all another round of drinks.

Our erratic behavior is often explained away by friends and family as "trying to be." If you're around Indians, you're trying to be white. If you're around white friends, you're trying to be Indian. Sometimes I feel like the blood in my veins is a deadly mixture of Rh positive and Rh negative and every cell in my body is on a slow nuclear melt-down.

As we approached America's statue of freedom, the only sound on the ferryboat was the muffled churning of its engines.

I thought about all the Indians huddled on reservations, the tired women-whores bound to their pimps, the Irish boxer, the poor Nigerian cab driver. I thought about our relationship to each other. Now almost two years have passed and still the images of those people have stayed with me through all the July Fourth hoopla and one-hundredth birthday celebration of the Statue of Liberty. Even though not one word was mentioned about America's natives, only about the immigrants who've been coming here because they believed our country was better than theirs, I've decided Emma Lazarus, who wrote the Statue's welcoming inscription, was really an Indian: "Give me your tired, your poor, your huddled masses yearning to breathe free . . ."

You did. Now where do we go from here?

A Callow Fellow of Jewish Descent

Masahiko Shimada

I

PERHAPS BECAUSE the first time I visited its psychiatry department to get myself examined I asked a nurse, "Do you have a professor of philosophy here?" I was stuck with the appellation "Tecchan"[1] at the hospital. Later, following my parents' strong wishes and my older brother's urgings, I went to Paris to study, where by chance I met Mr. Ludwig Penman, a Jewish Pole, and in introducing myself to him I said:

Enchanté. Je m'appelle Théchien.

I spent my one year in Paris as Théchien. During that period I rented a room in Mr. Penman's apartment and in time ended up forming something like a master-disciple relationship with him. Come to think of it now, he was the most outstanding engineer who improved my distorted thinking circuit more freely, more actively, than anyone else.

2

A small office called Refugee Stability was located above a pornographic movie theater called Film X in a corner of the Rue St. Denis. My brother worked there. Mr. Penman was the boss of that office. He used to work for a "migration agency" which helped prepare necessary paperwork for Jewish refugees from the Soviet Union and Eastern Europe and for Jewish residents in France who wanted to emigrate to Israel and other countries. But three years earlier he had become independent and expanded his business to handle not only Jews but refugees and those who wished to emigrate in general, regardless of race, providing guidance to such people as best he could. In short, he became a jack-of-all-trades in matters related to national borders. My brother was in charge of Japanese and Americans.

In fact, Refugee Stability was an exaggerated appellation, for the office rarely took up political matters. Still, Mr. Penman had done some things he could be proud of: he had helped an Armenian cellist defect; arranged to have a Turkish weight-lifter of Bulgarian nationality—a candidate for an Olympic gold medal—emigrate to Turkey; undertaken the work to deposit some of the Philippine President Marcos's secret assets in an under-

---

1. Any personal name that starts with "Tetsu" tends to take the diminutive form of "Tecchan." The narrator's confused query about a "tetsguaku no sensei" (professor of philosophy) at a psychiatric department prompted the nurse to play with this custom.

ground bank in Switzerland; and so forth. On his part, my brother did practically nothing but coordinate news coverage for Japanese TV stations and work as a tourist guide. His habitual complaint was that there was nothing as remote to the Japanese as refugees. He was not so busy as to need my help. As a result, I was shunted off to play the role of errand boy for Mr. Penman.

If I'd gone as far as Paris to train as an errand boy, I'd have to say I was being extravagant. The main purpose of my sojourn in Paris, though, was to treat my illness. Furthermore, that purpose was not my own but my parents'. No, come to think of it now, it was *their* conspiracy to kick a gloomy eccentric out of their home. My brother had written letters saying things like, "In Paris there's a gentle-hearted madame psychoanalyst called Christva. She's an old friend of Mr. Penman's, and he would be glad to introduce you to her. I envy you being examined by Christva. I ought to get ill, too." But whenever I tried to remind him of this, he'd look away and say something like, "Not many people may know this, but Mr. Penman is quite a distinguished doctor who developed an 'errand-boy treatment' for schizophrenics."

For the first half of my year, my life was like the Great Depression after 1929. Just by reminding myself of that period I can torture myself. My head was a balloon packed full of broken plates and bowls. Each time I pulsated or breathed, those broken pieces crashed into each other, almost exploding the balloon. My nerves and blood vessels were innumerable strings crazily out of tune, and each time I opened my mouth to say something, each time I took a step to walk, they resonated unbearable discordant sounds throughout my body. And my immune system was tattered, exhausted by its fight against invading germs and viruses. My body was full of holes like a box to keep insects in, and I felt coming in through those holes destructive, impulsive exhaust gases that tempted me to suicide or crime, or else smells of garlic, dust, and other particles. Total disorder! It seemed almost impossible to reassemble me, a jigsaw puzzle, into orderly shape. At any rate, I was hard pressed to shut off traffic with the outside world temporarily, to prevent myself from falling apart further.

What was I so afraid of? Now I can tell you: I was certain that I'd die soon. I was held by the illusion—it was more of a conviction—that something lurked in my body that was secretly plotting to drive me out of myself. What kind of basis was there for this? There was nothing like a basis. Suppose I was taking a walk in the Bois de Boulogne one late autumn afternoon and saw, about sixty feet away, a prostitute in a fur coat open her chest like a triptych, shaking out her breasts that tended to look away from each other. What was projected on the screen at my nerve center the next instant was not my genitals in her mouth, but my head hanging from a branch of a beautifully shaped tree. Or I would take a walk along the Rue St. Denis in the evening. Gradually my walk would slow down. This was because my consciousness and my body would slip away from each other. My consciousness would fall one step behind my body no matter how I tried, so that unless I stopped and corrected the slippage, I would not be able to take the next step ahead.

I better stop. Once I begin to talk about something like this, I can go on and on. In a healthy person's eyes my experience is like some bait for existentialism, and it is likely to be judged that the culprit for creating such illusions as I had was excessive self-defense.

At least until then my life had been a series of countless negative reactions. It wasn't only that I was constitutionally prone to food poisoning, that I was allergic to cedar pollen, or that I had weak resistance to pathogens. It had more profound meanings. In a word, I had inferior genes. However, I don't want to align myself with the view that genes are what makes an individual an individual. In defiance of that theory, I would assert:

"The genes are thinking only of themselves. My genes and myself have nothing to do with each other. My genes are using me, a machine, for their own survival. The moment they give up on me, I'll be a heap of scrap. That's why I'm keeping company with my genes, though very reluctantly. Besides, I have to protect them from germs and viruses. They're so *delicate*, compared with other superior genes, that they force me to have a negative reaction at the drop of a hat. It makes me mad to think they'll drive me like a slave until I die. It makes me madder to think they are my parents' genes synthesized."

The doctor who examined me two weeks before I left for Paris told my parents:

"As a patient, he attacks with considerable logic. He seems to recognize some personality in his own genes. He himself has a complex dual personality. His body is pushed around by what he thinks. This is a symptom common to schizophrenics. He doesn't have to be hospitalized yet, although he'll be welcome if you want him to be. But I'd suggest you let him travel before that. He needs to learn to turn his attention outside himself. If you let him travel, though, he'd better have someone to protect him."

I had realized that I was a little ill. I didn't dislike regularly visiting the psychiatry department. The place had an inexplicable restfulness and was excellent for doing things like reading. Among its patients was a beautiful woman of noble bearing; beside her practically all the nurses looked dingy. The most annoying thing was the male nurses. They were discriminators who secured their pride in one point: they were not patients. Following

Dante's classification, they'd have to live in Subdivision One, in Division Seven. That's where those who used violence against others and their possessions abide.

Fortunately, I merely wandered in the dark wood between Hell and Purgatory, and didn't have to become a settler in Hell. Incidentally, I learned about Christianity through Nietzche's writings. "Everyone has to go through a period when the outside world looks like a jungle inhabited by wild beasts," Mr. Penman once said to me. For me, who spent that particular period in Paris, Mr. Penman merged with Virgil, while my brother and parents, who enjoyed the progression of my illness as a bit of a joke, became beasts. And the Frenchmen, who regard it as a virtue to remain indifferent to others, were the trees in the wood.

Unfortunately, though, Mr. Penman and I had nothing in common. The languages he used were French, Polish, and Yiddish. He could also speak Russian. I spoke Japanese, a little bit of English, and pidgin French and Russian. Since he couldn't speak English at all, it was at first as if the fabled Asian combination of enemies, the dog and the monkey, had started communicating their thoughts to each other. Worse, he avoided speaking Russian as if it was a scourge. My brother later told me that his hatred of German was greater than that of Russian. It was a small revenge on his part. It appeared that Mr. Penman had suffered from both the Nazi persecution of Jews and imprisonment in concentration camps by the Russian SMERSH ("Death to the Spies") squad. He himself didn't say much, but the few words he did utter concerning those experiences became powerful curses. Take these words:

"If I had the slightest bit of human sentiment left in me, I wouldn't waste it in the form of love of fatherland, peace, or the spirit of self-sacrifice. People say the war's over, but I myself haven't signed any peace treaty with anybody. Has the Great Purge passed? Does that mean that I, who have survived it, am a remnant of the past? Fortunately, I left all my human sentiments in the concentration camps, so I can remain unconcerned about love of fatherland, morals, and faiths advocated by the peoples of the world as they wrangle with one another in friendly fashion."

I didn't know how to respond to someone with that kind of past, but as a matter of minimal courtesy, I put on a deferential expression when I heard such talk. I heard him through my brother's interpretation. When my brother wasn't around, I became exhausted by worries that Mr. Penman must find my presence unpleasant since I kept speaking pidgin Russian. That was one of the causes that worsened my illness. At no other time did I want to go back to that island of lovable philistines and peasants, that country of the rising sun. I should have taken an extreme step in the opposite direction and become a right-wing punk of the kind Mr. Penman would despise. And I should have habitually mouthed such inanities as "The Kwantung Army was right!" to distract myself a bit. But a combination of errand boy and right-winger would have been too much. In this regard I was a man of common sense, and chose to learn French and acquire information about the Jewish people, while cleaning Mr. Penman's apartment and serving him tea. And my curiosity about Mr. Penman— well, I was right to place it at the center of my life. The moment I did so, he automatically became my teacher.

Mr. Penman's apartment was located north of Montmartre, near the Jules-Joffrin Station. The fifth-floor flat, facing south, had a dining room, a kitchen, and five other rooms, two of which were occupied by books. I was given the smallest room, which faced west. The combination of a bed, a shoddily made closet, and a TV set was exactly like a room in a single-star hotel. Still, since I had a TV set for my exclusive use, I could spend all night doing nothing but playing computer games, paying no attention to anybody.

I was particularly devoted to a game called "The Divine Comedy," which, as the name suggests, told the story of Dante's journey through Hell and Purgatory as he observed things and made inquiries until he reached the Empyrean Heaven. On his way the player must seek out the guide, Virgil, or Beatrice, for advice in order to move up to the next stage. To climb up to the Empyrean Heaven, he must solve the riddles, get out of the labyrinth, and shake off those who cling to Dante's feet at each of the twenty-eight stages, thereby getting the specified number of points (called "sophia values"). To conquer the game, a player needs at least half a year, even spending two hours a day. As a result, the conquest of the game, like my curiosity about Mr. Penman, became a daily part of my life in Paris.

I don't remember when, but just about the time I got out of the body of Lucifer, who has three faces and six wings, and cleared Hell, Mr. Penman came into my room and asked me to let him play the game, too. He had secretly peeped into my room and seen me concentrating on it late at night. I took that as proof that he himself was curious about me, and grateful as I was for his act of peeping, I immediately translated the instruction manual of the game into French and taught him how to play it, step by careful step.

Nevertheless, Mr. Penman gave up playing at the entrance to Hell, in front of the River Acheron. His excuse was too severe for a mere game:

"If you call Jesus God, you must also call Marx and Freud Gods. I can't get myself to like the hierarchical structure of 'The Divine Comedy.' It's the same as a bureaucracy, isn't it? I'd stick to the earth and aim for a desert. What is there in the Heavens? The air gets thinner, that's all."

After my brother's interpretation, I took this to be a high-class joke and laughed, though it wasn't funny. With a stony expression that reminded me of the Ayatollah Khomeini, Mr. Penman continued:

"I shouldn't imagine, Théchien, that for some reason you think that life is a game, should I? A game surely has rules. But the rules of life aren't simple enough to be understood by a single human being. If you're planning to live your life as if its rules were the same as the game's, you'll remain a spoiled kid forever."

My brother asked, "What in the world have you done?" I had no choice but to turn myself into a single question mark and attach myself right behind the word "Jew": Jew?

Mr. Penman was never a crass, hysterical scholar. Rather, your impression was of a likable old bartender. He knew the name and the face of the guard at the opera house, and he even knew the backgrounds of the family who ran the store where I often went to buy fruit. I think he had acquired a special skill that couldn't be born of mere affability. It may have come from his profession. After all, an intermediary for refugees must be prepared to become a refugee himself at any time. A refugee, for the time being, has no choice but to support himself on a few things that are common to all countries, my brother said to me once. The observation must have been handed down to me straight from Mr. Penman, but it was persuasive. Among such common traits are affability, a quick sixth sense, a presentable body, aggressiveness, stamina, a driver's license—and, if I may add one more, being Jewish. Excepting the third trait, Mr. Penman met all the conditions. And having noted this, I must note I have none of them.

3

Half a year passed. Perhaps because the physical relationship between Paris and me became intimate, my negativism entered a period of lull. Then, a month later, by early March, I was free from the voodoolike thinking involving my genes. I had defeated my genes' despotic government, quelled the civil war at my nerve center, restored order, and successfully established a republic. Come to think of it now, I had been preoccupied with an utterly illogical persecution mania. In short, all I had been trying to do was to stubbornly protect my thinking circuit in its isolation.

My recovery from the illness fell on me just like a revelation. It was about the same time I conquered the game, "The Divine Comedy." The game was good for the rehabilitation of someone with schizophrenic tendencies.

As I entered the Heavenly Realm, I must have gotten what might be called a "player's high," and cleared one saint's test after another, climbed to the Ninth Heaven in three weeks, and met the Choir of Angels. I've heard that in this game it becomes difficult to get ahead once the player enters the Heavens, and that usually more than half the players give up after entering this realm. They never see what the Empyrean Heaven looks like. Beginning in the Sixth Heaven, you are given quite abstruse riddles by saints, angels, and Beatrice. At times you must have knowledge of astronomy, the basics of physics, and even a fair grasp of the history of Christianity. Besides, you aren't given optional answers, but are required to type up your own arguments in a hundred words or so. Each time this happened, I tirelessly checked the Larousse Encyclopedia (which was in Mr. Penman's library), translated the needed information into Japanese, and input it. As a result, my name was registered in the Empyrean Heaven. My intoxication at the time I finally entered it . . . I'd like to remember it as often as I can. After all, I had spent half a year just to find out how the images of the Empyrean Heaven might be displayed.

The Tenth Heaven I entered, guided by Beatrice, was so dazzling that I had to put on a pair of sunglasses. There it was no longer necessary to punch the keyboard. All I had to do was to stare at the images given as beneficences. The pleasure of stoicism brought on not by a drug but by an endurance lasting for half a year . . . at that moment my brain was as lucid as the night above a desert where countless stars flash. Beatrice, wearing only a robe of light, held out her hands. Around her were angels dancing wildly in a weaving motion like that of a roller coaster running on loops. They played the Paradise Song in Fauré's *Requiem*. Now one with Dante, I flitted like a butterfly from one pistil of white roses to another. There I saw the dear women I met in Purgatory, Rachel and Eudit. Next I met the Virgin Mary. A closeup of her face. Looking exactly like the picture of the Virgin Mary that Raphael is said to have painted with a baker's daughter as his model, she winked. The next moment Dante=I, along with Beatrice, was sucked into the Virgin Mary's crotch. Then began a memoir of Hell and Purgatory. The records of the journey, which took a total of three hundred hours, floated up one after another in flashes. Devils with rakes, usurers, snakes, jolly robbers, our friend Caserla who sang love songs for us, souls like invisible men praying in tears . . . Soon all of them showed up en masse on the screen and, bumping and falling, gradually turned into brilliantly colored marble patterns. Dante=I merged with Beatrice and melted into them.

These images were made to last forever and did not stop unless you turned the power off. For fully two hours I continued to watch them. If you punched the keyboard, the marble patterns changed into various shapes. Depending on what you thought, they looked like a nebula, a carnival scene, or an ugly monster. Sometimes a sexy Virgin Mary or a Beatrice with a funny face showed up; or all the patterns disappeared and something like a full moon casting pale blue light appeared; or the whole thing turned into purling electric waves like those you see after broadcasting on TV is over.

I saw God in the disorder.

Is it an exaggeration to say this? At least, I am certain that I thought a God with some shape or figure was cheap. The Jewish God is expressed with the four letters, Y, H, W, and H, but according to one of the ten commandments you can't chant "Yahweh" in vain, and you aren't allowed to make any image of him. In this regard I easily sympathize with the followers of Judaism who have no idols or icons, although I must say that my God is spelled WXY, which represents the female body, and is pronounced, "Gee, it stinks!" In telling Mr. Penman that I had conquered the game "The Divine Comedy," I said something like this:

"I thought that God and nature, God and disorder, were the same. God must be what is nothing and everything."

Mr. Penman showed a flicker of interest and said:

"In my boyhood I was taught that by a rabbi. Yes, from my childhood I thought it silly to revere Jesus as God. Seeing Jews insisting on The Law and trying to make its interpretations ever more complicated, that fellow made fun of them. This happened to please the dumb people. In personality Jesus was a man like Marx, Freud, or Einstein. Your game is made better than the original version of *The Divine Comedy*, if it educated you in such a way as to make you feel that."

"Monsieur Penman, does that mean Jesus criticized the followers of Judaism just as Nietzsche did Christians?"

"Well, that wasn't exactly the case, but you're more or less right. In the first place, Jesus had nothing to do with Christianity. He was no more than a man with a special constitution capable of wandering in a desert. Of course, he was smart and was of the sort that attracted people's interest. Just think. Which will people prefer—a scholar who sweats over the interpretation of each and every word and phrase of The Law, or a fellow who sums up in a word what's written in The Law? Those bastards who wrote the New Testament are to blame for everything."

Attracted by the way he said these things, I studied French with an intensity I hadn't had since the entrance examinations.

4

In April, in addition to the conquest of the game "The Divine Comedy," there was another event that made my health take a turn for the better: a vacation in Southern France. I managed sightseeing for the first time in my seventh month in France. There was no better rehabilitation than a ten-day tour of Nice, St. Paul, and Monaco. From the food on the plane, an airport bar, and a salon car made by Renault, to the curtains in a hotel room—everything made me lightheaded with the joy of discovering values that were plainly visible but not noticed till then. Does the strong sunlight give an aura to ordinary things? Quite aside from this, what this city mouse felt in visiting resort places was that most of the people there were children.

We—the five of us, that is: Mr. Penman; my brother; my brother's lover, Claudine; Mr. Penman's secretary, Marusha; and I—did things together during the day and separately during the night. My brother and Clau (he called her that) disappeared every other night, but the rest of us stayed in the mansion owned by Mr. Penman's friend (who was absent). In Nice, too, I was still an errand boy, and every morning I went out by bicycle to fetch croissants and whatever was needed for lunch that day. In cooking I offered almost all the ideas and skills, and the four others puttered about only when dishing things out. I made bouillabaisse and roasted fowl and, when so inclined, served thinly cut slices of raw flounder. Everyone recognized my talent as a cook.

Once, at Mr. Penman's request, I prepared a dinner consisting only of fried eggs, bread, and salad of green vegetables. It was the first night of Pesach. It appeared that the vacation had been planned to fall on Pesach. But with four heathens this Pesach ended up as a party to console Mr. Penman for his solitude.

"In the old days all the relatives used to get together and make a big celebration of it," Mr. Penman sighed as he rarely did. "Whenever this time of the year comes around, I regret I didn't have any children."

"How about adopting my brother?" said my brother in an insensitively jolly voice. "He tells me he'd like to prostrate himself before Judaism. He also respects you, Monsieur Penman."

Ever sensitive to French spoken with a Japanese accent, I bluntly expressed my view, "I don't like Judaism."

"I don't like it, either," Mr. Penman sneered with his nose, without changing his Ayatollah Khomeini expression. "If an anti-Semite riot took place in my heart, that would be because of the hard-headed followers of Judaism. Wherever I may be, I remain a Jew, but before that I'm a stranger. Just as Christ and Marx were strangers to their contemporary Jews."

"In my heart there's an anti-Japanese riot constantly," I said, borrowing Mr. Penman's expression. "At the same time, somewhere in my heart, I am an imperialist. I'd like to be freed from this aspect of being Japanese."

Mr. Penman suddenly exploded a husky laugh. "Théchien, you are some pacifist. Unfortunately, though, a half-hearted human being like you won't be taken seriously in any place. The best you can do is to try not to give unpleasant impressions to people, but to try to be loved. Neutralistic people arouse the most suspicion. Every human being alive in this world is somebody. For example, suppose you go to Israel and ask to be made a Jew. They'll tell you, first have a self-awareness as a Japanese. Only then can we become friends."

"But for the Jews," Claudine interjected, "heathen friends are also enemies, aren't they?" My brother put his mouth close to her ear and said, "Stop that."

"Discriminators are common to all countries. They are among the Jews and the French—though, if anything, there may be more of them among the French."

"I don't think it's a question of number. Everybody has a sense of discrimination, more or less. I find weird the notion that everybody should be friendly and equal. I prefer French women to Italian women. Japanese women are inferior to Chinese women. That's because in Japan there are few hybrids."

My brother had an absolutely low opinion of the Japanese. He hadn't come out of the Francomania of his student days, and as a seven-year settler in Paris, he affected the airs of a refugee. Still, his thinking wasn't too different from that of a Japanese "salaried man," for he said to me from time to time that he'd like to buy a good co-op within thirty minutes of commuting distance and settle down with Clau as soon as he could. Claudine was a clerk at the Museum of African and Oceanic Art. Intellectually Italian, sexually French—"If the reverse were the case, I'd have no complaint," my brother secretly grumbled, making me suspect that their marriage wouldn't go too well.

In the end, the four of us, excluding Mr. Penman, each came up with his own reason for celebration to keep Mr. Penman's company at Pesach. I celebrated the recovery from my illness, my brother counted the days since he met Clau and celebrated the 481st day since their encounter, and Marusha, the secretary, celebrated the health of her Polish father, who had defected.

We enjoyed cruising on the third and fourth day of our vacation, and on the fifth we went to the village of St. Paul. There we drank champagne watching Yves Montand playing *pétanque* with a large bet, and went to see a famous astrologer to have him tell us about our futures. It appeared that I was to encounter in the near future a big incident which might greatly change my life. When I asked whether the incident was going to be good or bad for me, I was told, "If you get deeper into it, you might run into some danger, but it's going to be good on the whole." As for Mr. Penman, he was told, "If you pay attention to your health and value your friends, you can get through the year without any problem. Two years from now, the inclination of your star will improve."

During the second half of our vacation, my brother and Clau disappeared, Marusha went to visit a friend, and Mr. Penman and I frequented a casino in Monaco. To return to Japan I had to make enough money for the airfare on my own, but the wage Mr. Penman's company paid me was 1,500 francs (less than ¥40,000) a month, not much more than a student loan. Unless I hit the jackpot at a casino, I would be forced to stay in Paris another six months.

However, whereas a casino is gentle to those who mean to play with coincidences in a healthy fashion, and gives some aid to those who attempt to find some inevitability in coincidences, it remains absolutely cold to those with a greedy bent who'd rush to a gold mine if they heard of one. I clung to roulette for five hours and lost 2,000 francs. Mr. Penman, who's shrewd in everything, continued to bet on zero for an hour and, when he happened to bet 1,000 francs, he won and triumphantly left, after giving me and the dealer 500 francs each.

On the last night of our vacation, Mr. Penman invited the four of us to a restaurant at the top of Ez. Ez is known to be the place where Nietzsche thought up and penned *Thus Spake Zarathustra*. Because there also was "Nietzsche's promenade," I offered this impression:

"The mountain where Zarathustra is said to have shut himself up may turn out to be as resorty as this, and when he got tired of writing, he may occasionally have come down to eat some tortoise soup, don't you think?"

Mr. Penman sniffed as usual and said: "There are no books on mountains and in deserts, are there? That's what's important. How to read nature and one's own body—that is the basis of philosophy. In this regard ancient Greeks were healthy. In contrast, we Jews have been unhealthy since the olden days. You see, even our daily life is tightly bound up by the Bible, Talmud, and Halakah. The body of a Jew is fettered with words. When you think of it, it may be we Jews who need a philosopher like Nietzsche—though he's German, and no Jew would read him seriously."

My brother, who showed great reluctance to serve as an interpreter, pleaded, "Would you refrain from talking any more about such complicated things?" But by then I could understand most of what Mr. Penman said without interpretation.

I suspect that Mr. Penman recognized me as his disciple and felt joy in imbuing me with his thoughts. The vacation in Southern France was meant to be a lesson to restore my consciousness to my body, as well as a stage for Mr. Penman to talk about his philosophy.

5

After returning to Paris I offered to translate Mr. Penman's writings into Japanese. I explained that, having conquered "The Divine Comedy," I wanted to have some work for times when I had nothing to do. His response wasn't too good, however.

"A publisher has been found for the records of the work we've done at Refugee Stability. But your brother is doing the translation into Japanese. I published my writings in the past, but for my own reasons I destroyed all of them. I'm writing a memoir now. When I've completed it, I'll give you a copy, too."

So I began to read some of the more notable titles I found in Mr. Penman's library, but I gave up on every one of them and left them unfinished. This was because as Japan's "Golden Week"[2] arrived I was forced to work as a guide for hordes of tourists from Japan. I received training under my brother for only three days and rushed tourist groups around the Louvre, Montmartre, the Pompidou Center, and the Garden of the Tuileries. This work gave me a good opportunity to sightsee Paris in a serious fashion. Pressed by the necessity, I learned to speak freely the kind of French needed for conducting daily business. When one of the tourists asked me to introduce him to a prostitute without AIDS, I gave him the telephone number of my brother's apartment, saying that he was a pimp specializing in Japanese.

While my brother and I were kept extremely busy with the guide work, Mr. Penman was working on two cases. One of them had to do with his acting as an agent for a French-Africaner family of the Republic of South Africa who'd decided to live in Paris. The other was finding work for an immigrant worker fresh from Portugal. When I asked him about the details of the work involved in these cases, Mr. Penman said, "So you want to steal the know-how of my work?" But he then followed the remark with a vivid explanation of the negotiations at the Immigration Office of the Ministry of Foreign Affairs and how to concoct the positions and arguments best suited for immigration. I was interested in the fees he would get, but he didn't give precise answers, making me guess the amounts by saying, "My fees are such that they don't make the defectors feel gratitude to me, but they don't make them hate me, either."

Until June the tour-guide work kept me busy; as a result, I was able to build a windfall fortune (though the amount was about the same as what Mr. Penman made at the casino). That was enough for me to get out of Paris. When I thought hard about it, though, I had by then acquired more detailed knowledge about the geography of Paris than that of Tokyo, and from the viewpoint of my closeness to my teacher and the range of friends and acquaintances I'd developed, it was more advantageous to stay on in Paris. My life in Tokyo was quite sequestered, as it was limited to my apartment, the hospital, and about three friends.

2. A week from the end of April to early May when national holidays occur every other day.

But the moment I decided to stay on in Paris for one more year or so, my brother meddled. For a long time he'd had the bad habit of using his younger brother like a possession of his own.

"You've cured your illness by coming to Paris, haven't you? I wouldn't say that was thanks to me, but you would give me some credit, too, wouldn't you? I have a special favor to ask. Will you do it for me?"

I said, "No," in anticipation of what was to come.

"Hey, I haven't said anything yet. It's a simple thing. All you do is go back to Tokyo. All I ask you to do is something you can do in two hours. I've decided to marry Clau. We'll have a wedding here in August. When I told this to Mom, she began to insist that we have the wedding ceremony in Tokyo. But Clau's parents are stubborn, too. They say lovers in Paris ought to live in Paris and get married in Paris. To get out of this bind, we've decided to go to Japan on a honeymoon around September and, to convince Mom, to have a wedding ceremony in Tokyo, too. Then we'll return to France on another honeymoon. An excellent plan, isn't it? So, I'd like you to return to Tokyo ahead of me and pick the places for the wedding and the party that follows, and make other arrangements. You mail the invitations, too. You'll do that, won't you? If you don't, I'll be in trouble. There are things you've got to do, like making reservations and figuring out the costs. Unless I'm nice to Pop and Mom, I can't expect them to give me any financial aid."

He tried to persuade me twice, three times. Finally I had to agree, though on condition that he give me round-trip airfare. When I told this to Mr. Penman, he sneered through his nose three times (unlike the usual two) and muttered—I couldn't tell whether it was a monologue or he was talking to me:

"A round-trip means you plan to come back here. You better live wherever you want to. There's no reason you shouldn't use that freedom."

After a while he asked how old I was. When he learned I was twenty-five, he did some counting on his fingers.

"You could have been my child when I was forty-one," he said. "You're still young. You can still become anything. I can't be any other thing than a Jew. It's too late now. The next time I'm reborn, I'd like to be Japanese."

Mr. Penman sank deeply into his sofa and turned his attention to the portrait of some rabbi hung on the wall.

6

On the day I left Paris, Mr. Penman handed me an envelope, telling me to translate it on the plane. Written in it were words of blessing that also whipped me.

To My Dear Son, Théchien,

You don't seem to have any consciousness other than curiosity. One can draw your portrait by simply rubbing this morning's newspaper on a pure-white wall. Faded stains of ink—that is all of you. There's nothing else. You are wonderfully zero. I envy you so. After all, you can always begin from zero. Yes, if equipped with curiosity, you can discard conventional morality, jealousies, and vengeful sentiments for something, simple comedies and faith in wooden idols, let alone joys, angers, sorrows, and pleasures that merely scatter noises about. There's nothing to worry. They are like germs and parasites, sometimes making human beings ferment, sometimes making them rot. Usually we evaluate a human being by the degree of his fermentation or rotting and judge who he is. But you are an exception. Because curiosity constantly pulls you outside yourself, you can't become anybody forever. The only certain thing is that you have a special constitution whose identity can't be ascertained. A single mistake, and you'll be an idiot; at best, a callow fellow or a bankrupt personality. You can continue to live only by getting food through other people's compassion or by being treated nicely by some teacher who's eager to teach you personal virtues, morality, and how to make it in the world. Fortunately, you are no fool. If things work out, you may become a man surpassing human beings. Don't misunderstand. By "a man surpassing human beings," mind you, I don't mean a superman. All I mean is that your special constitution can't be understood by a traditional view of human beings. If you have value beyond that, make it on your own as you like.

Your old disciple,
LUDWIG PENMAN

I wanted to think that this letter expressed the essence of Mr. Penman's thought. With the specimen called Théchien before him, he must have wondered how to explain it. Just as Mr. Penman was a stranger to me, I must have been the Sphinx's riddle to him. No game requires you more to use your head than an encounter with something whose identity can't be explained. In this regard, my encounter with him was a philosophical event.

At each person's nerve center swirls his own thinking circuit. The swirl is generated by group environments such as society, race, and nation, and the power relations among the morals, disciplines, education, and laws that are forced upon them; it is then individualized through the complex layering of information and knowledge that pours into it through mass media. A true teacher must be someone who pulls out to an airy spot the thinking circuit that tends to burrow into someplace closed. At the same time he must be someone who can distinguish things that are common to his own in his disciple's thinking circuit from things that are different from his.

In my true teacher Mr. Penman's letter, I sensed even a touch of jealousy for my youth, my half-heartedness, and my nonpersonality. I continued to marvel at the wonderful way he'd aged.

7

When I had finished the chores my brother asked me to do and was planning the time to return to Paris, I had a telephone call from my brother. He liked to throw out conventional jokes in serious guises. But this time he didn't sound like his usual self in reporting an incident: "Monsieur Penman was beaten up by a young Jew and has ended up in a hospital!"

He continued, crushing any opportunity for me to ask a question.

"I learned about the circumstances from the police today. It appears that Monsieur Penman is no Jew. That his youth was ruined by the Nazis and that he missed the chance to live his youth because of his imprisonment in Russian concentration camps were both lies, it seems. What are you going to do? He was from a bourgeois Polish family, and in the confusion right after the war decided to pretend to be Jewish. 'Shit, how can a fellow who isn't a Jew pretend to be one?' thought some poor Zionist of the religious sect who got hold of the information, it seems, and he resorted to a radical measure."

"Is Mr. Penman all right?"

"I hear he broke his collarbone. But he can leave the hospital in a week. I can't tell you how busy I am."

"Listen, is it a fact that Mr. Penman isn't a Jew? I can't believe it."

"You may believe it. Penman himself has confessed it. 'I'm not a Jew, but have become one by making efforts,' is what he said. In his business he can make more money and get more work by being a Jew than by being a Pole. Jews are said to be good businessmen, but Monsieur Penman, who took advantage of that, is an actor one cut above. Are you shocked?"

I think I was considerably shocked, for I suffered acute aphasia.

"But he's great, don't you think? To become Jewish he must have spent a considerable amount of time studying Yiddish and various customs. He may have been in Israel as a French spy. If he was, his current business must be a cinch for him. But the world is complicated, isn't it? There are a disgusting number of things *you* can't understand with your head. By the way, about our wedding in Tokyo, I heard you worked out everything all right. You saved me. At this end it's business as usual. Whether Monsieur Penman is Jewish or Polish has nothing to do with us for now. Everything will remain unchanged, as it has been. Look, we'll see you in Tokyo in September. Stay well. Write a letter to Monsieur Penman."

My humble Shangri-La illuminated by the Mediterranean sun and the dazzling light of the Empyrean Heaven was now surrounded by a desert. In this desert that suddenly opened up before my eyes lived Mr. Penman. Surely a resident of the same Shangri-La with me until yesterday, he had now left for the desert with new riddles.

I hesitated to step into this desert. Could I possibly bear the hell of translating myself into a Jew? At least at that moment I didn't want to think about anything like that.

Translated by Hiroaki Sato

GROWING UP
ELSEWHERE

Global Cultures are replete with stories of children who are born into their parents' cultural passage and must, as an extra burden and challenge to the usual human complexities of "developmental lines," become bicultural or poly-cultural negotiators—if they can, if their circumstances permit such an undertaking. I have chosen to glance at the multitude of issues involved in growing up elsewhere through three Spanish stories—one by a Peruvian, one by a Puerto Rican, one by a Uruguayan. To indicate the timelessness of this phenomenon, I selected one story—the Puerto Rican tale—written in the 1950s; the other two are from the 1980s, both by writers born during World War II. The younger writers have both been literature professors, and their stories are textured with literary references and literary devices. Pedro Juan Soto, on the other hand, cultivated the simple, pen-and-ink sketch style of social realism, the ironic, biting but sad style that is still so brilliantly in use by many of Latin America's political activist writers, like Sergio Ramirez, Nicaragua's former vice president.

The Peruvian **JULIO ORTEGA**, born in 1942, currently teaches Latin American literature at Brown University. He is a prolific essayist, and three books have also appeared in English, *Latin America in Its Literature* (1980), *Poetics of Change* (1984), and *Garcia Marquez and the Powers of Fiction* (1988). In addition to many volumes of literary criticism in Spanish, he has published the short story collection *Diario imaginario* (1988), where the story presented here first appeared. "Las Papas" is built upon a metaphor: Potatoes originated in Peru, like the author, and they have adapted well to life elsewhere—so well that they seem Irish to some, simply Idaho to others. Potatoes suggest, as Ortega himself noted in a commentary on this story, "cultural preservation in exile. . . . Cooking is not a melting pot if you care for flavors." As most transplanted people know, this cultural cooking lesson has to be communicated carefully to children, who grow up elsewhere without direct roots in the home culture that their parents remember so vividly.

PEDRO JUAN SOTO, novelist and playwright born in 1928, put children at the center of many of the short stories he wrote in the 1950s, particularly the stories, like "The Innocents," collected later in *Spiks* (Monthly Review Press, 1973). When Soto was a child growing up in Puerto Rico, he was taught in English because American citizenship had been imposed on the islanders in 1916. When he was an adolescent, he experienced the militant nationalist response to American imperialism; and as a young man he worked marginal jobs in New York before being drafted for the Korean War. His literary cohort, known as the Generation of 1940, used the short story—when in Spanish using the quite distinctive syncretistic Caribbean-Castilian-African-Puerto Rican Spanish—as their main medium for brilliantly capturing the contradictions between life in Americanized Puerto Rico and life in Spanish Harlem. Like so many of the writers represented in this anthology, they used domestic scenes, focusing on women and children, to tell political tales. In "The Innocents," subtly, indirectly, we receive the message that when a Puerto Rican family moves from the villages of the island into the cramped poverty of upper Manhattan, their ability to live humanely—to care for a child who has been brain damaged in an accident—is threatened. Innocents are slaughtered. Themes like this have been reworked by Pedro Juan Soto's literary heirs ever since, and they can be found, for example, in the present burgeoning literature by Puerto Rican women, in the fictions collected in *Reclaiming Medusa: Short Stories by Contemporary Puerto Rican Women* (Spinsters/aunt lute, 1988), and in the novels of the superbly talented Nicholasa Mohr (see *Nilda*, Arte Publico Press, 1973, a classic story of childhood in Spanish Harlem).

Uruguayan literature after World War II was dominated by a cohort known as the Generation of 1945, which, like the Puerto Ricans, cultivated the short story for talking about modern urban life—life mostly in Montevideo where a third of Uruguay's population was concentrated. The military government that came to power in 1973 clamped down on the fervent and rich Montevidean culture, and many of the Generation of 1945 went into exile. This is the background for **CHRISTINA PERI ROSSI**'s story, first published in 1985 in Spain where the author was living in exile—the literary daughter of a generation in exile. Peri Rossi was born in 1941 and was a professor of literature when she was expelled from the country in 1972 and ended up making her living as a journalist in Barcelona. In her story, she imagines a third generation, the next one, represented by a girl who was "born under the sign of resistance and endurance," daughter of a dreamy professor and an urban guerrilla mother who leaves her to make the revolution. The child is an organizer, a parent to her father, like so many children of immigrants and exiles, a girl of tough exterior, of tenacity and cunning—and of great sadness. In addition to seven collections of short stories, Peri Rossi has written three novels. The second, the only one available in English, *The Ship of Fools* (Readers International, 1989), has won her a reputation in Europe as one of the leading younger feminist literary figures. The story presented here appeared in an extraordinary collection, *You Can't Drown the Fire: Latin American Women Writing in Exile* (Cleis Press, 1988).

Las Papas

Julio Ortega

HE TURNED on the faucet of the kitchen sink and washed off the knife. As he felt the splashing water, he looked up through the front window and saw the September wind shaking the tender shoots of the trees on his street, the first hint of fall.

He quickly washed the potatoes one by one. Although their coloring was light and serene, they were large and heavy. When he started to peel them, slowly, using the knife precisely and carefully, the child came into the kitchen.

"What are you going to cook?" he asked. He stood there waiting for an answer.

"Chicken cacciatore," the man answered, but the child didn't believe him. He was only six, but he seemed capable of objectively discerning between one chicken recipe and another.

"Wait and see," he promised.

"Is it going to have onions in it?" asked the child.

"Very few," he said.

The child left the kitchen unconvinced.

He finished peeling the potatoes and started to slice them. Through the window he saw the growing brightness of midday. That strong light seemed to paralyze the brilliant foliage on the trees. The inside of the potatoes had the same clean whiteness, and the knife penetrated it, as if slicing through soft clay.

Then he rinsed the onions and cut into them, chopping them up. He glanced at the recipe again and looked for seasonings in the pantry. The child came back in.

"Chicken is really boring," the child said, almost in protest.

"Not this recipe," he said. "It'll be great. You'll see."

"Put a lot of stuff in it," the child recommended.

"It's going to have oregano, pepper, and even some sugar," he said.

The child smiled, approvingly.

He dried the potato slices. The pulp was crisp, almost too white, more like an apple, perhaps. Where did these potatoes come from? Wyoming or Idaho, probably. The potatoes from his country, on the other hand, were grittier, with a heavy flavor of the land. There were dark ones, almost royal purple like fruit, and delicate yellow ones, like the yolk of an egg. They say there used to be more than a thousand varieties of potato. Many of them have disappeared forever.

The ones that were lost, had they been less firmly rooted in the soil? Were they more delicate varieties? Maybe they disappeared when control of the cultivated lands was deteriorating. Some people say, and it's probably true, that the loss of even one domesticated plant makes the world a little poorer, as does the destruction of a work of art in a city plundered by invaders. If a history of the lost varieties were written it might prove that no one would ever have gone hungry.

Boiled, baked, fried, or stewed: the ways of cooking potatoes were a long story in themselves. He remembered what his mother had told him as a child: at harvest time, the largest potatoes would be roasted for everybody, and, in the fire, they would open up—just like flowers. That potato was probably one of the lost varieties, the kind that turned into flowers in the flames.

Are potatoes harvested at night in the moonlight? He was surprised how little he knew about something that came from his own country. As he thought about it, he believed *harvest* wasn't even the correct term. *Gathering? Digging?* What do you call this harvest from under the earth?

For a long time he had avoided eating them. Even their name seemed unpleasant to him, *papas*. A sign of the provinces, one more shred of evidence of the meager resources, of underdevelopment—a potato lacked protein and was loaded with carbohydrates. French-fried potatoes seemed more tolerable to him: they were, somehow, in a more neutralized condition.

At first, when he began to care for the child all by himself, he tried to simplify the ordeal of meals by going out to the corner restaurant. But he soon found that if he tried to cook something it passed the time, and he also amused himself with the child's curiosity.

He picked up the cut slices. There wasn't much more to discover in them. It wasn't necessary to expect anything more of them than the density they already possessed, a crude cleanliness that was the earth's flavor. But that same sense transformed them right there in his hands, a secret flowering, uncovered by him in the kitchen. It was as if he discovered one of the lost varieties of the Andean potato: the one that belonged to him, wondering, at noon.

When the chicken began to fry in the skillet, the boy returned, attracted by its aroma. The man was in the midst of making the salad.

"Where's this food come from?" the child asked, realizing it was a different recipe.

"Peru," he replied.

"Not Italy?" said the child, surprised.

"I'm cooking another recipe now," he explained. "Potatoes come from Peru. You know that, right?"

"Yeah, but I forgot it."

"They're really good, and there are all kinds and flavors. Remember mangoes? You really used to like them when we went to see your grandparents."

"I don't remember them either. I only remember the lion in the zoo."

"You don't remember the tree in Olivar Park?"

"Uh-huh. I remember that."

"We're going back there next summer, to visit the whole family."

"What if there's an earthquake?"

The boy went for his Spanish reader and sat down at the kitchen table. He read the resonant names out loud, names that were also like an unfinished history, and the man had to go over to him every once in a while to help explain one thing or another.

He tasted the sauce for the amount of salt, then added a bit of tarragon, whose intense perfume was delightful, and a bit of marjoram, a sweeter aroma.

He noticed how, outside, the light trapped by a tree slipped out from the blackened greenness of the leaves, now spilling onto the grass on the hill where their apartment house stood. The grass, all lit up, became an oblique field, a slope of tame fire seen from the window.

He looked at the child, stuck on a page in his book; he looked at the calm, repeated blue of the sky; and he looked at the leaves of lettuce in his hands, leaves that crackled as they broke off and opened up like tender shoots, beside the faucet of running water.

As if it suddenly came back to him, he understood that he must have been six or seven when his father, probably forty years old, as he was now, used to cook at home on Sundays. His father was always in a good mood as he cooked, boasting beforehand about how good the Chinese recipes were that he had learned in a remote hacienda in Peru. Maybe his father had made these meals for him, in this always incomplete past, to celebrate the meeting of father and son.

Unfamiliar anxiety, like a question without a subject, grew in him as he understood that he had never properly acknowledged his father's gesture; he hadn't even understood it. Actually, he had rejected his father's cooking one time, saying that it was too spicy. He must have been about fifteen then, a recent convert devoutly practicing the religion of natural foods, when he left the table with the plate of fish in his hands. He went out to the kitchen to turn on the faucet and quickly washed away the flesh boiled in soy sauce and ginger. His mother came to the kitchen and scolded him for what he had just done, a seemingly harmless act, but from then on an irreparable one. He returned to the table in silence, sullen, but his father didn't appear to be offended. Or did he suspect that one day his son's meal would be refused by his own son when he served it?

The emotion could still wound him, but it could also make him laugh. There was a kind of irony in this repeating to a large extent his father's gestures as he concocted an unusual flavor in the kitchen. However, like a sigh that only acquires some meaning by turning upon itself, he discovered a symmetry in the repetitions, a symmetry that revealed the agony of emotions not easily understood.

Just like animals that feed their young, we feed ourselves with a promise that food will taste good, he said to himself. We prepare a recipe with painstaking detail so that our children will recognize us in a complete history of flavor.

He must have muttered this out loud because the child looked up.

"What?" he said, "Italian?"

"Peruvian," he corrected. "With a taste of the mountains, a mixture of Indian, Chinese, and Spanish."

The child laughed, as if he'd heard a private joke in the sound of the words.

"When we go to Lima, I'll take you around to the restaurants," he promised.

The child broke into laughter again.

"It tastes good," said the child.

"It tastes better than yesterday's," the man said.

He poured some orange juice. The boy kneeled in the chair and ate a bit of everything. He ate more out of curiosity than appetite.

He felt once again that brief defenselessness that accompanies the act of eating one's own cooking. Behind that flavor, he knew, lurked the raw materials, the separate foods cooked to render them neutral, a secret known only to the cook, who combined ingredients and proportions until something different was presented to eyes and mouth. This culinary act could be an adventure, a hunting foray. And the pleasure of creating a transformation must be shared, a kind of brief festival as the eaters decipher the flavors, knowing that an illusion has taken place.

Later, he looked for a potato in the pantry and he held it up against the unfiltered light in the window. It was large, and it fit perfectly in his barely closed hand. He was not surprised that the misshapen form of this swollen tuber adapted to the contour of his hand; he knew the potato adapted to different lands, true to its own internal form, as if it occupied stolen space. The entire history of his people was here, he said to himself, surviving a territory overrun and pillaged several times, growing in marginal spaces, under siege and waiting.

He left the apartment, went down the stairs and over to the tree on the hillock. It was a perfect day, as if the entire history of daytime were before him. The grass was ablaze, standing for all the grass he had ever seen. With both hands, he dug, and the earth opened up to him, cold. He placed the potato there, and he covered it up quickly. Feeling slightly embarrassed, he looked around. He went back up the stairs, wiping his hands, almost running.

The boy was standing at the balcony, waiting for him; he had seen it all.

"A tree's going to grow there!" said the boy, alarmed.

"No," he said soothingly, "potatoes aren't trees. If it grows, it will grow under the ground."

The child didn't seem to understand everything, but then suddenly he laughed.

"Nobody will even know it's there," he said, excited by such complicity with his father.

Translated by Regina Harrison

The Innocents

Pedro Juan Soto

to climb up to the sun on that cloud with the pigeons without horses without women and not to have to smell the junk burning in the lot with no one to make fun of me

Dressed in a suit that had been made and sold to contain some other man, he could see from the window the pigeons fluttering about the eaves of the house opposite.

or with doors and windows always open to have wings

He began to flap his hands and coo like the pigeons when he heard a voice behind him.

"Baby, baby."

The woman, dried up by age, was seated at the table, underneath which stood the flimsy suitcase, a rope its only lock; she looked at him with her bright eyes, spread out over the chair like a hungry, abandoned cat.

"Bread," he said.

Her hands on the table, the woman pushed back her chair and went to the cupboard. She took out some bread that was lying unwrapped upon boxes of rice and gave it to the man, who was still gesticulating and mouthing sounds.

to be a pigeon

"Stop your noise, Pipe."

He crumbled the piece of bread on the windowsill, paying no attention to her.

"Stop your noise, baby."

Some men playing dominoes under the awning of the grocery store stared up at them.

He left off moving his tongue from side to side in his mouth.

with no one to make fun of me

"Walk in the square," he said.

"All right, Hortensia is coming now to take you for a walk."

"In the square."

"No, not in the square. They took it away. It flew away."

He pouted. His attention shifted again to the fluttering pigeons.

no more square

"It wasn't the pigeons," she said. "It was the evil one, the devil."

"Oh."

"Must ask Papa God to bring back the square."

"Papa God," he said, gazing upward, "bring back the square and the river . . ."

"No, no. Without opening your mouth," she said. "Kneel down and talk to Papa God without opening your mouth."

He knelt by the windowsill, joined his hands and stared out over the flat roofs.

I want to be a pigeon

She looked down at the men's Saturday morning idleness and the bustle of the women going to and from market.

Slowly, heavily, but erect, as if balancing a bundle on her head, she went into the room where, in front of the mirror, her daughter was removing hairpins from her hair and piling them on the dresser.

"Don't take him today, Hortensia."

The younger woman glanced at her out of the corner of her eye.

"Don't start that again, Mama. Nothing'll happen to him. They'll take good care of him and it won't cost us a cent."

Freed of its pins, her hair formed a black mass about her ears.

"But I know how to take care of him. He's my son. Who knows better than I?"

Hortensia, in the mirror, studied the small, lean figure.

"You're old, Mama."

In the mirror, one fleshless hand was raised.

"I'm not dead yet. I can still look after him."

"That's not the point."

The curls remained stubbornly tight, in spite of her efforts to loosen them with a comb.

"Pipe is innocent," the mother said, her words drawn from a sea of pity. "He's a baby."

Hortensia threw down the comb. She took a pencil from the purse that lay open on the dresser and began to darken her scanty eyebrows.

"There's no cure for that," she said to the mirror. "You know it. So the best thing . . ."

"In Puerto Rico this wouldn't have happened."

"In Puerto Rico things were different," said Hortensia over her shoulder. "People knew him. He could go out because people knew him. But in New York people can't be bothered and they don't know their neighbors. Life is hard. The years go by while I sew my life away and I'm still not married."

As she looked for her lipstick, she saw in the mirror her mother's despondent face.

"But that's not the reason either. He'll be better taken care of there."

"That's what you say," her mother replied.

Hortensia tossed eyebrow pencil, lipstick, and comb into her purse and snapped it shut. She turned around—a thin blouse, greasy lips, blackened eyebrows, tight curls.

"After a year here, we deserve something better."

"He's not to blame for what happens to us."

"But if he stays here he will be. Take it from me."

She darted to her mother, grasped her arm, and pushed up her sleeve to the elbow. On the thin corded flesh was a purple bruise.

"He's already raised a hand to you, and I'm never easy in my mind at the factory thinking what might be happening to you and to him. And if this has already happened . . ."

"He didn't mean to," the mother said, pulling down her sleeve and staring at the floor, at the same time twisting her arm to make Hortensia let go.

"He didn't mean to when he had you by the neck? If I hadn't grabbed the bottle, God knows what would have happened. There's no man here to stand up to him, and I'm worn out, Mama, and you're scared to death of him."

"He's a baby," the mother said in her gentle voice, withdrawing into herself like a snail.

Hortensia half-closed her eyes.

"Don't give me that. I'm young and I have my life before me, but he hasn't. You are worn out and if he went away you could live out the rest of your days in peace and you know it but you don't dare admit it because you think it's wrong but I'll say it for you *you're worn out* and that's why you signed the papers because you know they'll take better care of him in that place and then you can sit down and watch the people go by in the street and whenever you take the notion you can get up and go out and walk around like the rest but you'd rather think it's a crime and I'm the criminal so you can go on being the long-suffering mother and *you have been a long-suffering mother* no one can take that away from you but you've got to think of yourself and of me. What if the horse knocked him down when he was ten years old . . ."

The mother walked rapidly away, as if she were being pushed, as if the room itself were blowing her out, while Hortensia went on, ". . . and for the other twenty he's lived knocked down like that . . ."

And she turned to watch her mother go, not following, leaning her weight on the dresser upon which her fists beat out a rhythm for what was almost a scream: ". . . we've had to live all those years with him."

And in the mirror she could see the hysterical carnival mask that was her face.

and there's no roosters and there's no dogs and there's no bell and there's no wind off the river and there's no buzzer from the movie house and the sun doesn't come in here and I don't like it

"All right," the mother said, bending over to brush the crumbs off the windowsill. Below in the street, the boys were hitting a rubber ball and chasing it.

and the cold sleeps sits walks with you in here and I don't like it

"All right, baby, all right. Say amen."

"Amen."

She helped him to his feet and put his hat in his hand, for she saw that Hortensia was coming toward them, serious; her eyes red.

"Let's go, Pipe. Give Mama a kiss."

She put her purse on the table and bent over to pick up the suitcase. The mother threw herself around his neck—her hands like pincers—and kissed his burned hazelnut of a face, running her fingers over the skin she had shaved that morning.

"Let's go," Hortensia said, picking up purse and suitcase.

He pulled away from his mother's arms and walked toward the door, swinging the hand that carried his hat.

"Baby, put your hat on," his mother said, and blinked lest he see her tears.

Turning, he placed on his vaseline-coated hair that which on account of its smallness looked like a toy trying to compensate for the waste of cloth in the suit.

"No, he better leave it here," Hortensia said.

Pipe pouted. The mother kept her eyes fixed on Hortensia, her jaw trembling.

"All right," Hortensia said, "carry it in your hand."

Again he walked toward the door, the mother following, barely restraining herself from reaching out to him.

Hortensia barred the way. "Mama, they'll take care of him."

"Don't let them mistreat . . ."

"No. There are doctors. And you . . . every two weeks. I'll take you."

They were both making an effort to keep their voices steady.

"Go lay down, Mama."

"Tell him to stay . . . not to make any noise and to eat everything."

"Yes."

Hortensia opened the door and looked out to see if Pipe had waited on the landing. He was amusing himself by spitting over the stair rail and watching his saliva fall.

"I'll be back early, Mama."

The mother stood by the chair that was now one too many, trying to catch a glimpse of her son through the body that blocked the doorway.

"Go lay down, Mama."

Not answering, her hands clasped, she stayed rigid till chest and shoulders were shaken by a spasm, and, hiccuping, she began softly to weep.

Slamming the door, Hortensia ran downstairs with Pipe as fast as she could. Faced with the immense clarity of June midday, she longed for hurricanes, eclipses, blizzards.

Translated by Barbara Howes with the author

The Influence of Edgar A. Poe in the Poetry of Raimundo Arias

Christina Peri Rossi

I'VE BEHAVED, I swear it," said her father, looking straight at her. His eyes were the clear blue eyes of a small child. Later in life eyes darken. Alicia had observed that characteristic of eyes. Something in life cast shadows on them. They lost that color of a lake where geese can contemplate their own reflection. The quiet waters shook: internal currents coming from afar, from other horizons, from overseas, changed the rhythm and tonality of eyes. Then, children were no longer children, turned into men of dark eyes, men with no eyes to mirror anything. It became impossible to look inside as she could still do with her father's eyes. She liked to lean out on those waters. She could see sand dunes, marine animals, stones, bright spaces and the serene yet disturbing lunar geography of the sea. If he stopped being a child she could not look into his eyes and see the dangling Hippocampus navigating slowly, or the white-flowered plant with the golden stalk. She blew on the plant and the stalk moved. Her father closed his eyes.

"You've come back late," she said in her clear soprano voice, "thirty-five minutes, five seconds late. As a punishment: no dessert tonight." She didn't look at him to avoid watching those waters tremble.

"But, Alicia," he defended himself, "the traffic was very bad, there were a lot of people walking in the opposite direction, so many people that it was hard to walk two steps at a time. One had to carefully land on one foot, taking advantage of every little free spot, and keep the other foot in the air. This seems easy, I know it seems easy to you because you did not have to walk through that avenue this afternoon selling 'Wonder Soap: three bars for the price of one, they freshen up your life' but I assure you, it is a very difficult operation. Sometimes the foot suspended in the air got tired of being in that position. Remember, also, that a briefcase full of soap bars is very heavy. I tried to distract myself, to think about other things while I was holding my foot in the air, waiting for a small strip of blank sidewalk that I could use. One time I had a chance to finally put my foot on the ground but a man walking by me made an effort, moved his enormous square foot forward and reached the tile before I did."

"You should have moved him aside," the girl severely commented. Her father lowered his eyes. The soap briefcase was nearby; it was black. On its shiny leather a sign read: "Wonder Ltd. makes life more pleasant."

"It wouldn't have been easy," he defended himself. "That man was big, a stone lump; he was marching ahead decisively and quickly, ferociously propelled forward; he could have walked over me, smashing me as you smash an ant when you walk, inadvertently, with total indifference. That man and all the others were going somewhere, implacably, in a hurry." They had arrived in that country six months earlier but they had not found out yet the direction in which one was supposed to run. The father wasn't even sure that it was quite correct to run. "Where were they running?" asked Alicia with curiosity. "I don't know," he confessed. He tried furtively to light a cigarette, but she saw.

"Four," she brutally sentenced. "You have only one left."

"Three, I believe," he attempted to trick her. "If you remember, the one this morning I shared with you, and besides I couldn't enjoy it because I was in a hurry."

"Four," she repeated from her chair. Her blue dress and her long hair falling down her back made her resemble her mother. Her mother had never had a blue dress and always wore her hair short. According to the father those differences stressed the resemblance. Maybe the girl really looked like her mother's sister, but he wasn't quite sure. He had met her by coincidence at the supermarket; they had not been able to talk much because both were in a hurry. He had to feed the girl and write a paper on the influence of Edgar A. Poe on the poetry of a very famous writer nobody knew because he had never been out of his non-European country; she had to go immediately back to the hiding place of a guerrilla group for whom she was acting as a cover. She was a very nice young lady—he would never forget her red hair. It was surely a wig to better conceal her identity. He thought he would have liked enormously to show her his paper on the influence of Edgar A. Poe on the poetry of Raimundo Arias, even when she did not have time for those things; she looked at him with intelligence, intelligence devoured by passion, according to an expression of Raimundo Arias who, he was positive, had never met her yet he had intuited her.

She thought it was a pity that he was a bourgeois intellectual as her sister had said before abandoning him: he looked to be a tender and intelligent man.

In any case, he would never forget the red or blue or green or yellow hair of that young woman. "I should have gotten to know my wife's sister better," he reproached himself, but everybody was in a hurry: One had to make revolution, dinner, stand in line to buy bread, flour, rice, beans, oil, kerosene; one had also to run away from the assaults of the army, to take care of the little girl, product of a condom of the worst quality.

Besides he was going to write a novel about the revolution; sometimes the novel got ahead of the revolution, sometimes the revolution ran so fast that it managed to get ahead of the novel, and meanwhile, his wife had left him—she surpassed both the revolution and the novel; the girl stayed with him. They had reached an agreement; it was not convenient to enter the guerrilla movement with a very small girl so, to hide the truth from everybody, he said that his wife had run away with another man, to Czechoslovakia.

"I should have gotten to know my sister's husband better," she had thought, but there wasn't enough time; she had to work, she had to stand in line to buy milk, bread, flour, rice, beans, oil, kerosene, she had to make revolution and, besides, sometimes she got sleepy.

"How many soap bars have you sold today?" asked Alicia, without moving from her seat in front of a small wooden table covered with colorful stones and a crystal giraffe. That was all that they had been able to rescue in their escape, when they had to leave their country because he had been accused of professing the Marxist-Leninst faith and of writing articles that were real anthems attempting to undermine the fatherland and the prestige of national institutions. Then, he had taken his daughter's hand with great dignity.

"I'm not an object to be carried in your arms," she had said. He had picked up a few papers, some clothes, and they had boarded the ship, under police control.

"Why don't we kill him now?" one military corporal had asked another. "We'll say, as always, that he died while trying to run away from the forces of order."

"Nobody is waiting for us," said the girl once they had arrived.

"Dear daughter," he had answered, "I'm not a soccer player." Alicia had looked at her father's extremely thin legs in the only pair of slacks that he owned. She thought as a daughter she was not very lucky. Her father wasn't a soccer player, nor was he a ship owner, nor a well known singer. (The only song she had heard him sing was "A desalambrar,"[1] and he was always out of tune; she sounded better singing the "Do tremble tyrants . . ." verse of the national anthem, which had been banned by the government because of its subversive character.) She wasn't very lucky indeed; her father was not the owner of a corporation, or a film star. Resignation. Children do not choose their parents but parents get to choose their children: "I'll take this one, Alicia; I won't take this one, abortion, no name."

"I've sold twenty-six, plus one that I gave an old lady, twenty-seven.

---

1. A very popular song about revolution of land reform.

The truth is that I didn't give it to the lady for nothing, she gave me three oranges in return. She was selling red healthy oranges, La Rioja oranges."

"Twenty six," the girl reflected, "not much for a whole day."

"You should be more considerate, my daughter. I believe that in this country people only take a bath on Sunday morning; besides, you must take the competition into account: gel, salts, powder soaps, cleaning lotions, soap flowers, solid foam and foam that solidifies." Not only was there no one waiting for them in that country—or in any other country— but in fact, the reception was rather hostile. As soon as they arrived the authorities requested an extraordinary amount of documents: father's ID, daughter's ID, father's passport, daughter's passport, father's visa, daughter's visa, father's certificate of no criminal record, daughter's certificate of no criminal record, certificate of baptism for both, certificate of being single ("How do you expect me to have it if I'm married?"). Well then, daughter's certificate of being single . . . and your marriage certificate. Father's certificate of elementary school, of high school, of higher education. Certificates of vaccinations against hepatitis, tetanus, tuberculosis, rabies, polio, meningitis, asthma, measles, chicken pox. The girl handed the certificates to the authorities, one by one, yellow and black certificates. Afterward, the girl neatly put them back in their places: Her father was very untidy. They also asked for the wife to be present so the girl could enter the country.

"That is not possible," said the father. "My wife has not come with us."

"Then the girl cannot enter," stated the immigration officer.

"Why?" the man asked. "I'm her father and I'll be responsible for her."

"Who says you are the father of this girl? Only her mother knows it."

"What about the papers?" the man asked. "Don't the papers say it, huh?"

"Papers are not proof of paternity," asserted the officer. "In fact only the mother can say if you are the real father of this kid."

"I'm not a kid, I'm a potential woman," said Alicia, outraged (she had learned that from her textbook).

"Her mother will have to come to reassure us that this girl is the fruit of her marriage to you," concluded the officer, threatening. "You might be a criminal, a kidnapper, a child rapist and this girl, your hostage."

"Ask her!" complained the father.

"This man is my father," confirmed the girl a few seconds later. To tell the truth, she had had the idea of denying it; it was the first time that to be his daughter, or not, depended on her, not on her parents. She could have said, for instance: "No, by no means is this man my father, he's an impostor," or something like that, as she had seen in soap operas.

Then she could have chosen any father, or better, she could have become a sudden orphan, but she wasn't sure that solution was really the most adequate for her happiness. It was very hard to find a convenient father in your own country; abroad it could be even harder. To become an orphan started to be interesting only past eighteen, when one was allowed into R-rated movies, when one could buy and sell without authorization and pay taxes. One could have children much earlier, at twelve or thirteen; it surely must be something less important because one could do that even before opening an individual savings account.

The authorities finally decided to do a blood test to prove his paternity. It wasn't that bad, after all. (Even though he fainted, as he did every time he saw blood. His wife used to say, "Revolution cannot be made this way!") It wasn't bad at all because they were taken to a very nice clinic. They were given a free meal after one more pint of blood than necessary was extracted from him as was usually done to foreigners, just because they were foreigners. She ate with great appetite.

"You're eating my blood," he said. He was so dizzy after the extraction that he could barely take advantage of his cafe au lait. She then ate two rations of bread and butter and apricot marmalade. They called peaches "apricots" in that country. In the country she came from, apricots were called "peaches." Newspapers never reported news from their country of origin; both the girl and her father found that in very poor taste.

"I would like to know what happened to the four hours they stole from me in the ship," she said after the test results confirmed that he, or any other fellow with a type A blood, was the kid's father.

After their fourth day on the ship, the captain's order had come through the sound system, reminding the passengers to turn watches thirty minutes ahead. At first the girl had resisted. She had kept her watch at 12:00 while everybody else on the ship was turning the hands around the dials, an activity that, in Alicia's opinon, showed an extreme frivolity in the treatment of time. Her father had not forced her to change the time. He was an anarchist and believed in freedom.

"Eat your berry ice cream, who knows when we'll be able to eat again," her father reminded her. Berries were strawberries, strawberries were berries in the country they had chosen because they already spoke the same language. "And bear in mind, daughter, that any individual rebelliousness is bound for failure," he had decreed while undauntedly looking at the girl's watch, which kept functioning at the measured rhythm of minutes and seconds. It was a very nice watch with a blue dial and silver numbers. Her mother had left it for her before leaving, surely because in the place she was heading to time was measured in different dimensions and life was more intense. Alicia, her eyes filled with tears, looked at the blue dial of her small watch (it looked like a lake, its hands like necks of two swans floating slowly). She had said:

"I will not turn it ahead for anything in the world." When they descended from the ship her watch was four hours behind.

"It's not that I'm behind, they are ahead," she said, looking at the two enormous clocks in the square. Finally, once she agreed (against her conscience) to adjust her watch to the time in that part of the world, she started to miss the four hours that had been stolen from her on the ship.

"What have they done to my five thousand, seven hundred and sixty minutes?" She asked her father. He wasn't ready with that answer. In fact he wasn't ready with any answer. He had been a son, also, for many years. He had lived as he had been able to live, which was good enough, and he was used to being robbed. He had had much more than four hours stolen from him, and he had not been able to do much to change the state of things. The state of things was determined by the owners of things, so every individual act of rebelliousness was bound for failure . . . With respect to his wife, wherever she was, if she was still anywhere, she had also been a daughter for many years, she had lived as she had been able to live, which was good enough, and she had devoted her life to changing the state of things, but things were resistant to change.

"Daughter, when we go back, they'll return those hours to you, if we ever go back. If we go back by ship."

That answer did not comfort her. She did not care for long-term returns. She felt completely humiliated, cheated. What would they do with so many stolen hours? She thought about ships loaded with stolen hours, silent ships that went through the ocean with their secret cargo of time. She thought about ghostly ships, about men guarding those areas where stolen time had been stored; she imagined hour-dealers waiting for the ships in dirty, dark ports, to buy hours and sell them afterwards. She thought of desperate men buying small boxes of insignificant time, poor victims of speculation. In a given port, an anxious man sees a ship arriving, a blue box is unloaded and he buys half an hour, maybe less than that, he buys ten minutes stolen from the unsuspecting passengers of a ship, robbed from involuntary emigrants, taken from the exiled. A desperate man is waiting at the port, looking at the big oil stains on the water, anxiously looking both ways, watching the white side of the arriving ship, the blue box, the insignificant time, that portion of time that for some reasons he needs and then the implacable voice of the Captain repeating: "Dear passengers, please be so kind as to turn your watches half an hour ahead," and it is no longer twelve, no longer twelve at night on board the white ship that moves with the rhythm of the waves. It is no longer the dark sea night at twelve. The passengers, impotent from so many lost battles, follow the orders docilely, adjust their watches and suddenly, it is no longer twelve but twelve-thirty. Thirty minutes have disappeared from their lives to fatten the storage areas of ships, to make time-dealers even wealthier.

"Damn those motherfucking ships," the girl desperately cried out.

Twenty-six soap bars was not a big deal, even when they only ate nuts and milk. "They have lots of calories," said her father, who knew about those things thanks to a workshop in parenting he had attended before Alicia's birth. He had learned about calories in food. He had learned the ten suitable answers a parent should produce when children start showing signs of sexual curiosity; he had learned how to clean and sterilize a bottle and what to do before the doctor arrived; but he had not learned a thing about surviving with children in a foreign country. He therefore, kept silent contemplating the ceiling. It was a very ordinary ceiling, white, without significant geographical accidents. Alicia sighed, aware of her responsibilities. It was not a very nice job to have to be responsible for a father or a mother in those hard times. Even when her father was not very rebellious, he sometimes tried to make his own decisions and the enterprises he started from those decisions were almost sure to fail. Afterwards, she did not criticize him much because her father was very sensitive and she was afraid of discouraging him; it was necessary to stimulate his personal growth, even through those ill-fated initiatives. She had read a couple of manuals about adults and even when she did not completely agree with Freud (she preferred his rebellious disciple Lacan), she tried to avoid a worsening of her father's depressive neurosis. She was specially concerned for her father's sexual life; she thought it was too irregular and unstable. He could always find excuses to avoid discussing the subject. Sometimes he said he was too tired, other times, that he was not interested. When they walked the streets together and she made frequent comments on the women that passed by, he showed stubborn indifference. At first he alleged that he had to adapt his aesthetic standard, because the women there were very different from those in his country; later, he hinted something about the scarce use of soap; he finally praised the beauty of black women when everybody knew that in that country they had finished off the black people many, many years ago.

Alicia went to the box of French-made Chinese tea and checked its contents. There were a few coins left, all from different countries. They carried the portraits of various oppressors, almost none current. The bills were from the country they had left in the diaspora and no bank accepted them because they had no gold value whatsoever. She had thought of decorating the walls of that room with those blue bills but later she decided that it would have looked too folksy and she was a citizen of the world. Her father was not.

"We don't have any money,' she said unemphatically. She said the same almost every day. Then her father looked into the pockets of his only suit. He found the address book with names of friends and acquaintances; he carefully checked it, without any results, because most of those people had died, no longer lived at those addresses or were thousands of miles away. However, he seemed to like that ritual. Friends almost always leave useless addresses behind.

"I don't think we have anybody to borrow from, today," her father commented, also unemphatically. Alicia sighed and went to the big hat box that she had stuffed with clothes before starting their trip.

"Wait, I'll be back in three or four hours," she told her father as she usually did while getting ready to leave. He then watched her with melancholy. She didn't look bad with that Indian costume he had given her for a school festivity. The feathers were somehow worn out and she had lost many on the trip. Alicia had painted them again, with watercolors, trying to give them an exotic, typical look. There were blue, red, yellow, black and white feathers.

"Do you have any idea of the kind of feathers the Charrua Indians sported?" she had asked her father. No way; the Spaniards had killed up to the last Indian in their country and there was a sole descendant alive, who claimed to be 104 years old, but he could be either Indian or Afghan. Her father wasn't even sure that the Indians wore feathers, as Metro Goldwyn Mayer liked to suggest. "Today I'm gonna add three more yellow ones, nobody will notice the difference," Alicia said.

She took her brushes and started to paint her face, trying to make very horrible grimaces. Tomato sauce was very good but she had once had a problem with a cat that had jumped on her, excited by the smell. Her father silently watched her, in admiration. Her skin was too clear to look like an Indian, but Europeans did not really care for details; not, at least, the kind of Europeans that were ready to stop in the street and give an Indian girl a few coins.

"Beware of the old men, my daughter, they are usually very libidinous," her father advised her every time she left. "Don't let any of them approach you; they are given to defloration . . ."

"Especially with virgin Indian girls," Alicia concluded, reciting the part of the speech she had already memorized.

She watched herself in the mirror. This time she had painted a horrifying grimace around her mouth. Some shadows around her eyes, the painted age line, the blue on her eyebrows and a fake scar gave her an air of antiquity she had seldom fabricated before. While looking at the mirror she said:

"I don't know whether to carry a sign that reads 'Latin American Indian Girl' or one with the words 'Elderly Latin American Indian Midget.' "

"I'm not sure that there were any midgets among the Indians," her father replied.

"Me neither," she said. That ignorance about their ancestors was a terrible thing. It was not the rule in Europe. People in Europe were better educated; they could always name five or six of their previous ancestors; they did not have revolutions and almost every country had a parliament, some with two chambers, some different.

Only once she had had a small accident while exhibiting herself in the Latin American Indian Girl costume. A terrible Machiavellian small boy, a little younger than she, had approached her and, with all his might, had pulled on her only Indian braid. In that moment she forgot that she should have uttered unintelligible sounds, and instead insulted him in perfect Spanish (which she did not hesitate to attribute to the fact that the Spanish had colonized the indigenous civilizations of the La Plata River). The incident had ended with Alicia's perfect strike to his jaw, which sent him and the Mother Country down to the ground.

Her father used to look at her in some anguish but with great admiration. He thought that something had changed in the genes from one generation to the other; obscured modification in their inherited characters had allowed current children to be perfect parents to their progenitors. It was a different race, furnished with unusual resistance; they had assimilated in their mother's wombs the lessons of the most intimate, the darkest of defeats. They had learned sadness, failure and desolation right from their mother's uterus. Later, when they saw light, they already knew how to live despite everything. Conceived in bitter nights, in nights of persecution, uncertainty, misery and terror, conceived in houses that looked like jail cells or in jail cells that were tombs, in beds fit for coffins, the survivors of those nights of torture and pain were born under the sign of resistance and endurance.

Alicia looked at him before leaving. Her head was crowned with feathers and her straw skirt covered in part her very white legs. Her torso was nude, her incipient, discretely round breasts ending in tender soft pink nipples. She did not carry an arrow because her father could never buy her one; he was always short of money. Their eyes met, different, but transparent. They both knew how to decipher the codes of eyes. They had learned to do it at sea, during those long nights of insomnia, when not even the moon was shining. There, while smoking rationed cigarettes and plotting ways of grabbing a ham sandwich from the kitchen, they had learned to read the waters of eyes, quiet waters of the father, restless waters of the daughter's lake. Alicia looked at him and read; she read the mystification, the dreams, the sadness. So when she opened the door and disguised her voice to go along with her Latin-American-Indian-girl-lost-in-Europe costume, she told him clearly: "I'm positive that what you think about my generation is completely wrong."

Translated by Alicia Partnoy and Regina M. Kreger

EXILES

ROSE MOSS, born in 1937, was educated in South Africa and emigrated to America in 1961. She has written three novels, *The Family Reunion* (1974), *The Terrorist* (1979), and *The Schoolmaster* (1981), as well as a book about South Africa's politics, *Shooting at the Crocodile* (1990), which is more optimistic about the country than her earlier work. She also taught writing at Wellesley College in Massachusetts, a liberal arts college like the one where her central character in "Exile," Stephen Katela, a black South African composer, meets the kind Americans who can offer him hospitality but no comprehension of his life, his loss of home, his inability to write his music in a country with no ears for it, the "intractable troubles" of a refugee. "Exile" is a story—like so many others in Global Cultures—that is about both the lost homeland and the new land that is home but can never feel like home. It is a scathing indictment of South African *apartheid* rendered in the microcosm of one man's life, but it is also a lament for America, where the educated and privileged take freedom for granted and cannot imagine any dilemma of life that is beyond solution: "These Americans thought they could solve everything."

Instead of a single tormented, despairing consciousness, a social microcosm—"Exiles" in the plural—gives TONY EPRILE's stories, collected in *Temporary Sojourner* (1989), their noisy, cluttered, mordantly humorous street scene or bar scene quality. South African exiles of every sort populate his work: English-speaking Jews, blacks from the townships (Xhosa speakers), blacks from the homelands (Zulu speakers), coloreds from Capetown, Afrikaners. The only cultural form they share is the one Eprile's generation has internationalized—rock 'n' roll. Each individual has a story, each is in exile for different reasons, each is unassimilatable in America for different reasons. Tony Eprile's own story is that he was born in 1955 and grew up in South Africa, the son of the *Golden City Post's* editor, the white editor of the country's first nonwhite mass circulation newspaper. With an M.A. in writing from Brown University, he has worked as a writing teacher at a number of American universities—currently Northwestern. Like Rose Moss, nee Rappaport, Eprile is Jewish; that is, both authors come from the one white community in South Africa in which knowledge of what it is to be a victim of racism is not abstract.

Both of these writers remind their American readers that there are, in America, two South Africas—one is the country, in all its complexity, in all its political division and cultural hybridization, and one is the South Africa that many well-intentioned Americans use to understand themselves and "the American dilemma," American racism. This second South Africa is "us" in a wholly mythic manner: "If they cared at all, it was not for a country that had an independent existence, it was for a symbol of their own conflicts," is Stephen Katela's depressed assessment. But both writers also use their South African exiles to show Americans that racism in America has a very specific quality when it is directed toward, and felt by, Africans, emigrant peoples of color. In many of Global Cultures' stories, the writers are addressing two audiences simultaneously and equally, mingling languages and cultural markers; in these two stories, the primary audience is American.

Exile

Rose Moss

STEPHEN KATELA dozed at the back of the car. Occasionally he opened his eyes to look at the two dark heads in front of him, the kind white couple who were taking him to their home. Yesterday he had been at another college and had given a talk on African music, and another kind white couple had taken him home as their guest, and he had talked about South Africa. He closed his eyes. A theme kept palpitating under the surface of his attention, its outline blurred like a cat in a bag, like his own young body when he crept down to the bottom of his mother's bed and thought that no one could see him because it was dark under the blanket. His brother played with him there, a touch and move game in the shapeless dark, a hiding-go-seek without rules, until they started to wrestle and wriggled so fast they rolled off the bed on to the humourless floor. Then their mother scolded them while she fed another baby mealie pap with one hand and attended to the tea and remaining mealie pap on the stove with the other. Stephen and his brother went out to play until she called them in to breakfast. They ignored her injunctions to take soap and wash under the tap in the yard. Winter was too cold for washing. She would come out when the baby was fed and give them a slap and another scolding, would oversee their mutual lathering and squirming at the tap, and when the relics of their brief exploration had been washed off them— cinders of a brazier in which they had poked for coal, gritty smears if they had been examining the rubbish in the street—she would fold them into the bosomy warmth of the room. The reminiscent smell of early morning fires, the grey blue haze of the township, bit like an acrid, toxic gas into the tissue of Stephen's memory. He opened his eyes again to fill them with the two silhouettes in front of him, the white couple driving home through a heavy mist that the headlights held pale and solid, close to the car.

The road twisted and heaved. They had come off the smooth turnpike, homogeneous from Virginia to Maine, that made Stephen feel that his whole lecture tour was an hallucination in which distance had no more dimension than in a dream. Episodes that repeated the same obsessional pattern followed each other arbitrarily in settings that differed only like the scenery of an impoverished theatrical company. Every road was the same road. The arrangement played with slightly differing signs and overpasses, discreet banks of grass, and trees that only gradually and reluctantly admitted the grey agglomeration of cities whose suburbs had long been suppressed by the same green uniform as the countryside. At last, off the highway, an idiosyncratic thrust from the land moulded the road into a pliant index of fields and streams, pulled straight over flats, packed more densely in steep valleys and rises. The mist was so thick he could hardly see the vegetation. From the dancing swell of the road he could imagine himself back on the stretch between Mooi River and Pietermaritzburg where frequent mists nourished the land, and cattle condensed the airy whiteness into substances richly edible—for those who could afford to buy them.

But every now and then a leafy intrusion over the road caught his eye, the uneven bars of a wooden fence, or irregular stone globules of a wall, and Stephen was reminded by these foreign shapes and colours that he was not on that Natal road, he was somewhere in New England, going to spend the night in a strange house among strangers. These sights, like foreign substances grafted among the tissues of what he had seen, lived, and compounded into organic constituents of his own self, set up a resistance. Each reminder that he was not home accelerated an irritation, a process of rejection. His body, his perception, the accumulated chemicals of his own being barred these alien elements and tried to seal their pernicious proximity off from himself, to cast them off like a foreign skin or organ, to expel all toxic strangeness. He shut his eyes. He tried to lull himself. Let him not think that if he did not learn how to assimilate America there would be nothing left for him to see, no place where he could retain that dwindling self he felt to be his own. He thought of his brother and the dusty soccer field where they used to play when their mother went off with the baby and a bundle of washing wrapped in a sheet, to the white city where she worked until night came. How did that theme shape?

His host was also a composer. Stephen had heard a quartet by him. It had been played at one of the colleges where Stephen had contributed to a symposium on modern music. There had been lectures and workshops during the day. In the evening there was a concert and Ken Radley's String Quartet, cited as an example of some of the finest composition in the United States, was played to instruct an audience that might find such compositions hard to come by. To Stephen the quartet seemed unintelligible, thin, and boring, but he blamed his response on his own ignorance. Ken's quartet was one of the many signs, like billboards on the road, that said to Stephen, "We don't speak to you. We are not written in your language. You have nothing to say to us."

The car slowed, turned up a driveway, and they had come. "We're here," Janet announced smiling. This was her home. Stephen smiled to her. They were so kind. Ken opened the door and light flared out of the amber hall over damp steps. Inside there was more light.

"Why don't we wash and have a drink while Janet's preparing supper?" Ken suggested. "I'll show you your room," and he took Stephen's suitcase, which he had already fetched from the car. Stephen wondered whether it was right to let Ken carry his suitcase; or did he feel uncomfortable because Ken was white? "I'll take it." He reached for the handle. Ken let him take it and picked up another suitcase. He led the way up carpeted stairs, pointed out the bathroom, and gestured inside the doorway of a room at the end of the passage, "This is yours. See you downstairs." With a quick smile he indicated his confidence that Stephen could manage from this point. He could, in a manner of speaking. He had done it before. He took the smaller of two towels neatly waiting for him at the foot of the bed, and the cake of soap, still wrapped, and went to the bathroom. It retained the old-fashioned tub of an old house, but a combed sheepskin on the floor and a shelf over the tub for an ashtray, two detective stories and a small vase of brightly dyed star flowers indicated that it was not a room where Ken and Janet expected austere behaviour.

When he came back to the room they had given him Stephen noted the artefacts of someone else's life. A childhood unimaginably unlike his own surrounded him. Behind the bed hung a drawing of the beach. The sea was a properly undulating blue on whose conventional waves there sailed the black outline of a yacht, innocent of the relatively immense fish whose profile stood mute, motionless, and symbolic between it and the yellow and purple sand, where a green scribble suggested grass. In a low bookcase under the window, children's books about shells and birds, adventure stories, Webster's illustrated dictionary, a microscope under a plastic cover, indicated another layer of the American boy's life. The most recent stratum was evidenced near the dressing table where a poster of Humphrey Bogart ignored college pennants and the image of the alien in the mirror.

Stephen sat on the bed. He felt his knees under his palms. He insisted on his own undeniable life, on his own childhood in and out of the dusty location and the dusty mission school, on his skill to be as slick as a tsotsi who wore tight trousers and carried knives. He had been as mocking as a mosquito when he played the pennywhistle on street corners, when he demanded a penny, a tickey, a sixpence, baas. He went downstairs for a drink.

Janet was busy in the kitchen that was separated from the dining area and lounge by a wooden counter. He noticed that she was wearing a string of those grey seeds that white women didn't think smart in South Africa. Here they were favoured by the wives of college professors, like Janet, and girl students from good homes.

It was fine to sit in the same room as a busy woman preparing food. "Haven't you got some vegetables to peel?" he offered. In America it was all right to help like a piccanin.

"It's all done, frozen and sliced," she laughed, "very American." She untied her apron and hung it over a rail. "Come and have a drink."

How casually legal it seemed to her to offer him a drink. How legal and unremarkable to be alone with a black man. In South Africa when white women offered him drinks, he was wary. Even at mixed parties he felt his safety as sharp as a blade's edge. With Cynthia Barton he would drink; after dinner, meat and wine, she offered him brandy and liqueur. After slow talk and darkness he would wake to hear his heart slamming, police banging the door, and his brother crying, sick. When the police arrested David Msimang with a white woman and found out that he was a musician, they broke his eardrums, just for fun. After that, Stephen would not visit Cynthia alone any more, and on the phone she said, "For goodness' sake, don't *explain*. There's nothing to *explain*. If you don't want to come, don't come. You don't owe me anything. I'm not your white madam." She never allowed him to tell her about David Msimang.

In New York he went to some mixed parties given by Andrew Mohone. South Africans who had left with the cast of *King Kong*, after Sharpeville, after Mandela, after Sobukwe, after waves of arrests under the sabotage laws, after Vorster, on scholarships, on exit permits, on passports and family money, met each other at mixed parties and felt that the old risk and thrill could be recaptured. They repeated the gestures of defiance that here did not defy, and knew again that they were singly brave and free. Some of the whites at Andrew's parties were Americans—young reporters, instructors at Columbia and the Free School, churchmen with missionary acquaintances—a miscellaneous lot who, like the South Africans themselves, of different generations and concerns, seemed to have little in common but a geographically named node of feeling. By two o'clock in the morning the parties had usually divided into Siamese twin parties, one black, one white. In South Africa the mixture would have lasted all night. Mixed parties here missed the police.

Once or twice black separatists came instead of whites. They made remarks to Stephen like, "I can see you come from Africa. Your face is so proud." They had never heard his music. The mixed parties were easier. At first, the old South Africans asked him for news and gossip. "Do you know Diana Zindberg? . . . What's she doing now?"

"Didn't she marry an Englishman? I think she married an Oxford don," someone would supply. Or she was "on the West Coast now," or she had remained in South Africa.

A few people knew Cynthia Barton, and asked whether he knew her. "Yes, I think she's still in Johannesburg."

"Goli, hey! Good old Goli! Man, I still miss the place. Well Cynthia was a great gal," as though she had partially died, "just a great kid! I wish she'd come here."

Why? Stephen wondered, why did anyone wish that?

He imagined that in New York there were such parties given by White Russians, Serbians, Spanish anarchists, Palestinian Arabs, Ghanaians and Czechs. All exiles, all dying. When all his oxygen was exhausted he would also relish thin gossip about South Africa and the people of his generation, become a comfortable exile, a cell in the specific tissue of exiles and cosmopolitans who had by now become organically accepted and integral in the American metabolism.

Ken entered from another room. "There's a letter from Christopher. He says he'll stop by on his way to New York," he told Janet.

"Good. When'll that be?"

"Any time."

"Christopher's our son," she explained to Stephen. "He's been summering in the Hudson Bay area. He says there are some interesting algae there. Algae are his thing." She smiled fondly, indulgently.

The remoteness of these lives that he saw in midstream pressed in on Stephen. There was none of his own air left, none of the spacious sunlight, naïve and simple, by which he had learned to read the world. Here, existence was compounded into individual complex studies and specialized fields. Each man saw his own topic, noted its intricate interrelationships and structures, and guessed at the intricacies known by others. In South Africa he had written music, it seemed to him now, like a child. He had composed as though he could pour sound simply into the heart of another man, a heart unobstructed by perceptions evolved to assimilate incommunicable knowledge. Here his communications were defined. He was a practising composer, and an authority on the music of Southern Africa. He had become a curiosity devoted to curiosities, the speaker of an arcane language—composer, consequently, to no ear but his own. The longer he stayed the more arcane his music must become; it must breed into itself to retain that exotic worth that was supposed to give it value. It could not mate again with the sounds of his daily life, now American—that would breed an impurity into his sound, a new idiom into his voice. And then he would lose that now ghostly audience in South Africa who, when they listened to his music, thought that the earth sang and the cicadas chorused together, and did not know that their unique earth was quaint veld, their noon remote from others'.

Each of these Americans with his intricate knowledge constituted one cell of this complex society whose function was a life other than Stephen's, whose purpose was something he did not know, and could not, without destroying himself, adopt. If he did not adopt its purpose, America would shake him off as an intrusion, a piece of a foreign body, a cell or organ that lived by the principles of some othe body born under the Southern Cross.

Something of Stephen's loneliness emanated through to Janet. It prompted her to the inbred courtesy that required her to turn the topic of conversation to her guest's interests rather than her own. She reserved the subject of Christopher and his letter for later, for that conjugal conversation whose even tenor is like the even conversation a man conducts with the sights and texture of his belongings and his people. She would deal with Christopher in a time and a language from which Stephen felt sealed off as if from the air of life. She asked him questions about South Africa while they sipped gin and tonic with wedges of lime—a drink he had never known in South Africa, even at the mixed parties of Houghton and Northcliff, and certainly never in the shebeens. At last she came to the question that all these polite, interested Americans asked.

"Will you ever go back?"

"I can't. I got out illegally, without a passport. I'm a refugee."

"You mean they wouldn't give you a passport. Why on earth not?"

"They've had some bad experiences with the wrong people getting out and making propaganda against the government overseas. We Africans talk too much."

Ken liked his dryness. "And have you talked too much here?"

"I've been on a lecture tour." They laughed.

"Your topic's not very incendiary," Ken pursued.

"No," Stephen agreed, "but I do some damage in ordinary conversations like this. And then, most Afrikaners, especially those who deal with us, are ignorant. They're afraid of people like me because I'm not a simple kaffir."

"How did you get out?" Janet wanted to know.

"Oh, there's a sort of underground railroad, and a refugee centre in Dar-es-Salaam."

"Will you go back there?"

"I don't know what will happen to me." After he had spoken he heard the passive helplessness he had revealed. Ken heard it too.

"Why do you want to go back to South Africa?"

"I don't." But Ken ignored this reply. His waiting silence was as heavily palpable as a waking sensation that presses into sleep and breaks its integuments. And like a sleeper who begins to talk before he has quite shaken off sleep, and talks as truthfully as in a dream, Stephen continued.

"I can't work here. I say to myself that tomorrow, or next week I'll be able to, but I can't. I compose, but it's all false. I can't bear to listen to it. I don't think I can write outside South Africa."

"Then you must go back." Ken spoke the imperative that Stephen feared. He brought into it the auditory reality of an American accent with a resolute inflection that Stephen would never have invented in his own mind, the instruction that, like the ground bass of a passacaglia, had sounded without interruption in Stephen's feelings for weeks.

Stephen repeated, "I can't." Ken and Janet said nothing. "If I go back I'll be in prison within a year—not a nice comfortable prison where people can write their memoirs. I'll be in a South African jail where people get beaten up and tortured and go mad. I've been in prison. A pass offender gets kicked around. Sometimes he's sent to work on potato farms where he wears a potato sack, winter and summer. Sometimes he's beaten for not working hard enough. They knocked the eardrums out of a friend of mine because he was a musician. Some people get beaten to death. In the jail they put ten men in one cell, and give you one bucket that gets full long before morning. There are no beds. You sleep on the floor, as far away from the bucket as you can. And I'm not a pass offender. I can't expect such good treatment. I'm not likely to write much music there."

"Then you must learn how to write here."

"How? How can I learn anything like that?" Stephen breathed hard on his rage. These Americans thought they could solve everything. They had no respect for boulder weight, for things too heavy for a man to lift.

"I don't know. I guess it's easier to say than to do. Just give yourself time to hear what this country sounds like. You probably just need time."

"Yes," seconded Janet. "After all, you haven't been here very long."

Their unsuffering sympathy fed Stephen's rage. "I want to write in my own language. In South Africa that isn't allowed. An African has to speak English or Afrikaans, a composer has to learn the sonata form and the instruments of the European orchestra. They are what he must write for. There's an instrument we have in Lesotho—a bow and a string, and a gourd for resonance. It plays two notes. The person who plays it can hardly hear it himself, it's like a whisper, like a lover. In a world that's so quiet, there's room for an instrument like that. There are nothing but mountains, and one bad road. It keeps the cars out. The people are too poor for radios. All they can afford is the sound of a gourd, like the earth, like the sunlight, like being poor, like being black. You can't hear it in Johannesburg—even the Africans are too rich there, or their being poor is a cramping vice. That bow and gourd says what I want—but where could I play something like that in America? No one would hear it. Everything's so loud here, the cars, the radios, the fire trucks, planes. I can't hear anything human, alive. And even if anyone could hear my bow and gourd, what would they make of it? Two simple notes over and over, so monotonous. Not at all . . . psychedelic." He smiled at this disparaged word of praise, as if to overcome squeamishness at having used it. "I sound angry, but I'm not angry at Americans for being what they are. That's what they are. It's incurable. Like being an African. But it's at the other end of the world, and I can't make myself learn what to be again, like a baby. I don't start from nothing. I'm a man already."

Ken and Janet were embarrassed at this outburst. Their habitual withdrawal from involvement with strangers, especially strangers whose insoluble problems could grieve and fester in those whose pity held no power to remedy; an accepted training rooted in the manners of ancestors who knew that what is delicate must be protected (sometimes by deliberate ignorance), who would not mention rape, drunkenness or money in front of women; and a traditional stoicism that would not weep but fastened troubles to the self like a brace to keep men upright—all made them withdraw from Stephen's demand.

Ken spoke first. "I hope you'll take advantage of the musical opportunities in these parts. There'll be some interesting concerts in New York this fall, and other things too. I've got a notice from Hunter College. I'll look for it after supper. You will be in New York, won't you?"

"Yes." Stephen didn't tell him that he received his own notices, invitations, introductions.

"And I've got programmes for Lincoln Center. I can often get complimentary tickets . . ."

Stephen saw how the problems of the boy Christopher must have been kindly finessed away until he grew up into, not quite a man—for he was allowed no human, intractable troubles, only those his society could digest—but an expert on algae.

Christopher came home that night. Stephen heard him arrive, and the noise of welcome and explanation that a guest was sleeping in his room. "Then you must go back," Ken had said in an American voice with an unforeseen inflexion. "Then you must go back." The initial staccatos of greeting sank into long blurred sentences, and Stephen tried to fuse the reawakened rhythm of family discourse in his ear with the theme that had struggled forward during the drive through the mist, the song of playing with his brother in the morning. But he could not achieve the fusion, and fell asleep again.

He met Christopher at the breakfast table. Ken introduced him to the bony youth. "Steve's giving a paper on African music at Fenmore Hall this afternoon, and going to New York tomorrow."

"I think I'm in your room," Stephen said tentatively.

"I'm only camping here," Christopher assured him. "I'm going on to New York myself."

"Perhaps Chris can give you a ride down," Ken suggested. "Unless you'd rather fly . . ."

During the meal Christopher accompanied firm gestures that reached for butter or toast on the well-known table with stories about his summer. He talked about what his expedition had accomplished. "We collected hundreds of specimens that are probably new. How'd you like an alga named after you, Mother?"

"I'd have to see it first," she joked.

"I've got slides. Are you free tonight? Can we look at them?"

Janet drew him back to arrangements for the day. "I've been waiting all summer for you to help your father clear out the cellar."

"That'll be great," Christopher assented before Ken could protest.

Stephen wondered whether his help would be welcome or obtrusive. No, he'd work on the location theme, even though nothing would come of it.

While he was sitting at the desk the boy Christopher must have used, Stephen saw them walking through the grounds. Sometimes they stopped to examine a change or permanence. The two men walking among trees, their heads flickering among bright foliage, who lived in that world inhabited by squirrels and jays that he had sometimes read about in northern storybooks, were indeed men, not plastic surrogates produced by a society that forbade suffering and wanted only organs of perception, units of intelligence, consumers. These two were men, father and son, archetypal, and as mythical to Stephen as woods that harboured plentiful creatures, as strange as snows and blueberries and maples. Such familial affluence was unknown to him. His father had been one of the men who lived with his mother for a few years and then disappeared into the jails, into the labyrinth of townships around Johannesburg, or into the reserves. A series of men had played with him and the other children, in idle friendliness. Nostalgic for a life some of them had never known, they assessed him as a candidate for initiation, and told him stories to inspire warlike heroism, sagas of Zulu impis led by Chaka and Dingaan. But often they were irritable. The children seemed always underfoot, Sarah wanted more money to buy them clothes, and Stephen was always wasting candles at night when a man wanted darkness and Sarah's hard breathing.

Stephen and his brother knew the world directly, not by the mediation of fathers. There were not discrete worlds, one filled with talking animals and fairies for children, another with money and taxes and politics for adults. It was all one world. Grown men as frightened as children of policemen who, as irresistible as witchcraft, might bang on the door in the middle of the night to ask for a pass, or dig up the floor to look for skokiaan. It was all one world. In an acid dawn as pink as millions of pounds, neighbours climbed on to bicycles and rode into the city; on the way to the long queue at the bus-stop they stepped on the hoar that clung to wisps of dry grass and paper; some who had slept with braziers in closed rooms breathed the warm air too long and did not wake up in time for life. Nothing was omitted except this other world, inconceivable—the house set among wild trees and lavish grass, this world that the father and the son were revisiting, and had never altogether left, and this kind of humanity that grew among them. Stephen could never revisit his childhood. Now he must live in a world that his childhood had never guessed existed.

That night Christopher showed them slides of his expedition to the Hudson Bay. Beyond sight or sound of any other human life small villages grasped tight in dour friendliness. Granite boulders grew lichens like birthmarks, and in their brief summer thronged with silky flowers that looked like Karoo vygies. Pane after pane of light offered visions that Stephen could understand—emptiness, light, virginity—where he had expected only more that was alien, unassimilable. In a landscape like this one could play an instrument with two notes. But he was afraid to think of what he saw. Would he go to the Hudson Bay to try another kind of exile?

Being driven to New York, he asked about the expedition. "Didn't you feel lonely?"

"No. There were seven of us on the ship, and we got to know some of the village people quite well. Strangers are very welcome. And it's not as if there aren't any phones. I called my girl in New York twice a week. It's not half as bad as it'll be next year when we go to Lake Baikal, if we can arrange it. We might go to Antarctica instead. What's Cape Town like? They say it's beautiful."

"I've never been there. The government tries to keep us Africans out of Cape Town."

"Oh, I thought most of the population was Negro."

"In Cape Town there are a lot of people of mixed blood. They're called coloureds and are treated differently from us. Every shade of whiteness deserves a special degree of privilege."

"You must be really glad to be out of it."

"I am. Don't you ever get homesick when you go to these strange places?"

"I guess I've never been away long enough. It's no problem really. I could come back any time." They seemed to have come to a dead end. "Do you ever get homesick?"

"Sometimes."

"I guess people get homesick for the strangest things. One of our research team comes from Anatolia. He longs for sheep's eyes. Look for *that* in a supermarket!" Christopher laughed.

Stephen was silent.

"Mind if I turn on the radio?"

"Go ahead."

Sometimes they let the clamour of baroque music substitute for conversation. Sometimes they spoke through it.

"Why did you come to the States? To get out of South Africa?"

"Partly. And people always told me I should go overseas to finish my education. They said my composing needed to be finished." He smiled at the private irony.

"But your family's still there?"

"My mother."

"Have you got brothers, or sisters?"

"Most of them died as babies. One brother grew up with me, but he died when I was in high school."

"Your mother must miss you."

"I don't know. I wrote, but didn't get an answer. And I asked someone I knew to look for her, but I haven't heard from him either."

"Why don't you phone."

"We haven't got phones. In the locations, only white officials have phones."

Vivaldi gave way to Cimarosa by way of a commercial. How must it be to live in Christopher's world, where there was no sensual space, distance, silence, darkness? Stephen remembered reading that a night of darkness had come upon New York like a disaster. How must it be to live like that, deprived of any sense of the given light, and the given earth's autonomous being? How would it be to live in America and lose all stillness, loneliness, man-otherness, to live in a world where the whisper of a string in a gourd could never be heard, imagined? Christopher could hardly be five years younger than himself, but Stephen felt old, old-fashioned, old as the chameleon who first allowed the news of death to be brought into the world, old as death, incomprehensible to Christopher. Christopher lived in the new world. Was there any music Stephen could write for him? What was there in Christopher's life he could understand?

"What does your girl do?"

Christopher answered in sentences whose individual words were intelligible. It was the syntax, the meaning, that fled.

When they came to New York, the road lost all connection with the shape or look of the land. It dived, swung, curved, twisted back on itself, over other roads and under them. Buildings crowded nearer and nearer as in a kinetic hallucination of suffocation, claustrophobia and spacelessness. The commercials between symphonies gave way to a long newscast about Vietnam, New York, Turkey, Israel, Lindsay, Rockefeller and people whose roles and names Stephen could not identify. As usual there was nothing about South Africa. From here it seemed an almost non-existent country. The few Americans who had heard of it refracted it, distorted it, saw it as an image of their own problems. If they cared at all, it was not for a country that had an independent existence, it was for a symbol of their own conflicts. The little of South Africa that survived had been absorbed into the bloodstream of another system. And if he were to survive, he must learn who all these people were, must learn to become interested in them, must tutor himself in this system, this Vietnam, CORE, LSD, FBI, CIA, UCLA, this system of symbols and personalities in whom he had no interest. He must give up his self, and must become a self who could subsist in this vast artefact that offered hardly a blade of grass he could recognize from his own life.

They drove through Harlem. The stores advertised foods he had never eaten. Children played games with rules and passwords he had never known. He had been here, in a black world as foreign as the white, where people didn't understand his English and stared at his strangeness, this black Harlem whose language was as opaque as Spanish Harlem's, as whiteness, as the intelligent assurance of a youth like Christopher.

They left Central Park behind them and the big stores, and came to

Stephen's hotel. When Andrew Mohone and Ester Matimba had come to meet him at the airport and offered to help him find accommodation, they had been careful not to take him to Harlem. Andrew wore a loose, flowered costume that he had never worn in South Africa. He carried an airmail edition of the London *Times* under his arm. Later he explained that many had to masquerade to get a respect they could not otherwise achieve.

"Don't you feel funny to be an African pretending to be an African so that Americans will recognize you as the kind of African they recognize?"

"What sort of game is that, man? You've got to do it. Believe me, there are lots of tricks to learn."

Ester wore the expensive clothes of a performer offstage. Her bearing neither expected nor brooked contempt. And in their aura, Stephen had been able to rent a room out of Harlem.

When Christopher left him, with vaguely friendly American remarks about being glad to meet him, Stephen wondered whether to phone Ester. Or should he wait until this sombre mood lightened? He felt lethargic, almost inanimate. He opened the window of his room. It gave on to a dark airshaft. In a corner a heap of crates and cartons rotted and waited for someone to dispose of them. Lights from other rooms in the hotel glowed anonymously. A pale sky sagged against the building's dark bulk. The city's flaccid roar sank towards the rotting corners of the airshaft. Its hoarse wheeze breathed into his face. The outside air, like the air in his room and in the passages of the hotel, had been used so often that an impalpable grime hung in it, like wear in the face of an old prostitute. Any man who took comfort in its warmth breathed dying, as if he slept in a closed room where a brazier breathed.

He took out his notes for the theme of the game under the blanket. The whole affair seemed pitifully thin and worthless, but he tried to work on it. Every new idea seemed banal, false, either involuntarily reminiscent of a commercial, or masquerading like Andrew as an Africa he had never experienced, unnaturally bright and vigorous. Ai! the winter mornings had been cold, the air outside fierce, the water from the tap outside blinding. He and his brother in torn vests hid from the windy sun. Did Andrew tell stories about living in a jungle? Did he wear a different country in his memory and forget the location winters and the cracked European jackets of his native past? Stephen juggled the thin souvenir of those winters he dared not forget, devised harmonies and variations, and eventually put the sheets away. He phoned Ester.

"Stephen! It's good to hear you, man. How *are* you?"

"Okay. How're you?"

"I'm giving a party. Come."

"When? Now?"

"Yes now. I've got two people from Columbia who've heard your music and want to meet you. Have you done anything new?"

"No."

"Well, they like what they've heard."

"Okay."

"Are you all right, Stephen?"

"Yes. Why not?"

"I must be imagining. Too long since I've seen you. I'd like to see you myself, not just hand you over to those people from Columbia."

"Drop the party and come with me."

"I can't. TV people and journalists are here too. I want you to meet them, Stephen."

"I've just come back. I'm tired. Some other time."

"Stephen, you sound awfully depressed."

"Good-bye, Ester."

He was surprised to find Ester giving a party. Parties were one of Andrew Mohone's tricks, a habit of the exile community. Ester was surely not one of these. She did not make a special, trivial virtue of being South African and different. She met New York on its own terms. She worked. She did not talk about how much she had suffered at home, how rare and sensational her escape had been. She worked. Ken worked. Christopher worked. That was how they survived. But he could not work. He had lost a gear. He had become junk. He was like the rest of the South African clique. He might as well not despise their party.

He showered and changed. He looked in the mirror cynically. What had been the matter, man. He could still live.

He walked through the airless corridor into the streets. Stores offered enticements to millions of people with incomprehensible needs. Windows showed copper pots and wooden bowls, dyed hammocks, coloured glass spheres, ceramic fungus, leather waistcoats, books about Zen, posters, and records of Indian ragas. At best his music would cling to this sea ledge with other monstrous forms, curiosities, fads, psychedelia, and would be heard by these bedecked hermaphrodites whose fantastic forms pressed past him with insinuations of contempt, either at his clothes or blackness. This transient hallucination was yet another world, another language. He was lost in an infinity of variations, unconceived possibilities. They all extinguished him. All pressed suffocation. He was nothing. South Africa was nothing. What he had taken as the world omitted a world, an infinity of worlds.

He mounted a bus and rode it passively until the driver told him that he'd have to pay another fare—the bus had completed its route. He climbed off and walked among shabby and indefinite stores. Some scream-ing children ran in front of him and were rebuked by a screaming woman whose words he could not interpret. He stopped to stare at a window that displayed a French Provincial dining room and bar. Then he walked on again. A man who might have been drunk leaned towards him and asked the time, brother, but he didn't answer, and the man said, "Fuck you, nigger." He didn't answer that either. He was near another incessant high-way. It roared without rhythm. He came to an overpass. He stopped to stare at the rapid cars, the inhuman speed, the implacable concrete legs of another overpass, the din of America. There was only one way. He would accept America. He would throw himself into it, into the breathless air, the machine light. He tightened his hand on the railing and pulled up. The freeway rushed and fled beneath him. He leapt into it.

Exiles

Tony Eprile

THIS IS how Mark comes to meet Zach' Mahlope.

A friend of Mark's calls him one morning and says: "Clarissa really likes you. Why don't you ask her out?" Clarissa is the friend's sister, a small dark-haired girl with a sidelong pickerel smile. Mark had found her attractive when they talked at a recent party but felt that he had not made a very good impression. The thought that the girl might want to see him again is cheering, but it is almost two weeks before he can bring himself to dial her number. There is no answer. The instant he hangs up, however, his own phone rings and it is Clarissa, who happens to be at a phone booth a block away from his apartment.

After an afternoon spent wandering around the West Village, followed by dinner at an inexpensive Vietnamese restaurant that they discover together, they find themselves in the Sunfish Café, the local bar that Mark often stops in late at night on his way home from the darkroom. Mark has been at low ebb, uneasy except in the company of a few close friends—although more than four months have now passed since his breakup with Kylie. He feels good now as he banters lightly with this pretty young woman, whose black hair seems almost blue in the dim barroom light and whose pupils merge into the dark irises. Clarissa is saved from conventional petite prettiness by a strong, almost masculine chin and that strange, sly smile.

"Stop looking at me that way," she says, dimpling. "You're embarrassing me."

"I was wondering how you photograph . . ."

Fortunately this doesn't sound as stupid to her as it does to him, since she smiles at him with her eyes shuttered as she rises from the booth, saying, "I don't suppose this establishment has a ladies' room!"

He watches as she sidles past the bar stools toward the back room. It's not exactly the ideal place to bring a date, although the bar does attract a motley crowd of local workers, businessmen, and students. Nearby, the regular known as the Psycho Vet is holding forth in a loud voice. Mark had talked to him once when he sat on a neighboring stool at the bar counter, but he soon tired of the man's self-aggrandizing monologues and overt come-ons to any woman who passed within hearing range.

When he looks up again, Mark sees that Clarissa, who had stopped at the bar to order more drinks, is caught in conversation with the Psycho Vet and a black man wearing a peaked camouflage cap. Her head is tilted and he feels a rush of love at the vulnerability of her white nape, her neck as slim and strong as a gazelle's. Mark gets up and goes over to interpose himself between the P.V. and Clarissa. In the same moment, he realizes that he has misjudged the situation, for she is in fact happily looking at some photographs the black man has out on the counter.

"Cape Town," the man says. "My nephew sent them to me. Ag, they make me homesick."

Clarissa does not give Mark much chance to look at the photographs, but, pushing his drink at him, giggles: "Let's get drunk."

"Who's the South African guy?" Mark asked her.

"Jack. He's a custodian at NYU and he said he comes here just about every night. So you can talk to him another time. Right now, I've got dibs."

It is several days later before Mark again sets foot in the Sunfish Café. He has spent most of this time with Clarissa, and if anyone had asked how things were progressing with her, he would have had to reply: "Fast and slow." She stayed over at his apartment that first night, and each night since. They passed their time talking, making snacks, reading poetry aloud, and doing the *New York Times* crossword puzzle together, all punctuated by frequent hugging and caressing. It puzzles him that they have not made love, since it is clear they both want to. Mark wonders whether he has been trying too hard to avoid making the same mistakes he had made with Kylie. For in the process he has been making new mistakes: talking too much about his ex-love (a term which even now seems too harsh and final—he prefers to think of her as his "step-girlfriend") and there had been that awkward moment when Clarissa lifted one of his books out from the shelf and a note had fallen face up onto the bed. Kylie had been in the habit of secreting passionate letters to him all over the room. He thought he had found and filed away all of them, but apparently not . . . and this one read:

"M.
        I love you madly MAdly MADLY!!!
                                K."

Signs of her, he realizes, are still all over the room. There is the box he keeps his bills in: it has her name and his address emblazoned on its side. There is the photograph of her over the kitchen table, the pair of women's shoes in his closet . . .

Mark has forgotten about his compatriot in the bar until, coming back from the studio late one night, he notices the peaked cap sitting on top of some newspapers in the corner. He moves over to sit on the stool next to the papers and cap, just as their owner returns.

"Is your name Jack? My friend talked to you the other night . . ."

"Zach'. Who's your friend?"

"Small, dark-haired girl? Clarissa. You were showing her some photographs."

"Oh, the chippie. You're a lucky bloke. What's your name?"

"Mark, I'm from Jo'burg. At least, I was born there. I haven't been back in a pretty long time."

Mark wonders whether he should have immediately mentioned his birthplace. You never could tell what the response would be, and he didn't want to have to go through the "My dad used to work for the Institute" routine to prove he was okay. The previous summer he had been wearing a University of Witwatersrand T-shirt sent to him by a friend, when he went out to buy detergent at two in the morning. As he was waiting for the light to change, a young black man leaned out of a car on the opposite side of the street and yelled: "Is you from WITS?" pronouncing the guttural Afrikaans W and flat I: "Vuhts."

"No, a friend gave me the shirt."

"I'm from South Africa, man," he shouted. "And I hate that fucking school. Don't wear that T-shirt, you understand!"

Before Mark could cross the street and talk to the man, the light changed and the car roared off, the driver calling out once more: "You musn't wear that shirt, hey?"

Mark had been surprised. Wits was the most liberal university in the country and the first to integrate—albeit the percentage of nonwhite students and lecturers had always been small. Mark's older sister had gone there, and he has always assumed that if he had stayed in the country he too would have gone to Wits, the spawning ground for progressive thinking among South African whites.

Zach', in contrast, is delighted by Mark's admission. "You're from Joey, 'ey? I'll drink to that."

He has obviously been drinking much of the evening and is in a mood to tell someone *all* about his life. Introductions are barely over when Zach' launches into his narrative, the only interruptions coming when he orders them both more to drink, or leans over to murmur conspiratorially: "You understand what I'm talking about. I've tried talking to this lot"—indicating the crowd around the bar—"but they don't understand fuck-all. In fact, they're always wanting to tell *me* about South Africa."

. . . I'm from the Western Cape originally, a little town named Underhillsrus. Our nickname for the place was Under-hell-we-rust, because it was a real dorp with no way out. But my pa was a Bible-thumper and he at least made sure I got a good mission school education. I never did get the calling, though; so after I got my matric' I went off to a technical college near Cape Town. Olambane was a "mixed-race" techie, which means that along with a lot of Coloureds they let a few of us full-bloods in.

I did pretty well there and even had grand dreams of becoming an office clerk, or maybe even a primary-school teacher. Then two fateful things happened to me: I took a course with Dickie LeGrand and I started playing tennis. Dickie was a lecturer in sociology who'd spent some time in America. The main thing I learned from him was that it was possible for me to be good friends with a white . . . even one who had the power to fail me if he wanted. He not only didn't fail me, but he got me to fight my natural laziness and send out applications to study outside the country.

Tennis was where the real trouble started, I guess. I used to do battle every day with Lenrie Stoffels on the old cracked concrete squares that served as the school tennis courts. To this day I have scars on my knees from all the spills I took, but we got really good. I tell you . . . so good nobody could touch us. In fact, we got so good that we had the crazy idea of trying out for the intercollegiate championships once we discovered that there was nothing in the written rules to say a bush college couldn't compete. It's just that nobody had tried it before. All we needed was a letter from the Registrar to state that we were students in good standing, which turned out to be no minor obstacle. The Registrar was one of those craggy-faced Afrikaners who look like they've been carved from a chunk of the Drakensberg by an amateur. To complete the effect, he wore a pair of oversize steel-rimmed glasses mended at the rim with Scotch tape.

"You're asking me to stir up a wasps' nest, boys. Do you realize that?" he said to us.

"But, sir, all we want to do is play tennis," Stoffels replied, as though the question had not been rhetorical.

The Registrar ignored him. "Let's think ahead a little, yesss?" he said. "Suppose the teams from the white colleges agree to play you, and you win . . . what then? Do you really think anyone will let you play Sterkfontein, or, God forbid, out of Cape Province altogether? Of course most of the other teams will refuse to play you."

"Under the rules, sir, they would forfeit . . ."

"No, no, my laddie, I simply can't allow you to bring this kind of unwelcome attention—we're talking not just about you but Olambane as well."

We were pretty downcast when we left his office, and I was ready to give up right then. But not Stoffels. Most of the time he was a playboy who didn't care much about school and hardly had a thought for tomorrow, but once he got an idea in his head he stuck with it.

"The man's talking shit out of his hat, yesss," he said. "I really don't give a damn if we get to play tennis with a bunch of white boys or not, but I'm bloody sick and tired of being told what I can do and what I can't do. It's high time we stuck a firecracker up the Registrar's arse."

Stoffels put all his energy into creating that firecracker: a petition to the school's Board of Chancellors. It started out with the simple request that we get our letter, but once people started counting their grievances, they found a lot of them. Pretty soon the demands included an end to the seven o'clock curfew, subsidized books for the poorer students (which meant pretty much all of us), a course in "alternative" South African history—i.e., one that did not revel in Boer victories but told the story of how we had our land stolen from us, a reprimand for any teacher who referred to his students as "this girl" or "that boy," and so on. We had five single-spaced foolscap pages by the time we were done.

Stoffels wanted to be the one to present the petition, but Hendrickse, who had sat through the various meetings without saying a word, vetoed the idea. "Listen, Stoffels," he said. "There's no point your taking the petition to the Registrar. You're in scholastic trouble as it is. They'll just throw you out as a bad apple and forget the whole thing. But if Zach' and I present the petition . . ."

Of course, the university would have to take the grievances seriously if they were brought up by its two top students. Everyone had heard the rumor of how, only the other day, the Registrar had himself favorably mentioned Hendrickse's name at a meeting of the Chancellors.

He and I worked on the petition for a full day to tone it down, although there were still quite a few demands more than the tennis letter when it finally came time to hand it in to the Registrar. The response was swift. An emergency meeting of the Chancellors was called, and that same evening there was a knock at my door. The assistant to the Registrar stood outside, together with a burly white guy in a safari suit who smelled of police. They gave me a letter telling me that I'd been expelled for wanton and malicious conduct damaging to the best interest of Olambane College.

"Since you no longer have any reason to be in the area, you must immediately vacate the premises," the burly man said to me. He didn't give me any time to object but started pulling my clothes out of the closet and throwing them on the bed. I asked for some time to pack my things. He gave me one hour and told me he would wait outside the door until I was done. The worst thing was that only that very morning I had gotten a letter from Columbia University offering me a scholarship—providing I finished up the year in good stead.

I saw Hendrickse at the bus station . . . climbing onto a bus for Mafokeng or whatever little dorp he had sprung from. Stoffels I never saw again. One thing was clear: best student, worst student, it made no difference. They didn't give a damn about us; the only thing that counted was keeping your nose clean and your trap shut . . .

Later that week, Mark takes Clarissa to his favorite photo gallery, which, coincidentally, is holding a retrospective exhibit of South African photography. Each photograph strikes him as remarkable, as if someone has developed the plates of memory in his own mind. There are pictures of men drinking out of milk cartons, lining up on the pavement to show their passes, or sleeping in crowded vans on the way to work. There is a late-nineteenth-century picture of Hottentots playing Ping-Pong in Johannesburg. There is the well-known picture of a black woman recoiling from the bared teeth of a snarling German shepherd—its leash loosely held by a policeman who himself is rushing forward with raised whip and gleaming boots.

Mark spends a long time in front of each photograph. Clarissa soon appears to grow bored, more interested in Mark than in the photographs. He speeds up his viewing of the exhibit with a mental note to come by again and see it on his own. Then he stops in front of a picture taken in the 1960s. A white child is leaning far out of the window of an old black Humber to touch the hand of a black boy of about the same age. The child in the car is ash blond and wearing slightly faded pajamas: the other boy is wearing ragged shorts that are a little too large for him. Mark recognizes the narrow, winding streets near the Jo'burg market, where Zulu vendors would whistle shrilly through the gaps in their front teeth as they pushed along heavy barrows filled with pimply, denuded chicken carcasses or great slabs of meat.

"What are you looking at?" Clarissa asks, edging close to him.

"I think it's me," he says.

. . . You asked me about Dickie. I was pretty dispirited when I arrived home, and my parents weren't exactly helpful: my getting expelled was a bitter blow to them as well, and they really couldn't understand why, in my father's words, I had been so stupid. I got a couple of messages from Dickie at the Indian grocer's, which at that time housed the town's principal telephone, but I didn't call him back. Then he and his wife stopped by to see me while they were on a driving holiday. I'm ashamed to say I was aloof, which I could tell hurt him . . . but I just didn't want to be reminded of my failure. He kept telling me not to give up, to just make my way to America somehow or other. Once I was there, he said, no one would care whether I had finished up at the technical school or not.

Of course, there was a hitch—the authorities had their eye on me now, and after I applied for a passport I had regular visits from the local police sergeant. I won't bore you with the whole story, but there's one thing I still can't believe: that, even after everything, I thought they would just go ahead and give me my passport. It shows you how naive, how hopeful we still were in those days! I lost three months waiting to be told that permission was denied.

My next plan was to just get out of the country. I had heard that if I could get myself to Zambia, the ANC would help me get a plane to London and then I could get the Americans to help me from there. I sewed the letter into the lining of my jacket and got some false documents to show I was a migrant laborer from Malawi—no shortage of them! Someone got the wind up, though, and soon after we crossed into Rhodesia (this was before anyone had even thought of calling it Zimbabwe), they pulled me and a couple of other blokes off the train. Whoever forged my documents didn't do a very good job, since even the thickheaded local cop recognized something was wrong—my picture had practically peeled away from its backing. The customs officer must have been asleep to let me through.

Well, they found the letter in my jacket and they assumed I must have hit this Zach' Mahlope guy on the head and stolen it from him. They kept me awake for three days—and me trying to prove the whole time that I hadn't killed my very own self! Then they hauled me in front of a D.O. who gave me six months hard for traveling with falsified documents. Man, I was shit-scared. I was eighteen, a little pretty boy, and I was stuck in some work camp in the bush with a bunch of common criminals. I'd heard about rapes and stuff . . . how if you're young they make you the woman and everybody has his turn.

My first night in the prison hut. I was trembling all over trying not to look scared. There was this ugly older guy with a beard and one eye missing who kept looking at me. I thought I'd had it when he came over to me. "You from South?" he says. He was a political, from PAC. You know about the Pan African Congress, right? Hector Makhulo was his name, and he saved my skin. Once the crims saw I was with him, they didn't look at me again. There were a couple of rival gangs in there, and the leader of one of them got interested in the political education Hector was giving me. It was unnerving, the way these hoods would squat silently on their heels listening to us talk about means of production and the rise of the working class.

Hector had been in a lot tougher places than Malopindi Corrections Center. He'd even been on the Island where he'd gotten to wave to So- bukwe and Mandela. "Just stay out of the hands of Lynus Van Nickerk," he told me. We'd all heard about Van Nickerk: who liked to boast that he knew his prisoners better than their wives ever would. In fact, the only time I ever saw Hector look uncomfortable was when I asked if the rumors about the policeman were true and what that meant. He wouldn't answer, but just kept saying I had better get away before I ran the risk of finding out for myself. I knew I owed my survival at Malopindi to him, and I even started to dread the end of my prison stretch when I was to be deported back to S.A.

The day before I was released, Hector gave me the names of some PAC people in Gaberone and one final piece of advice. "When the train stops in Botswana, get up and walk out the door. I don't think they have any jurisdiction there."

I somehow kept my cool until we pulled into Gaberone, where I told the South African cop who was accompanying me that I needed to take a leak. He didn't even look up from his newspaper. I walked out the door like I knew exactly where I was going and, man, I just kept on going. Hec had made a smart guess. None of the countries involved wanted to go through extradition hearings: they simply relied on us to be good boys and sit quietly while we were carried back into the Republic. You know, Hector had a favorite saying: "A whipped dog doesn't know when its collar is off . . ."

Crossing the street one day, after he has dropped off Clarissa at her Chelsea apartment, Mark is almost run down by a familiar figure. It is Serge, his former roommate, recognizable anywhere by his question-mark shape: slight build, head hunched down, stomach thrust forward and shoulders and hips back. Serge is thirty-five but looks older; an Armenian refugee from Bulgaria, he is working as an intern in a lab at NYU while he studies for his medical boards. He is a self-proclaimed expert in "adaptogenics"—

drugs made from plants, such as Siberian ginseng and Schizandria, that are claimed to bolster the immune system. Serge was forever consuming pills of hard-packed vegetable matter and vials of evil-smelling liquid, but to little effect on his habitual jitteriness.

"I must eat *quickly*," Serge used to reply to his roommate's suggestion that he sit down to eat his dinner of Chef Boyardee or takeout lo mein. On weekend nights, Mark would come home late to find Serge lying in the dark on the living-room couch. Mark would be preparing a 2:00 A.M. snack in a last-ditch attempt to avoid the next day's hangover, when he would suddenly realize that there was a still but quite conscious and sentient body on the couch in the unlit living room. After a while he grew to expect, and even dread, this lonely nocturnal presence.

"Tell me something nice," Serge would say, heaving a deep sigh. Mark would describe the course of his day—the classes he had gone to, the customers who showed up at the processing lab, the friends he met in the evening, the movies he saw. "That's nice," Serge would interject periodically.

"Serge, how are things?" Mark now asks, pleased to see his former friend. Serge shrugs: What can one expect? ". . . And your father, is he still living with you?"

Mark had finally decided it was time to seek a new place to live when Serge's elderly father, a widower who was a slightly smaller replica of his son and had the same question-mark shape, moved in with them "temporarily." Father and son would have long debates in Armenian at the kitchen table. Once in a while, Serge would reach into his pocket and absentmindedly put a cigarette into his mouth; the old man would just as absentmindedly lean over and slap it to the floor before Serge had a chance to light it. Mark had been able to gauge the length of their conversation by the number of broken filter-tipped cigarettes lying in a half-circle around the table.

"He is still living with me. It is very bad. He said he would go out if I bring woman home, but where would he go?"

"What about your exams? And your paper . . . did you get it published?"

Serge had shown Mark the paper he was writing on plant pharmaceuticals. Serge's supervisor at NYU had told him to redo it, since the bulk of the paper consisted of lengthy quotes by various experts, followed by brief interpolations: *Dr. X of Y University writes . . . In disagreeing, Dr. Z. responds . . .*

"Terrible. All terrible. I am always writing. I am always studying." The answer comes forth in a spate of words, followed by a dramatic pause: "But I never give up. If I gave up, I would still be in Bulgaria."

Mark recalls with a blush how, when his finances were horrible and he was not sure if he would be able to pay the rent on his studio, he would cheer himself up by saying these very words.

"You're still in Bulgaria," Kylie had yelled at him one day.

It is Saturday night, and Mark, who has been unable to reach Clarissa all day, calls up his friend Gary to see if he has any plans. Gary, who knows Mark from California, invites him to a party that turns out to be held in a run-down building on Manhattan Avenue and 110th Street, a neighborhood marginal enough to make Mark wary of walking there at night. Gary, however, is very much part of the New York scene and never seems to much care what part of Manhattan he goes to or what comments and strange looks are elicited by his long blond ponytail. Mark's nervousness increases with the trouble they have finding the address because the numbers on most of the buildings have been totally or partially erased, but at last they find the right place. Mark notices that the lock to the front door is broken. Through the grease-smudged glass panes he can see the figures of two black men loitering in the lobby.

"I think we should wait a minute . . ."

"What for?" Gary asks, pushing his way into the building. "Come on, I think it's on the sixth floor."

The men in the lobby follow them silently with their eyes as they start up the unlit stairway. Mark feels his back muscles tighten and he only relaxes when he can at last hear music and see light filtering through the doorjamb of their destination. Later in the evening, he sees one of the men from the lobby again: the hostess, a short, attractive woman wearing a low-cut blouse, is hand-feeding him an empanada.

. . . I managed to find my way to the American Embassy with no trouble, and I called up the numbers Hector had given me. That was the easy part. The embassy wasn't sure whether I would be traveling to the United States as a student or a refugee; they kept telling me it would be easier if I had travel documents. I wound up sitting on my thumbs for six months, bored beyond words, before I was able to make all the arrangements to come here. If it wasn't for the PAC people, I would probably still be in Botswana while the embassy made up its mind. Then, when I got to this country, I called Columbia and they told me that my scholarship had been given to someone else because they hadn't heard from me.

I worked for PAC for about six months, going around the country giving lectures to various colleges about the evils of Apartheid. I started getting really fed up with the whole thing. Kids would always ask me if I'd been tortured; then they'd seem disappointed when I said no. It made me think of Hector, and I wondered how he'd feel if he became a profes-

sional exile on parade. You tell the same story over and over again, and after a while it becomes unreal. Finally I just packed it in. Needless to say: my friends at PAC were pretty angry. They called me a petit bourgeois, a traitor to the struggle, the whole thing. But I just couldn't face one more college student asking me: "So, how does it feel to be free?"

Mark is taking an advanced course in photography at Hunter College. He loves the hours in the darkroom—the sulfuric acid smell of the developer and the magical way an image would form on the white paper, spreading from the middle outward, rapidly, like some instant Shroud of Turin. He loves the warm red, womblike glow, the intimacy he forms with a girl who always wears the same fuzzy mohair sweater and seems to share his schedule. They often brush against each other as they move from the enlarging lamp to the chemicals, but to speak would break their bond.

The people in his class think Mark's black-and-white photographs of New York were taken in Johannesburg. One picture shows a bare-chested black man carrying a rolled-up carpet on his shoulders. Back-lit by bright sunlight, he looms enormous, his burden larger than himself. In another picture, a bearded and tangle-haired tramp gives the viewer a gap-toothed grin as he proffers an unlabeled fifth of some grain spirit. It is not only the subject matter that seems imported straight from South Africa. In the quality of the light, in the angles of shadows falling from abandoned buildings, in the stance and posture of the human parade, the camera chooses to fix those moments that mirror the lost reality of a distant land.

Mark calls Clarissa to see if she wants to go with him to Zach's fortieth birthday party. She tells him no; she is going to watch a baseball game with a friend in Brooklyn.

"This is your chance to see a bunch of South Africans get roaring drunk," Mark cajoles. "How can you pass up such an opportunity?"

"I can't miss the Mets! You know, the season's just started and I even went out and bought myself a cap to watch the game in."

"Another time, then?" Maybe when the season's over.

"Mmmh."

When Mark arrives at the party everyone else is already there, excitedly watching the game on a small black-and-white TV in the living room. He helps himself to a beer in the kitchen, then wanders over to the couch on the far end of the room to read an old copy of *Staffrider* that he found on a bookshelf. A young woman sits curled in an armchair nearby, her attention taken up by a sleepy cat that tolerates her caresses with mild ill temper. Her hair is long and straight and hangs down to hide her face as she leans forward to pet the cat; now and then the scrim parts to reveal large, pretty eyes and skin pitted with acne. Mark's thoughts turn sadly to Clarissa, who is probably sitting before a wide-screen in some Brooklyn bar—everybody's darling in her Mets cap, with a stein of beer clutched in her small fists.

"Is that a South African magazine?" the girl asks, awkwardly looking away from Mark.

"It's a literary magazine that I think's folded. The name comes from young African daredevils who would run along the roofs of moving trains."

She looks puzzled, so Mark adds, "Westerns are very popular in the township. The guy who rides on top of the wagon is said to be riding staff."

"Oh, I'll have to ask Simon if he ever did that."

The latter turns out to be her boyfriend, Simon Nxhlenge, a tall wiry fellow who is sitting directly in front of the television cheering on the Mets. "Soccer was always my game," he later tells Mark. "But I love watching baseball. There's this moment when the batsman looks in the pitcher's face and tries to figure out what he's going to throw. It's like when you're in a bar and you notice that some tough is looking at you. You don't know whether he's going to pull a knife or buy you a drink." He mimics the staring-down, the uncertainty on the victim's face.

Simon reveals that he is studying journalism through Columbia's General Studies program. His inspiration is Nat Nakasa, the young black journalist who founded *The Classic*, an important literary magazine in the sixties.

"I met him when I was a little kid. We gave him a ride to Durban," Mark reminisces. Nat was unlike any adult he had met before, keeping the children entertained with absurd jokes about parliamentarians and pumpkins and the difficulty of distinguishing between the two. Mark remembers Nat's "proof" for transmigration of the soul—that dogs understand Afrikaans. "If a dog hears me speaking Zulu, he'll run after me and bite me; but if I shout *voetsek* at him in Afrikaans, he will run away. You see, if an Afrikaner is very good in this life, then he gets reborn as a dog. But if a dog behaves badly, he has to come back as an Afrikaner."

"You met Nat? Whites have all the luck."

"He was a great guy. I can't believe he committed suicide."

"He didn't. He was pushed," Simon says with conviction. "The police had to kill him because he was too dangerous to be allowed to stay alive."

Simon returns to his seat in front of the television and Mark watches the screen from the back of the room. He tries to see it the way Simon does, but all he can discern are distant stick figures moving back and forth and the occasional close-up of a strong jaw vigorously chewing gum. His head feels heavy with beer, and he is relieved when Zach'—whom he did not notice leaving the house—reappears with several family-size buckets of Kentucky Fried Chicken. Someone else has bought two more cases of beer, and they all watch the Mets, gnaw on chicken bones, and drink from bottles that are icy from being in the freezer. Near Mark, a Xhosa named Johan and a Zulu named Solly are disparaging each other's tribal leaders with mock ferocity.

"That Matanzima, he put his own brother in jail. His own brother!"

"And Buth'? His brother picked up some white dollie in Sun City and moved her into the ancestral kraal."

"You'll be sorry when Buth' is running the country."

"Everyone will be sorry . . ."

The drinking continues unabated after the game is over. Mark knows he has reached his limit, though he is unable to resist taking another near-frozen bottle when the Mozambiquan whose name he has forgotten hands it to him with the words: "In my country, we call beer like this 'stupid with cold.' " There is a ring at the front door, followed by a loud banging in the hallway as a tall youth comes in tripping over his guitar case. He is dressed in jeans and denim jacket, has a remarkably friendly grin and long red hair braided into dreadlocks. His guitar case is plastered with stickers bearing the symbols of countries and towns—the Eiffel Tower, Copenhagen's Mermaid, elephants rampant from some indeterminate African game park.

"It's Julian," Zach' and Johan shout simultaneously. "Come on in, you Boer!"

"Zach', Johan, Solly, Si," Julian beams. Simon nods imperceptibly, intent on picking at the label of his Brahma beer, which has begun to separate from the bottle as moisture condenses underneath it. "Julian Visser," the redhead introduces himself, extending his hand toward Mark and in the process almost kicking over the low coffee table.

"He's an Afrikaner, but I had to teach him Afrikaans," Zach' roars, while Julian looks happily around him as if not knowing Afrikaans is an accomplishment.

"My mother is English," the youth explains. "Her and us kids staged a coup in our household—no Afrikaans. I almost didn't get my matric' because of it."

"The only songs Julian knew were bloody rubbish by Jackson Browne and Billy Joel," Zach' grins. "So I taught him 'Suikerbossie' and 'Sarie Marais'—"

"And 'Daar Kom die Ali Bama . . .' "

"Ja, but I'm not talking about the slave songs, I'm talking about the real *Rock* songs, the ones the old boer Rocks sing when they sit around the braai after a hard day of kicking kaffirs out in the fields."

"Zach' means my father," Julian responds. "He's a real *verkrampte*, a hard-liner. He couldn't believe it when he came to visit me and finds I'm sharing a flat with a black man."

"His dad walked in when we were all sitting around singing Afrikaans songs. He didn't know whether to shit or cry or just be happy that his son is finally learning *die taal*."

"*O bring my terug na die ou Transvaal*," Julian sings in a voice that is hoarse and untrained yet pleasant to the ear.

"Very touching," Simon cuts in. "If we can just get Botha and Mandela to sing 'Sarie Marais' together, we could forget Apartheid and all live happily ever after."

There is an embarrassed silence, broken at last by Zach' saying in slightly aggrieved tones: "Simon takes things too seriously. You can't hate a language: especially since it's us Coloureds who invented it . . . though I'll bet you the government would like to hang me for state terrorism for even suggesting that idea."

"I don't care if I never hear another word of Afrikaans in my life," Simon mutters.

"You spend too much time worrying about women," Zach' tells Mark when they are sitting in the Sunfish some weeks later. "You can't rely on someone else to give meaning to your life, you have to do it for yourself."

"What are you suggesting in their place? Drinking?" Annoyed, Mark almost adds "*Social activism?*" but thinks better of it.

"No . . . I suppose I'm jealous. Your obsessions are at least normal, the sign of a healthy ego. I can look at a pretty woman and feel attracted to her. I can lie all night in my bed and fantasize about her, or worry about why she rejected me, or just think of the nice time we might have had. But I can never forget who I am, that I am this displaced person with no roots and no reason for being here except that I can't go home. Sometimes I walk along the pavement and I feel it all slip away from me. I become disembodied, and I have to tell myself not to ignore the cars when I cross the street."

Zach's speech—which has the ring of something said or thought often —dispels what's left of Mark's irritability. "I don't know," he responds. "You seem to serve as a pretty solid peg for some people. Like Julian."

Zach' smiles. "Julian's a child, a naïf. He even tells me I'm his *true* father, as if you can choose to take on new parents. You know, he pitched up in New York with just his guitar and a little money, no plans."

"And he found his way to you."

"Ja, I was looking for a roommate and this bloke I know who deals with draft resistance passed him on to me." Zach' paused and smiled in remembrance. "A couple of months after he came here, Julian got busted in Penn Station with a bag of pot in his jacket pocket. He was high as a kite, picking over and over at the same chord on his guitar. I had one hell of a time stopping him from being deported. I can tell you that. We had to get half the bigwigs in Harlem to testify to his good character . . . and that includes this preacher I know. We told the judge, this boy left his country because he didn't want to fight against his black brothers. He's heartsick over the horrible things going on over there. That's why he smokes pot."

"The real reason we left South Africa," Charles Spiegelman used to tell the English and American guests to their London home, "was *not* that I had to witness the filthy hands of an Afrikaner policeman going through my wife's underwear. *Nor* that my principal achievement seemed to be in helping hitherto mildly discontented Africans educate themselves to the point where their only possible response to their own impotence was to become hopeless drunkards, outcasts in both the white world and their own. *Nor* even that I myself had to compromise my ideals every day so that I could keep the Institute open and be praised for my idealism. *But* that I did not want to see my sons grow up and be inducted into the South African army."

While this argument was invariably well received by their visitors, it was a constant source of annoyance to the adolescent Mark, who wondered why he had not been consulted in a decision that had been taken for his "own good." Charles was the only one in the family who truly found the move to England a positive one. Mark's impression was that his father's work was a pleasant round of reviewing grant proposals from altruistic researchers wishing to study the infinite range of ills brought on by racism, punctuated by the business lunches at the inner city's finer restaurants, whose details he would later recount at the dinner table. For the children, England was characterized by its oppressive crampedness. They had moved from the beginning of a South African summer into London at midwinter, and the large but dingy apartment and dull gray days made Mark long for a country that took on greater brightness with its ever-increasing distance.

Mark and Joel had been accepted into a prestigious high school run on public school lines; its headmaster had a habit of waiving the school's rigid entrance requirements for foreign children, taking the neo-Darwinist view that there must be some spark of intelligence in anyone whose parents had the good sense to leave their blighted countries for Blessed Albion. The rich blue of the school uniform announced to the world that the wearer was a member of the intellectual elite and made Mark and Joel's walk home through a rough neighborhood of poorer local schools even more perilous. After one particularly harassed journey home through a chilling mist of fine rain, Mark railed at his father: "You're always talking about how we left South Africa to gain freedom. Here, I'm afraid to go outside half the time. *I* was much freer there."

"What ever happened to Simon?" Mark asks Zach' one day, when they are once again bellying up at the Sunfish." He seemed like a nice guy."

Zach' gives him an ironical look. "Simon? *Nice?* There's nothing 'nice' about Simon."

"Interesting, then."

Zach' heaves a sigh, then replies: "That interesting, nice guy broke his sweet little girlfriend's jaw a couple of weeks ago. He used to beat her up something terrible—I can't tell you why. Maybe because she was white and rich and pretty and thought she loved him. Maybe because he just enjoyed doing it. Julian told me the story. I wanted to kill Simon . . . or at least knock some sense into him."

"What happened to the girl?"

"Oh, I don't know. She spent a night or two in the hospital and then they let her go. Her parents were plenty upset; I heard they got the police after him, but she persuaded them to drop the complaint. If he ever goes near her again, he'll be in big trouble—I can tell you that, boy."

"Is anyone in touch with him? He seemed so smart . . . even if he was angry."

"Actually, I did see him. Yesterday, in fact. He was sitting in one of those needle parks on Seventh Avenue yelling things at nobody. Just another crazy black man in New York City. I walked past him a couple of times but he didn't recognize me. Finally he looked up and said: 'You got a brother? He just walked by.' "

Although he senses it is a lost cause, Mark calls Clarissa several times, until she agrees to meet him in the evening after one of her summer classes in philosophy at Columbia. Her sister had already told Mark that Clarissa has three passions in life: men, Kierkegaard, and baseball ("or baseball, Kierkegaard, and men—the order varies"). She had also intimated that Mark has blown it, though she did not tell him this outright.

As Mark rides the No. 1 train up to Columbia, he reviews in his head all he plans to say to Clarissa when he sees her: that she should know he was simply distracted by his own confusion and not indifferent to her, that it is a misjudgment of the situation not to realize he *does* care for her, that they should give it another go.

He leaves the 116th Street station and walks over to the Columbia steps still muttering to himself his incontrovertible arguments. Although he is late for their rendezvous, she is later still and he seats himself beside the statue named Alma Mater to wait. A couple comes out of the Philosophy Building and stand in close conversation for a minute or two, then the girl detaches herself and hurries toward Mark with quick, light steps.

"Clarissa!" he calls out as she is about to walk past him.

"Hi. How are you?" Her face is set as if there is some task she feels she has to get through.

"I'm okay," he replies. "What do you feel like doing? It's such a nice night, maybe we should just take a walk?"

She shrugs assent and they start strolling back toward Broadway. Mark realizes that there is no point in saying any of his rehearsed thoughts, and he wishes he could just cancel out the evening and be back in his room with a book and his music, or in the Sunfish with Zach'. By the time they have bought ice-cream cones at Häagen Dazs and sauntered back onto campus, they have both thawed enough to be enjoying each other's company. Clarissa even laughs when he reads aloud some of the names carved above the library: "Demosthenes, Plato, Aristotle. I didn't realize the alumni were quite so famous."

They go and sit down in a grassy lot that is generally filled with sunbathing students during the daytime but is now quite empty. It is a perfect early summer night. The air is warm, but not uncomfortably so, and there is a floating diaphanous mist that lends a mood of magical unreality to the surroundings. Mark likes listening to Clarissa's half-humorous ragging on her classmates' pettinesses and stupidities—it is her "lovable brat" quality—and is glad now that they met here and not in some noisy anonymous bar. As he glances around, though, his eye is stopped by a ghostly movement in the grass some distance away. Peering harder into the surrounding darkness, he notices several more faint gray shapes moving around the lawn.

"Let's go," he says quietly. He stands up and holds out his hand to help Clarissa up.

"But it's so nice right here . . ." she says.

"Seriously, I think we should go."

They begin walking toward the nearest opening in the fence and still she has not noticed the gray shapes. But just as they step onto the path, a large rat dashes squeaking in front of them as it heads for shelter in the bushes.

"Ugh," Clarissa says, and suddenly shivers. "I hate those things. No matter how long I live in the city, I'll never get used to them."

"They're all over the lawn. They must have been hiding in their holes when we first walked in."

As if to herald the irrevocable breaking of their pleasant mood, a speaker in a nearby dorm blares out some very loud and indistinguishable heavy metal music.

"Do you ever feel," Mark muses, "as if you had slipped just a little bit out of time, maybe taken a right turn where you should have taken a left or gone back to check whether you'd turned off the light in your room when what you should have done is left the apartment right away . . . and now everything is just that little bit out of kilter and you'll never quite catch up?"

"No."

Mark has just finished working a half day at the photo lab and is about to head home when he sees Zach' coming toward him. Zach' is on his way to visit a musician friend of his and he invites Mark to accompany him. As they walk, Zach' mentions a program on poor Afrikaners that he has just seen.

"I used to hate Afrikaners before I came to this country," he says, "but from this distance I can finally have some grudging sympathy for them. Not for the government, of course, but for the ordinary, everyday worker who's terrified that someone of my complexion is going to steal his job. When I heard this woman talking about having to queue up to get milk for her kids, I felt such a rush of nostalgia. She sounded like my mother."

"It's funny, as an English speaker I was probably more insulated from Afrikaners than you, or even most Africans. We never really dealt with them except when we went on holiday and drove through small towns. In fact, for a lot of my friends, their first encounter with living with Afrikaners was in the army . . . which can't be the best way to get to know a people."

"Ja, from here you can see how much my culture and theirs have bled into each other," Zach' grins. "I guess I just miss what was familiar. If I ever went back, my sentimentality probably wouldn't last a day."

They stop to buy falafel at a Lebanese shop and go into a park just off Avenue A to eat their sandwiches. The park is deserted except for a few tramps sleeping on the benches and the ubiquitous drug dealers indifferently murmuring "Smoke? Smoke?" Mark initially feels nervous sitting there on the pigeon-fouled bench away from the bustle of the streets, but Zach's calm is contagious as he holds forth on his friend's musicianship ("He plays too much George Benson stuff, but his tone is outstanding").

They leave the park and walk down the far side of Avenue A, past a fenced-in construction site. A group of lean and muscled black teenagers are hanging about the fence, occasionally tossing a stone or can into the gaping hole left by the ground movers. One of them looks hard at Mark and Zach' and whispers to his companion. Zach' pays no attention and continues talking, but just when they seem safely past the gang, Mark detects a movement behind him. An arm snakes around his neck and he feels the sharp point of a knife blade pushed up against the base of his ear. He stands absolutely still while expert hands go through his pockets. Behind him there is the sound of scuffling feet and he hears Zach's voice, "Come on, brothers. We're not rich folk."

Mark starts to turn around, but the arm tightens around his throat and a quiet, firm voice behind his ear says, "Just be cool." There is a thump as something solid hits human flesh. The arm around his throat is suddenly withdrawn and Mark is given a shove that sends him staggering into the fence. Turning, he sees their assailants start to run off, but one of them stops and kicks hard at the head of the prostrate figure on the sidewalk. Once. Twice.

"I hate these fucking Africans," the youth says, before he too pivots and runs away. "They're always giving you shit."

Mark arrives at the hospital, where after two and a half days Zach' has just regained full consciousness. He has a subdural hematoma and is still having trouble with one of his eyes. When Mark walks in, Zach' has his eyes shut and Julian is asleep on the armchair where he has been sitting for the past forty-eight hours picking over and over again at the chords to "Sarie Marais." He has somehow charmed the nurses into letting him stay—despite his dirty bare feet that protrude from beneath his curled-up legs.

Zach' wakes up with a start. He takes a moment to regain focus before he recognizes Mark, who is relieved when Zach' smiles and it is clear he does not resent Mark's escaping unscathed.

"I'm glad he's asleep." He indicates Julian fondly. "He was beginning to drive me crazy with his boere songs."

"I'm told it's good medicine," Mark replies.

"I'm sure. The worst thing is I'm not allowed to laugh, or to cough. I can feel this tickle deep down inside me, but I have to suppress it." He closes his eyes and is silent for a few minutes, then he murmurs. "The real worst thing is that I only had about ten dollars on me. I have no idea what I was fighting for."

GOING HOME
AGAIN

AMA ATA AIDOO, born in 1942 in a town near the center of Ghana, fiction writer, poet, and playwright, is one of the leading voices of African feminism. Along with other wonderful women novelists of western Africa—particularly the Nigerians Buchi Emecheta, Flora Nwapa, and Adaora Lily Ulasi, and the Senegalese Mariama Ba—Ama Ata Aidoo has helped bring the literature of that area out into Global Cultures. She was educated at the University of Ghana in Legon, but also at Stanford University; she was taught in Ghana, Kenya, and Tanzania, but also at various American universities. In the 1980s, she was Ghana's secretary for education. Her first novel, *Sister Killjoy, or Reflections from a Black-eyed Squint* (1966), is a wry, strangely surrealistic, exuberant, confusing look at Africans studying in Europe, spinning webs of cultures, deflating imperialism with sarcasm. *Changes* was published in 1991. In "Everything Counts," her central character is an earnest economics professor who has come home from getting married abroad (*not* to a foreigner) to help with "the revolution." The term revolution refers to the Ghanian people's prolonged effort to recover from the anti-Western economic policies of their brilliant and ambiguous leader Kwame Nkrumah, who in 1966 was overthrown by a military government, which was itself overthrown in 1972, and so forth through much chaos ever since. She finds—like so many of the writers in Global Cultures—that the political battle of home, the battle to overcome imperialism, to create a peaceful nation, is being played out in a "battle of the sexes" and a battle of cultural identities as well.

Formulating a national identity has been a dream in the Philippines through successive imperialisms—Spanish, and, after 1898, American—and through successive attempts to unite the peoples of the populated areas (the Philippines consists of 7,000 islands, 70 language groups). Philippine literature has a rich tradition of novels and stories about exiles who come back home in search of that identity, having failed to find any way to live abroad without it. It also has a strong strain of works in English, in Tagalog (a relatively "national" vernacular), and in many local vernaculars that show how those who leave the country's agricultural-traditional communities for the cities—Philippine or American—become heartless, lost. **PAULINO LIM, JR.**, who writes in English, is a professor of English at California State University, Long Beach, although he has also taught in Taiwan. His story "Homecoming," from *Passion Summer* (New Day Publishers, Quezon City, 1988), won the 1985 *Asiaweek* Short Story Competition. It alludes to the dozen years that the central character has spent in America, a dozen years during which President Ferdinand Marcos, a president so unlike the progressives who have had streets named after them—Roxas and Magsaysay—declared martial law (1973) and then granted himself imperial powers for life, with American indulgence. The country became deeply corrupt, the poor got poorer, the rich got richer, the Communist Party carried on a tenacious guerrilla war—but none of this is spoken about directly between the two brothers. They speak, unknowingly, in a kind of code full of little daily events and irritations, one having his nostalgia punctured, the other his patriotic sentimentality pricked. The homecoming cannot happen—there is no agreement about where the "home" is.

The effects of American imperialism dominate modern Puerto Rican literature, too. **AURORA LEVINS MORALES** makes it a point when she prepares bibliographic material for her publishers to say that she was born in 1954, just a week before a group of Nationalist Party members, fighters for Puerto Rican independence, stunned the American people by staging an armed attack on the U.S. House of Representatives. She grew up in the coffee farming barrio of Indiera in western Puerto Rico, daughter of a Jewish father and a South Bronx–born Puerto Rican mother, both communists. Her mother, Rosario Morales, is herself a writer and has co-authored with her daughter *Getting Home Alive* (Firebrand Books, 1986). The family emigrated when Aurora Levins Morales was thirteen, and she now lives in the San Francisco Bay area, where she is active in Latina and lesbian and Latina lesbian cultural circles. The region of her birth, as her story shows, fell into decay as Puerto Rico's economy became more and more oriented around tourism. But her homecoming is, unlike so many in *Global Cultures*, one that produces a kind of peace, reconciliation: "I don't belong to Indiera. I never will. But Indiera belongs to me." The story, beautifully going back and forth between languages, tells of that reconciliation.

For the nameless characters in **REINALDO ARENAS's** "End of a Story," however, there is no ending to the grief, the pain, the loss. Arenas, born in 1943, was among the youngest of a brilliant generation of Cuban writers brought into being by Fidel Castro's guerrilla campaign against the Batista tyranny and then by the Cuban Revolution of 1959—a revolution of such promise and such contradictions. Arenas' fame was growing abroad—his second novel *El mundo alucinante* (1969) was already published in Mexico (in English: *Hallucinations*, 1976)—when he was arrested on a morals charge, spent a year in prison, and began his period of obscurity and peril in Cuba, where Castro's regime had no tolerance for homosexuals. He continued to be critical of the regime, and escaped it with the Mariel boatlift in 1980. In America, he published novels prolifically, but, tragically, his freedom was short-lived: He died of AIDS in 1990, leaving behind a last work published posthumously as *Before Night Falls* (1993). Unlike the friend in his story, Arenas' funeral remained in his new home; his ashes were not sent drifting back to the island he had loved and detested. "End of a Story" tells, kaleidoscopically, in a dizzying gazetteer of streets in New York and streets in Havana, the story of two lovers, one who has committed suicide and one who must decide how to tell their story. (Winston Leyland collected this story and a brilliant array of others in *My Deep Dark Pain is Love* (1983), the second anthology of Latin American gay writing issued by Gay Sunshine Press in San Francisco.)

Everything Counts

Ama Ata Aidoo

S H E   U S E D to look at their serious faces and laugh silently to herself. They meant what they were saying. The only thing was that loving them all as sister, lover and mother, she also knew them. She knew them as intimately as the hems of her dresses. That it was so much easier for them to talk about the beauty of being oneself. Not to struggle to look like white girls. Not straightening one's hair. And above all, not to wear the wig.

The wig. Ah, the wig. They say it is made of artificial fibre. Others swear that if it is not gipsy hair, then it is Chinese. Extremists are sure they are made from the hairs of dead white folk—this one gave her nightmares, for she had read somewhere, a long time ago, about Germans making lampshades out of Jewish people's skins. And she would shiver for all the world to see. At other times, when her world was sweet like when she and Fiifi were together, the pictures that came into her mind were not so terrible. She would just think of the words of that crazy *highlife* song and laugh. The one about the people at home scrambling to pay exorbitant prices for second-hand clothes from America . . . and then as a student of economics, she would also try to remember some other truths she knew about Africa. Second-rate experts giving first-class dangerous advice. Or expressing uselessly fifth-rate opinions. Second-hand machinery from someone else's junkyard.

Snow-ploughs for tropical farms.

Outmoded tractors.

Discarded aeroplanes.

And now, wigs—made from other people's unwanted hair.

At this point, tough though she was, tears would come into her eyes. Perhaps her people had really missed the boat of original thinking after all? And if Fiifi asked her what was wrong, she explained, telling the same story every time. He always shook his head and laughed at her, which meant that in the end, she would laugh with him.

At the beginning, she used to argue with them, earnestly. "But what has wearing wigs got to do with the revolution?" "A lot sister," they would say. "How?" she would ask, struggling not to understand.

"Because it means that we have no confidence in ourselves." Of course, she understood what they meant.

"But this is funny. Listen, my brothers, if we honestly tackled the problems facing us, we wouldn't have the time to worry about such trifles as wigs."

She made them angry. Not with the mild displeasure of brothers, but with the hatred of wounded lovers. They looked terrible, their eyes changing, turning red and warning her that if she wasn't careful, they would destroy her. Ah, they frightened her a lot, quite often too. Especially when she thought of what filled them with that kind of hatred.

This was something else. She had always known that in her society men and women had had more important things to do than fight each other in the mind. It was not in school that she had learnt this. Because you know, one did not really go to school to learn about Africa . . . As for this, what did the experts call it? War of the sexes? Yes, as for this war of the sexes, if there had been any at all in the old days among her people, they could not possibly have been on such a scale. These days, any little "No" one says to a boy's "Yes" means one is asking for a battle. O, there just are too many problems.

As for imitating white women, mm, what else can one do, seeing how some of our brothers behave? The things one has seen with one's own eyes. The stories one has heard. About African politicians and diplomats abroad. But then, one has enough troubles already without treading on big toes.

After a time, she gave up arguing with them, her brothers. She just stated clearly that the wig was an easy way out as far as she was concerned. She could not afford to waste that much time on her hair. The wig was, after all, only a hat. A turban. Would they please leave her alone? What was more, if they really wanted to see a revolution, why didn't they work constructively in other ways for it?

She shut them up. For they knew their own weaknesses too, that they themselves were neither prepared nor ready to face the realities and give up those aspects of their personal dream which stood between them and the meaningful actions they ought to take. Above all, she was really beautiful and intelligent. They loved and respected her.

She didn't work that hard and she didn't do brilliantly in the examinations. But she passed and got the new degree. Three months later, she and Fiifi agreed that it would be better for them to get married among a foreign people. Weddings at home were too full of misguided foolishness. She flew home, a month after the wedding, with two suitcases. The rest of their luggage was following them in a ship. Fiifi would not be starting work for about three months so he had branched off to visit some one or two African countries.

Really, she had found it difficult to believe her eyes. How could she? From the air-stewardesses to the grade-three typists in the offices, every girl simply wore a wig. Not cut discreetly short and disguised to look like her own hair as she had tried to do with hers. But blatantly, aggressively, crudely. Most of them actually had masses of flowing curls falling on their shoulders. Or huge affairs piled on top of their heads.

Even that was not the whole story. Suddenly, it seemed as if all the girls and women she knew and remembered as having smooth black skins had turned light-skinned. Not uniformly. Lord, people looked as though a terrible plague was sweeping through the land. A plague that made funny patchworks of faces and necks.

She couldn't understand it so she told herself she was dreaming. Maybe there was a simple explanation. Perhaps a new god had been born while she was away, for whom there was a new festival. And when the celebrations were over, they would remove the masks from their faces and those horrid-looking things off their heads.

A week went by and the masks were still on. More than once, she thought of asking one of the girls she had been to school with, what it was all about. But she restrained herself. She did not want to look more of a stranger than she already felt—seeing she was also the one *black* girl in the whole city . . .

Then the long vacation was over and the students of the national university returned to the campus. O . . . she was full of enthusiasm, as she prepared her lectures for the first few weeks. She was going to tell them what was what. That as students of economics, their role in nation-building was going to be crucial. Much more than big-mouthed, big-living politicians, they could do vital work to save the continent from the grip of its enemies. If only for a little while: and blah, blah, blah.

Meanwhile, she was wearing her own hair. Just lightly touched to make it easier to comb. In fact, she had been doing that since the day they got married. The result of some hard bargaining. The final agreement was that any day of the year, she would be around with her own hair. But she could still keep that thing by for emergencies. Anyhow, the first morning in her life as a lecturer arrived. She met the students at eleven. They numbered between fifteen and twenty. About a third of them were girls. She had not seen them walk in and so could not tell whether they had beautiful bodies or not. But lord, were their faces pretty? So she wondered as she stared, open-mouthed at them, how she would have felt if she had been a young male: She smiled momentarily at herself for the silliness of the idea. It was a mistake to stop the smile. She should just have gone on and developed it into a laugh. For close at its heels was a jealousy so big, she did not know what to do with it. Who were these girls? Where had they come from to confront her with their youth? The fact that she wasn't really that much older than any of them did not matter. Nor even that she recognised one or two who had come as first years, when she was in her fifth year. She remembered them quite clearly. Little skinny greenhorns scuttling timidly away to do her bidding as the house-prefect. Little frightened lost creatures from villages and developing slums who had come to this citadel of an alien culture to be turned into ladies . . .

And yet she was there as a lecturer. Talking about one thing or another. Perhaps it was on automation as the newest weapon from the industrially developed countries against the wretched ones of the earth. Or something of the sort. Perhaps since it was her first hour with them, she was only giving them general ideas on what the course was about.

Anyhow, her mind was not there with them. Look at that one, Grace Mensah. Poor thing. She had cried and cried when she was being taught to use knives and forks. And now look at her.

It was then she noticed the wigs. All the girls were wearing them. The biggest ones she had seen so far. She felt very hot and she who hardly ever sweated, realised that not only were her hands wet, but also streams of water were pouring from the nape of her neck down her spine. Her brassière felt too tight. Later, she was thankful that black women have not yet learnt to faint away in moments of extreme agitation.

But what frightened her was that she could not stop the voice of one of the boys as it came from across the sea, from the foreign land, where she had once been with them.

"But Sissie, look here, we see what you mean. Except that it is not the real point we are getting at. Traditionally, women from your area might have worn their hair long. However, you've still got to admit that there is an element in this wig-wearing that is totally foreign. Unhealthy."

Eventually, that first horrid lecture was over. The girls came to greet her. They might have wondered what was wrong with this new lecturer. And so probably did the boys. She was not going to allow that to worry her. There always is something wrong with lecturers. Besides, she was going to have lots of opportunities to correct what bad impressions she had created . . .

The next few weeks came and went without changing anything. Indeed, things got worse and worse. When she went home to see her relatives, the questions they asked her were so painful she could not find answers for them.

"What car are you bringing home, Sissie? We hope it is not one of those little coconut shells with two doors, heh? . . . And oh, we hope you brought a refrigerator. Because you simply cannot find one here these days. And if you do, it costs so much . . ." How could she tell them that cars and fridges are ropes with which we are hanging ourselves? She looked at their faces and wondered if they were the same ones she had longed to see with such pain, when she was away. Hmm, she began to think she was in another country. Perhaps she had come down from the plane at the wrong airport? Too soon? Too late? Fiifi had not arrived in the country yet. That might have had something to do with the sudden interest she developed in the beauty contest. It wasn't really a part of her. But there it was. Now she was eagerly buying the morning papers to look out for the photos of the winners from the regions. Of course, the winner on the national level was going to enter for the Miss Earth title.

She knew all along that she would go to the stadium. And she did not find it difficult to get a good seat.

She should have known that it would turn out like that. She had not thought any of the girls beautiful. But her opinions were not really asked for, were they? She just recalled, later, that all the contestants had worn wigs except one. The winner. The most light-skinned of them all. No, she didn't wear a wig. Her hair, a mulatto's, quite simply, quite naturally, fell in a luxuriant mane on her shoulders . . .

She hurried home and into the bathroom where she vomited—and cried and cried and vomited for what seemed to her to be days. And all this time, she was thinking of how right the boys had been. She would have liked to run to where they were to tell them so. To ask them to forgive her for having dared to contradict them. They had been so very right. Her brothers, lovers and husbands. But nearly all of them were still abroad. In Europe, America or some place else. They used to tell her that they found the thought of returning home frightening. They would be frustrated . . .

Others were still studying for one or two more degrees. A Master's here. A Doctorate there . . . That was the other thing about the revolution.

Homecoming

Paulino Lim, Jr.

PERHAPS, SOMEDAY I will know what really happened to my brother. I took him to the airport this morning. He turned as he entered the terminal, his face behind his thick bifocals showing no expression, lifted a hand and waved. It was a doll's goodbye, a child holding the hand and shaking it. I did not wave back. All that trouble that he caused, getting everybody excited about his homecoming, his *balikbayan*, and then acting the way he did. More accurately not acting at all, as if he were shell-shocked, benumbed by some undiagnosed injury.

What gets me is that, as far as I can see, nothing really happened. A threat maybe, but no harm. For a while I even saw it as a game, like betting a thousand pesos on the unfavored rooster at the cockpit. That was how I felt, when I heard his voice and saw five men circling him, the two suitcases at his feet, and he was shaking his head.

I edged my way through the crowd; my brother was handing out dollar bills to the men. When I saw the sampaguita garlands around his arm, I surmised that he first bought the flowers; then the young men went after him and asked for a "gift." Quite ordinary for me, but what followed during the next five minutes must have pushed him against his fears about coming home, after an absence of a dozen years.

I have always felt a softness in my brother's character, and the sampaguita garlands made me feel this way again. Where did he think he was? Hawaii? He must have fit the men's profile of a victim, a likely prey. He should have come with his wife and two children; she is tougher, and the children a better protection against evil than the sampaguita.

He took up law because that was what our father, now dead, wanted, but I'm sure he preferred music or philosophy. He married a nurse who landed a hospital job in Newport Beach and later got him to emigrate to the United States. He promised to take the California Bar Examination, but he did not write about passing the bar or working in a law office. Instead he wrote about his job in a newspaper office in Orange County. I would have been proud of him as a lawyer. Why would he want to trade a law office in the Philippines for a newspaper morgue in California? For a Toyota and a Buick in his garage. I'll keep my sturdy Tamaraw jeep, live near my brothers and sisters, and watch my nieces and nephews grow up, here in my own country where life spills into the streets and houses unable to contain it.

I did have that one day with my brother when he was his old self and wanted to visit places he knew as a student in Manila. He arrived a day earlier than his two suitcases did. From what he told me, I gathered that the flight from Los Angeles was delayed and the baggage could not be transferred to the connecting flight to Manila in time for the scheduled departure from Tokyo. But my brother insisted on another explanation and I did not want to contradict him.

"You know," he said, "on the flight from Tokyo to Manila, I sat between two pudgy Filipino nurses."

I thought I'd ask him when I had the chance, how he kept his weight, approaching middle age. No paunch, hardly any fat.

"They came from two different flights, one from Chicago and the other from New York. It's an education to see how the complexion of passengers changed from the flight to Tokyo and aboard the plane to Manila. From white, yellow, black and brown and then to almost all brown. Except for the Chinese . . . the Chinese are everywhere. I think there were a few Mormon missionaries aboard."

I chuckled at his observation but kept silent. I wanted to hear his version of why his luggage did not arrive with him.

"Do you know that the nurse from New York had six pieces of luggage."

"Six!"

"That's right, she told me, six. The airline allows you two and charges one hundred and seven dollars for each additional piece of luggage. Some enterprising Filipino took the maximum allowable size and made carboard boxes to fit. These are sold as *balikbayan* boxes in Filipino stores in the U.S. Zero weight, strong, disposable. And they stuff these with radios, cassettes, and Betamaxes."

"Well, you know how it is, Brother. You can't come home without gifts for relatives and friends, without *pasalubong*."

"And for checkers and porters and customs. I know, I know; just look what happened to my suitcases."

I was going to say, what's another day, but didn't.

"I must say I learned a lot from those two nurses. They told me how to fill out my customs declaration form. Just put 'personal effects,' they said. A tip here, a tip there and you might not have to open your bags."

"Well, at least, tonight you won't be as tired as you were yesterday. That was a long flight, wasn't it?"

"Yeah, eighteen hours, including two stopovers in Tokyo and Okinawa. The nurses told me that I must be careful about the transportation from the airport. They've heard of contract workers from Saudi Arabia who were waylaid by taxi drivers, and jumped upon by thugs, who stripped them of everything, even the clothes on their backs."

"An isolated case," I said, trying to allay his fears. "Besides we have secret marshalls in Manila, organized to fight crime."

"What good would that do? How's the jeepney passenger to know who's a mugger and who's a marshal?"

I was beginning to be irritated by my older brother, but did not want to offend him. I said, "I'm sure you have crime in Los Angeles, too."

"I know. Did I ever tell you that our house was burglarized? Twice. The same things were taken each time. My stereo system, tuner, record player, reel-to-reel, everything."

"Well, there you are. You can be a victim of crime in any part of the world, in Luneta or in California."

"It doesn't have to be in one's country. A homecoming should be an occasion for rejoicing, not stress."

My brother and his platitudes. Stress, he says, spare me. A tidal wave kills five thousand in Bangladesh. Children dying of starvation in the sugar regions of the country. A radio commentator is shot in front of his daughter at a May Day festival. And he talks of stress. I kept my mouth shut; I did not want to create more stress for him on his homecoming.

I took my brother to Quiapo, and Escolta. For lunch he wanted to go to a *mami* and *siopao* place he used to eat at when he studied in Santo Tomas.

"Well, what do you think of Manila?" I asked my brother, as soon as we were seated at the restaurant directly under a ceiling fan. I noticed my brother's face puffed up with sweat, his plastic bifocals cloudy. "Too hot for you, I see."

"It's not the heat. It's the humidity."

"What's that?"

"It's the moisture content in the air. It's what makes your skin sticky. And that's what makes you uncomfortable, not so much the heat."

I did not press him for further explanation. One sweats because one feels hot. It's as simple as that, but I guess my brother has to have a scientific explanation for everything.

"Well," I said, "what do you think of the city?"

"It seems dirtier and denser than when I lived here. But what really amazes me is the smoking. Look at you, how many cigarettes have you smoked these past two hours?"

I didn't quite like this; he was making me feel defensive. He was becoming too critical for one who hasn't been around to know what's really going on.

"It's strange. In America the impetus is to do away with smoking. There's even a move to ban smoking aboard planes, after a recent crash caused by a passenger who smoked in the toilet."

"Is that so?"

"It seems, however, that the United States unloads upon the Third World countries the tobacco it cannot sell in its own supermarkets. The way Japan dumps its unsold television sets in the States and sells them cheaper than in Hong Kong. At least you won't get cancer from watching TV. Stupid maybe, but not cancer."

Working in the newspaper morgue must have reduced my brother's view on things to capsule summaries.

After lunch he wanted to visit a bookstore.

"Let's go to Azcarraga."

"It's no longer Azcarraga, Brother. It's been renamed Claro M. Recto. Just as Dewey Boulevard is no longer Dewey. It's Roxas."

"A mistake," my brother said, shaking his head. "The sentiment's fine, but at what cost. I remember, after President Kennedy was assassinated in 1963, Cape Canaveral was renamed Cape Kennedy. It's a launching place for space ships. The residents protested and got it changed back to Cape Canaveral again. There are ways of honoring national heroes and statesmen without destroying the past, the tradition."

"What if the past reminds you of oppression?" I ventured an opinion.

"The more reason you should not forget, why you should not change the old Spanish and American place names to those of Filipinos."

"I think you're talking about a different kind of memory. And it's not history or tradition."

My brother looked at me, surprised. "What do you mean?"

"You are locked in your own nostalgia of what Azcarraga meant for you, a street where you searched for books when you were a student here. It's a special kind of memory, but very personal and distorted. A place name is a tradition, something that continues into the present, like a town fiesta. Tradition is memory kept alive. Nostalgia is frozen in time."

My brother smiled. "Is that what you teach your high school students?"

"No, Brother, I teach them English."

"Now, that's one tradition you should not change."

"We will not forget Dewey, but for my part I'd rather keep the memory of President Roxas or Magsaysay, than the man who delivered us from one kind of oppression to another. Didn't someone say, three-hundred years in a Spanish convent and fifty in Hollywood?"

I felt good to hear my brother laugh.

"So, you see, what you have, Brother, is nostalgia, not history. And your coming home is an attempt to recapture that nostalgia. You give up your country's history by choosing to live in another."

"I know a great deal of what's happening in this country," he protested.

"From newspaper accounts, no doubt. Simplified, easy to read on TV or over the radio but, as far as I'm concerned, dead."

"That's not fair. I bet I learn more about the political events in this country than what you can learn from the local newspapers."

"The foreign press, Brother, have their own bias. You cannot know everything from what you read in newspapers and magazines."

He had no response to this. I guess I matched his platitudes with mine and we had arrived at a stalemate. I took him to the National Bookstore near Far Eastern University. He liked the open-shelf arrangement, and bought novels by Santos, Tiempo and Sionil Jose, and essays by Constantino and San Juan.

That fateful night I took him back to the airport to meet his delayed luggage. We boarded the light-rail train on Avenida.

"This is nice," he said; "it's like the trolley from downtown San Diego to the Tijuana border in Mexico."

"The LRT is very convenient. It runs from Caloocan to Baclaran. Have you been to Mexico, Brother?"

"I have. I was going to say that the Philippines reminds me so much of Mexico. Some sections of Manila look like Tijuana."

I had nothing to say to this. My brother may have only nostalgia for his country, but he knows other people and other places, and he can compare. From the Baclaran station we took a cab to the international airport and got there about ten-thirty. We entered the office that issued passes to the terminal. The monitor in the office indicated that the flight from Tokyo, the last for the day, would arrive at 11:20 p.m.

The Filipina at the counter was soft-spoken and polite. "We can prepare the forms now, but we can't let you in until thirty minutes after the plane has landed."

"Thirty minutes!"

I looked at the man who said this, white-haired, dark, his skin wrapped tight around sturdy bones.

"Thirty minutes," he repeated; "by then my bag is on the carousel and someone else might pick it up."

"I'm sorry, sir, but that's the policy."

My brother handed the woman his passport and airline ticket. Another clerk copied information from the passport on a triplicate form, took this to an inner office for a woman in white uniform to sign. The clerk returned the passport to my brother, and asked for another ID card.

"What for?"

"So we're sure that you'll return the copy of the pass that we will give to you."

"My God!" I heard my brother mutter, as he pulled out his driver's license from his wallet.

"Why don't you have pity on us and give us our pass?" the old man cried. "It's not our fault that our baggage was delayed. Why do you do this to us?"

The clerk took my brother's license, clipped it to a folded copy of the pass, and put it on a filing tray.

"The plane has landed," the old man cried. "Give us our pass."

The woman in the inner office shouted. "If you don't shut up, we won't give it to you."

The old man whimpered as he sat on the bench against the wall, but it was because of him, I think, that at eleven thirty, just ten minutes after the plan landed, the clerk began giving out the passes.

My brother got his pass and quickly disappeared in the terminal. That was a mistake. We did not agree on a place to meet. I forgot to tell him that there were two exits, one for tourists and another for *balikbayans*. How was I to know that he'd come out of the tourist exit? I was sweating it out with the other welcomers, my face against the glass, looking at each passenger walk the gauntlet of customs officials, hawkers, taxi drivers, and sampaguita flower girls.

My brother had long since walked out, a leather suitcase in one hand and a canvas in the other, and walked back and forth from one exit to the other. He must have shown panic, wondering where I was, for when he shouted my name, I heard his terror.

That's when I came upon him, fending off the five men who orchestrated a dunning operation, pressing him for token sums he could very well afford.

As I approached, another man, bigger and older than the five, pointed to my brother and said, "He promised to take my car."

"For how much?" I asked.

"A hundred fifty pesos."

"That's too much. How about a hundred?"

"Okay, one hundred."

I picked up the canvas suitcase, one of the young men got the leather bag, and we followed him past the waiting cars and taxis. I sensed something was wrong. The man dropped the suitcase in the open trunk of an unmarked white car, but the engine was running and someone was behind the wheel.

"Brother," I screamed, "don't take the car!"

I saw him push the man aside and pull the suitcase out of the trunk. The man slammed the hood down, missed the suitcase, but caught the sampaguita hanging from my brother's wrist, scattering flowers on the pavement. We both started running back to the terminal and got into a taxi. On the dashboard, the driver's picture and license number were displayed and I felt fine. I wanted to laugh. I had won my one-thousand peso bet, but I noticed that my brother said nothing and had a strange look on his face.

I was about to give the driver the address of the cousin's house we stayed in the night before, but I heard my brother say in a tone I had not heard, "Take me to the Hilton."

I was puzzled but did not argue with him. To stay at the Hilton, even for one night, would be something to tell the folks back home. I leaned back, craving a smoke. I closed my eyes and listened to the taxi sputter diesel in the midnight air. I thought my brother was tired and would snap out of it after a good night's rest.

He never did. At the Hilton he sat on the edge of the bed, staring out the window. He could have been praying or meditating, but I doubt it. He cut a pathetic figure in his underwear, his back hunched. From the knees up, he looked like an inverted question mark.

"Are you all right?" I kept asking him.

"I'm all right."

"Do you want to send for a doctor?"

"I'm fine," he said in a very quiet voice. "I just want to go back to Los Angeles on the next available flight."

I became angry. I wasn't going to beg him to stay but I asked, "Don't you want to see our family in the province?"

"Some other time. I just want a few of my clothes back. You can take the two suitcases to them."

He left this morning.

Something must have pierced his mind and transfixed his vision, something in the midnight incident at the airport he had forgotten after a decade of absence, that struck him. I hope that it will free him from nostalgia and bring him closer to the reality of his homeland, to his country. For his sake, I hope it does, because that is the only way he can come home again. Now, I'm sorry I didn't wave goodbye, and thinking he may not return I feel like crying.

El bacalao viene de más lejos
y se come aquí

Aurora Levins Morales

Passports

1

I'VE BEEN packing for a month. Useless packing because I always end up taking the clothes out again to wear. Last week I bought a new suitcase. A small one. I decided to travel as light as I can. The weight of my own fears is more than enough for me. I've been coughing uncontrollably for three weeks, my chest too tight for breath. I keep on believing that one clear inhalation of that wet warm air will cure me, like stepping into a humidifier. I don't believe any of this is real. I panic regularly. I can't go! I don't want to go. I don't want to know the answers to my questions: will it be different? Do I belong? Is it home?

2

Now it's time for the ritual: the immigrant going home. Suddenly I become aware of us all, a little group of foreigners, all homesick, all exiles in San Francisco, a city of out-of-towners. Sitting in living rooms in last minute visits, everyone presses addresses into my hand, asks me to bring them . . . tokens, reminders, something to hold in the hand, keep on a shelf, taste. "Bring me a güiro, some panapén to cook, don't come back without something, anything, from Loíza Aldea." Proof that they can go back anytime, are going soon, probably next year, that they really want to, that they don't need to: a passport (I remember doing it myself), proof of a fading citizenship, an open door.

3

On the plane, the first plane, to New York, I write about sex, trying to measure off, summarize these last almost seven years, a period of my life that's ending with this journey home. I find myself making lists of lovers (as we fly over snowy mountains, the dusty plains, green cornfields) trying to remember which year, and was it April or May, and instead of getting analytical, trying to find out something revealing, see some pattern in my long list of dissatisfactions, I just list them and close the book, and close my eyes. Soon enough, after all, I'm in New York.

4

Early morning, winging southeast. I decided to watch the movie, to fill the time until Puerto Rico appears in the windows. I have to keep reminding myself to feel, to breathe, to stay alive. "I wish I had taken a picture of the people standing in line, that immigrant crowd with their bags and cardboard boxes and the children in pretty-for-abuelita dresses and tucked-in shirts. I was such a child in my organdies and checked shifts, and Ricardo all tucked and belted with this hair cut short, but that was the other journey: grandparents and tíos and tías in North and us going to visit . . ."

5

These must be the southern latitudes. I imagine the water is lighter, richer, carbonated with sunlight. I scan the dark lines in the distance: islands or cloud shadows? They hand out the hot towels and my ears begin to pop. I still can't see a thing. It must be under those rainfilled clouds. We stoop lower, circling. The humidity is condensing on the outside of the windows. Then at the last minute, the grey folds back: a patch of turquoise sea, a line of white surf, green palms, and far away, where the rain is falling, the mountains.

Esa Noche La Luna Caía En Gotas De Luz

Deperté, pensando que ya amanecía, que debía irme para que no me cogiera el día, ni los vecinos. Tito dormía. Poco a poco me desenredé de su cuerpo y me vestí a la luz de las voces roncas de los gallos. "¿Ya te vas?" Me recuerda de lo de la puerta, que hay que levantarla pá que no chille, y se duerme de nuevo. Afuera la luna se derrama en una llovizna finita. El cafetal, los guineos recién sembrados, la tierra roja del camino, mi piel recién acariciada: todo se empapa de luna. ¡Qué truca de la noche! Faltan horas todavía. Paso por paso, calladita, tomo el camino hasta mi casa por el aire florecido en la hora más secreta del barrio, cuando hasta los perros se esconden debajo de las casas. Quise cantar. Quise hablar en poesía, pero cuando llegué por fin a mi puerta, tenía la garganta amarrada de silencio y luz, y florecitas minúsculas de luna llena por toda mi piel.

Sí Los Escritores Son Así

I tell Lencho and Sefa I'm working on a book of stories. Sefa's sharp black eyes flash all over her wrinkled face. Snoot in the air and everything akimbo she says, "Hm! A mí no me vayas a poner ahí con mi nombre, nah! Don't you go putting me in there with my name." Lencho is reasonableness personified, explaining to the unenlightened . . . "But, Sefa, eso no es ná, ¿verdad que eso no es ná, Dori? There's nothing wrong with that." I say OK, I'll change your name. What name shall I give you? Lencho confirms that this is something writers do. César did the same thing when he wrote the novel about the crime in El 22. He says "Ponle Tomasa." Sefa bridles in mock indignation, smirks, looks at me challengingly. "Ay, Lori, you really are too much, tú sí que eres tremenda! Y que Tomasa!" Then, beginning to reminisce, "I knew an old lady named, Tomasa once. She used to wear one of those dresses de antes, from the old days, with a deso here, you know, of lace . . . *her* name was Tomasa . . ."

Lencho is delighted with the project. If he sees me writing he stands stock still, grinning, until I look up and catch the expression of delighted respect and pride on his face. Then he tiptoes out of the room. One night when he's drunk he asks me to dedicate a book to him. I promise. For the way his face lit up when I told him I was a writer. For his pride: "I passed the drivers' test first time round, even though I can't read. Some of those school kids have to take it three or four times before they pass." And of course for love.

Just like César is the refrain. Lencho is deeply proud of having known him. Once when he was waiting for his government pension settlement, after the accident to his leg, he complained to César about the delay. The next week César wrote it up in his column in the *Imparcial*, and the very next day Lencho got his check by special messenger. He's never forgotten this basic lesson on the power of journalism, and now . . . "Just like César . . . *he* used to take down everything you said, too. He asked me all sorts of things when he wrote *Cosas De Aquí* . . . César liked to get up early, too . . . but he liked sweets, y ésta no." He recognizes all the symptoms:

Meanwhile Sefa punctuates the conversation, exclaiming, "¡Mira si la nena no sabe ná! She doesn't know *much*, does she? ¡Mira si no sabe la nena!"

Algunas Cosas No Cambian

The first night I spend with Tito I am amazed at how easy it is. As if we were old lovers returning to a familiar bed. Later I prop myself on one elbow and ask: So what have you been doing for the last fifteen years? He tells me: school, a carpentry job, got married, time served in the north, washing dishes in New Jersey and two months in jail because he was stopped driving without a license and didn't speak English. Three children, a girl and two boys. More time in the north, this time in Brooklyn with his cousin Cuni. The marriage falling apart. Haydée living with her mother who looks after the kids. I tell my own story as succinctly: school, work, lovers, changes of address.

The miraculous thing is that it works. We're caught up. I've known Tito since I was six. He hasn't seen me in ten years, and it doesn't seem to matter at all. He tells me Don Paco's store is gone, did I notice, and his sister is living in New York. Remember Caín, you know, El Múcaro, he married a woman with five kids. He reminds me of how he used to steal kisses from me in the lunch line and I remind him of how my father threatened to cut his balls off if he didn't quit it.

This affair requires no courtship. It's all been done in advance. My first day back in the barrio I run into Tito at the store. He asks me if I'm married. I say nope. He says,

"You know how I've always felt about you."

"MmmHmm"

"We need to talk," he demands.

"OK, where?"

"The rock."

I grin. "Neutral territory, huh?"

"Exacto."

The big boulder between our houses where we used to eat stolen tangerines and plan trouble. OK, I say, just like I did when I was ten . . . I'll wait for you at the rock.

Vivir Es Un Peligro . . . Y Muerto No Se Puede Vivir

She was a beautiful girl. I remember her at twelve or thirteen, a quick, intelligent face. Bright. She was always in and out of César and Jane's house. They half adopted her, taught her to read, lent her books. Then Jane died and César moved back to the city with his son and Jane's mother Maga.

I asked Tito about her. "She's not pretty any more," was all he would say. She was one week under fourteen when she ran away with her·first man. He turned out to be a thief, got caught and went to jail. While he was inside she fell in love with his brother. The first one got out, got his own sister in trouble and took rat poison. He died in the road between her parents house and ours. Years ago I heard she was living in Cabo Rojo. Twenty-three years old, five kids.

Last week Carmen showed me a picture of her, surrounded by children in a living room somewhere in Massachussetts where she lives with her third husband. I didn't recognize her. This afternoon I was out driving with Lencho. We stopped at the place where the road widens before it becomes a razorback between two 500 foot ravines and winds down in to Bartolo. I asked him, "Do you remember Charo?" "¡Cómo no!" he said, "Muchacha inteligente." "She was beautiful, too, wasn't she?" Lencho gazed off toward the silhouette of the farm, a far away crest of pines in a distance his eyes can no longer reach. He sighed. "A flower . . . era una flor."

El Bacalao Viene de Más Lejos Y Se Come

1

I dream it's my childhood again. The house is as it used to be: none of the damage has been done. Glass sparkles in the windowpanes. The tiles are all in place in the floor, the wood solid and well painted. The trees stand back from the house and the garden is cleared. The drying platform is unbroken. Little yellow planes fly over, cute stubby ones, and Mami runs out to wave at them and they waggle their wings, just like they used to. Then I see that the house is ruined. The cement of the platform is crumbled and the wilderness has reclaimed everything. The whole barrio is overgrown. There are no houses, no paths, nothing but trees and vines. It's been abandoned for years and everything is gone. I know that now the little planes will be lost out at sea. They can't find their way back to land, and I can never return.

I wake sobbing in Tito's arms, pouring out my dream and all the grief of my loss. He strokes my hair and says yes, I know. I know how you feel. I know what you mean. Until I fall asleep again, no more an exile than Tito, living with his loneliness or Cheíto across the way or Haydée up the hill or Caín down the road, all of us grown here and watching it die. No more a stranger than anyone who grows up.

2

There are things I will always know and people who will always expect me to. The difference between a *niño* and a *chamaluco*. What an orange tastes like hot off the tree and eaten on the run. What Don Paco's store smelled like on a rainy day: rum, dust, damp wood, butchers paper, stale candy and the steaming road. I will always remember Angela Báez and Carmen Ana Ríos and Ofelia Ramos who lived in an old wooden house on the way to school. I will always recognize the taste of bacalao cooked up with onions and the look of geraniums planted in battered Sultan cans.

When I came back, I expected to be foreign. To have to introduce myself, explain. I found I was familiar, expected to show up sometime, as all the immigrant children of the barrio are expected. The barrio nodded its head to me, asked after my family, called by my name.

3

I didn't marry Tito. He wanted me to. He asked me about once a day. Now that I'm gone he writes:

I can't change how I feel. I understand. You have your whole life there and I know how important your writing is and your politics. I know you won't leave that. Let's not argue. Que el tiempo lo decida. Meanwhile, its raining here. A lizard has moved into our room. She looks at me as if she wanted to talk and I feed her sugar from my finger . . .

Sitting at a desk surrounded by the New England fall, I ask myself again . . . Do I belong? The understanding comes slowly. No. I don't belong to Indiera. I never will. But Indiera belongs to me.

End of a Story

Reinaldo Arenas

The Southernmost Point in the U.S.A. That's what the billboard says. How awful! And how would we say it in Spanish? *El punto más al sur en los Estados Unidos*, of course. But it's not the same. The sentence grows too lengthy; it loses precision and power. In Spanish it doesn't give the idea that you're in the southernmost place in the United States, but just at some spot in the south. But in English that brevity, that "Southernmost Point," with those "T's" sticking up at the end, indicates clearly to us that the world really does end right here, that once you leave this "point" and cross the horizon all you'll find is the Sargasso Sea, the dark ocean. Those "T's" aren't letters, they're crosses—look at the way they stick up—and they clearly signify that what lies behind them is death, or even worse, hell. And it does. But, anyhow, we're here now. I finally got you to come here. I wish you had come of your own free will; I wish you'd had a photograph taken of you beside that billboard, laughing; and I wish you could have sent that snapshot off right away, over there, over the Sargasso Sea (so that they'd all die of envy or of rage); I wish you had spit, just as I'm doing right now, into these waters, where hell begins. In short, I wish you had come to stay here, on this isolated key, one hundred and fifty-seven miles from Miami, and only ninety from Cuba, right in the middle of the sea, with the same seabreeze as down there, and the water the same colour, the same landscape, almost—and none of the horrors. I wish I could have brought you here—and not this way, almost dragging you—and not just for you to lose yourself in these waters, but so that you could have understood the good fortune of being on this side of them. But despite all my insistence—maybe because of it—you were never willing to come. You thought that what attracted me to the spot was just homesickness: the nearness of the island, isolation, discouragement, failure. You never understood anything—or, maybe, in your own way, you understood too much. Isolation, homesickness, memories—call them what you please—I feel all that, I suffer from it, but at the same time I enjoy it. Yes, I enjoy it. And, above all, what makes me come here is the sensation, the certainty, of experiencing a feeling of triumph . . . I can look southward, I can look at that sky that I love and hate so much, and let a punch loose at it; I can raise my arms and laugh and laugh; I can almost hear, from down there, from the other side of the sea, the mute, desperate shouts of all the ones who wish they were in my place: right here where I am, cursing, shouting, hating and really alone—not like there, where even being alone is prohibited and can get you bundled off to jail for being "anti-social." Here you can destroy yourself or find yourself, and nobody gives a damn where you're going. And, for those of us who know what the other "way" is like, that, too, is a blessing. You thought that I wasn't going to understand these advantages, that I wouldn't be able to make use of them, that I wouldn't be able to adapt. Yes, I know what you said. That I won't learn a word of English, that I won't ever write a single line again, that once you're here there are no more reasons or motives, that even the most lasting hatreds weaken and succumb to the inevitable impression that the supermarkets and 42nd Street make on you, or to the desperate need to find your niche in one of those towers around which the world spins, or to the security of knowing that we're no longer the objects of government concern or the subjects of secret dossiers . . . I know that they all thought that I was through, finished. And that you yourself agreed with their underhanded manoeuvres. I won't forget how you used to laugh, almost with satisfaction (mockingly, sadly), every time the telephone rang, and how you took advantage of every little opportunity to criticise my lack of discipline, my tendency to vagrancy. When I told you that I was

merely adjusting, adapting, or just simply living and in the process building up stories and plots, you looked at me pityingly, positive that I had
died of the new hypocrisy, the inevitable personal contacts, the harmful
effects of success or the intolerable talk-talk-talk . . . But it wasn't like that
at all, listen closely, twenty years of rôle-playing, of enforced cowardice
and humiliation can't be got rid of that easily . . . I won't forget how you
observed me, critically, judiciously—of course—waiting for me finally to
break down, to become part of the anonymous throng among the frozen,
clamorous tunnels or on these hostile streets swept by the winds of hell.
But it didn't happen like that, d'you hear? Those twenty years of crafty
hypocrisy, of that repressed terror, kept me from going under. And that
(too) is why I've dragged you here, to leave you defeated at last and at
peace—maybe even happy—and to show you—I can't hide my vanity—
that you are the one who went under.

As you can see, this spot looks a lot like Cuba, or, rather, like some
places in Cuba. Beautiful places, beyond a doubt, but I'll never visit them
again. Never! Did you hear me? Not even if the government falls and they
beg me to come back to have my profile engraved on a medal, or something
similar; not even if my return could prevent the whole island from sinking
into the sea; not even if they roll out a red carpet from the airplane for me
to march martially along to where the firing squad is waiting for me to
pump a merciful final bullet in the back of the dictator's neck. Never! Did
you hear me? Not even if they beg me on bended knee. Not even if they
crown me as they did Avellaneda and name me Beauty Queen of Guanabacoa Muncipality,[1] the most heavily populated with macho studs[2] . . .
I'm saying this last bit as a joke. But the part about not going back is really
in earnest. Are you listening? But you're different. You don't know how
to survive, how to hate, you can't forget. That's why, for some time now,
when I saw there was no cure for your homesickness, I've been wanting
you to come here, to this spot. But, as usual, you never paid the least attention to what I was saying. Maybe if you had listened to me, I wouldn't
have to be the one bringing you now. But you always were stubborn, set
in your ways, sentimental, humane. And those are qualities you pay a very
high price for possessing in life . . . Anyhow, now you're here, whether
you like it or not. D'you see? The streets are built so that people can walk
along them, there're sidewalks, galleries, arcades, old wooden houses with
decorated balconies, just like down there . . . We're not in New York any

1. Gertrudis Gómez de Avellaneda, prominent Cuban poet of the last century. Returning
to Cuba after a thirty-year absence, she was crowned with laurel at the theatre in recognition
of her talents. Guanabacoa is an eastern suburb of Havana.
2. In Spanish "bugarrones"—straight-identified men, who take only the active role when
fucking gays.

more, where everybody shoves you without looking at you or begs your pardon without touching you; we're not in Miami, where there are only horrible mad automobiles in asphalt parking-lots. Here everything is built on a human scale. Just like in the poem, there are female figures—and male ones, too—seated on the balconies. They look at us. Groups gather on corners. Can you feel the breeze? It's the seabreeze. Can you sense the sea? It's our sea . . . The young men walk around in shorts. There's music. You can hear it anywhere. Here you won't fry with the heat or freeze with cold, like up there. We're very close to Havana . . . I always told you that you should come, that I was inviting you to come, that there's even a little seafront promenade, not like the one down there, of course[3] (because it's the one over here), and trees and fragrant twilights and a sky filled with stars. But no way could I succeed in convincing you to come, and, what was worse, I couldn't manage to convince you to stay, either, and enjoy the things that can be enjoyed up there. At night, walking along the Hudson, how many times did I try to show you the island of Manhattan the way it really is, like a great medieval castle with electric light, an enormous lamp that was worthwhile exploring? But your soul was somewhere else, down there, in a quiet, sunny ward of a city with streets that have stone pavements, where people chat from one balcony to another, and you walk along and you understand what they're saying, because they are you . . . And what good did it do to tell you that I wanted to be there, too, inside that noisy, crowded bus that right now is probably crossing Harbour Avenue, going across the Ramp, or going into a public urinal where inevitably, at any moment, the police will arrive and ask me for my ID . . . But, listen closely to me, I'm never going to go back, not even if the continued existence of the world depended on my going back. Never! Look at that guy who went by on a bicycle. He looked at me. He stared. Haven't you noticed? Here people really look at you. If they like your looks, naturally. It's not like up there, where looking seems to be a crime. Or like down there, where it *is* a crime. "Anyone who looks at another individual of the same sex will be condemned to" . . . Hey! That other guy just looked at me, too. And so now you can't tell me anything. Cars even stop and honk their horns: suntanned young men stick their heads out the windows. *Where? Where?* But they'll take you wherever you say. Of course, we're right in the middle of Duval Street, where the action is, the hot street, as we used to say down there . . . That's another reason (I won't deny it) why I wanted to bring you here, so you could see that young men still look at me, so you wouldn't think your friendship was a

3. Havana possesses a particularly long and imposing seaside avenue and promenade, the Malecón.

special favour, a gracious concession that I had to preserve under any circumstances, so you'd see that I have my admirers here too, just like I had them down there. I think I already mentioned that to you, too. But none of that seemed to matter to you: not the possiblity of being two-timed, or even the (always more exciting) possibility of two-timing . . . I kept on talking to you, but your soul, your memory, whatever it was, seemed to be somewhere else. Why didn't you leave your soul back down there along with your book of food stamps, and your ID and *Granma* newspaper?[4] . . . Come on, walk through Times Square, take a chance and go into Central Park, take a train and enjoy the real Coney Island, I'm inviting you to. I'll even give you the money to go. You don't have to go with me. But you never went out, or if you did, you were back the next minute. It was too cold, it was too hot—you always had a reason for not seeing what you had right in front of your eyes. For being somewhere else . . . But look, look at those people milling around in spite of the bad weather (the weather's always bad here), look at those human figures braving the storm. Many of them are from other places, too (places that were theirs), places they can't go back to, either, places that maybe don't even exist any more. Listen: homesickness can also be a kind of consolation, a sweet sadness, a way of seeing things and even enjoying them. Our triumph is resisting. Our revenge is surviving. Put on blue jeans, a pull-over, a pair of boots and a leather belt; get a crew cut, wear leather clothes or aluminum clothes, put a ring through your ear, or a fluted hoop around your neck, and a spiked bracelet on your arm. Go out on the street in a dayglow loincloth, buy a motorcycle (here's the money), go punk, paint your skin sixteen different colours and find yourself an American black, or try out a woman. Do your thing, but forget Spanish and everything you ever gave a name to, heard or remember in that language. Forget me, too. Don't come back . . .

But in a few days, you're back. Dressed just as I recommended, with boots, jeans, pull-over and leather jacket. You drink a soft drink and you listen to the tape recorder that you were never able to own down there. But you're not really dressed the way your're dressed, you aren't really drinking that soft drink that you were never able to drink down there, you're not listening to that tape recorder playing, because you don't exist, the people around you give you no proof of your own existence, they can't identify you, and they don't know who you are, and they're not interested in knowing; you aren't part of all this, and it's really all the same if you go out dressed in those togs or wrapped in a hemp sack. All I had to do was look in your eyes to know that that's what you were thinking . . . And I couldn't tell you that I also thought the same things, that I also felt

4. Cuba's only newspaper, the official organ of the Communist Party.

the same way—no, a lot worse. At least *you* had somebody, me, trying to console you . . . but what arguments can you use to console somebody who still doesn't have the protective armour of a boundless hatred? How can a person survive when the place where he suffered most, and which no longer exists, is the only place that still keeps him going? Look—I insisted, because I'm pig-headed, and you know it—for the first time we're human beings now, what I mean is, we *can* hate, we can offend the people openly, and still we don't have to cut sugarcane . . . But I think you didn't even hear me. In your elegant sports clothes, you look in the mirror, and you see only your own eyes. Your eyes, searching for the street where the people cross, swinging their hips, entering a park where there are statues you can identify, figures, voices, and even bushes that seem to recognise you. You're about to sit down on a bench now, you sniff, you feel that indefinable transparency in the air, that sensation of a rainshower that has just fallen, of still wet vegetation and roofs. You look at the balconies covered with clothing stretched out to dry. The old colonial buildings are now like bright, floating sailboats. You go down. You want to lean over one of those balconies, looking at the people down below, who look up at you and greet you, in recognition. *A city of open balconies with clothes stretched out on them, a city of seabreeze and sun, with buildings that swell up and seem to sail* . . . Yes! Yes! I used to interrupt you, a city of propped-up old balconies and a million eyes watching you, a city of cut-down trees, of exported palm-groves, of waterpipes without water, of ice-cream parlours with no ice cream, of markets without any merchandise for sale, of closed-down baths, of forbidden beaches, of backed-up sewers, of constant blackouts, of multiplying jails, of buses that never run, of laws that make all life a crime—d'you hear me?—of policemen and orders. And what's even worse—listen to me—a city suffering all the horrors that these horrors bring with them . . . But you stayed there, floating, trying to get down and lean on that propped-up balcony, trying to go down and sit in that park where there'll surely be a police raid tonight . . . "Go south! Go south!" I said to you then—I repeated it— I was sure that in a place similar to that place you wouldn't feel lost in the clouds, or anywhere. "Go south!," I say, turning out the apartment lights to keep you from going on looking at yourself in the mirror, seeing yourself somewhere else. "To the southernmost point in the country, right to Key West, where I've invited you to come so many times, and you've refused to go, just to spite me! There you'll find places the same as, or better than, the ones you know. Beaches where you can see the sand under the clear water, houses surrounded by trees, people who don't seem to be always in a hurry. I'll pay for the trip and the expenses. And you don't have to go with me." And like always—without saying anything to

me, without taking the money either—you go out, we go out, on to the
street. You walk ahead of me, along Eighth Avenue. You turn on to 51st
Street. Further and further away, you enter the whirlpool of Broadway.
The birds, clouding a violet sky, are alighting now on the roofs and roof-
tiles of the National Theatre, the Inglaterra Hotel and the Isla de Cuba, of
the Camponamor movie theatre and the Social Club of Asturias. They take
shelter, in flocks, in the single silk-cotton tree of Fraternidad Park[5] and in
the few, severely trimmed trees of Havana's Central Park. The decorative
lighting of the Capitol building and of Aldama Palace has been turned on.
Young people stream along the sidewalk by the Payret movie theatre and
between the lions of El Prado Avenue,[6] toward the seafront promenade.
El Morro Castle[7] lighthouse flashes on the water, on the people crossing over to the docks, on the buildings of Harbour Avenue, on your face.
The evening heat has brought almost everyone out on the street. You see
them, you're there almost beside them. Invisible, hovering over the few
trees, you watch them, you listen to them. Now you're rousing the birds,
spying from the La Manzana de Gómez towers. You rise up and you see
the lighted city. Gliding over the beaches, you hear the music played by
people with transistors, the conversations (whispers) of those who want
to cross the sea, you observe the way the young men walk, almost grazing
you without seeing you, as they raise a hand. A boat enters the harbour,
slowly blowing its siren. You hear the waves breaking against the seawall.
You smell the smell of the sea. You contemplate the slow, shining waters
of the bay. From Cathedral Square the crowd scatters through the narrow,
badly-lit streets. You go down; you want to mingle with this crowd. To be
with them, to be them, to touch this street-corner, to sit down on just this
bench, to pull off that leaf and sniff it . . . But you're not there: you can
see, you can feel, you can hear, but you can't lose yourself in it, take part
in it, you can't go all the way down. Jumping from that lamppost, you
try to touch the ground and submerge yourself in the stone-paved street.
You leap. The cars—especially the taxis—stop you from going on. You
wait with the crowd for the "WALK" sign of the traffic light. You cross
50th Street and seem to vanish among the lights of the Paramount Plaza,
the Circus Cinema, the Circus Theatre and the huge illuminated fish of
Arthur Treacher's: now you're under the enormous billboard announcing

5. Formerly Campo de Marte, a landscaped park to the north of Havana's former Capitol
building.
6. Paseo del Prado, following the old city walls, formerly one of the most elegant avenues
of Havana, runs from the city's Central Park (near the Capitol and the National Theatre)
down to the seafront. It is flanked with marble lions.
7. El Morro Castle, with its lighthouse, stands on a rocky headland and guards the
northern side of the entrance to Havana and its port.

Oh Calcutta! today in Arabic and Spanish, you walk along with the people who pile up or scatter among voices hawking hot dogs, instant polaroid photographs for one dollar, real roses illuminated by batteries discreetly inserted in their stems, sweaters with slogans, glasses with mirror lenses, luminous medals, shiskebab, frozen food, plastic frogs that croak and stick out their tongue at you. Now the tumult of the taxis has turned all Broadway into a dizzying yellow river. Burger King, Chock Full O'Nuts, Popeye's Fried Chicken, Castro Convertibles, Howard Johnson's, Melon Liqueur, and you walk on. A man dressed as a cowboy, standing behind an improvised table, deftly shuffles cards, calling people to play; an Indian woman, in native Hindu dress, sells aphrodisiacal incenses and perfumes, spreading flames and smoke to prove the quality of her merchandise; a magician in a tall hat tries to force an egg into a bottle, as numerous people watch; another magician, in close competition with him, is promising to hypnotise a rabbit, which he shows the audience. "Girls! Girls! Girls!" shouts a mulatto in shorts by a lighted doorway, while a cheerful old drag queen, from her stand, proclaims herself an expert in the art of palmistry. A loud blonde in a bikini tries to take your arm, whispering something to you in English. In the midst of the multitude, a policeman with a loudspeaker announces that the next showing of *E.T.* will begin at nine forty-five, and a black, dressed all in black, with a high, round, black collar and a Bible in his hand, cries out his verses and quotations, while a mixed choir, directed by Friedrich Dürrenmatt himself, sings, "Take me, guide me by the hand" . . . A scalper is selling tickets for *Evita* at half-price. Another woman, in long sleeves and a long skirt, approaches you and gives you a booklet with "Twenty-one Amazing Predictions." Erotically charged young men of various races, in rubber trousers, cross the street on rollerskates in the opposite direction to the way we're going, patting their cocks promisingly. A multicoloured cluster of aerial balloons rises up now from the centre of the crowd and disappears into the night, while a picturesque band of musicians playing only marimbas breaks into a magnificent polyphonic concert. Someone dressed as a wasp comes up and gives you a piece of paper with which you can eat two hamburgers for the price of one. "Free love! Free love!" a man wearing a uniform recites in a loud, monotonous voice, handing out cards as he does. The sidewalk is covered with purple umbrellas, which a tiny woman is selling for only one dollar, predicting as she does so that a storm is going to break out at any moment. A blind man with a seeing-eye dog jingles coins at the bottom of a jar. A Greek sells china dolls with a tear on their cheeks. "Tonight Festa Italiana" announces the illuminated superscreen from the first tower of Times Square Plaza. Now you cross over opposite Bond and Disc-O-Mat, you look in the shop windows, full of every kind of merchandise, from a dwarf orange tree to portable dildos, from an Afghan shawl to a Peruvian llama. "Mariguana!" someone addresses you, ostensibly in Spanish. Everyone passes by in front of you, freely offering his merchandise or openly expressing his desires. Along O'Reilly Street, on Obispo, on Obrapia, along Teniente Rey, Muralla, Empedrado,[8] on all the streets leading to the bay, the people stroll, seeking the coolness of the sea air, after another monotonous, asphyxiating day, full of unavoidable responsibilities and unimportant, frustrated plans, small desires (a fruit drink, a pair of shoes that are the right size, a tube of toothpaste) that they weren't able to satisfy, and vast wishes (a trip, a bigger house), that it would even be dangerous to suggest. There they go, seeking at least the openness of the horizon, ill-fed, wearing their frumpy, look-alike clothes, thinking "Will the queue at the frozen meat counter be very long? Will the Pio-Pio be open?" . . . Faces that could be your own face, whispered complaints, curses never formulated in words: signals and gestures that you understand, because they're your signals and gestures, too. A loneliness, a wretchedness, a helplessness, a humiliation and a hatred that you too share. Great, shared horrors that would at least make you feel you were not alone. From the grilles of the Vice-Captain's Palace you try once again to submerge yourself among them, but you can't reach the street. You share their tragedy, but you can't be there, sharing their company too. The wail of an ambulance going down 42nd Street paralyses the traffic on Broadway. With no difficulty you slowly cross Times Square through the sea of cars; I follow, I almost overtake you: Avenue of the Americas, Fifth Avenue, down to the village, you walk on through the crowd, looking dourly at everything, with that expression of resentment, of impotence, of absence. But, listen, I feel like tapping you on the shoulder and asking you—"What other city besides New York could tolerate us, what other city could we tolerate?" . . . The Public Library, the ostentatious shop windows of Lord and Taylor, we go on walking. On 34th Street, you stop opposite the Empire State Building. And please note that I've pronounced the name perfectly correctly. Did you hear? Everything I've said in English up to now I've said marvellously well. Now, listen! Don't start making fun of my accent, or putting on that other expression of yours—half-pitying, half-weary. Naturally, you're not putting on any expression any more; maybe you're not interested in anything any more, not even in making fun of me, not even in contradicting my point of view, the way you always did. But, anyhow, I wanted to bring you here before we say goodbye; I wanted you to come along with me on this trip. I want you to get to know the whole town, to see that I was right, that there still is a place where you

8. These are all streets of Old Havana, the colonial centre of the city.

can breathe freely, and where people look at us with eyes of desire, or at least with curiosity. You see? There's even a Sloppy Joe's just like the one in Havana—what am I saying? Far better. All the artists have drunk in this one. Day and night you hear music, and you can enjoy the musicians (if you don't like listening to them, at least looking at them). Hemingway doesn't have to worry about old age here. Young men, young men everywhere, all of them wearing shorts, barefoot and shirtless, and suntanned, all of them showing off or hinting at the thing that they know (and they're so right) is their greatest treasure . . . It wasn't for nothing that Tennessee Williams set up winter barracks here; there's certainly no shortage of soldiers for them . . . Did you see the stained-glass windows of that old house? "Old Havana," they call it. And that gallery with wooden swings? It's called "Chez Emilio"—a bit Latin, at least. Look! A San Carlos Hotel, just like the one on Zulueta Street . . . From the Aquarium, we're only a hop, skip and jump away from the docks and the harbour. This is the promenade. It's not as wide or as high, but there's the same seabreeze as there, or almost . . . Oh, yeah, I know it isn't the same; everything here is tiny and flat, and those wooden buildings with their little balconies look like dovecotes, or doll's houses, and these streets aren't like the ones there, and this shitty little harbour can't even be compared with ours; you don't have to spell it out for me; you don't have to start your spiel again. I know that these beaches are garbage and that the air is much hotter, and there's no promenade, or anything like it, and even Sloppy Joe's is much smaller than the one down there. But look, look, listen to me, pay attention to me, down there doesn't exist any more, and this is here, with music and drinks and boys wearing shorts. Why do you have to look at people that way, as if they were to blame for something? Try to mingle with them, try to talk and move like them, try to forget and be them, if you can't, listen, enjoy your solitude, because homesickness can be a kind of consolation, a sweet sadness, a way of seeing things and even enjoying them. But I knew it was useless to repeat the same old song; you weren't going to listen to me and, besides, I wasn't even sure of the truth of what I was saying. That's why I chose to follow you silently through the long lobby of the Empire State Building. We took the elevator and, still not speaking, we went up to the top floor. Besides, conversation was the last thing you needed: the group of Japanese (or were they Chinese?) who went up with us were making so much noise you couldn't have heard me. We reached the observation terrace. Everybody scattered in four different directions. I'd never gone up on the Empire State Building at night before. The view is really something: rivers of light running to the end of space. And look up: you can even see the stars. Did I say "touch them"? No matter, whatever sentimental nonsense I said, you wouldn't hear it, even if you were by my side, the way you are now. Anyhow, you leaned out over the terrace to look down at the void where the city was gleaming. I don't know how long you stood there. It may have been hours. The elevator came back empty and went down laden with all the (seemingly) happy Japanese (or were they Koreans?). Someone spoke in French near me. I felt the childish pride of understanding the words, though they said nothing. Behind the windows of the tall look-out tower a beautiful blond kid was looking up at me. Unexpectedly, he made an ample, delightful, obscene gesture at me. Yes (don't think it was merely vanity—or senility—on my part). He really did. Although, then, I don't know why, he stuck out his tongue at me. But I really didn't pay too much attention to him. The temperature had dropped abruptly, and the wind was almost unbearable. We were alone on the tower by now, and all I wanted was for us to go down and eat. I called to you. Your answer was to signal me to come and stand beside you, by the guard-rail. I don't recall that you said anything. Did you? You just signalled me quickly to come, as if to see something extraordinary and, for that very reason, very fleeting. I leaned over and looked. I saw the Hudson stretching out and out till it was lost from sight. "The Hudson is so huge!" I said . . . "You fool!" you answered, and you kept on looking: a blue sea was breaking against the seawalls of the promenade. In spite of the altitude, you heard the roar of the waves and felt the inimitable coolness of that seabreeze. The waves were beating against the cliffs of Morro Castle, refreshing Harbour Avenue and the narrow streets of Old Havana. All along the lighted seawall, people were walking or sitting. Fishermen, after whirling their fishhooks almost ritually in the air, cast the line into the waves, generally hooking some fish. Sturdy, dark-skinned boys throw off their open shirts and leap from the wall, floating afterwards near shore in a tumult of foam and splashing. Groups of people stroll and talk along the wide seafront avenue. The statue of Jupiter on the top of the Commercial Exchange Building bends to salute the tower of the Fortress, which glows brightly. Of course the moon had come out to one side of the sea. Or was it only the Morro Castle lighthouse producing those flashes? Whichever of the two it was, the light poured down in torrents, illuminating all the ferry-boats too, full of passengers crossing the bay to Regla or Casablanca.[9] It seems to be opening night for an American movie at the Payret movie house: there's a huge line-up; from El Prado Avenue to San Rafael the people keep joining it, almost causing a riot . . . You were in ecstasy, watching it all. I saw you slip over the high railing and go down to the second terrace, where there's a sign that says "No Trespassing" or something like that. I don't think I tried to stop you, and, anyway, I'm

9. Suburbs of Havana.

sure you wouldn't have let me do anything, would you? Tell me! . . . Anyhow, I called to you, but you didn't even hear me. You leaned over and looked out into space again. In place of the dark, evil-smelling Hudson, a glittering sea rose up to that sky where the stars could not shine. On its waves now came the groves of palm trees, moving their fronds. Majestic and sonorous, they burst out over the whole West Side, which immediately disappeared, and they covered El Prado Avenue. Coconut palms, Indian laurels, taro, banana plants, *almásigos* and *yagrumas* came sailing in, effacing almost the whole island of Manhattan with its lofty towers and endless tunnels. A row of oil-palm plantations joined Riverside Drive to the beaches of Marianao.[10] From Paseo de la Rena to Carlos III was taken over by the *yagrumas. Salvaderas, ocujes*, Indian laurels, indigo-trees, *curujeyes* and seaside grapes buried Lexington Avenue as far as the Jesús del Monte road. The balconies of the buildings of Monserrate were hidden by coconut fronds—nobody could have imagined that that green, tropical avenue once bore the peculiar name of Madison Avenue. All Obispo Street was a garden. The waves cooled the roots of the tropical-almond trees, the *guasimas*, the tamarinds, the *jubabanes* and other trees and shrubs, weary, perhaps, after the long journey. A silk-cotton tree broke out in Lincoln Centre (which was still standing), turning it suddenly into Fraternidad Park. A *júcaro* tree curved its branches, and Cristo Park appeared beneath it. 23rd Street filled up with *nacagüitas*—who could imagine that that was once called New York's Fifth Avenue? At the bottom of the downtown area a huge liana dangled, its shade covering the Ramp and the National Hotel. From Old Havana to the East Side, which was disappearing now, from Arroyo Apolo to the World Trade Centre, which had become Chapel Hill, from Luyanó to the beaches of Marianao, all Havana was a huge arboretum, where the lights danced like great fireflies. Along the lighted paths the people walk, free-and-easy, join in little groups and separate; then they can be seen again, partially, under the foliage of some avenue. Others go to the seashore and let the motion of the waves lave their feet. The sounds of the city, alive with trees and conversation, filled you with contentment and coolness. You jumped. This time—I saw it in your face— you were sure you were going to get there, you would succeed in mingling with your people, in being you again. At that moment, I couldn't imagine that it could happen any other way. It couldn't—it shouldn't happen any other way. But the noise of that ambulance has nothing to do with the roar of the waves, and those people down below, like a polychrome anthill swarming around you, don't know you at all, they aren't your people. I went down. For the first time you had managed to make New York look

---

10. A suburb and beach resort to the west of Havana.

at you. Traffic was stalled all along Fifth Avenue. Sirens, whistles, dozens of police cars. A real spectacle. There's nothing more attractive than a disaster; a flying body is a magnet whose pull no one can resist; everyone has to get a look at it and investigate it. Don't think it was easy to get you back. But nothing material is hard to obtain in a world controlled by castrated, cretinised pigs. All you have to do is find the groove and insert the quarter into it. And I said "quarter"! Did you hear me? In perfect English! Just the way Margaret Thatcher herself would pronounce it, although I don't know if Thatcher has ever had occasion to pronounce that word . . . Fortunately, I had a bit of money (I've always been stingy, and you know it). I pronounced the words "cremation," "last wishes" and all those things beautifully. All I had to do was place you in your neat and narrow niche—you see? It's even good as a tongue-twister, the whole thing. But why should I leave you in that cold, dark, tiny place, along with so many finicky, meticulous, horrible people, along with so many old people? Who would care if a few ashes were or were not put in a hole? Who would even take the trouble to investigate such a ridiculous business? And, besides, who cared about you? I did. I always did. I was the only one that did . . . And I wasn't going to let them stick you in some nook in a wall along with people whose last names are written in reverse and who must be dreadful companions. Once again, I had to find the groove in the piggy bank and fill the pig's stomach.

I don't know if it's fashionable in New York to leave a cemetery with a suitcase in one's hand. What matters is, I did it, and nobody noticed anything. A taxi, a plane, a bus. And here we are, back in the *southernmost point in the U.S.A.* after having taken you for a walk through the whole of Key West—and please notice that I pronounce it perfectly. I didn't want to say goodbye to you without taking you for this walk first—without taking this walk with you, too. How many times did I tell you that this was the place for you, that there was a place that was similar, almost the same as everything down there? Why didn't you pay attention to me? Why didn't you want to come with me, each time I came? Maybe you did it just to annoy me, or so as not to be convinced, in order not to be so cowardly as to accept a half-solution, a kind of merciful, inevitable amputation, which would have allowed you to regain the use of some of your senses, to some extent—your sense of smell, perhaps, part of your sight, maybe. But your soul, your soul would surely have stayed on down there, where it always was (the place from which it couldn't ever leave), watching your shadow here wandering through noisy streets, among people who prefer you to touch anything but their car. "Don't touch the car! Don't touch the car!" But I will touch it! D'you hear me? And I'll kick them too, and I'll take a stick and I'll smash their car windows, and I'll make a short story out of this (I've almost finished it), so that you can see I can still write, and I'll speak Aramaic and Japanese and mediaeval Yiddish if I have to, in order never to return to a city with a seafront promenade, to a castle that has a lighthouse, and to an avenue with marble lions that lead down to the sea. Hear me well: I'm the one who's triumphed, because I've survived, and I will survive. Because my hatred is greater than my homesickness. Far, far greater. And it grows every day . . . I don't know if anybody on this key gives a good goddamn if I approach the open sea with a suitcase. If it were down there, I'd already have been arrested. Are you listening? With a suitcase, beside the sea, where I could get to a ship, or to some hidden rowboat, or to a rubber tire, or a board that would float and would take me away from hell. From the hell toward which you're going to return now. Did you hear me? Where you—I'm convinced now—want to end up. Are you listening? . . . I'm opening the suitcase. I'm taking the cover off the box which contains you, a bit of dark ash, almost bluish. I'm touching you for the last time. For the last time, I want you to feel my hands, as I know you feel them, touching you. For the last time, what we are will be joined together, we mingle with each other . . . Goodbye now. Fly, sail. Just like that. Let the waters take you and lead you on and take you back . . . Sargasso Sea, dark sea, divine sea, accept my treasure; do not reject the ashes of my friend; just as so many times down there we both asked you, desperate and enraged, to bring us to this spot, and you brought us. Take him now to the other shore, lay him down gently in the place which he hated so much, where they hurt him so much, which he left, fleeing, and apart from which he could not go on living.

THOSE WHO
STAY HOME

Global Cultures includes many stories about women and men who have been tempted to leave their homes—to make a better life, to escape persecution, to join the transnational cultural tribe—but who have decided that they must stay at home—to work for a better life for their people, to fight persecution, to cultivate their local, national, or regional cultures.

In **ROHINTON MISTRY**'s story collection *Swimming Lessons and Other Stories from Firozsha Baag* (Penguin, 1990), a gallery of characters appears, all residents of a single noisy, bustling apartment building in Bombay. Most members of the younger generation with education and aspiration want to leave India as soon as possible to take up the lucrative jobs available in the English-speaking Indian emigrant communities of Great Britain, Canada, and the United States. But in "Lend Me Your Light," a young idealist, Percy, bands together with his friend Navjeet to form a charitable agency supplying small farmers with funds they would otherwise have to get from scalping moneylenders. The young men work in rural Maharashtra, the predominantly Hindu province in western India of which Bombay is the capital. Their commitment seems incomprehensible to their schoolmates, who are headed for success abroad and convinced that India is so corrupt that "nothing could stop its downhill race towards despair and ruin."

Rohinton Mistry, born in 1952, once a bank clerk and parttime student of English and philosophy at Toronto University and now a full-time writer, studies the effects that their convictions and their life choices have on the young men of Firozsha Baag—and he does it as one who did not stay home. Like others of his literary generation, however, he often goes home. There is a new wave of Indian writers using English—after a period of reaction to British imperialism and celebration of India's 1947 independence in which Hindi and the many regional languages were preferred for literature—and most of them are cosmopolitans. For young writers like Shashi Tharoor, Amitav Ghosh (a Bengali), O.V. Vijayan (who translates his own work into English from Malayalam, a south Indian language), and Anita Desai, Salman Rushdie is the literary pioneer, and Bharati Mukherjee, whose stories encompass many immigrant groups other than Indians in Canada and America, is the exemplary transnationalist—the quintessential student of those who did not stay home.

A different kind of parting of the ways takes place in a "Letter from Gaza," which is addressed by the friend who stayed home to the one who went to California to make his fortune. The nameless letterwriter has to confront the "amputated town" in Gaza where he and his friend grew up, a refugee camp established during the 1948 War of Independence (as it is known in the state that resulted from it, Israel), when the Gaza Strip becomes one of the principal centers for displaced Palestinians. The town has been bombed repeatedly—once leaving his brother dead, more recently leaving his niece maimed, an amputee herself. The letter's author decides he must stay in very much the same spirit that **GHASSAN KANAFANI**, born in Palestine in 1936, a refugee by the age of thirteen, decided he had to commit himself to his people. He became one of the chief spokespersons for the Popular Front for the Liberation of Palestine and the editor of its weekly, *Al-Hadaf*, and he dedicated himself as a Marxist to the ideal of a social revolution throughout the Arab world. But his life was amputated when he was murdered in a booby-trapped car in July 1972, an explosion that his colleagues and his widow attributed to Israeli agents. Kanafani's stories are unabashedly polemical, and his widow issued after his death a statement of his that conveys why: "Self-sacrifice, within the context of revolutionary action, is an expression of the very highest understanding of life, and of the struggle to make life worthy of a human being . . . [His] understanding of life becomes a social virtue, capable of convincing the militant fighter that self-sacrifice is a redemption of his people's life. This is a maximum expression of attachment to life" (from the Introduction to *Men in the Sun and Other Palestinian Stories*, Three Continents Press, 1983 edition of a 1978 collection of Kanafani's work). Kanafani wrote five novels, five collections of stories, plays, and many studies of Palestinian literature.

Lend Me Your Light

Rohinton Mistry

> . . . your lights are all lit—then where do you go with your lamp?
> My house is all dark and lonesome,—lend me your light.
> Rabindranath Tagore, *Gitanjali*

WE BOTH left Bombay the same year. Jamshed first, for New York, then I, for Toronto. As immigrants in North America, sharing this common experience should have salvaged something from our acquaintanceship. It went back such a long way, to our school days at St Xavier's.

To sustain an acquaintance does not take very much. A friendship, that's another thing. Strange, then, that it has ended so completely, that he has erased himself out of our lives, mine and Percy's; now I cannot imagine him even as a mere bit player who fills out the action or swells a procession.

Jamshed was my brother's friend. The three of us went to the same school. Jamshed and my brother, Percy, both four years older than I, were in the same class, and spent their time together. They had to part company during lunch, though, because Jamshed did not eat where Percy and I did, in the school's drillhall-cum-lunchroom.

The tiffin carriers would stagger into the school compound with their long, narrow rickety crates balanced on their heads, each with fifty tiffin boxes, delivering lunches from homes in all corners of the city. When the boxes were unpacked, the drillhall would be filled with a smell that is hard to forget, thick as swill, while the individual aromas of four hundred steaming lunches started to mingle. The smell must have soaked into the very walls and ceiling, there to age and rancidify. No matter what the hour of the day, that hot and dank grotto of a drillhall smelled stale and sickly, the way a vomit-splashed room does even after it is cleaned up.

Jamshed did not eat in this crammed and cavernous interior. Not for him the air redolent of nauseous odours. His food arrived precisely at one o'clock in the chauffeur-driven, air-conditioned family car, and was eaten in the leather-upholstered luxury of the back seat, amid this collection of hyphenated lavishness.

In the snug dining-room where chauffeur doubled as waiter, Jamshed lunched through his school-days, safe from the vicissitudes of climate. The monsoon might drench the tiffin carriers to the bone and turn cold the boxes of four hundred waiting schoolboys, but it could not touch Jamshed or his lunch. The tiffin carriers might arrive glistening and stinking of sweat in the hot season, with scorching hot tiffin boxes, hotter than they'd left the kitchens of Bombay, but Jamshed's lunch remained unaffected.

During the years of high school, my brother, Percy, began spending many weekend afternoons at his friend's house at Malabar Hill. Formerly, these were the afternoons when we used to join Pesi *paadmaroo* and the others for our most riotous times in the compound, the afternoons that the adults of Firozsha Baag would await with dread, not knowing what new terrors Pesi had devised to unleash upon the innocent and the unsuspecting.

But Percy dropped all this for Jamshed's company. And when he returned from his visits, Mummy would commence the questioning: What did they eat? Was Jamshed's mother home? What did the two do all afternoon? Did they go out anywhere? And so on.

Percy did not confide in me very much in those days. Our lives intersected during the lunch routine only, which counted for very little. For a short while we had played cricket together with the boys of Firozsha Baag. Then he lost interest in that too. He refused to come when Daddy would take the whole gang to the Marine Drive *maidaan* on Sunday mornings. And soon, like all younger brothers, I was seen mainly as a nuisance.

But my curiosity about Percy and Jamshed was satisfied by Mummy's interrogations. I knew that the afternoons were usually spent making model airplanes and listening to music. The airplanes were simple gliders in the early years; the records, mostly Mantovani and from Broadway shows. Later came more complex models with gasoline engines and remote control, and classical music from Bach to Poulenc.

The model-airplane kits were gifts from Jamshed's itinerant aunties and uncles, purchased during business trips to England or the U.S. Everyone except my brother and I seemed to have uncles and aunties smitten by wanderlust, and Jamshed's supply line from the western world guaranteed for him a steady diet of foreign clothes, shoes, and records.

One Saturday, Percy reported during question period that Jamshed had received the original soundtrack of *My Fair Lady*. This was sensational news. The LP was not available in Bombay, and a few privately imported or "smuggled" copies, brought in by people like Jamshed's relatives, were selling in the black market for two hundred rupees. I had seen the records displayed side by side with foreign perfumes, chocolates, and cheeses at the pavement stalls of smugglers along Flora Fountain.

Sometimes, these stalls were smashed up during police raids. I liked to imagine that one day a raid would occur as I was passing, and in the mêlée and chaos of the clash, *My Fair Lady* would fly through the air and land at my feet, unnoticed by anyone. Of course, there wasn't much I could have done with it following the miracle, because our old gramophone played only 78 rpms.

After strenuous negotiations in which Mummy, Percy, and I exhausted ourselves, Percy agreed to ask his friend if I could listen to the album. Arrangements were made. And the following Saturday we set off for Jamshed's house. From Firozsha Baag, the direction of Malabar Hill was opposite to the one we took to go to school every morning, and I was not familiar with the roads the bus travelled. The building had a marble lobby, and the lift zoomed us up smoothly to the tenth floor before I had time to draw breath. I was about to tell Percy that we needed one like this in Firozsha Baag, but the door opened. Jamshed welcomed us graciously, then wasted no time in putting the record on the turntable. After all, that was what I had come for.

The afternoon dragged by after the sound-track finished. Bored, I watched them work on an airplane. The box said it was a Sopwith Camel. The name was familiar from the Biggles books Percy used to bring home. I picked up the lid and read dully that the aircraft had been designed by the British industrialist and aeronautical engineer, Thomas Octave Murdoch Sopwith, born 1888, and had been used during the First World War. Then followed a list of the parts.

Later, we had lunch, and they talked. I was merely the kid brother, and nobody expected me to do much else but listen. They talked of school and the school library, of all the books that the library badly needed; and of the *ghatis* who were flooding the school of late.

In the particular version of reality we inherited, *ghatis* were always flooding places, they never just went there. *Ghatis* were flooding the banks, desecrating the sanctity of institutions, and taking up all the coveted jobs. *Ghatis* were even flooding the colleges and universities, a thing unheard of. Wherever you turned, the bloody *ghatis* were flooding the place.

With much shame I remember this word *ghati*. A suppurating sore of a word, oozing the stench of bigotry. It consigned a whole race to the mute roles of coolies and menials, forever unredeemable.

During one of our rare vacations to Matheran, as a child, I watched with detachment while a straining coolie loaded the family's baggage on his person. The big metal trunk was placed flat on his head, with the leather suitcase over it. The enormous hold-all was slung on his left arm, which he raised to steady the load on his head, and the remaining suitcase went in the right hand. It was all accomplished with much the same approach and consideration used in loading a cart or barrow—the main thing was balance, to avoid tipping over. This skeletal man then tottered off towards the train that would transport us to the little hill station. There, similar skeletal beings would be waiting with rickshaws. Automobiles were prohibited in Matheran, to preserve the pastoral purity of the place and the livelihood of the rickshawallas.

Many years later I found myself at the same hill station, a member of my college hikers' club, labouring up its slopes with a knapsack. Automobiles were still not permitted in Matheran, and every time a rickshaw sped by in a flurry of legs and wheels, we'd yell at the occupant ensconced within: "Capitalist pig! You bastard! Stop riding on your brother's back!" The bewildered passenger would lean forward for a moment, not quite understanding, then fall back into the cushioned comfort of the rickshaw.

But this kind of smug socialism did not come till much later. First we had to reckon with school, school uniforms, brown paper covers for textbooks and exercise books, and the mad morning rush for the school bus. I remember how Percy used to rage and shout at our scrawny *ghaton* if the pathetic creature ever got in his way as she swept and mopped the floors. Mummy would proudly observe, "He has a temper just like Grandpa's." She would also discreetly admonish Percy, since this was in the days when it was becoming quite difficult to find a new *ghaton*, especially if the first one quit due to abuse from the scion of the family and established her reasons for quitting among her colleagues.

I was never sure why some people called them *ghatons* and others, *gungas*. I supposed the latter was intended to placate—the collective conferment of the name of India's sacred river balanced the occasions of harshness and ill-treatment. But the good old days, when you could scream at a *ghaton* that you would kick her and hurl her down the steps, and expect her to show up for work next morning, had definitely passed.

After high school, Percy and Jamshed went to different colleges. If they met at all, it would be at concerts of the Bombay Chamber Orchestra. Along with a college friend, Navjeet, and some others, my brother organized a charitable agency that collected and distributed funds to destitute farmers in a small Maharashtrian village. The idea was to get as many of these wretched souls as possible out of the clutches of the village moneylenders.

Jamshed showed a very superficial interest in what little he knew about Percy's activities. Each time they met, he would start with how he was trying his best to get out of the country. "Absolutely no future in this stupid place," he said. "Bloody corruption everywhere. And you can't buy any of the things you want, don't even get to see a decent English movie. First chance I get, I'm going abroad. Preferably the U.S."

After a while, Percy stopped talking about his small village, and they only discussed the concert program or the soloist's performance that evening. Then their meetings at concerts ceased altogether because Percy now spent very little time in Bombay.

Jamshed did manage to leave. One day, he came to say goodbye. But Percy was away working in the small village: his charitable agency had taken on the task full time. Jamshed spoke to those of us who were home, and we all agreed that he was doing the right thing. There just weren't any prospects in this country; nothing could stop its downhill race towards despair and ruin.

My parents announced that I, too, was trying to emigrate, but to Canada, not the U.S. "We will miss him if he gets to go," they told Jamshed, "but for the sake of his own future, he must. There is a lot of opportunity in Toronto. We've seen advertisements in newspapers from England, where Canadian Immigration is encouraging people to go to Canada. Of course, they won't advertise in a country like India—who would want these bloody *ghatis* to come charging into their fine land?—but the office in New Delhi is holding interviews and selecting highly qualified applicants." In the clichés of our speech was reflected the cliché which the idea of emigration had turned into for so many. According to my parents, I would have no difficulty being approved, what with my education, and my westernized background, and my fluency in the English language.

And they were right. A few months later things were ready for my departure to Toronto.

Then the neighbours began to arrive. Over the course of the last seven days, they came to confer their blessings and good wishes upon me. First was Bulsara Bookworm's mother, her hair in a bun as usual and covered with the *mathoobanoo*. She said, "I know you and Jehangir were never very good friends, but that does not matter at a time like this. He says best of luck." She put her arm over my shoulder in lieu of a hug and said, "Don't forget your parents and all they did for you, maintain your good name at all times."

And Tehmina, too, using the occasion to let bygones be bygones with Mummy and Daddy, arrived sucking cloves and shuffling in slippers and duster coat. Her cataracts were still a problem, refusing to ripen, she said.

Then one morning Nariman Hansotia stopped me in the compound. He was on his way to the Cawasji Framji Memorial Library, and I to the airline office for a final confirmation of my seat.

"Well, well," he said, "so you were serious when you used to tell everyone that you would go abroad. Who would have thought of it! Who would have imagined that Silloo Boyce's little Kersi would one day go to Canada. Knee high I had seen you, running around in the compound with your brother, trying to do everything he did. Well, lead a good life, do nothing to bring shame to you or the Parsi community. And don't just land there and say, where are the girls? like this other chap had done. Did I ever tell you that story?"

And Nariman launched into an anecdote: "A sex-crazy young fellow was going to California. For weeks he used to tell his friends about how the women there went around on the beaches with hardly any clothes on, and how easy it was to find women who would go with you for a little bit of this and that, and what a wonderful time he was going to have as soon as he got there. Well, when he landed at Los Angeles, he tried to joke with the immigration officer and asked him, 'Where are the girls?' What do you think happened then?"

"What, Nariman Uncle?"

"He was deported on the very next plane, of course. Never did find out where the girls were."

Good old Nariman Uncle. He would never stop telling his tales. We finally parted, and as he pulled out of the compound in his old Mercedes-Benz, someone called my name from the ground floor of A Block. It was Rustomji-the-curmudgeon, skulking in the shadows and waiting for Nariman to leave. He shook my hand and gruffly wished me well.

But as I slept on my last night in Bombay a searing pain in my eyes woke me up. It was one o'clock. I bathed my eyes and tried to get back to sleep. Half-jokingly, I saw myself as someone out of a Greek tragedy, guilty of the sin of hubris for seeking emigration out of the land of my birth, and paying the price in burnt-out eyes: I, Tiresias, blind and throbbing between two lives, the one in Bombay and the one to come in Toronto . . .

In the morning, Dr Sidhwa arrived and said it was conjunctivitis, nothing very serious. But I would need some drops every four hours and protective dark glasses till the infection was gone. No charge, he said, because he was going to drop by anyway to say goodbye and good luck.

Just before noon came Najamai. She must have been saving herself for an auspicious *chogeryooh*. She sympathized about my eyes before bringing forth her portable celebration kit: a small silver *thaali* holding a garland, and a tiny cup for the vermilion. They were miniatures of her regular apparatus which was too heavy to lug around. She put the garland round my neck, made a large, bright red *teelo* on my forehead and hugged me several times: "Lots and lots of years you must live, see lots of life, study lots, earn lots, make us all very proud of you."

Then Najamai succumbed to reminiscing: "Remember when you used to come upstairs with the meat? Such a good boy, always helping your mother. And remember how you used to kill rats, with your bat, even for me? I always used to think, how brave for such a small boy to kill rats with a bat. And one day you even ran after Francis with it! Oh, I'll never forget that!"

She left, and Daddy found me a pair of dark glasses. And thus was spent my last day in Bombay, the city of all my days till then. The last glimpses of my bed, my broken cricket bat, the cracks in the plaster, the chest of drawers I shared with Percy till he went away to the small village, came through dark glasses; the neighbourhood I grew up in, with the chemist's store ("Open Twenty-Four Hours"), the Irani restaurant, the sugar-cane juice vendor, the fruit-and-vegetable stall in Tar Gully, all of these I surveyed through dark glasses; the huddle of relatives at the airport, by the final barrier through which only ticket holders can pass, I waved to and saw one last time through dark glasses.

Tense with excitement I walked across the tarmac. The slight chill I felt was due to the gusting night winds, I convinced myself.

Then, eyes red with conjunctivitis, pocket bulging with the ridiculously large bottle of eye-drops, and mind confused by a thousand half-formed thoughts and doubts, I boarded the aircraft sitting white and roaring upon the concrete. I tried to imagine Mummy and Daddy on the visitors' gallery, watching me being swallowed up into its belly. I imagined them consoling each other and fighting back the tears (as they had promised me they would) while I vanished into the night.

After almost a year in Toronto I received a letter from Jamshed. From New York—a very neat missive, with an elegant little label showing his name and address. He wrote that he'd been to Bombay the previous month because in every single letter his mother had been pestering him to visit: "While there, I went to Firozsha Baag and saw your folks. Glad to hear you left India. But what about Percy? Can't understand what keeps him in that dismal place. He refuses to accept reality. All his efforts to help the farmers will be in vain. Nothing ever improves, just too much corruption. It's all part of the *ghati* mentality. I offered to help him immigrate if he ever changes his mind. I've got a lot of contacts now, in New York. But it's up to him to make up his mind," and on and on.

Finally: "Bombay is horrible. Seems dirtier than ever, and the whole trip just made me sick. I had my fill of it in two weeks and was happy to leave." He ended with a cordial invitation to New York.

What I read was only the kind of stuff I would have expected in a letter from Jamshed. That was the way we all used to talk in Bombay. Still, it irritated me. It was puzzling that he could express so much disdain and discontentment even when he was no longer living under those conditions. Was it himself he was angry with, for not being able to come to terms with matters as Percy had? Was it because of the powerlessness that all of us experience who, mistaking weakness for strength, walk away from one thing or another?

I started a most punctilious reply to his letter. Very properly, I thanked him for visiting my parents and his concern for Percy. Equally properly, I reciprocated his invitation to New York with one to Toronto. But I did not want to leave it at that. It sounded as if I was agreeing with him about Percy and his work, and about India.

So instead, I described the segment of Toronto's Gerrard Street known as Little India. I promised that when he visited, we would go to all the little restaurants there and gorge ourselves with *bhelpuri, panipuri, batata-wada, kulfi,* as authentic as any in Bombay; then we could browse through the shops selling imported spices and Hindi records, and maybe even see a Hindi movie at the Naaz Cinema. I often went to Little India, I wrote; he would be certain to have a great time.

The truth is, I have been there just once. And on that occasion I fled the place in a very short time, feeling extremely ill at ease and ashamed, wondering why all this did not make me feel homesick or at least a little nostalgic. But Jamshed did not have to know any of it. My letter must have told him that whatever he suffered from, I did not share it. For a long time afterwards I did not hear from him.

My days were always full. I attended evening classes at the University of Toronto, desultorily gathering philosophy credits, and worked during the day. I became a member of the Zoroastrian Society of Ontario. Hoping to meet people from Bombay, I also went to the Parsi New Year celebrations and dinner.

The event was held at a community centre rented for the occasion. As the evening progressed it took on, at an alarming rate, the semblance of a wedding party at Bombay's Cama Garden, with its attendant sights and sounds and smells, as we Parsis talked at the top of our voices, embraced heartily, drank heartily, and ate heartily. It was Cama Garden refurbished and modernized, Cama Garden without the cluster of beggars waiting by the entrance gate for the feast to end so they could come in and claim the dustbins.

My membership in the Society led to dinner invitations at Parsi homes. Many of the guests at these gatherings were not the type who would be regulars at Little India, but who might go there with the air of tourists, equipped with a supply of ohs and aahs for ejaculation at suitable moments, pretending to discover what they had always lived with.

These were people who knew all about the different airlines that flew to Bombay. These were the virtuosi of transatlantic travel. If someone inquired of the most recent traveller, "How was your trip to India?" another would be ready with "What airline?" The evening would then become a convention of travel agents expounding on the salient features of their preferred carriers.

After a few such copiously educational evenings, I knew what the odds were of my luggage getting lost if I travelled airline A. The best food was served on airline B. Departures were always delayed with airline C (the company had a *ghati* sense of time and punctuality, they said). The wash-rooms were filthy and blocked up on airline D (no fault of airline D, they explained, it was the low class of public that travelled on it).

Of Bombay itself the conversation was restricted to the shopping they'd done. They brought back tales of villainous shopkeepers who tried to cheat them because they sensed that here was the affluence of foreign ex-change: "Very cunning, they all are. God knows how, but they are able to smell your dollars before you even open your wallet. Then they try to fool you in the way they fool all the other tourists. I used to tell them"— this, in broken Hindi—"'go, go, what you thinking, I someone new in Mumbai? I living here thirty years, yes thirty, before going phoren.' Then they would bargain sensibly."

Others told of the way they had made a shrewd deal with shopkeepers who did not know the true value of brass and copper artifacts and knick-knacks, what did bloody *ghatis* know about such things anyway. These collectors of bric-a-brac, self-appointed connoisseurs of art and antiques, must have acquired their fancies along with their immigration visas.

But their number was small. And though they were as earnest about their hobbies as the others were, they never quite succeeded in holding the gathering transfixed the way the airline clique managed to. Art was not as popular as airlines were at these evenings.

Six months after Jamshed's trip to Bombay, I received a letter from my brother Percy. Among other things, he wrote about his commitment in the small village:

Our work with the farmers started successfully. They got interest-free loans in the form of seed and fertilizer, which we purchased wholesale, and for the first time in years they did not have to borrow from those bloodthirsty money-lenders.

Ever since we got there the money-lenders hated us. They tried to persuade us to leave, saying that what we were doing was wrong because it was upsetting the delicate balance of village life and destroying tradition. We in turn pointed out things like exploitation, usury, inhumanity, and other abominations whose time was now up. We may have sounded like bold knights-errant, but they turned to threats and said it would soon become so unhealthy for us that we would leave quickly enough.

One day when we were out visiting a loan applicant, a farmer brought news that a gang of thugs wielding sticks and cudgels was waiting at the hut—our office and residence. So we stayed the night with the loan applicant, and in the morning, escorted by a band of villagers who insisted on coming along, started for our hut. But all we found were smouldering embers. It had been razed to the ground during the night, and no one had dared interfere.

Now we're back in Bombay, and Navjeet and I are working on a plan for our return. We've spoken to several reporters, and the work is getting much publicity. We're also collecting fresh donations, so that when we go back we won't fail for lack of funds.

Having read this far, I put down the letter for a moment. There you were, my brother, waging battles against corruption and evil, while I was watching sitcoms on my rented Granada TV. Or attending dinner parties at Parsi homes to listen to chit-chat about airlines and trinkets. And it was no use wishing that we had talked more to each other about our hopes and visions and dreams. I thought of our school-days, trying to locate the point when the gulf had appeared between us. Did it grow bit by bit or suddenly happen one morning? I cannot remember, but it did throw everything into silence and secrecy.

The rest of the letter concerned Jamshed's visit to Bombay six months ago:

I wish he'd stayed away, if not from Bombay then at least from me. At best, the time I spent with him was a waste. I expected that we would look at things differently, but was not prepared for the crassly materialistic boor that he's turned into. To think he was my "best friend" in school.

No doubt he believes the highlight of his visit came when he took some of us to dinner at the Rendezvous—nothing but the most expensive, of course. It was a spectacle to surpass anything he'd done so far. He reminded us to eat and drink all we wanted without minding the prices and enjoy ourselves as much as we could, because we wouldn't get such a chance again, at least, not until his next visit.

When the soup came he scolded the waiter that it was cold and sent it back. The rest of us sat silent and embarrassed. He looked at us nonchalantly, explaining that this was the only way to handle incompetence; Indians were too meek and docile and should learn to stand up for their rights the way people do in the States.

We were supposed to be impressed by his performance, for we were in an expensive restaurant where only foreign tourists eat on the strength of their U.S. dollars. And here was one of our own, not intimidated within the walls of the five-star Taj Mahal Hotel. In our school-days we could only stand outside and watch the foreigners come and go, wondering what opulent secrets lay inside, what comforts these fair-skinned superior beings enjoyed. Here was one of our own showing us how to handle it all without feeling a trace of inferiority, and now we were ashamed of him.

We spent the evening watching Jamshed in disbelief, in silence, which he probably thought was due to the awesome splendour of our surroundings.

I was determined not to see him again, not even when he came to say goodbye on the day of his departure, and I don't intend to meet him when he visits Bombay the next time . . .

As I finished reading, I felt that my brother had been as irritated by Jamshed's presence as I had been by Jamshed's letter six months ago. But I did not write this to Percy. After all, I was planning to be in Bombay in four or five months. We could talk then. In just four months I would complete two years in Canada—long enough a separation, I supposed with a naive pomposity, to have developed a lucidity of thought which I would carry back with me and bring to bear on all of India's problems.

Soon it was time to go shopping for gifts. I packed chocolates, cheeses, jams, jellies, puddings, cake mixes, panty hose, stainless steel razor blades —all the items I used to see displayed in the stalls of the smugglers along Flora Fountain, always priced out of reach. I felt like one of the soldiers who, in wartime, accumulates strange things to use as currency for barter. What was I hoping to barter them for? Attention? Gratitude? Balm to soothe guilt or some other malady of the conscience? I wonder now. And I wonder more that I did not wonder then about it.

The suitcase I had come with proved insufficient. And although I bought a new one, an extra leather strap around each seemed wise, for they were both swelled to threatening dimensions.

Then, arms still sore from the typhoid and cholera inoculations, luggage bursting at the seams with a portable grocery store, and mind suffused with groundless optimism, I boarded the plane.

The aircraft was losing height in preparation for landing. The hard afternoon sun revealed the city I was coming back to after two years. When the plane had taken off two years ago, it had been in the dark of night, and all I saw from the sky through shaded and infected eyes were the airport lights of Santa Cruz. But now it was daytime, and I was not wearing dark glasses. I could see the parched land: brown, weary, and unhappy.

A few hours earlier the aircraft had made its scheduled landing in London, and the view from the air had been lush, everywhere green and hopeful. It enraged me as I contrasted it with what I was now seeing. Gone was the clearness with which I'd promised myself I would look at things. All that was left was a childish and helpless reaction. "It's not fair!" I wanted to stamp my foot and shout, "it's just not fair!"

Construction work was under way at the airport. The van transporting passengers from the aircraft to the terminal building passed improvised dwellings of corrugated metal, cardboard, packing crates, plastic sheets, even newspaper.

The van was reduced to a crawl in the construction zone. A few naked children emerged from the corrugated metal and cardboard and ran to keep up with us, screaming for money. When they came dangerously close to the van, the driver screamed back. On board was a group of four businessmen, and three of them tossed some change out the window. They sounded Australian. The fourth was the seasoned traveller, and the others hung on every word he said. He warned them, "If you try that when you're on the street, you'll create something like a bloody feeding frenzy of sharks." The children fell far behind when the construction zone ended and the van picked up speed.

Bombay seemed dirtier than ever. I remembered what Jamshed had written in his letter, and how it had annoyed me, but now I couldn't help thinking he was right. Hostility and tension seemed to be perpetually present in buses, shops, trains. It was disconcerting to discover I'd become unused to it. Now I knew what soldiers must experience in the trenches after a respite far behind the lines.

As if enacting a scene for my benefit with all the subtlety of a sixteenth-century morality play, a crowd clawed its way into a local train. All the players were there: Fate and Reality, and the latter's offspring, the New Reality, and also Poverty and Hunger, Virtue and Vice, Apathy and Corruption.

The drama began when the train, Reality, rolled into the station. It was overcrowded because everyone wanted to get on it: Virtue, Vice, Apathy, Corruption, all of them. Someone, probably Poverty, dropped his plastic lunch bag amidst the stampede, nudged on by Fate. Then Reality rolled out of the station with a gnashing and clanking of its metal, leaving in its wake the New Reality. And someone else, probably Hunger, matter-of-factly picked up Poverty's mangled lunch, dusted off a *chapati* which had slipped out of the trampled bag, and went his way. In all of this, was there a lesson for me? To trim my expectations and reactions to things, trim them down to the proper proportions?

I wasn't sure, but when I missed my bus an old instinctive impulse returned: to dash after it, to leap and join the crowd already hanging from the door rail. In the old days I would have been off and running. I used to pride my agility at this manoeuvre. After all, during rush hour it was the only way to catch a bus, or you'd be left at the bus-stop with the old and the feeble.

But while the first flush of confidence flowed through me, the bus had moved well into the stream of traffic. My momentary hesitation gave the game away. With the old and feeble was my place, as long as I was a tourist here, and not committed to life in the combat zone.

In Firozsha Baag things were still roughly the same, but Mrs Mody had died, and no one knew what Pesi was doing now. In fact, ever since he had been sent away to boarding school some years ago, Pesi's doing were not spoken of at all. My friend Viraf of A Block, whom I had been unable to say goodbye to two years ago because he was away in Kharagpur studying at the Indian Institute of Technology, was absent for my hello as well. He did not return to Bombay because he had found a job in nearby Calcutta.

Tehmina had at last rid herself of the cataracts. She was suddenly very spry, very sure of herself in all she did. Along with her cataracts she had also jettisoned her old slippers and duster-coat. Her new ensemble consisted of a long, flowing floral-patterned kaftan and a smart pair of *chappals* with little heels that rang out her presence on the stairs and in the hallway.

But Najamai had aged considerably. She kept asking me why I had not yet been to see her daughters even though she had given me their addresses: Vera was somewhere in Alberta, and Dolly in British Columbia.

My brother, Percy, wrote from the small village that he wanted to meet me, but: "I cannot come to Bombay right now because I've received a letter from Jamshed. He's flying in from New York, and has written about reunions and great times for all the old crowd. That's out of the question as far as I'm concerned. I'm not going to see him again."

I wrote back saying I understood.

Our parents were disappointed. They had been so happy that the whole family would be together again for a while. And now this. They could not understand why Percy did not like Jamshed any more, and I'm sure at the back of their minds they thought their son envied his friend because of the fine success he'd made of himself in America. But who was I to explain things, and would they understand even if I tried? They truly believed that Jamshed was the smart young fellow, and Percy the idealist who forgot that charity begins at home.

This trip was not turning out to be anything I'd hoped it would. Jamshed was coming and Percy wasn't, our parents were disappointed with Percy, I was disappointed with them, and in a week I would be flying out of Bombay, confused and miserable. I could feel it already.

Without any destination in mind I left the house and took the first empty bus to come along. It went to Flora Fountain. The offices were now closing for the day. The dirty, yellow-grey buildings would soon spill out typists and clerks and peons into a swelling stream surging towards bus-stops and train stations.

Roadside stalls were open for business. This would be their busy hour. They were lined up along the edge of the pavement, displaying their merchandise. Here a profusion of towels and napkins from shocking pink to peacock green; there, the clatter and gleam of pots and pans; further down, a refreshment stall selling sizzling *samosas* and ice-cold sherbet.

The pavement across the road was the domain of the smugglers with their stalls of foreign goods. But they did not interest me, I stayed where I was. One man was peddling an assortment of toys. He demonstrated them all in turn, calling out, "Baba play and baby play! Daddy play and

Mummy play!" Another, with fiendish vigour, was throwing glass bowls to the ground, yelling: "Un-ber-rakable! Un-ber-rakable!"

Sunlight began to fade as I listened to the hawkers singing their tunes. Kerosene lamps were lit in some of the stalls, punctuating at random the rows on both sides of the street.

Serenely I stood and watched. The disappointment which had overcome me earlier began to ebb. All was fine and warm within this moment after sunset when the lanterns were lit, and I began to feel a part of the crowds which were now flowing down Flora Fountain. I walked with them.

Suddenly, a hand on my shoulder made me turn around. It was Jamshed. "Bet you weren't expecting to see me in Bombay."

"Actually, I was. Percy wrote you were coming." Then I wished I hadn't volunteered this bit of information.

But there was no need to worry about awkward questions regarding Percy. For Jamshed, in fine fettle, had other thoughts he was anxious to share.

"So what are you doing here? Come shopping?" he asked jokingly, indicating the little stalls with a disdainful sweep of his hand. "Terrible, isn't it, the way these buggers think they own the streets—don't even leave you enough room to walk. The police should drive them off, break up their bloody stalls, really."

He paused. I wondered if I should say something. Something that Percy would love to hear me say. Like: these people were only trying to earn a meagre living by exercising, amidst a paucity of options, this one; at least they were not begging or stealing. But I didn't have a chance.

"God, what a racket! Impossible to take even a quiet little walk in this place. I tell you, I'll be happy when it's time to catch my plane back to New York."

It was hopeless. It was his letter all over again, the one he'd written the year before from New York. He had then temporarily disturbed the order I was trying to bring into my new life in Toronto, and I'd struck back with a letter of my own. But this time I just wanted to get away from him as quickly as possible. Before he made the peace of mind I was reaching out for dissipate, become forever unattainable.

Suddenly, I understood why Percy did not want to meet him again— he, too, sensed and feared Jamshed's soul-sapping presence.

Around us, all the pavement stalls were immersed in a rich dusk. Each one was now lit by a flickering kerosene lantern. What could I say to Jamshed? What would it take, I wondered, to light the lantern in his soul?

He was waiting for me to speak. I asked, perfunctorily, how much longer he would be in Bombay.

"Another week. Seven whole days, and they'll go so slowly. But I'll be dropping in at Firozsha Baag in a couple of days, tell Percy." We walked to my bus-stop. A beggar tugged at his sleeve and he mechanically reached in his pocket for change. Then we said good-night.

On the bus I thought about what to say if he asked me, two days later, why I hadn't mentioned that Percy was not coming.

As it turned out, I did not have to say anything.

Late next evening, Percy came home unexpectedly. I rushed to greet him, but his face revealed that he was not returning in this manner to give us a pleasant surprise. Something was dreadfully wrong. His colour was ashen. He was frightened and shaken, and struggled to retain his composure. He tried to smile as he shook my hand limply, but could not muster the effort to return my hug.

"What's the matter?" said Mother. "You don't look well."

Silently, Percy sat down and began to remove his shoes and socks. After a while he looked up and said, "They killed Navjeet."

No one spoke for the next few minutes. Percy sat with his socks dangling from his hands, looking sad, tired, defeated.

Then Mummy rose and said she would make tea. Over tea, he told us what had happened. Slowly, reluctantly at first, then faster, in a rush, to get the remembering and telling over with as soon as possible. "The money-lenders were ready to make trouble for us again. We didn't think they'd do anything as serious as the last time. The press was following our progress and had reported the arson in many newspapers. Yesterday we were out at the wholesaler's. Ordering seed for next year. But Navjeet had stayed behind. He was working on the accounts. When we returned he was lying unconscious. On the floor. His face and head were bleeding badly. We carried him to the makeshift clinic in the village—there is no hospital. The doctor said there was severe internal damage—massive head injuries—a few hours later he was dead."

There was silence again. Perhaps when we were together later, sharing our old room again, Percy would talk to me. But he lay on his bed in the darkness, wide awake, staring silently at the ceiling, tracing its old familiar cracks as I was, by the hints of streetlights straying through the worn curtains. Was there nothing to say? There had to be something I could do to help.

Strangely enough, it was Jamshed who provided this something the next day.

When he arrived in the evening, he presented Mummy with a box of chocolates and some cheese triangles. She asked him how he'd been enjoying his trip so far. He replied, true to form, "Oh Auntie, I'm tired of

this place, really. The dust and heat and crowds—I've had enough of it."
And Mummy nodded sympathetically.

Soon, the moment Percy had been dreading was at hand. Mummy asked
him to narrate, for Jamshed's benefit, the events which had brought him
home so suddenly. But Percy just shook his head, so she told the story
herself.

When she finished, we shifted uneasily. What was next? But Jamshed
could not contain himself. He heaved the sigh of the worldly-wise: "I
told you from the beginning, all this was a waste of time and nothing
would come of it, remember? Every time we met we would talk about it,
and you used to make fun of me wanting to go abroad. But I still think
the best thing for you is to move to the States. There is so much you
could achieve there. There, if you are good at something, you are appreciated, and you get ahead. Not like here, where everything is controlled by
uncle-auntie, and . . ."

When Jamshed concluded his harangue, Percy calmly turned to Mummy
and said in his quiet voice, "Could we have dinner right away? I have to
meet my friends at eight o'clock. To decide our next move in the village."

Five days later I was back in Toronto. I unpacked my suitcases, which were
quite flat on the return trip and had not required the extra leather straps. I
put my things away and displayed in the apartment the little knick-knacks
bought in handicraft places and the Cottage Industries store.

Gradually, I discovered I'd brought back with me my entire burden
of riddles and puzzles, unsolved. The whole sorry package was there,
not lightened at all. The epiphany would have to wait for another time,
another trip.

I mused, I gave way to whimsy: I Tiresias, throbbing between two lives,
humbled by the ambiguities and dichotomies confronting me . . .

I thought of Jamshed and his adamant refusal to enjoy his trips to India,
his way of seeing the worst in everything. Was he, too, waiting for some
epiphany and growing impatient because, without it, life in America was
bewildering? Perhaps the contempt and disdain which he shed was only
his way of lightening his own load.

That Christmas, I received a card from Jamshed. The Christmas seal,
postage stamp, address label were all neatly and correctly in place upon
the envelope, like everything else about his surface existence. I put it down
without opening it, wondering if this innocuous outer shell concealed more
of his confusion, disdain, arrogance.

Later, I walked out of the apartment and down the hallway, and dropped
the envelope down the chute of the garbage incinerator.

Letter from Gaza

Ghassan Kanafani

DEAR MUSTAFA,

I have now received you letter, in which you tell me that you've done everything necessary to enable me to stay with you in Sacramento. I've also received news that I have been accepted in the department of Civil Engineering in the University of California. I must thank you for everything, my friend. But it'll strike you as rather odd when I proclaim this news to you—and make no doubt about it, I feel no hesitation at all, in fact I am pretty well positive taht I have never seen things so clearly as I do now. No, my friend, I have changed my mind. I won't follow you to "the land where there is greenery, water and lovely faces" as you wrote. No, I'll stay here, and I won't ever leave.

I am really upset that our lives won't continue to follow the same course, Mustafa. For I can almost hear you reminding me of our vow to go on together, and of the way we used to shout: "We'll get rich!" But there's nothing I can do, my friend. Yes, I still remember the day when I stood in the hall of Cairo airport, pressing your hand and staring at the frenzied motor. At that moment everything was rotating in time with the ear-splitting motor, and you stood in front of me, your round face silent.

Your face hadn't changed from the way it used to be when you were growing up in the Shajiya quarter of Gaza, apart from those slight wrinkles. We grew up together, understanding each other completely, and we promised to on together till the end. But . . .

"There's a quarter of an hour left before the plane takes off. Don't look into space like that. Listen! You'll go to Kuwait next year, and you'll save enough from your salary to uproot you from Gaza and transplant you to California. We started off together and we must carry on. . . ."

At that moment I was watching your rapidly moving lips. That was always your manner of speaking, without commas or full stops. But in an obscure way I felt that you were not completely happy with your flight. You couldn't give three good reasons for it. I too suffered from this wrench, but the clearest thought was: why don't we abandon this Gaza and flee? Why don't we? Your situation had begun to improve, however. The Ministry of Education in Kuwait had given you a contract though it hadn't given me one. In the trough of misery where I existed you sent me small sums of money. You wanted me to consider them as loans, because you feared that I would feel slighted. You knew my family circumstances in and out;

you knew that my meagre salary in the UNRWA schools was inadequate to support my mother, my brother's widow and her four children.

"Listen carefully. Write to me every day . . . every hour . . . every minute! The plane's just leaving. Farewell! Or rather, till we meet again!"

Your cold lips brushed my cheek, you turned your face away from me towards the plane, and when you looked at me again I could see your tears.

Later the Ministry of Education in Kuwait gave me a contract. There's no need to repeat to you how my life there went in detail. I always wrote to you about everything. My life there had a gluey, vacuous quality as though I were a small oyster, lost in oppressive loneliness, slowly struggling with a future as dark as the beginning of the night, caught in a rotten routine, a spewed-out combat with time. Everything was hot and sticky. There was a slipperiness to my whole life, it was all a hankering for the end of the month.

In the middle of the year, that year, the Jews bombarded the central district of Sabha and attacked Gaza, our Gaza, with bombs and flame-throwers. That event might have made some change in my routine, but there was nothing for me to take much notice of: I was going to leave this Gaza behind me and go to California where I would live for myself, my own self which had suffered so long. I hated Gaza and its inhabitants. Everything in the amputated town reminded me of failed pictures painted in grey by a sick man. Yes, I would send my mother and my brother's widow and her children a meagre sum to help them to live, but I would liberate myself from this last tie too, there in green California, far from the reek of defeat which for seven years had filled my nostrils. The sympathy which bound me to my brother's children, their mother and mine would never be enough to justify my tragedy in taking this perpendicular dive. It mustn't drag me any farther down than it already had. I must flee!

You know these feelings, Mustafa, because you've really experienced them. What is this ill-defined tie we had with Gaza which blunted our enthusiasm for flight? Why didn't we analyse the matter in such a way as to give it a clear meaning? Why didn't we leave this defeat with its wounds behind us and move on to a brighter future which would give us deeper consolation! Why? We didn't exactly know.

When I went on holiday in June and assembled all my possessions, longing for the sweet departure, the start towards those little things which give life a nice, bright meaning, I found Gaza just as I had known it, closed like the introverted lining of a rusted snail-shell thrown up by the waves on the sticky, sandy shore by the slaughterhouse. This Gaza was more cramped than the mind of a sleeper in the throes of a fearful night-mare, with its narrow streets which had their peculiar smell, the smell of defeat and poverty, its houses with their bulging balconies . . . this Gaza!

But what are the obscure causes that draw a man to his family, his house, his memories, as a spring draws a small flock of mountain goats? I don't know. All I know is that I went to my mother in our house that morning. When I arrived my late brother's wife met me there and asked me, weeping, if I would do as her wounded daughter, Nadia, in Gaza hospital wished and visit her that evening. Do you know Nadia, my brother's beautiful thirteen-year-old daughter?

That evening I bought a pound of apples and set out for the hospital to visit Nadia. I knew that there was something about it that my mother and my sister-in-law were hiding from me, something which their tongues could not utter, something strange which I could not put my finger on. I loved Nadia from habit, the same habit that made me love all that generation which had been so brought up on defeat and displacement that it had come to think that a happy life was a kind of social deviation.

What happened at that moment? I don't know. I entered the white room very calm. Ill children have something of saintliness, and how much more so if the child is ill as a result of cruel, painful wounds. Nadia was lying on her bed, her back propped up on a big pillow over which her hair was spread like a thick pelt. There was a profound silence in her wide eyes and a tear always shining in the depths of her black pupils. Her face was calm and still but eloquent as the face of a tortured prophet might be. Nadia was still a child, but she seemed more than a child, much more, and older than a child, much older.

"Nadia!"

I've no idea whether I was the one who said it, or whether it was someone else behind me. But she raised her eyes to me and I felt them dissolve me like a piece of sugar that had fallen into a hot cup of tea. Together with her slight smile I heard her voice.

"Uncle! Have you just come from Kuwait?"

Her voice broke in her throat, and she raised herself with the help of her hands and stretched out her neck towards me. I patted her back and sat down near her.

"Nadia! I've brought you presents from Kuwait, lots of presents. I'll wait till you can leave your bed, completely well and healed, and you'll come to my house and I'll give them to you. I've bought you the red trousers you wrote and asked me for. Yes, I've bought them."

It was a lie, born of the tense situation, but as I uttered it I felt that I was speaking the truth for the first time. Nadia trembled as though she had had an electric shock, and lowered her head in a terrible silence. I felt her tears wetting the back of my hand.

"Say something, Nadia! Don't you want the red trousers?"

She lifted her gaze to me and made as if to speak, but then she stopped, gritted her teeth and I heard her voice again, coming from far away.

"Uncle!"

She stretched out her hand, lifted the white coverlet with her fingers and pointed to her leg, amputated from the top of the thigh.

My friend . . . Never shall I forget Nadia's leg, amputated from the top of the thigh. No! Nor shall I forget the grief which had moulded her face and merged into its traits for ever. I went out of the hospital in Gaza that day, my hand clutched in silent derision on the two pounds I had brought with me to give Nadia. The blazing sun filled the streets with the colour of blood. And Gaza was brand new, Mustafa! You and I never saw it like this. The stone piled up at the beginning of the Shajiya quarter where we lived had a meaning, and they seemed to have been put there for no other reason but to explain it. This Gaza in which we had lived and with whose good people we had spent seven years of defeat was something new. It seemed to me just a beginning. I don't know why I thought it was just a beginning. I imagined that the main street that I walked along on the way back home was only the beginning of a long, long road leading to Safad. Everything in this Gaza throbbed with sadness which was not confined to weeping. It was a challenge; more than that, it was something like reclamation of the amputated leg!

I went out into the streets of Gaza, streets filled with blinding sunlight. They told me that Nadia had lost her leg when she threw herself on top of her little brothers and sisters to protect them from the bombs and flames that had fastened their claws into the house. Nadia could have saved herself, she could have run away, rescued her leg. But she didn't.

Why?

No, my friend, I won't come to Sacramento, and I've no regrets. No, and nor will I finish what we began together in childhood. This obscure feeling that you had as you left Gaza, this small feeling must grow into a giant deep within you. It must expand, you must seek it in order to find yourself, here among the ugly debris of defeat.

I won't come to you. But you, return to us! Come back, to learn from Nadia's leg, amputated from the top of the thigh, what life is and what existence is worth.

Come back, my friend! We are all waiting for you.

Part Two

NEW NATIONS
National Liberations, Civil Wars, Apartheid

Parables

In Global Cultures, there are many texts of the sort that are known in the European literary tradition by the Greek word "parable," literally, something thrown down beside, *paraballein*. Behind a parable there is another story, one that will not fit into a brief compass, one that may defy words altogether, toward which the parable points. Often, the parable is in one tone or emotional register, and the hidden story—the reader senses—is in another. A witty story about a war would be offensive, but a parable about war is comparable to a bright light that guides a miner out of a shaft.

For the great generation of Nigerian writers born in the 1930s, especially for the Nobel laureate playwright and memoirist Wole Soyinka and the well-known political novelist Chinua Achebe (*Things Fall Apart*, 1958), Nigeria's brutal civil war, 1967–1970, became a galvanizing theme. Often as partisans, they wrote both during the war, while the secessionist region known as Biafra was the site of genocidal horrors, and later as historians. The literary description has continued with novels and story collections like the feminist Flora Nwapa's *Wives at War* (Tana Press [Nigeria], 1980) that show war in all its grisly, stark, military and domestic detail. Now a younger generation, including **ADEWALE MAJA-PEARCE**, born in 1953 and raised in London, who was a boy during the war years, is adding voices of more detached retrospection on that war. Maja-Pearce writes with a political impartiality unthinkable to his elders and with a large emotional range, which I will represent using the humorous parable below and then, in the next section, with a somber, haunting lamentation. Even in Nigerian literature, which is so rich with comic *groit* [village storyteller] strains and ironic styles, the humor in this tale is startlingly above the horrible fray.

MOACYR SCLIAR's humor is startling, too, but he does not sound like a *groit*—although there are allusions in his work to the Brazilian popular story form, the *cordel*. Instead, he sounds like a man who has studied Franz Kafka's *Parables*, but among Russian-Jewish emigres living in the southern Brazilian city of Porto

Alegere, learning to write in Portuguese. Scliar, born in 1937, a physician in public health, has a droll diagnostic sensibility. In his story collections and novels—
The Volunteers was translated in 1988, *The Strange Nation of Rafael Mendes* in 1987—he aims right at the absurdity of modern urban life and particularly at the wars and guerrilla operations about which modern urban people confabulate. Brazil, from the mid-1960s to the mid-1970s, sank into military authoritarianism and terrorism, both from the right and from the left. City streets became battlefields. Faced with this insanity, a virtual civil war, Scliar wrote a tale in *The Enigmatic Eye* (1989) about terrorism: His topic was a poor urban terrorist's malaise that set in as his task—blowing up people and stores—became a "tedious routine." In the story from the same collection presented here, the tedium of the unending urban warfare is also presented as a problem, but the central character has solved it—by cultivating "the unknown element of the future."

The traditions for parable-making in Global Cultures are enormously diverse, and each version has its own humor. When HWANG SUN-WON, born in 1915, was young, Korea was a Japanese colony. He went to Waseda University in Tokyo, but he took a degree in English literature. During the Second World War, when writing in Korean was forbidden by the Japanese, he wrote in secret. After the war, critical of the Communist regime in his northern home region, he lived as a refugee in the South. The Cold War's hot war, the Korean War, which broke out in 1950, left hundreds of thousands of Koreans dead and families split between North and South. The thirty-eighth parallel became a Berlin Wall. Proponents of democracy suffered in both societies. Through this terrible history, Hwang Sun-won, the dean of Korean letters, addressed politics indirectly. In "Masks," he portrays his homeland in a macabrely witty parable: A soldier is killed and reincarnated—he becomes a plant, an animal, and finally a man, in the form of the soldier who had once killed him. Both he and his enemy, his host body, were wounded. Where their wound is, on their upper body or their lower, whether it is a bullet hole or an amputation, depends upon your perspective—as could be said for the one land, Korea, North and South.

The history of El Salvador is full of conflict—with its neighbors, Guatemala, Nicaragua, and most recently Honduras (in 1969), and internally between the poor masses (backed by leftist activists) and the owners of vast coffee and sugar-growing estates (backed by military dictator after military dictator from 1931 onward). Between 1960 and 1979, there were surges of growth in popular parties and some reform, but a 1979 military coup reintensified the repression of political opposition and resulted in terrible human rights violations, in which the United States became heavily involved. ALFONSO QUIJADA URIAS, born in the town of Quezaltepeque in 1940, was part of a literary-political group that formed at the National University in 1956. It included Manlio Argueta, Roque Dalton (who was assassinated in 1975), and Otto Rene Castillo, among others, and allied itself with the peasants who opposed the military dictatorship then in power. Persecution and prison terms were their fate, and most of the survivors went into exile. Urias remained until 1978, when he went to Nicaragua, then to Mexico, then to Canada. In this story, like many of his, the life of "just ordinary people" appears in all its senseless suffering. The project of burying an old woman who has—like the nation—had many identities, who is "the mother of invention," who has survived everything, the project of getting her to rest in no peace whatsoever becomes ludicrous.

Loyalties

Adewale Maja–Pearce

I WAS twelve years old at the time. One afternoon my father came rushing home earlier than usual.

"Wife," he shouted to my mother who was out the back preparing food; "wife, have you not heard the news?" He was so excited he went rushing through the house. I followed him.

"Aren't you ashamed of yourself, a grown man like you rushing around like a small boy? What is it?" my mother said.

"Ojukwu has announced the new state of Biafra. We are no longer Nigerians, you hear? We are now Biafrans," he said and smiled.

"And what then?" my mother asked.

"Woman, don't you know what you are saying? Don't you realize this is an important day, an historic occasion?"

My mother stood up and put her hands on her hips. Her face was streaming from the heat of the fire.

"Whether we are in Nigeria or whether we are in Biafra we are almost out of firewood," she said.

My father raised his hands to the sky.

"Events of world importance are taking place and you are telling me about firewood. Trust a woman," he said and walked away.

That evening the schoolmaster and the barber and the man who owned the Post Office came to our house.

"Boy, come here," the schoolmaster called.

"Come and hear what teacher has to say," my father ordered.

"Seven nines are?"

"Sixty-three," I answered.

"Good. Now, if twenty Nigerian soldiers march into our village and five Biafran women attack them with saucepans who will win?" he asked, and the barber collapsed on the floor. My mother took me by the arm and we left the room. But I crept back and stood by the door.

"What was I telling you the other day? That Ojukwu is a real man, just the sort of leader we need to get things moving. Those dirty Nigerians will taste pepper if they try to attack us, let me tell you," my father was saying.

"That's the way to talk," the schoolmaster said. "Just let them try. Biafra stands supreme."

"They were saying on the news that five coutries have already recognized us," the postmaster said.

My mother called me. "Where were you? Must you always be sneaking about listening to what foolish men are saying? Biafra, Nigeria, what difference? Have we suddenly acquired two heads? Go and collect the goat and tie him up for the night," she said, and added: "After all, he is now a Biafran goat so we must take better care of it."

During the next few weeks everybody was talking about it. But as my mother kept saying, the only difference it made was the increased cost of food.

And then there was a rumour that Federal troops were marching towards us. Biafran soldiers appeared overnight. In their new uniforms and polished guns they looked smart. They drove up and down in their jeeps and raised dust everywhere. All my friends worshipped them.

One morning I woke up and heard gunfire in the distance. A plane flew overhead.

"Hurry, hurry, we are under attack," my father shouted.

"Where are we going?" my mother asked.

"Are you blind, woman, can't you see the others heading for the forest?" my father said.

"But what about our troops?" I asked.

"What troops? They ran away last night."

My mother rushed into the bedroom and started dragging clothes onto the bed.

"We have no time for that," my father said.

When we got outside I saw that it was true. The entire village was heading for the forest, the schoolmaster in the lead.

We spent two days and nights in the bush.

"So this is your great Biafra," my mother said. "Where is Ojukwu, I didn't see him?"

"Shut up, woman," my father said.

On the third day my father said to me: "Go and see if the soldiers are still there."

"You want to get the boy killed?" my mother said, reaching for me.

"Leave him, they won't harm a child," my father said; and to me: "I don't ask you to show yourself, you hear?"

I crept to the edge of the forest. The village was completely deserted, except for a few hens. And then I saw our goat. He was eating the food in front of the Post Office. I knew the owner would be angry. I forgot my father's warning and started running. Three armed Nigerian soldiers stepped out of the barber's shop, their rifles in their hands, and waited for me.

"Where are your people?" one of them asked. I pointed in the direction.

"Are they afraid of us?"

I nodded.

"Go and tell them we mean no harm."

As soon as I got back to the clearing everyone began talking at once. I told them what had happened. An argument began. Some wanted to stay and others wanted to go, but we were all hungry and there was no food left. Because of the mosquitoes no-one had slept well. So we went.

The soldiers kept to their word. By the next day everything had returned to normal. At the end of the week the soldiers pulled out.

One evening the barber, the schoolmaster and the man who owned the Post Office came to our house. My father sent me out to buy bottles of beer. When I returned my father was saying:

"Those dirty Biafrans, what did I tell you? As usual it was all talk. When it comes to talk there is nothing they cannot do."

The schoolmaster called me. "Boy, if the Biafran soldiers cover twenty miles a day how long will it take them to reach the Cameroons?"

The barber held his sides and groaned.

"Don't mind them," my father said. My mother called me from the back.

"Go and collect our Nigerian goat," she said.

Peace and War

Moacyr Scliar

BEING LATE for the war, I had to take a taxi. Much to my annoy-ance: with the recent increase in the taxi fares, this expense, unforeseen and ill timed, was a hole in my budget. However, I did make it, and was able to clock in just in the nick of time, thus averting further hassles. There was a long line of people waiting to get to the time clock: I wasn't the only latecomer. Walter, my partner in the trench, was there, too, muttering: Like me, he had been forced to take a taxi. We were neighbors and we had joined the war roughly at the same time. Every second Thursday of each month we would take a bus at an intersection of our street in order to take part in the war activities.

I'm sick and tired of the whole shebang, said Walter. Me, too, I replied. Sighing, we clocked in and headed for the quartermaster's depot, where the locker room was temporarily (but this had been so for over fifteen years) located. Aren't you late today? asked the youth in charge of the locker room. We made no reply. He handed us the keys to our lockers. Quickly, we changed out of our clothes and into our old fatigues; then, grabbing the rifles and the ammunition (twenty cartridges), we headed for the line of battle.

The setting for the armed conflict was a stretch of prairie land on the outskirts of the city. The battlefield was surrounded by a barbed-wire fence with signs saying WAR, KEEP OUT. An unnecessary warning: hardly anybody went there, to that site of bucolic granges and small farms.

We, the soldiers, occupied a trench roughly two kilometers long. The enemy, whom we had never seen, were about a kilometer away from us, and they, too, were entrenched. The terrain between the two trenches was littered with debris: wrecked tanks and other destroyed armored vehicles lay jumbled together with skeletons of horses—reminders of a time when the fighting had been fierce. But now the conflict had reached a stable phase—of upkeep, in the words of our commander. Battles were no longer fought. But even so, our orders were not to leave the trench. Which posed a problem to me: My youngest son wanted me to get him an empty shell fired from a howitzer, but there was no way I could get one. My kid kept pestering me about it, but there was nothing I could do.

We—Walter and I—climbed down to the trench. The place wasn't totally lacking in amenities. It was furnished with tables, chairs, a small stove, kitchen utensils, not to mention a sound system and a portable television set. I suggested that Walter and I play a game of cards. Later, he said. With a wrinkled forehead and an air of dissatisfaction, he was examining his rifle: This fucking thing doesn't work anymore, he stated. But after all, I said, it is more than fifteen years old, it has seen better days. Then I offered him my own weapon: I had no intention of ever firing a shot. Just then we heard a detonation and a bullet came hissing over our heads. That was a near miss, I said. The idiots, muttered Walter, one of these days they'll end up hurting someone. Grabbing my weapon, he rose to his feet and fired two shots in the air. That's a warning to you, he shouted, and sat down again. A manservant appeared holding a cordless telephone: Your wife, Senhor Walter. What the devil, Walter cried out, not even here will this woman leave me in peace. He took the phone.

"Hello! Yes, that's me. I'm fine. Of course I'm fine. No, nothing has happened to me, I've already told you, I'm fine. I know you get nervous, but there's no reason why you should. Everything's okay, I'm well sheltered, it isn't raining. Did you hear me? Everything's okay. There's no need to apologize. I understand. A kiss."

What an utter bore, this woman, he said, handing the phone back to the manservant. I said nothing. I, too, had a problem with my wife, but of a different nature. She didn't believe that we were at war. Her suspicion was that I was spending the day in a motel with someone else. I would like to explain to her the nature of this war, but in fact, I myself didn't know. Nobody knew. It was a very confusing thing; so much so that a committee had been set to study the situation of the conflict. The chairman of this committee would sometimes visit us, and then he would complain about the car he had been given to go on these inspection trips: a jalopy, according to him. It was, in fact, a very old car. To practice economy, his superiors wouldn't change it for a newer model.

The morning went by serenely; somebody from our side fired a shot, somebody from the other side fired back, and that was all. At noon we were served lunch. A green salad, roast beef, rice prepared in the Greek style; for dessert, an insipid pudding. This is really going downhill, Walter grumbled. The waiter asked him if he thought this place was a restaurant or what. Walter made no reply.

We lay down for a nap and slept peacefully. When we woke up, night was falling. I think I'll go home now, I said to Walter. He couldn't leave with me: He was on duty that night. I went to the locker room and changed. How was the war? the smart-alecky youth asked me. Good, I replied, really good. I dropped by the administration office, got my paycheck from a sour-looking employee, and signed all three copies of the receipt. And I arrived at the bus stop just in the nick of time.

At home, my wife, dressed in a leotard, was waiting for me. I'm ready, she said dryly. I went to the bedroom to get my sweatshirt. We went to the fitness gym and mounted the exercise bicycles. Where exactly were we? I asked. You never seem to know, she answered in a reproachful tone. Picking up the map, she studied it for a moment, then said: "Bisceglie, on the Adriatic coast."

We started pedaling vigorously; when we stopped two hours later, we were approaching Molfeta, still on the Adriatic coast. We figure it will take us a year to complete the circuit of Italy. Then, we'll wait and see. I dislike making long-term plans; because of the war, of course, but mostly because the unknown element of the future is for me a source of constant excitement.

Masks

Hwang Sun-won

WOUNDED BY a bullet in the leg, the soldier fell. As he tried to lift himself, a bayonet pierced his chest. In the instant he lost consciousness, the face of his attacker was imprinted on his eyes as though burned there. The blood from the soldier's chest flowed into the yellow earth of this desolate battlefield. It was at the foot of a hill far from his home, yet it resembled the land around his own village.

His blood soaked into the earth and became earth. The dead soldier had been a farmer, and for him soil was life itself. At first this soil was a deeper shade than the rest, but gradually it became all one color.

The roots of a purple eulalia reed furtively sipped the soldier's life, and he became reed.

A jumble of combat boots trampled the reed and moved on. In winter, boots heavier than before trod upon the snow-covered reed. Time after time they trampled it and left, but the plant did not die. After the boots had moved on, the reed was blown by the breezes in spring, bathed in sunbeams, washed by rain and dew, covered with snow, and blown once again by the spring breezes. In the late spring the reed was cut down by a farmer's scythe and carried to a stable.

Here the reed became a bull. Just as the dead man had done when he was a farmer, the bull's owner cared for it as if it were the most important member of his family. Now the soldier worked hard alongside the farmer. He worked until his skin was bruised and swollen, but keeping the farm alive from year to year was not easy. Then a flood swept away the fields, and one night that autumn the farmer stifled the sound of his own crying as he stroked the scruff of the soldier's neck. The soldier passed through the market, then went by train to the slaughterhouse. He was hung up in a butcher's in the city, where meat was cut and sold from his carcass. There he saw someone he knew—the one who had pierced his chest with a bayonet at the foot of the hill. He was begging for food. He ate a piece of the meat from scraps he had begged at a restaurant, and the soldier entered this man.

The man tossed away his empty begging tin and hoisted himself up, one sleeve of his worn-out work clothes dangling where he had no arm. He went toward the iron foundry where he had worked as a lathe operator before the war took his arm. He strode inside and approached his former boss.

"Good day."

The foundry master's face showed his displeasure. He crushed out his cigarette with the toe of his shoe.

"Don't worry, I haven't come here to badger you, sir. I've come here to work as I did before."

The master cast an uncomfortable glance at the armless sleeve.

"What are you looking at?" The man eyed the master squarely and continued, "I was wounded in the leg by a bullet, but does that mean I can't operate a lathe?"

The man shifted his body as he spoke, his empty sleeve dangling at his side.

Translated by Martin Holman

In the Shade of a
Little Old Lady in Flower

Alfonso Quijada Urias

A DEMENTED sun twisting like a snake in the orphaned, turbulent landscape. Each day's noisy confusion, the city under siege. Thousands of building eyes pondering: How long? The mute history of organized every-dayness. State of siege. Demented states. Sirens of Ulysses, driver for the fire department. People walking fast, complaining about the heat and the crush in the sardine can buses. Deadly feelings of dread. Fear of dying while walking along these San Sivar Streets, these España and Delano Roosevelt Avenues. Dead air that I breathe as I live. Bullets whistle. Cannons bleat. The demented sun fires a sweaty heat. Brash. The radio in the Flower of Paris Shoestore at full blast: the national anthem as main course. A gloomy voice from the bottom of a well announcing the state of siege. All days meet their end on the tin roofs, cultivated by the sun. Flowering coins covering the city. Clouds on the horizon. Flocks of black sheep on the steep slope, bleating. Weeping mourners.

That's how things are here. Behind that apparent calm in the cafeterias, behind that fake calm a whirlwind—turmoil. And suddenly the cars spin around. They come back in the opposite direction. Crash. Twist around each other. Nobody pays attention to traffic lights. Shots. Gunfire. Flight of frightened pigeons. Terrified. "It's on San Miguelito," shouts the real estate salesman. "They went into the bank." All four dead. ("Terrorists" the *Daily Devil* will say. On page one.) Later it was learned that one of them was a pastor of the Latter Day Saints. Another was found with a "Don Quixote" notebook containing love poems. Celia heard the same story. The cab driver told her all the gory details. He was cornered, sweating like a pig on a corner of San Miguelito. That's how they tell the thousand and one stories about that infernal day.

That same afternoon. At the age of one hundred, moving straight from eternity to eternity, the mother of invention died. She died. What a bright idea at her age, to die pre-cise-ly during these days. Black days.

She died because she felt like it, because she no longer liked this world. This infernal world. Sordid. She was the grandma of the neighborhood. Of the district. Of life. Was there anyone who didn't know her? She fought the pimps with her stiletto. She got drunk on weekends and holidays. A voracious reader of Eugene Sue, Vargas Vila, and Genoveva de Brabante. She played card games and Chinese checkers with astounding skill. There were times when she got itchy feet or was plagued by unshakeable, obsessive ideas and would travel by mule to the mountains of Honduras. She would go off with her ornate boxes, porcelain treasures, magnet stones, laces, patent leather slippers, gold coins, silkalines, needles, enchanted birds, song books, magic powders, devotionals—and so many other things that had their proper place in a complete inventory.

That day (all days meet their end) her funeral service was held. Decent just as she dreamed it would be. Everybody was there, congregated. Legendary family legions. Generations of generations. Origin of her species. Incredibly distant relatives. So distant they seemed invisible, unnameable. That entire universe spoke about her: Great saintly woman. Without a navel. Without sin. Pure as a white parchment womb. Cauliflower vagina.

What was the matter? Where was the problem? Without a birth certificate there is no death certificate, to certify the journey. The document of her birth had been lost. Seed of her origin.

Afterward Adam told the story of that mess. We had to consult dignitaries, magistrates, ailing old men. Create a great flight of pigeons. Knock on thousands of doors, walk across salons, impenetrable houses. Patios filled with brilliant flowers and leaves. We sat with the doctors of the law, interrogated the greatest great-grandfather of them all. It took us forever to find out. To discover the original version. The grand old man solved it at last. Her name was Cleotilde Barrios. Not Isadora Cartagena as she called herself. She was born on a Thursday, the third of March 1899, in La Vega District. "Said information attested to by the father of the child in the presence of the Municipal Secretary." Whose signature was affixed to the present document.

After all that trouble came the burial, which was even more complicated because of having to cross the city in wartime. We had to take the risk. Of course. Tides of war broke against the wall of the Sisters of Charity. The quiet trees, the green leaves of translucent jade. His eye is on the sparrow. We had to give her a holy burial. Take the risk of the difficult pilgrimage. Go up Arce. Cross España. Turn on to Dario. Come out on El Calvario and then straight ahead on Cementerio General. And bury her at last. Yes. With all due speed. Give her a holy burial in this time of war. Apocalyptic sorrow. Trumpets of Jericho. Wailing Wall. Mother of mine.

And there we go. Behind the hearse, black, solemn. How serious they are, the dead and those who bury them. The ones in the funeral procession. The little man with his black suit and his account book. The driver and his Charlie Chaplin moustache. And those peculiar odors: a mortal breath, lilies, cologne, chemical decomposition of the body, wreaths of flowers. Between the scent of life and of death. And us—remembering, ceremoniously thoughtful, those days of our great mother. Remembering the times when she drank her "cane spirits." Her elixir of life. And sang and cursed half the world. She advised her daughters to forget all that crap about virginity. Gave advice about everything. At night she recounted her old adventures. Her stories about when she enlisted as purveyor of provisions in the armed forces of General Mendieta, in '26. Or else her countless love affairs. We went back to the pure fountain. To the original patio. To the cosmic return of the great mother. And we saw her as she was on that day of her return from the war in Honduras with her spoils of war—two trucks full of liquor, four juke boxes, three freezers, two bars, five sets of living-room furniture, six dining rooms, two pool tables, and more junk than could fit into an account book. All of us. That beautiful day we went out to meet her, moved, patriotic. That was a fiesta without end. Six weeks when the tremendous din of the music did not stop. Night and day. Day and night.

"Listen," I said to the driver, "try not to go through the center of town. There's always trouble around the post office." But he thought he knew it all, and his only answer was to wiggle his tiny Charlie Chaplin moustache. "Look," I insisted again, "it's better to avoid any problems. It's better for you to take the side streets going toward Plazuela Barrios or Policía Street." But the man continued straight ahead with his wooden face. Expressionless. His nothing's-going-on-here face.

And so we moved at a snail's pace, through that peaceful central district, following the black car; having premonitions of disaster. We passed along Arce: the little square of San José. Second-hand book stalls. Shoeshine boys. Pigeons. Flocks of pigeons cleaning the dirty hot four o'clock air with their whiteness. Water ice and ice cream stands. Schoolgirls, blue and white, faces painted in the style of the latest *Vanidades*. Tigresses and vampires. Just ordinary people. The lady with elephantiasis at the foot of the General Electric building. And further on, drunkards and tourists coming out of Chico's Bar and the New World Hotel. Old bars filled with old binges.

There. Right then. That's when the trouble began. Like the roar of the sea. People scattering. Then the sound of sirens and gunfire, and the cars began to spin around, to lose their sense of direction. Crashing. Motors turning off. Accelerating, bellowing, doors slamming. That's how the trouble began. After the gunfire came the panic. Everybody running, jumping, looking for a way out. A safe place just as the heavy grates of the bakeries, the shops, the cafeterias came slamming down. Because after fire and disaster come the devouring locusts. Looting—base, shameless. "Another student massacre. The ones who occupied the cathedral," shouted a woman in terror. "Monsignor just came out." Everything is red. Red-hot. Sunsets and roses. Blood of our blood. The massacred will be avenged. Rio Lempa 1930 and twice as bloody. Steps covered with blood, skin, brains. Another funeral pyre.

In the distance, scattered spots. Multitudes like heads of pins. Dots running in every direction, through the smoke and ashen explosions of the afternoon. A bus enveloped in flames on the corner of Dragón.

Through great vicissitudes, with the ancient and astute instinctive logic of the fox, we escaped from danger. From the labyrinth, the disastrous confusion, the hecatomb. Far from the fire zone. Making our way, retreating, advancing. We plunged into alleys, ancient passageways, ruined mansions, old places in a San Salvador that was anonymous, primitive. Remains of railroads, wagons. Way stations for mules. Old and solemn barbershops like The Little French Girl and Figaro. Yes, escaping by twists and turns. Finally we reach the cemetery. Scattered. Terrified. Coming to the main gate from different directions. All of us. Except the hearse. Except the remains of one who had once been. Just one of those things.

There we are. Nervous. Cigarette after cigarette of not finding the thread of the matter. Ariadne's thread. Whacanyado? We waited for things to settle down so we could look for the coffin. Lost ark. Urn of our empress.

Other stories began to surface. No less bizarre. Could the hearse have been run down by the immense sardine can bus? Or did they pick up the driver as a suspect? With the car and all? Opinions surfaced. The most desperate: We would have to call the Red Cross or the Fire Department. Another one. Pay for an announcement on Radio KL asking for information regarding the whereabouts of a solemn funeral hearse—'66 Chevrolet, four door, license number 26000. Bearing the mortal remains of Cleotilde Barrios, known far and wide as The Bandit.

But it was all in vain. Vanity of vanities. While we thought and thought again the shadows were falling. Chinese. Ink blots on the white mausoleums, on the graves, on the dark earth. And as they closed the gate, creaking of plaintive doors, the hearse turned the corner. Twice as black. Sepulchral. And then came a terrible absurd joy with shouts of *hurrah* and *Viva*! Stony astonishment afterward. Black spring.

We were in a rush to bury her. To leave her once and for all in the peace or war of her holy sepulcher. Then came the tears, seas of weeping, gnashing of teeth, sighs, fainting, hearts pounding. We had to pay the funereal little man. The custodian who refused to open—regulations in hand—the portentous portals. We cursed frantically at the stubborn driver and were ready to lynch him for having put us through moments of such crisis. And so. At last. He gave in to our pleas. The skinny little man opened the great gate again.

Leaping. Almost falling flat on our faces over tombstones and mauso-leums we finally came to her grave. Empty as a round O. As the mouth of nothingness. Mouthful of smoke. Lowering the varnished mortuary ark with straps, coffer of what once was, to the bottom of the earth. Wood creaking. We left them. Her remains. Ready. Deposited in the dark king-dom of eternity. Then came the earth. Spongy—falling hard and heavy, loose and dark over the glass and wood. Producing a muffled noise, of drums. The lugubrious drum that bids farewell to the dead. The tom-tom of death. And again, of course, seas of weeping, hurricanes of sighs, jungles of shouts and laments.

At last. All days meet their end. The funereal urn lost in its funeral kingdom. Sealed under a thousand and one blankets of earth, very deep. Packed down by earth: hard, compact, black and loose. We were in a great rush to bury her. A great rush before the night grew any deeper.

When we reached home our mother was there. Behind the curtain. In her wicker rocking chair, with a glass of "spirits" in her hand. Rocking. As if nothing at all had happened. Nothing at all.

Translated by Edith Grossman

PEOPLE IN WAR

"Our ancestors created their myths and legends and told their stories for a human purpose," wrote the Nigerian Achebe in his essay collection *Morning Yet on Creation Day* (1975), adding that he thought that, for now, "any good story, any good novel should have a message, should have a purpose." The message in many of Achebe's stories, and a constantly recurring theme everywhere in Global Cultures, is about how war corrupts. Two stories from Nigeria, the most populous African country, and one with an archetypal postcolonial political history, and one from its neighbor to the south, Cameroon, can provide a sustained look at just one region where war and military dictatorships stamped themselves on people's lives.

Nigerian literature was one of the first postcolonial literatures to be influential in Global Cultures, a process that began when the West hailed **CHINUA ACHEBE**'s novel *Things Fall Apart* (1958), which he, an Ibo, wrote in English. Achebe, born in 1930, had an international reputation when a predominantly Ibo eastern state, Biafra, seceded in 1967 after years of tribal conflict during which the Ibo had been ravaged. He could work effectively for Biafra as its chief liaison and diplomatic missionary to the English-speaking world. Unlike his friend Christopher Okigbo, considered by many Nigeria's greatest poet, who joined the Biafran army and was killed, Achebe survived the war to become one of its most unrelenting, acerbic chroniclers. The title story of *Girls at War and Other Stories* (1972) is a short fictional reflection, but he has also written poetry about the war (*Beware, Soul Brother*, 1971) and, much later, *Anthills of the Savannah* (1987).

Nigeria was and is a country with complex colonial political and cultural legacies, tribal-regional struggles for power, cultural and religious differences. The country has southern Christians, northern Muslims, and many types of traditional believers; altogether it has some 250 distinct ethnicites. There are vast economic inequities and international involvement in the form of weapons trafficking and superpower interest in Nigeria's oil. The war produced one class, known as "big men," who flourished as profiteers, who made graft a way of life, and another class of people, like the girl in Achebe's "Girls at War," who survived by parasiting on the "big men." Many of Achebe's war texts wonder over who can stay human in a war zone, over what core or human feeling can survive—and how.

Many younger Nigerians, who did not know the war, concentrated their attention on postwar opportunities in a country quickly reconstructed by way of a petro-dollar boom but still morally and politically in ruins. They rejected their elders' anticolonialism and socialism, their parents' support for tribal languages (Achebe, for example, had founded a bilingual journal of Ibo culture) and subversive use of English; but not **ADEWALE MAJA-PEARCE**, whose parable "Loyalties" appeared in the last section. His obsession with the war and its long-term effects on modern Nigeria is represented by "An Easy Death," whose central character is a hero of the Nigerian victory over secessionist Biafra, a man who has been honored enormously for his participation in a war that cost so many Biafran lives and left Nigeria itself deeply divided, corrupted, and tied to military regimes.

In contrast to Nigeria, the Cameroon, Nigeria's neighbor to the south, has had a relatively peaceful postindependence and is now, although not unified, relatively prosperous on its agricultural base. The regime that took control in 1961 might be called a somewhat enlightened authoritarianism, and no civil war broke out, although there are a number of lines of fissure. The chief division is between the Muslim north and the Christian south, but there are divisions among the 150 ethnicities and between English-speakers and French-speakers as well. The outstanding anticolonialist writers of Achebe's generation, like Mongo Beti and Ferdinand Oxono, were francophone. But in the next generation, there are many English writers, like **NDELEY MOKOSO**, who has been a journalist, and industrialist, and a politician.

One succession crisis gripped Cameroon in the early 1980s, and it lies in the background of Mokoso's story "No Escape." The postindependence President Ahidjo handed over his power to his constitutionally designated successor, but a coup attempt in 1984 by the former president's loyalists caused the new government to tremble. Mokoso uses this episode, fictionalizing it, to study the weaknesses—so magnified in neighboring Nigeria—of the political process. In this situation, a callous, self-serving man without scruples can find himself, finally, headed for his death, arrested by—a version of himself. Unfaithfulness, called treason by whomever is in power at the moment, is the common coin.

Girls at War

Chinua Achebe

THE FIRST time their paths crossed nothing happened. That was in the first heady days of warlike preparation when thousands of young men (and sometimes women too) were daily turned away from enlistment centres because far too many of them were coming forward burning with readiness to bear arms in defence of the exciting new nation.

The second time they met was at a check-point at Awka. Then the war had started and was slowly moving southwards from the distant northern sector. He was driving from Onitsha to Enugu and was in a hurry. Although intellectually he approved of thorough searches at road-blocks, emotionally he was always offended whenever he had to submit to them. He would probably not admit it but the feeling people got was that if you were put through a search then you could not really be one of the big people. Generally he got away without a search by pronouncing in his deep, authoritative voice: "Reginald Nwankwo, Ministry of Justice." That almost always did it. But sometimes either through ignorance or sheer cussedness the crowd at the odd check-point would refuse to be impressed. As happened now at Awka. Two constables carrying heavy Mark 4 rifles were watching distantly from the roadside leaving the actual searching to local vigilantes.

"I am in a hurry," he said to the girl who now came up to his car. "My name is Reginald Nwankwo, Ministry of Justice."

"Good afternoon, sir. I want to see your trunk."

"O Christ! What do you think is in the trunk?"

"I don't know, sir."

He got out of the car in suppressed rage, stalked to the back, opened the trunk and holding the lid up with his left hand he motioned with the right as if to say: After you!

"Are you satisfied?" he demanded.

"Yes, sir. Can I see your pigeon-hole?"

"Christ Almighty!"

"Sorry to delay you, sir. But you people gave us this job to do."

"Never mind. You are damn right. It's just that I happen to be in a hurry. But never mind. That's the glovebox. Nothing there as you can see."

"All right, sir, close it." Then she opened the rear door and bent down to inspect under the seats. It was then he took the first real look at her, starting from behind. She was a beautiful girl in a breasty blue jersey, khaki jeans and canvas shoes with the new-style hair-plait which gave a girl a defiant look and which they called—for reasons of their own—"air force base"; and she looked vaguely familiar.

"I am all right, sir," she said at last meaning she was through with her task. "You don't recognize me?"

"No. Should I?"

"You gave me a lift to Enugu that time I left my school to go and join the militia."

"Ah, yes, you were the girl. I told you, didn't I, to go back to school because girls were not required in the militia. What happened?"

"They told me to go back to my school or join the Red Cross."

"You see I was right. So, what are you doing now?"

"Just patching up with Civil Defence."

"Well, good luck to you. Believe me you are a great girl."

That was the day he finally believed there might be something in this talk about revolution. He had seen plenty of girls and women marching and demonstrating before now. But somehow he had never been able to give it much thought. He didn't doubt that the girls and the women took themselves seriously; they obviously did. But so did the little kids who marched up and down the streets at the time drilling with sticks and wearing their mothers' soup bowls for steel helmets. The prime joke of the time among his friends was the contingent of girls from a local secondary school marching behind a banner: WE ARE IMPREGNABLE!

But after that encounter at the Awka check-point he simply could not sneer at the girls again, nor at the talk of revolution, for he had seen it in action in that young woman whose devotion had simply and without self-righteousness convicted him of gross levity. What were her words? We are doing the work you asked us to do. She wasn't going to make an exception even for one who once did her a favour. He was sure she would have searched her own father just as rigorously.

When their paths crossed a third time, at least eighteen months later, things had got very bad. Death and starvation having long chased out the headiness of the early days, now left in some places blank resignation, in others a rock-like, even suicidal, defiance. But surprisingly enough there were many at this time also who had no other desire than to corner whatever good things were still going and to enjoy themselves to the limit. For such people a strand of normalcy had returned to the world. All those nervous check-points disappeared. Girls became girls once more and boys boys. It was a tight, blockaded and desperate world but none the less a world—with some goodness and some badness and plenty of heroism which, however, happened most times far, far below the eye-level of the people in this story—in out-of-the-way refugee camps, in the damp tatters, in the hungry and bare-handed courage of the first line of fire.

Reginald Nwankwo lived in Owerri then. But that day he had gone to Nkwerri in search of relief. He had got from Caritas in Owerri a few heads of stockfish, some tinned meat, and the dreadful American stuff called Formula Two which he felt certain was some kind of animal feed. But he always had a vague suspicion that not being a Catholic put one at a disadvantage with Caritas. So he went now to see an old friend who ran the WCC depot at Nkwerri to get other items like rice, beans and that excellent cereal commonly called Gabon gari.

He left Owerri at six in the morning so as to catch his friend at the depot where he was known never to linger beyond 8:30 for fear of air-raids. Nwankwo was very fortunate that day. The depot had received on the previous day large supplies of new stock as a result of an unusual number of plane landings a few nights earlier. As his driver loaded tins and bags and cartons into his car the starved crowds that perpetually hung around relief centres made crude, ungracious remarks like "War Can Continue!" meaning the WCC! Somebody else shouted "Irevolu!" and his friends replied "shum!" "Irevolu!" "shum!" "Isofeli?" "shum!" "Isofeli?" "Mba!"

Nwankwo was deeply embarrassed not by the jeers of this scarecrow crowd of rags and floating ribs but by the independent accusation of their wasted bodies and sunken eyes. Indeed he would probably have felt much worse had they said nothing, simply looked on in silence, as his trunk was loaded with milk, and powdered egg and oats and tinned meat and stockfish. By nature such singular good fortune in the midst of a general desolation was certain to embarrass him. But what could a man do? He had a wife and four children living in the remote village of Ogbu and completely dependent on what relief he could find and send them. He couldn't abandon them to kwashiokor. The best he could do—and did do as a matter of fact—was to make sure that whenever he got sizeable supplies like now he made over some of it to his driver, Johnson, with a wife and six, or was it seven? children and a salary of ten pounds a month when gari in the market was climbing to one pound per cigarette cup. In such a situation one could do nothing at all for crowds; at best one could try to be of some use to one's immediate neighbours. That was all.

On his way back to Owerri a very attractive girl by the roadside waved for a lift. He ordered the driver to stop. Scores of pedestrians, dusty and exhausted, some military, some civil, swooped down on the car from all directions.

"No, no, no," said Nwankwo firmly. "It's the young woman I stopped for. I have a bad tyre and can only take one person. Sorry."

"My son, please," cried one old woman in despair, gripping the door-handle.

"Old woman, you want to be killed?" shouted the driver as he pulled away, shaking her off. Nwankwo had already opened a book and sunk his eyes there. For at least a mile after that he did not even look at the girl until she finding, perhaps, the silence too heavy said:

"You've saved me today. Thank you."

"Not at all. Where are you going?"

"To Owerri. You don't recognize me?"

"Oh yes, of course. What a fool I am . . . You are . . ."

"Gladys."

"That's right, the militia girl. You've changed, Gladys. You were always beautiful of course, but now you are a beauty queen. What do you do these days?"

"I am in the Fuel Directorate."

"That's wonderful."

It was wonderful, he thought, but even more it was tragic. She wore a high-tinted wig and a very expensive skirt and low-cut blouse. Her shoes, obviously from Gabon, must have cost a fortune. In short, thought Nwankwo, she had to be in the keep of some well-placed gentleman, one of those piling up money out of the war.

"I broke my rule today to give you a lift. I never give lifts these days."

"Why?"

"How many people can you carry? It is better not to try at all. Look at that old woman."

"I thought you would carry her."

He said nothing to that and after another spell of silence Gladys thought maybe he was offended and so added: "Thank you for breaking your rule for me." She was scanning his face, turned slightly away. He smiled, turned, and tapped her on the lap.

"What are you going to Owerri to do?"

"I am going to visit my girlfriend."

"Girlfriend? You sure?"

"Why not? . . . If you drop me at her house you can see her. Only I pray God she hasn't gone on weekend today; it will be serious."

"Why?"

"Because if she is not at home I will sleep on the road today."

"I pray to God that she is not at home."

"Why?"

"Because if she is not at home I will offer you bed and breakfast . . . What is that?" he asked the driver who had brought the car to an abrupt stop. There was no need for an answer. The small crowd ahead was looking upwards. The three scrambled out of the car and stumbled for the bush, necks twisted in a backward search of the sky. But the alarm was false. The sky was silent and clear except for two high-flying vultures. A humourist in the crowd called them Fighter and Bomber and everyone laughed in relief. The three climbed into their car again and continued their journey.

"It is much too early for raids," he said to Gladys, who had both her palms on her breast as though to still a thumping heart. "They rarely come before ten o'clock."

But she remained tongue-tied from her recent fright. Nwankwo saw an opportunity there and took it at once.

"Where does your friend live?"

"250 Douglas Road."

"Ah! That's the very centre of town—a terrible place. No bunkers, nothing. I won't advise you to go there before 6 p.m.; it's not safe. If you don't mind I will take you to my place where there is a good bunker and then as soon as it is safe, around six, I shall drive you to your friend. How's that?"

"It's all right," she said lifelessly. "I am so frightened of this thing. That's why I refused to work in Owerri. I don't even know who asked me to come out today."

"You'll be all right. We are used to it."

"But your family is not there with you?"

"No," he said. "Nobody has his family there. We like to say it is because of air-raids but I can assure you there is more to it. Owerri is a real swinging town and we live the life of gay bachelors."

"That is what I have heard."

"You will not just hear it; you will see it today. I shall take you to a real swinging party. A friend of mine, a Lieutenant-Colonel, is having a birthday party. He's hired the Sound Smashers to play. I'm sure you'll enjoy it."

He was immediately and thoroughly ashamed of himself. He hated the parties and frivolities to which his friends clung like drowning men. And to talk so approvingly of them because he wanted to take a girl home! And this particular girl too, who had once had such beautiful faith in the struggle and was betrayed (no doubt about it) by some man like him out for a good time. He shook his head sadly.

"What is it?" asked Gladys.

"Nothing. Just my thoughts."

They made the rest of the journey to Owerri practically in silence.

She made herself at home very quickly as if she was a regular girl friend of his. She changed into a house dress and put away her auburn wig.

"That is a lovely hair-do. Why do you hide it with a wig?"

"Thank you," she said leaving his question unanswered for a while. Then she said: "Men are funny."

"Why do you say that?"

"You are now a beauty queen," she mimicked.

"Oh, that! I mean every word of it." He pulled her to him and kissed her. She neither refused nor yielded fully, which he liked for a start. Too many girls were simply too easy those days. War sickness, some called it.

He drove off a little later to look in at the office and she busied herself in the kitchen helping his boy with lunch. It must have been literally a look-in, for he was back within half an hour, rubbing his hands and saying he could not stay away too long from his beauty queen.

As they sat down to lunch, she said: "You have nothing in your fridge."

"Like what?" he asked, half-offended.

"Like meat," she replied undaunted.

"Do you still eat meat?" he challenged.

"Who am I? But other big men like you eat."

"I don't know which big men you have in mind. But they are not like me. I don't make money trading with the enemy or selling relief or . . ."

"Augusta's boyfriend doesn't do that. He just gets foreign exchange."

"How does he get it? He swindles the government—that's how he gets foreign exchange, whoever he is. Who is Augusta, by the way?"

"My girlfriend."

"I see."

"She gave me three dollars last time which I changed to forty-five pounds. The man gave her fifty dollars."

"Well, my dear girl, I don't traffic in foreign exchange and I don't have meat in my fridge. We are fighting a war and I happen to know that some young boys at the front drink gari and water once in three days."

"It is true," she said simply. "Monkey de work, baboon de chop."

"It is not even that; it is worse," he said, his voice beginning to shake. "People are dying every day. As we talk now somebody is dying."

"It is true," she said again.

"Plane!" screamed his boy from the kitchen.

"My mother!" screamed Gladys. As they scuttled towards the bunker of palm stems and red earth, covering their heads with their hands and stooping slightly in their flight, the entire sky was exploding with the clamour of jets and the huge noise of homemade anti-aircraft rockets.

Inside the bunker she clung to him even after the plane had gone and the guns, late to start and also to end, had all died down again.

"It was only passing," he told her, his voice a little shaky. "It didn't drop anything. From its direction I should say it was going to the war front. Perhaps our people who are pressing them. That's what they always do. Whenever our boys press them, they send an SOS to the Russians and Egyptians to bring the planes." He drew a long breath.

She said nothing, just clung to him. They could hear his boy telling the servant from the next house that there were two of them and one dived like this and the other dived like that.

"I see dem well well," said the other with equal excitement. "If no to say de ting de kill porson e for sweet for eye. To God."

"Imagine!" said Gladys, finding her voice at last. She had a way, he thought, of conveying with a few words or even a single word whole layers of meaning. Now it was at once her astonishment as well as re-proof, tinged perhaps with grudging admiration for people who could be so light-hearted about these bringers of death.

"Don't be so scared," he said. She moved closer and he began to kiss her and squeeze her breasts. She yielded more and more and then fully. The bunker was dark and unswept and might harbour crawling things. He thought of bringing a mat from the main house but reluctantly decided against it. Another plane might pass and send a neighbour or simply a chance passerby crashing into them. That would be only slightly better than a certain gentleman in another air-raid who was seen in broad daylight fleeing his bedroom for his bunker stark-naked pursued by a woman in a similar state!

Just as Gladys had feared, her friend was not in town. It would seem her powerful boyfriend had wangled for her a flight to Libreville to shop. So her neighbours thought anyway.

"Great!" said Nwankwo as they drove away. "She will come back on an arms plane loaded with shoes, wigs, pants, bras, cosmetics and what have you, which she will then sell and make thousands of pounds. You girls are really at war, aren't you?"

She said nothing and he thought he had got through at last to her. Then suddenly she said, "That is what you men want us to do."

"Well," he said, "here is one man who doesn't want you to do that. Do you remember that girl in khaki jeans who searched me without mercy at the check-point?"

She began to laugh.

"That is the girl I want you to become again. Do you remember her? No wig. I don't even think she had any earrings . . ."

"Ah, na lie-o. I had earrings."

"All right. But you know what I mean."

"That time done pass. Now everybody want survival. They call it number six. You put your number six; I put my number six. Everything all right."

The Lieutenant-Colonel's party turned into something quite unexpected. But before it did things had been going well enough. There was goat-meat, some chicken and rice and plenty of home-made spirits. There was one fiery brand nicknamed "tracer" which indeed sent a flame down your gullet. The funny thing was looking at it in the bottle it had the innocent appearance of an orange drink. But the thing that caused the greatest stir was the bread—one little roll for each person! It was the size of a golf ball and about the same consistency too! But it was real bread. The band was good too and there were many girls. And to improve matters even further two white Red Cross people soon arrived with a bottle of Courvoisier and a bottle of Scotch! The party gave them a standing ovation and then scrambled to get a taste. It soon turned out from his general behaviour, however, that one of the white men had probably drunk too much already. And the reason it would seem was that a pilot he knew well had been killed in a crash at the airport last night, flying in relief in awful weather.

Few people at the party had heard of the crash by then. So there was an immediate damping of the air. Some dancing couples went back to their seats and the band stopped. Then for some strange reason the drunken Red Cross man just exploded.

"Why should a man, a decent man, throw away his life. For nothing! Charley didn't need to die. Not for this stinking place. Yes, everything stinks here. Even these girls who come here all dolled up and smiling, what are they worth? Don't I know? A head of stockfish, that's all, or one American dollar and they are ready to tumble into bed."

In the threatening silence following the explosion one of the young officers walked up to him and gave him three thundering slaps—right! left! right!—pulled him up from his seat and (there were things like tears in his eyes) shoved him outside. His friend, who had tried in vain to shut him up, followed him out and the silenced party heard them drive off. The officer who did the job returned dusting his palms.

"Fucking beast!" said he with an impressive coolness. And all the girls showed with their eyes that they rated him a man and a hero.

"Do you know him?" Gladys asked Nwankwo.

He didn't answer her. Instead he spoke generally to the party.

"The fellow was clearly drunk," he said.

"I don't care," said the officer. "It is when a man is drunk that he speaks what is on his mind."

"So you beat him for what was on his mind," said the host, "that is the spirit, Joe."

"Thank you, sir," said Joe, saluting.

"His name is Joe," Gladys and the girl on her left said in unison, turning to each other.

At the same time Nwankwo and a friend on the other side of him were saying quietly, very quietly, that although the man had been rude and offensive what he had said about the girls was unfortunately the bitter truth, only he was the wrong man to say it.

When the dancing resumed Captain Joe came to Gladys for a dance. She sprang to her feet even before the word was out of his mouth. Then she remembered immediately and turned round to take permission from Nwankwo. At the same time the Captain also turned to him and said, "Excuse me."

"Go ahead," said Nwankwo, looking somewhere between the two.

It was a long dance and he followed them with his eyes without appearing to do so. Occasionally a relief plane passed overhead and somebody immediately switched off the lights saying it might be the Intruder. But it was only an excuse to dance in the dark and make the girls giggle, for the sound of the Intruder was well known.

Gladys came back feeling very self-conscious and asked Nwankwo to dance with her. But he wouldn't. "Don't bother about me," he said. "I am enjoying myself perfectly sitting here and watching those of you who dance."

"Then let's go," she said, "if you won't dance."

"But I never dance, believe me. So please, enjoy yourself."

She danced next with the Lieutenant-Colonel and again with Captain Joe, and then Nwankwo agreed to take her home.

"I am sorry I didn't dance," he said as they drove away. "But I swore never to dance as long as this war lasts."

She said nothing.

"When I think of somebody like that pilot who got killed last night. And he had no hand whatever in the quarrel. All his concern was to bring us food . . ."

"I hope that his friend is not like him," said Gladys.

"The man was just upset by his friend's death. But what I am saying is that with people like that getting killed and our own boys suffering and dying at the war fronts I don't see why we should sit around throwing parties and dancing."

"You took me there," said she in final revolt. "They are your friends. I don't know them before."

"Look, my dear, I am not blaming you. I am merely telling you why I personally refuse to dance. Anyway, let's change the subject . . . Do you still say you want to go back tomorrow? My driver can take you early enough on Monday morning for you to go to work. No? All right, just as you wish. You are the boss."

She gave him a shock by the readiness with which she followed him to bed and by her language.

"You want to shell?" she asked. And without waiting for an answer said, "Go ahead but don't pour in troops!"

He didn't want to pour in troops either and so it was all right. But she wanted visual assurance and so he showed her.

One of the ingenious economics taught by the war was that a rubber condom could be used over and over again. All you had to do was wash it out, dry it and shake a lot of talcum powder over it to prevent its sticking; and it was as good as new. It had to be the real British thing, though, not some of the cheap stuff they brought in from Lisbon which was about as strong as a dry cocoyam leaf in the harmattan.

He had his pleasure but wrote the girl off. He might just as well have slept with a prostitute, he thought. It was clear as daylight to him now that she was kept by some army officer. What a terrible transformation in the short period of less than two years! Wasn't it a miracle that she still had memories of the other life, that she even remembered her name? If the affair of the drunken Red Cross man should happen again now, he said to himself, he would stand up beside the fellow and tell the party that here was a man of truth. What a terrible fate to befall a whole generation! The mothers of tomorrow!

By morning he was feeling a little better and more generous in his judgments. Gladys, he thought, was just a mirror reflecting a society that had gone completely rotten and maggoty at the centre. The mirror itself was intact; a lot of smudge but no more. All that was needed was a clean duster. "I have a duty to her," he told himself, "the little girl that once revealed to me our situation. Now she is in danger, under some terrible influence."

He wanted to get to the bottom of this deadly influence. It was clearly not just her good-time girlfriend, Augusta, or whatever her name was. There must be some man at the centre of it, perhaps one of these heartless attack-traders who traffic in foreign currencies and make their hundreds of thousands by sending young men to hazard their lives bartering looted goods for cigarettes behind enemy lines, or one of those contractors who receive piles of money daily for food they never deliver to the army. Or perhaps some vulgar and cowardly army officer full of filthy barrack talk and fictitious stories of heroism. He decided he had to find out. Last night he had thought of sending his driver alone to take her home. But no, he must go and see for himself where she lived. Something was bound to reveal itself there. Something on which he could anchor his saving operation. As he prepared for the trip his feeling towards her softened with every passing minute. He assembled for her half of the food he had received at the relief centre the day before. Difficult as things were, he thought a girl who had something to eat would be spared, not all, but some of the temptation. He would arrange with his friend at the WCC to deliver something to her every fortnight.

Tears came to Gladys's eyes when she saw the gifts. Nwankwo didn't have too much cash on him but he got together twenty pounds and handed it over to her.

"I don't have foreign exchange, and I know this won't go far at all, but . . ."

She just came and threw herself at him, sobbing. He kissed her lips and eyes and mumbled something about victims of circumstance, which went over her head. In deference to him, he thought with exultation, she had put away her high-tinted wig in her bag.

"I want you to promise me something," he said.

"What?"

"Never use that expression about shelling again."

She smiled with tears in her eyes. "You don't like it? That's what all the girls call it."

"Well, you are different from all the girls. Will you promise?"

"O.K."

Naturally their departure had become a little delayed. And when they got into the car it refused to start. After poking around the engine the driver decided that the battery was flat. Nwankwo was aghast. He had that very week paid thirty-four pounds to change two of the cells and the mechanic who performed it had promised him six months' service. A new battery, which was then running at two hundred and fifty pounds was simply out of the question. The driver must have been careless with something, he thought.

"It must be because of last night," said the driver.

"What happened last night?" asked Nwankwo sharply, wondering what insolence was on the way. But none was intended.

"Because we use the headlight."

"Am I supposed not to use my light then? Go and get some people and try pushing it." He got out again with Gladys and returned to the house while the driver went over to neighbouring houses to seek the help of other servants.

After at least half an hour of pushing it up and down the street, and a lot of noisy advice from the pushers, the car finally spluttered to life shooting out enormous clouds of black smoke from the exhaust.

It was eight-thirty by his watch when they set out. A few miles away a disabled soldier waved for a lift.

"Stop!" screamed Nwankwo. The driver jammed his foot on the brakes and then turned his head towards his master in bewilderment.

"Don't you see the soldier waving? Reverse and pick him up!"

"Sorry, sir," said the driver. "I don't know Master wan to pick him."

"If you don't know you should ask. Reverse back."

The soldier, a mere boy, in filthy khaki drenched in sweat lacked his right leg from the knee down. He seemed not only grateful that a car should stop for him but greatly surprised. He first handed in his crude wooden crutches which the driver arranged between the two front seats, then painfully he levered himself in.

"Thank sir," he said turning his neck to look at the back and completely out of breath.

"I am very grateful. Madame, thank you."

"The pleasure is ours," said Nwankwo. "Where did you get your wound?"

"At Azumini, sir. On the tenth of January."

"Never mind. Everything will be all right. We are proud of you boys and will make sure you receive your due reward when it is all over."

"I pray God, sir."

They drove on in silence for the next half-hour or so. Then as the car sped down a slope towards a bridge somebody screamed—perhaps the driver, perhaps the soldier—"They have come!" The screech of the brakes merged into the scream and the shattering of the sky overhead. The doors flew open even before the car had come to a stop and they were fleeing blindly to the bush. Gladys was a little ahead of Nwankwo when they heard through the drowning tumult the soldier's voice crying: "Please come and open for me!" Vaguely he saw Gladys stop; he pushed past her shouting to her at the same time to come on. Then a high whistle descended like a spear through the chaos and exploded in a vast noise and motion that smashed up everything. A tree he had embraced flung him away through the bush. Then another terrible whistle starting high up and ending again in a monumental crash of the world; and then another, and Nwankwo heard no more.

He woke up to human noises and weeping and the smell and smoke of a charred world. He dragged himself up and staggered towards the source of the sounds.

From afar he saw his driver running towards him in tears and blood.

He saw the remains of his car smoking and the entangled remains of the girl and the soldier. And he let out a piercing cry and fell down again.

An Easy Death

Adewale Maja–Pearce

And they had no comforter, and they were not able
to resist their violence, being destitute of help from any.
(*Ecclesiastes*: 4; I).

HE WAS one of those people who seemed to have everything: money, exceptional intelligence, and good looks. By contrast I was poor, an average student, and looks that could only be called nondescript. I suppose I envied him.

In our second year at University he had the room next to mine, which is how I got to know him. It all happened fairly quickly: one day we were on nodding terms and the next he was confiding in me. I never understood why he took me up, but I was spending more and more time in his company. Our talk was mainly about women, of whom he had more than his fair share.

At the end of the year he won the prize for the highest marks obtained in the examinations. The day before we broke up for the long vacation he handed me an invitation. His parents were throwing a party for his twenty-first birthday. Of course I was flattered, and also impressed by the gilt-edged card.

"Everyone of any importance will be there," he said. "If you play it right you'll be able to make contacts." Then he looked at my clothes. "And don't worry, I can lend you a suit if you want."

On the morning of the party a long American car appeared outside my parents' house. A man in a white uniform and a white cap called one of the children to fetch me. Our neighbours were impressed, especially when they saw me enter it.

When I got to his parents' house a steward showed me to his room. In one corner there was a stereo record player and a huge stack of records, and in another an enormous wardrobe, which stood open and was crammed with clothes.

"Pick something out and try it on," he said. "We're about the same build, aren't we?"

Later, we went downstairs. I sat and watched him supervise the proceedings. I wondered how much it was costing his parents. Food was supplied by one of the more expensive hotels and crates of drinks filled the cellar from floor to ceiling. In the garden a band was getting ready.

By the time the party began I was dazzled. I had never seen so many beautiful women in one place. I ate and drank until I was nearly sick, and finally I found the courage to ask for a dance. She was a pretty half-caste and she told me that she had just returned from a trip to Europe. She asked me how I had met our host and I told her.

"Isn't he something? Just look at him! The women can't keep their hands off him, and I don't blame them. He'll be a catch for the one who marries him, that's for sure, though she'll loose sleep worrying about her rivals."

It may have been the music, or the atmosphere, or the perfume she wore. Either way I was intoxicated and forgot myself. I held her closer.

"I like you," I said.

"Do you?" she said and laughed.

"Yes," I said. I tried to kiss her but she gently pushed me away. I should have taken the hint. Instead I tried again. This time she became angry.

"Just leave me alone, who do you think you are?" she said.

I tried to apologize but she walked off. The rest of the evening was a nightmare. I was reminded of my own status. These people were different from me, and I had been foolish to imagine otherwise. Suddenly I hated the suit I was wearing, and I even fancied everyone was laughing at me. As soon as I could I fled, back home to where I belonged.

During our third and final year I used the excuse of work to avoid him. At first I could see he was hurt, but he quickly adopted someone else and before long we were back on nodding terms. By the time we finished University we had drifted apart altogether.

With a brilliant degree he entered one of the Ministries as a high-ranking Civil Servant; I became an ordinary clerk in an obscure office. I found a place to live, married a girl my parents had chosen for me, and settled down to educate my younger brothers and sisters.

Meanwhile I continued to hear about him in the gossip columns of the daily papers. He travelled abroad regularly on conferences, and he was seen about with society women.

And then the civil war came. While others rushed to join up I stayed at home. I wanted nothing to do with it: I had other responsibilities, as far as I was concerned greater ones. The war had been caused by greed and the lust for power by businessmen and politicians, and only fools couldn't see that by fighting their own people, with whom they had no argument, they were merely playing into the hands of others. When it was all over they would only be worse off than before. But in the general hysteria they were blinded.

When the war had been going on for a year I heard that he, too, had joined. He was an officer with his own command, and to believe the reports he was doing very well. By the end of the war he had been decorated three times and his name had become synonymous with victory. He returned to Lagos a hero, and there was a song written about him by one of the local bands and was played on the radio continuously for a whole month. The man had everything, nobody could deny that.

Five years passed. My younger brothers and sisters had finished school or got married and I had children of my own. I had bought a small house and I was doing quite well at my job. The civil war had been almost forgotten and life had resumed as before.

One day I was out shopping with my family. My eldest son was about to start school and he needed new clothes. Since I had nothing better to do I went along with them. As we entered one of the Department Stores I caught sight of a man in a pair of shabby trousers. He was standing at a counter idly flicking through a magazine. For a moment I did not recognize him, and then with a shock I realised who it was. I would have passed on but my curiosity got the better of me. I went up to him.

"Don't you remember me?" I asked.

He looked at me vacantly. He had not shaved in a week and his shirt collar was grubby. And then he smiled.

"Of course I remember you. How are you keeping?" We shook hands.

"Not too bad. What of yourself?"

He shrugged. "Not too bad," he said, and then: "No, that's a lie. To tell you the truth not well at all." There was a profound sadness in his look.

"Let's go somewhere for a drink," I said, and he agreed. I told my wife I would see her back at the house and we went to a nearby restaurant.

"What happened to you?" I asked when we had sat down. "From what I heard everything was going your way."

He sighed and lit a cigarette. "That's what everyone thought, including me. Now look at me: no job and my wife has left me for another man. I've still got my house and my father left me some money when he died, but when that runs out I don't know what I'll do."

The waiter brought our drinks.

"So what happened?" I asked again.

He was silent for a moment, and then he looked straight at me. "I'll tell you. It was during the war. For months we had been fighting to get control of the city of N——. It was the Rebels' last stronghold, and once we captured it we would have won the war. You can imagine the resistance they put up: it was stupendous. Day and night we shelled them, from the ground and from the air, but every time we thought we had finally broken through they would come back at us. They were putting everything they had into the defence of the city and it began to look as if we would have to destroy every last building in the place before we could take it. And all the while there was international pressure on us: they said we were committing genocide, but they didn't know the half of it.

"Anyway, we finally captured it. We went wild. If you had been there you would understand. Most of my original force had been wiped out and we were exhausted.

"The night of our victory I went drinking with some of my officers. I got drunker than I've ever been in my life and I passed out. When I woke up I was lying in bed with a woman. It was horrible, I'll never forget it as long as I live. There was a terrible smell in the room, and it was incredibly bare and dirty. The bed itself was infested with lice and the woman was thin and ugly. I got up and hurriedly started to pull my clothes on when she woke up and threw herself at me.

" 'Help me, I haven't eaten in three days,' she said. 'Please, help me before I die.'

" 'Get away from me,' I shouted, horrified, and kicked her. She went sprawling across the floor, where she lay. I thought I had killed her, but presently she began moaning. It was an inhuman sound that came from her lips, the cry of someone who has come face to face with absolute evil, someone who has suffered as much as it is possible to suffer and yet lived. And still the smell that pervaded everywhere. I was about to flee when I noticed a bundle in the corner to which the woman was now reaching. I kept telling myself that I must go but I had to see what was in that bundle. I went over to it, and gently lifted the cover."

He was so agitated he could no longer smoke the cigarette he held. He crushed it out and tried to take a drink but choked on it.

"What was it you saw?" I asked.

"In the war I saw many things, I can tell you, but up until then there was never a sense of personal involvement. But this time . . ."

"What was it?"

"The body of a child, no more than a few months old and dead for God knows how long. It was putrefying away in the corner of the room and the mother could not or would not dispose of it. I do not know how long I stood there gaping at it: the spell was finally broken by the woman's hand on my leg. That did it. I ran."

I signalled the waiter for fresh drinks. He was quiet for a long time as he re-lived it. I wanted to say so many things to him but none of them seemed appropriate. He started talking again.

"The war ended soon after I came home. I took up my former job and settled down to raise a family. But it was no good. My nights were haunted by what I had seen in that room. I would wake up screaming, the sheets soaking. I lost interest in everything. My wife and friends tried to help me but it was no use. And I don't blame my wife for leaving me. She stuck it out for three years before she left. And then I lost my job."

"What have you been doing since then?" I asked.

"Nothing, nothing at all."

"And the nightmares, do they still trouble you?"

"Yes. They won't go away. I feel I'm going mad and I can't do anything about it."

"I would like to help you if I can." I said. He shook his head.

"Nobody can help me. It's too late for that."

Months passed and I did not see him again. At first our meeting depressed me, and then angered me, and finally left me perplexed. I wanted to do something for him, but what? And then I would recall how kind he had been to me at the University even if I had rejected his friendship, and I would feel guilty about my inactivity.

A year later I read about his death in one of the daily papers. It was only a short article. It said he had been out hunting and accidentally shot himself. I knew at once that it had been suicide, and this was confirmed by a dream I had a few days later. We were standing in a forest. I was dressed for work and he was in combat uniform. He was walking towards me, pointing the gun to his forehead and saying, "I'm sorry, but I have to do it, you understand, don't you?" and I kept on trying to say something but the words wouldn't come and I tried to go to him but my legs wouldn't move. He pulled the trigger. As he fell it seemed to me that he was smiling.

No Escape

Ndeley Mokoso

"WE ARE going to teach these bastards a lesson. A lesson they will never forget; that will go down in history. For all our endeavours and sacrifices over the years to bring this country to its present state of development, we will not stomach any more insults from undeserving, wanton and ungrateful idiots. I count on you all to execute this sacred mission. And remember it is now or never."

The speaker paused thoughtfully. He surveyed the small group of soldiers whose assignment it was to seal off a section of the capital city of Yaounde and prevent possible movements of contending troops and reinforcements.

"Any questions?" There was a silence—an uneasy calm. Then one of them ventured: "This is a rebellion, isn't it, Captain?" The other thought for a moment before he replied. "Er-r-r, No. Not exactly. It is called a coup d'état, you don't only rebel but you also seize power."

"And if we fail . . . I mean the consequences." The Captain frowned. "Don't ask such silly questions," he blurted harshly. "We are an army of liberation, destined to win. And who said soldiers make such mistakes; what do you think we learn strategy for; bloody fools we should call ourselves if we fail! In any case, civilians have never been known to hold out against the military." His tone was agitated and sarcastic.

Having concluded, he stared with fierce concentration at the questioner.

That settled it. The rest of his listeners looked at each other and nodded in agreement. The embarrassed questioner was for some moments lost in thought.

So this was the beginning of disunity and instability! His country had known peace since the early turbulent years immediately after independence, although surrounded by neighbours who had tasted the effects and aftermath brought about by the inordinate ambitions of their own citizens; for him, this was a completely new trend in the country's politics! He was not fighting for a cause—certainly not in defence of the motherland!

He had a young wife and two children. And an old mother. What would happen to them if he got killed? The idea of the triumphal entry into heaven did not impress him; neither did the amulet he wore under his shirt containing a parchment of the "holy book," believed to neutralise the deadly shock of bullets.

Then suddenly certain lines in the second verse of the National Anthem struck him forcibly. He recited them in silent prayer:

Muster thy sons in close union around thee
Mighty as the Buea Mountain be their team
Instil in them the love of gentle ways
Regret for errors of the past
Foster for mother Africa (Cameroon) a loyalty
That true shall remain to the last.

He did not recite the refrain but ended with a sigh. He had realised it was now too late; the explosion was inevitable.

Captain Dewa was content within himself, stimulated by his mission, the excitement, the belief of the rightness of it all, the promise of it all, and the hopes, BIG HOPES. At thirty, he had been tipped as the likely military Governor of the South West Province after the successful overthrow of the civilian Government. If he had a choice of residence on taking command, he would prefer the "Schloss"—the celebrated German Governor's residence in Buea. The civilian Government's idea of designating it a public monument, he thought stupid and wasteful.

Dewa was not a particularly bright student while training at the Armed Forces Training Centre at Ngaundere (CIFAN), the Training and Proficiency Centre at Ngaoundal (CEFAN), the Specialist Centre in Yaounde (CISA) and the Military Academy, Yaounde (EMIA). His progress had been rapid and over that of his better qualified colleagues who were destined to climb their "tree" the hard way owing to a policy of *avancement aux choix*. Qualifications meant nothing; talent meant nothing; merit meant nothing!

The previous evening he had been summoned to a meeting of the presidential guard top-brass for the final briefing, and the delegation of specific powers after the coup. The scheme of manoeuvres, the movement and storming action of the troops on the strategic and sensitive establishments; those to be taken as hostages, communication between the "attacking forces" by walkie-talkie on a secret frequency—all these were discussed in detail. It was revealed that special combat uniforms for the mission were not ready. This had been due to a re-scheduling of D–day as a result of certain government measures which included the deployment of members of the presidential guard. It had been decided to wear red armbands for identification purposes.

Two lists had been prepared: The Black List which contained those who were thought potentially dangerous. These would be eliminated or detained immediately. The White List, of those who might be counted upon to cooperate and help.

The possible reaction of the civilian population—favourable or otherwise—was then discussed; they had to count on their support! It was
argued that a swift but smooth takeover would certainly shock the civilian
population into complete acceptance of a situation brought about by what
they called the "recklessness and planlessness of the civilian regime." If
the capital territory fell, it would be easy to woo the numerous "chorus
groups" to send the first messages of support and solidarity. The ensuing
"avalanche" from the rest of the regions would crown it all. That was the
consensus.

The national radio network came in here for mention. It must be taken
over and guarded at all costs. For the effective coverage and dissemination
of information and proclamations, it was imperative that the residences of
all senior technical and news staff of the radio be located and put under
round-the-clock surveillance. The public relations committee was to see
to that.

Then the conduct of the rebellion was agreed upon: No indiscrimi-
nate killings; contending forces must be ruthlessly crushed; take no
prisoners; shoot all deserters and looters; no harrassment of the civilian
population; minimum destruction of the infrastructure; password—
OPERATION HYENA.

The logistics expert and strategist, an expatriate technical adviser, was
congratulated for the brief and comprehensive report presented. It showed
that the military hardware in their possession greatly outweighed that of
the government forces both in quantity and sophistication. These included
French, Belgian, Russian and Israeli made automatic firearms. His intelligence machinery reported that, so far, the coup plot had remained a secret
thus maintaining that important element of surprise in military tactics—
catching the enemy with their pants down. He predicted that barring any
unforeseen circumstance, Yaounde would fall in a matter of hours.

The assembly then moved into the Operations Centre. In the middle
was a giant map of Yaounde and its environs. There were areas shaded in
green and red with arrows and coloured flagged pins indicating the movements and the tactical positioning of the storming troops led by mecha-
nised units including armoured vehicles into blocking positions. Here the
expert pounded home the operation objectives.

Other plans included the jamming of the military communications system to prevent any contact with regional commands, the severing of telephone links and the taking over of power and water installations.

The text of the proclamation presented at the meeting was considered
verbose, uninspiring and not reflecting the spirit and the revolution. It
had, for instance, omitted the suspension of the constitution and its institutions, the respect by the new regime of the obligations and commitments

of the deposed regime, and a warning to Foreign diplomatic missions to restrain from any action that tended to undermine the sovereignty and territorial integrity of the nation. The guidelines for the final text were given and a drafting committee of three, one senior military official and two top civil servants, was charged with its redrafting.

The meeting came to a conclusion. The leader of the group assured his listeners of complete victory over what he called "forces of disunity." The hard part, he said, was to gain the position of authority, and once that was attained the rest would be easy. "The more power you have the easier it is to find solutions to any problems. You merely surround yourself with the right people, the right brains—they come up with the answers and the solutions. The credit and glory will be ours." That sounded quite sensible! They clapped enthusiastically. There was a lot of back-slapping as the leader moved round, chatting freely with everyone.

Dewa was meeting the commander-in-chief for the first time. He stood a good six foot plus. He had a substantial physique but his voice was too mellow for a senior military officer.

Dewa stood stiffly at attention throughout their brief encounter. He finally shook his hand with a graceful bow of the head, his left hand behind his back. Here he was among the trusted ones—one of those to rule and direct the affairs of the nation after the takeover! His trend of thought was interrupted by the thud of clicking-boots. All came to attention as the commander-in-chief left the hall, his right hand raised high up above his head in the "thumbs-up" signal. They all raised their hands in unison, and saluted as the jeep departed.

The tense and hushed atmosphere in the room now gave place to light-hearted banter.

The time was 2.30 a.m. thirty tense and anxious minutes to ZERO HOUR. Dewa himself took the roll-call. There were fifty soldiers under his command. They all sat restless as he paced the corridor, giving last minute instructions. A couple of them were already experiencing the effects of the combat "shots" and were keyed up for the battle.

Earlier he had carried out a kit inspection, insisting that iron rations must be carried; he thought they might come in handy.

The minutes and seconds ticked away. Transport vehicles had lined up with troops at the ready, their engines running as they awaited the orders to strike. Then a tense voice crackled over the rebel communication system. "This is OPERATION HYENA Operation Headquarters OB calling. Are you receiving me? Come in LION, over." "Receiving you clean and clear, Sir, over." "Come in SCORPION, over." "Ever ready Sir, over." "Come in TORTOISE, over." "Receiving you Sir, over." The final instructions then followed.

"This is operation headquarters, OBILI, calling all loyal units. This is the start of the people's revolution. Remember it is now or never. I count on your support and loyalty. Good luck to you all."

The revolution had begun. The Hyena Lion commanded by Dewa had taken the strategic positions at the city's centre, blocking all the main access roads with barbed wire entanglements. The road blocks were each manned, visibly, by two soldiers armed with sub-machine guns, while about ten others stayed in the background, completely out of view.

Although explosions and periodical short bursts of gun fire were heard all over Yaounde, most inhabitants did not learn what had happened until late afternoon the following day. The troop movements had been mistaken for military training exercises.

The progress of the fighting was being monitored and coordinated from field operation reports communicated by units. Operations Centre reported the taking over of the national radio, the airport, power and water installations. There had been no resistance. The proclamation had been broadcast nationwide and relative calm had been reported. Stiff resistance in the siege of the presidential palace was reported in morale-boosting language.

Captain Dewa relayed the good news to his comrades. There were hopes, big hopes for those who would live after the takeover.

The battle situation remained relatively the same until the airforce helicopters and transport planes took to the skies. As Dewa's group decided to take cover, one of the helicopters roared low over the Obili Barracks. There were loud explosions. All attempts by Captain Dewa to contact operations headquarters after the attack had failed—the secret radio communications system had been silenced.

"This is a very serious situation," Dewa told his comrades. "I cannot now contact headquarters. I don't know what's happening." No one replied but he sensed a tinge of desperation on their faces. He thought this unsoldierly behaviour for "heroes"—the elite arm of the regular forces.

Minutes later, a member of his group disappeared. Dewa knew he would not have gone far. He moved stealthily, straining his ears for any sounds. Suddenly a bareheaded figure in battle-dress and unarmed emerged about thirty yards away. He wore no red armband. This was the deserter. He raised his rifle. The conduct of the rebellion permitted this. He pulled the trigger. There was only a muffled scream as the escaping soldier threw up his arms and fell on his back—a shuddering mass of flesh. A *coup de gráce* was not necessary. The sprawling corpse was left where it had fallen.

The explosions from the direction of the Obili Barracks continued and now and then the noise of steady small-arms gun fire came closer. Two armoured cars rumbled in their direction bristling with machine guns. The rebels made a courageous attempt to stop them. They succeeded in disabling one of them by shooting at the tyres. Although it finally came to a halt, its guns blazed away in all directions taking a considerable toll of lives. The other continued, smashing its way through the road blocks with ease.

Captain Dewa knew the end of the rebellion had come. Here he was surrounded by the dead, the dying and the wounded. He moved forward trying to ignore their moans and feeble cries for help. He felt a hand weakly grasp his trousers but fell away at the next step. He told himself, he must not stop for anything or anybody. He had to escape. He started weeping for his mother, wife and child. He wondered what would be said later about him. A deserter, killed in action or reported missing? He knew what would happen to him if he was caught—face a charge of high treason, felony and murder and finally the firing squad. He thought of giving himself up. A good soldier never surrendered; too cowardly, he told himself.

He thought of Mariatu, his girlfriend, living at Briquterie. He could take refuge there? No, he told himself again and again. They were likely to search for him there.

The Operation HYENA had gone awry. It was a fiasco. Logistically it had appeared a relatively simple operation. A quick mop-up victory had now escalated into a much more complicated affair. The mistake had been the underestimation of the foe. The fight to martyrdom was lost.

The only option now was escape. But through what route? The following were open to him: southwards through Mbalmayo, Sangmelima on to Bertoua, Batouri, Yokadouma, Molundu into the Central African Republic. The second through Ebolowa, Kribi and Campo into Equatorial Guinea. The third by train to Douala, Tiko, Limbe, by boat to Oron in Nigeria. The fourth was through Bafia, Bafoussam, Dschang through Mbo country into Mamfe, then on to Ekok and Abakaliki in Nigeria.

The first three routes he considered unsafe. He knew there would be a round the clock vigil at all the main routes out of Yaounde for escaping rebels. He preferred the Yaounde–Bafoussam route through Mbo country along bush-paths to Mamfe. He judged that in the Western Region where the inhabitants had lived through a turbulent post independence era, people would normally prefer to go about their lawful business of harvesting and planting coffee than bother themselves with the antics of government. To them nothing else would matter as long as they sold their coffee. He was sure they did not even know that a rebellion was taking place!

Dewa's first problem was how to obtain some clothes. He had remained in hiding in a sparsely built-up area dominated by government offices, around the municipal lake. He had earlier watched a man hanging clothes on a line to dry. These included a pair of blue jeans and a Bastos "T" shirt. As soon as it was getting dark he came out of hiding and stole the clothes. The jeans fitted nicely. Soon he had discarded his camouflage uniform and all except a sum of five hundred thousand francs, the initial sum he had been paid the day before, for his participation in the rebellion. He finally dumped his German-made HK21 rifle into the lake and walked on to the road.

There were not many people about and he gathered from scraps of conversation that fighting was still going on. His heart thumped with great excitement. There were hopes that he could make the trip by road via Bafia before the security forces spread their drag-net.

He took the first lorry he found bound for Bafoussam carrying a cargo of cement. The journey was long, bumpy and uneventful; he had slept for most of the time. Bafoussam was quiet—"asleep"—except for one or two late taxis which honked time and again for no apparent reason, and the distant noise of blaring loudspeakers playing Makossa music.

He was not hungry. The iron rations had sustained him for nearly twenty-four hours. He had to get out of Bafoussam before dawn to avoid being caught in a security check; he had no identification papers. As he walked quickly along the road he came on a drove of cattle being herded for the long trek. What luck, he thought. He could join the drovers disguised as one of them! That was it. He soon found the three and spoke in the language they understood. They listened to his story; apparently they had heard nothing about the rebellion.

They provided him with a white flowing robe and a skull-cap to match, a spear and a sheathed dagger. They then shaved his thick hair down to the skin of his skull. The disguise was perfect. They told him the trail was long. He said he did not mind. He had been accustomed to road-treks during his training.

They were out of Bafoussam just as the first rays of the sun peeped from the east. They entered the trail along little hamlets and villages and left the hustle and bustle of the town behind. They halted to say their prayers while the cows moved freely cropping the green wet grass.

The first night Dewa's mind went through the events of the past few days. That bloody traitor of a logistic expert had failed them. He had messed things up. But all along he'd been so optimistic about it all! Now the military governor designate of the South West Province was on the run—a fugitive! He hoped he would make the Nigerian border and declare himself a political refugee under the United Nations Human Rights Declaration. He felt completely exhausted both mentally and physically, his nerves almost numb by the haunting horrors Operation HYENA had held. The moans and cries of the maimed and dying, the din of sporadic gun fire, even the overwhelming smell of bloating corpses. He was now far away from the scene. He slept as he had never slept before.

For five days they trekked over predominantly grasslands at an altitude that made trekking less exhausting with little or no menace from the tse-tse fly. From Dschang they went over the Mbo Plains into Fontem, Atebong, Tali and Bakebe into Mamfe. Here, news of the abortive coup was discussed everywhere, bluntly and freely. He heard ridiculous accounts and rumours about everything, including an impending invasion by Libyan and Moroccan mercenaries. There was outright condemnation of the "plotters and enemies of peace." There were calls for more vigilance and maximum punishment for those who they said had introduced "ganster politics." He was disappointed by those who said a military regime would not have done any better! Throughout the trek he had remained in the background while the haggling with the dealers and butchers went on.

They found a long queue of transport vehicles. Armed security officials swarmed all over the place, like hornets, interrogating and demanding identity papers from nervous passengers. A few of them had left their papers at home. That was no excuse, they were told. They were detained for further questioning.

The cows and their four drovers continued their long trek past the check-point. They all looked so innocent—ordinary Cameroonians going about their lowly occupation. "Get moving, you there," one of the soldiers ordered, waving his hand. The cows and the men continued their journey towards the Nigerian border. Dewa felt the cold sweat on his brow and neck. What luck! What a relief! 130 kilometres and he would be out of Cameroon and on to FREEDOM! They looked at each other. No one spoke.

They stopped about two miles away from the check-point. They said their prayers. Dewa prayed for himself and the family he had left behind.

He had fallen asleep soon after, quite oblivious of everything else around him. Then he dreamt he'd been making love to Mariatu and woke up suddenly, feeling quite spent and an ugly sticky wetness around his loins.

Now, where was he? He looked around, giving his eyes a good rub. He soon realised he was in strange surroundings. Then his mind became alert; he was now alone! What had happened to the cows and his kinsmen? They had thought it best to abandon and desert him!

A wave of hot anger swept through him. Then he shook with rage. "The damned, bloody bastards," he fumed. He wished he were armed; that would have settled it; shot them in the back. He gathered himself and picked up the trail.

Dewa had calmed down by the time he caught up with them. They only nodded a welcome and one of them explained that they did not wish to disturb his deep slumber. He did not reply. He was a rebel run-away soldier, and should do nothing that would erode his chances of escape. He thought of paying them some "hush" money but he had finally suppressed the urge to do so. His life could be in great danger if they discovered he had money on him.

They had arrived at the border-town of Ekok, where there had been a lull in business activities; the Nigerian Military Government had ordered the closure of their borders in their historic operation—*New Naira for old*. Security officials swarmed everywhere like locusts. They searched, interrogated, checked identification papers and even scrutinised faces. In the mean time, the identities of the coup leaders had been established and were rightly classified as "wanted persons." A nation-wide man-hunt, compared only to the pre- and post-independence era of the *Maquisard*, had commenced. There were long queues of vehicles and persons waiting to take their turns before the screening panels at road-blocks and check-points.

Dewa's three companions had checked-out, but he was asked to wait with the rest who had no identification papers. They were "herded" to an area and closely watched by armed soldiers.

He did not panic like most of them. His "particulars" had been lost. He thought over it again. "Lost" would give the impression of carelessness on his part. No. That would not do. "Stolen," he thought. Yes, that was the right word. He would say he had reported the loss to the police, who had advised him to renew them as soon as possible. As soon as possible also meant at the earliest opportunity! The opportunity had not presented itself! That was his defence. There was nothing to fear! He still had good cover. He looked like an ordinary herdsman—hair shaved down to the skull, filthy-looking boubou with skull-cap to match, prayer kettle and beads, a bow and quiver full of poison-tipped arrows and a six-inch dagger. He was convinced the disguise would go by.

"Now, get a move on and see about the fellows without papers," the officer said to his second-in-command. Then he announced without any fuss for all to hear. "We are sorry for the inconvenience, but the now uncertain situation of the country warrants the measures being taken to safeguard life and property, and in the overall interest of the nation. You all know, as well as I do, that every Cameroonian *must* carry a National Identity Card on his person; too bad if you left it at home."

A long ripple of suppressed tittle-tattle, passed through the little crowd. The majority of them were harmless, ordinary peasants, who only remembered to carry their papers when they travelled to the city. Others, the petty-traders, whose love for making money transcended other considerations including civic obligations, were ready to bribe their way through.

Dewa had taken the hint given earlier in the warning by the officer-in-charge of the operation. He edged his way through from the top of the queue. How would he explain his being in possession of five hundred thousand francs? He thought of handing over the money to one of the traders for safe-keeping; but how could he do this with everyone watching? and what would happen if the trader disappeared with the money? No. He was not prepared to take the risk. But he was a herdsman who sold cows as he travelled from one place to the other. Was he also not a trader?

He tried to absolve himself of total blame. He told the soldier that his papers had been stolen; he intended to renew them as soon as possible.

"You talking bull-shit. What you mean 'as soon as possible'; as soon as possible means what? Do you think I'm here to listen to that shit . . . ? Next."

Dewa moved on. There were two other soldiers, a captain and a second-lieutenant sitting side by side. The one with the sun-shades seemed to fix his gaze on Dewa as he walked over and sat down in front of them. The other fired him with questions—when and where he was born, the names of his parents, where he went to school, etc. The other in the glasses just sat there, his arms folded across his chest, saying nothing, just looking, looking and looking. Dewa could feel his eyes boring right through him.

Why didn't he say something? Why wouldn't he take off those damn glasses so he could guess what was on his mind? And what the hell was he after?

The two conferred briefly. Then the one in the glasses stood up and asked Dewa to follow. He followed and acted as ordered. He unshouldered the quiver and emptied it. There were ten iron-tipped arrows. "They are all poisoned, you know," he warned, as he put them back carefully, one by one, not touching the tips. The other did not reply. He ordered Dewa to raise his hands. He then frisked him expertly. But that was a stupid order—raise your hands. Who told the bastard he was prepared to surrender! He found the dagger. Then he felt his hands moving deftly up his right thigh. They stopped; an object strapped there! "Well, let's see what's here . . . if it's marijuana, then you're in for something really bad." The soldier unwrapped the little bundle and found the money. Dewa would have liked to watch the expression on his face; he still had his glasses on.

"The spoils of war," he muttered as he put the money away into his pocket. Perhaps they would set him free! Let him get on to safety through the border. That was his prayer; and hadn't they just taken ransom money?

The interrogation commenced once more. There was no mention of the money recovered from him. The soldier in the dark glasses said nothing; he just sat looking, looking and looking straight at him. The questioner had changed his tactics. He was now being buffetted and badgered incessantly with questions. "I put it to you . . . I put it to you that . . ."

They finally took him to another room. There were three others seated as he walked in. They all stood up and saluted. Then the senior of the three addressed him. "Captain Dewa, in the name of the President of the Republic, I am taking you into lawful custody." The lieutenant in the dark glasses walked in with the hand-cuffs. He took off the glasses just before he clicked the hand-cuffs shut. "Mon capitaine," he said sadly, "Vous êtes dans le foyer de trahison . . . c'ést domage, mon capitaine."

Dewa recognised him. He was the little truant who spent some time in his unit. That was a long time ago, he remembered. He simply nodded recognition.

Dewa realised the game was up. There on the wall were blown-up photographs of his other colleagues who headed the rebellion. There was now no escape. How he wished he had died in the heat of the battle, fighting for the cause. Yes, he thought; to take his rightful place among the *faithful*.

THE GENERATIONAL
CIRCUIT OF VIOLENCE

The literature of war in Global Cultures is not war stories. It is not about soldiers soldiering, pilots flying. It is about people at war, and it is about war in people's lives, especially in the lives of women and children—those left at home, those whose homes are the battlefield, those who are widowed and orphaned, those who grow up wounded.

Guatemalan writers pay particular attention to what their country's bloody recent history has meant for its children and the environment they live in. The talented generation born at the end of the Second World War, for example, includes the guerrilla fighter Mario Payeras, whose memoir *Days of the Jungle* has appeared in English (1983), a man who has written children's literature but also an acclaimed book on ecology in Guatemala. These writers were children in 1954, when a military dictatorship, backed with American aid and troops, suppressed the leftist, land reform-oriented government that had tried to return to the Guatemalan people the plantations owned by the United Fruit Company, an American enterprise. In the mid-1960s, the Guatemalan government, with the help of American troops stationed in the country to train for anti-Cuban missions, began a campaign of repression against its own people, and some one hundred and fifty thousand have since been killed or "disappeared." In Guatemala, the highest maternal mortality rate in Central America goes along with a staggering infant mortality rate—40 per cent of urban children and 60 per cent of rural children do not live to the age of the central character in **ARTURO ARIAS**'s poignant story, which focuses on a child who was born in the same year as the author, 1950. Arias, from Guatemala City, has published a short story collection and two novels in Spanish. He is best known outside of Central America for his work on the film script for *El Norte*, a study of the misery and danger refugees from Central America face as illegal immigrants going over the Mexican border and into America.

In two South African stories, Miriam Tlali's "Point of No Return" and Najabulo Ndebele's "Death of a Son," we meet one family being torn apart by the father's commitment to anti-apartheid struggle and another family torn by a sudden explosion into their lives of apartheid's always simmering violence. One child will be fatherless; one dies, leaving his father and mother helpless even to recover his body.

MIRIAM TLALI, born in 1933, lives in Soweto and has written interviews under the title "Soweto Speaking" for *Staffrider*, the most influential literary-political magazine in Johannesburg (see Tony Eprile's story in this volume). Until 1985, her two novels, *Muriel at Metropolitan* (1975) and *Amandla* (1980), were censored or banned in South Africa. In 1984 she was able to publish a collection of her stories, which are widely read and anthologized, for white readers as well as for black, although she insists that she writes "with a black audience in mind." In the volume where she made this remark, *Sometimes It Rains: Writings by South African Women* (1987), Tlali published an interview she did in 1979 with Albertina Sisulu, whose husband Walter was a leader with Nelson Mandela of the African National Congress. At the time of the interview, Walter Sisulu had served twenty-four years of his life imprisonment sentence. Reflecting an experience like the one Tlali had imagined in her "Point of No Return" a few years before, Ms. Sisulu explained: "He used to tell me that he doesn't belong to the family and that he would be sent to Robben Island [prison]. As early as only a few years after we were married [in 1944], he used to tell me that his time with us was going to be very short, and that his destiny was that of a man determined to strive for the liberation of his people. He prepared me for what was to come."

"Our literature," NJABULO NDEBELE wrote, "ought to seek to move away from an easy preoccupation with demonstrating the obvious existence of oppression. It exists. The task is to explore how and why people can survive under such harsh conditions." In his collection *Fools and Other Stories* (1983), he has taken up this task, and in the many essays he has written as lecturer in African, African-American, and English literature at University College of Roma, Lesotho, he has explored the political implications of South African literature.

Many stories in Global Cultures reflect on why and how parents send their children off to fight in wars. Much can be learned about the purposes wars serve for those who fight them—as opposed to those who declare them—from these reflections. The shoeshine man in ABDELAL EL HAMAMSSY's "Dust" is bitter from being gypped out of his inheritance of land by his own brother, then losing his wife and watching his older son go bad. He has only his younger son as solace, and this boy is off with the Egyptian Army in the Suez, an army embittered by the inconclusive Suez War of 1956 and the disastrous loss to Israel in 1967, an army bent on redemption. The fearful father wants his son home, desperately—until the Egyptian victory is announced and he, too, is in a delirium of familial and patriotic pride. The story ends with this joy undiminished. But the war ended differently—with its Third Army trapped on the eastern side of the canal, Egypt agreed to negotiate. Abdelal el Hamamssy was born in 1932 and writes in Arabic, although a collection of his stories has been published in English—*This Voice and Others* (Cairo, 1979). He is of a generation of Egyptian intellectuals who could see very clearly the disasters resulting from the delusions of victory that have been entertained throughout the Middle East.

Guatemala 1954 —
Funeral for a Bird

Arturo Arias

MÁXIMO SÁNCHEZ crawled into the light. He had been hiding with his mother under the big old desk. Now that the bombs had stopped, he could see the world. He wanted to see the things his mother had told him about: elephants, houses, spiders and streets. Maybe he would hear someone call his name, and if he did he could answer. His mother had told him this, and his age too. He was five years old and already knew so much! Well, he was four and a half in truth, but Máximo felt bigger if he said five. He said so with scars on his cheeks. They were scars from something called welts. Everything had its name. Máximo went through the zigzagging streets, between the ruins of the houses. He looked for everything, and its name.

There were bodies all around him. These were called corpses. His mother had told him not to touch, because they were filled with nasty worms. He had asked his mother if there were worms in him too, but she said they were just in the dead. Poor little corpses. He wanted to play. It was a pity they were dead. But they stank so much! They deserved to die for smelling so badly. He continued to walk with one hand over his nose and the other over his belly. And his father? Would he smell too? No! His father wouldn't stink. He wasn't dead—only maybe. His mother had told him that his father had disappeared. Maybe now that the bombs had stopped, his father would return. Máximo remembered his father's handsome mustache. Will you come back Father? Soon? Will you come back?

Máximo could walk in any direction unless the streets were blocked by corpses or fallen walls. That was called freedom. But the air wasn't free of the stench, and this freedom had its limitations. He lifted one foot, balanced lightly on the other leg, and leaped, arms open, over a puddle of blood in the street. Despite that, everything seemed possible. To fly, to float, to wash, to run here, to run there, to run always. He felt free.

Then it began to rain, softly at first. One drop followed another, with plenty of time between one drop and the next. He could feel each drop caress his hair, and see their explosions against the remains of the old walls. Inside the drops he saw red and blue colors. Drops crisscrossed and absorbed yellow until they touched the grey dust ground. Then they ran together in colorful furrows, and grew like a spider's web. Where was

Father? Playing the spider? The drops fell more forcefully, falling with-out end. Máximo got cold and wet, pursued the colors, caught shades of marine blue spilling behind violets. He ran through the streets, goose bumps forming on his skin instead of welts. He passed smiling corpses, mouths open, and feared they would bite at his heels. His mother had told him they wouldn't move, but Máximo wasn't sure. He studied a cock-roach scurrying from one of the open mouths. Were they born inside a dead person? How would they know when they were born? Something struck him on the forehead and fell in the mud.

A bomb? He searched for it and found something like a cold piece of glass that melted. More of these began falling on every side. A big one hit his shoulder. He had to find a place to hide. It was cold. It had never been cold under the desk. He hoped his mother would still be waiting there with her white hair and toothless mouth. Would she still be bent? Maybe he ought to go back. Then another hit him. And he went on without knowing its name. Maybe he ought to go back?

There it is! Look at it!

He was in a very narrow alley. In its center, there was a dead bird. So he was not the only one! Children of all sizes were there shouting.

A dead bird! A dead bird!

He had never seen a bird, dead or alive, except in photos from old magazines at home. He had looked at them all the time. This bird was smaller than he had imagined it, silently crossing the sky with bombs under its wings.

A dead bird! A dead bird!

The children ran toward him, and he ran too. He didn't see the headless body behind the pile of mossy bricks. He stumbled on it and got his belly full of mud. Blood dripped from scratches on his arm, but he didn't cry. Instead, in a fit of anger, he kicked the corpse, his foot sinking through the body as though it were a cotton sock. Corpses, corpses at every turn! Then he remembered the bird.

Look at it!

Soon a circle of children surrounded it, and the eldest watched that no one got too close. Careful there! Don't step on it! Brutes! One of the littlest boys started to cry. But Máximo wouldn't do that. In sepulchral silence, the eldest kneeled, facing the body. Poor bird. He touched it and trembled. Murmurs. He extended his middle finger to stroke its tiny breast. The murmurs grew. Someone pushed through the group to see, and stepped on Máximo's foot. But at this moment, only the bird mattered. Poor bird. Let's touch him too. No. Such a delicate body would be torn to pieces. Poor bird. Its rounded breast was covered with dots white and soft as the drops of rain. Its wings pressed down around its body as if in protection from the cold. Its neck was long, almost too long, and ended in the head where a big black eye and open beak protruded. Stiff feet stretched directly upward. You think the hail killed him? No. When something hits, it leaves marks. Look at what the bombs did. But this is different, bombs explode. Why shoud this be different? They kill don't they? Yes, but they kill differently. Maybe he broke his neck? Maybe. The eldest crouched down, and carefully took the head of the bird between his forefinger and thumb. He lifted it a little. Everybody bent down to be able to see better. What are we going to do with him? He laughed, already knowing they had to bury it. Of course, everybody shouted. We must bury the bird. Poor bird. Máximo saw the beautiful bird, as he had seen the colors fleeing from the dead walls. All the birds were gone.

Everyone ran towards the ruins to look for objects for the funeral. Máximo didn't know what to look for. He had never been to a funeral. He hadn't heard anything about them. He had seen pictures, but wondered what a funeral could be. The eldest said they should bring pretty things, but Máximo knew he couldn't grasp the colors. Nevertheless, he searched for something, something that glowed, and he began to dig through the ruin closest to him.

Beautiful things. I only want beautiful things!

One of the boys brought a board. Another brought a colorful cloth. One found a picture of a rose. A tall freckled boy rang a silver bell. Someone had tallow candles. There was a watch. An oilcloth slipper. A medal from the air force. Two pairs of pants. A yellowed laundry ticket. Máximo was the last to arrive. I found a ring! A precious ring, he shouted. The circle of children parted so he could pass and place his offering at the feet of the dead bird. He was proud of his discovery. And it was truly precious. Solid gold with a delicious aquamarine mounted exactly in the center. The finger it encircled also seemed beautiful.

Was it the finger of a woman? Look at the fingernail. Maybe. But it isn't painted. Some women don't paint them. Maybe it's a Martian finger—it's half green. No, that's because it's rotting. It isn't rotting, it's only half burned, if it were rotting it would stink. Perhaps then it would smell good? You haven't by chance smelled a corpse, ever?

"Okay, enough," said the eldest. "We have to bury the bird. Is everyone in agreement? Good." With everyone pushing for a good view, he crouched before the body and gathered it up in cupped hands. He put it on the board, and some of them applauded. "Good. Now you cover it with this cloth," he ordered, "and we'll put the insignia above the head. Like that. The great dead pilot. Put the ring at the feet, finger and all. It's the finger of its owner."

The freckled boy with the little bell led the procession. Stopping on each corner, he rang it shouting, "There is a dead bird! A dead bird!" A line of pious boys carried candles and followed the photograph of the rose held high in the air so that everyone could see. Two boys hung the trousers on pointed sticks like flags. One brought the golden crucifix without any body. The board with the deceased, carried on the shoulders of the six eldest boys, came next, with the youngest children, Máximo among them, scrambling into the rear of the line. The rain continued falling. But the bird was dead. They would have to bury it in the rain.

They decided to bury the bird by an intersection in a vacant lot. The youngest ones dug the hole with sticks, the oilcloth slipper, an old broom. The land was soft and moist, and in almost no time at all they had a large enough hole.

The trousers were put in place at the bottom. On top of them, the photo of the rose, face upward. And after that the board with the body and its precious adornments. Everyone stood in a circle around the grave, with their eyes fixed on the lifeless feathery body. The only movement was the murmuring rain. The oldest boy took the crucifix and let it fall on the body. Good. Cover it. All at once, they dug into the mud, each trying to throw more dirt than the others. No one saw the old man who approached.

"Children, hey, you over there! What's going on?" They all whirled around. Máximo saw the old man, black coat dragging in the mud, legs bent and half useless. He was leaning on a wooden stick, and there was mud and food on his filthy gray beard. His pallid skin was covered with splotches of welts, especially on either side of his broad nose. His jaw bone shook.

"What are you doing?" he asked.

They stood there paralyzed, afraid. The smallest one cried again. Another one ran away. Soon, very soon, there was an avalanche of boys pushing, elbowing, scratching, all to get away from the place as fast as possible.

"Don't leave! Don't leave! I just asked what you were doing!"

Máximo was the only one left. He scrutinized the old man. Could this be his father? No. The old man had no mustache. If he were his father, he would have a mustache. This is how he had always seen him in pictures. His mother had also mentioned that the gringos had no mustaches, but his father did. He wondered why everyone else had run away. And this old man—why were his hands trembling? His feet twisted? Why did he have hair in his ears? Should he have fled also? Maybe the old man only wanted to talk. Why should he be scared?

"Hey there little fellow! Will you come here?"

Máximo was scared. "I have to go home. My mother is waiting for me under the desk."

"Don't worry my boy, this old man isn't going to hurt you."

"I have to go. It's simple."

The old man shouted to the other boys. "I see you! There you go! You act like rats scurrying around the ravines. There—by the Street of Illusions and Street of Sighs."

Máximo looked. Street of Illusions. Street of Sighs. For the first time he realized that the streets, like people, have names. Máximo had a lot to learn.

"By the bones of my grandmother!"

The old man hobbled over to Máximo.

"What were you rascals doing here anyway?"

"A bird died. We were burying it."

"A funeral for a bird?" said the old man.

"Yes. We found it on the street and couldn't leave it there. It was so beautiful and soft. Someone might have stepped on it."

"Of course. Did you find it on that street? The Street of Sighs?"

"Yes, that one. Then we decided to bury it here. We dug a hole in the dirt and put it inside. Then we covered it."

"You did this and nothing more? You didn't leave something to accompany it and to protect it from the cold?"

"Yes we did. We had a procession, and gave it a ring and a medal of gold."

"Well, you made an effort, but this isn't how to bury the dead. Of course, it wasn't your fault. I'm sure none of you have had experience in the matters of death. But let me continue. When you have the bird on the board, you must burn it with incense. Then sprinkle the body with flowers of death and some drops of *indita*.[1] This helps the soul on the road to infinity. Of course, these days you couldn't have located any *indita*. But you could have improvised. And there's one more thing. When you lift the board, you must give three turns to the right and four to the left. Seven in all. This is to confuse the soul so that it can't return to this life of misery. Imagine if the poor thing had to live life all over again? Of course, you wouldn't understand." The old man opened his mouth to laugh. But nothing came out of it.

Translated by Ann Koshel

---

1. Guatemalan Spanish, meaning "small Indian woman"; also the name of a strong drink, said to have an "indita" in the bottle.

The Point of No Return

Miriam M. Tlali

S'BONGILE STOPPED at the corner of Sauer and Jeppe streets and looked up at the robot. As she waited for the green light to go on, she realized from the throbbing of her heart and her quick breathing that she had been moving too fast. For the first time since she had left Senaoane, she became conscious of the weight of Gugu, strapped tightly on her back.

All the way from home, traveling first by bus and then by train from Nhlanzane to Westgate station, her thoughts had dwelt on Mojalefa, the father of her baby. Despite all efforts to forget, her mind had continually reverted to the awesome results of what might lie ahead for them, if they (Mojalefa and the other men) carried out their plans to challenge the government of the Republic of South Africa.

The incessant rumbling of traffic on the two intersecting one-way streets partially muffled the eager male voices audible through the open windows on the second floor of Myler House on the other side of the street. The men were singing freedom songs. She stood and listened for a while before she crossed the street.

Although he showed no sign of emotion, it came as a surprise to Mojalefa when one of the men told him that a lady was downstairs waiting to see him. He guessed that it must be S'bongile and he felt elated at the prospect of seeing her. He quickly descended the two flights of stairs to the foyer. His heart missed a beat when he saw her.

"*Au banna!*" he said softly as he stood next to her, unable to conceal his feelings. He looked down at her and the baby, sleeping soundly on her back. S'bongile slowly turned her head to look at him, taken aback at his exclamation. He bent down slightly and brushed his dry lips lightly over her forehead just below her neatly plaited hair. He murmured, "It's good to see you again, Bongi. You are *so* beautiful! Come, let's sit over here."

He led her away from the stairs, to a wooden bench farther away opposite a narrow dusty window overlooking the courtyard. A dim ray of light pierced through the windowpanes making that spot the only bright area in the dimly lit foyer.

He took out a piece of tissue from his coat pocket, wiped off the dust from the sill and sat down facing her. He said:

"I'm very happy you came. I . . ."

"I *had* to come, Mojalefa," she interrupted.

"I could not bear it any longer. I could not get my mind off the quarrel. I could not do any work, everything I picked up kept falling out of my hands. Even the washing I tried to do I could not get done. I *had* to leave everything and come. I kept thinking of you . . . as if it was all over, and I would not see you nor touch you ever again. I came to convince myself that I could still see you as a free man, that I could still come close to you and touch you. Mojalefa, I'm sorry I behaved like that last night. I thought you were indifferent to what I was going through. I was jealous because you kept on telling me that you were committed. That like all the others, you had already resigned from your job, and that there was no turning back. I thought you cared more for the course you have chosen than for Gugu and me."

"There's no need for you to apologize, Bongi. I never blamed you for behaving like that and I bear you no malice at all. All I want from you is that you should understand. Can we not talk about something else? I am so happy you came."

They sat looking at each other in silence. There was *so* much they wanted to say to one another, just this once. Yet both felt tongue-tied; they could not think of the right thing to say. She felt uneasy, just sitting there and looking at him while time was running out for them. She wanted to steer off the painful subject of their parting, so she said:

"I have not yet submitted those forms to Baragwanath. They want the applicants to send them in together with their pass numbers. You've always discouraged me from going for a pass, and now they want a number. It's almost certain they'll accept me because of my matric certificate. That is if I submit my form *with the number* by the end of this month, of course. What do you think I should do, go for registration? Many women and girls are already rushing to the registration centers. They say it's useless for us to refuse to carry them like you men because we will not be allowed to go anywhere for a visit or buy anything valuable. And now the hospitals, too . . ."

"No, no wait . . . Wait until . . . Until after this . . . After you know what the outcome is of what we are about to do."

Mojalefa shook his head. It was intolerable. Everything that happened around you just went to emphasize the hopelessness of even trying to live like a human being. Imagine a woman having to carry a pass everywhere she goes; being stopped and searched or ordered to produce her pass? This was outrageous, the ultimate desecration and an insult to her very existence. He had already seen some of these "simple" women who come to seek work from "outside," proudly moving in the streets with those plastic containers dangling round their necks like sling bags. He immediately thought of the tied-down bitch and it nauseated him.

S'bongile stopped talking. She had tried to change the topic from the matter of their parting but now she could discern that she had only succeeded in making his thoughts wander away into a world unknown to her. She felt as if he had shut her out, aloof. She needed his nearness, now more than ever. She attempted to draw him closer to herself; to be *with* him just this last time. She could not think of anything to say. She sat listening to the music coming from the upper floors. She remarked:

"That music, those two songs they have just been singing. I haven't heard them before. Who composes them?"

"Most of the men contribute something now and again. Some melodies are from old times, they just supply the appropriate words. Some learn 'new' tunes from old people at home, old songs from our past. Some are very old. Some of our boys have attended the tribal dancing ceremonies at the mines and they learn these during the festivities. Most of these are spontaneous, they come from the feelings of the people as they go about their work; mostly laborers. Don't you sometimes hear them chanting to rhythm as they perform tasks; carrying heavy iron bars or timber blocks along the railway lines or road construction sites? They even sing about the white foreman who sits smoking a pipe and watches them as they sweat."

S'bongile sat morose, looking toward the entrance at the multitudes moving toward the center of town and down toward Newtown. She doubted whether any of those people knew anything of the plans of the men who were singing of the aspirations of the blacks and their hopes for the happier South Africa they were envisaging. Her face, although beautiful as ever, reflected her depressed state. She nodded in halfhearted approval at his enthusiastic efforts to explain. He went on:

"Most of the songs are in fact lamentations—they reflect the disposition of the people. We shall be thundering them tomorrow morning on our way as we march toward the jails of this country!"

With her eyes still focused on the stream of pedestrians and without stopping to think, she asked:

"Isn't it a bit premature? Going, I mean. You are *so* few; a drop in an ocean."

"It isn't numbers that count, Bongi," he answered, forcing a smile. How many times had he had to go through that? he asked himself. In the trains, the buses, at work . . . Bongi was unyielding. Her refusal to accept that he must go was animated by her selfish love, the fear of facing life without him. He tried to explain although he had long realized that his efforts would always be fruitless. It was also clear to him that it was futile to try and run away from the issue.

"In any case," he went on, "it will be up to *you*, the ones who remain behind, the women and the mothers, to motivate those who are still dragging their feet; you'll remain only to show them why they must follow in our footsteps. That the future and dignity of the blacks as a nation and as human beings is worth sacrificing for."

Her reply only served to demonstrate to him that he might just as well have kept quiet. She remarked:

"Even your father feels that this is of no use. He thinks it would perhaps only work if all of you first went out to *educate* the people so that they may join in."

"No, father does not understand. He thinks we are too few as compared to the millions of all the black people of this land. He feels that we are sticking out our necks. That we can never hope to get the white man to sit round a table and speak to us, here. All he'll do is order his police to shoot us dead. If they don't do that, then they'll throw us into the jails, and we shall either die there or be released with all sorts of afflictions. It's because I'm his only son. He's thinking of *himself*, Bongi, he does not understand."

"He *does* understand, and he loves you."

"Maybe that's *just* where the trouble lies. Because he loves me, he fails to think and reason properly. We do not agree. He is a different kind of person from me, and he can't accept that. He wants me to speak, act, and even think like him, and that is impossible."

"He wants to be proud of you, Mojalefa."

"If he can't be proud of me as I am, then he'll never be. He says I've changed. That I've turned against everything he taught me. He wants me to go to church regularly and pray more often. I sometimes feel he hates me, and I sympathize with him."

"He does not hate you, Mojalefa; you two just do not see eye to eye."

"My father moves around with a broken heart. He feels I am a renegade, a disappointment; an embarrassment to him. You see, as a preacher, he has to stand before the congregation every Sunday and preach on the importance of obedience, of how as Christians we have to be submissive and tolerant and respect those who are in authority over us under all conditions. That we should leave it to 'the hand of God' to right all wrongs. As a reprisal against all injustices we must kneel down and pray because, as the scriptures tell us, God said: 'Vengeance is Mine.' He wants me to follow in his footsteps."

"Be a priest or preacher, you mean?"

"Yes. Or show some interest in his part-time ministry. Sing in the church choir and so on, like when I was still a child." He smiled wryly.

"Why don't you show *some* interest then? Even if it is only for his sake? Aren't you a Christian, don't you believe in God?"

"I suppose I do. But not like *him* and those like him, no."

What is *that* supposed to mean?"

"What's the use of praying all the time? In the first place, how can a slave kneel down and pray without feeling that he is not quite a man, human? Every time I try to pray I keep asking myself—if God loves me like the Bible says he does, then why should I have to carry a pass? Why should I have to be a virtual tramp in the land of my forefathers, why? Why should I have all these obnoxious laws passed against me?"

Then the baby on Bongi's back coughed, and Mojalefa's eyes drifted slowly toward it. He looked at the sleeping Gugu tenderly for a while and sighed, a sad expression passing over his eyes. He wanted to say something but hesitated and kept quiet.

Bongi felt the strap cutting painfully into her shoulder muscles and decided to transfer the baby to her lap. Mojalefa paced up and down in the small space, deep in thought. Bongi said:

"I have to breast-feed him. He hasn't had his last feed. I forgot everything. I just grabbed him and came here, and he didn't cry or complain. Sometimes I wish he would cry more often like other children."

Mojalefa watched her suckling the baby. He reluctantly picked up the tiny clasped fist and eased his thumb slowly into it so as not to rouse the child. The chubby fingers immediately caressed his thumb and embraced it tightly. His heart sank, and there was a lump in his throat. He had a strong urge to relieve S'bongile of the child, pick him up in his strong arms and kiss him, but he suppressed the desire. It was at times like these that he experienced great conflict. He said:

"I should never have met you, Bongi. I am not worthy of your love."

"It was cruel of you Mojalefa. All along you knew you would have to go, and yet you made me fall for you. You made me feel that life without you is no life at all. Why did you do this to me?"

He unclasped his thumb slowly from the baby's instinctive clutch, stroking it tenderly for a moment. He walked slowly toward the dim dusty window. He looked through into the barely visible yard, over the roofs of the nearby buildings, into the clear blue sky above. He said:

"It is because I have the belief that we shall meet again, Bongi: that we shall meet again, in a free Africa!"

The music rose in a slow crescendo.

"That song. It is so *sad*. It sounds like a hymn."

They were both silent. The thoughts of both of them anchored on how unbearable the other's absence would be. Mojalefa consoled himself that at least he knew his father would be able to provide the infant with all its needs. That he was fortunate and not like some of his colleagues who had been ready—in the midst of severe poverty—to sacrifice all. Thinking of some of them humbled him a great deal. S'bongile would perhaps be accepted in Baragwanath where she would take up training as a nurse. He very much wanted to break the silence. He went near his wife and touched her arm. He whispered:

"Promise me, Bongi, that you will do your best. That you will look after him, please."

"I *shall*. He is our valuable keepsake—your father's and mine—something to remind me of you. A link nobody can destroy. All yours and mine."

He left her and started pacing again. He searched hopelessly in his mind for something to say; something pleasant. He wanted to drown the sudden whirl of emotion he felt in his heart when he looked down at S'bongile, his young bride of only a few weeks, and the two-month-old child he had brought into this world.

S'bongile came to his rescue. She said:

"I did not tell my mother that I was coming here. I said that I was taking Gugu over to your father for a visit. He is always so happy to see him."

Thankful for the change of topic, Mojalefa replied, smiling.

"You know, my father is a strange man. He is unpredictable. For instance, when I had put you into trouble and we realized to our horror that Gugu was on the way, I thought that he would skin me alive, that *that* was now the last straw. I did not know how I would approach him, because then it was clear that you would also have to explain to your mother why you would not be in a position to start at Turfloop. There was also the thought that your mother had paid all the fees for your first year and had bought you all those clothes and so forth. It nearly drove me mad worrying about the whole mess. I kept thinking of your poor widowed mother; how she had toiled and saved so that you would be able to start at university after having wanted a whole year for the chance. I decided to go and tell my uncle in Pretoria and send *him* to face my father with that catastrophic announcement. I stayed away from home for weeks after that."

"Oh yes, it was nerve-racking, wasn't it? And they were all so kind to us. After the initial shock, I mean. We have to remember that all our lives, and be thankful for the kind of parents God gave us. I worried *so* much, I even contemplated suicide, you know. Oh well, I suppose you could not help yourself!"

She sighed deeply, shaking her head slowly. Mojalefa continued:

"Mind you, I knew something like that would happen, yet I went right ahead and talked you into yielding to me. I was drawn to you by a force so great, I just could not resist it. I hated myself for weeks after that. I actually despised myself. What is worse is that I had vowed to myself that I would never bring into this world a soul that would have to inherit my servitude. I had failed to 'develop and show a true respect for our African womanhood,' a clause we are very proud of in our disciplinary code, and I remonstrated with myself for my weakness."

"But your father came personally to see my people and apologize for what you had done, and later to pay all the *lobola* they wanted. He said that we would have to marry immediately as against what you had said to me—why it would not be wise for us to marry, I mean."

"That was when I had gone through worse nightmares. I had to explain to him why I did not want to tie you down to me when I felt that I would not be able to offer you anything, that I would only make you unhappy. You know why I was against us marrying, Bongi, of course. I wanted you to be free to marry a 'better' man, and I had no doubt it would not be long before he grabbed you. Any man would be proud to have you as his wife, even with a child who is not his."

He touched her smooth cheek with the back of his hand, and added:

"You possess those rare delicate attributes that any man would want to feel around him and be enkindled by."

"Your father would never let Gugu go, not for anything. Mojalefa. He did not name him 'his pride' for nothing. I should be thankful that I met the son of a person like that. Not all women are so fortunate. How many beautiful girls have been deserted by their lovers and are roaming the streets with illegitimate babies on their backs, children they cannot support?"

"I think it is an unforgivable sin. And not all those men do it intentionally, mind you. Sometimes, with all their good intentions, they just do not have the means to do much about the problem of having to pay *lobola*, so they disappear, and the girls never see them again."

"How long do you think they'll lock you up, Mojalefa?" she asked, suddenly remembering that it might be years before she could speak to him like that again. She adored him, and speaking of parting with him broke her heart.

"I do not know, and I do not worry about that, Bongi. If I had you and Gugu and they thrust me into a desert for a thousand years, I would not care. But then I am only a small part of a whole. I'm like a single minute cell in the living body composed of millions of cells, and I have to play my small part for the well-being and perpetuation of life in the whole body."

"But you are likely to be thrust into the midst of hardened criminals, murderers, rapists and so on."

"Very likely. But then that should not deter us. After all most of them have been driven into being like that by the very evils we are exposed to as people without a say in the running of our lives. Most of them have ceased to be proud because there's nothing to be proud of. You amuse me, Bongi. So you think because we are more educated we have reason to be proud? Of what should we feel proud in a society where the mere pigmentation of your skin condemns you to nothingness? Tell me, of what?"

She shook her head violently, biting her lips in sorrow, and with tears in her eyes, she replied, softly:

"I do not know, Mojalefa."

They stood in silence for a while. She sighed deeply and held back the tears. They felt uneasy. It was useless, she thought bitterly. They had gone through with what she considered to be an ill-fated undertaking. Yet he was relentlessly adamant. She remembered how they had quarreled the previous night. How at first she had told herself that she had come to accept what was about to happen with quiet composure, "like a mature person" as they say. She had however lost control of herself when they were alone outside her home, when he had bidden her mother and other relatives farewell. She had become hysterical and could not go on pretending any longer. In a fit of anger, she had accused Mojalefa of being a coward who was running away from his responsibilities as a father and husband. It had been a very bad row and they had parted unceremoniously. She had resolved that today she would only speak of those things which would not make them unhappy. And now she realized with regret that she was right back where she had started. She murmured to herself:

"Oh God, why should it be us, why should we be the lambs for the slaughter? Why should you be one of those handing themselves over? It's like giving up. What will you be able to do for your people in jail, or if you should be . . ."

She could not utter the word *killed.*

"*Somebody* has got to sacrifice so that others may be free. The *real* things, those that really matter, are never acquired the easy way. All the peoples of this world who were oppressed like us have had to give up *something,* Bongi. Nothing good or of real value comes easily. Our freedom will never be handed over to us on a silver platter. In our movement, we labor under no illusions; we know we can expect no handouts. We know that the path ahead of us is not lined with soft velvety flower petals; we are aware that we shall have to tread on thorns. We are committed to a life of service, sacrifice and suffering. Oh no, Bongi, you have got it all wrong. It is not like throwing in the towel. On the contrary, it is the beginning of something our people will never look back at with shame. We shall never regret what we are about to do, and there is no turning back. We are at the point of no return! If I changed my mind now and went back home and sat down and deceived myself that all was all right, I would die a very unhappy man indeed. I would die in dishonor." He was silent a while.

"Bongi, I want to tell you my story. I've never related it to anyone before because just *thinking* about the sad event is to me a very unpleasant and extremely exacting experience . . ." He was picking his way carefully through memories.

"After my father had completed altering that house we live in from a four-roomed matchbox to what it is now, he was a proud man. He was called to the office by the superintendent to complete a contract with an electrical contractor. It had been a costly business and the contractor had insisted that the final arrangements be concluded before the City Council official. It was on that very day that the superintendent asked him if he could bring some of his colleagues to see the house when it was completed. My father agreed. I was there on that day when they (a group of about fifteen whites) arrived. I had heard my parents speak with great expectation to their friends and everybody about the intended 'visit' by the white people. Naturally, I was delighted and proud as any youngster would be. I made sure I would be home and not at the football grounds that afternoon. I thought it was a great honor to have such respectable white people coming to *our* house. I looked forward to it and I had actually warned some of my friends . . .

"After showing them through all the nine rooms of the two-story house, my obviously gratified parents both saw the party out along the slasto pathway to the front gate. I was standing with one of my friends near the front veranda. I still remember vividly the superintendent's last words. He said: 'John, on behalf of my colleagues here and myself, we are very thankful that you and your kind *mosade* allowed us to come and see your beautiful house. You must have spent a *lot* of money to build and furnish it *so* well. But, *you should have built it on wheels*! And the official added, with his arms swinging forward like someone pushing some imaginary object: 'It should have had *wheels* so that it may *move* easily! And they departed, leaving my petrified parents standing there agape and looking at each other in helpless amazement. I remember, later, my mother trying her best to put my stunned father at ease, saying: '*Au, oa hlanya, mo lebale; ha a tsebe hore ontse a re'ng. Ntate hle!*' ('He is mad; just forget about him. He does not know what he is saying!')

"As a fifteen-year-old youth, I was also puzzled. But unlike my parents, I did not sit down and forget—or try to do so. That day marked the turning point in my life. From that day on, I could not rest. Those remarks by that government official kept ringing in my mind. I had to know why he had said that. I probed, and probed; I asked my teachers at school, clerks at the municipal offices, anyone who I thought would be in a position to help me. Of course I made it as general as I could and I grew more and more restless. I went to libraries and read all the available literature I could find on the South African blacks.

"I studied South African history as I had never done before. The history of the discovery of gold, diamonds and other minerals in this land, and the growth of the towns. I read of the rush to the main industrial centers and the influx of the Africans into them, following their early reluctance, and sometimes refusal, to work there, and the subsequent laws which necessitated their coming like the vagrancy laws and the pass laws. I read about the removals of the so-called 'black spots' and why they were now labeled that. The influenza epidemic which resulted in the building of the Western Native and George Goch townships in 1919. I dug into any information I could get about the history of the urban Africans. I discovered the slyness, hypocrisy, dishonesty and greed of the lawmakers.

"When elderly people came to visit us and sat in the evenings to speak about their experiences of the past, of how they first came into contact with the whites, their lives with the Boers on the farms and so forth, I listened. Whenever my father's relations went to the remote areas in Lesotho and Matatiele, or to Zululand and Natal where my mother's people are, during school holidays, I grabbed the opportunity and accompanied them. Learning history ceased to be the usual matter of committing to memory a whole lot of intangible facts from some obscure detached past. It became a living thing and a challenge. I was in search of my true self. And like Moses in the Bible, I was disillusioned. Instead of having been raised like the slave I am, I had been nurtured like a prince, clothed in a fine white linen loincloth and girdle when I should have been wrapped in the rough woven clothing of my kind.

"When I had come to know most of the facts, when I had read through most of the numerous laws pertaining to the urban blacks—the acts, clauses, subclauses, regulations, sections and subsections; the amendments and subamendments—I saw myself for the first time. I was a prince, descended from the noble proud house of Monaheng—the true kings of the Basuto nation. I stopped going to the sports clubs and the church. Even my father's flashy American Impala ceased to bring to me the thrill it used to when I drove round the townships in it. I attended political meetings because there, at least, I found people trying to find ways and means of solving and overcoming our problems. At least I knew now what I really was . . . an underdog, a voiceless creature. Unlike my father, I was not going to be blindfolded and led along a garden path by someone else, a foreigner from other continents. I learned that as a black, there was a responsibility I was carrying on my shoulders as a son of this soil. I realized that I had to take an active part in deciding (or in insisting that I should decide) the path along which my descendants will tread. Something was wrong: radically wrong, and it was my duty as a black person to try and put it right. To free myself and my people became an obsession, a dedication.

"I sometimes listen with interest when my father complains. Poor father. He would say: 'Mojalefa *oa polotika*. All Mojalefa reads is politics, politics, politics. He no longer plays football like other youths. When he passed matric with flying colors in history, his history master came to my house to tell me how my son is a promising leader. I was proud and I moved around with my head in the air. I wanted him to start immediately at university, but he insisted that he wanted to work. I wondered why because I could afford it and there was no pressing need for him to work. He said he would study under UNISA and I paid fees for the first year, and they sent him lectures. But instead of studying, he locks himself up in his room and reads politics all the time. He has stopped sending in scripts for correction. He is morose and never goes to church. He does not appreciate what I do for him!' Sometimes I actually pity my father. He would say: 'My father was proud when Mojalefa was born. He walked on foot rather than take a bus all the way from Eastern Native Township to Bridgman Memorial Hospital in Brixton to offer his blessings at the bedside of my late wife, and to thank our ancestors for a son and heir. He named him Mojalefa. And now that boy is about to sacrifice himself—for what he calls "a worthy cause." He gives up all this . . . a house I've built and furnished for twenty-one thousand rand, most of my money from the insurance policy my good old boss was clever enough to force me to take when I first started working for him. Mojalefa gives up all this for a jail cell!' "

There were tears in the eyes of S'bongile as she sat staring in bewilderment at Mojalefa. She saw now a different man; a man with convictions and ideals; who was not going to be shaken from his beliefs, come what may. He stopped for a while and paused. All the time he spoke as if to some unseen being, as if he was unconscious of her presence. He went on:

"My father always speaks of how his grandfather used to tell him that as a boy in what is now known as the Free State (I don't know why) the white people (the Boers) used to come, clothed only in a 'stertnem,' and ask for permission to settle on their land. Just like that, barefooted and with cracked soles, begging for land. My father does not realize that *he* is now in a worse position than those Boers, that all that makes a man has been stripped from under his feet. That he now has to *float in the air*. He sits back in his favorite comfortable armchair in his living room, looks around him at the splendor surrounding him, and sadly asks: 'When I go, who'll take over from me?" He thinks he is still a man, you know. He never stops to ask himself: 'Take *what* over . . . a house on wheels? Something with no firm ground to stand on?' " He turned away from her and looked through the dusty windowpane. He raised his arms and grabbed the vertical steel bars over the window. He clung viciously to them and shook them until they rattled. He said:

"No, Bongi. There is no turning back. Something has *got* to be done . . . something. It cannot go on like this!"

Strange as it may seem, at that moment, they both had visions of a jail cell. They both felt like trapped animals. He kept on shaking the bars and shouting:

"Something's *got* to be done . . . Now!"

She could not bear the sight any longer. He seemed to be going through great emotional torture. She shouted:

"Mojalefa!"

He swung round and faced her like someone only waking up from a bad dream. He stared through the open entrance, and up at the stairs leading to the upper floor where the humming voices were audible. They both stood still listening for a while. Then he spoke softly yet earnestly, clenching his fists and looking up toward the sound of the music. He said:

"Tomorrow, when dawn breaks, we shall march . . . Our men will advance from different parts of the Republic of South Africa. They will leave their passbooks behind and not feel the heavy weight in their pockets as they proceed toward the gates of the prisons of this land of our forefathers!"

Bongi stood up slowly. She did not utter a word. There seemed to be nothing to say. She seemed to be drained of all feeling. She felt blank. He thought he detected an air of resignation, a look of calmness in her manner as she moved slowly in the direction of the opening into the street. They stopped and looked at each other. She sighed, and there were no tears in her eyes now. He brushed the back of his hand tenderly over the soft cheeks of the sleeping Gugu and with his dry lips, kissed S'bongile's brow. He lifted her chin slightly with his forefinger and looked into her eyes. They seemed to smile at him. They parted.

Death of a Son

Njabulo S. Ndebele

A T L A S T we got the body, Wednesday. Just enough time for a Saturday funeral. We were exhausted. Empty. The funeral still ahead of us. We had to find the strength to grieve. There had been no time for grief, really. Only much bewilderment and confusion. Now grief. For isn't grief the awareness of loss?

That is why when we finally got the body, Buntu said: "Do you realize our son is dead?" I realized. Our awareness of the death of our first and only child had been displaced completely by the effort to get his body. Even the horrible events that caused the death: we did not think of them, as such. Instead, the numbing drift of things took over our minds: the pleas, letters to be written, telephone calls to be made, telegrams to be dispatched, lawyers to consult, "influential" people to "get in touch with," undertakers to be contacted, so much walking and driving. That is what suddenly mattered: the irksome details that blur the goal (no matter how terrible it is), each detail becoming a door which, once unlocked, revealed yet another door. Without being aware of it, we were distracted by the smell of the skunk and not by what the skunk had done.

We realized something too, Buntu and I, that during the two-week effort to get our son's body, we had drifted apart. For the first time in our marriage, our presence to each other had become a matter of habit. He was there. He'll be there. And I'll be there. But when Buntu said: "Do you realize our son is dead?" he uttered a thought that suddenly brought us together again. It was as if the return of the body of our son was also our coming together. For it was only at that moment that we really began to grieve; as if our lungs had suddenly begun to take in air when just before, we were beginning to suffocate. Something with meaning began to emerge.

We realized. We realized that something else had been happening to us, adding to the terrible events. Yes, we had drifted apart. Yet, our estrangement, just at that moment when we should have been together, seemed disturbingly comforting to me. I was comforted in a manner I did not quite understand.

The problem was that I had known all along that we would have to buy the body anyway. I had known all along. Things would end that way. And when things turned out that way, Buntu could not look me in the eye. For he had said: "Over my dead body! Over my dead body!" as soon as we knew we would be required to pay the police or the government for the release of the body of our child.

"Over my dead body! Over my dead body!" Buntu kept on saying.

Finally, we bought the body. We have the receipt. The police insisted we take it. That way, they would be "protected." It's the law, they said.

I suppose we could have got the body earlier. At first I was confused, for one is supposed to take comfort in the heroism of one's man. Yet, inwardly, I could draw no comfort from his outburst. It seemed hasty. What sense was there to it when all I wanted was the body of my child? What would happen if, as events unfolded, it became clear that Buntu would not give up his life? What would happen? What would happen to him? To me?

For the greater part of two weeks, all of Buntu's efforts, together with friends, relatives, lawyers and the newspapers, were to secure the release of the child's body without the humiliation of having to pay for it. A "fundamental principle."

Why was it difficult for me to see the wisdom of the principle? The worst thing, I suppose, was worrying about what the police may have been doing to the body of my child. How they may have been busy prying it open "to determine the cause of death"?

Would I want to look at the body when we finally got it? To see further mutilations in addition to the "cause of death"? What kind of mother would not want to look at the body of her child? people will ask. Some will say: "It's grief." She is too grief-stricken.

"But still . . . ," they will say. And the elderly among them may say: "Young people are strange."

But how can they know? It was not that I would not want to see the body of my child, but that I was too afraid to confront the horrors of my own imagination. I was haunted by the thought of how useless it had been to have created something. What had been the point of it all? This body filling up with a child. The child steadily growing into something that could be seen and felt. Moving, as it always did, at that time of day when I was all alone at home waiting for it. What had been the point of it all?

How can they know that the mutilation to determine "the cause of death" ripped my own body? Can they think of a womb feeling hunted? Disgorged?

And the milk that I still carried. What about it? What had been the point of it all?

Even Buntu did not seem to sense that that principle, the "fundamental principle," was something too intangible for me at that moment, something that I desperately wanted should assume the form of my child's body. He still seemed far from ever knowing.

I remember one Saturday morning early in our courtship, as Buntu and I walked hand-in-hand through town, window-shopping. We cannot even be said to have been window-shopping, for we were aware of very little that was not ourselves. Everything in those windows was merely an excuse for words to pass between us.

We came across three girls sitting on the pavement, sharing a packet of fish and chips after they had just bought it from a nearby Portuguese cafe. Buntu said: "I want fish and chips too." I said: "So seeing is desire." I said: "My man is greedy!" We laughed. I still remember how he tightened his grip on my hand. The strength of it!

Just then, two white boys coming in the opposite direction suddenly rushed at the girls, and, without warning, one of them kicked the packet of fish and chips out of the hands of the girl who was holding it. The second boy kicked away the rest of what remained in the packet. The girl stood up, shaking her hand as if to throw off the pain in it. Then she pressed it under her armpit as if to squeeze the pain out of it. Meanwhile, the two boys went on their way laughing. The fish and chips lay scattered on the pavement and on the street like stranded boats on a river that had gone dry.

"Just let them do that to you!" said Buntu, tightening once more his grip on my hand as we passed on like sheep that had seen many of their own in the flock picked out for slaughter. We would note the event and wait for our turn. I remember I looked at Buntu, and saw his face was somewhat glum. There seemed no connection between that face and the words of reassurance just uttered. For a while, we went on quietly. It was then that I noticed his grip had grown somewhat limp. Somewhat reluctant. Having lost its self-assurance, it seemed to have been holding on because it had to, not because of a confident sense of possession.

It was not to be long before his words were tested. How could fate work this way, giving to words meanings and intentions they did not carry when they were uttered? I saw that day, how the language of love could so easily be trampled underfoot, or scattered like fish and chips on the pavement, and left stranded and abandoned like boats in a river that suddenly went dry. Never again was love to be confirmed with words. The world around us was too hostile for vows of love. At any moment, the vows could be subjected to the stress of proof. And love died. For words of love need not be tested.

On that day, Buntu and I began our silence. We talked and laughed, of course, but we stopped short of words that would demand proof of action.

Buntu knew. He knew the vulnerability of words. And so he sought to obliterate words with acts that seemed to promise redemption.

On that day, as we continued with our walk in town, that Saturday morning, coming up towards us from the opposite direction, was a burly Boer walking with his wife and two children. They approached Buntu and me with an ominously determined advance. Buntu attempted to pull me out of the way, but I never had a chance. The Boer shoved me out of the way, as if clearing a path for his family. I remember, I almost crashed into a nearby fashion display window. I remember, I glanced at the family walking away, the mother and the father each dragging a child. It was for one of those children that I had been cleared away. I remember, also, that as my tears came out, blurring the Boer family and everything else, I saw and felt deeply what was inside of me: a desire to be avenged.

But nothing happened. All I heard was Buntu say: "The dog!" At that very moment, I felt my own hurt vanish like a wisp of smoke. And as my hurt vanished, it was replaced, instead, by a tormenting desire to sacrifice myself for Buntu. Was it something about the powerlessness of the curse and the desperation with which it had been made? The filling of stunned silence with an utterance? Surely it ate into him, revealing how incapable he was of meeting the call of his words.

And so it was, that that afternoon, back in the township, left to ourselves at Buntu's home, I gave in to him for the first time. Or should I say I offered myself to him? Perhaps from some vague sense of wanting to heal something in him? Anyway, we were never to talk about that event. Never. We buried it alive deep inside of me that afternoon. Would it ever be exhumed? All I vaguely felt and knew was that I had the keys to the vault. That was three years ago, a year before we married.

The cause of death? One evening I returned home from work, particularly tired after I had been covering more shootings by the police in the East Rand. Then I had hurried back to the office in Johannesburg to piece together on my typewriter the violent scenes of the day, and then to file my report to meet the deadline. It was late when I returned home, and when I got there, I found a crowd of people in the yard. They were those who could not get inside. I panicked. What had happened? I did not ask those who were outside, being desperate to get into the house. They gave way easily when they recognized me.

Then I heard my mother's voice. Her cry rose well above the noise. It turned into a scream when she saw me. "What is it, mother?" I asked, embracing her out of a vaguely despairing sense of terror. But she pushed me away with an hysterical violence that astounded me.

"What misery have I brought you, my child?" she cried. At that point, many women in the room began to cry too. Soon, there was much wailing in the room, and then all over the house. The sound of it! The anguish! Understanding, yet eager for knowledge, I became desperate. I had to hold onto something. The desire to embrace my mother no longer had anything to do with comforting her; for whatever she had done, whatever its magnitude, had become inconsequential. I needed to embrace her for all the anguish that tied everyone in the house into a knot. I wanted to be part of that knot, yet I wanted to know what had brought it about.

Eventually, we found each other, my mother and I, and clasped each other tightly. When I finally released her, I looked around at the neighbors and suddenly had a vision of how that anguish had to be turned into a simmering kind of indignation. The kind of indignation that had to be kept at bay only because there was a higher purpose at that moment: the sharing of concern.

Slowly and with a calmness that surprised me, I began to gather the details of what had happened. Instinctively, I seemed to have been gathering notes for a news report.

It happened during the day, when the soldiers and the police that had been patrolling the township in their Casspirs began to shoot in the streets at random. Need I describe what I did not see? How did the child come to die just at that moment when the police and the soldiers began to shoot at random, at any house, at any moving thing? That was how one of our windows was shattered by a bullet. And that was when my mother, who looked after her grandchild when we were away at work, panicked. She picked up the child and ran to the neighbors. It was only when she entered the neighbor's house that she noticed the wetness of the blanket that covered the child she held to her chest as she ran for the sanctuary of neighbors. She had looked at her unaccountably bloody hand, then she noted the still bundle in her arms, and began at that moment to blame herself for the death of her grandchild . . .

Later, the police, on yet another round of shooting, found people gathered at our house. They stormed in, saw what had happened. At first, they dragged my mother out, threatening to take her away unless she agreed not to say what had happened. But then they returned and, instead, took the body of the child away. By what freak of logic did they hope that by this act their carnage would never be discovered?

That evening, I looked at Buntu closely. He appeared suddenly to have grown older. We stood alone in an embrace in our bedroom. I noticed, when I kissed his face, how his once lean face had grown suddenly puffy.

At that moment, I felt the familiar impulse come upon me once more, the impulse I always felt when I sensed that Buntu was in some kind of danger, the impulse to yield something of myself to him. He wore the look of someone struggling to gain control of something. Yet, it was clear he was far from controlling anything. I knew that look. Had seen it many times. It came at those times when I sensed that he faced a wave that was infinitely stronger than he, that it would certainly sweep him away, but that he had to seem to be struggling. I pressed myself tightly to him as if to vanish into him; as if only the two of us could stand up to the wave.

"Don't worry," he said. "Don't worry. I'll do everything in my power to right this wrong. Everything. Even if it means suing the police!" We went silent.

I knew that silence. But I knew something else at that moment: that I had to find a way of disengaging myself from the embrace.

Suing the police? I listened to Buntu outlining his plans. "Legal counsel. That's what we need," he said. "I know some people in Pretoria," he said. As he spoke, I felt the warmth of intimacy between us cooling. When he finished, it was cold. I disengaged from his embrace slowly, yet purposefully. Why had Buntu spoken?

Later, he was to speak again, when all his plans had failed to work: "Over my dead body! Over my dead body!"

He sealed my lips. I would wait for him to feel and yield one day to all the realities of misfortune.

Ours was a home, it could be said. It seemed a perfect life for a young couple: I, a reporter; Buntu, a personnel officer at an American factory manufacturing farming implements. He had traveled to the United States and returned with a mind fired with dreams. We dreamed together. Much time we spent, Buntu and I, trying to make a perfect home. The occasions are numerous on which we paged through *Femina, Fair Lady, Cosmopolitan, Home Garden, Car,* as if somehow we were going to surround our lives with the glossiness in the magazines. Indeed, much of our time was spent window-shopping through the magazines. This time, it was different from the window-shopping we did that Saturday when we courted. This time our minds were consumed by the things we saw and dreamed of owning: the furniture, the fridge, TV, videocassette recorders, washing machines, even a vacuum cleaner and every other imaginable thing that would ensure a comfortable modern life.

Especially when I was pregnant. What is it that Buntu did not buy, then? And when the boy was born, Buntu changed the car. A family, he would say, must travel comfortably.

The boy became the center of Buntu's life. Even before he was born, Buntu had already started making inquiries at white private schools. That was where he would send his son, the bearer of his name.

Dreams! It is amazing how the horrible findings of my newspaper reports often vanished before the glossy magazines of our dreams, how I easily forgot that the glossy images were concocted out of the keys of typewriters, made by writers whose business was to sell dreams at the very moment that death pervaded the land. So powerful are words and pictures that even their makers often believe in them.

Buntu's ordeal was long. So it seemed. He would get up early every morning to follow up the previous day's leads regarding the body of our son. I wanted to go with him, but each time I prepared to go he would shake his head.

"It's my task," he would say. But every evening he returned, empty-handed, while with each day that passed and we did not know where the body of my child was, I grew restive and hostile in a manner that gave me much pain. Yet Buntu always felt compelled to give a report on each day's events. I never asked for it. I suppose it was his way of dealing with my silence.

One day he would say: "The lawyers have issued a court order that the body be produced. The writ of *habeas corpus*."

On another day he would say: "We have petitioned the Minister of Justice."

On yet another he would say: "I was supposed to meet the Chief Security Officer. Waited the whole day. At the end of the day they said I would see him tomorrow if he was not going to be too busy. They are stalling."

Then he would say: "The newspapers, especially yours, are raising the hue and cry. The government is bound to be embarrassed. It's a matter of time."

And so it went on. Every morning he got up and left. Sometimes alone, sometimes with friends. He always left to bear the failure alone.

How much did I care about lawyers, petitions and Chief Security Officers? A lot. The problem was that whenever Buntu spoke about his efforts, I heard only his words. I felt in him the disguised hesitancy of someone who wanted reassurance without asking for it. I saw someone who got up every morning and left not to look for results, but to search for something he could only have found with me.

And each time he returned, I gave my speech to my eyes. And he answered without my having parted my lips. As a result, I sensed, for the first time in my life, a terrible power in me that could make him do anything. And he would never ever be able to deal with that power as long as he did not silence my eyes and call for my voice.

And so, he had to prove himself. And while he left each morning, I learned to be brutally silent. Could he prove himself without me? Could he? Then I got to know, those days, what I'd always wanted from him. I got to know why I have always drawn him into me whenever I sensed his vulnerability.

I wanted him to be free to fear. Wasn't there greater strength that way?

Had he ever lived with his own feelings? And the stress of life in this land: didn't it call out for men to be heroes? And should they live up to it even though the details of the war to be fought may often be blurred? They should.

Yet it is precisely for that reason that I often found Buntu's thoughts lacking in strength. They lacked the experience of strife that could only come from a humbling acceptance of fear and then, only then, the need to fight it.

Me? In a way, I have always been free to fear. The prerogative of being a girl. It was always expected of me to scream when a spider crawled across the ceiling. It was known I would jump onto a chair whenever a mouse blundered into the room.

Then, once more, the Casspirs came. A few days before we got the body back, I was at home with my mother when we heard the great roar of truck engines. There was much running and shouting in the streets. I saw them, as I've always seen them on my assignments: the Casspirs. On five occasions they ran down our street at great speed, hurling tear-gas canisters at random. On the fourth occasion, they got our house. The canister shattered another window and filled the house with the terrible pungent choking smoke that I had got to know so well. We ran out of the house gasping for fresh air.

So, this was how my child was killed? Could they have been the same soldiers? Now hardened to their tasks? Or were they new ones being hardened to their tasks? Did they drive away laughing? Clearing paths for their families? What paths?

And was this our home? It couldn't be. It had to be a little bird's nest waiting to be plundered by a predator bird. There seemed no sense to the wedding pictures on the walls, the graduation pictures, birthday pictures, pictures of relatives, and paintings of lush landscapes. There seemed no sense anymore to what seemed recognizably human in our house. It took only a random swoop to obliterate personal worth, to blot out any value there may have been to the past. In desperation, we began to live only for the moment. I do feel hunted.

It was on the night of the tear gas that Buntu came home, saw what had happened, and broke down in tears. They had long been in the coming . . .

My own tears welled out too. How much did we have to cry to refloat stranded boats? I was sure they would float again.

A few nights later, on the night of the funeral, exhausted, I lay on my bed, listening to the last of the mourners leaving. Slowly, I became conscious of returning to the world. Something came back after it seemed not to have been there for ages. It came as a surprise, as a reminder that we will always live around what will happen. The sun will rise and set, and the ants will do their endless work, until one day the clouds turn gray and rain falls, and even in the township, the ants will fly out into the sky. Come what may.

My moon came, in a heavy surge of blood. And, after such a long time, I remembered the thing Buntu and I had buried in me. I felt it as if it had just entered. I felt it again as it floated away on the surge. I would be ready for another month. Ready as always, each and every month, for new beginnings.

And Buntu? I'll be with him, now. Always. Without our knowing, all the trying events had prepared for us new beginnings. Shall we not prevail?

Dust

Abdelal el Hamamssy

LIFE PROCEEDS according to its normal rhythm: the congestion, calls of the vendors, honking of automobiles, voices of people passing by . . . nothing new. A newspaper vendor cries out the results of yesterday's game. The line at the cooperative store extends all the way to the sidewalk in front of as-Samar coffee shop in Giza Square. Women crowd around the nearby Bata shoe store. At the door of the coffee shop stands Biyumi the shoeshine man from Upper Egypt with his box fastened by a cord to his shoulder. On his face is a frown which long years of toil and deprivation have dug there with zigzag furrows. His glances fly in all directions through the coffee shop on the lookout for any request. He is not in the habit of approaching a customer until actually summoned by him.

Ishaq, the elderly waiter, is on the run, carrying things from his counter to the tables. Nothing new at all. Suddenly, the radio interrupts its normal transmission to broadcast a military bulletin from the supreme military command. Everyone rushes to cluster together under the set, jostling for position with people who had been out in the street. The coffee shop is crammed from corner to corner with masses of people all hanging on the words of the announcer.

"At one-thirty p.m. today the enemy launched an attack on our forces in the two regions of az-Za'farana and as-Sukhna in the Gulf of Suez, employing a number of squadrons from its air force, while some of its naval vessels approached the west coast of the Gulf. Our forces are currently resisting the aggressors."

The normal rhythm has changed, even though the announcer's voice was unusually calm, with none of the emotion customary in announcements of that type. At once, there are comments everywhere critical of the long stalemate. What's the use of resisting? The years of dishonor have lasted too long. We're about to expire. Let's reclaim our land and honor, come hell or high water. The commander promised a decisive year of making war or peace; so let him do it, come what may.

Biyumi the shoeshine man scrutinizes the people's faces around him, trying to understand what their comments imply. They wish for death when each family has lost someone. The withdrawal has left a martyr in every household and a wound in every heart. Grief presses Biyumi's heart. Fears spread throughout him. Delight of my heart, where are you? You who compensate for the toil and humiliation, for a lifetime lost in the dust . . . Mahrus' last letter said he was there . . . in az-Za'farana, the place the announcement mentioned. His letter had mentioned nothing but his longings and desires . . . and the toughness of the boys on the alert in the trenches with the promise to fulfil the promise.

"Tomorrow the war will be over, Father. We will clear away the nightmare choking Egypt. I'll get you whatever you want. You'll have the small store to run. You can recover from all your hustling around and suffering. My one dream is to live to repay some part of it to you."

I don't want anything, Mahrus. As long as you're safe, nothing else matters. Indeed, everything else has become insignificant. You plunge into the quagmires of mud and bring forth a flower. I will sacrifice my life if you can have a chance to enjoy your youth and return.

His procession of sufferings parades before his mind. Ever since he came from his home in Upper Egypt, fleeing from poverty and need, and from the shadow of a crime which tempted him—to kill the usurper of his land who had put on the deed of sale the signature of his unconscious father, using as witnesses some bad men. He had been deprived of his right to the feddan and a half left from their ancestral lands. Conscience forced him to flee from the dishonor of killing his brother, even though this brother was the usurper. All Cairo had done for him was to turn its back on him.

The city's modern buildings intimidated him and wore away his stratagems. But he was not going to return home defeated, and so he set off to tour with his box, wiping the dirt from other people's shoes with shoe polish.

The men sit down again and resume their games and chatter, but there is a wave of expectation in the air. Biyumi is torn apart inside by his worries. Az-Za'farana stretches out before him wherever he looks. It is part of his every sensation and of all his surroundings. He pretends not to notice more than one request. He is not in a receptive mood. When Mr. Abd Rabbih calls to him again, bristling with disapproval at his having ignored his first call, Biyumi almost shouts back at him: Shut up! My son's over there. He does not say it, but the old man Ishaq can discern it in his agitated looks. He glances at him compassionately. When Biyumi's eyes meet his, Ishaq underscores the look by saying with a burst of optimistic encouragement. "Right now Mahrus is plowing through those dirty rascals. I promise you, Biyumi, that the day he returns victorious, I'll get you a bride as beautiful as the moon. You'll be like a young man again with her, Biyumi, you father of Mahrus."

He tries to smile at Ishaq's teasing, but Ishaq has scraped the scab off a deep-seated, old wound, one which has never stopped bleeding inside. He does not want to be paired with a bride at this late date after his youth has vanished leaving only aches. Ishaq, who could take the place of Zuhayra? Who is equal even to a clipping from her fingernail? It is fifteen years since Zuhayra passed away. She was a model wife, perfect. She shared in his hardships and poverty with a spirit which accepted graciously what was inevitable. At first she gave him a child who did not turn out well. Then came Mahrus. He was flawless, a true descendant of his grandfathers. Some years later she breathed her last in another childbirth that had complications. She left him alone forever. He dedicated his life to Mahrus. He was his mother, father, and friend. When he was a child he carried him on his shoulder as he made his rounds of the coffee-houses, curbs, and shops. The young boy was well-behaved and pleasant-tempered, unlike the older one who was a discipline problem. He was soon lured away into a life in the streets. When Mahrus asked his father to buy him a box and some tins of polish so he could join the profession and help him, Biyumi gave him a blow that almost broke his ribs. "You're going to be something else, you son of ancient heroes."

He, to this very day, hates Zubayda, the midwife of al-Manawati alley, blindly, because she offered to get Mahrus a job as a servant in the home of a rich woman. She told him that Mahrus would be well provided for, while he, as Mahrus' father, collected the generous salary every month. Satan himself could not have glared at her more ferociously when he screamed at her, "We sons of Upper Egypt may scratch away at stones, but we don't work in people's houses, woman."

Music and patriotic songs are being broadcast. Before the announcer can get his first words out, all the people jam together under the set again.

"In response to the treacherous aggression of the enemy against our forces, both in Egypt and Syria, some of our air force squadrons are currently engaged in bombing the enemy's bases and military targets in the occupied lands." When the announcer falls silent, Biyumi looks at the faces around him. All the eyes say it is not just a question of a brief attack followed by a retaliatory raid. It seems the matter goes beyond this. His heart is beating irregularly. Mahrus is there. Will he return? He remembers his son's last words: "If we go to war this time, we'll win, Father. The situation is totally different. We've learned from experience. The age of panic and confusion is over. Everything is carefully planned and evaluated now."

His eyes are wet with tears he tried to confine to his heart. May God preserve you, my boy; you are so young. For five years you have been with the best of the young men of Egypt in the trenches exposed to fiery heat, blowing sand, and the agony of waiting; while every day, my heart has been dying.

He leaves the coffee-house to roam around the streets. Fears and worries rage within him. He sees a bunch of people gathered at a juice stand. He hurries over to pick up the latest news.

"Supplementing announcement number two: the planes of our air force have successfully completed their missions and scored hits on enemy positions. All of our planes have returned safely to their bases except for one."

"This is really turning out to be something, men," says one of the people standing there. His statement inspires various predictions and comments. The day has come. It's come. The predictions of good news are going to come true. We were told there would be something decisive, and here it is. When the way was clear, he really did it. That's the way Egypt is; she keeps quiet until people think she has lost her voice. Egypt's like that. She's patient to the point they think she's died. When she does speak, thunder rolls down. Lava flies far and wide. When she gets moving, impossible odds are overcome.

"We are all ready to sacrifice our lives so Egypt may live," said a girl wearing a blue school uniform and holding a book bag in front of her. Faces smile and light up. Biyumi does not smile. The comments bore into him. They bring him face to face with danger. "We will all die so Egypt may live," the young girl said. I would die a thousand times for the sake of Egypt, but let Mahrus live. You are my dream, my life. What else remains? The other boy has entered a life of crime, lost in the night, saddled with his previous offenses and prison record. He sold out his birthright. You are the authentic heir. He was an offspring for Satan. You carry on the proud line of your grandfathers.

He returns once more to the coffee house. He tries to bury his worries in the shoe polish, unsuccessfully. Mahrus and az-Za'farana and fear of the unknown . . .

One communiqué follows another. Each one grabs hold of his heart and squeezes it. He feels ashamed whenever he sees the glowing love for Egypt in everyone's eyes. All these people crowding around the radio have sons there, and brothers or relatives. Why are you the only one who is listless and depressed? Is Mahrus the only worthy son Egypt has produced? How do I know? Perhaps inside they are like me: drained, or they are thinking only of the nation. But do they not have as much invested in their children as I do in Mahrus? He remembers Mahrus' words when he told him of his fears after the commander-in-chief had said this year would be decisive—either for war or peace. At that time, the word 'war' had tormented him. His son, a chip off the old block, had told him, "If we all thought this way, Father, Egypt wouldn't be Egypt. Egypt owes its continued existence to the fact that generation after generation we have given our blood to defend its soil. Each of us can only be true to himself insofar as he is true to his nation." He had not understood the words at that time. But he sensed they were true and expressed a reality. All the same he could not accuse his emotions of being any less real.

From inside the coffee house, he looks at the automobiles whizzing through the streets driven by trendy young men with long flowing hair and dangling chains. He asks himself why they don't round up all these pests and send them off to the front. Why should Mahrus from al-Manawati alley—after his father shed blood so he could get a diploma—why should he defend people like these? If Mahrus had been there beside him now, he would have asked him. Perhaps he would have considered this question illogical too?

All the prognostications become irrelevant. Reality shows her face. The decisive announcement bursts forth.

"Our forces have succeeded in crossing the Suez Canal in numerous sectors and have gained control over the enemy's fortified positions there. The Egyptian flag has been raised over the eastern bank of the Canal."

The crowds do not wait for the conclusion of the announcement. Joy roars out. We've crossed. We've crossed. Hearts embrace hearts, and tears hug tears. Words swarm out of the Egyptian consciousness. It is a return of the spirit. The spirit has returned. The hour has drawn nigh, and the moon split as on Judgment Day.

The infectious joy spreads to Biyumi. He wants to scream at all of them, "It's my son who made the crossing. Mahrus is there. My boy." But he suppresses the eager desire. Everyone there has some personal tie to the event. It is not just Mahrus who crossed.

Ishaq the elderly waiter makes his way through the throngs of people to where Biyumi is standing. He embraces him. "Mahrus crossed, Biyumi. Mahrus is in Sinai, you father of Mahrus." He says that and goes back inside. He takes the picture of the commander-in-chief down from the wall.

He waves it in front of the swarms of people who shout out in victory. Then he puts it back in its place.

Biyumi feels a longing to go to his room in the Manawati alley to embrace the picture of Mahrus hanging over his bare bed. The alley has come to life again. Trills of joy greet him when he appears at the entry. They are the same trills which burst out in joy the day Mahrus succeeded in getting a diploma in commerce. That day the people in the neighborhood handed out soft drinks in honor of Biyumi who had fathered a son equal to those of the upper classes.

Ashraf, a friend of Mahrus, comes up to him and embraces him merrily. He says, "I'd give my whole life to be there now beside Mahrus, Uncle Biyumi. They wouldn't take me. They used my heart ailment as an excuse and deprived me of the moment of a lifetime. They discharged me after a year of military service. And here's my heart roaring like a lion's."

He goes into his room and presses his face against everything related to Mahrus. He lets his tears flow. When he goes out into the neighborhood, he finds the children going around in processions singing:

> My country, my country, my love and heart are yours.
> Egypt, Mother of all lands, it is you I seek and desire.

Kamal the barber says to him, "The boys have turned out to be men and that's a fact, Biyumi. They've raised high Egypt's head." A passerby in the alley says, "We're not worthy of wiping the dust from their feet."

Biyumi closes his eyes so he can picture the sons of Egypt and Mahrus with them, plunging forward through the muck of the destroyed defense line. He sees them in the midst of hellish danger planting the flag. He can not suppress his emotions. Taking the people of the area as his witnesses, men, women, and children, he points to the shoeshine box in his hand and says, "By the tomb of Zuhayra, people, when the boys come home safe, I'll clean their shoes myself. Yes, I must polish Mahrus' army shoes myself. I'm his father."

He sees before him the face of Mahrus protesting. His boy had never given him the chance to do it. Although he polished everyone else's shoes, his high-minded son thought it wrong for a father to polish his son's shoes, even if that was his trade. "Some things just aren't done, Father." He resolves in his heart that he will do it this time. He himself will clean Mahrus' army boots. "It's not just for your sake this time, son."

Part Three

CULTURE CLASH
Modernization, Urbanization, Westernization

PARABLES

In Global Cultures you can learn several things about "Third World development" very quickly—most quickly in the form of parables. First, development is not for little people. For small farmers and peasants, for workers, it is either a dream—as in the story "Clamor of Innocence"—or a nightmare—as in "Close to the Earth." Second, it divides people, extending and rigidifying class differences, separating men and women, putting unimaginable modern educations between parents and children. Third, words like "capitalism" do not do justice to its irrationalities. (As **MOACYR SCLIAR** implies in his "A Brief History of Capitalism," the word hardly covers the situation wherein the owners of property are so insecure and crazy that they try to destroy their property and the workers rise to the occasion to *prevent* them—without even getting paid for their trouble.) Fourth, "Third World development" inspires further developments that enlarge local and regional mistakes and messes into global ones, as in "And We Sold the Rain."

A collection of **SALONI NARANG**'s stories, *The Colored Bangles*, was issued by Three Continents Press in 1983. Narang, the daughter of a Kashmiri mother and a Punjabi father, is one of the few writers from the north Indian state of Uttar Pradesh to be published in America. Her writing language is English, which she learned in the Irish Convent School of the Loretto Order and the University of Delhi, and she travels frequently in the United States. But this cosmopolitan is also deeply connected to traditional Indian story-telling. "Though these stories," she has said of her collection, "pick up echoes only from the Northern half of India, this Northern half which colors my imagination is a varied canvas, and my backdrops shift from the Westernized sitting rooms of the educated elite to the thatch atop the mud huts of rural India; from an anglicized manager of a West Bengal tea estate face to face with the horror of Naxalite [Communist] terrorism to the emotional volatility of pastoral Punjab." "Close to the Earth" is based upon a true story from this pastoral Punjab.

Like so many of the brilliant generation of Central and South American writers born circa 1930–1940—like the Brazilian Moacyr Scliar, born in 1937, whose biography I sketched briefly in the last section—**CARMEN NARANJO**, from Cartago, Costa Rica, born in 1931, is a very public figure. She has often been honored by her government, one that has been consistently stable and open enough to admit satire of the sort in "And We Sold the Rain." Naranjo has published novels, volumes of short stories, poetry, plays, essays, all known throughout Central America, where she has been active as Secretary of Cultural Affairs for Costa Rica and as head of the Editorial Universitaria Centroamericana, the most important publishing organization in Central America. Her *There Never Was a Once Upon a Time* appeared in English in 1989.

Of the same generation is **LYZANDRO CHAVEZ ALFARO**, from Bluefields, Nicaragua, born in 1929, who is both a writer and a political activist. His first novel, *Tragame terra* (1969), won him literary prizes and fame in Central America and Spain, but it—like two volumes of short stories and two of his poems—has yet to be translated into English. He grew up under the dictatorial regimes of the Somoza family (1937–1979), but he was allied with their revolutionary successors, the Sandinistas, who were committed to social and land reform, and he served that government as ambassador to Hungary. In "Clamor of Innocence," the narrator reminisces about the period between the Second World War and the Korean War, when he was an adolescent, and recaptures a fantasy of modernization, a fantasy about how his peasant family, his backward country, might be lifted miraculously into mechanization. Written from the standpoint of an older, wiser, and disillusioned man, the story is a parable of the harsh realities that really did face Nicaraguans when they took their destiny into their own political hands after the Somozas.

A Brief History of Capitalism

Moacyr Scliar

MY FATHER was a Communist and a car mechanic. A good Communist, according to his comrades, but a lousy mechanic according to consensus. As a matter of fact, so great was his inability to handle cars that people wondered why he had chosen such an occupation. He used to say it had been a conscious choice on his part; he believed in manual work as a form of personal development, and he had confidence in machines and in their capability to liberate man and launch him into the future, in the direction of a freer, more desirable life. Roughly, that's what he meant.

I used to help my father in his car repair shop. Since I was an only son, he wanted me to follow in his footsteps. There wasn't, however, much that I could do; at that time I was eleven years old, and almost as clumsy as he was at using tools. Anyhow, for the most part, there was no call for us to use them since there wasn't much work coming our way. We would sit talking and thus while away the time. My father was a great storyteller; enthralled, I would listen to his accounts of the uprising of the Spartacists, and of the rebellion led by the fugitive slave Zambi. In those moments his eyes would glitter. I would listen, deeply affected by his stories; often, my eyes would fill with tears.

Once in awhile a customer appeared. Usually a Party sympathizer (my father's comrades didn't own cars), who came to Father more out of a desire to help than out of need. These customers played it safe, though: It was always some minor repair, like fixing the license plate securely, or changing the blades of the windshield wipers. But even such simple tasks turned out to be extraordinarily difficult for Father to perform; sometimes it would take him a whole day to change a distributor point. And the car would drive away with the engine misfiring (needless to say, its owner would never set foot in our repair shop again). If it weren't for the financial problems (my mother had to support us by taking in sewing), I wouldn't have minded the lack of work too much. I really enjoyed those rap sessions with my father. In the morning I would go to school; but as soon as I came home, I would run to the repair shop, which was near our house. And there I would find Father reading. Upon my arrival, he would set his book aside, light his pipe, and start telling me his stories. And there we would stay until Mother came to call us for dinner.

One day when I arrived at our repair shop, there was a car there, a huge, sparkling, luxury car. None of the Party sympathizers, not even the wealthiest among them, owned a car like that. Father told me that the monster car had stalled right in front of the shop. The owner then left it there, under his care, saying he would be back late in the afternoon. And what's wrong with it? I asked, somewhat alarmed, sensing a foul-up in the offing.

"I wish I knew." Father sighed. "Frankly, I don't know what's wrong with it. I already took a look but couldn't find the defect. It must be something minor, probably the carburetor is clogged up, but . . . I don't know, I just don't know what it is."

Dejected, he sat down, took a handkerchief out of his pocket, and wiped his forehead. Come on, I said, annoyed at his passivity, it's no use your sitting there.

He got up and the two of us took a look at the enormous engine, so clean, it glittered. Isn't it a beauty? remarked my father with the pleasure of an owner who took pride in his car.

Yes, it was a beauty—except that he couldn't open the carburetor. I had to give him a hand; three hours later, when the man returned, we were still at it.

He was a pudgy, well-dressed man. He got out of a taxi, his face already displaying annoyance. I expected him to be disgruntled, but never for a moment did I imagine what was to happen next.

At first the man said nothing. Seeing that we weren't finished yet, he sat down on a stool and watched us. A moment later he stood up; he examined the stool on which he had sat.

"Dirty. This stool is dirty. Can't you people even offer your customers a decent chair to sit on?"

We made no reply. Neither did we raise our heads. The man looked around him.

"A real dump, this place. A sty. How can you people work amid such filth?"

We, silent.

"But that's the way everything is," the man went on. "In this country that's the way it is. Nobody wants to do any work, nobody wants to get his act together. All people ever think of is booze, women, the Carnival, soccer. But to get down to work? Never."

Where's the wrench? asked Father in a low, restrained voice. Over there, by your side, I said. Thanks, he said, and resumed fiddling with the carburetor.

"You people want nothing to do with a regular, steady job." The man sounded increasingly more irritated. "You people will never get out of this filth. Now, take me, for instance. I started at the bottom. But nowadays I'm a rich man. Very rich. And do you know why? Because I was clean, well organized, hardworking. This car here, do you think it's the only one I own? Do you?"

Tighten the screw, said Father, tighten it really tight.

"I'm talking to you!" yelled the man, fuming. "I'm asking you a question! Do you think this is the only car I own? That's what you think, isn't it? Well, let me tell you something, I own two other cars. Two other cars! They are in my garage. I don't use them. Because I don't want to. If I wanted, I could abandon this car here in the middle of the street and get another one. Well, I wouldn't get it myself; I would have someone get it for me. Because I have a chauffeur, see? That's right. I drive because I enjoy driving, but I have a chauffeur. I don't *have* to drive, I don't *need* this car. If I wanted to, I could junk this fucking car, you hear me?"

Hand me the pipe wrench, will you? said Father. The small one.

The man was now standing quite close to us. I didn't look at him, but I could feel his breath on my arm.

"Do you doubt my word? Do you doubt that I can smash up this car? Do you?"

I looked at the man. He was upset. When his eyes met mine, he seemed to come to his senses; only for a moment, though; he opened his eyes wide.

"Do you doubt it? That I can smash up this fucking car? Give me a hammer. Quick! Give me a hammer!"

He searched for a hammer but couldn't find one (it would have been a miracle had he found one; even we could never find the tools in our shop). Without knowing what he was doing, he gave the car door a kick; soon followed by another, then another.

"That's what I've been telling you," he kept screaming. "That I'll smash up this fucking car! That's what I've been telling you."

Ready, said Father. I looked at him; he was pale, beads of sweat were running down his face. Ready? I asked, not getting it. Ready, he said. You can now start the engine.

The man, panting, was looking at us. Opening the car door, I sat at the steering wheel and turned on the ignition. Incredible: The engine started. I revved it up. The shop was filled with the roar of the engine.

My father stood mopping his face with his dirty handkerchief. The man, silent, kept looking at us. How much I owe you? finally he asked. Nothing, said my father. What do you mean, nothing? Suspicious, the man frowned. Nothing, said my father, it costs you nothing, it's on the house. Then the man, opening his wallet, pulled out a bill.

"Here, for a shot of rum."

"I don't drink," said my father without touching the money.

The man replaced the bill in his wallet, which he then put into his pocket. Without a word he got into his car, and, revving the engine, drove away.

For a moment Father stood motionless, in silence. Then he turned to me.

"This," he said in a hoarse voice, a voice that wasn't his, "is capitalism."

No, it wasn't. That wasn't capitalism. I wished it were capitalism—but it was not. Unfortunately not. It was something else. Something I didn't even dare to think about.

Close to the Earth

Saloni Narang

I T I S a beautiful country, my country. Never has nature manifested herself with such abandoned pride, never has the earth borne the traces of passionate love with such splendour. Caressed, repudiated, and loved in turn, my country stands: lushly verdant, heart-breakingly arid, and awesomely majestic. Many-hued is my country, and many-hued are my people. Creamy white, honey skinned, ebony black, and golden brown are my people, and the earth is alive with echoes of their many moods. It echoes their gaiety, their sorrow, their anger, their restraint. Lush green vies with sombre brown, awesome white towers above the rush of blue waters. It is a beautiful country, my country.

And in my country there is a land in which the earth sings with a pride unequalled by any land. It is the land of the five rivers, the land of plenty, the land of a strong and virile people. Hot-blooded, sentimental, simple-hearted people, these people of the land of the Punjab.

This is the story of the most sentimental, the most virile and the most hot-blooded of them all. A man named Sawan Singh. He was a big powerful man, whose fifty-two years sat lightly on his shoulders. His strength was proverbial, as was his generosity. Laughter came to him easily, so did a quick rush of anger. He was proud of his land, proud of his birth, and, most of all, he was proud of his family.

A small family, his. Only two stalwart sons. He had married a gentle, fragile girl in his youth, and had loved her with all the fiery passion that only a hot blooded Punjabi can give. She was the only one who never fell prey to his volatile temper. With her, he was unfailingly gentle and tender, and she returned his passion with unquestioning adoration. Too shy to voice her love, she let her eyes speak for her, and he basked in the adoration of those eyes, becoming increasingly self-confident, dynamic, and successful day by day. She presented him with two sons, then, two years later, she died. He never remarried. Mistresses he had in plenty. He drained the cup of life with enjoyment, like a true connoisseur, but his ardent, sentimental heart could never conceive of enthroning another woman in place of his deeply mourned wife.

Left to him were his sons: a cherished legacy. He brought them up with stern discipline, watered by an abundance of love. Boys to be proud of— broad of shoulder, tall, good-looking—fine strapping lads. Very alike in looks, but totally different in temperament. The younger son, Atma Singh, had his father's flashing eyes, quick temper, a penchant for trouble, and a positive genius for arousing his father's wrath. He revolted early from his father's uncompromising discipline, incurred many a beating, and returned unscathed to the battlefield. Strong willed, like his father, he asserted his untamed, independent spirit at every opportunity. But in spite of frequent clashes the father could not but feel a joy in this son. He seemed to fill the house, this younger son. With his buoyant step, engaging laugh, and easy familiarity, he had an irresistible charm. There was a contagious joyousness about him. He was impetuous, easily ignited, warm, loving and generous.

As a foil to this impetuous brother, was the older son, Ram Singh. Gentle, thoughtful and considerate was this son, and his quiet goodness was the pivot of their home. Fearless, armed with his understanding and sympathy, he used his innate sympathy and understanding as a mediator between the two impassioned hotheads he loved so dearly. But for his gentle, almost imperceptible control, the father and younger son would have caused irreparable injury to each other. He had that rare gift of communication, where just to talk to him was to understand oneself better. He accepted his father's whims and dictates with typical grace. Yielding caused him so little discomfort and gave his father so much satisfaction. Not that he couldn't, on occasion, bend his father's will to his own. He did it with such gentle tack, that the father was scarcely aware of the manipulation. But it was seldom that Ram Singh sought to influence his father, and certainly never for himself did he wield this influence. He did it only to extricate his turbulent brother from his father's wrath or to benefit some worthy petitioner. No one who sought his help left disappointed, no petitioner left unheard. Quiet, self-effacing, he was nevertheless a pillar of strength to his father, who consulted him at every turn. Towards his younger brother, Ram Singh had an almost fatherly love, and watched and protected him with true parental concern. He took his mother's place, this gentle son, and reaped a rich harvest of love from his family.

It came about that Atma Singh, being brilliant, won a scholarship to the Agricultural Institute in the big city. Ram Singh married a quiet, efficient woman, who in time presented him with three children and looked after his father and himself with admirable efficiency.

The house seemed empty without Atma Singh. The shouts of laughter, the heated discussions on irrelevant matters, that turbulence in the atmosphere, was all gone. Even the colourful, volatile father seemed subdued. He had got too used to the constant clash of wills, and deprived of a satisfactory opponent, vented his spleen on the farmhands. The fields rang with his imaginative, vivid abuses, and many a vocabulary was enriched in consequence.

In the evenings, sitting in the stilled silence of the dying day, soothed by the gurgle of his hookah, the sentimental father's eyes would fill with tears when he thought of his younger son, with his bold, flashing eyes, in a far off city. He dreamed of the day his son would return and he and his boys would work together. He had already chosen a girl for his son— a high-spirited beauty, his best friend's daughter. In her he will meet his match, he chuckled to himself agreeably. Besides, she is a strong girl and will give him many children.

And puffing contentedly, he dreamed away the many evenings till his son's return. At last the day dawned, and Atma Singh returned, his new big-city confidence draped about him with elegance. The father's pride knew no bounds as he watched this self-assured stranger alight from the train. Atma Singh touched his father's feet with grave respect, then gravity abandoned, he flung his arms around, first his father, then his brother, hugging them in turn, laughing, jubilant, his eyes shining, his face glowing with all his transparent happiness at being home again. Old friends, relatives, servants, they were all there, crowding around, voicing their joy, being affectionately hugged and punched in turn. The whole crowd rolled, like one large body, homeward, to continue the long-planned, long-awaited celebration. The little township rang with merry-making. The fatted calf was killed. Good food, good wine, had never flowed so freely. Never had men seen such celebration, or witnessed such gaiety. The night vibrated to the intoxicating beat of the bhangra and the men danced till dawn. The wedding date was set, the dowry agreed upon to mutual satisfaction.

The father's cup of joy had overflowed. Then began the clashes. First it was the question of the tractor, then it was the aerial spraying of the crops with insecticide. One disagreement after another. In the fields, in the house, frayed tempers, a total disinclination to compromise; father and son simply could not work together amicably. To begin with, the father willed himself with superhuman forbearance, to listen to his son's new-fangled ideas. But to listen, and to listen only once, was all that he could school himself to do.

The young coxcomb! He wanted to replace the well-tried and so obviously successful methods of his forefathers with some ridiculous, untried, classroom techniques. And not only replace, but replace without any consideration to the cost involved. Twenty thousand rupees for a tractor! And his fields to be sprayed with poison gas. Impossible. This pitiful little spawn of his loins sought to instruct him on the profession he had followed from his infancy. God in heaven. This was too much for his self-acknowledged superhuman patience! In vain did Ram Singh reason, pacify and beseech. In vain did he marshall all his mediating skill. They were both equally tactless. The inevitable happened. Beside himself with anger, Sawan Singh partitioned the land of his forefathers and banished his recalcitrant son from his sight. The marriage celebrations were suspended, the intended bride married another.

In vain did Ram Singh plead.

"Father, he is young. For many years he has been saturated with those ideas so alien to you. Give him understanding. Surely, it was for these very new ideas that you let him be torn away from the family hearth. Surely, it was for this very learning he spent those lonely years in an unfriendly city. Now would you deny him his learning? Would you turn him out for justifying his years of hard work? He is young. Time will sift the impractical ideas and leave him with an ideal synthesis of the old and the new. Give him time. With a little understanding he will inevitably bow to your will."

"Silence!" thundered the implacable father. "I forbid the mention of his name in my house. He who acknowledges his existence is my enemy. From now on I have only one son."

And so it was that the house fell silent again. The father's terrible wrath lodged in every nook and corner, forbidding disobedience. Atma Singh might never have existed. Except in memory. The father's stubborn pride ignored his wounded heart, and the ignored wound festered to bitterness. True to his word, he never mentioned his son or his bitterly hurt pride, but he never ceased to think of both. Ram Singh, in turn, longed for the sight of the brother he had loved, protected, and reared with such brotherly pride. He loved his volatile young brother no less than he loved his stormy father. He felt heartrendingly torn in two. Habit kept him obedient and ever mindful of his father's wishes, but his heart inspired him to constant effort at mending this tragic breach.

Troubled and distressed, Ram Singh was walking home one evening, and walking home, met his brother. Not to acknowledge him was out of the question. They embraced again and again, and loathe to lose this heaven-sent opportunity, they went to the nearby cinema together in search of a little privacy.

In a small town can any act remain undetected?

Ram Singh returned to face, for the first time, his father's unreasoned, uncontrolled anger. Ever since he had heard of this act of perfidy, Sawan Singh's blood had been pounding in his head. His hands had been itching to shake his traitorous son like the rat he had proved to be. With redoubled fury he watched Ram Singh approach. Disloyalty, and from this son! What a contemptible hypocrite this son had turned out to be. All that seeming obedience while he betrays me the moment my back is turned. This is how he has repaid my love. Make me the laughing stock of the whole town, will he? I'll show them how I treat a traitor. Die traitor! And with blind, insane rage, the father lifted his kirpan and slashed at the traitor in front of him.

It was the compassion in those dying eyes that jerked him back to sanity. With horror he watched the ebbing life of his favourite son. The enormity of his anguish hit him like a blow, and he knelt. Gently, gently, he cradled his child. His life, his whole future lay in those dimmed eyes, and he watched the light of those eyes fade forever.

It is a hot-blooded land, the land of the Punjab, where anguished remorse stalks silently behind pride, and where a father died that day with his son, leaving an empty shell to walk, talk, and tend the silent fields; an empty shell to live among men, and gaze with unseeing eyes at the beautiful land he had once loved so well.

Clamor of Innocence

Lizandro Chávez Alfaro

TOWARD THE end of the trip, after we had crossed the bay under several downpours and the glare of the sun was drying the moisture from his sombrero, Don Abelino said that all this would be changing soon, unless the devil himself pulled some impossible Axis counteroffensive out of his hat.

In spite of my adolescent confusion, I understood that "all this" meant these miserable six-hour crossings: half a day of slow sailing exposed to the elements, reduced to the austerity of a weather-beaten rowboat, the entire weight of our sluggish motion pressing on our very bones.

His fervor and concentration made it unmistakably clear which approaching change he meant: he was referring to the imminent victory of the Allies, who were pleasurably occupied just then with the demolition of Munich and Cologne.

What I still couldn't grasp was what connection could bridge the distance between those victories and this grim advance into a headwind toward his little dominion of swampland.

Innocently figuring, I tried to make out the hidden common denomi-

nator of these two terms and me, or of these two terms and him; the only
thing I got was a feeling of stupidity, a feeling that everything was fragile.

I saw the shore approaching, brimming with green, with no border-
line between water and vegetation; the overhanging branches touching the
waves presented a façade that looked impenetrable. In back of me, past
the man who worked the oar, the humidity blurred the contours of the
jutting rocks, and the opposite shore was lead grey and spattered with
white at the furthermost point where the harbor lay.

From the prow came the faint odor of tobacco in Don Abelino's pipe,
which he had put out and relit a hundred times. He was calmly anchored
in another of those withdrawn moods that separated his orders or his rare
outbreaks of enthusiasm, always expressed with only a marginal interest in receiving an answer, much less in making himself understood. Up
to that time he had granted me placid glances and wandering talk, both
subject to his strict rule of concealing affection. I had granted him my
involuntary imitation and an ever-sincere expectancy for his breaks in the
silence: a kind of distant watchfulness.

We were entering the channel: a narrow waterway of little depth,
hacked out of the mangrove swamp, which lay between a creek and the
supposedly solid ground. All the work of men with axes, machetes, and
shovels kept getting lost in the renovations imposed there by time; the
shores were filled with crayfish, the water with toadfish, which raised little
clouds of mud as they fluttered away. It was a winding strait, still-subdued
by the pride of a natural order that bore no relation to machines. The stability of this primitive, contemptuous indifference was shaken somewhat
when Don Abelino, his voice resonating through the swamp, proclaimed
his scheme of widening the channel so that in the abundant postwar era
an amphibious boat could sail in and out.

I kept staring at the muck on the shore through which crayfish had
bored, but Don Abelino's compelling scheme forced me to recall quickly
what few facts I had gathered thus far about amphibious boats: they had
a propeller and tires, a rudder and a steering wheel, an anchor and brakes,
a keel and a chassis—to which I added the roar of its motor, penetrating
the swamp like an announcement that even our little backwater would be
visited by Victory.

At the landing I stayed behind to pet all the dogs on the property while
he went off across the level, hard-packed sand, a knot of insects whirling
around his head. The main house was built on stakes, narrow, mold-
covered posts, which aimed to save it not only from the water but from the
swarms of gnats. From its elevated corridors I could see the cattle grazing
in complete accord with this semiaquatic life, the horizon of palm trees

growing in floodwaters, and the overwhelming image of the mechanical prodigy rolling around, sailing, unstoppable; land and water mastered by a single invention, something heretofore found only in foreign lands, the protagonist of remote troop landings and patrol operations. Transposed from news reports, where I had seen it fixed on black and white paper, to that plane of existence corresponding to the rhythm of my breath, the amphibian reached its state of perfection, if not its absolute reality. As I imagined it hurling jets of mud and water into the air before or below me, it left the realm of possibility to become something necessary, inevitable. The scattered events of war found their precise form; until then I had understood them only as the vague repercussions of a clash of numbers—30 divisions, say, against 27,400 prisoners or dead. El Alamein, Saint-Lo, Guadalcanal, Stalingrad—the geography of fantasy was transfigured, trembling under a soundless explosion. Don Abelino called out to me from his room. Sitting in an armchair, he paused from reading his magazine, On Guard. With the same hand that slipped his bifocals onto the bridge of his nose, he indicated the pile of loose papers I ought to read and contemplate—thereby participating in the devotion and painstaking care with which he had separated them with a razor blade and perhaps even arranged them in order of presentation.

I withdrew to a corner where I could better immerse myself in the collection of articles and prints, sensing that beneath his cold offering he was proposing to share something that I was now in line to inherit. I learned that he had been following the amphibian since it had first appeared, that with these clippings I was receiving the illustrated history of a dream: conceived in the esoteric regions of eternity, definitively passed on through a compilation of fragments, preserved in material form for this album dedicated to a heroic kinsman. Restrained by our unspoken rule against getting carried away by emotion, we read separately, at the distance demanded by habit, but holding out new lines of contact on behalf of the amphibian, viewed here from every angle, described in each of its capacities—above all, so full of promise, like one betrothed. The anticipated re-uses of so much war material included flamethrowers for fighting plagues of insects, engines of every class of horsepower, hangars convertible to silos or stables, parachute cloth available for anyone who would still want to travel by sailboat, and sparklers for Christmas celebrations.

But out of this splendid inventory, we coveted only this one vehicle made to order for our swampy coastal terrain. Without taking out the pipe wedged between his loose, yellowed teeth, he asked me what I thought about all this; yes, I said, we would have to wait for the final stroke of victory, and then there would be public auctions in some marketplace of the victorious world.

It had been Don Abelino's custom to maintain the solitude of his walks around the estate. Laconic, rigid, he would rebuff any suggestions of companionship and suggest instead that I could more fittingly befriend the swamps roundabout. Quite studious in my lonely apprenticeship, I would improvise spears and fishhooks, watching him askance as he went off in his cowhide gaiters with his machete in a sheath, riding on a sluggish horse as he skillfully skirted the quagmires. Yet during this vacation—perhaps believing that I was showing acceptable signs of growth, or thinking that we were now fellow communicants partaking of a common desire— we went out together almost daily to fulfill our uncertain task of invoking the future. We scattered phrases into air exposed to abrupt occupations of sun and rain: the DUKW now showing advantages over the LVT in dense brush; the tires of one versus the spiked treads of the other; how the former had performed in Isigny and the latter in Guadalcanal. We speculated about geological similarities between Luzon and the muck on which we stood, sometimes with water up to our chests. When there remained no other task to ascribe to our pacified amphibian, we would lapse into silence like addicts sunken in vice, although each of us would continue polishing his part of the hallucination.

Shortly before my vacation ended we returned to the port town. Berlin had fallen. The ceremony for the opening of the school year included a solemn expression of celebration. On the stage of the auditorium a board was set up with a brief column of numbers, corresponding to the hymns we would sing in praise. Five hundred lowered heads with eyes closed, we gave thanks for the heavenly designs invoked in the minister's prayer. Then the enormous structure of mortised wood revealed its fine acoustical properties. The glass in the open windows rattled at the choir's mercy: deep voices, frail voices, my own voice stubborn, propelled by the force of simplicity, proud to be setting out over the bay in company with this multitude, to spread over its stagnant waters another surge of words poured out in solidarity. And my heart shook with joy, certain that the words sung mattered less than to participate without holding back. We sang and sang again, grasping our red-covered hymnals; I, immersed in this opportunity to exceed my bounds.

The resonance of good fortune gave way to the voice of our principal, a woman walled in by her aggressive but feeble manner. Probably anything would have appeared clumsy to me after our flights of song, but it was her chubby pink legs that offended me most, quivering from repressed vehemence in the center of the stage. I barely managed to hear her rambling remarks about the meaning of victory; the last echoes of my musical reverie left me only when she announced an upcoming public ceremony, a student assembly to which we were all to bring a fold-up wooden V, something built with care, with an eye for beauty and for the good name of our school. She stipulated the size, but as for the method, each of us would be free to produce it according to his own imagination.

Don Abelino found me sandpapering a pair of rulers which were decorated with a clover design at one end. He rewarded me with that smile of his that always left me wondering which state of calm he was in—tolerant or treacherous. I placed a circle of white enamel in the center of each clover and added a blue stripe going the length of each ruler and outlining the clover shape. The final varnish brought out the mahogany's blood-red color. A screw joining the two rulers at the base created the folding V: it was something stirring and brilliant, my homage to the sign of victory but in some veiled way also an allusion to the amphibious boat.

On the appointed day I arrived at school in my starched uniform with the V placed between the shirt and the waistband, whether to take away some of its solemnity or from sloth or plain shyness. Perhaps it was the latter feeling that hinted to me that there was something ostentatious and vaguely servile in all the pomp and circumstance of this kind of mass meeting.

We marched to the park, nearly flayed alive under the midmorning sun. There the entire student body of the town was formed into columns, converging on the spot that the authorities (collaborating with the trees that dominated the other half of the park) had declared to be the front of the bandstand, supplied for the occasion with a microphone and loudspeakers. First the vendors of fruit drinks and ices passed through, shielded from the sun by steaming sombreros, shoving their pushcarts among the parched columns of people and hawking their wares discreetly, with lowered voices. Next came the speakers; they too were shaded under the Victorian bandstand. And there I was, waiting for the opulent presentation of our many V signs, raised up with one unanimous cry, displayed in a single gesture which—minimizing our own sacrifice under the sun— would usher in the powerful reality of a new era soon to begin with the auctioning-off of war surplus. At the end of her long peroration, the decrepit voice of an old Englishwoman exerted itself to cry out "God save the Queen," and some of us thought that this might be the signal. I hastened to raise up my unfolded V. To my right I saw another V made with drum-sticks; up ahead, another made from ornately carved boards: three blundering V's held up against the heavy sun.

One August we heard the news from Japan. Hiroshima had been pulverized by a single weapon. The atomic bomb. The entire city. Not a single part of it spared. Hiroshima. I heard about it during the break between two classes. "They blew the whole thing up with one shot," said a classmate of mine, the gold fillings in his thick set of teeth sparkling with a drool of satisfaction. The explosion kept reverberating in that far-off, inconceivably dead land, but for me it was a nameless feeling that gnawed inside, amounting to a premonition of the end of the world, which would render useless even my yearning for the amphibious boat. But such a sudden leap landed me in an unfamiliar fog, and I would immediately seize once more upon the blissful expectation of new things to come.

I lived in constant vigilance, facing out to sea, facing the river; then again, the cargoes might arrive by air, consigned to some customs agent who would open his storeroom to the delights of a public auction. My nights were charmed by the far-off rumblings of an incoming vessel, the foghorn's gruff signal once more forcing me to imagine what pristine cargo the ship's tonnage might be carrying stowed deep to its very waterline. I examined Don Abelino's reading matter, certain that in his mute dedication to reading hovered the key which I would one day fish out between the lines. Walking along the banks of the port town, I wanted to sound the depth of the change I felt. Cautiously, I began to notice the gradual disappearance of the wartime boom: half-deserted wharves and warehouses, vacant waters that were once the landing place of barges equipped with massive outboard motors, their metal hulls painted yellow, the red and green glass of their lanterns, their stowage black with great clumps of rubber—a pure memory scattered across layers of purple clouds as evening fell.

The frustration that follows from mockery survived my capacity to forget. With boundless self-pity I played the destitute child who is fully prepared to perish except that he has a grand idea of being some titanic child-god, bestower of all favors save those lost in the mazes of oblivion.

The following year I was once more in Don Abelino's care during the months when the sun shines fourteen hours a day, when the marshes dry up and their dry beds crack but still retain enough underground moisture for planting rice. One afternoon he invited me to accompany him in burning a vast palm grove that was roasting from exposure to the sun. Sharing silence, we went off at an easy pace to determine the wind's direction; positioning ourselves at one end of the grove, we made torches from little *yolillo* palms; starting from a single match we ran in opposite directions, tossing flames into the overgrown foliage until we had kindled a wall of fire half a kilometer long; panting, we met up again further out. By that time the blaze was well along but contained, creating an immense howling composed equally of crackling branches and the calling of animals, of male to female caught in midcopulation, of herd to herd fleeing at a slower pace than the great chain of fire, of terror to terror as the scorching heat crept forward, flying, fed from one moment to the next by the dry brush and the fuel of fruits and leaves—a vast profile outlined here by monkeys singed in the impossible, fleeting act of leaping into the sky, there by vipers holding themselves upright on the utmost branch with the utmost vertebra: superimposed onto air that was also fire.

We sat on a fallen trunk for hours, taking in the howling and the stinking smoke. I broke the fervor of this undisturbed pose of rapt contemplation by venturing to ask what would become of the amphibious boat. In answer, Don Abelino flashed me the vertical lines of a constricted frown: blunt knife edges, frozen even in the midst of fire.

Years later—years well acquainted with genuine separations, excuses, strained relations, occasional letters exchanged across the distance of several countries—I came upon a news report about the battle of Inchon, the Korean War's masterpiece, in which fifteen hundred amphibious boats had formed the core of a coastal invasion. I clipped it carefully and sent it to him, as from a son to a credulous parent, not needing to add a letter of my own for him to catch the allusion to this new opportunity for hope: the amphibious boat might yet be auctioned off somewhere within reach of his yearning. In return I received in the mail an elongated parcel which likewise contained no letter, nothing more than the V with the clover design, as from a father to an insolent son, enough for me to hear his laconic, cutting voice telling me: You too were once a believer, *carajito*. Little fool.

Translated by Dan Bellm

And We Sold the Rain

Carmen Naranjo

"THIS IS a royal fuck-up," was all the treasury minister could say a few days ago as he got out of the jeep after seventy kilometers of jouncing over dusty rutted roads and muddy trails. His advisor agreed: there wasn't a cent in the treasury, the line for foreign exchange wound four times around the capital, and the IMF was stubbornly insisting that the country could expect no more loans until the interest had been paid up, public spending curtailed, salaries frozen, domestic production increased, imports reduced, and social programs cut.

The poor were complaining. "We can't even buy beans—they've got us living on radish tops, bananas and garbage; they raise our water bills but don't give us any water even though it rains every day, and on top of that they add on a charge for excess consumption for last year, even though there wasn't any water in the pipes then either."

"Doesn't anyone in this whole goddamned country have an idea that could get us out of this?" asked the president of the republic, who shortly before the elections, surrounded by a toothily smiling, impeccably tailored meritocracy, had boasted that by virtue of his university-trained mind (Ph.D. in developmental economics) he was the best candidate. Someone proposed to him that he pray to La Negrita; he did and nothing happened. Somebody else suggested that he reinstate the Virgin of Ujarrás. But after so many years of neglect, the pretty little virgin had gone deaf and ignored the pleas for help, even though the entire cabinet implored her, at the top of their lungs, to light the way to a better future and a happier tomorrow.

The hunger and poverty could no longer be concealed: the homeless, pockets empty, were squatting in the Parque Central, the Parque Nacional, and the Plaza de la Cultura. They were camping along Central and Second Avenues and in a shantytown springing up on the plains outside the city. Gangs were threatening to invade the national theater, the Banco Central, and all nationalized banking headquarters. The Public Welfare Agency was rationing rice and beans as if they were medicine. In the market-place, robberies increased to one per second, and homes were burgled at the rate of one per half hour. Business and government were sinking in sleaze; drug lords operated uncontrolled, and gambling was institutional-ized in order to launder dollars and attract tourists. Strangely enough, the prices of a few items went down: whiskey, caviar and other such articles of conspicuous consumption.

The sea of poverty that was engulfing cities and villages contrasted with the growing number of Mercedes Benzes, BMWs and a whole alphabet of trade names of gleaming new cars.

The minister announced to the press that the country was on the verge of bankruptcy. The airlines were no longer issuing tickets because so much money was owed them, and travel became impossible; even official junkets were eliminated. There was untold suffering of civil servants suddenly un-able to travel even once a month to the great cities of the world! A special budget might be the solution, but tax revenues were nowhere to be found, unless a compliant public were to go along with the president's brilliant idea of levying a tax on air—a minimal tax, to be sure, but, after all, the air was a part of the government's patrimony. Ten *colones* per breath would be a small price to pay.

July arrived, and one afternoon a minister without portfolio and with-out umbrella, noticing that it had started to rain, stood watching people run for cover. "Yes," he thought, "here it rains like it rains in Comala, like it rains in Macondo. It rains day and night, rain after rain, like a theater with the same movie, sheets of water. Poor people without umbrellas, without a change of clothes, they get drenched, people living in leaky houses, without a change of shoes for when they're shipwrecked. And here, all my poor colleagues with colds, all the poor deputies with laryngitis, the president with that worrisome cough, all this on top of the catastrophe itself. No TV station is broadcasting; all of them are flooded, along with the newspaper plants and the radio stations. A people without news is a lost people, because they don't know that everywhere else, or almost everywhere else, things are even worse. If we could only export the rain," thought the minister.

Meanwhile, the people, depressed by the heavy rains, the dampness, the lack of news, the cold, and their hunger and despair without their sitcoms and soap operas, began to rain inside and to increase the baby population—that is, to try to increase the odds that one of their progeny might survive. A mass of hungry, naked babies began to cry in concert every time it rained.

When one of the radio transmitters was finally repaired, the president was able to broadcast a message: He had inherited a country so deeply in debt that it could no longer obtain credit and could no longer afford to pay either the interest or the amortization on loans. He had to dismiss civil servants, suspend public works, cut off services, close offices, and spread his legs somewhat to transnationals. Now even these lean cows were dying; the fat ones were on the way, encouraged by the International Monetary Fund, the AID and the IDB, not to mention the EEC. The great danger was that the fat cows had to cross over the neighboring country on their way, and it was possible that they would be eaten up—even though they came by air, at nine thousand feet above the ground, in a first class stable in a pressurized, air-conditioned cabin. Those neighbors were simply not to be trusted.

The fact was that the government had faded in the people's memory. By now no one remembered the names of the president or his ministers; people remembered them as "the one with glasses who thinks he's Tarzan's mother," or "the one who looks like the baby hog someone gave me when times were good, maybe a little uglier."

The solution came from the most unexpected source. The country had organized the Third World contest to choose "Miss Underdeveloped," to be elected, naturally, from the multitudes of skinny, dusky, round-shouldered, short-legged, half-bald girls with cavity-pocked smiles, girls suffering from parasites and God knows what else. The prosperous Emirate of the Emirs sent its designée, who in sheer amazement at how it rained and rained, widened her enormous eyes—fabulous eyes of harem and Koran delights—and was unanimously elected reigning Queen of Underdevelopment. Lacking neither eyeteeth nor molars, she was indeed the fairest of the fair. She returned in a rush to the Emirate of the Emirs, for she had acquired, with unusual speed, a number of fungal colonies that were taking over the territory under her toenails and fingernails, behind her ears, and on her left cheek.

"Oh, Father Sultan, my lord, lord of the moons and of the suns, if your Arabian highness could see how it rains and rains in that country, you would not believe it. It rains day and night. Everything is green, even the people; they are green people, innocent and trusting, who probably have never even thought about selling their most important resource, the rain. The poor fools think about coffee, rice, sugar, vegetables, and lumber, and they hold Ali Baba's treasure in their hands without even knowing it. What we would give to have such abundance!"

Sultan Abun dal Tol let her speak and made her repeat the part about the rain from dawn to dusk, dusk to dawn, for months on end. He wanted to hear over and over about that greenness that was forever turning greener. He loved to think of it raining and raining, of singing in the rain, of showers bringing forth flowers . . .

A long distance phone call was made to the office of the export minister from the Emirate of the Emirs, but the minister wasn't in. The trade minister grew radiant when Sultan Abun dal Tol, warming to his subject, instructed him to buy up rain and construct an aqueduct between their countries to fertilize the desert. Another call. Hello, am I speaking with the country of rain, not the rain of marijuana or cocaine, not that of laundered dollars, but the rain that falls naturally from the sky and makes the sandy desert green? Yes, yes, you are speaking with the export minister, and we are willing to sell you our rain. Of course, its production costs us nothing; it is a resource as natural to us as your petroleum. We will make you a fair and just agreement.

The news filled five columns during the dry season, when obstacles like floods and dampness could be overcome. The president himself made the announcement: We will sell rain at ten dollars per cc. The price will be reviewed every ten years. Sales will be unlimited. With the earnings we will regain our independence and our self-respect.

The people smiled. A little less rain would be agreeable to everyone, and the best part was not having to deal with the six fat cows, who were more than a little oppressive. The IMF, the World Bank, the AID, the Embassy, the International Development Bank and perhaps the EEC would stop pushing the cows on them, given the danger that they might be stolen in the neighboring country, air-conditioned cabin, first class stable and all.

Moreover, one couldn't count on those cows really being fat, since accepting them meant increasing all kinds of taxes, especially those on consumer goods, lifting import restrictions, spreading one's legs completely open to the transnationals, paying the interest, which was now a little higher, and amortizing the debt that was increasing at a rate only comparable to the spread of an epidemic. And as if this were not enough, it would be necessary to structure the cabinet a certain way, as some ministers were viewed by some legislators as potentially dangerous, as extremists.

The president added with demented glee, his face garlanded in sappy smiles, that French technicians, those guardians of European meritocracy, would build the rain funnels and the aqueduct, a guarantee of honesty, efficiency and effective transfer of technology.

By then we had already sold, to our great disadvantage, the tuna, the dolphins, and the thermal dome, along with the forests and all Indian artifacts. Also our talent, dignity, sovereignty, and the right to traffic in anything and everything illicit.

The first funnel was located on the Atlantic coast, which in a few months looked worse than the dry Pacific. The first payment from the emir arrived—in dollars!—and the country celebrated with a week's vacation. A little more effort was needed. Another funnel was added in the north and one more in the south. Both zones immediately dried up like raisins. The checks did not arrive. What happened? The IMF garnisheed them for interest payments. Another effort: a funnel was installed in the center of the country, where formerly it had rained and rained. It now stopped raining forever, which paralyzed brains, altered behavior, changed the climate, defoliated the corn, destroyed the coffee, poisoned aromas, devastated canefields, dessicated palm trees, ruined orchards, razed truck gardens, and narrowed faces, making people look and act like rats, ants, and cockroaches, the only animals left alive in large numbers.

To remember what we once had been, people circulated photographs of an enormous oasis with great plantations, parks, and animal sanctuaries full of butterflies and flocks of birds, at the bottom of which was printed, "Come and visit us. The Emirate of Emirs is a paradise."

The first one to attempt it was a good swimmer who took the precaution of carrying food and medicine. Then a whole family left, then whole villages, large and small. The population dropped considerably. One fine day there was nobody left, with the exception of the president and his cabinet. Everyone else, even the deputies, followed the rest by opening the cover of the aqueduct and floating all the way to the cover at the other end, doorway to the Emirate of the Emirs.

In that country we were second-class citizens, something we were already accustomed to. We lived in a ghetto. We got work because we knew about coffee, sugar cane, cotton, fruit trees, and truck gardens. In a short time we were happy and felt as if these things too were ours, or at the very least, that the rain still belonged to us.

A few years passed; the price of oil began to plunge and plunge. The emir asked for a loan, then another, then many; eventually he had to beg and beg for money to service the loans. The story sounds all too familiar. Now the IMF has taken possession of the aqueducts. They have cut off the water because of a default in payments and because the sultan had the bright idea of receiving as a guest of honor a representative of that country that is a neighbor of ours.

Translated by Jo Anne Engelbert

DEVELOPERS

All accounts of successful development projects undertaken by people concerned for the welfare of villagers, their ancestral lands, their traditions and cultures, must be solely in grant and loan proposals to the acronymed agencies listed by Carmen Naranjo in "And We Sold the Rain"—"IMF, the World Bank, the AID, the Embassy, the International Development Bank and perhaps the EEC . . ."—for they are certainly not to be found in Global Cultures. The absence of success stories is the most striking thing about all the attention given to development and developers by contemporary short fiction writers. The second striking aspect about the short fictions devoted to criticizing development—to naming exploitation—is the enormous range of emotion and literary technique employed. Of the four stories below, two are satiric, one is in a complex, very Latin American, magical/realistic vein, and one is in an earthy cartoonish manner immediately recognizable as "Pacific Islands." Two are somber, the first a meditative tale, a modern folktale, from Trinidad, and the second a brutal chronicle, like an anthropological documentary, from the southern Philippines.

AUGUSTO MONTERROSO, born in 1921 in Guatemala but living for most of his adult life in Mexico, is acknowledged as the leading Latin American writer of short satires and fables. Of his fourteen volumes, only *The Black Sheep and Other Fables* has appeared in English (in 1971), but he is widely anthologized. The story of "Mr. Taylor" hinges upon allusions to the Yankee obsession with business efficiency. It particularly mocks late nineteenth-century industrializing methods like the "Taylor system," named after Frederick Winslow Taylor (1856–1915), author of *Principles of Scientific Management* and the man who made the assembly line a key feature of American factories.

LEONCIO P. DERIADA, born in 1940 in the southern Philippines, writes in most of the languages spoken by the characters in his story "Daba-Daba." His native tongue is Hiligaynon, and he is appreciated by readers of Cebuano, another southern language, but he is nationally known in English and Tagalog, the main language of the most populous city, Manila, which many Philippine people feel has been imposed as a national language. In his story, the linguistic hierarchy of the country is reflected in the development hierarchy. The small farmer and his family are Bagobo, from near Davao on the southernmost island of Mindanao, and are Hiligaynon speakers—a family just like the author's own—and the children's friends are Ilongo and Cebuano. All the southern groups get along. The Bagobo are tenants for Mr. Ventura, a Vasayan, whose name alludes to the northern city of Ventura. He is a Christian, while the tenants are Muslim. Two of Mr. Ventura's hired guns are foreigners and urban dwellers, a Tagalog speaker and an Ilocano from the northernmost province of Luzon, whose language is unknown to the villagers; the third is a local Cebuano speaker, an interpreter—a traitor. It is necessary for Deriada to fill his story with precise descriptions of everyone's group and language, everyone's weapons, because the story's entire purpose depends upon these details, this roster. This is not a story of imperialist developers—at least not immediately—but of intra-Philippine class war and north-south regional conflict, of exploitation and rebellion. It shows graphically how recruits for a guerrilla army are created through the actions of the exploiters.

MICHAEL ANTHONY, born in Mayaro, Trinidad, in 1932, grew up on that island and in the San Francisco area, then made his way as a factory worker in Trinidad and in England where he wrote most of his stories. He is best known on the island and, through the Heinemann Caribbean Writers Series, in the English-speaking world for his stories and novels of childhood, his growing up tales like *The Year in San Fernando* (1970). He writes with more nostalgia for old ways than many younger Caribbean authors, and his critique of modernization is less Marxist than most, but his tales are very affective.

EPELI HAU'OFA, born in 1938, is from Papua New Guinea, the son of missionary parents from Tonga, a tiny kingdom made up of 150 tiny islands to the northeast of the Australian coast near Sydney. He has a Ph.D. in social anthropology from the Australian National University, Canberra, and has studied in Montreal, Canada, as well. He has taught at various South Pacific universities, but he has also served as the director of the Rural Development Centre in Tonga; that is, he has served the cause of development that he mocks so delightfully in his *Tales of the Tikongs* (1983), an even dozen ribald, high-spirited, strung-together jokes.

Mister Taylor

Augusto Monterroso

"SOMEWHAT LESS strange, although surely more exemplary," the other man said then, "is the story of Mr. Percy Taylor, a headhunter in the Amazon jungle.

"In 1937 he is known to have left Boston, Massachusetts, where he had refined his spirit to the point at which he did not have a cent. In 1944 he appears for the first time in South America, in the region of the Amazon, living with the Indians of a tribe whose name there is no need to recall.

"Because of the shadows under his eyes and his famished appearance, he soon became known as 'the poor gringo,' and the school children even pointed at him and threw stones when he walked by, his beard shining in the golden tropical sun. But this caused no distress to Mr. Taylor's humble nature, for he had read in the first volume of William C. Knight's *Complete Works* that poverty is no disgrace if one does not envy the wealthy.

"In a few weeks the natives grew accustomed to him and his eccentric clothing. Besides, since he had blue eyes and a vague foreign accent, even the president and the minister of foreign affairs treated him with singular respect, fearful of provoking international incidents.

"He was so wretchedly poor that one day he went into the jungle to search for plants to eat. He had walked several meters without daring to turn his head when, by sheerest accident, he saw a pair of Indian eyes observing him intently from the undergrowth. A long shudder traveled down Mr. Taylor's sensitive spine. But Mr. Taylor intrepidly defied all danger and continued on his way, whistling as if he had not seen anything.

"With a leap, which there is no need to call feline, the native landed in front of him and cried: 'Buy head? Money, money.'

"Although the Indian's English could not have been worse, Mr. Taylor, feeling somewhat ill, realized the Indian was offering to sell him an oddly shrunken human head that he was carrying in his hand.

"It is unnecessary to say that Mr. Taylor was in no position to buy it, but since he pretended not to understand, the Indian felt horribly embarrassed for not speaking good English and gave the head to him as a gift, begging his pardon.

"Mr. Taylor's joy was great as he returned to his hut. That night, lying on his back on the precariously balanced palm mat that was his bed, and interrupted only by the buzzing of the passionate flies that flew around him as they made love obscenely, Mr. Taylor spent a long time contemplating his curious acquisition with delight. He derived the greatest aesthetic pleasure from counting the hairs of the beard and moustache one by one and looking straight into the two half-ironic eyes that seemed to smile at him in gratitude for his deferential behavior.

"A man of immense culture, Mr. Taylor was contemplative by nature, but on this occasion he soon became bored with his philosophical reflections and decided to give the head to his uncle, Mr. Rolston, who lived in New York and who, from earliest childhood, had shown a strong interest in the cultural manifestations of Latin American peoples.

"A few days later, Mr. Taylor's uncle wrote to ask him (not before inquiring after the state of his precious health) to please favor him with five more. Mr. Taylor willingly satisfied Mr. Rolston's desire and—no one knows how—by return mail he 'was very happy to honor your request.' Extremely grateful, Mr. Rolston asked for another ten. Mr. Taylor was 'delighted to be of service.' But when in a month he was asked to send twenty more, Mr. Taylor, simple and bearded but with a refined artistic sensibility, had the presentiment that his mother's brother was making a profit off of the heads.

"And, if you want to know, that's how it was. With complete frankness Mr. Rolston told him about it in an inspired letter whose strictly business-like terms made the strings of Mr. Taylor's sensitive spirit vibrate as never before.

"They immediately formed a corporation: Mr. Taylor agreed to obtain and ship shrunken heads on a massive scale while Mr. Rolston would sell them as best he could in his country.

"In the early days there were some annoying difficulties with certain local types. But Mr. Taylor, who in Boston had received the highest grades for his essay on Joseph Henry Silliman, proved to be a politician and obtained from the authorities not only the necessary export permit but also an exclusive concession for ninety-nine years. It was not difficult for him to convince the chief executive warrior and the legislative witch doctors that such a patriotic move would shortly enrich the community, and that very soon all the thirsty aborigines would be able to have (whenever they wanted a refreshing pause in the collection of heads) an ice cold soft drink whose magic formula he himself would supply.

"When the members of the cabinet, after a brief but luminous exercise of intellect, became aware of these advantages, their love of country bubbled over, and in three days they issued a decree demanding that the people accelerate the production of shrunken heads.

"A few months later, in Mr. Taylor's country, the heads had gained the popularity we all remember. At first they were the privilege of the wealthiest families, but democracy is democracy, and as no one can deny, in a matter of weeks even schoolteachers could buy them.

"A home without its own shrunken head was thought of as a home that had failed. Soon the collectors appeared, and with them, certain contradictions: owning seventeen heads was considered bad taste, but it was distinguished to have eleven. Heads became so popular that the really elegant people began to lose interest and would only acquire one if it had some peculiarity that saved it from vulgarity. A very rare one with Prussian whiskers, that in life had belonged to a highly decorated general, was presented to the Danfeller Institute, which, in turn, immediately donated three and a half million dollars to further the development of this exciting cultural manifestation of Latin American peoples.

"Meanwhile, the tribe had made so much progress that it now had its own path around the Legislative Palace. On Sundays and Independence Day the members of Congress would ride the bicycles the company had given them along that happy path, clearing their throats, displaying their feathers, laughing very seriously.

"But what did you expect? Not all times are good times. Without warning the first shortage of heads occurred.

"Then the best part began.

"Mere natural deaths were no longer sufficient. The minister of public health, feeling sincere one dark night when the lights were out and he had caressed his wife's breast for a little while just out of courtesy, confessed to her that he thought he was incapable of raising mortality rates to the level that would satisfy the interests of the company. To that she replied he should not worry, that he would see how everything would turn out all right, and that the best thing would be for them to go to sleep.

"To compensate for this administrative deficiency it was indispensable that they take strong measures, and a harsh death penalty was imposed.

"The jurists consulted with one another and raised even the smallest shortcoming to the category of a crime punishable by hanging or the firing squad, depending on the seriousness of the infraction.

"Even simple mistakes became criminal acts. For example: if in ordinary conversation someone carelessly said 'It's very hot,' and later it could be proven, thermometer in hand, that it really was not so hot, that person was charged a small tax and executed on the spot, his head sent on to the company, and, it must be said in all fairness, his trunk and limbs passed on to the bereaved.

"The legislation dealing with disease had wide repercussions and was frequently commented on by the diplomatic corps and the ministries of foreign affairs of friendly powers.

"According to this memorable legislation, the gravely ill were given twenty-four hours to put their papers in order and die, but if in this time they were lucky enough to infect their families, they received as many month-long stays as relatives they had infected. The victims of minor illnesses, and those who simply did not feel well, earned the scorn of the fatherland, and anyone on the street was entitled to spit in their faces. For the first time in history the importance of doctors who cured no one was recognized (there were several candidates for the Nobel Prize among them). Dying became an example of the most exalted patriotism, not only on the national level but on that even more glorious one, the continental.

"With the growth achieved by subsidiary industries (coffin manufacture in particular flourished with the technical assistance of the company) the country entered, as the saying goes, a period of great economic prosperity. This progress was particularly evident in a new little flower-bordered path on which, enveloped in the melancholy of the golden autumnal afternoons, the deputies' wives would stroll, their pretty little heads nodding yes, yes, everything was fine, when some solicitous journalist on the other side of the path would greet them with a smile, tipping his hat.

"I remember in passing that one of these journalists, who on a certain occasion emitted a downpour of a sneeze that he could not explain, was accused of extremism and put against the wall facing the firing squad. Only after his unselfish end did the intellectual establishment recognize that the journalist had one of the fattest heads in the country, but once it was shrunken it looked so good that one could not even notice the difference.

"And Mr. Taylor? By this time he had been designated as special adviser to the constitutional president. Now, and as an example of what private initiative can accomplish, he was counting his thousands by the thousands; but this made him lose no sleep, for he had read in the last volume of the *Complete Works* of William C. Knight that being a millionaire is no dishonor if one does not scorn the poor.

"I believe that this is the second time that I will say that not all times are good times.

"Given the prosperity of the business, the time came when the only people left in the area were the authorities and their wives and the journalists and their wives. Without much effort Mr. Taylor concluded that the only possible solution was to start a war with the neighboring tribes. Why not? This was progress.

"With the help of a few small cannons, the first tribe was neatly beheaded in just under three months. Mr. Taylor tasted the glory of expanding his domain. Then came the second tribe, then the third, the fourth and the fifth. Progress spread so rapidly that the moment came when, regardless of the efforts of the technicians, it was impossible to find neighboring tribes to make war on.

"It was the beginning of the end.

"The little paths began to languish. Only occasionally could one see a lady taking a stroll or some poet laureate with his book under his arm. The weeds once again overran the two paths, making the way difficult and thorny for the delicate feet of the ladies. Along with the heads the bicycles had thinned out, and the happy optimistic greetings had almost completely disappeared.

"The coffin manufacturer was sadder and more funereal than ever. And everyone felt as if they had awakened from a pleasant dream—one of those wonderful dreams when you find a purse full of gold coins, and you put it under your pillow and go back to sleep, and very early the next day, when you wake up, you look for it and find emptiness.

"Nevertheless, business, painfully, went on as usual. But people were having trouble going to sleep for fear they would wake up exported.

"In Mr. Taylor's country, of course, the demand continued to increase. New substitutes appeared daily, but nobody really believed in them, and everyone demanded the little heads from Latin America.

"It happened during the last crisis. A desperate Mr. Rolston was continually demanding more heads. Although the company's stocks suffered a sharp decline, Mr. Rolston was convinced that his nephew would do something to save the situation.

"The once daily shipments decreased to one a month, and they were sending anything: children's heads, ladies' heads, deputies' heads.

"Suddenly they stopped completely.

"One harsh, gray Friday, home from the stock exchange and still dazed by the shouting of his friends and their lamentable show of panic, Mr. Rolston decided to jump out the window (rather than use a gun—the noise would have terrified him). He had opened a package that had come in the mail and found the shrunken head of Mr. Taylor smiling at him from the distant wild Amazon, with a child's false smile that seemed to say 'I'm sorry; I won't do it again.'"

Translated by Edith Grossman

Daba-Daba

Leoncio P. Deriada

DANSIG IS seven years old. He is a Bagobo. His father is Asan. His mother is Anyaw.

Dansig's parents grew up on the plateau. It is called Tamugan, one of the most beautiful places in old Daba-Daba. Daba-Daba is now called Davao.

Dansig is not like the Ata children. He is not dark. He is fair and handsome, even handsomer than his older brother. Masaglang is sixteen. He is brave and strong like a durian tree. His face is like the durian, too. It is rough with pimples.

Dansig's family lives in a house made of bamboo and cogon. The house stands on the edge of the plateau. The house is overlooking the big Tamugan River. Dansig loves this river as much as he loves the forests and his father's house and the tall durian tree that Asan's great-grandfather planted long ago. The tree stands on the cliff a camote patch away from the house. It is so tall that it almost touches the sky. Once in a while, the huge bird that eats monkeys perches on the topmost branch and whistles to its mate.

Asan works in the abaca plantation of Mr. Ventura. Mr. Ventura is a rich Visayan who owns the whole plateau on the other side of Tamugan River. He is tall and fair with a mustache and a cigar. Dansig cannot understand why a stranger like Mr. Ventura owns a big abaca plantation. Datu Elid, a powerful old man with hanging earlobes, does not even own a stripping machine. Neither does Datu Duyan, the chief of the tribes in the forests and mountains beyond Panigan River, on the northern side of Tamugan Plateau.

When it is not the stripping season of abaca, Asan plants crops around the house, like camote and gabi and cassava. Anyaw plants vegetables. Then Dansig's sister keeps the chickens away. Ogaret is four years old. She has long wavy hair. When she grows up, she will be married to Anani, one of Datu Elid's numerous grandsons. Anani is eight years old, and he can speak some words in English. He has been in Grade One for two years at Gumalang Elementary School.

Dansig's family owns a carabao, two goats, a dozen hens, three cocks, and a hunting dog named Ul-ul. One of the cocks has been trained to fight in Malagos. Every morning Dansig takes the carabao to pasture. He rides on Tibak, the carabao, and joins the Cebuano and Ilongo boys on the grassy side of the plateau. Tibak has a wire ring in his nose. A strong abaca rope is attached to the ring, and as Dansig pulls the rope while guiding Tibak towards Tamugan River, he feels like Datu Elid riding his horse to visit Datu Baguio or to attend the cockfights in Malagos.

Masaglang does not work in the abaca plantation. He has a kaingin just below the durian tree, along the tortuous path to Tamugan River. He alternately plants palay and corn in the kaingin. Now the corn ears are just sprouting hair and Masaglang expects an abundant harvest before the heavy rains flood Tamugan River.

Tamugan River floods easily. A downpour in the mountains in the west swells the river in a couple of hours. The onrush of the brown water—washings of the fertile mountainsides and plateaus—makes the river both monstrous and magnificent. Dansig and the Visayan boys always enjoy watching the oncoming flood from a precipice beside Masaglang's kaingin. Five of them—Dansig, Kalaw, Nardo, Onyot, and Mundo—give out whoops as the dark-brown swell from the river's tributaries at the foot of Mt. Apo push downwards the clear water. After watching the flood's coming many times, Nardo, who is an Ilongo, has given up the hope of seeing a gigantic monkey leading the brown current. Dansig and the other boys laugh at this fairy tale. Ilongos are so superstitious, Onyot the Cebuano says. Yet Onyot is mortally afraid of some creatures in the dark like the *wakwak* and the *sigbin*.

One afternoon, while Anyaw is alone digging camote and Ogaret is feeding Asan's fighting cock, three men come. One has a long gun. The other two are carrying a roll of barbed wire.

The men do not say anything, but they start putting up the fence. The barbed wire fence runs across Anyaw's camote patch. For a long while, Anyaw stands gaping, not knowing what to do.

"But—but this is our land," Anyaw protests at last. "You are building a fence on our land!"

"This is not yours anymore," the man with the gun says gruffly. He is a Tagalog.

"Not ours anymore? Why—why?" Anyaw is about to cry.

"Mr. Ventura has just bought it," says the darker one of the barbed wire men. He is unmistakably an Ilocano.

"Bought? From whom? We haven't sold our land!"

"*Samok 'ning bayhana,*" the third man says in Cebuano. "This woman asks too many questions."

Anyaw is now on the other side of the fence, separated from her co-gon house. She crawls under the barbed wire and faces the men, her body trembling in anger and confusion.

"This land is ours," Anyaw is now crying. "Please remove the fence. My husband will be very angry."

"And what will your husband do, ha?" snarls the gunman. "Scare us away?"

"We'll be back tomorrow," says the Cebuano. "Tell your man to behave, or else . . ."

The three men leave the woman beside the wire fence. Anyaw wipes her face with the flared sleeve of her multicolored blouse. She breathes deeply then calls her sons, her voice shrill but strong, penetrating the still afternoon. In the west the sun is bloody red above Mt. Apo.

Soon Dansig comes, riding Tibak like Datu Elid's horse. Behind him is Ul-ul, barking and playfully biting Tibak's hind legs. The carabao trots awkwardly towards the house but suddenly stops, arrested by the newly constructed fence.

Before he can ask questions, his brother Masaglang is beside him. Masaglang looks dirty after working in the kaingin the whole day. The brothers stand by the fence, their mother on the other side.

And Anyaw tells them everything about the three men and Mr. Ventura.

Masaglang spits on the ground in intense anger. Then he draws his big bolo slung on his waist and cuts the barbed wires. The taut metal lines resist stubbornly but soon they snap and curl with a hiss towards the closest wooden stake. Dansig picks up a piece of raw branch and strikes each wooden stake until the stake loosens from the ground. Then he and his brother pull out each pointed wood and hurl it into the tall cogon beside the camote patch.

Before dark Asan comes home from the abaca plantation on the other plateau. It is Saturday and he has just received his weekly wages. He has dropped by Eng Nga's store and has bought some cans of sardines, a kilo of salt and two of sugar, some dried fish, and pieces of coconut candy wrapped in colored paper.

Around their supper laid on the bamboo floor that evening, the family talk about the men who put up the fence.

The next day, Sunday, the men do not come. They must have gone to Calinan to visit their church where a white priest mumbles strange words at the foot of the altar. Or they must have attended the cockfights in Malagos.

On Monday, Asan does not report for work. He stays at home and sharpens his *panumbahay* and *taksiay*. The panumbahay is a huge but light blade used to cut abaca trunks close to the base. An expert has to strike only thrice and the plant crashes to the ground with a rich thud somehow cushioned by the wide, thick leaves. The taksiay is a doubled-edged knife shaped like the tip of a spear. It is used to strip the abaca stalk of the fiber-rich outer layer. Aside from their function in the abaca plantation, the panumbahay and the taksiay are deadly weapons.

The family do their accustomed chores without a word. Anyaw resumes her work in the camote patch, digging up the fat yellow tubers and depositing them in a bamboo basket. Masaglang goes back to his kaingin. Among his blossoming corn plants he feels something odd—an anticipation of some terrible happening. Ogaret keeps the chickens away from the vegetables, her lips red with the coconut candy wrappers she has used as lipstick. Dansig brings Tibak to pasture, but now, he does not join the Visayan boys.

In the afternoon, just as the shadow of the house touches the nearer margin of the camote patch, the three men come. On Tibak's back, Dansig sees them climbing up the twisting path from Tamugan River. Dansig whistles. From his kaingin, Masaglang hears the signal and hurries home to his appointed place behind the house. On the cogon wall are two spears and a dozen tusked boar skulls—trophies of the previous year's abundant hunt.

The three men face Anyaw. The scared woman freezes. Ogaret runs towards her. The girl trembles, clutching her mother's soiled *patadiong*.

The Tagalog still has the long gun. The other two men do not have guns but they are just as armed. The Ilocano has a long jungle bolo dangling from his waist. On the Cebuano's side Anyaw can see the hilt of some knife the kind of which she has not seen before.

"What have you done to our fence?" demands the Tagalog who is obviously the leader.

The woman opens her mouth but cannot say anything.

"Didn't we tell you to behave?" says the Cebuano. "Now tell your husband and sons to put back our fence."

The Ilocano says something in his language. Anyaw does not understand him.

The woman is trembling now, but the sight of her husband coming from the house steadies her. Asan is in double steps, the huge scabbard of the panumbahay ominous on his side.

"Put back the fence," the Tagalog orders Asan. Mr. Ventura's man stands solid on the ground, his right hand holding the gun like a support.

"This is my land," Asan's voice is soft but keen in primitive fury. "You cannot drive me away from my land."

"*Pisti!*" the Cebuano hisses through his stained teeth. "You don't own this land anymore. Didn't your woman tell you?"

The Ilocano utters something incoherent. From his place behind the house, Masaglang can see how dark the Ilocano's nape is, like the color of any Ata warrior.

The Tagalog steps forward, his hand strong around the barrel of the gun. Asan does not move an inch. His legs are spread straight and firm on the earth like a pair of lanzones trunks.

"Get out of this land!" the Tagalog is shouting now. "Get out, you brute, or you'll have a taste of this!" the gunman raises his arms and Asan feels the butt of the gun on his chest.

The Bagobo falls to the ground, in the Tagalog's shadow. From where he is among the creeping creatures of the field, he looks at the towering figure above him. With the instincts of a beast that can see every detail of the enemy at one sweep of the eyes, Asan glares as the gunman moves closer, pushing his shadow in front of him. First Asan notes the rubber boots, then the tight khaki pants that hug the legs sensually, showing generous folds where the sex is. Asan's eyes linger in a split second at the slim waist where a belt of ammunition clings loosely. The man's body is tough and hairy: the unbuttoned shirt shows a chest that has both power and cruelty. Were the face gentle, it could be handsome—but now there is no beauty there, not even a trace of humanity. The Tagalog leers with an awareness of the strength in both his chest and his gun.

From the ground Asan looks at the towering body that is both menacing and vulnerable.

The man raises his arms again and Asan anticipates the blinding closeness of the gun butt. Quick as a jungle beast, the Bagobo springs to a crouching position, his right hand tight around the sarimanok hilt of the panumbahay. With all the might of the arm that has felled countless abaca trees, Asan attacks the human trunk in front of him. A single swish of the large, light blade finds its way sure and clean across the groin that is both sensual and vulnerable. Red, warm blood spills into Asan's face and the Bagobo has a momentary taste of salt.

The man shrieks and drops the gun. He shrieks again, clasping his front. Then he falls . . .

The Bagobo is on his feet now. Cursing, sweating, panting and bloodthirsty like a hunting dog, he kneels between the fallen man's legs, clasps the panumbahay sarimanok with both hands, and with all the anger in his body and soul, plants the lethal tool in the Tagalog's heart.

"Aieeee!" Anyaw screams, her hands scratching the afternoon wind. Ogaret clings to her mother's sleeves, mute with terror.

Momentarily stunned by the happening, the two men find their senses now. As if on cue, both pull their weapons. The Ilocano brandishes his jungle bolo above his head, and from behind, Masaglang finds him funny like an inept *huramentado*.

Asan has pulled his blade from the Tagalog's heart. Hotter than ever, he faces the two, this time with a fiercer heart and a firmer hand.

Masaglang lets go his spear. The javelin hisses in the air to find its target. The spear—killer of a dozen boars in the mossy valleys of Tamugan River—hits the bull's-eye: the Ilocano's nape. The dark Northerner crashes to the ground with a thud somehow cushioned by the thick, purplish camote tops. The spear's blade has shot through the man's neck. The Ilocano grimaces darkly, then expires.

"Aieeee!" Anyaw screams again. This time Ogaret joins her.

The dog Ul-ul, whose instincts have been sharpened by the numberless boar hunts, rushes to the fallen quarry, but sensing the impaled body unmoving and lifeless, foregoes the customary bite in the throat. Instead, the dog licks the blood on the spear tip, then points his nose to the sky and howls his canine joy.

The Cebuano turns towards the cogon house. Masaglang is poising the second spear, but before the hunter releases the bamboo-bodied lance, the third man darts blindly towards the snaky path to Tamugan River, leaving his almost inhuman shout behind him.

Meanwhile, farther in the west, rain is falling in the forests of the smaller mountains at the foot of Mt. Apo. The sun has darkened.

Dansig jumps off Tibak and joins his family around the intruders sprawled over the camote patch. Wordlessly, each stares at the bloody bodies. Dansig feels his heart pumping wildly inside his little breast—awed by the bravery of his elders and terrified by his first experience of death. He looks at his father's face and there he sees the valor that must have been in the face of the most illustrious *bagane* among Datu Elid's ancestors.

Suddenly, anxiety covers Asan's face. Fear begins to take shape in his eyes. He and his son have just killed two men.

"Go! Go!" he gasps. "Go back to the house. Let's get out of here!"

His wife and children understand him. Anyaw picks up her basket of tubers and drags Ogaret to the house. Dansig goes back to Tibak and ties the carabao to a *kamansi* tree. Masaglang pulls his spear from the Ilocano's neck. The spearhead offers some trifling resistance. Masaglang strengthens his pull. The dead man's face upturns and its mouth opens into an obscene grin.

Asan stands on the edge of the plateau. The path is empty. He looks down into the valley below, at the river. Clearly, he can see the Cebuano fording the Tamugan in maddening hurry.

The sky has darkened. Asan looks at the west. The rain in the mountains at the foot of Mt. Apo has become heavier.

Ul-ul has left the two bodies in the camote patch. Now the flies are hovering over them.

Asan goes back to the two bodies. He stands above them for a moment. He is no longer shaking with anger. Instead, pity and fear have taken possession of him and he shakes anew. The Tagalog's face has become serene in death; indeed the face is handsome. The Ilocano is still grinning and his eyes are open. Flies are now humming over the dead.

Asan picks up the men's weapons and hurries to the house. His family are huddled in the main room, anxious and afraid.

Asan strikes the huge agong by the door. He strikes it loud and long, with a regularity of beat that is at once a call and a signal. The full sound of the brass instrument echoes in the cliffs of Tamugan and into the *marang* and lanzones woods beyond. In a short while, Asan's relatives, and Anyaw's, too, will come.

Asan has decided now: they have to leave.

The next hour finds the family speechless and busy. In Asan's inner eye, he sees the Cebuano climbing up the other tortuous path from the river, towards Mr. Ventura's plantation. With the mental precision of one who has been working according to the clock, he knows that it will take the Cebuano twenty-five to thirty minutes of frenzied speed to reach the plantation house. He sees the man screaming through the abaca fields, running in horror towards Mr. Ventura's iron gates. It will take him five minutes to be understood: that his companions have been murdered by a mere Bagobo and his son. The father is one of those dirty laborers in the plantation. Then Mr. Ventura will strut out of the house, biting his cigar, to call his security guards and other armed protectors. One of the men will drive the service jeep to the police outpost in Calinan. The nearer outpost is in Gumalang, but it is most unlikely that the lone policeman is at the station. He must be at home training his fighting cocks. It will save time to drive to Calinan instead.

The police and Mr. Ventura's men will not come before sunset. But Asan is sure of one thing: the flood caused by the rains in the smaller mountains at the foot of Mt. Apo will swell the Tamugan within an hour.

The flood will stop the police and Mr. Ventura's men from crossing the river. There will be enough time to leave the cogon house and the camote patch and the durian tree for a safer place in the mountains beyond Panigan River. It will be safe to join Datu Duyan's men.

Asan knows. There will be no mercy from these Christian landgrabbers. The only wise thing to do is flee. He and his son have killed two of them in actual combat. In ancient time, that was more than enough to make him a bagane, a hero, a protector of home and tribe. But now, he is afraid.

From their own homes in the various parts of the plateau come Asan's relatives and friends. Old man Garong is with his teen-age son Masteda. Masteda is newly tattooed and he would like everybody to see the snake-skin design around his wrists and biceps. Then Asan's cousin Dumpit arrives panting, one hand gripping a Muslim *kampilan*. More relatives and friends come: Atoy and Amolong and Rasid and Anggawod. And Anyaw's brothers and uncles: Bunglay and Unday and Amilhasa and Kurokudo.

Even the bastard Mikoto is there. Mikoto's father was a Japanese gardener who turned out to be an officer of the Imperial Army during the War. His mother was Anyaw's unmarried sister who drowned in Panigan River during a December flood.

Asan stops beating the agong and addresses the excited relatives and friends.

"We cannot fight them," Old Man Garong says, shaking his white head. His distended, pierced earlobes shake, too.

"We are men of peace," says Dumpit, fondling the blade of his kampilan. "But if they push us farther, we will fight."

"They have guns!" Anyaw gasps. She has now bundled her clothes of brightly dyed hemp woven with *dumdum* beads.

"And money and power," continues old man Garong. "They will kill you, *us*! So, leave now while there is time. Go and join Datu Duyan's men. You will be safe there."

Suddenly from the river's direction comes a muffled, rolling sound. The flood has come. Asan cocks his ears, mentally measuring the swell of the Tamugan. He smiles. The river is too deep and too swift for any man to cross. Those Christians with guns will not dare defy the flood.

"We'll help you carry your things across the Panigan," Dumpit says. "Nobody should be here when those men arrive."

"No," answers Asan bitterly. "Nobody will be here. Nothing will be here. For I will burn this house and destroy all my plants. They can have my land but not my animals and my trees. I'll destroy them first!"

Anyaw weeps loudly, shamelessly. Ogaret cries with her.

Asan gives Dansig the Ilocano's jungle bolo. "Go!" he orders the boy. "Destroy the tree!"

Dansig stares at his father in horror. He looks at his father long until he sees again the bagane in that face. He understands.

The boy runs to the tree at the edge of the cliff. In the camote patch, more flies are hovering over the dead men. Dansig looks at them momentarily, and in his bitterness, he spits on them.

Below the cliff, the Tamugan is moaning steadily. It is late afternoon.

Dansig looks at the durian tree looming above him. It is so tall that it seems to touch the sky. The first blossoms of the season crowd the branches of the tree. In the pale, purple flowers, the boy pictures the future fruit. And on the topmost branch he pictures, too, the huge bird that catches monkeys for its food. The bird is whistling to its mate.

Anyaw's anguished cry startles the boy. He looks towards the direction of the house. Asan has set it on fire. Flame and smoke curl upwards like an offering to the ancient gods on Mt. Apo. Under the kamansi tree to which Dansig has tied Tibak, are piled the simple wealth of the house: baskets and mats and agongs and bolos and spears. There are assorted bundles of clothes and sacks of grain. And also Masaglang's hunting trophies of boar skulls and tusks.

Ul-ul barks at the fire.

Dansig squirms at the sight. He feels his heart jump and his muscles tense. His little hand is tight around the bolo's hilt. With all his little man's frustration and pristine rage, the boy strikes the tree. The bark gives way and soon the boy has made a ring around the massive trunk. He makes another ring under the first. A final stroke of the bolo's point removes the bark between the two rings until the tree has a fatal wound around its trunk.

Again, Dansig looks at the burning house and then at the tree looming above him. He sees the pale, purple blossoms. A few days from now, all of them will fall. Then the glossy leaves, too, will fall. He sees the tree sapless and dead, its gnarled branches clawing the sky, a sinister sentinel on the highway of the spiral winds . . .

He cries.

The Girl and the River

Michael Anthony

T H E R E   I S nobody in all Ortoire who cannot remember the ferry. None save those too young to understand or too old to remember anything at all. For it had been plying the wide river even before the village itself sprang up, in those remote times when men said the river was too wide to take a bridge.

But today there is no ferry any more. No more the precarious platform which took people and vehicles from bank to bank. Nor the winch and cable which drew the ferry across the river. Indeed, if you were travelling that way you'd be amazed by the steel bridge which towers where the ferry used to be. And you'd have been as overjoyed as I was when I was commissioned to build that bridge.

I was overjoyed and excited only until the work began. For at that point the anger of the whole village was unleashed upon me.

Everyone was bitterly opposed to me because of the ferryman. They said I was trying to chase him off the river. They said the ferryman belonged right here in the village and had been working the ferry before I was born. Now I had come—they did not know from where—and I found the ferry not good enough. They would see how far I'd get.

I kept quiet but I was determined to carry on with the work. For I needed a project of this size and the Ortoire river needed a bridge. I could not let the villagers frighten me away. We began by laying the foundations on the banks, driving piles in the riverbed, and cutting back the mangrove. All the time we worked the villagers hurled abuses at us and in the end they threatened to stop us if we did not stop.

We were scared, but fortunately they were never as good as their word and we pushed on with the job. We kept on going relentlessly for we were anxious to finish in the shortest time possible and clear out. We sweated from dawn till dusk and at night we stayed tensely in camp. We had no friends but the river itself, and the crabs of the mangrove, and the birds of passage that came and went.

When after many months the structure began taking shape across the river and the end of our labours drew in sight I began growing so excited I could hardly sleep at nights. And it was not only because I was anxious to be rid of this place. Each time I laid my head down I had visions of opening ceremonies and great crowds, and miles of cars queueing to drive over the bridge. My bridge. This was my first opportunity and I wanted to leave something on the face of the land. I wanted people to see it and know that I had built it and I wanted them to say it was the best in this part of the world. I grew so nervous for the completion that in my spare hours I had to go far from the bridge to find peace inside me. I did not dare show myself in the village so at such times I would take our little boat and row down river, losing myself in the green wilderness beyond the village.

Down river there was a tributary where some of the village folk came to wash clothes. The water was very clear in this part and there was a big, flat stone on the bank. I often came here and sat on the stone—when no one was around—and I would let my mind wander from place to place: to Port of Spain, my home-town; to the problems of this place; and to where and what I'd be sent to next. Very often my thoughts would dwell on this village here, and I would wonder what it was really like, and I would ask myself whether these angry people would change their minds and be pleased when the bridge was finished. I would think about all these things, and after about an hour or so I would get back into the boat and row towards the mother river again, then upstream towards the bridge.

One day, arriving at the stone earlier than usual, I met a young woman scrubbing clothes. I was going to turn back but she looked up and saw me, so I said, "Afternoon."

"Afternoon, Mr Danclar."

I could not remember seeing the face before, but the young lady knew my name. They all knew my name in the village, it seemed.

"Doing some hard work?"

"Yes," she said.

She was poorly dressed and she seemed anxious for me to leave. But it was the closest I had got to one of these villagers for a long time, and as she seemed the gentle type I wanted to talk. I was interested to know whether she, too, thought the bridge the work of the Devil.

I said, "The water clean here, eh?"

"That's why we does wash clothes here," she said.

This drew my attention to the large heap of clothes she had washed already, but there was a still larger heap waiting to be done.

"You could do all this today?"

"Might," she said, "but if not, I'll have to come back tomorrow." She paused a little, her hands frothy with soap. She looked at the remaining bundle, and she looked round at the vast waters stirring about her.

I said, "Tide coming in."

"It look so. It must be getting late. I'd better finish, to go."

She resumed washing and I pretended that I did not notice in her words the invitation for me to leave. I would not leave until I had asked her about the bridge.

She took up another piece of clothes from the bundle. I looked at the heap. She really seemed to be confronting a heavy task and I thought if I could say anything to make it lighter I would. I looked at her. She was busily washing and not looking at me but I could see she was conscious of my being there.

I said, "You know, I wish I was you. This place is so quaint—so quiet. I like this. I like to work in quietness and peace."

She said, "In Ortoire it have too much quietness and peace."

"Too much quietness and peace? That's what I'm looking for."

"I don't mean so," she chuckled. "I mean the place itself—you know."

"But tell me, you find here too dull? What's the village like?"

"Well there's nothing much to do in Ortoire. But I like here."

Now I brought the boat right up to the stone and as I stepped onto the bank, she said anxiously, "Mr Danclar!"

I was quickly back into the boat and about to push off. She couldn't help laughing at me.

I said, "It's all right. I don't want you to get in any trouble for me. I have enough myself already."

She said, "No, it's not that. It wouldn't look good if anybody see you here. You know what people give. And especially . . ."

"I know, I know. Especially as they want my head in the village. You think I don't know what the position is?"

She couldn't stop laughing. Then she said, "Don't think I'm against you. I realize you only doing your job."

"Well, thank you very much. Thanks a lot. Because nobody else seems to realize that."

She said nothing. I continued, "After all, I'm only a Government servant come to build a bridge. I don't want to put anybody out of work."

She kept on washing. "Don't worry about that," she said. And after a while she added, "I see you nearly finish."

"Praise God," I said, feeling relief.

She chuckled. "I know how happy you'll be to leave here."

"Aha? I'm not so sure about that. Strange, but this place seem to be growing on me. I like this sort of life—trees, river, birds . . . Somehow I'm growing to like this wilderness," I said, "once the Ortoire people leave me alone."

She smiled. She was rinsing out the clothes now. She said quietly, "I, too. This place growing on me, too."

"So you don't belong here, then?" I was surprised.

"Well, yes and no. I from here but I spend almost my whole life in Sangre Grande. But since Pa isn't working now, I'm back here helping him out."

"But couldn't you work in Sangre Grande and still help him out?"

She hesitated a little and said, "But I want to be here, too. He's so depressed." She was looking at the river.

"And where you work now?"

"Right here."

I just looked at her and could not say anything. Inside, I felt shocked. At first I thought that this young lady was just the elder sister in a family, taking charge of the week's washing. I did not know that she washed other people's clothes so that she and her father could live!

After a few moments I left the girl and her washing and with a depressed feeling I rowed down into the mother river, and then up to our quarters. I watched the great structure towering across the river before me and for once I did not feel any pride.

Why was life so ironical? I thought. Here across the river rose an engineer's dream of success, and yet on this very river there was also the distress and even humiliation of a young girl.

That night, as I began telling my foreman the story of the girl, I noticed he fell into an unusual silence.

"What's the matter?"

"You know the girl?"

"No, but that doesn't make any difference. I just feel that for a young person the life she's leading is hell."

"So you having regrets?"

"Regrets about what? I mean I don't get your point."

My foreman turned and looked at me and said, "Now don't give me that, Shallo. Don't try to play you don't know what's happening."

"You mean something special happening? Something besides . . ."

He was laughing heartily. Afterwards he said, "Anyway, the point is, we came here to build a bridge and we almost finish it. This place more than need a bridge and even the ferryman himself will realize this in the end. Although everybody vex like hell now. But to come back to this girl— I can't believe you don't know her because she belong to right over there. In a sense she's doing that job because of the bridge. But what the hell. The old man won't last long and she can go back to Sangre Grande and look for a job. Let's face it, the old man couldn't do that job much longer anyway. Just imagine your father—a man of about eighty—pushing a big donkey of a plank across a river!"

The Tower of Babel

Epeli Hau'ofa

"TIKO CAN'T be developed," Manu declared, "unless the ancient gods are killed."

"But the ancient gods are dead. The Sabbatarians killed them long ago," countered the ancient preacher.

"Never believe that, sir. Had they died Tiko would have developed long ago. Look around you," Manu advised.

The ancient preacher looked around and saw nothing; he looked at himself, his tattered clothes, his nailed-in second-hand sandals, and nodded rather dubiously. He wished to be developed. "And how do you slay the ancient gods?" he inquired cautiously.

"Never try, sir, it's useless," Manu replied. "Kill the new ones." And that, in short, is what Manu does. He wants to keep the ancient gods alive and slay the new ones. He pedals his bicycle to the International Night-light Hotel, to the Bank of Tiko, and all over Tulisi, shouting his lonely message against Development, but the whole capital is as a cemetery.

And Manu shouted at the Doctor of Philosophy recently graduated from Australia. The good Doctor works on Research for Development. He is a portly man going to pot a mite too soon for his age; and he looks an oddity with an ever-present pipe protruding from his bushy, beefy face. The Doctor is an Expert, although he has never discovered what he is an expert of. It doesn't matter; in the balmy isles of Tiko, as long as one is Most Educated, one is Elite, an Expert, and a Wise Man to boot.

One starry evening the portly Doctor walked down a dusty Tulisi street. He walked the walk of those who would build Tiko higher than the Tower of Babel. The good Doctor walked loftily. Then out of the blue, on this clear and starry night, a piercing voice sliced the stillness with, "WHY ARE YOU DESTROYING MY COUNTRY?" It was Manu, who knows how to pierce.

Manu also shouted at the Great Secretary, a young man with an enormous mop on his head. The Secretary is a Most Important Person, an Expert, Elite, and a Wise Man to boot. This happy combination of four great elements in the person of one so young has turned the Secretary into a Man of Substance with a bright and prosperous future in the development of his country.

One sunny day he was driving through the main street of downtown Tulisi, waving to all and sundry, who waved back, impressed with his Friendliness and Humility. With Wise Men like him, say all and sundry, the development of the realm is in Good Hands. The Secretary was driving to the Bank of Tiko to draw $50,000 for the funding of a Great Development Project. He was very pleased with himself. Then suddenly a slashing voice split the steamy asphalt: "TIKO HATES YOU!" The Secretary was so surprised he ran his automobile into an old raintree outside the Bank of Tiko. The voice was Manu's, and Manu knows how to drive a man up a tree.

Tiko can't be developed, said Manu with the certainty of someone who knows. But the Wise Men of Tiko want to develop everything; everything, that is, except sex. Sex is too developed already; why else would Tiko have the highest population growth rate in the Pacific? Furthermore, was not sex responsible for the Fish Cannery Project fiasco?

The great cannery project revolved around the fishing vessel, the *Mau-mau Taimi*, which originated in Japan and had a refrigerated compartment to hold one hundred tons of tuna. In Japanese hands it operated well around the Pacific waters for twenty years before the owners decided that instead of converting it into scrap metal they would send it to Tiko as aid to needy foreign friends.

The *Hata Maru*, as it was known in Tokyo, was crewed by Japanese men none of whom was younger than sixty-five. The elderly hands, whose sex drive had long gone dry, as they say around the dockyards of the Orient, would go out for three or four months until the one-hundred-ton hold was filled to the hatch with tuna.

When the Japanese envoy presented the vessel at Tulisi to His Excellency's Government he did not reveal this clever operating method, because the Japanese, whose country is managed by a gerontocracy, did not wish to let it be known that their old men are of little value to women. They did not want to lose face.

The vessel's arrival created high expectations that Tiko would shortly become a Nation with a Fish Cannery. The *Maumau Taimi* has been around for ten years now, but there is still not a cannery. The vessel could have long ago been passed on to New Zealand as a foreign-aid item, but the Wise Men at the Thinking Office do not want to lose face.

And what's behind this failure? "Sex!" said Manu without hesitation. And he is right. The vessel's arrival coincided with a period of much anxiety concerning the too many young men walking the streets of Tulisi; doing nothing, according to high officialdom. In actual fact the young men had been doing many, many things, like looking for a bit of sex most of the time; but the Appropriate Authorities did not let this be known, for fear of losing face. And the Appropriate Authorities persuaded the young men to crew the newly acquired vessel as a way of doing something and as part of their contribution to the development of Tiko.

The first of their projected ninety days at sea was very nice, and the next few days at sea were also very nice. But by the end of the second week the much deprived youths wanted desperately to set for home and a bit of sex. On the third week nothing would keep them away and the vessel headed home with only four tons of tuna. The operating costs for the trip ran close to $8000 and the sale of the catch brought in not quite $2000. It's been that way since the *Maumau Taimi* ventured forth on its Tikong maiden voyage. No one says anything, no one does anything, for no one dares lose face.

In developing the realm into a Nation with a Fish Cannery it was necessary to develop not only the Top but also the Bottom, in order to get a proper balance. "A well-rounded Bottom below a well-rounded Top is beauty well worth having," Manu declared, not thinking of tinned fish.

The responsibility for Bottom Development went to one Alvin (Sharky) Lowe of Alice Springs, Australia. Mr Lowe, a matey-matey sort of bloke who wanted to be known simply as Sharky, was a Great Expert with lifelong experience in handling natives in New Guinea, Thursday Island, and in a certain humpy settlement outside his gentle hometown of Alice

Springs. He had developed a good feel for the Grassroots, demonstrating it by grabbing every frightened, small-time, part-time fisherman on the beaches of Tulisi and forcing him ever so gently to accept $4000 in Development Loans from the Appropriate Authorities. And, like the Great Shepherd of Nazareth, Sharky converted many frightened fellows into fishermen.

One such frightened, small-time, part-time fisherman was Ika Levu, who happened also to be a small-time, part-time gardener. His dual occupation meant that Ika worked whenever he felt like it; and he had very little money, which bothered him not at all. Ika never felt miserable until Sharky laid hands on him. It was his most urgent duty to help develop his country, said Sharky.

Mr Lowe had originally found him on a beach one day caulking a leaky old dinghy. "Hello there. I'm Sharky, and I'm the Fisheries Grassroots Development Adviser. Do you speak English?"

"Eh, a leetol bit."

"You no can speak English good?" Sharky switched to the language he used when talking to simple natives.

"Eh, a leetol bit."

"Whassat name belong you?"

"Eh, a leetol bit."

"Leetol bit? You no leetol bit! You beeg fela bit! Look, me try one more time yet." Sharky took a deep breath, then resumed speaking, very slowly and very clearly this time. "Now, me like savvy name belong you. All right? Name belong you Joe? or Jack? or . . ."

"Oi, me Ika Levu."

"Good fela name, Ika. Me like it too much. You go catch fish sometime?"

"Eh, a leetol bit."

"Good, good. Now suppose you help me develop country belong you, me help you catch plenty big fela fish. You savvy?"

Ika didn't quite get it so he shrugged and turned away. Sharky grabbed his shoulders, turned him around, and put all his salesmanship into operation. "Now is duty belong you to help Tiko come up rich fela country. Suppose you help Tiko, me help you too. Like me help you get one big fela loan, na you can buy new boat, na fishing nets, na lines, na hooks, na floats. Plenty something you can buy. Then you go catch big fela fish, na you sell em, na you get plenty money, na you can buy six fela Marys inside International Nightlight Hotel, pushpush no stop all time good! Me think think you clever fela man. You strong up there, you strong down below like four fela Brahmin bullmacow. Now you me work allgather onetime like brothers. Me big brother, you little brother. You me help Tiko come up all same big fela rich country. Plenty plenty ice cream, sweet sweet all same lollies from Heaven. All right?"

"Me doan know."

"You no can savvy? Gawd! Me talk talk all same simple something na you no can savvy! Whassamatter? Me think think head belong you too much dumdum na full up shit something no good true! All right, me all same try one more time yet, na you try savvy good or I'll bloody well bash your coon head in, O.K.?"

So with the infinite patience and gentleness of an expert native handler Sharky went through the whole routine a few more times until Ika got the message. Ika was thoroughly frightened and confused. He was also flattered. No Important Person had ever before sought his help, let alone talked to him. And although he was full of doubt Ika prayed to God for guidance and consented to accept the loan.

With Sharky's help Ika acquired a twelve horse-power Rendo outboard motor, an eighteen-foot imported dinghy, six big nets, and dozens of lines and hooks, all of which came from certain firms in Japan and Australia which Sharky represented.

When Ika was properly equipped and properly launched for a lifetime of catching the big fish, Sharky moved on to the next fisherman, and to the next. By the time his tour of duty ended Sharky had equipped and launched one thousand fishermen with one thousand Rendo outboard motors, one thousand imported dinghies, six thousand big nets, and tens of thousands of lines and hooks. Sharky had also established a Fishermen's Aid Post furnished with spare parts and a stock of Rendo motors, imported dinghies, and big nets, all of which came from those certain companies in Japan and Australia of which he was the sole South Pacific Representative. In helping the development of Tiko, Sharky had helped the development of himself and his companies most generously.

And what of Ika, the frightened little man embarked on his solemn duty toward the development of his country? As soon as he got his fishing equipment, and got himself thoroughly in debt, Sharky dropped him and forgot about his existence. No one thought of guiding him, so he remained a small-timer and part-timer in everything. Like other such fishermen Ika never met the Appropriate Authorities: they simply could not be seen.

The first time Ika tried to see them he was so nervous that he stood outside the office door for twenty minutes before he could summon sufficient courage to knock; and his knock was so gentle that it hardly made a sound. Another twenty minutes went by before he mustered enough courage to open the door ever so slightly and peek in. A plumpish receptionist was sitting at a desk only ten feet away, talking to a fellow-worker. Ika coughed a bit to attract their attention.

"What do you want?" asked the receptionist, obviously annoyed with the interruption. She had just resumed duty that morning after two-months' maternity leave.

"Please miss. I want to talk to someone . . ."

"He's not here. Come back tomorrow."

"Forgive me, miss, I think it's important. It's about the payments of a loan I got from this office."

"Well, come right in then; I won't eat you. Do you have the instalment on you?"

"That's what I want to talk to someone about. You see, I haven't got anything with me."

"I see. You'd better discuss that with the Assistant Secretary. Mele!" she called out to someone in the main office behind her, "is the A.S. in?"

"No. He's gone to Wellington to attend a conference. He'll be back in two weeks."

"How about the Director then?"

"He's gone with the Minister to Geneva. They'll be back next month after meetings in Rome, Tel Aviv, New Delhi, Djakarta, and Sydney. Lucky pigs; their pockets won't be big enough to hold their travel allowances. Why can't they send us sometime for a change?"

"And Dau Yali?"

"That idiot is in London on a six-month training course. He has no brains, but he's the Director's cousin. They're all overseas, the whole bloody lot of them."

"But who's holding the fort?"

"Who do you think but the likes of us?"

The receptionist turned to Ika. "Well, you heard what the situation is. Go home and come back in a month's time. Don't look so depressed, for goodness' sake. It's nothing new. Look, I'll try the crowd downstairs. They may be able to help you."

She picked up the telephone and dialed a number. "Seini? Susana. Very well thanks; and you? That's good, but don't overdo it. Look, is Vakarau Dro in?"

"No," came the voice from the other end, "he's in bed with gout and won't be in for the rest of the week."

"But he'll be back next week, won't he?"

"Sort of. He'll come in to pick up his papers and then he's off straight-away to a seminar in Kuala Lumpur. From there he goes to Tokyo to represent the Ministry at the Tayashita Year of the Biggest Sales Celebrations, and then to San Francisco for his three-months' leave. Sorry, you'll just have to pine for him; it's your own fault. I warned you not to fall for people like that; they're always on the go, and who knows who they shack up with overseas."

"You're a bitch, Seini. Anyway, what about Big Ben himself?"

"Haven't you heard? You must be the only one. Well, Big B's in a critical condition at the hospital. He went to the Russian Ambassador's cocktail party the other night, got absolutely drunk, and attacked his own wife. That was a near-fatal mistake; the missis got him on the head with an empty whisky bottle. Serves him right, I say. A lot of other things happened at that cocktail party, you know. The Director of Manpower also got drunk and swore at his Minister who smashed him on the kisser and then got himself kneed in the balls by the Director's wife. Those high-class women are pretty dangerous. And then that old billy goat, Henry Coles; took off with Mrs. Cohen to God knows where. Mr. Cohen is in Suva conducting a four-week training course. People shouldn't go overseas so often, leaving their wives behind. I don't blame the poor bitches getting it on the sly; they hardly get it straight, poor things. I'd do it myself if I were them."

"You'll never be one of them," said Susana, and put down the phone. "I'm very sorry. There's no one downstairs either. Come back in a month's time."

Ika went back after a month but couldn't get to see anyone. He returned once more, then gave up trying to see the Appropriate Authorities. And, because of official inaccessibility and his own predilections, Ika fell behind in paying back the loan. He fell so far behind that one day he ceased being frightened, took out his imported dinghy, the Rendo motor, and the six big nets, went two miles out to sea, pulled out an axe and hacked a huge hole in the bottom of the boat. Then he swam slowly ashore, cool and relaxed for the first time in months and months.

He wrote short letters to the Appropriate Authorities and reported regretfully that his boat and equipment were at the bottom of the ocean owing to a most unfortunate accident. Since he had neither money nor anything worth confiscating, and since he could not be held on any legal grounds, no one tried to touch him. His name was simply added to a long, long list of unreliable persons not worth aiding in the future. Ika couldn't care less, and today you will find him on a certain beach in Tulisi patching up an old dinghy and talking happily with his friends. Not all are so fortunate.

One such less fortunate person was Toa Qase, who was a successful small-time market gardener and banana grower until he switched to big-time chicken farming under the Poultry Development Scheme funded by an agency of the Great International Organisation. Toa abandoned all forms of gardening, obtained a loan, and built a big shed to house six thousand infant chickens flown in from New Zealand.

The chickens grew large and lovely, and Toa's fame spread. Everyone knew he had six thousand chickens and everyone wanted to taste them. A well-bred Tikong gives generously to his relatives and neighbours, especially one with thousands of earthly goods. But under the guidance of a Development Expert, who was Elite and a Wise Man to boot, Toa aimed to become a Modern Businessman, forgetting that in Tiko if you give less you will lose more and if you give nothing you will lose all. And Toa's chickens began to disappear, a dozen on the first night filched by his underpaid chicken-farmhands, two dozen the second night filched by the same underpaid farmhands plus their friends, and so on. Word spread that Toa's chickens were fast disappearing so why not help yourself before they were all gone. Thus everyone who happened to walk by the road at night helped himself to Toa's large and lovely chickens before they were all gone.

As for Toa, he gave up his dream of becoming a wealthy Modern Businessman, bade Godspeed to the Development Expert, and went to his clergyman for consolation and advice. The said Man of God reached for the Good Book, opened at St. Matthew and read, "Lay not up for yourselves treasures upon earth where moth and rust doth corrupt, and where thieves break through and steal." Yes, Toa remembered, and vowed he would never again be so greedy for earthly goods.

Since then, as Manu tells it, Toa has devoted all his time to developing for himself vast treasures in Heaven where live neither thieves nor experts.

COUNTRYSIDE
AND CITY;
FAMILY
FOREIGNERS

The theme that is so clear in Saloni Narang's parable "Close to the Earth" occurs often in the Global Cultures literature on development and modernization. A child or young person goes off to the city from the countryside to live with relatives, to go to school, to attend university, or simply to be able to make a living when the countryside has been afflicted with drought, economic downturn, or enterprises that have displaced the local agriculture. The one who goes away changes and becomes mysterious to those at home. Sometimes the one who goes away is lost forever, sometimes not. All of the themes in stories about a person of the colonies going abroad to the metropolis, to the colonializing country—covering vast geographical and cultural distances—are played out in these stories in temporal terms. Those who leave go into an unimaginable future, not so much to another people as to "our people" in another century. The Ghanian writer **AMA ATA AIDOO** (whose story "Everything Counts" is in Part 1) tells one variation on this tale: A girl who has refused to go on in school (we don't learn why) is placed outside the family to learn domestic skills; but she has dropped out of contact, and a brother has now (after an unexplained delay of twelve years) been dispatched to the city to look for her. The whole story is full of mysteries, which the village people cannot grasp, and the narrative technique lets these stand—to the reader's puzzlement. A generational saga flashes by so fast—"in the cutting of a drink"— it is uninterpretable.

In "The Homecoming Stranger," twenty years have been lost. They dropped out of the life of a girl named Lanlan, beginning when she was five and her father was arrested, and ending when she, while training to be a teacher, unexpectedly gets him back. While China's revolution has been underway, he has been in the timeless limbo of a prison camp for being an "offender against the people," but now he has been exonerated, rehabilitated, by the very same Theatre Association that once turned him over to the Maoist authorities. ("The Homecoming Stranger" was first published in 1978, which would set the father's arrest in 1958 if we translate into actual historical time; consequently he was in a camp and not on the collective farms established to re-educate officials during the Cultural Revolution, 1965–1976.) The grown-up daughter has to learn to accept this stranger, who feels to her like a traitor. To do so, she must receive a political education to understand what happened to the family and an emotional education to understand how she got sealed into her childhood sense of abandonment and purely personal loss.

In 1965, when the Cultural Revolution began in China, the story's author, the poet BEI DAO ("Northern Island," pen name of Zhao Zhenkai, b. 1949), was sixteen. He was being educated in a prestigious school for just that government bureaucracy and managerial elite which the revolutionaries wanted to demolish. His initial enthusiasm for Maoism waned as the Revolution became more tyrannical and more factionalized, and he began to write poetry and fiction, which he could only publish freely with the liberalization that arose two years after Mao's death, that is, with the 1978 "Democracy Wall Movement." While making his living as a construction worker, Bei Dao co-edited a literary magazine, *Today*, which was renowned for containing real literature, not propaganda. He was deeply skeptical about the modernization undertaken by the Communist Party between 1978 and 1988, particularly after *Today* was closed down in 1980. Separated from his family—including his own young daughter—Bei Dao has been in involuntary exile from China since 1989 when he organized a protest against the arrest of one of the 1978 Democracy Movement's leaders. Recently he has restarted *Today* in his country of exile, Norway.

In the Cutting of a Drink

Ama Ata Aidoo

I SAY, my uncles, if you are going to Accra and anyone tells you that the best place for you to drop down is at the Circle, then he has done you good, but . . . hm . . . I even do not know how to describe it . . .

"Are all these beings that are passing this way and that way human? Did men buy all these cars with money . . . ?"

But my elders, I do not want to waste your time. I looked round and did not find my bag. I just fixed my eyes on the ground and walked on . . . Do not ask me why. Each time I tried to raise my eyes, I was dizzy from the number of cars which were passing. And I could not stand still. If I did, I felt as if the whole world was made up of cars in motion. There is something somewhere, my uncles. Not desiring to deafen you with too long a story . . .

I stopped walking just before I stepped into the Circle itself. I stood there for a long time. Then a lorry came along and I beckoned to the driver to stop. Not that it really stopped.

"Where are you going?" he asked me.

"I am going to Mamprobi," I replied. "Jump in," he said, and he started to drive away. Hm . . . I nearly fell down climbing in. As we went round the thing which was like a big bowl on a very huge stump of wood, I had it in mind to have a good look at it, and later Duayaw told me that it shoots water in the air . . . but the driver was talking to me, so I could not look at it properly. He told me he himself was not going to Mamprobi but he was going to the station where I could take a lorry which would be going there . . .

Yes, my uncle, he did not deceive me. Immediately we arrived at the station I found the driver of a lorry shouting "Mamprobi, Mamprobi." Finally when the clock struck about two-thirty, I was knocking on the door of Duayaw. I did not knock for long when the door opened. Ah, I say, he was fast asleep, fast asleep I say, on a Saturday afternoon.

"How can folks find time to sleep on Saturday afternoons?" I asked myself. We hailed each other heartily. My uncles, Duayaw has done well for himself. His mother Nsedua is a very lucky woman.

How is it some people are lucky with school and others are not? Did not Mansa go to school with Duayaw here in this very school which I can see for myself? What have we done that Mansa should have wanted to stop going to school?

But I must continue with my tale . . . Yes, Duayaw has done well for himself. His room has fine furniture. Only it is too small. I asked him why and he told me he was even lucky to have got that narrow place that looks like a box. It is very hard to find a place to sleep in the city . . .

He asked me about the purpose of my journey. I told him everything. How, as he himself knew, my sister Mansa had refused to go to school after "Klase Tri" and how my mother had tried to persuade her to go . . .

My mother, do not interrupt me, everyone present here knows you tried to do what you could by your daughter.

Yes, I told him how, after she had refused to go, we finally took her to this woman who promised to teach her to keep house and to work with the sewing machine . . . and how she came home the first Christmas after the woman took her but has never been home again, these twelve years.

Duayaw asked me whether it was my intention then to look for my sister in the city. I told him yes. He laughed saying, "You are funny. Do you think you can find a woman in this place? You do not know where she is staying. You do not even know whether she is married or not. Where can we find her if someone big has married her and she is now living in one of those big bungalows which are some ten miles from the city?"

Do you cry "My Lord," mother? You are surprised about what I said about the marriage? Do not be. I was surprised too, when he talked that way. I too cried "My Lord" . . . Yes, I too did, mother. But you and I have forgotten that Mansa was born a girl and girls do not take much time to grow. We are thinking of her as we last saw her when she was ten years old. But mother, that is twelve years ago . . .

Yes, Duayaw told me that she is by now old enough to marry and to do something more than merely marry. I asked him whether he knew where she was and if he knew whether she had any children—"Children?" he cried, and he started laughing, a certain laugh . . .

I was looking at him all the time he was talking. He told me he was not just discouraging me but he wanted me to see how big and difficult it was, what I proposed to do. I replied that it did not matter. What was necessary was that even if Mansa was dead, her ghost would know that we had not forgotten her entirely. That we had not let her wander in other people's towns and that we had tried to bring her home . . .

These are useless tears you have started to weep, my mother. Have I said anything to show that she was dead?

Duayaw and I decided on the little things we would do the following day as the beginning of our search. Then he gave me water for my bath and brought me food. He sat by me while I ate and asked me for news of home. I told him that his father has married another woman and of how last year the *akatse* spoiled all our cocoa. We know about that already. When I finished eating, Duayaw asked me to stretch out my bones on the bed and I did. I think I slept fine because when I opened my eyes it was dark. He had switched on his light and there was a woman in the room. He showed me her as a friend but I think she is the girl he wants to marry against the wishes of his people. She is as beautiful as sunrise, but she does not come from our parts . . .

When Duayaw saw that I was properly awake, he told me it had struck eight o'clock in the evening and his friend had brought some food. The three of us ate together.

Do not say "Ei," uncle, it seems as if people do this thing in the city. A woman prepares a meal for a man and eats it with him. Yes, they do so often.

My mouth could not manage the food. It was prepared from cassava and corn dough, but it was strange food all the same. I tried to do my best. After the meal, Duayaw told me we were going for a night out. It was then I remembered my bag. I told him that as matters stood, I could not change my cloth and I could not go out with them. He would not hear of it. "It would certainly be a crime to come to this city and not go out on a Saturday night." He warned me though that there might not be many people, or anybody at all, where we were going who would also be in cloth but I should not worry about that.

Cut me a drink, for my throat is very dry, my uncle . . .

When we were on the street, I could not believe my eyes. The whole place was as clear as the sky. Some of these lights are very beautiful indeed. Everyone should see them . . . and there are so many of them! "Who is paying for all these lights?" I asked myself. I could not say that aloud for fear Duayaw would laugh.

We walked through many streets until we came to a big building where a band was playing. Duayaw went to buy tickets for the three of us.

You all know that I had not been to anywhere like that before. You must allow me to say that I was amazed. "Ei, are all these people children of human beings? And where are they going? And what do they want?"

Before I went in, I thought the building was big, but when I went in, I realized the crowd in it was bigger. Some were in front of a counter buying drinks, others were dancing . . .

Yes, that was the case, uncle, we had gone to a place where they had given a dance, but I did not know.

Some people were sitting on iron chairs around iron tables. Duayaw told some people to bring us a table and chairs and they did. As soon as we sat down, Duayaw asked us what we would drink. As for me, I told him *lamlale* but his woman asked for "Beer" . . .

Do not be surprised, uncles.

Yes, I remember very well, she asked for beer. It was not long before Duayaw brought them. I was too surprised to drink mine. I sat with my mouth open and watched the daughter of a woman cut beer like a man. The band had stopped playing for some time and soon they started again. Duayaw and his woman went to dance. I sat there and drank my *lamlale*. I cannot describe how they danced.

After some time, the band stopped playing and Duayaw and his woman came to sit down. I was feeling cold and I told Duayaw. He said, "And this is no wonder, have you not been drinking this women's drink all the time?"

"Does it make one cold?" I asked him.

"Yes," he replied. "Did you not know that? You must drink beer."

"Yes," I replied. So he bought me beer. When I was drinking the beer, he told me I would be warm if I danced.

"You know I cannot dance the way you people dance," I told him.

"And how do we dance?" he asked me.

"I think you all dance like white men and as I do not know how that is done, people would laugh at me," I said. Duayaw started laughing. He could not contain himself. He laughed so much his woman asked him what it was all about. He said something in the white man's language and they started laughing again. Duayaw then told me that if people were dancing, they would be so busy that they would not have time to watch others dance. And also, in the city, no one cares if you dance well or not ...

Yes, I danced too, my uncles. I did not know anyone, that is true. My uncle, do not say that instead of concerning myself with the business for which I had gone to the city, I went dancing. Oh, if you only knew what happened at this place, you would not be saying this. I would not like to stop somewhere and tell you the end ... I would rather like to put a rod under the story, as it were, clear off every little creeper in the bush ...

But as we were talking about the dancing, something made Duayaw turn to look behind him where four women were sitting by the table ... Oh! he turned his eyes quickly, screwed his face into something queer which I could not understand and told me that if I wanted to dance, I could ask one of those women to dance with me.

My uncles, I too was very surprised when I heard that. I asked Duayaw if people who did not know me would dance with me. He said "Yes." I lifted my eyes, my uncles, and looked at those four young women sitting round a table alone. They were sitting all alone, I say. I got up.

I hope I am making myself clear, my uncles, but I was trembling like water in a brass bowl.

Immediately one of them saw me, she jumped up and said something in that kind of white man's language which everyone, even those who have not gone to school, speaks in the city. I shook my head. She said something else in the language of the people of the place. I shook my head again. Then I heard her ask me in Fante whether I wanted to dance with her. I replied "Yes."

Ei! my little sister, are you asking me a question? Oh! you want to know whether I found Mansa? I do not know ... Our uncles have asked me to tell everything that happened there, and you too! I am cooking the whole meal for you, why do you want to lick the ladle now?

Yes, I went to dance with her. I kept looking at her so much I think I was all the time stepping on her feet. I say, she was as black as you and I, but her hair was very long and fell on her shoulders like that of a white woman. I did not touch it but I saw it was very soft. Her lips with that red paint looked like a fresh wound. There was no space between her skin and her dress. Yes, I danced with her. When the music ended, I went back to where I was sitting. I do not know what she told her companions about me, but I heard them laugh.

It was this time that something made me realize that they were all bad women of the city. Duayaw had told me I would feel warm if I danced, yet after I had danced, I was colder than before. You would think someone had poured water on me. I was unhappy thinking about these women. "Have they no homes?" I asked myself. "Do not their mothers like them? God, we are all toiling for our threepence to buy something to eat . . . but oh! God! this is no work."

When I thought of my own sister, who was lost, I became a little happy because I felt that although I had not found her, she was nevertheless married to a big man and all was well with her.

When the band started to play again, I went to the women's table to ask the one with whom I had danced to dance again. But someone had gone with her already. I got one of the two who were still sitting there. She went with me. When we were dancing she asked me whether it was true that I was a Fante. I replied "Yes." We did not speak again. When the band stopped playing, she told me to take her to where they sold things to buy her beer and cigarettes. I was wondering whether I had the money. When we were where the lights were shining brightly, something told me to look at her face. Something pulled at my heart.

"Young woman, is this the work you do?" I asked her.

"Young man, what work do you mean?" she too asked me. I laughed.

"Do you not know what work?" I asked again.

"And who are you to ask me such questions? I say, who are you? Let me tell you that any kind of work is work. You villager, you villager, who are you?" she screamed.

I was afraid. People around were looking at us. I laid my hands on her shoulders to calm her down and she hit them away.

"Mansa, Mansa," I said. "Do you not know me?" She looked at me for a long time and started laughing. She laughed, laughed as if the laughter did not come from her stomach. Yes, as if she was hungry.

"I think you are my brother," she said. "Hm."

Oh, my mother and my aunt, oh, little sister, are you all weeping? As for you women!

What is there to weep about? I was sent to find a lost child. I found her a woman.

Cut me a drink . . .

Any kind of work is work . . . This is what Mansa told me with a mouth that looked like clotted blood. Any kind of work is work . . . so do not weep. She will come home this Christmas.

My brother, cut me another drink. Any form of work is work . . . is work . . . is work!

The Homecoming Stranger

Bei Dao

PAPA WAS back.

After exactly twenty years of reform through labor, which took him from the Northeast to Shanxi, and then from Shanxi to Gansu, he was just like a sailor swept overboard by a wave, struggling blindly against the undertow until miraculously he is tossed by another wave back onto the same deck.

The verdict was: it was entirely a misjudgment, and he has been granted complete rehabilitation. That day, when the leaders of the Theater Association honored our humble home to announce the decision, I almost jumped up: when did you become so clever? Didn't the announcement that he was an offender against the people come out of your mouths too? It was Mama's eyes, those calm yet suffering eyes, that stopped me.

Next came the dress rehearsal for the celebration: we moved from a tiny pigeon loft into a three-bedroom apartment in a big building: sofas, bookcases, desks, and chrome folding chairs appeared as if by magic (I kept saying half-jokingly to Mama that these were the troupe's props): relatives and friends came running in and out all day, until the lacquer doorknob was rubbed shiny by their hands, and even those uncles and aunts who hadn't shown up all those years rushed to offer congratulations . . . all right, cheer, sing, but what does all this have to do with me? My Papa died a long time ago, he died twenty years ago, just when a little four- or five-year old girl needed a father's love—that's what Mama, the school, kindhearted souls, and the whole social upbringing that starts at birth told me. Not only this, you even wanted me to hate him, curse him, it's even possible you'd have given me a whip so I could lash him viciously! Now it's the other way round, you're wearing a different face. What do you want me to do? Cry or laugh?

Yesterday at dinner time, Mama was even more considerate than usual, endlessly filling my bowl with food. After the meal, she drew a telegram from the drawer and handed it to me, showing not the slightest sign of any emotion.

"Him?"

"He arrives tomorrow, at 4:50 in the afternoon."

I crumpled the telegram, staring numbly into Mama's eyes.

"Go and meet him, Lanlan." She avoided my gaze.

"I have a class tomorrow afternoon."

"Get someone to take it for you."

I turned toward my room. "I won't go."

"Lanlan." Mama raised her voice. "He is your father, after all!"

"Father?" I muttered, turning away fiercely, as if overcome with fear at the meaning of this word. From an irregular spasm in my heart, I realized it was stitches from the old wound splitting open one by one.

I closed the composition book spread in front of me: Zhang Xiaoxia. 2nd Class. 5th Year. A spirited girl, her head always slightly to one side in a challenging way, just like me as a child. Oh yes, childhood. For all of us life begins with those pale blue copybooks, with those words, sentences, and punctuation marks smudged by erasers: or, to put it more precisely, it begins with a certain degree of deception. The teachers delineated life with halos, but which of them does not turn into a smoke ring or an iron hoop?

Shadows flowed in from the long old-fashioned windows, dulling the bright light on the glass desktop. The entire staff-room was steeped in drowsy tranquillity. I sighed, tidied my things, locked the door, and crossing the deserted school grounds walked toward home.

The apartment block with its glittering lights was like a huge television screen, the unlit windows composing an elusive image. After a little while some of the windows lit up, and some went dark again. But the three windows on the seventh floor remained as they were: one bright, two dark. I paced up and down for a long time in the vacant lot piled with white lime and fir poles. On a crooked, broken signboard were the words: "Safety First."

Strange, why is it that in all the world's languages, this particular meaning comes out as the same sound: Papa. Fathers of different colors, temperaments, and status all derive the same satisfaction from this sound. Yet I still can't say it. What do I know about him? Except for a few surviving old photographs retaining a childhood dream (perhaps every little girl would have such dreams): him, sitting on an elephant like an Arab sheik, a white cloth wound round his head, a resplendent mat on the elephant's back, golden tassels dangling to the ground . . . there were only some plays that once created a sensation and a thick book on dramatic theory which I happened to see at the wastepaper salvage station. What else was there? Yes, add those unlucky letters, as punctual and drab as a clock: stuck in those brown paper envelopes with their red frames, they were just like death notices, suffocating me. I never wrote back, and afterward, I threw them into the fire without even looking at them. Once, a dear little duckling was printed on a snow-white envelope, but when I tore it open and looked, I was utterly crushed. I was so upset I cursed all ugly ducklings, counting up their vices one by one: greed, pettiness, slovenliness . . . because they hadn't brought me good luck. But what luck did I deserve?

The elevator had already closed for the day, and I had to climb all the way up. I stopped outside the door to our place and listened, holding my breath. From inside came the sounds of the television hum and the clichés of an old film. God, give me courage!

As soon as I opened the door, I heard my younger brother's gruff voice: "Sis's back." He rushed up as if making an assault on the enemy, helping me take off my coat. He was almost twenty, but still full of a childish attachment to me, probably because I had given him the maternal love which had seemed too heavy a burden for Mama in those years.

The corridor was very dark and the light from the kitchen split the darkness in two. He was standing in the doorway of the room opposite, standing in the other half of darkness, and next to him was Mama. The reflection from the television screen flickered behind their shoulders.

A moment of dead silence.

Finally, he walked over, across the river of light. The light, the deathly white light, slipped swiftly over his wrinkled and mottled neck and face. I was struck dumb: was this shriveled little old man him? Father. I leaned weakly against the door.

He hesitated a moment and put out his hand. My small hand disappeared in his stiff, big-jointed hand. These hands didn't match his body at all.

"Lanlan." His voice was very low, and trembled a little.

Silence.

"Lanlan," he said again, his voice becoming a little more positive, as if he were waiting eagerly for something.

But what could I say?

"You're back very late. Have you had dinner?" said Mama.

"Mm." My voice was so weak.

"Why is everyone standing? Come inside," said Mama.

He took me by the hand. I followed obediently. Mama turned on the light and switched off the television with a click. We sat down on the sofa. He was still clutching my hand tightly, staring at me intently. I evaded his eyes and let my gaze fall on the blowup plastic doll on the window-sill.

An unbearable silence.

"Lanlan," he called once again.

I was really afraid the doll might explode, sending brightly colored fragments flying all over the room.

"Have you had your dinner?"

I nodded vigorously.

"Is it cold outside?"

"No." Everything was so normal, the doll wouldn't burst. Perhaps it would fly away suddenly like a hydrogen balloon, out the window, above the houses full of voices, light, and warmth, and go off to search for the stars and moon.

"Lanlan." His voice was full of compassion and pleading.

All of a sudden, my just-established confidence swiftly collapsed. I felt a spasm of alarm. Blood pounded at my temples. Fiercely I pulled back my hand, rushed out the door into my own room, and flung myself headfirst onto the bed. I really felt like bursting into tears.

The door opened softly: it was Mama. She came up to the bed, sat down in the darkness and stroked my head, neck, and shoulders. Involuntarily, my whole body began to tremble as if with cold.

"Don't cry, Lanlan."

Cry? Mama, if I could still cry the tears would surely be red, they'd be blood.

She patted me on the back. "Go to sleep, Lanlan, everything will pass." Mama left.

Everything will pass. Huh, it's so easily said, but can twenty years be written off at one stroke? People are not reeds, or leeches, but oysters, and the sands of memory will flow with time to change into a part of the body itself, teardrops will never run dry.

. . . a basement. Mosquitoes thudded against the searing light bulb. An old man covered with cuts and bruises was tied up on the pommel horse, his head bowed, moaning hoarsely. I lay in the corner sobbing. My knees were cut to ribbons by the broken glass: blood and mud mixed together . . .

I was then only about twelve years old. One night, when Mama couldn't sleep, she suddenly hugged me and told me that Papa was a good man who had been wrongly accused. At these words hope flared up in the child's heart: for the first time she might be able to enjoy the same rights as other children. So I ran all around, to the school, the Theater Association, the neighborhood committee, and the Red Guard headquarters, to prove Papa's innocence to them. Disaster was upon us, and those louts took me home savagely for investigation. I didn't know what was wrong with Mama, but she repudiated all her words in front of her daughter. All the blame fell on my small shoulders. Mama repented, begged, wished herself dead, but what was the use? I was struggled against, given heavy labor, and punished by being made to kneel on broken glass.

. . . the old man raised his bloody face: "Give me some water, water, water!" Staring with frightened eyes, I forgot the pain, huddling tightly into the corner. When dawn came and the old man breathed his last, I fainted with fright too. The blood congealed on my knees . . .

Can I blame Mama for this?

2

The sky was so blue it dazzled the eyes, its intense reflections shining on the ground. My hair tied up in a ribbon. I was holding a small empty bamboo basket and standing amidst the dense waist-high grass. Suddenly, from the jungle opposite appeared an elephant, the tassels of the mat on its back dangling to the ground: Papa sat proudly on top, a white turban on his head. The elephant's trunk waved to and fro, and with a snort it curled round me and placed me up in front of Papa. We marched forward, across the coconut grove streaked with leaping sunlight, across the hills and gullies gurgling with springs. I suddenly turned my head and cried out in alarm. A little old man was sitting behind me, his face blurred with blood: he was wearing convict clothes and on his chest were printed the words "Reform Through Labor." He was moaning hoarsely. "Give me some water, water, water . . ."

I woke up in fright.

It was five o'clock, and outside it was still dark. I stretched out my hand and pulled out the drawer of the bedside cupboard, fumbled for cigarettes, and lit one. I drew back fiercely and felt more relaxed. The white cloud of smoke spread through the darkness and finally floated out through the small open-shuttered window. The glow from the cigarette alternately brightened and dimmed as I strained to see clearly into the depths of my heart, but other than the ubiquitous silence, the relaxation induced by the cigarette, and the vague emptiness left by the nightmare, there was nothing.

I switched on the desk lamp, put on my clothes, and opened the door quietly. There was a light on in the kitchen and a rustling noise. Who was up so early? Who?

Under the light, wearing a black cotton-padded vest, he was crouching over the wastepaper basket with his back toward me, meticulously picking through everything: spread out beside him were such spoils as vegetable leaves, trimmings, and fish heads.

I coughed.

He jumped and looked round in alarm, his face deathly white, gazing in panic toward me.

The fluorescent light hummed.

He stood up slowly, one hand behind his back, making an effort to smile. "Lanlan, I woke you up."

"What are you doing?"

"Oh, nothing, nothing." He was flustered and kept wiping his trousers with his free hand.

I put out my hand. "Let me see."

After some hesitation he handed the thing over. It was just an ordinary cigarette pack, with nothing odd about it except that it was soiled in one corner.

I lifted my head, staring at him in bewilderment.

"Oh, Lanlan," beads of sweat started from his balding head, "yesterday I forgot to examine this cigarette pack when I threw it away, just in case I wrote something on it: it would be terrible if the team leader saw it."

"Team leader?" I was even more baffled. "Who's the team leader?"

"The people who oversee us prisoners are called team leaders." He fished out a handkerchief and wiped the sweat away. "Of course, I know, it's beyond their reach, but better to find it just in case . . ."

My head began to buzz. "All right, that's enough."

He closed his mouth tightly, as if he had even bitten out his tongue. I really hadn't expected our conversation would begin like this. For the first time I looked carefully at him. He seemed even older and paler than yesterday, with a short grayish stubble over his sunken cheeks, wrinkles that seemed to have been carved by a knife around his lackluster eyes, and an ugly sarcoma on the tip of his right ear. I could not help feeling some compassion for him.

"Was it very hard there?"

"It was all right, you get used to it."

Get used to it! A cold shiver passed through me. Dignity. Wire netting. Guns. Hurried footsteps. Dejected ranks. Death. I crumpled up the cigarette pack and tossed it into the wastepaper basket. "Go back to sleep, it's still early."

"I've had enough sleep, reveille's at 5:30." He turned to tidy up the scattered rubbish.

Back in my room, I pressed my face against the ice-cold wall. It was quite unbearable to begin like this, what should I do next? Wasn't he a man of great integrity before? Ah. Hand of Time, you're so cruel and indifferent, to knead a man like putty, you destroyed him before his daughter could remember her father's real face clearly . . . eventually I calmed down, packed my things into my bag, and put on my overcoat.

Passing through the kitchen, I came to a standstill. He was at the sink, scrubbing his big hands with a small brush, the green soap froth dripping down like sap.

"I'm going to work."

"So early?" He was so absorbed he did not even raise his head.

"I'm used to it."

I did not turn on the light, going down along the darkness, along each flight of stairs.

3

For several days in a row I came home very late. When Mama asked why, I always offered the excuse that I was busy at school. As soon as I got home, I would dodge into the kitchen and hurriedly rake up a few leftovers, then bore straight into my own little nest. I seldom ran into him, and even when we did meet I would hardly say a word. Yet it seemed his silence contained enormous compunction, as if to apologize for that morning, for his unexpected arrival, for my unhappy childhood, these twenty years and my whole life.

My brother was always running in like a spy to report on the situation, saying things like: "He's planted a pot of peculiar dried-up herbs." "All afternoon he stared at the fish in the tank." "He's burned a note again" . . . I would listen without any reaction. As far as I was concerned, it was all just a continuation of that morning, not worth making a fuss about. What was strange was my brother, talking about such things so flatly, not tinged by any emotion at all, not feeling any heavy burden on his mind. It was no wonder: since the day he was born Papa had already flown far away, and besides, in those years he was brought up in his Grandma's home, and with Mama's wings and mine in turn hanging over Grandma's little window as well, he never saw the ominous sky.

One evening, as I was lying on the bed smoking, someone knocked at the door. I hurriedly stuffed the cigarette butt in a small tin box as Mama came in.

"Smoking again, Lanlan?"

As if nothing had happened I turned over the pages of a novel beside my pillow.

"The place smells of smoke, open a window."

Thank heavens, she hadn't come to nag. But then I realized that there was something strange in her manner. She sat down beside the small desk, absently picked up the ceramic camel pen-rack and examined it for a moment before returning it to its original place. How would one put it in diplomatic language? Talks, yes, formal talks . . .

"Lanlan, you're not a child anymore." Mama was weighing her words.

It had started; I listened with respectful attention.

"I know you've resented me since you were little, and you've also resented him and resented everyone else in the world, because you've had enough suffering . . . but Lanlan, it isn't only you who's suffered."

"Yes, Mama."

"When you marry Jianping, and have children, you'll understand a mother's suffering . . ."

"We don't want children if we can't be responsible for their future."

"You're blaming us, Lanlan," Mama said painfully.

"No, not blaming. I'm grateful to you, Mama, it wasn't easy for you in those years . . ."

"Do you think it was easy for him?"

"Him?" I paused. "I don't know, and I don't want to know either. As a person, I respect his past . . ."

"Don't you respect his present? You should realize, Lanlan, his staying alive required great courage!"

"That's not the problem, Mama. You say this because you lived together for many years, but I, I can't make a false display of affection . . ."

"What are you saying!" Mama grew angry and raised her voice. "At least one should fulfill one's own duties and obligations!"

"Duties? Obligations?" I started to laugh, but it was more painful than crying. "I heard a lot about them during those years. I don't want to lose any more, Mama."

"But what have you gained?"

"The truth."

"It's a cold and unfeeling truth!"

"I can't help it," I spread out my hands, "that's how life is."

"You're too selfish!" Mama struck the desk with her hand and got up, the loose flesh on her face trembling. She stared furiously at me for a moment, then left, shutting the door heavily.

Selfish, I admit it. In those years, selfishness was a kind of instinct, a means of self-defense. What could I rely on except this? Perhaps I shouldn't have provoked Mama's anger, perhaps I should really be a good girl and love Papa, Mama, my brother, life, and myself.

4

During the break between classes, I went into the reception office and rang Jianping.

"Hello. Jianping, come over this evening."

"What's up? Lanlan?" he was shouting, over the clatter of the machines his voice sounding hoarse and weary.

"He's back."

"Who? Your father?"

"Clever one, come over and help: it's an absolutely awful situation."

He started to laugh.

"Huh, if you laugh, just watch out!" I clenched my fists and banged down the receiver.

It's true, Jianping has the ability to head off disaster. The year when the production brigade chief withheld the grain ration from us educated youth, it was he who led the whole bunch of us to snatch it all back. Although I normally appear to be quite sharp-witted, I always have to hide behind his broad shoulders whenever there's a crisis.

That afternoon I had no classes and hurried home early. Mama had left a note on the table, saying that she and Papa had gone to call on some old friends and would eat when they returned. I kneaded some dough, minced the meat filling, and got everything ready to wrap the dumplings.

Jianping arrived. He brought with him a breath of freshness and cold, his cheeks flushed red, brimming with healthy vitality. I snuggled up against him at once, my cheek pressed against the cold buttons on his chest, like a child who feels wronged but has nowhere to pour out her woes. I didn't say anything, what could I say?

We kissed and hugged for a while, then sat down and wrapped dumplings, talking and joking as we worked. From gratitude, relaxation, and the vast sleepiness that follows affection, I was almost on the verge of tears.

When my brother returned, he threw off his work clothes, drank a mouthful of water, and flew off like a whirlwind.

It was nearly eight when they got home. As they came in, it gave them quite a shock to see us. Mama could not then conceal a conciliatory and motherly smile of victory; Papa's expression was much more complicated. Apart from the apologetic look of the last few days, he also seemed to feel an irrepressible pleasure at this surprise, as well as a precautionary fear.

"This is Jianping, this is . . ." My face was suffocated with red.

"This is Lanlan's father," Mama filled in.

Jianping held out his hand and boomed, "How do you do, Uncle!"

Papa grasped Jianping's hand, his lips trembling for a long time. "So you're, so you're Jianping, fine, fine . . ."

Delivering the appropriate courtesies, Jianping gave the old man such happiness he was at a loss what to do. It was quite clear to me that his happiness had nothing to do with these remarks, but was because he felt that at last he'd found a bridge between him and me, a strong and reliable bridge.

At dinner, everyone seemed to be on very friendly terms, or at least that's how it appeared on the surface. Several awkward silences were covered over by Jianping's jokes. His conversation was so witty and lively that it even took me by surprise.

After dinner, Papa took out his Zhonghua[1] cigarettes from a tin cigarette case to offer to Jianping. This set them talking about the English method of drying tobacco and moving on to soil salinization, insect pests

1. Zhonghua: a trademark of one of the best cigarettes in China.

among peanuts and vine-grafting. I sat bolt upright beside them, smiling like a mannequin in a shop window.

Suddenly, my smile began to vanish. Surely this was a scene from a play? Jianping was the protagonist—a clever son-in-law, while I, I was the meek and mild new bride. For reasons only the devil could tell, everyone was acting to the hilt, striving to forget something in this scene. Acting happiness, acting calmness, acting glossed-over suffering. I suddenly felt that Jianping was an outsider to the fragmented, shattered suffering of this family.

I began to consider Jianping in a different light. His tone, his gestures, even his appearance, all had an unfamiliar flavor. This wasn't real, this wasn't the old him. Could strangeness be contagious? How frightening.

Jianping hastily threw me an inquiring glance, as if expecting me to re-pay the role he was playing with a commending smile. This made me feel even more disgusted. I was disgusted with him, and with myself, disgusted with everything the world is made of, happiness and sorrow, reality and sham, good and evil.

Guessing this, he wound up the conversation. He looked at his watch, said a few thoroughly polite bits of nonsense, and got to his feet.

As usual, I accompanied him to the bus stop. But along the way, I said not a single word, keeping a fair distance from him. He dejectedly thrust his hands in his pockets, kicking a stone.

An apartment block ahead hid the night. I felt alone. I longed to know how human beings survive behind these countless containers of suffering, broken families. Yet in these containers, memory is too frightening. It can only deepen the suffering and divide every family until everything turns to powder.

When we reached the bus stop, he stood with his back to me, gazing at the distant lights. "Lanlan, do I still need to explain?"

"There's no need."

He leaped onto the bus. Its red taillights flickering, it disappeared round the corner.

5

Today there was a sports meet at the school, but I didn't feel like it at all. Yesterday afternoon, Zhang Xiaoxia kept pestering me to come and watch her in the 100 meter race. I just smiled, without promising any-thing. She pursed her little mouth and, fanning her cheeks, which were streaming with sweat, with her handkerchief, stared out the window in a huff. I put my hands on her shoulders and turned her round. "I'll go then, all right?" Her face broadening into dimples, she struggled free of me in embarrassment and ran off. How easy it is to deceive a child.

I stretched, and started to get dressed. The winter sunlight seeped through the fogged-up window, making everything seem dim and quiet, like an extension of sleep and dreams. When I came out of my room, it was quiet and still: evidently everyone had gone out. I washed my hair and put my washing to soak, dashing busily to and fro. When everything was done. I sat down to eat breakfast. Suddenly I sensed that someone was standing behind me, and when I looked round it was Papa, standing stiffly in the kitchen doorway and staring at me blankly.

"Didn't you go out?" I asked.

"Oh, no, no, I was on the balcony. You're not going to school today?"

"No. What is it?"

"I thought," he hesitated, "we might go for a walk in the park, what do you think?" There was an imploring note in his voice.

"All right." Although I didn't turn round, I could feel that his eyes had brightened.

It was a warm day, but the morning mist had still not faded altogether, lingering around eaves and treetops. Along the way, we said almost nothing. But when we entered the park, he pointed at the tall white poplars by the side of the road. "The last time I brought you here, they'd just been planted." But I didn't remember it at all.

After walking along the avenue for a while, we sat down on a bench beside the lake. On the cement platform in front of us, several old wooden boats, corroded by wind and rain, were lying upside down, dirt and dry leaves forming a layer over them. The ice on the surface of the water crackled from time to time.

He lit a cigarette.

"Those same boats," he said pensively.

"Oh?"

"There're still the same boats. You used to like sitting in the stern, splashing with your bare feet and shouting. 'Motorboat! Motorboat!" The shred of a smile of memory appeared on his face. "Everyone said you were like a boy . . ."

"Really?"

"You liked swords and guns: whenever you went into a toy shop you'd always want to come out with a whole array of weapons."

"Because I didn't know what they were used for."

All at once, a shadow covered his face and his eyes darkened. "You were still a child then . . ."

Silence, a long silence. The boats lying on the bank were turned upside down here. They were covering a little girl's silly cries, a father's carefree smile, soft-drink bottle-tops, a blue satin ribbon, children's books and toy guns, the taste of earth in the four seasons, the passage of twenty years . . .

"Lanlan," he said suddenly, his voice very low and trembling, "I, I beg your pardon."

My whole body began to quiver.

"When your mother spoke of your life in these years, it was as if my heart was cut with a knife. What is a child guilty of?" His hand clutched at the air and came to rest against his chest.

"Don't talk about these things," I said quietly.

"To tell you the truth, it was for you that I lived in those years. I thought if I paid for my crime myself, perhaps life would be a bit better for my child, but . . ." he choked with sobs, "you can blame me, Lanlan. I didn't have the ability to protect you. I'm not worthy to be your father . . ."

"No, don't don't . . ." I was trembling, my whole body went weak, all I could do was wave my hands. How selfish I was! I thought only of myself, immersed myself only in my own sufferings, even making suffering a kind of pleasure and a wall of defense against others. But how did he live? For you, for your selfishness, for your heartlessness! Can the call of blood be so feeble? Can what is called human nature have completely died out in my heart?

". . . twenty years ago, the day I left the house, it was a Sunday. I took an afternoon train, but I left at dawn: I didn't want you to remember this scene. Standing by your little bed, the tears streaming down, I thought to myself: 'Little Lanlan, shall we ever meet again?' You were sleeping so soundly and sweetly, with your little round dimples . . . the evening before as you were going to bed, you hugged my neck and said in a soft voice, 'Papa, will you take me out tomorrow?' 'Papa's busy tomorrow.' You went into a sulk and pouted unhappily. I had to promise. Then you asked again, 'Can we go rowing?' 'Yes, we'll go rowing.' And so you went to sleep quite satisfied. But I deceived you, Lanlan, when you woke up the next day, what could you think . . ."

"Papa!" I blurted out, flinging myself on his shoulder and crying bitterly.

With trembling hands he stroked my head. "Lanlan, my child."

"Forgive me, Papa." I said, choked with sobs. "I'm still your little Lanlan, always . . ."

"My little Lanlan, always."

A bird whose name I don't know hovered over the lake, crying strangely, adding an even deeper layer of desolation to this bleak winter scene.

I lay crying against Papa's shoulder for a long time. My tears seeped drop by drop into the coarse wool of his overcoat. I seemed to smell the pungent scent of tobacco mingling with the smell of mud and sweat. I seemed to see him in the breaks between heavy labor, leaning wearily against the pile of dirt and rolling a cigarette staring into the distance through the fork between the guard's legs. He was pulling a cart, struggling forward on the miry road, the cartwheels screeching, churning up black mud sods. The guard's legs. He was digging the earth shovelful after shovelful, straining himself to fling it toward the pit side. The guard's legs. He was carrying his bowl, greedily draining the last mouthful of vegetable soup. The guard's legs . . . I dared not think anymore, I dared not. My powers of imagining suffering were limited after all. But he actually lived in a place beyond the powers of human imagination. Minute after minute, day after day, oh God, a full twenty years . . . no, amidst suffering, people should be in communication with one another, suffering can link people's souls even more than happiness, even if the soul is already numb, already exhausted . . .

"Lanlan, look," he drew a beautiful necklace from his pocket. "I made this just before I left there from old toothbrush handles. I wanted to give you a kind of present, but then I was afraid you wouldn't want this crude toy . . ."

"No, I like it." I took the necklace, moving the beads lightly to and fro with my finger, each of these wounded hearts . . .

On the way back, Papa suddenly bent over and picked up a piece of paper, turning it over and over in his hand. Impulsively I pulled up his arm and laid my head on his shoulder. In my heart I understood that this was because of a new strangeness, and an attempt to resist this strangeness.

Here on this avenue, I seemed to see a scene from twenty years earlier. A little girl with a blue ribbon in her hair, both fists outstretched, totters along the edge of the concrete road. Beside her walks a middle-aged man relaxed and at ease. A row of little newly planted poplars separates them. And these little trees, as they swiftly swell and spread, change into a row of huge insurmountable bars. Symbolizing this are twenty years of irregular growth rings.

"Papa, let's go."

He tossed away the piece of paper and wiped his hand carefully on his handkerchief. We walked on again.

Suddenly I thought of Zhang Xiaoxia. At this moment, she'll actually be in the race. Behind rises a puff of white smoke from the starting gun, and amid countless faces and shrill cries falling away behind her, she dashes against the white finishing tape.

Part Four

CULTURE CREATION
Women Writing

PARABLES

Again and again, the contemporary women who are writing about and for women, telling their stories, return to two interrelated themes: how women are called upon to sacrifice for their families and societies, and how they are constricted by their familial and societal roles. These themes are woven into the following two stories by two African women of the same literary generation—Grace Ogot was born in 1930, Bessie Head in 1937—with very similar commitments to folk traditions and tales but of completely different life courses. **GRACE AKINYE OGOT,** a Kenyan, was trained as a nurse and midwife, but she has also worked as a journalist for the British Broadcasting Corporation in London and as one of Kenya's delegates to the United Nations and UNESCO. Ogot has told the history of rural western Kenya and the Luo people in a novel, *The Promised Land* (East African Pub. House, 1966)—the first novel in English by a Luo writer. A second novel, *The Graduate*, appeared in 1980, and she has three story collections. Like her countryman James Ngugi, now known as Ngugi wa Thiong'o, who has written many novels about the impact of Western education and political unrest on his people, the Kikuyu, Ogot argues for preserving tribal traditions and languages and urges exiled and self-exiled Kenyan intellectuals to return to their country.

BESSIE HEAD, the woman writer from Africa best known in Global Cultures, was born in Pietermaritzburg, South Africa. Head was born in an asylum where her mother had been committed by her English parents when they discovered that she was pregnant by their black stable boy. The mother committed suicide when Head was a year old. Growing up, Bessie Head always felt like an outcast among the whites who cared for her and, later, among the Africans who considered her a "colored" (not fully black). She was still in search of an emotional home when she emigrated in 1964 to Botswana, South Africa's neighbor to the northwest, a relatively peaceful and un-Europeanized land, a refuge to many victims of South Africa's apartheid. Before she died suddenly of hepatitis in 1986, Bessie Head wrote two complex, highly psychological novels, *Maru* (1971) and *A*

Question of Power (1974), that explore racism between whites and people of color and among people of color in their native settings and as refugees. "The Lovers" is an instance of another of her great themes—a collision between traditional village mores demanding submission to the group's identity and an individual's quest for freedom, love. This theme, particularly in the lives of women, animates the stories in *The Collector of Treasures and Other Botswana Village Tales* (1977).

The Rain Came

Grace Ogot

THE CHIEF was still far from the gate when his daughter Oganda saw him. She ran to meet him. Breathlessly she asked her father, "What is the news, great Chief? Everyone in the village is anxiously waiting to hear when it will rain." Labong'o held out his hands for his daughter but he did not say a word. Puzzled by her father's cold attitude Oganda ran back to the village to warn the others that the chief was back.

The atmosphere in the village was tense and confused. Everyone moved aimlessly and fussed in the yard without actually doing any work. A young woman whispered to her co-wife, "If they have not solved this rain business today, the chief will crack." They had watched him getting thinner and thinner as the people kept on pestering him. "Our cattle lie dying in the fields," they reported. "Soon it will be our children and then ourselves. Tell us what to do to save our lives, oh great Chief." So the chief had daily prayed with the Almighty through the ancestors to deliver them from their distress.

Instead of calling the family together and giving them the news immediately, Labong'o went to his own hut, a sign that he was not to be disturbed. Having replaced the shutter, he sat in the dimly lit hut to contemplate.

It was no longer a question of being the chief of hunger-stricken people that weighed Labong'o's heart. It was the life of his only daughter that was at stake. At the time when Oganda came to meet him, he saw the glittering chain shining around her waist. The prophecy was complete. "It is Oganda, Oganda, my only daughter, who must die so young." Labong'o burst into tears before finishing the sentence. The chief must not weep. Society had declared him the bravest of men. But Labong'o did not care anymore. He assumed the position of a simple father and wept bitterly. He loved his people, the Luo, but what were the Luo for him without Oganda? Her life had brought a new life in Labong'o's world and he ruled better than he could remember. How would the spirit of the village survive his beautiful daughter? "There are so many homes and so many parents who have daughters. Why choose this one? She is all I have." Labong'o spoke as if the ancestors were there in the hut and he could see them face to face. Perhaps they were there, warning him to remember his promise on the day he was enthroned when he said aloud, before the elders, "I will lay down life, if necessary, and the life of my household, to save this tribe from the hands of the enemy." "Deny! Deny!" he could hear the voice of his forefathers mocking him.

When Labong'o was consecrated chief he was only a young man. Unlike his father, he ruled for many years with only one wife. But people rebuked him because his only wife did not bear him a daughter. He married a second, a third, and a fourth wife. But they all gave birth to male children. When Labong'o married a fifth wife she bore him a daughter. They called her Oganda, meaning "beans," because her skin was very fair. Out of Labong'o's twenty children, Oganda was the only girl. Though she was the chief's favorite, her mother's co-wives swallowed their jealous feelings and showered her with love. After all, they said, Oganda was a female child whose days in the royal family were numbered. She would soon marry at a tender age and leave the enviable position to someone else.

Never in his life had he been faced with such an impossible decision. Refusing to yield to the rainmaker's request would mean sacrificing the whole tribe, putting the interests of the individual above those of the society. More than that. It would mean disobeying the ancestors, and most probably wiping the Luo people from the surface of the earth. On the other hand, to let Oganda die as a ransom for the people would permanently cripple Labong'o spiritually. He knew he would never be the same chief again.

The words of Ndithi, the medicine man, still echoed in his ears. "Podho, the ancestor of the Luo, appeared to me in a dream last night, and he asked me to speak to the chief and the people." Ndithi had said to the gathering of tribesmen, "A young woman who has not known a man must die so that the country may have rain. While Podho was still talking to me, I saw a young woman standing at the lakeside, her hands raised, above her head. Her skin was as fair as the skin of young deer in the wilderness. Her tall slender figure stood like a lonely reed at the riverbank. Her sleepy eyes wore a sad look like that of a bereaved mother. She wore a gold ring on her left ear, and a glittering brass chain around her waist. As I still marveled at the beauty of this young woman, Podho told me, "Out of all

the women in this land, we have chosen this one. Let her offer herself a
sacrifice to the lake monster! And on that day, the rain will come down
in torrents. Let everyone stay at home on that day, lest he be carried away
by the floods."

Outside there was a strange stillness, except for the thirsty birds that
sang lazily on the dying trees. The blinding midday heat had forced the
people to retire to their huts. Not far away from the chief's hut, two guards
were snoring away quietly. Labong'o removed his crown and the large
eagle head that hung loosely on his shoulders. He left the hut, and instead
of asking Nyabog'o the messenger to beat the drum, he went straight and
beat it himself. In no time the whole household had assembled under the
siala tree where he usually addressed them. He told Oganda to wait a
while in her grandmother's hut.

When Labong'o stood to address his household, his voice was hoarse
and the tears choked him. He started to speak, but words refused to leave
his lips. His wives and sons knew there was great danger. Perhaps their
enemies had declared war on them. Labong'o's eyes were red, and they
could see he had been weeping. At last he told them. "One whom we love
and treasure must be taken away from us. Oganda is to die." Labong'o's
voice was so faint, that he could not hear it himself. But he continued.
"The ancestors have chosen her to be offered as a sacrifice to the lake
monster in order that we may have rain."

They were completely stunned. As a confused murmur broke out,
Oganda's mother fainted and was carried off to her own hut. But the other
people rejoiced. They danced around singing and chanting, "Oganda is the
lucky one to die for the people. If it is to save the people, let Oganda go."

In her grandmother's hut Oganda wondered what the whole family
were discussing about her that she could not hear. Her grandmother's
hut was well away from the chief's court and, much as she strained her
ears, she could not hear what was said. "It must be marriage," she concluded. It was an accepted custom for the family to discuss their daughter's
future marriage behind her back. A faint smile played on Oganda's lips as
she thought of the several young men who swallowed saliva at the mere
mention of her name.

There was Kech, the son of a neighboring clan elder. Kech was very
handsome. He had sweet, meek eyes and a roaring laughter. He would
make a wonderful father. Oganda thought. But they would not be a good
match. Kech was a bit too short to be her husband. It would humiliate
her to have to look down at Kech each time she spoke to him. Then she
thought of Dimo, the tall young man who had already distinguished himself as a brave warrior and an outstanding wrestler. Dimo adored Oganda,
but Oganda thought he would make a cruel husband, always quarreling

and ready to fight. No, she did not like him. Oganda fingered the glittering chain on her waist as she thought of Osinda. A long time ago when she was quite young Osinda had given her that chain, and instead of wearing it around her neck several times, she wore it round her waist where it could stay permanently. She heard her heart pounding so loudly as she thought of him. She whispered, "Let it be you they are discussing, Osinda, the lovely one. Come now and take me away . . ."

The lean figure in the doorway startled Oganda who was rapt in thought about the man she loved. "You have frightened me, Grandma," said Oganda laughing. "Tell me, is it my marriage you were discussing? You can take it from me that I won't marry any of them." A smile played on her lips again. She was coaxing the old lady to tell her quickly, to tell her they were pleased with Osinda.

In the open space outside the excited relatives were dancing and singing. They were coming to the hut now, each carrying a gift to put at Oganda's feet. As their singing got nearer Oganda was able to hear what they were saying: "If it is to save the people, if it is to give us rain, let Oganda go. Let Oganda die for her people, and for her ancestors." Was she mad to think that they were singing about her? How could she die? She found the lean figure of her grandmother barring the door. She could not get out. The look on her grandmother's face warned her that there was danger around the corner. "Grandma, it is not marriage then?" Oganda asked urgently. She suddenly felt panicky like a mouse cornered by a hungry cat. Forgetting that there was only one door in the hut Oganda fought desperately to find another exit. She must fight for her life. But there was none.

She closed her eyes, leapt like a wild tiger through the door, knocking her grandmother flat to the ground. There outside in mourning garments Labong'o stood motionless, his hands folded at the back. He held his daughter's hand and led her away from the excited crowd to the little red-painted hut where her mother was resting. Here he broke the news officially to his daughter.

For a long time the three souls who loved one another dearly sat in darkness. It was no good speaking. And even if they tried, the words could not have come out. In the past they had been like three cooking stones, sharing their burdens. Taking Oganda away from them would leave two useless stones which would not hold a cooking pot.

News that the beautiful daughter of the chief was to be sacrificed to give the people rain spread across the country like wind. At sunset the chief's village was full of relatives and friends who had come to congratulate Oganda. Many more were on their way coming, carrying their gifts. They would dance till morning to keep her company. And in the morning they would prepare her a big farewell feast. All these relatives thought it a great honor to be selected by the spirits to die, in order that the society may live. "Oganda's name will always remain a living name among us," they boasted.

But was it maternal love that prevented Minya from rejoicing with the other women? Was it the memory of the agony and pain of childbirth that made her feel so sorrowful? Or was it the deep warmth and understanding that passes between a suckling babe and her mother that made Oganda part of her life, her flesh? Of course it was an honor, a great honor, for her daughter to be chosen to die for the country. But what could she gain once her only daughter was blown away by the wind? There were so many other women in the land, why choose her daughter, her only child! Had human life any meaning at all—other women had houses full of children while she, Minya, had to lose her only child!

In the cloudless sky the moon shone brightly, and the numerous stars glittered with a bewitching beauty. The dancers of all age groups assembled to dance before Oganda, who sat close to her mother, sobbing quietly. All these years she had been with her people she thought she understood them. But now she discovered that she was a stranger among them. If they loved her as they had always professed why were they not making any attempt to save her? Did her people really understand what it felt like to die young? Unable to restrain her emotions any longer, she sobbed loudly as her age group got up to dance. They were young and beautiful and very soon they would marry and have their own children. They would have husbands to love and little huts for themselves. They would have reached maturity. Oganda touched the chain around her waist as she thought of Osinda. She wished Osinda was there too, among her friends. "Perhaps he is ill," she thought gravely. The chain comforted Oganda—she would die with it around her waist and wear it in the underground world.

In the morning a big feast was prepared for Oganda. The women prepared many different tasty dishes so that she could pick and choose. "People don't eat after death," they said. Delicious though the food looked, Oganda touched none of it. Let the happy people eat. She contented herself with sips of water from a little calabash.

The time for her departure was drawing near, and each minute was precious. It was a day's journey to the lake. She was to walk all night, passing through the great forest. But nothing could touch her, not even the denizens of the forest. She was already anointed with sacred oil. From the time Oganda received the sad news she had expected Osinda to appear any moment. But he was not there. A relative told her that Osinda was away on a private visit. Oganda realized that she would never see her beloved again.

In the late afternoon the whole village stood at the gate to say good-bye and to see her for the last time. Her mother wept on her neck for a long time. The great chief in a mourning skin came to the gate barefooted, and mingled with the people—a simple father in grief. He took off his wrist bracelet and put it on his daughter's wrist saying, "You will always live among us. The spirit of our forefathers is with you."

Tongue-tied and unbelieving Oganda stood there before the people. She had nothing to say. She looked at her home once more. She could hear her heart beating so painfully within her. All her childhood plans were coming to an end. She felt like a flower nipped in the bud never to enjoy the morning dew again. She looked at her weeping mother, and whispered, "Whenever you want to see me, always look at the sunset. I will be there."

Oganda turned southward to start her trek to the lake. Her parents, relatives, friends and admirers stood at the gate and watched her go.

Her beautiful slender figure grew smaller and smaller till she mingled with the thin dry trees in the forest. As Oganda walked the lonely path that wound its way in the wilderness, she sang a song, and her own voice kept her company.

> The ancestors have said Oganda must die
> The daughter of the chief must be sacrificed.
> When the lake monster feeds on my flesh.
> The people will have rain.
> Yes, the rain will come down in torrents.
> And the floods will wash away the sandy beaches
> When the daughter of the chief dies in the lake.
> My age group has consented
> My parents have consented
> So have my friends and relatives.
> Let Oganda die to give us rain.
> My age group are young and ripe,
> Ripe for womanhood and motherhood
> But Oganda must die young,
> Oganda must sleep with the ancestors.
> Yes, rain will come down in torrents.

The red rays of the setting sun embraced Oganda, and she looked like a burning candle in the wilderness.

The people who came to hear her sad song were touched by her beauty. But they all said the same thing. "If it is to save the people, if it is to give us rain, then be not afraid. Your name will forever live among us."

At midnight Oganda was tired and weary. She could walk no more. She sat under a big tree, and having sipped water from her calabash, she rested her head on the tree trunk and slept.

When Oganda woke up in the morning the sun was high in the sky.

After walking for many hours, she reached the *tong'*, a strip of land that separated the inhabited part of the country from the sacred place (*kar lamo*). No layman could enter this place and come out alive—only those who had direct contact with the spirits and the Almighty were allowed to enter this holy of holies. But Oganda had to pass through this sacred land on her way to the lake, which she had to reach at sunset.

A large crowd gathered to see her for the last time. Her voice was now hoarse and painful, but there was no need to worry anymore. Soon she would not have to sing. The crowd looked at Oganda sympathetically, mumbling words she could not hear. But none of them pleaded for life. As Oganda opened the gate, a child, a young child, broke loose from the crowd, and ran toward her. The child took a small earring from her sweaty hands and gave it to Oganda saying, "When you reach the world of the dead, give this earring to my sister. She died last week. She forgot this ring." Oganda, taken aback by the strange request, took the little ring, and handed her precious water and food to the child. She did not need them now. Oganda did not know whether to laugh or cry. She had heard mourners sending their love to their sweethearts, long dead, but this idea of sending gifts was new to her.

Oganda held her breath as she crossed the barrier to enter the sacred land. She looked appealingly at the crowd, but there was no response. Their minds were too preoccupied with their own survival. Rain was the precious medicine they were longing for, and the sooner Oganda could get to her destination the better.

A strange feeling possessed Oganda as she picked her way in the sacred land. There were strange noises that often startled her, and her first reaction was to take to her heels. But she remembered that she had to fulfill the wish of her people. She was exhausted, but the path was still winding. Then suddenly the path ended on sandy land. The water had retreated miles away from the shore leaving a wide stretch of sand. Beyond this was the vast expanse of water.

Oganda felt afraid. She wanted to picture the size and shape of the monster, but fear would not let her. The society did not talk about it, nor did the crying children who were silenced by the mention of its name. The sun was still up, but it was no longer hot. For a long time Oganda walked ankle-deep in the sand. She was exhausted and longed desperately for her calabash of water. As she moved on, she had a strange feeling that something was following her. Was it the monster? Her hair stood erect, and a cold paralyzing feeling ran along her spine. She looked behind, sideways and in front, but there was nothing, except a cloud of dust.

Oganda pulled up and hurried but the feeling did not leave her, and her whole body became saturated with perspiration.

The sun was going down fast and the lake shore seemed to move along with it.

Oganda started to run. She must be at the lake before sunset. As she ran she heard a noise coming from behind. She looked back sharply, and something resembling a moving bush was frantically running after her. It was about to catch up with her.

Oganda ran with all her strength. She was now determined to throw herself into the water even before sunset. She did not look back, but the creature was upon her. She made an effort to cry out, as in a nightmare, but she could not hear her own voice. The creature caught up with Oganda. In the utter confusion, as Oganda came face to face with the unidentified creature, a strong hand grabbed her. But she fell flat on the sand and fainted.

When the lake breeze brought her back to consciousness, a man was bending over her. ". . . . . !!" Oganda opened her mouth to speak, but she had lost her voice. She swallowed a mouthful of water poured into her mouth by the stranger.

"Osinda, Osinda! Please let me die. Let me run, the sun is going down. Let me die, let them have rain." Osinda fondled the glittering chain around Oganda's waist and wiped the tears from her face.

"We must escape quickly to the unknown land," Osinda said urgently. "We must run away from the wrath of the ancestors and the retaliation of the monster."

"But the curse is upon me. Osinda, I am no good to you anymore. And moreover the eyes of the ancestors will follow us everywhere and bad luck will befall us. Nor can we escape from the monster."

Oganda broke loose, afraid to escape, but Osinda grabbed her hands again.

"Listen to me, Oganda! Listen! Here are two coats!" He then covered the whole of Oganda's body, except her eyes, with a leafy attire made from the twigs of *Bwombwe*. "These will protect us from the eyes of the ancestors and the wrath of the monster. Now let us run out of here." He held Oganda's hand and they ran from the sacred land, avoiding the path that Oganda had followed.

The bush was thick, and the long grass entangled their feet as they ran. Halfway through the sacred land they stopped and looked back. The sun was almost touching the surface of the water. They were frightened. They continued to run, now faster, to avoid the sinking sun.

"Have faith, Oganda—that thing will not reach us."

When they reached the barrier and looked behind them trembling, only a tip of the sun could be seen above the water's surface.

"It is gone! It is gone!" Oganda wept, hiding her face in her hands.

"Weep not, daughter of the chief. Let us run, let us escape."

There was a bright lightning. They looked up, frightened. Above them black furious clouds started to gather. They began to run. Then the thunder roared, and the rain came down in torrents.

The Lovers

Bessie Head

T H E   L O V E affair began in the summer. The love affair began in those dim dark days when young men and women did not have love affairs. It was one of those summers when it rained in torrents. Almost every afternoon towards sunset the low-hanging, rain-filled clouds would sweep across the sky in packed masses and suddenly, with barely a warning, the rain would pour down in blinding sheets.

The young women and little girls were still out in the forest gathering wood that afternoon when the first warning signs of rain appeared in the sky. They hastily gathered up their bundles of wood and began running home to escape the approaching storm. Suddenly, one of the young women halted painfully. In her haste she had trodden on a large thorn.

"Hurry on home, Monosi!" she cried to a little girl panting behind her. "I have to get this thorn out of my foot. If the rain catches me I shall find some shelter and come home once it is over."

Without a backward glance the little girl sped on after the hard-running group of wood gatherers. The young woman was quite alone with the approaching storm. The thorn proved difficult to extract. It had broken off and embedded itself deeply in her heel. A few drops of rain beat down on her back. The sky darkened.

Anxiously she looked around for the nearest shelter and saw a cavern in some rocks at the base of a hill nearby. She picked up her bundle of wood and limped hastily towards it, with the drops of rain pounding down faster and faster. She had barely entered the cavern when the torrent unleashed itself in a violent downpour. Her immediate concern was to seek its sanctuary but a moment later her heart lurched in fear as she realized that she was not alone. The warmth of another human filled the interior. She swung around swiftly and found herself almost face to face with a young man.

"We can shelter here together from the storm," he said with a quiet authority.

His face was as kind and protective as his words. Reassured, the young woman set down her bundle of sticks in the roomy interior of the cavern and together they seated themselves near its entrance. The roar of the rain was deafening so that even the thunder and lightning was muffled by its intensity. With quiet, harmonious movements the young man undid a leather pouch tied at his waist. He spent all his time cattle-herding and to while away the long hours he busied himself with all kinds of leather work, assembling skins into all kinds of clothes and blankets. He had a large number of sharpened implements in his pouch. He indicated to the young woman that he wished to extract the thorn. She extended her foot towards him and for some time he busied himself with this task, gently whittling away the skin around the thorn until he had exposed it sufficiently enough to extract it.

The young woman looked at his face with interest and marvelled at the ease and comfort she felt in his presence. In their world men and women lived strictly apart, especially the young and unmarried. This sense of apartness and separateness continued even throughout married life and marriage itself seemed to have no significance beyond a union for the production of children. This wide gap between the sexes created embarrassment on the level of personal contact; the young men often slid their eyes away uneasily or giggled at the sight of a woman. The young man did none of this. He had stared her directly in the eyes; all his movements were natural and unaffected. He was also very pleasing to look at. She thanked him with a smile once he had extracted the thorn and folded her extended foot beneath her. The violence of the storm abated a little but the heavily-laden sky continued to pour forth a steady downpour.

She had seen the young man around the village; she could vaguely place his family connections.

"Aren't you the son of Rra-Keaja?" she asked. She had a light chatty voice with an undertone of laughter in it, very expressive of her personality. She liked above all to be happy.

"I am the very Keaja he is named after," the young man replied with a smile. "I am the first-born in the family."

"I am the first-born in the family, too," she said. "I am Tselane, the daughter of Mma-Tselane."

His family ramifications were more complicated than hers. His father had three wives. All the first born of the first, second and third house were boys. The children totalled eight in number, three boys and five girls, he explained. It was only when the conversation moved into deep water that Tselane realized that a whole area of the young man's speech had eluded her. He was the extreme opposite of her light chatty tone. He talked from deep rhythms within himself as though he had specifically invented language for his own use. He had an immense range of expression and feeling at his command; now his eyes lit up with humour, then they were absolutely serious and in earnest. He swayed almost imperceptibly as he talked. He talked like no one she had ever heard talking before, yet all his utterances were direct, simple and forthright. She bent forward and listened more attentively to his peculiar manner of speech.

"I don't like my mother," he said, shocking her. "I am her only son simply because my father stopped cohabiting with her after I was born. My father and I are alike. We don't like to be controlled by anyone and she made his life a misery when they were newly married. It was as if she had been born with a worm eating at her heart because she is satisfied with nothing. The only way my father could control the situation was to ignore her completely . . ."

He remained silent a while, concentrating on his own thoughts. "I don't think I approve of all the arranged marriages we have here," he said finally. "My father would never have married her had he had his own choice. He was merely presented with her one day by his family and told that they were to be married and there was nothing he could do about it."

He kept silent about the torture he endured from his mother. She hated him deeply and bitterly. She had hurled stones at him and scratched him on the arms and legs in her wild frustration. Like his father he eluded her. He rarely spent time at home but kept the cattle-post as his permanent residence. When he approached home it was always with some gift of clothes or blankets. On that particular day he had an enormous gourd filled with milk.

The young woman, Tselane, floundered out of her depth in the face of such stark revelations. They lived the strictest of traditional ways of life; all children were under the control of their parents until they married, therefore it was taboo to discuss their elders. In her impulsive chatty way and partly out of embarrassment, it had been on the tip of her tongue to say that she liked her mother, that her mother was very kind-hearted. But there was a disturbing undertone in her household too. Her mother and father—and she was sure of it due to her detailed knowledge of her mother's way of life—had not cohabited for years either. A few years ago her father had taken another wife. She was her mother's only child. Oh, the surface of their household was polite and harmonious but her father was rarely at home. He was always irritable and morose when he was home.

"I am sorry about all the trouble in your home," she said at last, in a softer, more thoughtful tone. She was shaken at having been abruptly jolted into completely new ways of thought.

The young man smiled and then quite deliberately turned and stared at her. She stared back at him with friendly interest. She did not mind his close scrutiny of her person; he was easy to associate with, comfortable, truthful and open in his every gesture.

"Do you approve of arranged marriages?" he asked, still smiling.

"I have not thought of anything," she replied truthfully.

The dark was approaching rapidly. The rain had trickled down to a fine drizzle. Tselane stood up and picked up her bundle of wood. The young man picked up his gourd of milk. They were barely visible as they walked home together in the dark. Tselane's home was not too far from the hill. She lived on the extreme western side of the village, he on the extreme eastern side.

A bright fire burned in the hut they used as a cooking place on rainy days. Tselane's mother was sitting bent forward on her low stool, listening attentively to a visitor's tale. It was always like this—her mother was permanently surrounded by women who confided in her. The whole story of life unfolded daily around her stool: the ailments of children, women who had just had miscarriages, women undergoing treatment for barren wombs—the story was endless. It was the great pleasure of Tselane to seat herself quietly behind her mother's stool and listen with fascinated ears to this endless tale of woe. Her mother's visitor that evening was on the tail-end of a description of one of her children's ailments; chronic epilepsy, which seemed beyond cure. The child seemed in her death throes and the mother was just at the point of demonstrating the violent seizures when Tselane entered. Tselane quietly set her bundle of wood down in a corner and the conversation continued uninterrupted. She took her favoured place behind her mother's stool. Her father's second wife, Mma-Monosi, was seated on the opposite side of the fire, her face composed and serious. Her child, the little girl, Monosi, fed and attended to, lay fast asleep on a sleeping mat in one corner of the hut.

Tselane loved the two women of the household equally. They were both powerful independent women but with sharply differing personalities. Mma-Tselane was a queen who vaguely surveyed the kingdom she ruled, with an abstracted, absent-minded air. Over the years of her married life she had built up a way of life for herself that filled her with content. She was reputed to be very delicate in health as after the birth of Tselane she had suffered a number of miscarriages and seemed incapable of bearing any more children. Her delicate health was a source of extreme irritation to her husband and at some stage he had abandoned her completely and taken Mma-Monosi as his second wife, intending to perpetuate his line and name through her healthy body. The arrangement suited Mma-Tselane. She was big-hearted and broad-minded and yet, conversely, she prided herself in being the meticulous upholder of all the traditions the community adhered to. Once Mma-Monosi became a part of the household, Mma-Tselane did no work but entertained and paid calls the day long. Mma-Monosi ran the entire household.

The two women complemented each other, for, if Mma-Tselane was a queen, then Mma-Monosi was a humble worker. On the surface, Mma-Monosi appeared as sane and balanced as Mma-Tselane, but there was another side of her personality that was very precariously balanced. Mma-Monosi took her trembling way through life. If all was stable and peaceful, then Mma-Monosi was stable and peaceful. If there was any disruption or disorder, Mma-Monosi's precarious inner balance registered every wave and upheaval. She hungered for approval of her every action and could be upset for days if criticized or reprimanded.

So, between them, the two women achieved a very harmonious household. Both were entirely absorbed in their full busy daily round; both were unconcerned that they received scant attention from the man of the household for Rra-Tselane was entirely concerned with his own affairs. He was a prominent member of the chief's court and he divided his time between the chief's court and his cattle-post. He was rich in cattle and his herds were taken care of by servants. He was away at his cattle-post at that time.

It was with Mma-Monosi that the young girl, Tselane, enjoyed a free and happy relationship. They treated each other as equals, they both enjoyed hard work and whenever they were alone together, they laughed and joked all the time. Her own mother regarded Tselane as an object to whom she lowered her voice and issued commands between clenched teeth. Very soon Mma-Tselane stirred in her chair and said in that lowered voice: "Tselane, fetch me my bag of herbs."

Tselane obediently stood up and hurried to her mother's living-quarters for the bag of herbs. Then another interval followed during which her mother and the visitor discussed the medicinal properties of the herbs. Then Mma-Monosi served the evening meal. Then the visitor departed with assurances that Mma-Tselane would call on her the following day. Then they sat for a while in companionable silence. At one stage, seeing that the fire was burning low, Mma-Tselane arose and selected a few pieces of wood from Tselane's bundle to stoke up the fire.

"Er, Tselane," she said. "Your wood is quite dry. Did you shelter from the storm?"

"There is a cave in the hill not far from here, mother," Tselane replied. "And I sheltered there." She did not think it wise to add that she had shared the shelter with a young man; a lot of awkward questions of the wrong kind might have followed.

The mother cast her eyes vaguely over her daughter as if to say all was in order in her world; she always established simple facts about any matter and turned peacefully to the next task at hand. She suddenly decided that she was tired and would retire. Tselane and Mma-Monosi were left alone seated near the fire. Tselane was still elated by her encounter with the young man; so many pleasant thoughts were flying through her head.

"I want to ask you some questions, Mma-Monosi," she said eagerly.

"What is it you want to say, my child?" Mma-Monosi said, stirring out of a reverie.

"Do you approve of arranged marriages, Mma-Monosi?" she asked earnestly.

Mma-Monosi drew in her breath between her teeth with a sharp, hissing sound, then she lowered her voice in horror and said: "Tselane, you know quite well that I am your friend but if anyone else heard you talking like that you would be in trouble! Such things are never discussed here! What put that idea into your head because it is totally unknown to me?"

"But you question life when you begin to grow up," Tselane said defensively.

"That is what you never, never do," Mma-Monosi said severely. "If you question life you will upset it. Life is always in order." She looked thoroughly startled and agitated. "I know of something terrible that once happened to someone who questioned life," she added grimly.

"Who was it? What terrible thing happened?" Tselane asked, in her turn agitated.

"I can't tell you," Mma-Monosi said firmly. "It is too terrible to mention."

Tselane subsided into silence with a speculative look in her eye. She understood Mma-Monosi well. She couldn't keep a secret. She could always be tempted into telling a secret, if not today then on some other day. She decided to find out the terrible story.

When Keaja arrived home his family was eating the evening meal. He first approached the women's quarters and offered them the gourd of milk.

"The cows are calving heavily," he explained. "There is a lot of milk and I can bring some home every day."

He was greeted joyously by the second and third wife of his father who anxiously inquired after their sons who lived with him at the cattle-post.

"They are quite well," he said politely. "I settled them and the cattle before I left. I shall return again in the early morning because I am worried about the young calves."

He avoided his mother's baleful stare and tight, deprived mouth. She never had anything to say to him, although, on his approach to the women's quarters, he had heard her voice, shrill and harsh, dominating the conversation. His meal was handed to him and he retreated to his father's quarters. He ate alone and apart from the women. A bright fire burned in his father's living-quarters.

"Hello, Father-Of-Me," his father greeted him, making affectionate play on the name Keaja. Keaja meant: I am eating now because I have a son to take care of me.

His father doted on him. In his eyes there was no greater son than Keaja. After an exchange of greetings his father asked: "And what is your news?"

He gave his father the same information about the cows calving heavily and the rich supply of milk; that his other two sons were quite well. They ate for a while in companionable silence. His mother's voice rose shrill and penetrating in the silent night. Quite unexpectedly his father looked up with a twinkle in his eye and said: "Those extra calves will stand us in good stead, Father-Of-Me. I have just started negotiations about your marriage."

A spasm of chill, cold fear almost constricted Keaja's heart. "Who am I to marry, father?" he asked, alarmed.

"I cannot mention the family name just yet," his father replied cheerfully, not sensing his son's alarm. "The negotiations are still at a very delicate stage."

"Have you committed yourself in this matter, father?" he asked, a sharp angry note in his voice.

"Oh, yes," his father replied. "I have given my honour in this matter. It is just that these things take a long time to arrange as there are many courtesies to be observed."

"How long?" the son asked.

"About six new moons may have to pass," his father replied. "It may even be longer than that. I cannot say at this stage."

"I could choose a wife for myself," the son said with deadly quietude. "I could choose my own wife and then inform you of my choice."

His father stared at him in surprise.

"You cannot be different from everyone else," he said. "I must be a parent with a weakness that you can talk to me so."

His father knew that he indulged his son, that they had free and easy exchanges beyond what was socially permissible; even that brief exchange was more than most parents allowed their children. They arranged all details of their children's future and on the fatal day merely informed them that they were to be married to so-and-so. There was no point in saying: "I might not be able to live with so-and-so. She might be unsuited to me," so that when Keaja lapsed into silence, his father merely smiled indulgently and engaged him in small talk.

Keaja was certainly of a marriageable age. The previous year he had gone through his initiation ceremony. Apart from other trials endured during the ceremony, detailed instruction had been given to the young men of his age group about sexual relations between men and women. They were hardly private and personal but affected by a large number of social regulations and taboos. If he broke the taboos at a personal and private level, death, sickness and great misfortune would fall upon his family. If he broke the taboos at a social level, death and disaster would fall upon the community. There were many periods in a man's life when abstinence from sexual relations was required; often this abstinence had to be practised communally as in the period preceding the harvest of crops and only broken on the day of the harvest thanksgiving ceremony.

These regulations and taboos applied to men and women alike but the initiation ceremony for women, which Tselane had also experienced the previous year, was much more complex in their instruction. A delicate balance had to be preserved between a woman's reproductive cycle and the safety of the community; at almost every stage in her life a woman was a potential source of danger to the community. All women were given careful instruction in precautions to be observed during times of menstruation, childbirth and accidental miscarriages. Failure to observe the taboos could bring harm to animal life, crops and the community.

It could be seen then that the community held no place for people wildly carried away by their passions, that there was a logic and order in the carefully arranged sterile emotional and physical relationships between men and women. There was no one to challenge the established order of things; if people felt any personal unhappiness it was smothered and subdued and so life for the community proceeded from day to day in peace and harmony.

As all lovers do, they began a personal and emotional dialogue that excluded all life around them. Perhaps its pattern and direction was the same for all lovers, painful and maddening by turns in its initial insecurity. Who looked for who? They could not say, except that the far-western unpolluted end of the river where women drew water and the forests where they gathered firewood became Keaja's favoured hunting grounds. Their work periods coincided at that time. The corn had just been sowed and the women were idling in the village until the heavy soaking rains raised the weeds in their fields, then their next busy period would follow when they hoed out the weed between their corn.

Keaja returned every day to the village with gourds of milk for his family and it did not take Tselane long to note that he delayed and lingered in her work areas until he had caught some glimpse of her. She was always in a crowd of gaily chattering young women. The memory of their first encounter had been so fresh and stimulating, so full of unexpected surprises in dialogue that she longed to approach him. One afternoon, while out wood gathering with her companions, she noticed him among the distant bushes and contrived to remove herself from her companions. As she walked towards him, he quite directly approached her and took hold of her hand. She made no effort to pull her hand free. It rested in his as though it belonged there. They walked on some distance, then he paused, and turning to face her told her all he had on his mind in his direct, simple way. This time he did not smile at all.

"My father will arrange a marriage for me after about six new moons have passed," he said. "I do not want that. I want a wife of my own choosing but all the things I want can only cause trouble."

She looked away into the distance, not immediately knowing what she ought to say. Her own parents had given her no clue of their plans for her future; indeed she had not had cause to think about it but she did not like most of the young men of the village. They had a hang-dog air as though the society and its oppressive ways had broken their will. She liked everything about Keaja and she felt safe with him as on that stormy afternoon in the cavern when he had said: "We can shelter here together from the storm . . ."

"My own thoughts are not complicated," he went on, still holding on to her hand. "I thought I would find out how you felt about this matter. I thought I would like to choose you as my wife. If you do not want to choose me in turn, I shall not pursue my own wants any longer. I might even marry the wife my father chooses for me."

She turned around and faced him and spoke with a clarity of thought that startled her.

"I am afraid of nothing," she said. "Not even trouble or death but I need some time to find out what I am thinking."

Of his own accord he let go of her hand and so they parted and went their separate ways. From that point onwards right until the following day, she lived in a state of high elation. Her thought processes were not all coherent; indeed she had not a thought in her head. Then the illogic of love took over. Just as she was about to pick up the pitcher in the late afternoon, she suddenly felt desperately ill, so ill that she was almost brought to the point of death. She experienced a paralysing lameness in her arms and legs. The weight of the pitcher with which she was to draw water was too heavy for her to endure.

She appealed to Mma-Monosi.

"I feel faint and ill today," she said. "I cannot draw water."

Mma-Monosi was only too happy to take over her chores but at the same time consulted anxiously with her mother about this sudden illness. Mma-Tselane, after some deliberation, decided that it was the illness young girls get in the limbs when they are growing too rapidly. She spent a happy three days doctoring her daughter with warm herb drinks, for Mma-Tselane liked nothing better than to concentrate on illness. Still, the physical turmoil the young girl felt continued unabated; at night she trembled violently from head to toe. It was so shocking and new that for two days she succumbed completely to the blow. It wasn't any coherent thought processes that made her struggle desperately to her feet on the third day but a need to quieten the anguish. She convinced her mother and Mma-Monosi that she felt well enough to perform her wood gathering chores. Towards the afternoon she hurried to the forest area, carefully avoiding her gathering companions.

She was relieved, on meeting Keaja, to see that his face bore the same anguished look that she felt. He spoke first.

"I felt so ill and disturbed," he said. "I could do nothing but wait for your appearance."

They sat down on the ground together. She was so exhausted by her two-day struggle that for a moment she leaned forward and rested her head on his knee. Her thought processes seemed to awaken once more because she smiled peacefully and said: "I want to think."

Eventually, she raised herself and looked at the young man with shining eyes.

"I felt so ill," she said. "My mother kept on giving me herb drinks. She said it was normal to feel faint and dizzy when one is growing. I know now what made me feel so ill. I was fighting my training. My training has told me that people are not important in themselves but you so suddenly became important to me, as a person. I did not know how to tell my mother all this. I did not know how to tell her anything yet she was kind and took care of me. Eventually I thought I would lose my mind so I came here to find you . . ."

It was as if, from that moment onwards, they quietly and of their own willing, married each other. They began to plan together how they should meet and when they should meet. The young man was full of forethought

and planning. He knew that, in the terms of his own society, he was starting a terrible mess, but then his society only calculated along the lines of
human helplessness in the face of overwhelming odds. It did not calculate
for human inventiveness and initiative. He only needed the young girl's
pledge and from then onwards he took the initiative in all things. He was
to startle and please her from that very day with his forethought. It was
as if he knew that she would come at some time, that they would linger
in joy with their love-making, so that when Tselane eventually expressed
agitation at the lateness of the hour, he, with a superior smile, indicated a
large bundle of wood nearby that he had collected for her to take home.

A peaceful interlude followed and the community innocently lived out
its day-by-day life, unaware of the disruption and upheaval that would
soon fall upon it. The women were soon out in the fields, hoeing weeds
and tending their crops, Tselane among them, working side by side with
Mma-Monosi, as she had always done. There was not even a ripple of
the secret life she now lived; if anything, she worked harder and with
greater contentment. She laughed and joked as usual with Mma-Monosi
but sound instinct made her keep her private affair to herself.

When the corn was already high in the fields and about to ripen, Tselane realized that she was expecting a child. A matter that had been secret
could be a secret no longer. When she confided this news to Keaja, he
quite happily accepted it as a part of all the plans he had made, for as
he said to her at that time: "I am not planning for death when we are so
happy. I want it that we should live."

He had only one part of all his planning secure, a safe escape route
outside the village and on to a new and unknown life they would make
for themselves. They had made themselves outcasts from the acceptable
order of village life and he presented her with two alternatives from which
she could choose. The one alternative was simpler for them. They could
leave the village at any moment and without informing anyone of their
intentions. The world was very wide for a man. He had travelled great
distances, both alone and in the company of other men, while on his hunting and herding duties. The area was safe for travel for some distance.
He had sat around firesides and heard stories about wars and fugitives
and other hospitable tribes who lived distances away and whose customs
differed from theirs. Keaja had not been idle all this while. He had prepared all they would need for their journey and hidden their provisions in
a secret place.

The alternative was more difficult for the lovers. They could inform
their parents of their love and ask that they be married. He was not sure
of the outcome but it was to invite death or worse. It might still lead to
the escape route out of the village as he was not planning for death.

So after some thought Tselane decided to tell her parents because as she pointed out the first plan would be too heartbreaking for their parents. They therefore decided on that very day to inform their parents of their love and name the date on which they wished to marry.

It was nearing dusk when Tselane arrived home with her bundle of wood. Her mother and Mma-Monosi were seated out in the courtyard, engaged in some quiet conversation of their own. Tselane set down her bundle, approached the two women and knelt down quietly by her mother's side. Her mother turned towards her, expecting some request or message from a friend. There was no other way except for Tselane to convey her own message in the most direct way possible.

"Mother," she said. "I am expecting a child by the son of Rra-Keaja. We wish to be married by the next moon. We love each other . . ."

For a moment her mother frowned as though her child's words did not make sense. Mma-Monosi's body shuddered several times as though she were cold but she maintained a deathly silence. Eventually Tselane's mother lowered her voice and said between clenched teeth: "You are to go to your hut and remain there. On no account are you to leave it without the supervision of Mma-Monosi."

For a time Mma-Tselane sat looking into the distance, a broken woman. Her social prestige, her kingdom, her self-esteem crumbled around her.

A short while later her husband entered the yard. He had spent an enjoyable day at the chief's court with other men. He now wished for his evening meal and retirement for the night. The last thing he wanted was conversation with women, so he looked up irritably as his wife appeared without his evening meal. She explained herself with as much dignity as she could muster. She was almost collapsing with shock. He listened in disbelief and gave a sharp exclamation of anger.

Just at this moment Keaja's father announced himself in the yard. "Rra-Tselane, I have just heard from my own son the offence he has committed against your house, but he desires nothing more than to marry your child. If this would remove some of the offence, then I am agreeable to it."

"Rra-Keaja," Tselane's father replied. "You know as well as I that this marriage isn't in the interests of your family or mine." He stood up and walked violently into the night.

Brokenly, Keaja's father also stood up and walked out of the yard.

It was her husband's words that shook Mma-Tselane out of her stupor of self-pity. She hurried to her living quarters for her skin shawl, whispered a few words to Mma-Monosi about her mission. Mma-Monosi too sped off into the night after Rra-Keaja. On catching up with him she whispered urgently: "Rra-Keaja! You may not know me. I approach you because we now share this trouble which has come upon us. This matter will never be secret. Tomorrow it will be a public affair. I therefore urge you to do as Mma-Tselane has done and make an appeal for your child at once. She has gone to the woman's compound of the chief's house as she has many friends there."

Her words lightened the old man's heavy heart. With a promise to send her his news, he turned and walked in the direction of the chief's yard.

Mma-Monosi sped back to her own yard.

"Tselane," she said, earnestly. "It is no light matter to break custom. You pay for it with your life. I should have told you the story that night we discussed custom. When I was a young girl we had a case such as this but not such a deep mess. The young man had taken a fancy to a girl and she to him. He therefore refused the girl his parents had chosen for him. They could not break him and so they killed him. They killed even though he had not touched the girl. But there is one thing I want you to know. I am your friend and I will die for you. No one will injure you while I am alive."

Their easy, affectionate relationship returned to them. They talked for some time about the love affair, Mma-Monosi absorbing every word with delight. A while later Mma-Tselane re-entered the yard. She was still too angry to talk to her own child but she called Mma-Monosi to one side and informed her that she had won an assurance in high places that no harm would come to her child.

And so began a week of raging storms and wild irrational deliberations. It was a family affair. It was a public affair. As a public affair, it would bring ruin and disaster upon the community and public anger was high. Two parents showed themselves up in a bad light, the father of Tselane and the mother of Keaja. Rra-Tselane was adamant that the marriage would never take place. He preferred to sound death warnings all the time. The worm that had been eating at the heart of Keaja's mother all this while finally arose and devoured her heart. She too could be heard to sound death warnings. Then a curious and temporary solution was handed down from high places. It was said that if the lovers removed themselves from the community for a certain number of days it would make allowance for public anger to die down. Then the marriage of the lovers would be considered.

So appalling was the drama to the community that on the day Keaja was released from his home and allowed to approach the home of Tselane, all the people withdrew to their own homes so as not to witness the fearful sight. Only Mma-Monosi, who had supervised the last details of the departure, stood openly watching the direction in which the young lovers left the village. She saw them begin to ascend the hill not far from the home of Tselane. As darkness was approaching, she turned and walked back to her yard. To Mma-Tselane, who lay in a state of nervous collapse in her hut, Mma-Monosi made her last, sane pronouncement on the whole affair.

"The young man is no fool," she said. "They have taken the direction of the hill. He knows that the hilltop is superior to any other. People are angry and someone might think of attacking them. An attacker will find it a difficult task as the young man will hurtle stones down on him before he ever gets near. Our child is quite safe with him."

Then the story took a horrible turn. Tension built up towards the day the lovers were supposed to return to the community life. Days went by and they did not return. Eventually search parties were sent out to look for them but they had disappeared. Not even their footmarks were visible on the bare rock faces and tufts of grass on the hillside. At first the searchers returned and did not report having seen any abnormal phenomena, only a baffled surprise. Then Mma-Monosi's precarious imaginative balance tipped over into chaos. She was seen walking grief-stricken towards the hill. As she reached its base she stood still and the whole drama of the disappearance of the lovers was re-created before her eyes. She first heard loud groans of anguish that made her blood run cold. She saw that as soon as Tselane and Keaja set foot on the hill, the rocks parted and a gaping hole appeared. The lovers sank into its depths and the rocks closed over them. As she called, "Tselane! Keaja!" their spirits arose and floated soundlessly with unseeing eyes to the top of the hill.

Mma-Monosi returned to the village and told a solemn and convincing story of all the phenomena she had seen. People only had to be informed that such phenomena existed and they all began seeing them too. Then Mma-Tselane, maddened and distraught by the loss of her daughter, slowly made her way to the hill. With sorrowful eyes she watched the drama re-create itself before her. She returned home and died. The hill from then onwards became an unpleasant embodiment of sinister forces which destroy life. It was no longer considered a safe dwelling place for the tribe. They packed up their belongings on the backs of their animals, destroyed the village and migrated to a safer area.

The deserted area remained unoccupied from then onwards until 1875 when people of the Bamalete tribe settled there. Although strangers to the area, they saw the same phenomena, they heard the loud groans of anguish and saw the silent floating spirits of the lovers. The legend was kept alive from generation unto generation and so the hill stands until this day in the village of Otse in southern Botswana as an eternal legend of love. Letswe La Baratani, The Hill of the Lovers, it is called.

MEMORIES, FANTASIES, MADNESSES

Among the women writers in Global Cultures, there are many who, like Bessie Head, are pioneering in psychological studies of women. The literature being created by these women is rich with explorations of how women living in oppressive, sexist families and societies remember their lives before marriage, fantasize escapes that they cannot make in reality, and, sometimes, drift into socially induced or abetted madness. With the current generation, in which international feminism is taking root, there will undoubtedly be a literature of political activism and perhaps critiques of the rich vein of nostalgia and fantasy in these stories, which come from women isolated from any political culture or solidarity.

Growing old in societies that once venerated the aged but now find them a burden is especially a challenge for widows (as can be seen in a later story from Syria, "The Women's Baths"). The Taiwanese writer AI YA, born in 1945, describes a grandmother, longing for company during long days at home alone, wishing for a dog and, when her daughter objects, purchasing a little machine that makes dog sounds. In another key, the heroine of "Pilar, Your Curls," under her hairdryer in the beauty parlor, settles for reading romances and talking with her fantasy lover—if only reality would not intrude. CARMEN LUGO FILIPPI, born in Ponce, Puerto Rico, is a professor of French at the University of Puerto Rico.

The story called "Solitude of Blood" is by the second oldest writer in this anthology, the Chilean MARTA BRUNET who was born in 1897. Along with her slightly younger and more cosmpolitan contemporary Maria Luisa Bombal, Brunet is considered the outstanding woman novelist of her generation and one of South America's finest portraitists of rural life. The story's central character seems timeless, however, as she makes for herself a little oasis of pleasure and sensuality—enough to live for—in the midst of a marriage and a house where she is a slave. Writing in Egypt in the 1980s, ALIFA RIFAAT, from the generation born in the 1930s, creates a character in "The Long Night of Winter" who does not have such an oasis—except, perhaps, as the ending of the story ambiguously implies, in the physical presence of her young maidservant. Rifaat, like Marta Brunet, wrote entirely from within her world, which in her case was a traditional Islamic culture in provincial Egypt. She has no university education and speaks and writes only in Arabic, unlike many of her contemporaries who are much more Westernized and influenced by international feminism. Like Brunet, Rifaat is frank about her character's sexual frustration, and she effectively presents the woman's husband in his brutal indifference; but in this story, like the others in her collection *View from a Distant Minaret* (1983), the traditional right of a Muslim man to rule his wife is not questioned—the oppressiveness women suffer is assigned, rather, to the irreligious, disrespectful way men play their assigned role.

The quiet strength that keeps Brunet's and Rifaat's characters from going insane—though both feel near insanity—is not available to the characters in Yuko Tsushima's "The Marsh" or Khalida Hussain's "Story of the Name." The Japanese protagonist has stepped outside the bounds of propriety by rejecting traditional notions of marriage and motherhood. Although she does find an ally in another single mother, a woman who has spent time in a psychiatric ward, the protagonist slowly sinks into a "half-mad" marsh of her own fantasy and believes that she is an evil spirit who seduces human men. YUKO TSUSHIMA, born in 1947, a prolific and prize-winning writer, has had two of her novels published in English, *Child of Fortune* (1982) and *The Shooting Gallery* (1988). But KHA-LIDA HUSSAIN, born in 1938 in Pakistan, is represented in English only by this story, from a 1983 anthology of Urdu stories published in Islamabad and distributed by Oxford University Press. This story, which is indebted to the 1930s literary movement that brought realistic short fiction into Pakistani letters, where the traditional tales were magical and fantastical, is unusual in its specific focus, which is on the disease Western psychiatry knows as anorexia nervosa in combination with bulimia. The central character, apparently jilted or somehow disappointed in love, experiences the "sweet contentment" of starvation and incessant, mindless work. She is able to forget the name—her name—that she has been obsessively trying to recapture. So she stops looking for her self, for someone other than the "Sister," "Aunty," that she is for her family; at which point she becomes ravenous, balloons up, and feels, again, the need to find her self "inside the mounds of her flesh."

Whistle

Ai Ya

S H E N E V E R imagined that whistling could be so difficult. After puckering her lips and blowing—*phui phui*—for some strange reason she felt she had to urinate. But she could hardly be blamed for that, since she went *phui* whenever she tried to get little Hsiung-hsiung to pee. That was sure no whistle. She really and truly did not know how to whistle.

But no, she had to learn how, she just had to!

"I want a dog, a tiny little dog." She pleaded her case very tentatively to Ta-fa, who responded emphatically and, it seemed, without even considering her request,

"No!"

She tried to explain that she was lonely, especially after Ta-fa and his wife had left for work in the morning, leaving her alone at home from half past seven in the morning until six in the evening. It was so lonely being in such a big house all by herself. Mei-fang, who hadn't said a word all the time she was talking, banged one of the teacups hard against the tray—*clang*—as she was picking up the tea service, and her meaning was clear: Lonely? If you're so lonely, why don't you keep Hsiung-hsiung home with you and take care of him yourself? Mei-fang had said—in a roundabout way—that sending Hsiung-hsiung to a baby-sitter every day cost them well over a hundred dollars a month, which, when the cost of milk powder and baby food was added in, went up to nearly two hundred. But she wouldn't agree to it. She knew that at her advanced age the pudgy little boy, with all that energy, would be too much for her to handle. She didn't dare agree to it.

"Mama," Mei-fang reasoned with her, "you're not as spry as you used to be, and who's going to take care of feeding and cleaning up after the dog? Besides, the neighbors would complain about the dog's barking."

She was right, you can't keep a dog in an apartment building. Then, one day she noticed the little grade-school boy from across the way standing on the stairs whistling. Each whistle was answered by a series of barks—*arf, arf, arf*. What was going on here? The boy told her it was something called an "echo key-finder," invented for people who were forever misplacing their keys. All they had to do was whistle, which produced a series of barks in the echo sounder attached to the key, thereby giving away its location.

She asked the boy to buy one for her. It was a small thing, no bigger than a cigarette lighter. She called it "doggie" and pretended it was her very own dog. All she had to do was whistle and it would answer her, just like a real dog.

But she never imagined that whistling could be so difficult.

Pilar, Your Curls

Carmen Lugo Filippi

M A Y B E S H E should consider wearing glasses. She felt slightly dizzy as she watched the words swim across the page, and she was able to straighten them out only if she concentrated. But it really didn't require that much concentration because the words before her exercised a strange fascination. Sometimes her hypnotic trance reached the point where she forgot about everything but that rapid succession of related meanings.

The incessant chatter in the background was a counterpoint to her thoughts, weaving in and out intermittently against the sound of warm air around her head. The other sounds around her were the constant hum of three hairdryers and the screeching of the city buses in the distance.

She didn't let any of this noise bother her because she was able to turn it into a make-believe curtain that became part of the scenery. It was just like wearing false eyelashes: they feel a little heavy the first couple of days, but then you get used to them.

The only thing that got on her nerves was having to read while sitting in such a conventional position. She preferred to lie curled up on a couch or stretched out in an exotic feline pose that many of her friends liked to criticize, but who cares, she liked it. She couldn't even file her nails while sitting under the dryer—and, let's face it, they were starting to look like a washerwoman's. She turned the pages slowly, savoring each line. Why did they insist on making these paperbacks so ridiculously small— ten inches by six—when so many readers had requested better bindings and larger print?

This time she had rushed in late and, what with the line of customers and all, she had grabbed one that had a somewhat uninspired title: *You Shall Return*. She'd picked it out from a stack of magazines and paperbacks because she liked the picture on the cover—was it a picture or a drawing?—it made her think of that picture of her when she was only seventeen. She had dimples and hair that was pretty straight which she wore in a pageboy cut that won her the nickname "Suzanne Pleschette." Some of the nasty ones changed it to "Fleshette."

She glanced at the cover again while smoothing out her skirt—she had to remember to let down the hem one of these days. She opened the book and was pleased to see lots of dialogue. She liked the first few lines right away: "Walking into the darkened bedroom she noticed the rumpled bed . . . Duke had been looking rather pale these days . . . his hair was sprinkled with gray." Dramatic lines, these, with just the right touch of intimacy. "Sissy was overwhelmed by a storm of indescribable emotions."

Wear glasses? The idea intruded on her thoughts. Why not? It all depends on what kind of glasses you pick out. Those huge tinted ones . . . Maurice would take one look at her and . . . She could imagine herself hiding her face and Maurice walking in with that slightly clumsy gait of his that reminded her a little of Marlon Brando.

"You're looking lovely tonight, my dear. You have the air of a French intellectual fresh from her morning bath. Those black pajama pants with that crimson sash are stunning."

But wait . . . no. Maybe the glasses would make her look . . . old? Even if he didn't utter a word, she would know. Besides, neither Kate nor Betty, not even Sylvie wore glasses: they all had large brown dreamy eyes. Dreamy eyes? What are dreamy eyes? Probably a little humid-looking with just a hint of sadness. As if they were contemplating horizons . . . distant horizons?

She turned to her page and read about Sissy. "She was thin almost to a fault, with violet eyes." But even Elizabeth Taylor's were, what? Blue? No, *Cosmopolitan* said they were violet. That was in the article about that huge rock Richard Burton gave her "to match the lovely violet of her eyes." Violet eyes with glasses on, she whispered. An odd combination, perhaps, but one that Maurice would probably like. He also preferred older women. Remember, Maurice, the time you scolded me at that dance for being jealous without any reason? I was twenty-four and feeling old, especially since I was surrounded by all those young girls with their silly innocent faces. You put your arm around me and reassured me that you wouldn't trade me for a hundred young girls, not then, not ever—not ever, you said! And then you kissed me, you kissed me deeply.

She felt a weakness in her knees and crossed her legs, carefully covering her thighs. Whenever she let herself get into one of her sensuous reveries the same thing happened. She went from one mirror image to another and another and round and round till she was almost dizzy.

This time she avoided losing herself totally in that labyrinth and returned to her reading, slightly annoyed at having lost her place. But she knew the same thing had happened to her before. She probably should buy herself a bookmark, maybe one in mother-of-pearl with her initials engraved "P.A."

". . . searing violet eyes." Yes, that's where she'd been.

How did Sissy Biter meet Duke LeMoin? In Cocke County. In that small town—a burg really—on a day like any other. Who introduced them? It was all so vague. No one would have guessed how it was all to turn out, not even her. For Sissy it was all so routine and yet so suggestive . . . he had overpowered her . . . handsome, distant, sullen, he'd swept her off her feet. It was like floating on a still lake and suddenly having waves . . .

It was just like with Maurice. You arrived at the party early and were just about to order a Manhattan from the overly solicitous waiter when, as luck would have it, your girlfriend came over with Maurice in tow, calling out to you, "Pilar, this is Maurice. You know, the friend I've been telling you about." You stretched out your hand nervously, saying, "Pleased to make your acquaintance."

Then it was just like in a dream. He asked you to dance and in that half-joking flirtatious way of his, he asked if you were having a good time. You looked up at him and, in a voice that surprised you with its brazenness, you said, "Are you?" He was already steering you towards a dark corner of the dance floor, moving gracefully to the slow melody of a . . . a fox-trot? You never could tell slow dances apart. It's just a matter of rocking gently to music, moving your body against his . . . But you'll never forget the words to the song they were playing. You christened it "Our Magic Meeting Song." Remember? The song's words are etched in your memory. You have often thought since then that the author—was it the singer?—had an incredible sensitivity very similar to your own. You would repeat the words over and over to yourself—you've always had a good memory for song lyrics. "Your breasts like two young roes that feed amongst the lilies."

Then someone told you it was entitled "Chapter Twenty-Four" and you thought, "What a dull title for a song," as if it were just one more blade of grass, when in fact that song was full of spiritual, melancholy things. Sometimes song writers do that just to attract attention with their eccentricities. That's the way artists are. That's life. Just look at jet setters when they're about to get married. What scandalous behavior! Like that Mick or is it Mike? Jagger and his Bianca. *People* said her dress was cut down to her bellybutton and that she showed up at the St. Tropez chapel dressed that way. How could the priest put up with that? I'll never understand it in a million years. But she did look so chic in that picture they took of her. She had that big hat on, with her hair so straight and long, so natural . . .

You know, the more natural you look the better, like this Sissy here with her black pants "and her black wool sweater, with black boots. Dressed that way she might have looked just the slightest bit masculine but instead, the contrast made her look extremely feminine. Besides, with that silky black hair of hers . . ."

Maybe she'd wear black tonight for Maurice. It was such a classic color, so elegant. He would love her in black.

"How do I look, love? Is this little number becoming? It's from Francoise. You know, that new boutique in the mall. Maybe it's just a little too see-through, but I have a feeling you do like it. If not, say so and I'll return it."

That's Maurice, for you. Possessive to a fault, demanding in his taste and final in his decisions.

She just loved his firm "No!" You couldn't change his mind when he uttered one of those. Sometimes she'd try to find a little gap that she could work her way into, gnawing away at it like a tiny ant, finding a way to change his mind ever so slightly. But that "No!" of his was made of steel. She had to admit, though, that she got a kick out of reliving those scenes when he would utter his final pronouncement on an issue. She could feel her legs weaken as she remembered the last time . . .

Sissy Biter didn't seem to be such a sharp heroine after all. In Chapter X she still couldn't seem to understand Duke LeMoin's complex personality: a tender man who hides his true feelings under a cover of harshness.

" 'Do you find me a bit rough, Sissy?'

'Yes,' she sighed.

He wrapped his arms around her fervently as they rolled over each other onto the rug. He was breathing heavily, leaning hard onto her slender body . . ."

She's really a silly one, that Sissy. She just doesn't know how to handle a man psychologically. If Maurice were to try to force himself on me that way . . .

She went from the heat of the hairdryer to a garden path overhung with jasmine and roses. Maurice was there with her, leaning his body onto hers against a column . . .

"Now, Maurice, honey, you promised you wouldn't until after the wedding. I'm saving myself for you. Sweet, sweet Maurice, I know you would never force yourself on . . . Maurice! Take it easy, honey, you've had too much to drink, Maureeeeeeeee—"

She stretched her legs out to keep the woman under the dryer next to her from guessing what was on her mind. She closed her eyes in order to enjoy the full flavor of the growing dizziness that was enticing her to open her legs slightly.

Suddenly she heard the beauty parlor owner yelling, forcing her to open her eyes.

"Pilar, that was for you. Come out from under the dryer a sec. It was Juan on the phone and was he mad! He said you've taken too long so he's leaving the kids at the neighbor's because it's his night out with the boys. He said not to wait up."

Pilar pulled her head out from under the dryer and started taking off the curlers.

"It's the same old story, Millie. I'll come by tomorrow so you can comb me out. Hand me that brush."

"Take it easy, honey. Just take it one day at a time."

It was the tone in her voice that made Pilar feel even more depressed.

Solitude of Blood

Marta Brunet

THE BASE was made of bronze, with a drawing of lacework flowers. The same flowers were painted on the reservoir glass, and a white spherical shade interrupted its extremities to allow the chimney to pass through. That lamp was the showpiece of the house. Placed in the center of the table, on top of a meticulously elaborate crocheted table cover, it was turned on only when there was a dinner guest, an unexpected, remote occurrence. But it was also lighted on Saturday night, every Saturday, because that eve of a worry-free morning could be celebrated in some way, and nothing could be better then, than to have the lamp spreading its brightness over the vivid tangle of paper that covered the walls, over the china cabinet so symmetrically decorated with fruit plates, soup tureens and formal stacks of dishes; over the doors of the cupboard, with decorative panels and the iron latch and its lock speaking of the same times as the grating that protected the window on the garden side of the house. Yes, every Saturday night, the lamplight traced out for the man and the woman a little hollow of intimacy, generally peaceful.

From living in contact with the earth, the man seemed made of telluric elements. In the south, in the mountains, looking at their reflection in the translucent eye of the lakes, the trees, polished by wind and by water, had strange shapes and startling qualities. In that wood worked by the pitiless harsh weather the man was carved. The years had made furrows in his face, and from that fallow field sprouted his beard, moustache, eyebrows, eyelashes. And his tangled mat of hair, coal black, crowned his head with a rebellious shock, which was always escaping over his forehead and which he would push back into place with a characteristic mechanical gesture.

Now, in the brightness of the lamplight, the large hands carefully shuffled a deck of cards. He spread the cards out over the table. Absorbed in the game of solitaire, slow and meticulous, because he was about to win, his features swelled with a kind of pleasantness. He hardly had any cards left in his hand. He drew one. He turned it over and suddenly the pleasantness turned into harshness. He gazed at the cards with rapt attention, the new card in his hand. He put down his remaining cards and tossed the big shock back, sinking and fixing his fingers in his hair. The pleasantness spread over his face again. He lifted his eyelids, and his eyes appeared like grapes, azure-blue. A cautious glance that became fixed on the woman, that found the woman's eyes, grey, so clear that in certain light or from a distance they gave the unsettling sensation of being blind.

"Just imagine that I'm not looking at you and go on with your trick . . . ," said the woman with a voice that sang.

"Will it turn out really badly? asked the man.

"If it does, it does."

"It always fails to work for me! Come on, for God's sake! I'll do it again!" And he gathered the cards together to shuffle them.

Sometimes the game of solitaire "came out." Other times it "turned stubborn." But always at ten o'clock, the hours resonating in the corridor as they fell from the old clock, the man pulled himself up, looked at the woman, came toward her until he could put a hand on her head, and he caressed her hair, again and again, to conclude by saying, as he said that night:

"Until tomorrow, little one. Don't stay up for a long time, be sure the lamp is completely out and don't make a lot of noise with your phonograph. Let me drop off to sleep first . . ."

He left, closing the door. She heard his long strides through the corridor. Then she heard him go out onto the patio, saying something to the dog, turning around, going back and forth through the bedroom; she heard the bed creak, his heavy shoes falling one after the other, the bed creaking again, the man turning over, becoming quiet. The woman had abandoned the knitting in her lap. She was scarcely breathing, her mouth partially open, her whole self gathering in the sounds, separating them, classifying them, her auditory perception fine-tuned to such a point that all her senses seemed to have been transformed into one big ear. Tall, strong, her naturally brown skin tanned by the sun, she might have been any ordinary creole woman if her eyes had not set her apart, creating for her a face that memory, immediately, put in a place all by itself. Tension caused a little bead of perspiration to break out on her forehead. That was all. But she felt her chilled skin and, with an unconscious gesture, passed her hand slowly over it. Then, just as absent-mindedly, she looked at that hand. With every moment she seemed more tense, more like an antenna to receive signals. And the signal came. From the bedroom, and in the form of a snoring sound, which was followed, arrhythmically, by others.

Her muscles went limp. Her senses opened up into an exact five-pointed star, each one doing its particular job. But the woman still remained motionless, with her expanding pupils fixed on the lamp.

When had she bought that lamp? One time when she went to the town, when she sold her habitual dozen children's outfits, knitted between one household chore and another, between chores that were always the same, methodically distributed over days that were indistinguishable one from another. She bought that lamp as she had bought the china cabinet, and the wicker furniture, and the wardrobe with the mirror, and the quilted eiderdown comforter. Yes, as she had bought so many things, so much . . . Of course, over so many years! How many years had it been? Eighteen. She was thirty-six now, and she was eighteen when she got married. Eighteen and eighteen. Yes . . . The lamp. The china cabinet. The wicker furniture . . . She never believed, of this she was sure, that by knitting she could earn money not only to dress herself, but to give herself household conveniences.

He said, no sooner had they gotten married:

"You have to be enterprising in order to establish your own little business and earn money for your necessities. Raise chickens or sell eggs."

She answered:

"You know I'm ignorant about these things."

"Look for something that you know how to do then. Something they taught you in school."

"I could sell candy."

"Give up on selling in this god-forsaken place. It ought to be something that can be carried all together once a month to the town."

"I could knit."

"That's not a bad idea. But it's necessary to buy wool," he added, suddenly uneasy. "How much would you need to get started?"

"I don't know. Let me check prices. And ask around in the store, to see if people are interested in knitted articles."

"If it doesn't come out being really expensive . . ."

And it did not turn out to be expensive, and it was definitely a good business enterprise. The wife of the store owner himself bought the first completed item for her son, which was merely a sample. A lovely little suit, such as no child had ever had in that "god-forsaken place," where the people handled money and acquired tasteless things in shops in which the barrel of fat was next to the bottles of perfume and the cheap woolens were next to the medicinal balm. Her business was a big success. People placed orders with her. She knitted for the whole region. She was able to raise her prices. She never had enough supplies for the orders that were pending. When he saw that she was prospering, he said one day:

"It's a good idea for you to give me back the ten pesos I lent you to begin your knitting. And don't spend all the money that you earn just on things for yourself. Of course I'm not going to tell you to give me this money, it's yours, yes, you've well earned it, and I'm not going to tell you to hand it over to me." He always repeated what he had just expressed, insisting, wanting to impress the idea on his own mind. "But now you see, now it's necessary to buy a big kettle and to fix the cellar door. You could easily assume responsibility for the household affairs, now that you have so much money at your disposal. Yes . . . , so much money."

She bought the big kettle, she had the cellar door repaired. And then, she bought, and she bought . . . Because it represented happiness to her to be converting that mess of a country house, eaten up by neglect, into what it was now, a house like hers there in the north, in the little town shaded by willows and acacias, with the river singing or rumbling down the valley, and the Andes right there, ever present, background for the little houses that seemed like toys: blue pink, yellow, with wide entrance halls and a jasmine bush perfuming the siestas, and facing the patio gate, a painted green bench, inviting casual conversation in the early evening, when the birds and the angelus were taking flight through the skies in the same air, and the peaks took on violent pinks and gentle violet colors, before falling asleep beneath the blanket of watchful gleaming stars.

She closed her eyelids, as if she too should fall asleep in the shelter of that vigilance. But she opened them again right away and listened again, certain of hearing the rhythm of the one who was sleeping. Then she picked herself up and with silent movements opened the cupboard, and from the highest shelf she went about taking down and placing on the table an old phonograph, improbably shaped, like a little cabinet whose open main doors revealed a set of zither strings, at an oblique angle over the mouth of the receiver, which was nothing but a small open circle in the sound chamber. Below, other doors, smaller, afforded a view of the green turntable. That phonograph was her own luxury item, not like the lamp, luxury of the house, but hers, hers. Purchased when the señora from "los Tapiales," passing through the town, had found her in the store and seen her knitted articles and asked her if she could make some overcoats for her little girls. What a beautiful woman, with a mouth so large and tender and a voice that dragged out her "rr's," as if she were a French lady; but she wasn't, and that really made her laugh. What a workload she had that summer! That was when she saw fulfilled her longing to have a phonograph with records and everything. He permitted her to buy it. That was what she earned all that money for!

"Just buy it, my dear. What's yours is yours, of course, but it would be good if you could also see about buying a poncho for me, for the wool flannel one is wearing through. Because the poncho is a real necessity, and since I have to get together money for another pair of oxen, it's not a matter of squandering funds, and since you are earning so much . . . But it's clear, yes, that you'll buy yourself the phonograph too, and before anything else . . ."

First she bought the poncho and immediately afterwards the phonograph. Never greater was her pleasure than being back at home, the phonograph set up on the table, listening insatiably to the cadence of the waltz or the march that was abruptly interrupted to let the sound of tolling bells be heard. They had sold it to her with the right to two records that she might choose carefully; yet he was impatient on seeing her indecisive after choosing the first one—which was the one with waltz and the march on it—having to try out a whole album one record after another. Until he said, getting more and more impatient:

"It's getting late. Look how the sun is going down. We've got to go, yes. Night will catch us here if we don't. Take that one that you have set aside, and this one. One because you like it, and the other let's leave up to chance . . . ," and he pulled out at random a record from the box.

Which turned out to have Spanish songs filled with laments, which neither he nor she liked and which she tried in vain to exchange. And when, some time later, she hinted timidly at the idea of buying more records, he—with the claylike expression that he was accustomed to wearing when he was being negative—answered severely:

"No more fuss in the house. What you've got is enough and with that you can get along."

She never insisted. When she was alone, when he and his laborers were in the field working, she would take out the phonograph and in a standing position, with a vague uneasiness that she was "wasting time"—as he said—her hands together and a spiral of joy beginning to stir in her breast, she let herself sink sweetly into the music.

He did not like at all this "wasting time." She knew this well and did not allow herself to be carried away by the overwhelming desire to hear the waltz or to hear the march. But out of that habit of telling him, in minute detail, whatever she had done during the day, a habit to which he had made her accustomed since the beginning of their married life, she said, her eyelids open and her pupils dilated:

"I ground the flour for the workers, I mended your coat, I kneaded dough for the house . . ." She paused imperceptibly and added very gently: "I listened to the phonograph for a while and that's all . . ."

"Wanting to waste time . . . , time that's useful for so many things that bring in money, yes, to waste it . . ." He said it in different tones of voice, sometimes ascertaining a weakness in the woman, gently protective and condescending; sometimes absent-minded, mechanical, tossing back the rebellious shock of hair, troubled by another idea; sometimes stern, wooden and frightening her, she who had never been able to prevail over a dark, instinctive submissiveness of female animal to male, who in former years humiliated herself to her father and in the present, to her husband.

When she, without any hinting, bought that leather jacket for him, shiny as if it were waxed, black and long, which the storekeeper said was for a mechanic and which the rain could not seep into, like that which might fall in the stubborn downpours of the region; when she bought it and mysteriously brought it home and left the package in front of his place at the table—so that he might find it by surprise—the man, his mood softening on seeing it, passed his big hand over her soft hair, done up in braids and raised like a tiara on her head.

"You're a good old gal. Hard-working, like women ought to be, yes. And listen, little one, tonight since its Saturday, light the lamp, and that way I can do my solitaire better. And when I go off to bed, you'll stay for a little while longer and play your phonograph. Yes, you'll play it, but when I'm sound asleep. You should have your pleasure too . . ."

Thus the custom was born.

She lowered the lamp's light a little. She went on tiptoes to the window and opened it, letting in the night and its silence. She went back to the table, carefully wound up the phonograph, put her hands together and waited.

Ta-ta . . . , ta-ta . . . , ta-ta-dum . . .

The march. And suddenly everything around her was blotted out; it disappeared submerged in the stridency of the trumpets and the roll of the drums, dragging her back through time, until leaving her in the plaza of the northern town, after eleven o'clock mass on a rainless Sunday, the drum major spinning the baton around and following after him, marching in step, the band taking the final turn along the parade route, with the children swarming in front, and a dog mixed in among their racing feet, while the ladies on their traditional bench commented on petty problems, the gentlemen talked about the wine harvest, and they—she and her sisters, she and her friends, arm in arm, with their braids uneasily sliding over breasts that were already swelling with sighs—passed and passed again in front of the grown-ups, crossing through groups of boys, who seemed not to see them, and on fixing their gaze on their surroundings only looked at one of them, absorbing them as if thirsty for fresh water, from a real spring, mouths avid, grown large with desire.

It was the occasion when new clothes were shown off. Sometimes they were pink or celestial blue. Sometimes they were red or sea colored, and this meant that throughout a sky of faded blue a few clouds shed their fleece and that the wind had carried away the last leaf of dark gold. She particularly remembered a red overcoat, with a round collar of white fur, curly and soft against her face and a muff like a little barrel, hanging from the collar by a cord, also white. And the warning from the mother:

"Put your hands in the muff and don't you take them out again. Of course, you can say hello to people . . . ," she added after a thoughtful pause.

They went back and forth, arm in arm. They whispered incomprehensible things, inaudible confidences that drew their heads together, murmurs scarcely articulated and that suddenly shook them in long bursts of laughter that left the trees perplexed, because it wasn't nesting season, or they stirred the trees to nod approvingly during that other time of year when the birds tried to add their own comments to those musical sounds. Sometimes, no, once, she raised her face to better catch the laughter that always seemed to fall on her from above, and from this foreshortened perspective, her pupils found the gaze of a pair of green eyes, as green as new grass and in the face of a boy darkened by the sun, strong and like a freshly sprouting field. Only an instant. But an instant to be carried home and treasured and placed in the depths of her heart, and to feel that a pang of anguish and a feeling of warmth and a vague desire to cry and pass soft fingertips over her lips suddenly tormented her, in the middle of reading, a chore, or a dream. To see him again. To have the feeling impressed on her again that life was stopping in her veins. For that second in which the green gaze of the boy fixed on her was the reason for her existence. Who was he? Was he from the town? No. Someone familiar? No. Perhaps a summer vacationer from a nearby area. She guarded her secret treasure. She talked less, she rarely laughed. But her pupils seemed to become enlarged, to flood her face in that search for the vigorous silhouette, dressed as the boys from the town did not dress. He arrived in a tiny car. It left him beside the club. He went to mass. She observed him from a distance, attentive and circumspect, in the presbytery, a little on the fringe of the group of men. When mass was over, he went to the candy store, filled the car up with packages, then took a walk around the plaza in order to go to the post office, retraced his steps, got into the car and left.

It was obvious that the other girls had noticed him. And dying of laughter over what he was wearing, in his golf or riding pants, they called him "Baggy Pants." To her hidden desperation.

The march continued filling the house with harmonious sounds. The bells burst in. As if pealing. Like on certain Sundays, when there was High Mass; but these were more sonorous bells, more harmonious, as if while they were pealing, pulsations of untapped joy were mixed with them.

The march ended. She shifted the needle, wound it again, turned the record over, and now the waltz began to spin around the table, music that seemed to be dancing, a beat that created soap bubbles, sometimes slowly, sometimes rapidly, radiating their colors.

She never found out what his name was, who he was, where he was from. One Sunday he didn't appear. Or the next. Or any other. A young girl raised the point:

"I wonder what's become of 'Baggy Pants'?"

"La Calchona, the Witch, has probably eaten him up," answered another, and they burst out laughing.

Her chest ached, and the sharp claw of sorrow dug at her throat. The corners of her mouth drew taut, and her eyes, like never before, filled her face. Once in the house, she sought out the most secluded corner, in the storage room, between the piano box and a pile of mattresses, and there she released her sorrow, she opened her heart, allowing her pain to escape and envelop her in its viscous mantle, adhering to her like new skin, moist and painful. The tears rained down her face. Never to see him again. The sobbing became stronger. What gaze was going to hold that magic for her? That burning that raged within her, she did not know where, as if waiting longingly for some unknown happiness. His name? . . . Enrique . . . Juan . . . José . . . Humberto . . . And if his name was Romualdo, like her grandfather's? It did not matter. She would always love him, whatever his name was . . . She would love him . . . Love him . . . Love him the way a woman loves, because she already was a woman and her fifteen years were ripening in her budding breasts, bringing a downy softness to her intimate zones and giving her voice a sudden dark tremolo. She would love him forever. She seemed to disintegrate into weeping. And suddenly she became still, sighing and still, without tears, her sorrow diluted, formless and distant. She sighed again. She wiped her eyes. And she found herself thinking that probably they were looking for her all over the house, that she ought to go wash her tear-scorched face, that . . . Yes, it was shameful to confess it, but she was hungry. And she went out gently from among the stored items, watching carefully in order to leave without being seen and to go refresh her face in the courtyard water tank. Her mother stared at her occasionally, seeming confused, and would murmur repeatedly:

"What a woman my little girl's become . . ."

The father was more definitive in his conclusion and said at the top of his voice:

"Look, Maclovia, we have to marry this one off as soon as possible."

For years she wept her sorrow between the piano box and the stack of mattresses. Nobody ever found out anything. They lifted up her braids, which since then she wore like a tiara around her head. They lowered the hems of all her dresses. No one said that she was pretty. But there wasn't a man who did not become startled on seeing her, lost in the contemplation of her grey eyes, experiencing something akin to vertigo in the presence of her mouth, fleshy, intensely red. Her appearance was courteous and in-different. She had to protect her memory, to keep her dream-fantasy safe, and only in a land of silence could she do this. Men looked at her, they stopped right next to her, but all of them, unanimously, went after other girls who were more accessible to their courtship.

The father introduced the future husband one day. He was from lands to the south, proprietor of a ranch, part of the estate of an old family in the region. Already an older man, of course not a "veteran"; this is what her mother said. As she also added: "A good catch."

Indifferent, she allowed them to interpret her acquiescence among them-selves and they married her off. This man or another, it made no difference to her. For not a one of them was hers, the one she loved, that green gaze that filled her blood with tenderness. This one? The other one? What did it matter? And she had to get married, according to what her mother said, smiling and persuasive, and according to what her father ordered with his thundering voice that did not accept dissenting opinions.

She remembered the discomfort of her bridal gown, the crown that pressed against her temples and her terrible fear of ripping the veil. The groom whispered:

"It was so expensive . . . , be careful with it . . ."

The waltz ended. For a moment silence filled the house, a silence so complete that it was injurious. Because it was so complete that the woman began to sense the presence of her heart, and terror forced open her mouth, and then she heard the panting sound of her breathing. But she also per-ceived the snoring in the other room, broken off when the music was interrupted and which a soothed subconscious mind imposed again upon the sleeping man. Then she heard a cricket in the courtyard. She raised herself up slowly and looked, outside, at the black and spacious field that she knew was flat, without anything in the distance but the ring of the horizon. Flat. A plain. And in the midst of it herself and her vigil, intercepting memories, caressing the past. Lost on the plain. With no one for her tenderness, to look at her and kindle within her that passion that had moved through her blood before and made her mouth shudder under the trembling touch of her fingers. Alone.

She went back to the phonograph. She would have liked to repeat the magical experience. To spread out again the melodic canvas in order to project the images there once more. But no. The clock struck once. Ten thirty. If he were to wake up . . .

With the same caution as someone who handles living, fragile creatures, she put away the phonograph and the records, she closed the cupboard, and she put the key in her pocket. From the china cabinet she took out a small candle stick and lit the candle.

Then she turned off the lamp.

And she went out to the corridor, following after the light's mysterious glow, pursued by nightmarish shadows impinging on one another.

When she carried the rice pudding to the dining room, she believed she had made the last trip of the evening and that then she could sit down to wait for the guest to leave. But the two men, the lamp between them, dug in their spoons happily, like children, and once they had cleaned their plates, they both raised their heads and sat staring at her, eagerly, their mouths watering.

"Serve yourselves a little more," she said, bringing the platter up beside them.

"Of course, patrona; it's really a pleasure to eat this!" admitted the guest.

"It's that the old gal has a good hand for these things!" And the man added in a confidential manner, because the wine was spreading through his body: "Things that they taught her in school; its worth the trouble to have an educated wife, friend; yes, I'm telling you, and believe me."

She waited, uncomfortable in her chair, her hands placed politely on the tablecloth. During the day they had eaten abundantly from a side of beef and the wine in the big jug was almost gone. It would be a matter of waiting around for awhile for the obligatory after dinner conversation and then the guest would leave. For his house was far away and the night was becoming windy, and over a background of pale stars enormous threatening clouds were creating shapes and then destroying them.

The man's voice caught her attention:

"And that coffee? Hurry, for the train won't wait . . ." And he laughed at his statement, hitting the table with his fist and making the lamp wobble back and forth.

Her trips to the kitchen weren't over . . . She went out to the corridor, thinking, disheartened, that the fire was probably already out and to revive it was a task that would take awhile. But under the ashes the red throbbing of the embers made her almost smile, and the water promptly boiled, and the coffee pot, important-looking with its two tiers, was on the tray, and she was once again walking through the darkened house, for the light of the reflector only seemed to thicken the blackness in the corners.

In the dining room the two men deliberated, sparing their words, their creole sullenness still in effect, because that meal was designated to close a deal for the purchase of some pigs that the guest had come from the town to see, and the afternoon had been spent in calculations, "I'll ask for this and offer you that," and they still were not arriving at anything concrete.

"On Monday I'll send you a messenger with the answer," said the guest.

"It's that tomorrow, Sunday, I have to give an answer to one of the parties that's also interested, and I can't put it off any longer, you understand, certainly; it's not good to just leave him waiting and to have him back out and you too and I lose a good buyer . . ."

"It's that you insist on such prices . . ."

"What the pigs are worth, friend; you won't find any better ones. There's not another litter like this anywhere around here, as you well know, yes . . ."

The woman had brought out the cups, the sugar; now she served them the coffee. Let them settle their business quickly and have the guest be on his way! And she sat down again, in the same position as before, so identical to, so like a cardboard cut-out and placed there, so erect, inexpressive and mysterious that, suddenly, the two men turned around to look at her, as if attracted by the ecstatic force that emanated from her.

The guest said:

"The patrona is so quiet!"

And the man, vaguely uncomfortable without knowing why:

"Serve some aguardiente, then."

She got up again, but this time not to go to the kitchen. She opened the cupboard and stood on her tiptoes to reach up above her the bottle that was stuck away in a corner behind the phonograph. The guest, who was watching her do it, asked solicitously:

"Do you want me to help you, patrona? The bottle is pretty high up for you."

"Look at it, how troublesome the bottle is . . . , just like a woman. But that's what I'm here for, yes . . . ," exclaimed the man, and he reached up to take it down.

His hands bumped into the phonograph, and he added, delighted to find another token of respect to offer the guest:

"Let's tell the patrona to play the phonograph for us a little. I call it 'her noisemaker,' because you've got to see how it squawks; but she likes it and I let her get her pleasure out of it. That's the way I am, yes. Play something for my friend to hear. Put on what's prettiest. But first you'll serve us something, yes . . ."

He placed the bottle and the phonograph on the edge of the table. The woman had remained quiet, listening to what the man was saying. But when the big hands seized the little cabinet, a kind of resentment began to stir in her breast, slowly, hardly at all at first. The phonograph was her own property and nobody had any right to it. Never had anyone operated it, except for herself with her own hands, which were loving, as if for touching a child. She swallowed hard and then clenched her teeth, revealing the hard edge of her jaw, just like her father's and just like that of the distant grandfather who had come from the Basque Country. She thought that the aguardiente would make them forget the music and instead of the little glasses, green and deceiving, into which a thimbleful of liquid hardly fit, she set out the other big wineglasses and filled them halfway. The men sniffed the aguardiente, then raised their eyes at the same time as they clinked the glasses, and in union said:

"To your health!"

And they emptied their contents in one gulp.

"This is aguardiente!" the man said.

The guest answered with a whistle that seemed to get stuck in his puckered mouth, a gesture of stupor, because something was beginning to dance in his muscles without any intervention of his will, and this left him in this state, perplexed and so happy on the inside.

"Let's talk about the deal again," the man proposed. "It's a good idea now to get it decided, yes; my price is reasonable, as you well know and you know you're getting pigs that'll bring double the price, yes; fattened up in the feed pen and the boar almost a purebred, outstanding pigs for ham . . ."

The other man smiled leisurely and nodded his assent.

"It's a deal, then?" asked the man. "It's a deal?"

"The aguardiente's good; one doesn't drink any better around here, not even in the Piñeros' hotel."

It was strange what he was feeling: still that sort of muscular movement that now was polarizing in his knees and was hurling his legs in every direction, irreducibly, just like a clown. And he was so happy!

"Good aguardiente, of course, yes . . . ; it's a gift from my father-in-law, who's from the vineyard region and he trades in wines. Of the best quality. The deal is set?"

"What deal?" he asked stupidly, attentive to his desire to laugh, to the impossibility of his laughing and to the disconsolate feeling that was beginning to inundate him. And his legs under the table dancing, dancing . . .

"The deal about the pigs, yes . . ."

"Oh! Really . . . But wasn't the patrona going to play the . . . , how did you call it . . . , the . . . , well . . . the phonograph?"

The woman hated him with a violence that might have destroyed him on becoming tangible. All the bad words that she had heard in her existence, and that she never said, suddenly came to her memory and they felt so alive to her that she was astonished they did not turn around to look at her, terrified and speechless in the face of this rude avalanche.

"It's a deal?"

"Music . . . , music . . . , life is short and one must enjoy it . . ."

But instead of reaching her hand out to the phonograph, the woman had extended it toward the bottle and again she served them, causing the wine glasses to overflow. And since each one, absorbed in his own thoughts, had not seen that the glass had been set in front of him, it was she who said, suddenly cordial:

"Serve yourselves!" And she made an inconclusive gesture of invitation, a kind of greeting that stayed in the air, paralyzed, while she watched them drink: "To your health!" And the hoarse sound of her voice saying the toast surprised her.

"It's a deal?" insisted the man, his tongue tangled in his consonants.

The other man did not hear a thing but only felt the tide of distress growing, at the same time as in his ears a cicada began its steady mid-afternoon sawing. And why were his legs dancing?

"Brother, I'm a good man . . . I don't deserve this . . ." And the distress spilled over into a hiccough. "I don't want my legs to dance, my legs are mine, mine . . . Music . . . ," he shouted suddenly and he got up halfway, but he lost his momentum and fell down on top of the table.

The woman watched them, silent, with her eyes so open and inexpressive, so bright, so enormous in their greyness. They were not to come near her phonograph again, they were not to have it; it was hers; therein resided her inner life, her deliverance from colorless days. Outwardly she was similar to the plain, flat, with her husband's will cutting her level like the wind; but just as the current of water in all its forms passes under the layers of the earth, so she had within herself her singing water saying things from the past. The music belonged to her. To her, and pity anyone who came near it!

But the guest extended a heavy hand and placed it on the little doors of the phonograph, trying to open them. But he did not open them, because she, standing up violently and grabbing his hand harshly, said—also harshly:

"No. It's mine."

The guest looked at her, with his mouth curled up and trying to think some thought that he had just forgotten. Suddenly he remembered. And again he stretched out the hand that she had removed from the little door latch.

"I'm telling you, no!"

"Look how she's insulting me, brother . . ."

The man insisted greedily:

"It's a deal?"

"Music . . . ," answered the guest, stubbornly.

"Why don't you play something? Go ahead and raise a ruckus, little one, yes; something you like. Don't you see that we're going to close the deal?"

He would not put his hands on the phonograph. Not that, never. The guest had picked himself up and this time his muscles did obey him. But the woman prevented the attack and put herself in-between, defensively. The other man reeled about the dining room, until bumping into the wall, and he turned around, inflamed with a criminal impulse, blinded to everything that was not his own idea.

"Music . . . , music . . ."

"Has she gone crazy? What's happening to her?" asked the man.

The guest was on top of her and she on top of the phonograph, defending it with her whole body. They struggled. The man looked at them for an instant, stunned, repeating:

"Has she gone crazy? Has she gone crazy?"

But when the guest gave a sharp cry because the woman's teeth were ripping into his hand, he rushed forward to separate them, to defend his friend, to defend his transaction, his deal already almost completed.

She kicked and bit them, behaving like an animal, furious, the way a puma in the wild might defend her cubs. The men did not know why they were getting punched, why they were rolling on the floor, why the table was reeling and the lamp was shifting its light back and forth in a swaying movement that was worse than the sensation in their stomachs. The phonograph fell with a crash and the strings reverberated, like the lament of a grove of trees whose leaves are ripped off by a strong wind. The guest was sitting on the floor, bewildered, and suddenly his cry broke into sobs that interrupted his hiccoughs. The man leaned against the window, astonished by everything and looking at the woman, her clothing in shreds, the magnificence of her hairdo undone, with a long slash on her face, cleaning herself off with the apron that was red with blood, her blouse stained, stubbornly intent on gathering from the floor the pieces of the broken records, looking at them and sobbing, cleaning the blood off herself, sobbing and looking for more pieces and cleaning off the blood and sobbing.

But the guest diverted his attention with his enormous hiccoughs.

"Brother . . . , I thought I was in the home of a brother . . . I've been insulted . . . I have . . . ," he lamented, stumbling as he spoke.

"Don't cry anymore, brother." And suddenly back to his idea and full of solicitude and tenderness: "It's a deal?"

"Swine, that's just what you are: swine . . . ," shouted the woman, and with her armload of pieces she left the dining room, closing the door with a resounding bang that startled the rats in the loft and caused the dog to gaze at her steadily, its sequin eyes sparkling in the gloom.

Outside the wind's mane was whipping about, unleashed in a frenetic gallop. The clouds had pressed themselves tightly together, dense and black, imparting a dark tint to the environs and not allowing the outline of a single thing to be seen. As if the elements had not yet been set apart. A cricket was giving witness, immutably, to its existence.

She fled, pressing the shattered records against her chest as she went, feeling the flow of the blood through the wound, warm and sticky on her neck, making its way inside to the fine skin of her chest. She walked with her head down, breaking through the blackness and the wind. She walked. The house was far away, not just erased by the darkness. The cricket, imperceptible, was left behind tenaciously useless. She could be out on the plain and be the living center of her desolate surroundings; she could be in a valley bounded by rivers and precipices; she could walk, walk, endlessly, until she fell exhausted upon the hard earth, being grown over evenly with identical weeds; she could suddenly slide down the slope of the ravine and go crashing onto the smooth stones of a river engorged with reddish sand; she could . . . Anything could happen in this blackness of chaos, confusing and dreadful. For to her nothing mattered.

To end it all. To die against the earth. To be destroyed in the ravine. Not to feel any more that corrosive ardor, bitter to her mouth and clawing around inside her. To end it all. Not to make an effort any more to know what characteristic a certain day had, stubbornly persisting in extracting from the blurry sum a date to differentiate it. Not to live like a machine amidst the daily shuffle and the knitting, longing for Saturday to come in order to eat the crumb of memories that was incapable of satiating her heart's craving for tenderness. To put an end to the sordidness surrounding her, with its disguise of "do as you wish, but . . . ," of meticulousness, of concealed vigilance. To be no more. Never again to return to the house and find herself reporting what she had done and what it had yielded, listening to the insinuation regarding what had to be bought and what needed to be earned. To not get callouses on her hands pounding wheat, neither with her eyes weepy from the smoke of the oven, nor feeling her midsection aching in front of the laundry tub. Never to take pains with painting a little board and making a shelf, nor wallpapering the rooms, bedecking them with flowers like an imitation garden. Never. Nor ever again to feel him heaved over on top of her, panting and sweaty, heavy and without awakening any sensation in her other than a passive repugnance. Never.

The injury, which the air was turning cold, ached like a long stab wound. She touched it and found within the blood a hard point. A piece of glass. A spike-sized sliver from a broken glass that had buried itself there during the struggle, she did not know when. With a sort of insensitivity to the pain, she wiggled it to pull it out. She let out a groan. But furious with herself, in an abrupt tug that ripped her flesh more deeply, she pulled it out and tossed it away.

The blood was running through her fingers, around her neck, over her breasts. All stained and sticky, she kept going. To vanish. But first to sob, to shout, to howl. The wind, with its gusts, seemed to push its way inside her through her open flesh and make the pain intolerable. Greater still, sharper than the other pain which was destroying her feeling. Suddenly the hand that was gripping the apron, still holding the broken records, opened up and everything tumbled out over the ground. She took a few more steps and then fell face down sobbing, the sounds of which the wind seized with its strong hand and scattered throughout the surrounding area.

It was as if the water of those clear eyes could at last be water. She had the sensation that her mouth was opening for her, and she felt the strange noises being hurled from her throat and the scorched eyelids and wrinkled forehead and the salt from her weeping. And a hand clutching the wound, violently painful, and the blood running between her fingers and a braid of hair that must surely be soaked through and dampening her back. She raised herself up on one elbow; she turned her head. And she gave a sharp cry because a breath made her face feel warm and something inhuman terrified her to the point of losing consciousness.

The dog alternated periodically between sniffing her noisily, licking her hands, and sitting down—with his head raised on high, his snout stretched out toward mysterious omens—to deliver a long howl to the moon. He licked her face when the woman came to, and she knew instantaneously that it was the dog, although she did not know where she was. She sat up suddenly, and also suddenly she remembered her immediate situation.

It was as if she had not lived it. So strange, so alien to her. Almost like the sensation of the nightmare that had just become submerged in her subconscious. Was she fleeing from a dream; was she returning from some reality? A movement, on trying to stroke the dog, who was circling around her uneasily, gave her the exact shape of the facts. She groaned and the dog sought out her face again. But she pushed it aside, forcing it to lie down beside her. She pressed on the wound, which was oozing blood again, burning her as if she were being scalded.

She could bleed to death. To remain as she was, still in the night, in the cordial proximity of the dog until her blood went draining away and with it her life, that abhorrent life that she did not want to preserve for the benefit of another. Eliminating it, she avenged her constant state of humiliation, the animosities that had accumulated wordlessly, the resentment of a frustrated existence. To remove herself from the midst of things so that solitude might be the punishment for the man who would not have anyone to work, to produce and give an accounting of deeds and thoughts; the machine for his pleasure would have vanished and he would have to pay dearly to find another one so perfect as she. Not to see him again. Never to put in front of him the medium-done meat and see him chew with his surprisingly white teeth. Nor to see his gaze becoming clouded over, when desire made him reach out his hand to her futilely elusive body. Not to know that he was tangled up in subterranean calculations: "You'll buy this, because this little sum of money is to be stashed away and used to buy whenever possible the Urriolas' field, who are deep in debt and will finally have to sell, yes; or the field belonging to Valladares' widow, who with so many kids is not going to prosper, and they're going to put it up for auction, for the mortgage payments . . ." Waiting like a vulture, patiently, for the moment to take off with the prey. Land. Everything in him was reduced to that. To sell. To negotiate. To bring in money. And buy land, land.

To be no more. To think no more. To feel how the blood was slipping away through her fingers, running stickily over her chest, collecting in her lap, dampening her thighs.

The dog whined softly now, more and more restless. The woman, all of a sudden, opened her eyes, which no longer held any water other than that of their own clear irises, and she came face to face with a truth: to die was also never again to take out the memories of the past, that treasure chest with its images of tenderness. Never again to remember . . . To remember what? And in a rapid and incoherent superposition of images, snatches of scenes, fragments of sentences, she saw her mother sitting in front of the big gate, she saw herself with her sisters arm in arm, she saw the doves flying through the fragrant air of the garden. She perceived so exactly the smell of the jasmines that she inhaled longingly. But other images appeared: Herself crying between the piano box and the pile of mattresses; herself silent in the night under the moon's medallion in the bottom of the water tank; herself in front of the mirror, pinning a sprig of basil and some carnations into her braids, because Easter was an obstinately hopeful time; herself with her face turned around by the laughter and her eyes snaring the green gaze that stirred up a timid pigeon in her chest, so warm, so tender, so absolutely alive, that the surprise for her hand was not finding it sweetly nested there . . . All of that, never again. To die was also to renounce all of that.

Suddenly she stood up. Her legs felt unstable and little particles were dancing before her eyes. She closed them tight. She forced herself to hold herself erect. And also firmly she pressed the apron to her face, for she did not want the blood to flow through the wound, for she did not want the blood to abandon her, for death to leave her like an outspread rag in the middle of the field, on top of the mustard weeds, abandoned in the blackness with only the dog's protective custody. She wanted life, she wanted her blood, the branchwork of her blood, laden with memories.

She pressed the apron even harder against her cheek. She stared keenly into the night. Then she called the dog. She took it by its collar. And she said:

"Let's go home," and she followed it into the darkness.

Translated by Elaine Dorough Johnson

The Long Night of Winter

Alifa Rifaat

IN AN instant between sleep and wakefulness, an instant outside the bounds of time, that gave the sensation of being eternal, the sounds of night, like slippery fishes passing through the mesh of a net, registered themselves on Zennouba's hearing, filtering gradually into her awakening consciousness: the machine-like croaking of frogs, and the barking of dogs in the fields answered by the dogs of the village on the other bank in a never-ending exchange of information in some code language.

All at once she realized that she was in bed and that she was alone. The only other live things in the room were the leaping shapes on the peeling wall made by the dying wick in the kerosene lamp that looked down from the small aperture. She knew with certainty that she would now sleep no longer that night, and she longed for the day to come with the call to dawn prayers.

As she waited for the return of her husband, memories of the past took over from the sounds of night, and as on many such a night she guided herself back to the days of her childhood, to that closed society that children effortlessly set up for themselves, days of security in a house where love and tenderness were a child's right and did not have to be earned, where death was without dominion and sorrow never lasted beyond a night. She would play in the lanes of the village with her friends, coming and going as she pleased, and sometimes, on moonlit nights, she would walk in the fields with a group of young girls, singing songs charged with meanings that she only vaguely and deliciously understood, songs like: "The winter's night is long. Hug me and I'll hug you in the long winter's night," which they sang over and over again tirelessly, clapping their hands to its rhythm. Then, suddenly, with puberty pushing her sprouting breasts against the rough calico of her *galabia*, she was torn, like a foetus from the womb's warmth, out of her world of childish freedom and prevented from playing with her companions. Soon afterwards she was married to her cousin, Hagg Hamdan, so that the land might stay in the family, and she moved from her home among the closely-packed village houses to the lonely mansion that lay on her husband's lands on the other bank, with its two high storeys and the north-facing reception rooms paved with stone, and the winter rooms with their wooden floors, and its fruit and vegetable gardens, the whole surrounded by a high mud wall topped by pieces of broken glass. She particularly remembers, on her wedding day when they first took her through the wide gateway, the large camel painted in red against the white-washed wall, symbolizing the owner's pilgrimage, and the red palms of hands to ward off the evil eye.

And so had come the night when Hagg Hamdan had taken her to this same bed. It had been a night of violence and pain, utterly unrelated to any previous experience she had had. Since then it had been repeated hundreds of times, with the element of pain replaced by that of repugnance at the rough hands that kneaded her body, and the evil-smelling breath and spittle of a *habitué* of the blue smoke of hashish. In compliance to her husband, and for the sake of the children, she had submitted to the role of wife and mother, a woman protected by marriage and by the home that she would leave only when they bore her to her grave.

She recalled the first night she had woken to find that he was no longer beside her, and how she had got up to look for him and had found him lying on the stone bench above the oven with the young servant girl. When he had returned with her to their room, her hatred and bitterness had been so great that, contrary to all teachings and traditions, she had demanded a divorce. He had turned his back on her, saying: "Why should I divorce you? Why don't you go and ask your mother about your father who spent so much of his time on his prayer mat? Go to sleep and let's not have any more trouble." The following day he had brought her a pair of gold earrings and had kissed her head affectionately. Yet, with the passing of time, such nights were repeated and gifts of gold jewellery were made to her, while the girl servants came and went at his bidding without apparent reason, for he was the master of the house.

The doubts concerning her father, born of her husband's remark on that fateful night, continued to assail her. Could there be any truth in the insinuation about the dignified and pious man who had such influence in the village, that man with the kindly, bearded face who would sometimes take her on his knee and tell her stories from the Qur'an about the prophets, then, when he thought she had fallen to sleep, would carry her to bed? The mere touch of his *aba*, with its heavy smell of musk as she buried her face in its folds, gave her comfort and assurance that her father was good and that all was well with the world.

She re-enacted to herself that morning when her mother had visited her, coming from the village and crossing the bridge on a donkey and accompanied by a servant laden down with baskets of pies and pastries. It was on the morning of the eve of the Feast and the old lady had been to visit her husband's grave in the cemetery and had then completed her journey to her daughter's house. Between sips of tea her mother poured out the news of the village. At last Zennouba took courage and asked the question that had been in her mind for so long. Her mother lowered her gaze to the glass of tea in her hand and said:

"All men are like that."

"Even my father?"

The mother sipped noisily at her tea before answering:

"Daughter, he too was a man. Allah have mercy on him and show him His favours."

She would have liked to draw her mother out further. Had her mother suffered the same sort of nightmare of a life as she did? Was this the fate of all women? Her mother, though, had given her a glance that had silenced her, a warning not to tread on forbidden territory. Then her mother had broken into a recital of the Fatiha for the soul of her husband and Zennouba had repeated the words after her. Now her mother too was dead.

Zennouba's husband had reached the same age as her father when he had died, and his joints creaked and cracked as he prayed. Even so, he would still disappear of nights and she would still receive presents of jewellery from him. Surely there must come a time when he had had his fill? For a short time, she thought that he had at last changed. Then, suddenly, the girl servant had started to become insolent, to refuse to accept her orders, and she knew the reason instinctively. Her hopes frustrated, she had at last asserted herself and insisted that the girl be sent back to her village, and only a few days ago another one, little more than a child, had been brought to the house and had spent her first two days crying for her mother. Where else could he now be except with her? Was it possible?

As she stared at the glow from the dying coals in the earthenware fire at the foot of the bed, undecided whether to rise and go downstairs, she heard his hesitant, shuffling footsteps, and closed her eyes. He lay down quietly beside her, drew the covering over himself and almost immediately fell asleep.

She moved slightly in the bed, avoiding him, her own body tense. The pent-up hatred against him had long ago changed to a cold contempt; the hopes that things would change had now gone, but the ache to love and be loved was still there, as physically part of her as her sight or sense of smell. The lamp spluttered and she looked up at the small aperture and saw the first greyness of dawn seeping into the room. Holding her breath, she sidled off the bed and made her way, hands outstretched before her, out of the room, then, finding the bannisters, went downstairs to where the girl slept over the oven.

Nargis raised her head.

"Nothing wrong, lady Zennouba?"

"Nothing, Nargis," she said. "Nothing at all. Get up and bring hot water—I want a bath."

She returned to the room. Her husband was still fast asleep. Collecting up her towel, also the earthenware fire, she went out to the bathroom. She put down the fire and blew at the coals, bringing them to life, then took down the oval tin basin that was leaning against the wall.

Nargis came carrying a large jug of hot water to which she had added some drops of rose water. Zennouba took off her nightrobe and stepped into the basin. As she looked at Nargis, the other turned her face away.

"Don't be afraid, Nargis," she said. "Take off your nightdress so you can wash my back."

Turning round, Nargis drew her dress over her head, then faced her mistress. Zennouba looked at the girl's body and the thought occurred to her that she too had once been as beautiful. She was about to say so to the girl, then decided against it. Instead she said:

"I hope you'll be happy here, Nargis. God willing, you'll stay a long time in this house." Then she squatted down in the basin so that the girl would pour the water over her back.

"Scrub my back with the loofah," she said, and as the girl leant over her, Zennouba was aware of the taut breasts brushing against her shoulder.

"Scrub harder," she said. "Harder, harder." And the rough loofah scraped painfully across her back.

The Marsh

Yuko Tsushima

"IT'S CALLED the Round Marsh because it's round. That's all there is to its name," he told me.

His explanation made me think of a marsh I remember called the Small Marsh. This marsh was on top of a hill, right next to a larger marsh, which was naturally called the Big Marsh. I saw these two marshes years ago when I was in middle school. It was summer, and I was spending a few days near the marshes with my friend and her family.

Although I recall their names, I've forgotten what the Big Marsh looked like. I do remember the Small Marsh, though I haven't had any reason to think about it until now, when I suddenly find myself fascinated by the memory of it as if I had never forgotten about it, not even for a day.

The Small Marsh was also round. It had dark, still water at the bottom of its cone-shaped landform and its rim was slightly elevated. It was small enough for children to walk around easily; in fact it looked like a big puddle. I learned that the water from the nearby Big Marsh seeped underground and welled up to form the Small Marsh. Before this was discovered, people were mystified by the source of its water. Having grown up in the city, I couldn't understand what was so mysterious about water appearing in the middle of a mountain. At the time I listened to the explanations absent-mindedly, but now I realize what an impression the marsh made on me.

My friend's family told me that we were heading for the Small Marsh, but when I actually saw it from high up on the mountain path, I felt something that I couldn't explain. Even now I clearly remember the feeling that I had seen something I shouldn't have, something monstrous.

It was very quiet around the marsh and the scene was desolate. There were no trees or plants nearby, only black mud and turbid water. The stillness of the water reminded me of mercury. For a moment I was overcome by the belief that the marsh had the power to suck things in and swallow them whole. I wanted to run in the other direction.

Of course my fear was only momentary, and soon I was racing down the path toward the marsh with my friend. We ran all around it. It was in fact a popular sightseeing spot and there were a lot of people there that day. It wasn't a place where one should feel scared. The water was calm with occasional ripples breaking its surface. Still, because the bank was wet, there was some danger of slipping into the mud. Perhaps this was the main reason there were no restaurants, not even benches for people to sit on, although it was a part of the sightseeing route. We didn't stay there very long. The marsh was too small to make me feel nervous for long, and I quickly grew accustomed to its sight.

Probably because of the unknown origin of its water, there was a legend about the Small Marsh's guardian spirit. After all, it wasn't the kind of place where one wants to swim, and it didn't appear as though any fish or shellfish lived there. It didn't seem strange, therefore, that people imagined some mysterious creature living at the bottom of this barren-looking marsh. Certainly there might be one or two creatures which would grow to look like monsters after living in such a place.

The legend I was told at the time was quite an ordinary one. It went like this: The guardian spirit of the marsh fell in love with a man, and in order to live with him it changed its appearance to that of a woman. After the marsh spirit gave birth to a child, her true identity was revealed to her husband, and she was forced to return to the marsh, leaving her child behind. I thought at the time that it was an ordinary, uninteresting story, not unique to this marsh. I was more fascinated by the possibility that some grotesque creature might live at the bottom of the water.

The Small Marsh that I recall now, however, cannot be separated in my mind from the legend. I cannot think of it without hearing the suppressed breathing of a creature who longs for a human male.

I can see another marsh from the northern window of my apartment building. Since quite a few carp swim in the water and a few large stepping stones are arranged for a decorative effect, one should perhaps call this a pond, but I suspect it used to look more like a marsh before someone built it up. The pond is long and skinny, formed by the accumulation of water in the V-shaped crack at the bottom of a cliff. It is hard to tell where the water comes from, but it is probably the same source that feeds the other similar marshes in the neighborhood—those in the park which was formerly someone's estate, in the shrine's compound, and on the University campus. These marshes lie at the bottom of some cliffs which divide the hills and the lowlands.

One part of the marsh I see from my apartment is in the garden of a mansion where many generations of a family have been living. The marsh's center is in front of a newly built high-rise condominium; the rest stretches out like a tail along the land where a company dormitory stands. The cliff is at the south end of the marsh, blocking the sun. The water doesn't seem to be deep since even a small amount of rain makes it muddy. I can see from my window only the tail-like part by the dormitory. Plastic bags, styrofoam cups and other pieces of trash float on the surface of the water. Still, there are a few carp and crayfish in the water, and I often see the custodian shouting at the neighborhood boys as they try to sneak onto the grounds to catch them.

My building is in a neighborhood where small houses and apartments line the narrow, winding streets. But if I lean my head out while sitting on the sill of the north window of my room on the second floor, I can see the marsh. Every time I see the water of the marsh shining with dull light, I find it surprising. Walking along the streets, one would never suspect a marsh is hidden nearby. The high-rise condominium and the large estate face the sunny side of the hill, which gives no hint of water. When I walk by this hill to go to the train station and the neighborhood grocery stores, it's hard to picture the marsh on the other side.

Perhaps it is because of the marsh that I feel uneasy in my room. I can't get rid of the feeling that the building might sink into the water. My children are also afraid of the marsh. When my six-year-old daughter refuses to listen to me, I sometimes open the north window and call, "Mr. Kappa [1] over there, do you want a little girl?" She becomes frightened and cries, hiding behind my back. My two-year-old gets scared, too, and he retreats to the corner of the room crying, "I don't like kappas." Often an ominous feeling comes over me. Not just my children but I, too, cannot look down at the marsh for long.

And yet it was because of the marsh that I rented this apartment. I was surprised at my decision. I had just found out that I was pregnant with my second child. I knew that my lover's wife, also pregnant at the time with her second child, knew nothing of her husband's affair with me. I was upset with myself for wanting to keep the child, for trying to keep

---

1. A toad-like, imaginary creature which often appears in Japanese folk tales.

the child's father from leaving me by getting pregnant. I decided to move away without telling him. As long as I stayed where I was he would continue to come and see me, unable to resist his own desire, and I, for my part, would dream of having his babies as soon as he held me in his arms again. I wanted to live with him, to be in the same place and breathe the same air. But the more I became used to his body, the more he became a stranger to me. I was divorced and raising my daughter. I thought that if he, who had a life with his wife and child elsewhere, was a normal human being then I, whose existence was unknown, unseen and unacceptable to his family, had to be a creature without human form, like an evil spirit that inhabits the mountains and rivers. The thought that the man I loved didn't belong to the world I lived in filled me with despair. I couldn't resist thinking that if I bore his child, I would become one of his kind.

In my mind's eye the man's pregnant wife was my own mother. Just after I was born my mother learned that there was another woman about to have a child by my father. Shortly after this discovery, my father died, leaving my mother no chance to understand her relationship with him. Nonetheless, my mother didn't forget anything. For thirty years she has been obsessed with that other woman, whom she believes is the evil spirit of the mountains and rivers. What could the child of this evil spirit and her husband be like, and how could she, the legitimate wife, have given birth to his child as if nothing had happened? My mother has been endlessly haunted by these questions.

As for myself, when I learned of my second pregnancy I pictured this scene: upon finding out about my pregnancy, my lover's wife throws herself in front of a moving train, or from the top of a tall building. I was filled with fear that this scene would come true.

I felt obsessed with this vision and began living my days as if in a dream. I was looking for a new apartment in my dream, and one day I was shown a room facing a narrow alley. It was a dark room with the neighbors' wall blocking the sun, but the rent was cheap. When I opened the window on the north side, I immediately wanted to live there. The marsh I saw from the window was the one I had once seen, at another time.

Four years ago, there was no condominium or company dormitory there, just a large, empty lot. Because it was surrounded by tall walls, one couldn't tell that behind them was a wide open space.

I had just become friends with a woman. It was shortly after my husband and I had separated, and she and I each had two-year-old daughters. The father of my friend's daughter never appeared, but I didn't ask what had happened to him. She had apparently stopped seeing him before her daughter was born; it wasn't clear if he even knew about his child. Perhaps to him my friend was like the evil spirit of mountains and rivers, but to me she was a valued ally who taught me that mourning the loss of my child's father was silly. She was six years younger than I was, only twenty-two.

My friend and I saw each other almost every day. Sometimes I went to stay with her; other times she came to my apartment to spend the night. On weekends we went out with our daughters and walked around town. Then one day we discovered the vacant lot where the marsh was. We were excited about our discovery and immediately began exploring the place. Although we were a bit scared at the vastness of the space and the thick tangle of grasses growing there, we were as thrilled as our daughters. We laughed as we saw hydrangeas in bloom and laughed again as we took turns climbing up a large garden rock. Since there were overgrown shrubs all around, we could explore only a small area of the place. But when we forced our way through some tall bushes and sorrel vines, we found a long, skinny marsh. Beyond the bushes we saw a cliff, and at the bottom of the cliff was a body of dark water. We saw something move in the water. Terrified, we fled, making sure we didn't make any noise. When we reached the other side of the concrete wall, we found ourselves on an ordinary street. We heaved big sighs of relief, escaping what we had just seen. We thought that the marsh must be quite old and that the creature must have lived there for a long time—so long that it now looked like a monster. How big could it be and what did it look like? We talked about it for a while.

Our excitement lasted for some time. We promised each other we'd go back, but then I became involved with the father of my second child and I had little chance to see my friend. Around that time she began feeling anxious about her sexuality, and started acting strangely. She became afraid of the evil spirit of the mountains and rivers, which she felt was stirred up inside her as various men came in and out of her life. She was put into the psychiatric ward of a hospital by people who were alarmed by her behavior. It was difficult to visit her but we frequently talked on the phone. When I decided to move to my present apartment, I called her first.

"It's true, I can see our marsh from the back window," I told her. "A condominium and some company's dormitory stands on the lot now, and it looks quite different. But the marsh is still there. They probably wanted to fill it in but they couldn't. That's my guess. No, it doesn't look as if anything strange lives there; carp are swimming about instead. Compared to the time we saw it, it looks quite ordinary. But don't you think it's exciting that I can see it from my window? I want you to come and see it as soon as you can get permission to go out. It's no fun looking at it by myself. Only you and I knew about it. Right?"

It wasn't for quite a while, however, that she was able to come to my apartment. Even when she had permission to go out, she was required to spend the night at her parents' house.

Although I had managed to move away without telling the father of my baby, I couldn't change my job, and so within a week he found me and came to see me at my new apartment. Once he forced his way back into my life, I had no choice but to dream I could keep him as my own. His second child by his wife was born and, six months later, I also had my second child. He came to see how I was getting on with this newborn, and when he saw that I was becoming increasingly clinging and half-mad, he left me for good.

My baby has grown steadily. It's been more than two years since I moved to this room. More than a few people stopped being my friends when I had my second child, but I have made some new friends. I was a spirit of the mountains and rivers when I gave birth to this child but the child turned out to be a normal human being.

About a year and a half ago my friend was released from the hospital and returned to her parents' house. She sold insurance for awhile and then took the exams to become a nutritionist and a hygienic technician. She failed both exams. A few months ago she found work as a "lunch lady," a temporary position cooking at a school cafeteria. She seemed better suited to this job than anybody had expected. Her life became normal, and she began visiting me on Saturdays. She would stay until evening and then she'd go back to her parents' for supper. She almost always came to visit without advance notice. Sometimes I was out, and her visit would be wasted; other times her unexpected arrival would upset my plans. I found this irritating, but whenever I saw her plump face, I found myself smiling at her.

"This job is great for me," she told me the other day while she was playing with my younger child.

"I'm surprised how much I like it. The other lunch ladies are all older than me, and they pamper me. I get there an hour earlier than the others. No, I don't do anything in particular, I just wait for the rest to come. A big change for me, don't you think? Since I only work till four, my son doesn't have to wait for me too long when he gets home from school. I have no complaints now. I sometimes wonder if I should have some, though. I feel so comfortable. I don't seem to have a desire to change anything. No one will ever be seriously interested in me anyway. I can't think of marriage at this point, you know. My mother arranged for me to see this guy the other day. He's almost fifty years old, with three kids. His wife's dead, he told me. He didn't want to marry me though. "You're young and pretty, you must have plenty of offers," he said. A compliment perhaps. The age doesn't matter to me, but I don't feel like having a relationship with a man now. I think about our days a lot, though. Nowadays, I guess I'm what people call an education mama. Don't you think it's funny? I make my son take piano and swimming lessons. I nag him to study, although I myself watch television a lot. It somehow feels good to shout at your kid, you know. But I attend P.T.A. meetings regularly. I put makeup on and dress nicely. It's really interesting, because those mothers are so serious; they're always putting on airs. Most of the time I keep quiet, but once in a while I just have to let my true self out and say something. There was a meeting the day before yesterday, and some woman started talking about how she didn't know what to say when her kid kept asking about babies, how they are born, and so on. Everybody talked about it for a while. One person said it's too early to give them any facts, and the others looked so uncomfortable. I felt like teasing them and so I spoke up without thinking. It's an important issue, and we ought to give them accurate information, I said. I should've stopped there. But they were nodding their heads, you know. So I went ahead and told them how I would open my legs to let my kid see what's between them. I let him see the hole and told him that he came out of it, I told them. It's the same hole where men stick their penises and pour in this thing that makes babies. It's the hole that blood comes out of when babies are not made. I said I told my son all these things. They looked at me with shocked faces. Don't you think it's strange? I got a bit scared afterward and felt depressed. I felt I had said something silly again . . ."

When she talked like this, I enjoyed listening. Ever since I heard about the Round Marsh, I've been wanting to ask her something. I want to ask her about the spirit of the marsh who falls in love with a human male and changes her appearance to have his child. Why is it that the spirit's true identity must be revealed? I don't understand why she has to leave. Besides, why does she have to leave her child behind? You and I keep our children, I want to tell my friend.

It is no longer clear to me whether we are the evil spirits of the mountains and rivers, or if the spirits are our lovers. Whichever they are, the children who were born are growing up normally, unconcerned with the questions I keep asking.

I heard about the Round Marsh from a man who happened to find it while he was driving through the mountains. He told me he was surprised by his discovery. The marsh he spotted at a distance down from the road looked quite desolate and forbidding. He had never heard that there was a marsh in that area, and because it looked so quiet he felt a bit uneasy. There is an old inn by the marsh, he said. It was quite dark around the inn, even during the day, because it was deep in the forest. How would one feel staying overnight at such an inn? he asked me. He also told me that he found out the name of the marsh afterward.

Since then I have been thinking about the Round Marsh, which lies even deeper in the mountain than the Small Marsh.

Somewhere high up in the mountain is a road, shining in the sun. I see a small dot on the road, a white car driven by the man who told me about the Round Marsh. Perpendicular to the road is the mountain, which stretches all the way up from the road and down. The surface of the mountain is smooth, and it looks as if the slope is spiraling down into the marsh. The water of the marsh shines darkly. The surrounding virgin forest gives off a sound like the moaning of a person in pain, and by the water's edge is the creature of the marsh. From a distance it looks like a house, and it crouches, longing for a human male.

I want to go to see the Round Marsh. My longing is getting stronger every day, but I haven't been able to tell the man who described it to me that I want to visit it with him. I am merely gazing at this man, with whom I became acquainted on some unexpected occasion.

Story of the Name

Khalida Hussain

W H A T   C O U L D she have said to anyone now? First of all this story of forgetting the name was so strange. The letters were all there, and put together still formed a name. She was cognisant of it. But the problem was that at first she was herself this word. And now it was only a sheath. She was not there within it. She no longer knew if the real name was that sheath or it was herself who had ceased to have a name. That is how all things had come to a stop. Or was it for this that this event took shape. For a long time perhaps she had a feeling for her name. For instance, when Jamil left her she was always conscious of her name. She existed apart from other people as a definite word, for others had separated her from themselves. Thus, asleep or awake, in darkness and light someone whispered this word into her ears.

The strange thing about this word was that she had to keep alert. The moment she was thoughtless the name caught her in its claws. She tried a hundred and one things to escape its grip. She busied herself in preparing Nuzhat's marriage dresses, and needlessly kept awake for nights, unnecessarily embroidering the clothes and tucking laces on them; then she took the responsibility of sewing the clothes of the whole family, washing, ironing, needle work, on her own shoulders. But the moment she stopped for a little rest, someone would whisper that word into her ears. Everything would suddenly acquire a face, and only one word would remain alone; and she would be glued to her own eyes. There was an unknown terror in that word so that if she laughed, her heart began to sink, as though an evil spirit in a nightmare was running after her but her legs were paralysed by some magic and she could not move.

But when she came to stay with Nuzhat, strange things began to happen. For hours together she would not remember that word. For one thing, Nuzhat's Billo, Gitto, and Munno kept her busy with their tedious jobs: get them ready for school, give them breakfast, keep account of clothes, see to the cleaning and dusting of rooms, or to Nuzhat's sewing, like Nasim's shirts. Sometimes she did not get even a minute's respite. Morning turned to night in the winking of an eye. At times that word would pass caressing by her like the breeze somewhere in the space between sleep and waking. But then the chain of Gitto's sweaters and Munno's dolls would unravel itself and the day would dawn in no time.

This concatenation of chores was like a magic world. How many chores lay spread over the earth? She would sometimes prepare a list of these chores in her mind, and wonder how so many of them had come into being. Then she would get involved in the creation of new and newer chores: embroidering on canvas with woollen thread; tacking small bits of cloth together into curtains and bed-spreads; novel pieces of decoration. Time passed in such occupations, and the distance between morning and evening disappeared. Chores were the machine for abolishing Time and Space, as a blotter was for removing ink.

With work there was hunger, a blind incision that stretched inside, within which a fire roared. But in the roaring of the fire there was tranquility. At such moments she would feel her belly glued to her back; her fingers would count the bony ribs; and she would see every bone in her body like her own x-ray. She would find sweet contentment in this.

"For God's sake, Sister, cast this work away, have something to eat," Nuzhat would ask her constantly.

"I am just coming—" But she would sit there for hours drunk on hunger, wasting body and growing bones.

"You have greed for work, Sister," Nuzhat would grumble; and she would go out to see someone or other on Nuzhat's insistence. But all the time she would feel that chores were disappearing from the world, and disappearance of chores was the greatest calamity.

Then it happened unawares that the act of sunset became longer. She saw the pale sunlight linger on the parapet walls and move slowly inch by inch. The sun remained suspended for hours; and Time joined hands with neither day nor night. Earlier on the whole day used to pass, but now it was difficult to pass the time. Even after it was ended, it lingered somewhere near the parapet, which reminded her of the bowl of water which was kept out on the roof to watch the eclipse of the sun. The water would remain refractory for hours, then calm down and the shadow of the darkening sun would swim in it. Seeing the shadows she would feel that she was sleep-walking, and things would become long, or shrink, flatten out or keep stretching. The day had also become like that now. It would neither rise from the heavens nor even set, like the water in the bowl wandering sleepily—long, flattened, stretched out.

So, on the passing of the day she had no feeling now of a line obliterated, as before. That is why the chores became longer like a dirty elastic that keeps stretching and stretching. Even otherwise, having finished a chore she would be filled with doubt if it was really done. Like the days the chores had also ended in the past—getting the children ready for school, washing, ironing, needle-work at noon. And so quickly would the work and days end and be drowned in sleepy exhaustion at night.

Even the sleep of those days was different from the present. It started and ended on time; but now it had neither beginning nor end. When she thought she was awake and working, she felt suddenly that in spite of moving the hands did not move, that the soap suds in the tub had no soapiness, the clothes had no touch or substance, and yet she was washing them. She would be filled with wonder at this, then realise that she slept while sitting. She would mumble to herself and draw water from the pump, fill the tub and start washing. The clothes would keep on being washed, the line go on being choked. Still she would feel that she was sleeping as she sat. The two ends of sleep and waking had joined and become one.

She would sometimes vaguely think that things were clean and alive at that time, and endless chains of memories encircled them. But now rarely did a part of an image or unconnected pictures appear from somewhere and join up. A voice from the past, a golden queue, scattered cloth clippings on the slate-coloured floor, the glittering brass bin, were all like that, as were different smells. They would startle from some deep dark sleep within the inward spreading incision and in that space between waking and sleeping would come like the perfume of out-of-season flowers which, on waking, would seem only just imagination. In the past things and smells came woven in chains of incidents; but now without those links they swam in bits and pieces in a haze.

There was nothing disquieting about the swimming of smells, things, and voices thus in a haze. She was not alarmed for a long time by anything. The problem arose one evening as she was combing the knotted hair of Munno, while Billo and Gitto were playing on the lawn with Mr. Qureishi's children. Nuzhat and Nasim were also sitting out on the lawn. Inside, all the rooms, done up and dusted, were lying empty. Munno's hair smelt freshly washed and of soap. Her hands were deftly disentangling her tangled hair. But neither the hair nor the comb, not even the chair she was sitting on, had any substance. It was then that her gaze was fixed all of a sudden on her hands. On dry, colourless skin stood out swollen blue veins, fingers protruding like dead branches holding that dented piece in which hair was entangled. Then slowly her swimming gaze came to rest on her wrist, and she was amazed at the thought how for years she had been living with that wrist and hand. These two reminded her of the other members of her body which had been her constant companions from the very beginning. She felt that she was wrapt up in sleep and in the utter darkness all directions were obliterated. She did not know which side, which direction she was in. All known things had merged into the dark. Years ago it had happened that she would suddenly be startled and all at once lose all sense of direction and place. Experiencing this now in broad daylight she was quite bewildered, as though she had arrived there walking in sleep. She tried to recall where she started, whither she had come. But behind her and in front, everywhere, a dusty haze surrounded her.

She came to realise that she did not exist before. From the beginning to this day she had lived thus, a comb held in her hand, disentangling Munno's hair. But Munno was small, only about five. And she cast another glance at her decaying wrists. She had an intense feeling of the passage of time. Yet she noticed how the sun had been setting for hours on end, and pale sunlight was creeping ever so slowly over the parapet walls and never crossed them. From the morning, since when she did not know, the sun had been going in and out. It was neither day nor night, and all chores, unfinished, were stretching away into the distance.

"Hai, Aunty stop!" Unconsciously she had pulled Munno's hair while disentangling it.

"All right—" And she put the comb down on the dressing table. Munno jumped up and ran away outside.

"The king's key was stolen, was stolen—" The children were shouting in play.

"Sister, come outside." Nuzhat called out to her. But she had so much to do. She started stitching Nuzhat's blouse. Only after two stitches, she started feeling sleepy, and remembered she had not slept the whole day. And blouse in her lap she went to sleep, back resting against wall. Sleeping thus she recalled that other sleep of long, long ago which had brought an all-enfolding sense of non-existence. She was standing on the scorching roof in blazing sunlight, and the darkening shadows of the sun were dancing in the refractory water of the bowl. Nuzhat was falling right over the bowl in dimentia, while two tightly done-up pleats of hair dangled over her ears. She herself bent over the bowl, and her own image swam in the ruffled water. Then the bowl started expanding, and expanded to the length and breadth of the roof; and the expanding, burning brass of the bowl started pressing her against the walls, so that she went inside the wall, becoming one brick of its many dirt-coloured bricks, wholly indistinct. She wished to know if she was asleep. At this she sat up wide awake. And on waking up she saw that she had been stitching the blouse all the time, and that only a little work now remained.

This wide-awake sleep was amazing. In the beginning she tried to remember the old, old things, such as what clothes she had worn until then, the oldest shirts and shoes. One by one they swam into her consciousness from their dim haziness. Then the smells and ornaments: They were all there. But events were non-existent. The events had been lost. That is why she herself was missing. How could anyone exist without events?

Sometimes Nuzhat related things of the past to Nasim: "Mother and Father had the greatest awe of Sister. As for me, I was always punished."

She would marvel at people who had died. There was a photograph of mother and father in Nuzhat's room. But those semblances were nothing but sheaths. The meaning of real human beings had disappeared long ago. She would sometimes stop before those pictures in amazement, wondering where the pictures had vanished from the frames. Then she would notice that the pictures were all there; yet now for years she had not noticed even the emptiness of those once full frames. So she gave up the effort of remembering things, and found freedom from the name for ever.

In the past when the day had a beginning and an end, chores shortened the length of time. And now the day stretched like a dirty elastic, and chores stood still. The stretching of day and the stillness of chores made her feel greatly hungry.

"Thank God, Sister, your appetite has returned." Nuzhat was really happy. Hunger would now divide time into lengths. But like sleep, hunger was also astonishing. It had neither beginning nor end. Even after eating she would feel she had eaten nothing. To convince herself she would eat many times. Slowly the softness of flesh began to fill the space between her thin belly and the back, and the bones started getting covered over. Her old frame was disappearing, and when she touched herself she felt it was someone else she was touching.

Everything had its own taste before, saltish, sweet, harsh, bitter. But as hunger increased tastes started disappearing. Only one taste remained, just like that waking sleep, which perhaps was no taste. In fact, it was the tongue from head to toe, devoid of all tastes.

Nuzhat saw her eat and felt alarmed. "Are you all right, Sister? Do you feel well?" She would reach her hand to take away the rolls of bread from her plate, then stop short. "Yes. Why?" She would say indifferently.

"It's nothing." Nuzhat would restrain herself from saying more. And she would go on filling her sheath with tasteless substance, which would remain empty even after being full.

She noticed that her bones were covered over with thick layers of flesh, and she lost all sense of recognition. She had changed, and become someone else. Then she started feeling the weight of flesh separate from her body, as though she were a chunk of maunds of flesh.

"You are ill, Sister. Come to the Doctor. Putting on so much weight is not right." Nuzhat was very worried. She was astonished at this. What was the meaning of putting on weight? All this was the whole body, as always. She then looked at her body, then around herself. She did not know what time of day it was. Everything stood still, bathed in a hazy light. A dense feeling hung like a sheath. A sleepy noise arose from the road. Numerous voices and words intermingled and turned into a drawn-out cry of pain: "Black bricks, black boulders . . ."

A dim light of recognition of this pain awoke within her. She looked out of the window towards the road. Romping groups of children, ringing brass cups, faces raised towards the sky, were shouting loudly:

"Send down rain in heavy downpours . . ."

And among the dancing, jumping group of children far away, surfaced the image of a little girl. She tried to recognise her, and while moving close to the window, she stopped suddenly before the mirror: Maunds of flesh wrapt in awkward clothes, graying hair on a decaying face. Her eyes came to rest on the eyes of the image. The dots and lines of a word stirred and swam in them. She wanted to run away; but her feet became paralysed with some magic. It was only a distance of one step which, broadening, narrowing, stretched right into the skies.

Translated by Orooj Ahmed Ali

PERSONAL REBELLIONS

From two different generations—Luisa Mercedes Levinson of Argentina was born in 1914, and Bertalicia Peralta of Panama in 1939—come two stories with a remarkably similar core of violent feeling. The Jamaican woman in the third story, by Hazel Campbell, does not rebel directly or violently; she simply, slowly, over time, makes herself economically self-sufficient by taking in sewing and makes herself emotionally self-sufficient by dedicating herself to her church. Her feckless husband can be ignored; he does not need to be killed. The women who rebel against their husbands in these stories act alone. They are, one might say, pre-political.
LUISA MERCEDES LEVINSON was a cosmopolitan, a woman of upperclass Buenos Aires who often traveled abroad. She associated with the great short story master Jorge Luis Borges, and the collaboration resulted in the story collection *La hermana de Eloisa* (1955), which is quite Borgesian. But many of her stories invoke her childhood home on a ranch in a subtropical province of northern Argentina, Entrerrios, and the furious *machista* of the men in this wild west. BERTALICIA PERALTA, who is director of information at the University of Panama and a newspaper columnist, has written many volumes of poetry and children's books, and one collection of short stories, including "A March Guayacán," which won the Panamanian National Institute of Culture's literary prize. HAZEL D. CAMPBELL has been involved with an innovative Kingston, Jamaica, publishing venture, Savacou Co-operative, which has done two of her short story collections. She is not as well known in Global Cultures as Velma Pollard (b. 1937), whose story "My Mother" appears later, or Olive Senior (b. 1943), but she has done a great deal to develop English-language publishing in Jamaica and the Caribbean generally, especially for Caribbean readers.

The Clearing

Luisa Mercedes Levinson

IN THE midst of the clearing, half overrun by vegetation, on the land belonging to the Basque Mendihondo, stands a miserable shack consisting of two rooms, a porch and a zinc roof that the tropical sun was trying to melt.

The clearing, about a mile in diameter, was surrounded by the jungle of Misiones in northern Argentina, a primeval force that threatened to strangle the open space with its green noose. The clearing looked like a dry island crossed only by some ostriches or monkeys or, once in a great while, by an errant Indian who, like myself, was running away from his own poverty by venturing out into the jungle and the red desert.

At one time the shack wore a coat of white paint and a few cows grazed on the clearing. A deep water well with a mule tied to the *noria* provided the only source of water. From the high beams on the porch hung a Paraguayan-style hammock, and stretched out in it lay the body of a copper-skinned woman with short but well-rounded limbs who was cooling herself with a fan made out of reeds. In spite of her dark skin she did not look like a local girl; the exaggerated use of kohl made her eyes look exotic. The flimsy dress accentuated the heavy outline of her body. The hammock swayed a little, weighted down by the compact figure. An amorphous vapour hung about her like a halo, but it just might have been an undulating cloud of mosquitos.

The boss, Alcibiades, had brought her one night when returning from Oberá, and she had stayed on. He never called her by her name, only: "Hey, say, look." She had a name that was difficult to pronounce. She had thought that this bearded stranger with the expressionless eyes, limber movements and the gaucho belt covered with silver coins, would take her to cities where the ferris wheels at the fair would lift her up to the sky or where music can be heard from a distance while the bottle made its round among the men at sundown.

But they just stayed on the clearing without as much as a dog or a guitar. Then the man hired Ciro to be the peon. Ciro watered the cattle, he castrated and skinned animals, prepared food, served mate tea and washed the clothes. He also carried the hammock from one end of the porch to the other in search of shade, sometimes with the woman inside of the net. He seldom spoke. At night he squatted next to the porch pillar, unobtrusive and silent. Since he did not smoke, his face remained invisible. His eyes shone although not as brightly as the stars in the deep night.

In the dark Alcibiades threw away his cigarette butt and approached the hammock. He stood there for quite a while: suddenly he picked up the woman and carried her to his room.

Early in the morning Ciro prepared the mate in the gourd. The woman was back in the hammock as if she had never left it, fanning herself without stopping, fresh kohl around her eyes. The expression on her face equalled that worn by many women in the subtropical land: a mask depicting melancholia or tedium, and behind the mask, nothing.

Ciro served her the mate gourd from his crouched position on the red earth; he also offered her cigars made of dried corn leaves, fruits or sometimes a partridge that he had caught at a lake fifteen miles from there. The boss looked at them from the shack while putting on his belt with the silver pieces. The boy certainly was a hard worker and he had come to like him.

One morning while the woman was eating fruit from some far-away palm trees, she spotted a rattle snake. She shot its head off as she had done so many times with the gun that she kept in the hammock.

That brought out Alcibiades. "Hey, good shot. You deserve something for that aim of yours. I'm going to town and taking a few steers along. I'll bring you a blouse."

"You want me to come along, boss?" asked Ciro.

"No."

Alcibiades pointed at the gun. "There's one bullet left. That should be enough for you."

He left. The mask in the hammock remained unchanged.

Ciro mounted the mare and made his usual rounds: he brought three straying cows back from the jungle, he wormed a calf, cured the scabies and scraped the larvae off others and mended the wooden fence. When he returned to the shack, he began his domestic chores: he started a fire to barbecue some meat while the wind was blowing dust in his face. Stooped over the red earth he shot a glance at the woman. She stretched and then began to unbutton her blouse as if the buttons were constricting her chest. She continued to lie in the hammock fanning herself while the face remained completely expressionless; only her body seemed to be swaying in the net, shimmering like so many multi-colored fish twisting and turning in the monstrous deep. She exuded sparks of a remote and yet aggressive sort of beauty. Ciro, still on his knees, moved slowly and silently closer to the woman and began to caress the hand hanging down from the hammock. Her hand moved up to the breast carrying along Ciro's hand. Ciro jumped onto the net, feverish and desperate, the blood singing in his veins. His warm sweat ran into a deep, female saltiness; the woman opened her lips wide. A milky peacefulness settled on the lonely reddish earth from which even the birds had departed. Suddenly the woman's cry broke the silence, and Ciro's body fell onto the hard ground underneath the hammock.

"Didn't expect me back so soon now, did you? At least I didn't make him bleed all over you, you should thank me for that."

Alcibiades came closer, shoved the revolver under his belt and began to use his lassoo like a thread, sewing up the net from top to bottom. The woman lay very still, completely quiet, her eyes wide open without actually looking at anything while the rope was closing the net over her face and body. He concentrated hard on his work and very neatly tied the rope into a final double knot over her feet.

She still did not realize what had happened. The rope lay across her face and cut into her breasts. A scent rose from the ground, a mixture of gun powder and sex and other things that seemed far away and hidden. Contorting her body she made the hammock swing and her face turned to the ground. There lay the dead body: a bullet had shattered the forehead, the nose looked slightly crooked, and the mouth represented a sweet and grateful wound, the lips of a boy who had just been kissed.

The woman's senses were still dulled by the apparent peacefulness that gradually ebbed away. She did not understand how fear worked. She only knew that what was to come could hardly be worse than what had been before. She had touched bottom a long time ago. Happiness for her would never be more than a confused memory of a fleeting moment. A little while ago she had come to know a profound joy, possibly for the first time; and, in spite of what had just happened, a wave of well-being invaded her, pushing aside reality and transporting her in time, keeping her locked in a present that no longer existed. In the whorehouse of Doña Jacinta she had come to know the need of many men, but nothing ever happened to make her recover the preciousness of remote things: her childhood, a ship, a certain song. Her breasts and belly began to weigh her down like some gigantic rocks. She opened her eyes. Ciro was but a quiet, elongated figure on the ground. As she twisted in the net a stony, grey hatred that seemed to have seeped out of the red earth began to inundate and overwhelm her. Scraping her hips she managed to turn sideways. Her hatred had nothing to do with the anguish or frustration of finding herself humiliated, a prisoner caught in the roped net. Her hatred was directed against the man who represented power and oppression, the boss, Alcibiades, standing next to the pillar, the very same place that had given shelter to hope, patience, poverty and love: Ciro's place.

The woman's face had become a mask again. But behind it she relived a scene from the past when the bearded man had appeared in Doña Jacinta's patio late one afternoon, his boots squeaking, his heavy figure eclipsing the light as he looked over the girls: Zoila, so fragile that she seemed on the verge of breaking in two, Wilda with her kinky hair, thick lips and greenish eyes, and all the others. And then he had picked her and made her lie down with her hands clutching her neck, and a wave of revulsion had risen in her, something that never happened before. Then he promised to take her to the big cities and plied her with corn-leaf cigars, and she forgot her loathing and went with him, leaving a heap of clothes for the other girls. She was going to get a brand new outfit, even real light-blue silken underwear. And then they ended up at the clearing, and life was not better than in that patio, and the days went by, nothing changed, dawn turned into dusk and night into day, and always the same heat.

The hatred was choking her now, erupting deep inside of her, similar to her revulsion when Alcibiades had kissed her for the first time as she arched her back. Something dormant within her, like a stagnant pond, was spilling over her mind and body, sweeping along incongruent, astonishing images. She felt now cleansed from all previous contamination, lucid and determined to carry out her revenge. She could hear him walking around inside, counting his silver coins, opening a suitcase and putting clothes and the poncho from the bed in it. He was leaving her, leaving her to be sucked up by the sun that was about to hit the porch while a cloud of greenish, sticky flies zoomed up to her from the bloody head on the ground. Far away the buzzards and crows were waiting. Her tongue felt like straw and her stomach was growing a hundred claws, but she was not conscious of suffering hunger pains or, above all, thirst. Her hatred had erased everything else. A soft smell arose from the ground. It was a sweetish smell, not unlike that produced by two sweaty bodies in the act of making love.

Alcibiades, suitcase in hand, stopped next to the pillar, a sort of grin spreading over his taut lips. He did not quite know how to measure the consequences of his act, but in a way he admired himself for his decision. He had killed a man, the boy, and he had clearly gotten rid of something that bothered him. Now he had to flee. That was a bother too, and he did not quite know what to do next. It was hot and time to take a siesta.

The woman looked like a jaguar, short limbs and a bulky chest and belly, reddish spots appearing on her skin under the sun-flooded net. Her body started to twist. The sun was hitting her right shoulder and hip. She had turned her back to the dead body and the sun shone on her heavy breast partly covered by the rope. A purplish nipple was sticking out through one of the squares of the net. Her abundant hair was spread over her face and barely allowed her eyes to shine through. She began to let out a repetitious, hoarse moan; it sounded a little like a lullaby. At the same time an instinctive knowledge arose from somewhere within and filtered through to her brain. All she had to do was to utter the right sounds and the man would come closer, throw himself on her, undo the knot and slip out the rope, and the hammock would open up. It would also mean the triumph of the female: and life, power and revenge would be hers.

Alcibiades acted ill at ease standing next to the pillar. He put the suitcase down, came a step closer and stopped.

"Hey, that sun is roasting you," he said in a strange, thick voice.

Her body began to twist again and she let out a groan. He spoke slowly now, as if he had trouble getting the words out: "Now nobody will bother us, not even the sun."

He was coming closer, stopping and starting again. She saw his body growing, towering. Any moment now he would make the final jump. Maybe in his hurry he would cut the knot with his hunting knife.

The twisting of the woman's body had changed its pace; there was a new trembling that the man failed to notice. The hatred hit her in successive, quick waves, taking over, conquering her shrewdness, her indolence, her physical needs, all that she had been until now. The waves of boiling hatred engulfed her total being. Her hatred was more impatient and impulsive than his lust. Her awareness of self-preservation was being swept away, her revenge could wait no longer. The feeling of hatred had become ferocious, tyrannical, all-consuming. She could no longer stop it . . . the gun in her hand went off.

"Bitch," mumbled the man through his clenched teeth. His body turned and fell backwards onto the ground. He clutched his chest with one hand while spitting out some confused oaths.

In the hammock the revolver remained empty, useless. This had been the last bullet, the last roar to break the hum, the heaviness and the thirst. It was the last noise of the world to reach her. That man, Alcibiades, stretched out on the ground, his body still trembling, loomed darkly, like a shadow against the light, swearing and dying. And finally, it was all over, death under the pillar, next to the bulging, old suitcase. A thread of blood was making a design on the grimy, whitish shirt partly hidden by the black beard.

The woman now yielded herself to the sun that possessed her completely. Now that her hatred had been stilled, it abandoned her like a man—she became submerged in a sort of opaque, profound peace, a sense of peace very much like the one she had experienced as an aftermath of her love-making. But this new peace was going to be endless.

Bearing down on the red earth of the clearing the sun was concentrating with tenacity on the humid body under the net that was drying up little by little. The buzzing cloud of flies moved from the sun into the shade and back, settling on the bodies of the dead men and then on her, without making any distinction between the punctured forehead, the oozing blood on the chest and her thirsty body. Her hatred had been kept alive at the expense of the thirst, and something inside of her had been fulfilled, sated. For a while she lay there, drowsy. Suddenly she bit into the net with despair. One little square broke, then another. Her skin, her eyelids and her lips were on fire. Everything around her was burning although night was falling, as heavy as a hundred men on top of her. The jungle came to life at a distance, crawling at first, then galloping furiously, closing in on the clearing, strangling it. She was blinded by the reflection of faraway lakes and treacherous rivers that advanced and retreated. Night, sun, night again. She gnawed at the threads of fear and solitude. Her own screams engendered silent echoes that took on shapes, surrounded her, scared her, and thundered on into the night. Then silence enveloped her and the lassoo's knot over her feet grew larger, unreachable, all-powerful.

The jungle rushes onwards. Shadows, sticky wings slap her face, beaks peck at her thighs and hips, splattering her with blackness and death:

"Wilda and Zoila are asleep under the mosquito net. The customers are here! Doña Jacinta is going to get angry. My legs are caught in a vine, and the men's hands are squeezing the girls' breasts filled with a yellow and bitter milk to deceive the men's thirst. Little mother! My entrails are on fire. The palm trees and the snakes are burning. Down below the silver coins and the black beard are consumed by the fire: everything is a brakish liquid . . .

"Wheels rolling through towns. Ciro, Ciro, cut me loose from this wheel! There below, in the patio filled with jasmine, stand the soldiers in their pretty blue uniforms. And angels fly through the air singing. He is bringing silk blouses for all the girls. Let's all pray to the Virgin for a miracle: pretty underwear and a man around the house. The jungle is covering me, hiding me in its leaves. Vegetation, jungle . . . little Virgin, air creature, don't blind me with your light . . ."

The hammock, suspended in midair like a bridge or a murmuring dream, was softly swinging over death when I, the poor Indian traveller, arrived.

A March Guayacán

Bertalicia Peralta

THE NIGHT was steamy, and the air that passed through the openings in the wall came in hot, hot like the blood of the townspeople. Dorinda wasn't asleep. She was thinking, wasn't dreaming. Sometimes she dreamed. Dreamed about the beautiful and sweet things she never had. She wasn't dreaming now. Nor sleeping. Just thinking. And the thoughts turned tumbleweeding in her mind, parched her mind; then suddenly they made the black almond eyes shine. She moved on the cot. It was a light movement. Even so, the man at her side seemed to feel it because he curled up tighter and tried to snuggle up. Dorinda cringed away. She felt an awesome loathing for that tough, sweaty body that for so many years had stayed on top of hers, against hers, squeezing the breasts, thighs, panting over her belly, ripping her sex, opening her always, opening her, trying to destroy her, she thought. She moved to the other end of the cot.

"Let's go dance," he had said one day some time before. She just looked at him. What did he want? "Let's go," he insisted.

She didn't go. Who would take care of the three little angels she had in the house? There were more than a few stories in the town about irresponsible mothers who had gone dancing, abandoned their children, left them alone, and then something terrible happened to them. Some were hurt. One had a house burn down with the little ones locked up inside for safety's sake; some brute knocked up a child only five or six. No. She didn't go. She had to take care of the children.

But other dances came along, other get-togethers. He was always after her. She felt a distrust in the very beginning which became a sort of habit. She got used to his being around, even though there were many things she didn't like about him. His habit of fighting with her kids, who were not his. His resentment when he saw them, when he spoke to them. And then his guile and cunning attitude to pretend when he could see she had noticed he was coming up with the same old story. It was like playing the fox and the hen. She felt he wanted her for himself, and so he would deceive her, showing her that he liked the kids. But she knew he didn't.

And the booze. When he was sober he worked hard. He took the lumps. He even had his good-natured moments of tenderness—languid eyes that preceded getting into her on some wooded hill, the pleasures under a cloudless sky, the tussles and horseplay quite a distance from the house. He liked it this way. Until he maneuvered his way into her house, and they lived together and were very happy. No. Dorinda laughed under her breath. "And they lived happily ever after" was the ending to stories they always read in school, many years ago when she was a child and her grandmother sent her to school up to the second grade. Happy, yes, let's not deny it, sometimes, a little. When he got paid, when they went to some dance, and when he embraced her gently before he drank himself under the table. But it lasted too briefly. As he drank, he'd go out of his head, squashed her between his arms, only to keep from falling, the good-for-nothing. And he was jealous of all the other men. At some arbitrary moment she'd have to go home alone and wait for him to arrive, a brute, to drop on her without feeling, going soft, falling asleep because he was so drunk. He didn't stir until the day was in full swing with the sun on high.

Dorinda got up and left the house. It was cooler outside. March made a hot terrain, a hot breeze, hot blood. She looked for a little water in a jar. It was cool in terra cotta. The worst was when he made up the thing about children. Now he wanted children—*his* children because the others were not. And she knew he hated them. Above all the little girl. And she was not about to have more children. She had found out all the details at the clinic. The doctor had counseled her, and now she knew what she had to do. But though she tried hard not to, she became pregnant again. She didn't tell him anything, but he could tell. Her belly started to stretch, the breasts to fill, the eyes to sink deeper. He knew. And he told the whole world. Then he went on a week-long binge.

"So we are going to have more children in the family, Dorinda?" asked her neighbors.

"Don't believe him, they are just stories," she had said.

"Hmm, and what about that swelling in the belly? About three months along, No?"

She answered, "No, I say. I won't have any more."

Dorinda breathed in the night's cool breeze. The sky was dark, not a single star. A splendid darkness covered the entire land as she gathered her hair into a topknot.

"Why did you spread the news?" she asked the man. "I won't have any more children. I'm going to abort." She said this haltingly, pensively. The other three were outside the house. He was stretched out in the hammock, smoking. She ground corn, slowly, rhythmically, her belly rubbing against the rim of the basin. Her arms lifted and fell with strength, with certainty.

"Are you crazy?" And without giving her a chance to suspect it, he leaped up looming over her, grabbed her by the shoulders, whirled her around, and with his eyes ablaze, looking at her like a beast, he said: "Are you crazy? If you go through with it, I'll kill you. I'll kill you," and off he went.

He got soused that night, once again. And he touted on and on. For the first time Dorinda felt afraid. He would do it. He was a brute, and he would go through with it. He was a brute, and he couldn't see that there wasn't enough of anything around the house. That she worked all day and practically all night. It didn't matter to him. "Anyway, they're not my kids," he'd always say. And the kids grew, and they'd have to go to school. All of it. It wasn't true that they were going to be ignoramuses like he and she. She started to think. She calculated day and night. She began to take stock of the advantages she had with him. She had none. To the contrary. She had aged ten years in the two gone by since the first night he'd moved into her house.

Dorinda set out slowly by herself, headed for the creek in the gorge drying up in the summer heat. She did everything as she'd been told. The creek took away the blood flowing from her sex while she strained squatting.

Then she lay on the grass to regain her strength. Impetuous tears spilled uncontrollably, blurred her sight, burned her eyes as if salt had been thrown into them. She screamed. She felt such a deep sadness—something between grief and shame—so intensely hers, a sadness that had always been there, so much so she had never noticed it. She cried until she felt free. She got up and took her time getting back to the house.

The man was sleeping. She had set it up this way. Not even a fire would rouse him. The kids weren't there. They'd been sent to her sister's "so they could get to know their cousins better," as if this were a necessity of some kind. Dorinda approached the cot. The man was sweating. She recalled the times he had sweated over her, trying to get at her very guts. She wouldn't be missed at all. She had never been needed, truly, within his reality. She knew him well. He was a tough character. If he said he'd kill her, he would do it. But she wasn't going to let him. No. Not anymore. Now at this point, Dorinda would no longer permit some things in life. Not a soul knew any of this. She approached the man. She poked him. She tugged at him. She pushed him. He felt lifeless. But she knew he was alive. He was just out cold.

Calmly she went into the kitchen. She picked up a knife and gripped it firmly by the handle. She thrust it into the heart of the man more than once. The blood ran in torrents, first streaming, then more slowly until it stopped. A lot of blood. It smelled. She made sure he was dead. She thrust the knife three more times into the body.

The night was still hot and dark. Then she closed the windows and turned on a lamp very low. She tried to move the corpse, but she realized that it was too heavy for her alone. She relaxed and began to carve up the body. First the head, then the arms, the legs. Piece by piece. When she had all of it in small pieces, she stuffed them into a hemp sack and tied it up with bejuco reed. She dragged it outside the house. She went after the horse and strapped on the cinch. Mounting the horse, she pulled the hemp sack to the pasture over the hill.

When she got there her face was cool. Her deep-set eyes had their usual mysterious brilliance. She dug out a hole as deep as she could. Her body was used to the hard work of the countryside, and it obeyed her cerebral impulses. She put the hemp sack into the ground and threw dirt on it. She planted a *guayacán* and went back to the house. She spent the rest of the night cleaning up every spot of blood very carefully. She was bothered by the odor that seemed to permeate the dirt floor, the walls and cot.

Morning came clear and radiant. Dorinda was up early and went to the creek in the gorge to wash her sheets. She met other women there.

"Dorinda, what about the little baby?" one of them asked.

"Didn't I tell you that was pure gossip," she answered. "There's not a man who's going to make me pregnant."

"And Jacinto?" they asked, only to go on talking about something while beating the clothes against the rocks.

"He left at daybreak," said Dorinda. "He told me he was going to see if he could find work in the Canal Zone. If he doesn't find anything, he'll hop a ship as a seaman. Perhaps, he'll never come back."

Since it was March and Dorinda hoped the *guayacán* would grow tall and full of flowers, every day she went with her children to water the small tree.

Translated by Zoë Anglesey

The Thursday Wife

Hazel D. Campbell

SHORTLY AFTER Bertie and Mary got married, things started to get very bad.

Bertie had been a waiter working the hotels in Montego Bay but he had been laid off soon after the wedding and they decided to move to Kingston.

They had enough money to pay the first month's rent for their one room and to buy food for a while. But as the days passed and Bertie could get no work at all, starvation began to stare them in the face.

Still Bertie insisted that his young wife could not go out to work. She was so pretty, he thought, with her light colour skin and brown curly hair, anywhere she went to work the men would want to touch her, and that would cause him to kill. So when somebody told her that she could get a job as a store clerk in one of the Syrian stores downtown, he forbade her even to think about it.

Things went from bad to worse for them. The final blow came when Bertie got food poisoning from the can of sardines they shared over a two-day period. The young wife didn't know that she shouldn't leave the sardines in the can overnight and on the second day made a sandwich for her husband with it. The left-overs weren't enough to share so she pretended that she had already eaten when he came home weary and hungry after another futile day looking for work.

That night as she held the chamber pot for his vomit and watched him writhing in pain, the thought that he might die and leave her penniless in the big, hostile city filled her with great fear. So the next day when he was better but still too weak to contradict her too violently, she suggested that it might be better if she went back to her country, the country from which he had taken her a mere six months before. She could stay with her sister. They would give up the room and he could move in with his cousin until he found a job. Then, when things got better she would come back and they would start again.

They parted reluctantly because they really liked each other and the young love was still burning hotly in their veins, but it couldn't be helped.

For six months Mary fretted in her sister's house. They were all very kind to her and she made herself useful in the house and the shop, but it was not the same. She longed for her husband and her own home once more. And he didn't write. Much later she would find out that he was barely literate and that it wouldn't occur to him to write her a letter. And although she thought about him constantly, she didn't even know his cousin's address to write to him.

One Sunday morning as she was washing her hair in the basin under the pear tree in the back yard, her sister came to tell her, mysteriously, that she had a "gentleman visitor." Mary didn't want to see anyone. Of late, some of the country gentlemen aware of her lonely status had been trying to "talk her up." She wasn't interested in any of them. So she took her time drying and combing her hair and when she went upstairs she nearly died of shock, because there, sitting on the veranda talking to her sister, was her husband Bertie.

He had come for her. Things had improved. He had found a job, rented another room and got a few things together. So once again Mary left her country home and went with her husband to start a new life in Kingston.

There was only one thing about the new life that Mary did not like. Bertie had a live-in job. He worked for some white people up on top of a hill and had to stay on the premises for he was chauffeur, babysitter, watchman and waiter for their numerous parties—whatever they might ask him to do. He worked hard all week and was only allowed a half-day on Thursdays and that was all the time he had to be at home with Mary. For most of the rest of the week, she saw him only in snatches. Whenever he could, he would sneak away while on some errand with the car and drop in for a quick visit. But on Thursday evening Bertie came home to spend the night, free until six o'clock the next morning.

And on Thursday evenings Mary bloomed. Early Thursday morning she would wash her hair and plait it, twisting it around her head, the way Bertie liked it. She would thoroughly clean their room and the little veranda which served as kitchen and dining room on occasion. She would also make sure that the vase on the bureau was ready, for he always brought her some flowers from the white people's garden. Then she would cook his favourite meal, stewed peas and rice. When everything was ready, she would wash herself carefully and change all her clothes and rest a while so that by two o'clock when he came home she was as fresh as a new bride.

Her heart would lift in anticipation as she heard him whistling as he entered the yard. He would stop and greet anybody who happened to be about, then he would step loudly on to the little veranda, then rap—pam pa pam pam on their door. And, pretending that she didn't know it was he, she would call, "Who's that?" and he would answer, "Who you expecting?" Then she would open the door and he would haul her into his arms and on to their bed and ravish her in the most rewarding ways. Later he would say, as if they were just meeting, "So how you do?" and she would answer shyly, "All right you know."

Then they would eat and dress and he would take her to a movie or to visit his cousin or they would go downtown after the shops had closed and walk through the quiet streets and stop for a while at the seaside at the bottom of King Street laughing at the antics of the little boys diving in and out of the water as naked as the day they were born.

Afterwards they would stop at a little parlour and buy patties and ice-cream and then they would go home for another bout of lovemaking, falling asleep in each other's arms until the clock alarmed at five o'clock next morning and he jumped up to race to catch the first bus so that he wouldn't be late for work—until the next Thursday.

And so it went on month after month. One year passed, two, three, four years. Their love continued bright and shining, fanned into flame on Thursday and smouldering during the rest of the week. No children came to spoil their duet, but Mary was not unhappy.

During this time she had learned how to cope with her loneliness. For one thing there was the church, nearly all day Sunday, two nights during the week with an extra night once a month for women's meeting.

Also she was a visiting sister which meant that many mornings she spent the time visiting the sick and the shut-ins, encouraging them spiritually and doing what she could to help their physical needs.

Since all her husband's domestic chores were taken care of at his work place, she had a lot of time on her hands. She washed and cooked and kept house only for herself, and as Bertie gave her generously from his pay, small though it was, she could always manage to find a little something to take for those poorer than herself and earned a name as an Angel of Mercy. Mary was well satisfied with her life.

The lustfulness of her husband and his liking for the movie house and a drink or two bothered her Christian principles from time to time. But he was so good to her, she felt that she owed it to him to do whatever he wanted on the one day of the week when he could be with her. In fact she took almost sinful pleasure in breaking the church rules without having a guilty conscience. Wasn't she merely being submissive to her husband as the Bible taught?

Then one Sunday morning, just as she was getting ready for church, without any warning, Bertie descended on her in a taxi carrying all his clothes and belongings. Bertie had come home. He had left the job in the white people's mansion and had got a better-paying one working as a waiter in a restaurant in a hotel uptown. Now he would be with her every day of the week and not just Thursdays any more.

"Isn't it wonderful?" he asked her, enthusiastically. He had kept it as a surprise for her.

Mary agreed that it was wonderful but it was with regret that she stopped dressing for church for they had a visiting evangelist who was hot with the Holy Ghost and made the church walls shake with his message and the strong amens it brought forth.

However, her husband had come home, so she helped him to settle in and set about preparing Sunday dinner, a thing she rarely did, since she had nobody to cook for but herself. And she was happy, as she thought that for the first time since she was married she would truly have her husband by her side. She might even get him to go to church with her.

A couple of weeks passed before Mary began to admit that she was uneasy. At first she couldn't think why. The first time she thought that it might be because Bertie was around so much, she pushed the thought aside. How ungrateful to think such a thing!

But her life had been drastically changed by his continuous presence.

First, there was the problem of accommodating him and his possessions. She had to squeeze up her good clothes in the wardrobe and make room for his clothes in one of the bureau drawers. She had to find place for his shoes and personal things like shaving set and cologne—he was quite a sweet man, she thought. The room looked quite crowded now and was more difficult to keep clean and tidy, but he insisted on tidiness at all times so that it seemed she was always dusting and straightening or putting things away.

He was miserable about his clothes, she found herself complaining to a church sister. He had even threatened to box her because she hadn't ironed his merinos. She didn't iron these because they stretched out so easily that she had folded them neatly and put them in his drawer. But he had taken them all out and thrown them about the room shouting and calling her a lazy woman. She had been so ashamed, for the neighbours could hear every word he said.

He was miserable about his food too, but fortunately he was allowed to eat at the restaurant, so she didn't have to cook for him too often.

Then she had to curtail many of her activities. The first Tuesday night after he came home, she had dressed herself as usual to go to prayer meeting but when she was putting on her hat, he came into the room and asked her where she thought she was going. Now that he was home, he said, she didn't have to worry with all them church foolishness any more. Mary was so upset she couldn't speak and after that she could only go out on the nights when he was on the late evening shift because if he came home before her he would always quarrel.

When she tried to explain to the parson why she was no longer as diligent in her church duties as before, he was very unsympathetic and thundered at her.

"Sister Mary, God first! Everything else comes after."

Bertie laughed at her friends.

"Where you know all them meek and mild pious woman from?" he would tease her. "Them walk like them can't mash ants, but I bet you everyone of them is as sinful as Satan."

One day he embarrassed her beyond words by ordering them to be quiet in his house. She hadn't been feeling well and three sisters had come to visit her, but when they raised a hymn he had shut them up so violently that they had hastened away without even praying for her.

"Can't stand that damn croaking and wailing," he told Mary irritably, when she tried to protest.

Yet he expected her to be nice to his friends. Every now and then some of his friends who Mary was meeting for the first time would drop by and she would have to fetch ice and fix drinks while they chatted and laughed.

That was the men.

One evening a woman came to see him. A woman whom he hugged affectionately and brought in to sit on the good chair in their room.

Mary was wary of her from the beginning. But he explained the association innocently enough. She was the house-girl where he used to work and she had washed and cooked for him.

Mary and Bertie sat on the bed while Bertie and the woman reminisced and laughed.

"You remember the day when Miss Levy couldn't find her brown wig to go to the party and how we search down the whole place till we finally find it outside and all the dog them playing with it?" the woman said—Corrine was her name.

"And how them used to leave salt fish for we dinner when them wasn't eating in, but we used to tek out steak and cook it," Bertie added his story.

"Remember, the day we was going on outing to Ocho Rios and we cook and tek away so much things Miss Levy couldn't help but notice. But we swear it wasn't we but must be her beg beg sister who did come up and tek them."

Bertie didn't laugh so heartily at this. In fact he glanced a little nervously at the very quiet Mary who had started to wonder what else Corrine had done for him besides washing and cooking.

The way they laughed and joked together made Mary feel like an outsider, that she didn't know her husband.

Corrine, it seemed, was tired of working for the white people and Bertie had promised to get her a job at the hotel so she had come to find out what was happening.

Mary couldn't help but notice how Corrine's eyes darted around the room as if she was taking notes about how they lived. Mary decided that she didn't like her.

When she was ready to leave Bertie offered to walk her to the bus stop and Mary made up her mind to ask him point-blank about her suspicions. But Bertie didn't return and Mary seized the opportunity to sneak away to her church service. When she returned, Bertie was in bed, but strangely he didn't ask her where she had been nor did he fuss about not finding her at home when he got back.

Shortly after that, Bertie began to stay away from home one night in a week or a fortnight, then one night per week regularly, then two and three nights every week. He told Mary that the hotel restaurant at which he worked had started closing very late especially on weekends and that they had set aside two rooms for the staff to sleep rather than have them travel home in the wee morning hours.

Mary said nothing. Not even after the night when she suddenly became ill and on the way to the hospital in a taxi, she begged the neighbour who was accompanying her to stop at the hotel to tell Bertie.

The neighbour was told that Bertie had left for home long ago as the restaurant closed at ten o'clock.

She never asked him about this.

Gradually Mary found that life had returned to its old pattern of regular church-going as Bertie was either not at home or showed no interest in her comings and goings.

Things were like this for some time before it finally dawned on Mary that he was now coming home only once or twice each week. And that since he wasn't wearing the clothes he had there, she had little washing and ironing to do and she didn't have to be constantly cleaning and straightening the house. In fact she was a Thursday wife once more—almost.

And still she didn't say anything, for hadn't the parson insisted—"God first and all things after"? If this was God's way of giving her the time to serve Him, then she would accept it without murmur or complaint.

When Bertie began to make excuses for not paying the rent or for not giving her any money, she used her savings to buy a sewing machine and went to the Singer classes to refresh her memory. A long time ago she used to sew when she was in the country.

Mary started taking in sewing. She spoiled a few dresses but slowly got the hang of it, and soon enough between the church sisters and others she had more work than she could handle. So between serving the Lord and earning a living she had little time to be lonely and was often surprised when she returned from church to find Bertie in bed on the nights he chose to come to her.

He rarely attempted to make love to her any longer and she was glad because for both of them it was now a joyless exercise.

This pattern continued. Mary didn't know what he did with his time, and she didn't ask him any questions. But one afternoon when she returned home after being out most of the day on a mission of mercy, her neighbour told her that a woman with two small children had been looking for her and had waited some hours hoping to see her. When she asked what the woman looked like, she realised that it was Corrine, who had visited them some years before. Corrine who used to wash and cook for Bertie. Instinctively she knew that this was the reason why he had all but left her. She wondered what Corrine wanted from her. Why she had visited her.

Mary brooded on this for some days so that the next time Bertie came to visit her, she broke her vow of silence and told him about the woman's visit.

She could not quite understand Bertie's reaction. At first he seemed frightened, then angry, then embarrassed and when Mary said, "I wonder what she want?" he shrugged his shoulders and said, "I tired. I going to bed."

Mary sat in the best chair, worn now and faded like her marriage. She sighed. He wasn't even interested enough for them to have a quarrel. Since he was there she couldn't use the machine so what could she do to pass the time? It was too early to go to bed, she thought.

She sighed again and got up to fetch her sewing. At least she could do some handwork.

She sighed another time as she sat down and looked across the room at him lying on the bed in his underwear.

He wasn't even handsome any longer, she thought. Middle age was creeping up on him. Then she acknowledged with surprise that she didn't have any feelings for him any longer. She didn't love him. She didn't even like him. It wasn't that he was no longer physically attractive, for she too had put on weight and her stomach had started its middle-age swell. It was more the fact that he was a stranger to her. As if she had never ever been truly married to him. She didn't know him.

She wondered when he would make up his mind to leave her altogether. She didn't know why he bothered to keep up the pretence.

She could not know that Bertie was not asleep. That he lay there wondering how he had got himself into so much confusion. That most of all he was wondering how he had left this good woman to get involved first with Corrine and now with the devil who was out to mash up his life.

He thought of Corrine and her two children and how lately she had started nagging him, and how the children were getting on his nerves as they always seemed to be crying.

And he thought of Mary, patient Mary, who through all the years had never even questioned him when many other women would have made a stink. He thought how she always welcomed him, never turned him away even though she had more than good reason to do so.

He thought also of the other woman who had recently begun to pursue him. He had met her at the restaurant. She was a customer. She had invited him out after work and he had accepted. At first it was exciting to be with this superior, polished lady, but lately the things she wanted him to do in bed made him feel rebellious.

Corrine, he thought, had come to see Mary because she was wondering why he was staying out so often.

What a mess! he thought. The best thing to do, perhaps, was to come

back to his wife Mary. He was getting tired of those other demanding women.

"Cho! Mary," he said, turning around suddenly and startling her. "Turn
off the light now, and come to bed."

Mary, dutiful as ever, sighed. She hoped he had no amorous thoughts.
That night more than ever she would not be able to accommodate him.

Perhaps she wouldn't ever be able to accommodate him again.

MOTHERS

In Global Cultures, stories of daughters in struggle with or in rebellion against their mothers—a theme so familiar in Europe and America—seem to be quite rare. Rare, too, are stories about struggling against or rejecting motherhood. When this theme does emerge, it is usually tied to rebellion against an unsatisfactory husband, as in the stories in the previous section. This connection is epitomized by the ultimate good-bye note that an exhausted wife writes in a wry story by Amryl Johnson of Trinidad: "Boy, I gone. I not coming back. They is your children too." However, mothers are very often characters in women's fictions of Global Cultures, and the role that they most frequently play is as the bearer of great burdens—of child care, of work, of social responsibility, and of abuse. From three different angles of vision, this theme sounds in three stories—one from Costa Rica, one from Chile, and one from Jamaica.

CARMEN LYRA, pen name for Maria Isabel Carvajal, who was born in Costa Rica in 1888, is the oldest writer represented in this anthology; but her story, "Estefanía," feels as though it could have been written yesterday. The narrator in the tale makes up a story, moves in and out of the made-up story, and in the narrating motion weaves a picture of a woman, a mother, tossed from one relationship of exploitation to the next. Carmen Lyra was known for her collection of realist stories for children and adults, Los Cuentos de Mi Tia Panchita, but she also pioneered as a founder of innovative, progressive school programs for young children. She died in 1951 while exiled in Mexico. After a brief civil war in 1948, followed by a brief clash between Costa Rica and Nicaragua, a number of communist intellectuals were forced to flee Costa Rica, and Carmen Lyra was among them.

LAKE SAGARIS, by contrast, is the youngest writer represented in this anthology. She was born in 1957 in Santiago, Chile, but attended the University of British Columbia. Sagaris was an adolescent when Salvador Allende Gossens was the first Marxist to be elected (1970) by popular vote the president of a Latin

American country. She was seventeen when the Marxist regime was ended (1973) by a military coup that launched a reign of terror during which thousands of Chileans were executed, "disappeared," or went into exile. When she returned to Chile from Canada in 1981, she published poems and stories there as well as translated contemporary North American literature into Spanish.

VELMA POLLARD, born in 1937 in Jamaica, is, like Hazel Campbell (whose story "Thursday's Wife" appeared in the last section), part of a publishing revolution in Jamaica. Her stories *Considering Women* (1989), in which "My Mother" first appeared, was published by Women's Press—an institution that signals the enormous role women are now playing in Jamaican and, more generally, Caribbean literature. She is also a lecturer in the School of Education, University of the West Indies, in Kingston, where she has interests in teaching English in a creole-speaking environment and in the language of the Jamaican Rastafari.

Estefanía

Carmen Lyra

O N   T H E deserted, interminable beach that runs from Barra del Tortuguero to Barra del Colorado, we found the driftwood cross, once painted black, now almost completely faded. Along the arms was a name and perhaps the first letter of a surname, the rest of which was completely illegible: Estefanía R. Rojas maybe; perhaps Ramirez or Ramos.

We'd covered many miles without coming across anything to break the monotony of the landscape: sea and sky to the right, the sandy beach in front of us, and to the left the vegetation of cocoa plum, almond, and coconut trees. The afternoon fell within that immense solitude. And suddenly, that blackish cross stuck there in the sand, its arms extended out against the vast blue sky. The sea had carried it this far.

Estefanía R . . .

What would the woman who bore this name have been like?

And a row of feminine silhouettes, like those one might encounter on the beaches or in the banana fields, began to parade through my imagination: pallid figures, withered, scorched by the sun, fevers, and the sensuality of man, amoral and innocent like animals. There is one who stands out in this sorrowful frieze. Would she be the one called Estefanía? The name has been erased from memory. The face a dark triangle in the midst of a tumult of dark hair, her skin toughened, her teeth very white, her feet bare, strong, and vinelike, her arms elongated.

How would she have arrived at the banana fields from the highlands of Revantazón or Parismina? Her life had brought her wandering from Guanacaste. I believe that in Santa Cruz she first had a little boy, by the judge most recently appointed an honorable magistrate of the Court of Justice, when she had barely reached adolescence. And, of course, the esteemed gentleman would not remember such an insignificant occurrence later. She left her infant son at the first suitable home and began to drift. Then another, whose name she couldn't remember very well, left her pregnant, and she continued wandering, wandering. A little girl was born. She became like one of those branches that flows in a river's current. Life deposited her with all her belongings and a daughter on a banana plantation in the Atlantic region. And thus she continued, from farm to farm, man to man, today with one, tomorrow with another, even with a Chinese commissary owner and always with the baby girl clinging to her like fungus on a fallen branch.

On one occasion she got involved with a Honduran, and she accompanied him to a ranch where normally only single men were admitted. This girl was the only woman they'd seen there. The laborers got together one night and attacked the Honduran's house to take the woman away from him. They stabbed him and did with her as they wished. No one knows why they didn't just get rid of the little girl, who would have been about three years old at the time. On the ranch where I knew her as a cook, she was as faithful as a dog to the son of the owner. The young man was handsome and friendly—she would have died for him. He came to the ranch every month to check on how the farming was going; these visits made her as happy as an angel's visits from heaven would make a saint. For him she'd even put up with being kicked by the ranch foreman during his drunken binges, just as he'd kick his own daughter and his dog; and for him she'd see that not a nickel was misspent in the commissary, that not an egg was out of place, that not a stick of kindling was carried off. Meanwhile, in the city, the profits reaped at the ranch paid for the membership of both the owner and his son at the Union Club; made it possible for the Señora, with her corns and bunions, never to leave her automobile; and enabled their daughter to dress very chic and go to Europe or the United States every year, bringing back the finest outfits and underwear, which left her best friends envious.

She put in a few years there, but when she was stricken with malaria, no one did anything for her. She had to grab her daughter and her few belongings and leave for the San Juan de Dios Hospital. Who knows how she could have done it with the little girl . . . because I don't believe that in charitable institutions of that sort they'd admit her with everything and the little one too. And in the city, the young son of the ranch owner didn't even remember the poor, sick servant. As for the lady with the bunions and her distinguished daughter, they were unaware of the very existence of that poor woman who had taken great pains to see that the ranch didn't lose an egg or a nickel; whose efforts contributed humbly toward paying for that automobile, those foreign trips, and that fine, fine underwear for the daughter.

The last time I saw her was upon her return from the hospital, on one of those trains on the branch lines that leave from Siquirres, in a car full of black men laughing riotously, black women dressed in all colors, chattering with the soft voices of Nicaraguan parrots. And always the little girl clinging to her, already withered like an old person, and so serious that you began to wonder whether or not a smile had ever played upon her lips. It was really distressing to see this little girl, whose eyes were hard as stones and whose dry mouth led you to think of earth that has never felt rain. The mother was dressed in sky blue and her daughter in yellow— such brilliant fabrics. Why had they put on these showy outfits? Between the two of them, the sadness of their life together had acquired a painful absurdity.

Who would have thought that this woman had just turned twenty-five? She was so thin that she seemed to be sucking on her cheeks; on her bruised, discolored skin her sclerosis shone with a sinister yellowish tone; and on her cheeks, shoulder blades, and elbows the bones tore at her skin. When speaking, she made a grimace that uncovered her decaying gums where her illness had begun to uproot her beautiful, white teeth with the same indifference that one would pluck away the petals of a daisy.

Upon arriving at the terminal she descended painfully, supported by her daughter, and was confused by the crowd awaiting the train's arrival. From there she went to look for a space along with the other passengers on one of the open, mule-drawn platform carts, used primarily in fruit transport, which ran on rails, bisecting the nearby fields. Where was she going? She sat down with her little daughter amidst a pile of sacks and crates. You could see she was having difficulty breathing. It's not surprising that she was tubercular.

The driver cracked his whip and the mule took off at a trot, pulling the cart on rails behind it. At the end of the alley where the train ran trembled the living spot formed by the outfits of mother and daughter, who were going off again into the banana plantations.

From which humble cemetery of those villages along the line had a flooding river or the waves of the sea uprooted this humble cross?

Estefanía R . . .

One of so many women who have passed through the banana ranches. Behind us the cross remained planted in the sand, its arms spread open toward the immensity of the sea upon which twilight was beginning to fall.

Translated by Sean Higgins

The March

Lake Sagaris

S H E   S T A R T E D up out of her sleep, like a mother who has lost her child. She rubbed her eyes with unaccustomed force and looked around her, feeling the unusual silence of the place. Where was she? Shreds of dreams and memory clung to her and she had trouble knowing which was which.

She stared at the canvas walls, hastily put together, eyes of light peering at her through the holes. Then she remembered something. Tito! Where was he?

She scrambled up off the floor and only then did she realize how stiff and bruised she felt. What had happened? She went outside. The tent crouched with a hundred others, grey, weatherbeaten, huddled together as if a wolf were stalking the horizon.

A shadow of voices murmuring, the clatter of pots and pans and the smell of beans for breakfast (the same odor which had followed them from home to here, the big city, the capital, the President's house . . . ah, that was it, the President). But where was Tito? Her dark-eyed, skinny son, with two dimples so deep it looked like his smile had been nailed on. Indeed, his three-year-old eyes expressed an anguish that made his smile unreal, irrelevant.

"Tito!" she cried. "Tito! Where are you? Come here." A gust of empty wind darted past her, but nothing more, no answer, no footsteps, no voices whispered in the dry canvas, hot under the midday sun.

She saw her old shawl, now a clumsy tent door, and remembered trying to decide whether to take it or not. She heard Chavela's voice calling her: "Rosamaría! Ven pu'h! Nos vamos ahora mismo," and she remembered grabbing Tito's hand and hurrying after her friend.

That was it, of course. That's why there was no one here. They had risen early to go downtown to see the President, to tell him everything, to ask for help.

"But I went with them," she thought, confused. With little Tito beside me, his thin legs agile as a spider's even though he's only three years old.

She remembered the time he'd gone wandering and got locked behind the heavy wooden door where they parked the mine vehicles. Less than a year old and he'd pulled and crawled his way up the door. She had turned at the sound of his plaintive "ma—ma," only to see his head disappear abruptly as he lost his grip and fell.

She could hear him crying as she threw herself against the rough boards, trying to get to him. And then she was rolling on the ground, her son beside her, the security guard who had opened the door laughing down at them. His laughter was rain-fresh. She looked at her wandering son and she too began to laugh. A sudden smile chased the tears from Tito's face.

He's a tough one, she thought proudly, as hard and dark as the coal they tear from the mines, with the same fire glowering inside.

Perhaps this is a dream, she thought. Perhaps they had only just arrived and, exhausted from the long march she was sleeping, dreaming. But she remembered the morning. Where had they all gone? Where had they taken the morning?

She looked down the dusty road that stumbled uncertainly into the city and remembered Chavela: "Ya, Rosamaría. Ven acá. We're going to see the president. We're going to explain about the strike, the prices, the company store, how the children . . ."

While she listened to her friend's confident voice, she watched his thin legs flash in the sun as he kicked a stone down the hill, and ran after it.

Dreaming or waking she walks down the hill and with each step the city moves toward her, its paved streets hold her feet, the hot air burns her face, she sees again the people's eyes, turned toward them, this raggle-taggle mob of women and children who've come to see the President, come to explain why the strike, why the men won't go back to work until the company—

"Tito," she calls. And searches among the dirty children playing on the cracked sidewalk. Tito, she calls again, unconsciously tracing the same route, following the morning, Chavela, her son's legs, the sturdy arms and backs of neighbors and friends, the white blouses clouded with dust, the dark hair streaked with grey and a hunger for justice hidden behind the wrinkled mouths, cared for by the rough hands, like a weak child, all the more loved because its time is so short.

Asleep, or awake, she follows the memory of movements down the main street toward the palace, remembers her husband's grey, gritty kiss, his eyes red from coal dust and lack of sleep, alive with something she'd never seen before. There was exhaustion, attraction, and something new, surprise, as if she were a stranger, this woman, this wife, who suddenly left the daily ticking of their life to go out and meet the President, to argue for justice for her husband, her son, for all the miners on strike. And Tito marched along beside her, or rode majestic on her broad shoulders. She remembered her husband watching her, that new expression on his face, on all the strikers' faces, their husbands, their brothers, their fathers, waiting at home for the women who left for the city.

And here she was, dreaming awake in the city, her hand full of the memory of Tito's hand, her eyes full of the memory of all those backs and steady arms, heads held high, marching to the palace gates, calling the President, calling and calling, a hundred voices, a hundred women's voices, the children laughing, a thousand voices crying out for their daily bread, not pleading, not begging, claiming the daily bread earned in the daily struggle in the mines. She had never been down a mine, but she knew it intimately. Her husband filled their house with it every night, and took it away with him when he went to work every morning.

But the road she was traveling stopped abruptly in a wooden barricade, guarded by soldiers.

"Where are you going?" one asked, stepping in front of her, his machine gun cradled in his arms.

"I want my son," she said. "We came by here. I remember."

He looked at her. A shadow crossed his face. He pushed her away.

"Move along, lady. The road to the palace is closed. You can't pass."

She had been at the end of the long line of women. Tito had wandered off; she remembered seeing him kick a stone and run and then a line of soldiers, and then the thunder of bullets as if the whole world had caved in. And she was running toward her son, and someone beside her fell and clutched her leg. Chavela grabbed her arm and dragged her away screaming, from the President, the shiny clean palace, the soldiers calmly firing. Chavela fell and she had run and run and run, forgetting everything except the time Tito fell off the wooden door, the security guard laughing, his gun a toy in friendly hands, Tito's dimples so deep, like two nails, his hands, the time Tito fell before the soldiers, his dimples obliterated by the sharp teeth of hungry bullets, chewing his face until it was nothing but blood and grey, spongy thoughts that might have been love or mother or one day the mine—

And she was running toward him, ducking under the barricade, past police cars, tanks, ambulances, somewhere here here her son, Chavela, she had to take them home, she had to tell the President, she had to tell the men on strike, the President—! the company—!

The machine gun fire.

And no more memories. No more dreams.

My Mother

Velma Pollard

For Marjorie

THE LEXINGTON Avenue train raced into Fourteenth Street station like a runaway horse and miraculously came to a stop; belching forth such an army of fast-moving bodies that I flattened myself against the stair-rails in sheer terror. But I survived, and after the first flight of stairs, stood near a tiny candy shop in the station, to let them all pass.

I stared, but only at the blacks—the strangers whom this heartless machine had rushed out of Harlem, out of the safety of the familiar 125th Street and into this alien city; to dingy stores and tiny disorganised offices or to other vague connections: Canarsie, Long Island, Jamaica, etc. They were all running, in some way or other—in careless abandon or in crisp, short, overbred paces; the women's girdles and eventually their coats, controlling the obviousness of the movement; the men's coat tails flapping at the inevitable slit below the rump.

The men, whether they were briefcase types or lunchpan types, all wore little hats with short brims. It was a cold morning. In New York twenty-three degrees is considered cold. The women didn't need hats. Cheap, curly wigs hugged their temples protecting their black youthfulness and hiding their kinky strands. Fifty acknowledging thirty, needs a wig. For some reason the real hairline tells a story even when it is dyed black. And here the merciful cold allowed for the constant sweater or the little scarf that covers the tell-tale neck.

Everybody was running and everybody looked frightened. But you could see that all this had become natural. This speed was now normal and because they couldn't see their own frightened faces, they couldn't recognise their fright. When you answer long enough to a name that for one reason or another is wrong, and when you live long enough with a face that is always wrong, a frightened look grows on you and becomes an inseparable part of you. I looked at them and became numb with a kind of nameless grief. For I had seen my mother for the first time in all those tense women's faces, in all those heads hiding their age and gentleness beneath the black, curly wigs.

The little journey was a ritual. Very early, the first or second Saturday morning of the month, my grandmother and I would walk to Anne's Ridge and get in the line at the bank. I would sign my name on the money order made out to me and we would soon move from the Foreign Exchange line to the Savings line. I never knew how much money came, for the exchange from dollars to pounds was too much for me to handle; and I never knew how much was saved. But I always felt, one Saturday every month, that we were rich.

Sometimes we stopped in the big Anne's Ridge stores in town and bought a new plate or two, sometimes dress material and v-e-r-y occasionally, shoes. Then we stopped in the market for the few things Gran didn't plant and Mass Nathan's shop didn't stock.

The journey home was less pleasant. I never ever noticed the hills on the way back; not because they were so much less green but because it took all my energy to think up little stories to help me block out Gran's monthly lecture. It always had to do with ingratitude. I'm not sure now how she knew the extent of my ingratitude long before I even understood the concept of gratitude. It had to do with the faithfulness of her daughter working hard in America to support me so I could "come to something" and my not trying to show thanks. I was no great writer; but Gran saw to it that I scratched something on an airletter form to my mother every month and that something always included thanks for the money.

Gran never made it clear in what non-verbal ways I should express thanks. I had to do well at school; but the teachers had a sort of foolproof mechanism for assuring that—those were the days of the rod and I meant to be a poor customer for that. So school was okay. But the guidelines at home were less clear. An action that one day was a sign of ingratitude was, next day, a normal action. It seemed that the assessment of my behaviour was a very arbitrary and subjective exercise and depended partly on Gran's moods.

Now I understand what Gran's dilemma was like. She herself did not know what she had to produce from the raw material she was given if her daughter's sacrifice was not to be meaningless. She had been set a great task and she was going to acquit herself manfully at all costs; but she was swimming in very strange waters. And her daughter could only work and send money; she couldn't offer guidelines either—only vague hints like the necessity for me to speak properly, however that should be.

Every year we expected my mother home on vacation and every year she wrote that she was sorry she couldn't make it. But she always sent, as if to represent her, a large round box that people insisted on calling a barrel. It was full of used clothes of all sorts, obviously chosen with little regard for my size or my grandmother's size. I never went to the collecting ceremony. This involved a trip to Kingston and endless red tape. I merely waited at the gate till the bus turned the curve, gave its two honks and slid along the loose stones to a halt to let my grandmother out. Then the sideman would roll the barrel along the top of the bus and shove it to his comrade. Immediately the bus would honk again and move on.

Nothing smells exactly like my mother's boxes. It was a smell compounded from sweat and mustiness and black poverty inheriting white cast-offs. I still remember one of those dresses from the box. With today's eyes I can see that it was a woman's frock; a woman's short voile frock for cocktail parties or an important lunch. And I was nine or ten then. But I wore it with pride, first to the Sunday School Christmas concert and then to numerous "social" events thereafter. And even now, that low-slung waist or anything resting lightly on the hips has particular charm for me whether or not the beholder's eye shares my judgement . . . There were blouses and shoes and hats; something to fit almost everyone in my grandmother's endless chronicle of cousins. We accepted our ill-fitting fits and wore them with surprising confidence.

Every year we expected my mother home on vacation. But she never came. The year I was in third form they flew her body home. I hadn't heard that she was ill. I felt for months afterwards that my very last letter should have said something different, something more; should have shown more gratitude than the others. But I could not possibly have known that that would be the last.

When the coffin arrived it was clear that nobody from Jamaica had touched that coffin. Sam Isaacs may have kept it a few days but that was all. The whole thing was foreign—large, heavy, silvery, straight from the USA. And when they opened the lid, in the church, so she could lie in state and everybody could look and cry, it was clear that my mother too had been untouched by local hands. She had come straight from the USA.

When my mother left Jamaica I couldn't have been more than five or six, so any memory I had of her was either very vague or very clear and original—carved out of my own imagination with patterns all mixed up, of other people's mothers and of those impersonal clothes in the annual barrel. The woman in the coffin was not my mother. The woman in the purple dress and black shoes (I didn't even know they buried people in shoes), the highly powdered face, framed by jet black curls and covered lightly with a mantilla, was not like any of the several images I had traced.

The funeral couldn't be our funeral. It was a spectacle. I don't suppose more than half the people there had actually known my mother. But it was a Sunday, and the whole week that had elapsed between the news of her death and the actual funeral made it possible for people from far and near to make the trip to our village. Those who were from surrounding districts but had jobs in the city used one stone to kill two birds—visit the old folks at home, and come up to "Miss Angie daughter funeral."

It wasn't our funeral. It was a spectacle.

The afternoon was hot; inside the church was hotter. Outside, I stood as far as I could from the grave and watched several of them pointing at me, their eyes full of tears: "Dats de little wan she lef wid Miss Angie." Near to me was a woman in a fur hat, close fitting, with a ribbon at the side. She wore a dress of the same yellow gold as the hat, and long earrings, costume jewellery, of the same yellow gold.

I could hear the trembling voices from the grave—

> *"I know not oh I know not*
> *What joys await me there . . ."*

—and fur hat, beside me, trying to outdo them so her friend could hear her:

"A didn't know ar but a sih dih face; is fat kill ar noh?" (My mother was rather busty but that was as far as the fat went.)

She didn't wait for an answer but continued: "A nevva sih wan of dese deds that come back from England yet." (No one had taken the trouble to tell her it was America not England.)

"But de reason why a come to see ar is becaaz I was dere meself an a always seh ef a ded, dey mus sen mih back. Is now a sih ow a woulda look! But tengad a lucky a come back pon me own steam . . . An you sih dis big finneral shi have? she wouldn't have get it in Englan' you know. Since one o'clock she woulda gaan an' if they cremate ar, while we drinking a cuppa tea, she bunnin'."

"Wat?" asked her audience at last. "Deh gives tea? an peeple siddung?"

"Man, deh put dem in someting like ovin, an by dih time we jus' drink dih tea, you get dih ashes an' you gaan . . ."

They had stopped singing about my mother's joys; the slow heavy dirge was now "Abide with me," sung with the Baptist rhythm sad and slow, though I hardly think it is possible for that particular song to be anything but sad and slow, Baptist or no Baptist. I looked towards the crowd. They were supporting my grandmother. I knew she wasn't screaming. She was never given to screaming. She was just shaking as great sobs shook her body and her hands seemed to hold up her stomach. It was pointless my trying to comfort her; they wouldn't let me. Two old women were holding her, Miss Emma, her good friend, and Cousin Jean who was more like a sister than a cousin.

Next day I went alone to my mother's grave to push my own little bottle with maiden-hair fern into the soft, red earth. When all their great wreaths with purple American ribbons had long faded, my maiden-hair fern started to grow.

I had never known my mother. I had known her money and her barrels and my grandmother's respect for her. I had not wept at her funeral. But that morning, in the subway station at Fourteenth Street, in the middle of nowhere, in the midst of a certain timelessness, I wept for her, unashamedly, and for the peace at Anne's Ridge that she never came back to know, after the constant madness, after the constant terror of all the Fourteenth Street subway stations in that horrifying work-house.

I saw my tears water the maiden-hair fern on her grave to a lush green luxuriance. I was glad I was a guest in the great USA and a guest didn't need a wig. I would take no barrels home with me. I saw my mother's ancient grave covered again with its large and gaudy wreaths. Like the mad old man in Brooklyn, I lifted from a hundred imaginary heads a hundred black and curly wigs and laid them all on the ancient grave. And I laid with them all the last shapeless, ill-fitting clothes from the last barrel. The last of the women had hurried away. I wept for my mother. But I rejoiced that the maiden-hair fern was lush and that we had no longer need for gaudy wreaths.

ELDERS

Among the contributions that women are making to Global Cultures, there are many stories that present a young woman's—often a girl's—learning from an older woman, someone of her grandmother's generation. Struggles against the constrictions of traditions, the oppression of patriarchy, are very frequently directed at the parental generation, while the old people—though they may be, in many respects, purer representatives of the old ways and may be quite marginalized within households (like the grandmother in Ai Ya's "The Whistle")—are allowed to hand down their wisdom.

ULFAT AL-IDLIBI, born in Damascus, Syria, in 1912, is the grandmother of modern Syrian literature. From a wealthy family, and thus educated beyond any standard available to women of the emergent commercial middle class, she began publishing in the 1950s, pioneering with collections of realistic short stories and works of literary criticism. **ROBERTA FERNÁNDEZ**, on the other hand, is a daughter of the Chicana community in Laredo, Texas. She has had teaching appointments at various American universities in women's studies and Afro-American studies. In addition to her stories and stories for young adults, she has recently published a novel in six stories entitled *Intaglio* (Arte Publico, 1990) and curated an exhibition at the University of Texas on twenty-five years of Hispanic literature in the United States.

The Women's Baths

Ulfat al-Idlibi

OUR HOUSEHOLD was troubled by an unusual problem: my grandmother, who had passed the age of seventy, insisted on taking a bath at the beginning of every month at the public baths, or market baths as she used to call them.

In my grandmother's opinion the market baths had a delicious ambience about them which we, who had never experienced it, could not appreciate.

For our part we were afraid that the old lady might slip on the wet floor of the baths—this has often happened to people who go there—and break her leg, as her seventy years had made her bones dry and stiff; or she might catch a severe chill coming outside from the warm air of the baths and contract a fatal illness as a result. But how could we convince this stubborn old lady of the cogency of these arguments?

It was quite out of the question that she should give up a custom to which she had adhered for seventy years, and she had done so without ever once having been stricken with the mishaps we feared. Grandmother had made up her mind that she would keep up this custom as long as she was able to walk on her own two feet, and her tenacity in clinging to her point of view only increased the more my mother tried to reason with her.

Yet Mother never tired of criticizing her mother-in-law, arguing with her and attempting to demonstrate the silliness of her views, even if only by implication. Whenever the subject of the public baths came up my mother proceeded to enumerate their shortcomings from the standpoints of health, of society, and even of economics.

The thing which really annoyed Mother was that my grandmother monopolized our only maid from the early morning onward on the day she went to the baths. She would summon her to her room to help her sweep it and change the sheets and do up the bundles to take to the baths. Then she would set out with her and would not bring her back until around sunset, when our maid would be exhausted and hardly able to perform her routine chores.

In our house I was the observer of a relentless, even though hidden, struggle between mother-in-law and daughter-in-law: between my grandmother, who clung to her position in the household and was resolved under no circumstances to relinquish it, and my mother, who strove to take her place.

Although girls usually side with their mother, I had a strong feeling of sympathy for my grandmother: old age had caught up with her since her husband had died some time before and left her a widow, and little by little her authority in the home shrank as my mother's authority gradually extended. It is the law of life: one takes, then one hands over to another in one's turn. But that does not mean we obey the law readily and willingly.

I used to feel a certain prick of pain when I saw Grandmother retire alone to her room for long hours after being defeated in an argument with Mother. I would sometimes hear her talking bitterly to herself, or I would see her monotonously shaking her head in silence, as though she were rehearsing the book of her long life, reviewing the days of her past, when she was the unchallenged mistress of the house, with the last word. I would often see her vent the force of her resentment on her thousand-bead rosary as her nervous fingers told its beads and she repeated the prayer to herself:

"Oh merciful God, remove this affliction!"

And who could this "affliction" be but my mother?

Then little by little she would calm down and forget the cause of her anger. There is nothing like the invocation of God for purifying the soul and enabling it to bear the hardships of life.

One day when I saw my grandmother getting her things ready to go to the market baths I had the idea of accompanying her, thinking that perhaps I might uncover the secret which attracted her to them. When I expressed my wish to accompany her she was very pleased, but my mother did not like this sudden impulse at all, and said, in my grandmother's hearing, "Has the craze for going to the market baths affected you as well? Who knows—you may catch some infection, like scabies or something, and it will spread around the family."

Thereupon my father broke in with the final word: "What is the matter with you? Let her go with her grandmother. All of us went to the public baths when we were young and it never did any of us any harm."

My mother relapsed into a grudging silence, while my grandmother gave an exultant smile at this victory—my father rarely took her side against my mother.

Then Grandmother led me by the hand to the room where her massive trunk was kept. She produced the key from her pocket and opened the trunk in my presence—this was a great honor for me, for the venerable trunk had never before been opened in the presence of another person—and immediately there wafted out of it a strange yet familiar scent, a scent of age, a smell of the distant past, of years which have been folded up and stored away. Grandmother drew out of the depths of the trunk a bundle of red velvet, the corners of which were embroidered with pearls and sequins.

She opened it in front of me and handed me a wine-colored bathwrap decorated with golden stars. I had never set eyes on a more beautiful robe. She also gave me a number of white towels decorated around the edges with silver thread, saying "All these are brand new; no one has ever used them. I have saved them from the time I was married. Now I'm giving them to you as a present, since you are going to the baths with me. Alas . . . poor me. Nobody goes with me now except the servants."

She gave a deep, heart-felt sigh. Then she called the servant to carry the bundle containing our clothes and towels, and the large bag which held the bowl, the soap, the comb, the sponge-bag, the loofah,[1] the soil of Aleppo,[2] and the henna which would transform my grandmother's white hair to jet black. She put on her shawl, and we made our way toward the baths, which were only a few paces from our house. Times without number I had read the words on the little plaque which crowned the low, unpretentious door as I passed by: "Whoever the Divine Blessing of health would achieve, should turn to the Lord and then to the baths of Afif."

We entered the baths.

The first thing I noticed was the female "intendant." She was a stout woman, sitting on the bench to the right of persons coming in. In front of her was a small box for collecting the day's revenue. Next to it was a *nargileh*[3] decorated with flowers. It had a long mouthpiece which the intendant played with between her lips, while she looked at those around her with a proprietorial air. When she saw us she proceeded to welcome us without stirring from her place. Then she summoned Umm Abdu, the bath attendant. A woman hastened up and gave us a perfunctory welcome. She had pencilled eyebrows, eyes painted with *kohl*,[4] and was dressed very neatly. She had adorned her hair with two roses and a sprig of jasmine. She was very voluble, and was like a spinning-top, never motionless, and her feet in her Shabrawi clogs made a rhythmic clatter on the floor of the baths. Her function was that of hostess to the bathers. She came up to my grandmother and led her to a special bench resembling a bed. Our maid hastened to undo one of our bundles, drawing out a small prayer rug which she spread out on the bench. My grandmother sat down on it to get undressed.

I was fascinated by what I saw around me. In particular my attention was drawn to the spacious hall called *al-barani*.[5] In the center of it

1. The fibrous pod of an Egyptian plant, used as a sponge.
2. A kind of clay, found around Aleppo, which is mixed with perfume used in washing the hair.
3. An eastern tobacco pipe in which the smoke passes through water before reaching the mouth.
4. A powder, usually of antimony, used in eastern countries to darken the eyelids.
5. The outer hall of a public bath.

was a gushing fountain. Around the hall were narrow benches on which were spread brightly-colored rugs where the bathers laid their things. The walls were decorated with mirrors, yellowed and spotted with age, and panels on which were inscribed various maxims. On one of them I read, "Cleanliness is part of Faith."

My grandmother urged me to undress. I took off my clothes and wrapped myself in the wine-colored bath-wrap, but as I was not doing it properly Umm Abdu came and helped me. She secured it around my body and then drew the free end over my left shoulder, making it appear like an Indian sari.

Then she helped my grandmother down from her bench, and conducted us toward a small door which led into a dark corridor, calling out at the top of her voice, "Marwah! Come and look after the Bey's mother!"

With a sigh a shape suddenly materialized in the gloom in front of me: it was a grey-haired, emaciated woman of middle age with a face in which suffering had engraved deep furrows. She was naked except for a faded cloth which hung from her waist to her knees. She welcomed us in a nasal tone, prattling on although I could not catch a single syllable of what she was saying, thanks to the babble of discordant voices which filled my ears and the hot thick steam which obstructed my sight; and there was a smell which nearly made me faint, the like of which I had never encountered in my life before. I felt nauseous, and was almost sick, leaning against the maid for support.

Nevertheless, in a few moments I grew accustomed to the odor and it no longer troubled me; my eyes, also, became accustomed to seeing through the steam.

We reached a small hall containing a large stone basin. A number of women circled around in it, chatting and washing at the same time. I asked my grandmother: "Why don't we join them?"

She replied: "This is the *wastani*;[6] I have hired a cubicle in the *juwani*.[7] I am not accustomed to bathing with the herd."

I followed her through a small door to the *juwani*, and found myself looking with confused curiosity at the scene that presented itself. There was a large rectangular hall, at each corner of which stood a large basin of white marble. Women sat around each one, busily engrossed in washing, scrubbing, and rubbing, as though they were in some kind of race. I raised my eyes to look at the ceiling, and saw a lofty dome with circular openings, glazed with crystal, through which enough light filtered to illuminate the hall. The uproar here was at its worst—there was a clashing of cans, the splashing of water, and the clamor of children.

6. The middle hall of a public bath.
7. The inner hall of a public bath.

My grandmother paused for a moment to greet a friend among the bathers, while I found myself following a violent quarrel which had arisen between two young women. I understood from the women around them that they were two wives of a polygamous marriage, who had met face to face for the first time at the baths. The furious quarrel led at length to an exchange of blows with metal bowls. Luckily a spirit of chivalry among some of the bathers induced them to separate the two warring wives before they could satisfy their thirst for revenge.

As we advanced a little way the howling of a small child drowned the hubbub of the hall. Its mother had put it on her lap, twisting one of its legs around her and proceeding to scrub its face with soap and pour hot water over it until its skin was scarlet red. I averted my gaze, fearing the child would expire before my eyes.

We reached the cubicle, and I felt a sense of oppression as we entered it. It consisted of nothing but a small chamber with a basin in the front. Its one advantage was that it screened those taking a bath inside from the other women.

We were received in the cubicle by a dark, stout woman with a pock-marked face and a harsh voice. She was Mistress Umm Mahmud. She took my grandmother from the attendant Marwah, who was being assailed by shouts from every direction:

"Cold water, Marwah, cold water, Marwah!"

The poor woman set about complying with the bathers' requests for cold water, dispensing it from two big buckets which she filled from the fountain in the outer hall. She was so weighed down with the buckets that she aroused pity in those who saw her struggle.

I turned back to Grandmother and found her sitting on the tiled floor in front of the basin. She had rested her head between the hands of Umm Mahmud, who sat behind her on a sort of wooden chair which was only slightly raised above the level of the floor. She proceeded to scour Grandmother's head with soap seven consecutive times—not more, not less.

I stood at the door of the cubicle, entertained by the scene presented by the bathers. I watched the younger women coming and going, from time to time going into the outer hall for the sake of diversion, their fresh youthfulness showing in their proud swaying gait. In their brightly colored wraps decorated with silver thread they resembled Hindu women in a temple filled with the fragrance of incense. Little circles of light fell from the dome onto their tender-skinned bodies, causing them to glisten.

I found the sight of the older women depressing: they sat close to the walls chatting with one another, while the cream of henna on their hair trickled in black rivulets along the wrinkles of their foreheads and cheeks, as they waited impatiently for their turn to bathe.

Suddenly I heard shrill exclamations of pleasure. I turned toward their source, and saw a group of women gathered around a pretty young girl, loudly expressing their delight at some matter.

Mistress Umm Mahmud said to me: "Our baths are doing well today: we have a bride here, we have a woman who has recently had a child, and we have the mother of the Bey—may God spare her for us!"

It was no wonder that my grandmother swelled with pride at being mentioned in the same breath with a bride and a young mother.

I enjoyed standing at the door of the cubicle watching the bride and her companions. Then I caught sight of a fair well-built woman enveloped in a dark blue wrap, giving vent to overflowing joy with little shrieks of delight. I realized from the words she was singing that she must be the bride's mother:

> "Seven bundles I packed for thee, and the eighth in the
>   chest is stored;
> To Thee, Whom all creatures need, praise be, oh
>   Lord!"

A young woman, a relative or friend of the bride, replied:

> "Oh maiden coming from the *wastani*, with thy towel all
>   scented.
> He who at thy wedding shows no joy, shall die an infidel,
>   from Paradise prevented!"

The bride's mother continued the song:

> "The little birds chirp and flutter among the trellis'd leaves;
> How sweet the bride! The bath upon her brow now pearly
>   crowns of moisture weaves.
> Thou canst touch the City Gate with thy little finger tip,
>   though it is so high;
> I have waited long, long years for this day's coming nigh!"

But the best verse was reserved for the bridegroom's mother:

> "Oh my daughter-in-law! I take thee as my daughter!
> The daughters of Syria are many, but my heart only desires
>   and wishes for thee!
> Pistachios, hazels and dates: the heart of the envious has
>   been sore wounded;
> Today we are merry, but the envious no merriment shall
>   see!"

The singing finished as the bride and her companions formed a circle around a tray upon which had been placed cakes of Damascene mincemeat, and a second one filled with various kinds of fruit. The bride's mother busied herself distributing the cakes right and left, and one of them fell to my share also!

In a far corner a woman was sitting with her four children around a large dish piled with *mujaddarah*[8] and pickled turnips, their preoccupation with their meal rendering them completely oblivious to what was going on around them in the baths. When the dish had been emptied of food the mother took from a basket by her side a large cabbage. Gripping its long green leaves, she raised it up and then brought it down hard on the tiled floor, until it split apart and scattered into fragments. The children tumbled over each other to snatch them up and greedily devoured them, savoring their fresh taste.

Then my attention was diverted by a pretty girl, about fifteen or sixteen years old, sitting on a bench along the wall of the boiler-house. She seemed impatient and restless, as though she found it hard to tolerate the pervasive heat. She was surrounded by three women, one of whom, apparently her mother, was feverishly fussing over her. She began to rub over her body a yellow ointment which exuded a scent of ginger (it was what was called "strengthening ointment"). My grandmother explained to me that it reinforced the blood vessels of a new mother, and restored her to the state of health she had enjoyed before having her child.

The attendant Umm Abdu came up to us and inquired after our comfort. She brought us both glasses of licorice sherbet as a present from the intendant. Then she lit a cigarette for my grandmother, who was obviously regarded as a patron of distinction.

It was now my turn. My grandmother moved aside, and I sat down in her place, entrusting my head to the attentions of Umm Mahmud for a thorough rubbing. After I had had my seven soapings I sat down before the door of the cubicle to relax a little. I was amused to watch the bath attendant Marwah scrubbing one of the bathers. Her right hand was covered with coarse sacking, which she rubbed over the body of the woman sitting in front of her. She began quite slowly, and then sped up, and as she did so little grey wicks began to appear under the sacking, which quickly became bigger and were shaken to the floor.

After we had finished being loofah-ed and rubbed, Umm Mahmud asked me to come back to her to have my head soaped an additional five times. I surrendered to her because I had promised myself that I would carry out the bathing rites through all their stages and degrees as protocol dictated, whatever rigors I had to endure in the process!

8. A Syrian dish of rice, lentils, onions, and oil.

I was not finished until Umm Mahmud had poured the last basinful of water over my head, after anointing it with "soil of Aleppo," the scent of which clung to my hair for days afterwards.

Umm Mahmud rose, and standing at the door of the cubicle, called out in her harsh voice: "Marwah! Towels for the Bey's mother!"

With a light and agile bound Marwah was at the door of the *wastani*, calling out in a high-pitched tone, like a cockerel: "Umm Abdu! Towels for the Bey's mother!" Her shout mingled with that of another "Mistress" who was standing in front of a cubicle opposite ours, likewise demanding towels for her client.

Umm Abdu appeared, clattering along in her Shabrawi clogs, with a pile of towels on her arm which she distributed among us, saying as she did: "Blessings upon you . . . Have an enjoyable bath, if God wills!"

Then she took my grandmother by the arm and led her to the *barani*, where she helped her to get up onto the high bench, and then to dry herself and get into her clothes.

Grandmother stood waiting her turn to pay her bill. There was a heated argument going on between the intendant and a middle-aged woman who had three girls with her. I gathered from what was being said that the usual custom was for the intendant to charge married women in full, but that widows and single women paid only half the normal fee. The lady was claiming that she was a widow, and her daughters were all single. The intendant listened to her skeptically, and obviously could not believe that the eldest of the girls was single, in that she was an adult and was very beautiful. But at last she was forced to accept what the woman said after the latter had sworn the most solemn oath that what she was saying was the truth.

My grandmother stepped forward and pressed something into the intendant's hand, telling her: "Here's what I owe you, with something extra for the cold water and the attendance."

The intendant peered down at her hand and then smiled; in fact she seemed very pleased, for I heard her say to my grandmother: "May God keep you, Madam, and we hope to see you every month."

Then my grandmother distributed tips to the attendant, the "Mistress," and Marwah, as they emerged from the *juwani* to bid her good-bye.

I have never known my grandmother to be so generous and open-handed as on the day which we spent at the market baths. She was pleased and proud as she listened to the blessings called down on her by those who had received her largesse. Then she gave me an intentionally lofty look, as if to say: "Can you appreciate your grandmother's status now? How about telling your mother about *this*, now that she's begun to look down her nose at me?"

As she left the baths there was a certain air of haughtiness in her step, and she held herself proudly upright, although I had only known her walk resignedly, with a bent back, at home.

Now she was enjoying the esteem which was hers only when she visited the market baths. At last I understood their secret . . .

Amanda

Roberta Fernández

T R A N S F O R M A T I O N W A S definitely her specialty, and out of georgettes, piques, poie de soie, organzas, shantungs and laces she made exquisite gowns adorned with delicate opaline beadwork which she carefully touched up with the thinnest slivers of irridescent cording that one could find. At that time I was so captivated by Amanda's creations that often before I fell asleep I would conjure up visions of her workroom where luminous whirls of lentejuelas de conchanacar would be dancing about, softly brushing against the swaying fabrics in various shapes and stages of completion. Then amidst the colorful threads and telas de tornasol shimmering in a reassuring rhythm, she would get smaller and smaller until she was only the tiniest of grey dots among the colors and lights and slowly, slowly, the uninterrupted gentle droning of the magical Singer and her mocking whispering voice would both vanish into a silent solid darkness.

By day whenever I had the opportunity I loved to sit next to her machine observing her hands guiding the movement of the fabrics. I was so moved by what I saw that she soon grew to intimidate me and I almost never originated conversation. Therefore, our only communication for long stretches of time was my obvious fascination with the changes that transpired before my watchful eyes. Finally she would look up at me through her gold-rimmed glasses and ask, "¿Te gusta, muchacha?"

In response to my nod she would proceed to tell me familiar details about the women who would be showing off her finished costumes at the Black and White Ball or some other such event. Rambling on with the reassurance of someone who has given considerable thought to everything she says, Amanda would then mesmerize me even further with her provocative chismes about men and women who had come to our area many years ago. Then as she tied a thread here and added a touch there I would feel compelled to ask her a question or two as my flimsy contribution to our lengthy conversation.

With most people I chatted freely but with Amanda I seldom talked since I had the distinct feeling that in addition to other apprehensions I had about her by the time I was five or six, she felt total indifference towards me. "¡Qué preguntona!" I was positive she would be saying to herself even as I persisted with another question. When she stopped talking to concentrate fully on what she was doing I would gaze directly at her, admiring how beautiful she looked. Waves of defeat would overtake me, for the self-containment which she projected behind her austere appearance made me think that she would never take notice of me, while I loved everything about her.

I would follow the shape of her head from the central part of her dark auburn hair pulled down over her ears to the curves of the chongo which she wore at the nape of her long neck. The grey shirtwaist with the narrow skirt and elbow-length sleeves she wore day in and day out, everywhere she went, made her seem even taller than she was. The front had tiny stitched-down vertical pleats and a narrow deep pocket in which she sometimes tucked her eyeglasses. She always seemed to have a yellow measuring tape hanging around her neck and a row of straight pins with big plastic heads down the front edge of her neckline. Like the rest of the relatives she seemed reassuringly permanent in the uniform she had created for herself.

Her day lasted from seven in the morning until nine in the evening. During this time she could dash off in a matter of two or three days an elaborate wedding dress or a classically simple evening gown for someone's coming-out party which Artemisa would then embroider. Her disposition did not require her to concentrate on any one outfit from start to finish and this allowed her to work on many at once. It also meant that she had dresses everywhere, hanging from the edge of the doors, on a wall-to-wall bar suspended near the ceiling and on three or four tables where they would be carefully laid out.

Once or twice Amanda managed to make a bride late to her own wedding, when at the last minute she had to sew-in the zipper by hand while the bride was already in the dress. Somehow people didn't seem to mind these occasional slip-ups, for they kept coming back, again and again, from Saltillo and Monterrey, from San Antonio and Corpus Christi, and a few even from far-off Dallas and Houston. Those mid-Texan socialites enjoyed practicing their very singular Spanish with Amanda, and she used to chuckle over her little joke, never once letting on that she really did speak perfect English.

As far as her other designs went, her basic dress pattern might be a direct copy from *Vogue* magazine or it could stem from someone's dearest fantasy. From then on the creation was Amanda's and every one of her clients trusted the final look to her own discretion. The svelte Club Campestre set from Monterrey and Nuevo Laredo would take her to Audrey Hepburn and Grace Kelly movies to point out the outfits that they wanted, just as their mothers had done with Joan Crawford and Katharine Hepburn movies. Judging from their expressions as they pirouetted before their image in their commissioned artwork she never failed their expectations, except perhaps for that occasional zipper-less bride. She certainly never disappointed me as I sat in solemn and curious attention, peering into her face as I searched for some trace of how she had acquired her special powers.

For there was another aspect to Amanda which only we seemed to whisper about, in very low tones, and that was that Amanda was dabbling in herbs. Although none of us considered her a real hechicera we always had reservations about drinking or eating anything she gave us, and whereas no one ever saw the proverbial muñequitos we fully suspected that she had them hidden somewhere, undoubtedly decked out in the exact replicas of those who had ever crossed her in any way.

Among her few real friends were two ancianas who came to visit her by night, much to everyone's consternation, for those two only needed one quick stolen look to convince you that they were more than amateurs. Librada and Soledad were toothless, old women swarthed in black or brown from head-to-toe and they carried their morral filled with hierbas and potions slung over their shoulders just as brujas did in my books. They had a stare that seemed to go right through you, and you knew that no thought was secret from them if you let them look even once into your eyes.

One day in the year when it rained more than in the previous four years and the puddles swelled up with more bubbles than usual I found myself sitting alone in the screened-in porch admiring the sound of the fat raindrops on the roof when suddenly I looked up to find Librada standing there in her dark brown rebozo, softly knocking on the door.

"La señora le manda un recado a su mamá," she said while my heart thumped so loudly that its noise scared me even further. I managed to tell her to wait there, by the door, while I went to call my mother. By the time that mother came, Librada was already inside, sitting on the couch, and since the message was that Amanda wanted mother to call one of her customers to relay a message, I was left alone with the old woman while mother went to make the call. I sat on the floor pretending to work on a jig-saw puzzle while I really observed Librada's every move. Suddenly she broke the silence asking me how old I was and when my eighth birthday would be. Before I could phrase any words, mother was back with a note for Amanda, and Librada was on her way. Sensing my tension mother suggested that we go into the kitchen to make some good hot chocolate and to talk about what had just happened.

After I drank my cup, I came back to the porch, picked up one of my *Jack and Jill's* and lay down on the couch. As I rearranged a cushion my left arm slid on a viscous greenish-grey substance and I let out a screech which had mother at my side in two seconds. Angry at her for having taken so long to come to my aid, I was wiping my arm on the dress and screaming, "Mire lo que hizo la bruja." She very, very slowly took off my dress and told me to go into the shower and to soap myself well. In the meantime she cleaned up the mess with newspapers and burned them outside by the old brick pond. As soon as I came out of the shower she puffed me up all over with her lavender-fragranced bath powder and for the rest of the afternoon we tried to figure out what the strange episode had meant. Nothing of great importance happened to anyone in the family during the following wet days and mother insisted we forget the incident.

Only I didn't forget it for a long time. On my next visit to Amanda's I described in detail what had happened. She dismissed the entire episode as though it weren't important, shrugging, "Pobre Librada. ¿Por qué le echas la culpa de tal cosa?" With that I went back to my silent observation, now suspecting that she too was part of a complex plot that I couldn't figure out. Yet, instead of making me run, incidents like these drew me more to her, for I distinctly sensed that she was my only link to other exciting possibilities which were not part of the every-day world of the others. What they could be I wasn't sure of but I was so convinced of the hidden powers in that house that I always wore my scapular and made the sign of the cross before I stepped inside.

After the rains stopped and the moon began to change colors I began to imagine a dramatic and eery outfit which I hoped Amanda would create for me. Without discussing it with my sisters I made it more and more sinister and finally when the toads stopped croaking I built up enough nerve to ask her about it.

"Oye, Amanda, ¿me podrías hacer el traje más hermoso de todo el mundo? ¿Uno como el que una bruja le diera a su hija favorita? ¡Que sea tan horrible que a todos les encante!"

"¿Y para qué diablos quieres tal cosa?" she asked me in surprise.

"Nomás lo quiero de secreto. No creas que voy a asustar a los vecinos."

"Pues, mire usted, chulita, estoy tan ocupada que no puedo decirle ni sí ni no. Uno de estos días, cuando Dios me dé tiempo quizás lo pueda considerar, pero hasta entonces yo no ando haciendo promesas a nadie."

And then I waited. Dog days came and went, and finally when the lechuza flew elsewhere I gave up on my request, brooding over my having asked for something which I should have known would not be coming. Therefore the afternoon that Artemisa dropped off a note saying that la señora wanted to see me that night because she had a surprise for me, I coolly said that I'd be there only if my mother said that I could go.

All the time that I waited to be let in I was very aware that I had left my scapular at home. I knew this time that something very special was about to happen to me, since I could see even from out there that Amanda had finally made me my very special outfit. Mounted on a little-girl dress-dummy a swaying black satin cape was awaiting my touch. It was ankle length with braided frogs cradling tiny buttons down to the knee. On the inside of the neckline was a black fur trim. "Es de gato," she confessed, and it tickled my neck as she buttoned the cape on me. The puffy sleeves fitted very tightly around the wrist, and on the upper side of each wristband was attached a cat's paw which hung down to the knuckles, on top of each hand. Below the collar on the left side of the cape was a small stuffed heart in burgundy-colored velveteen and, beneath the heart, were tear-shaped red translucent beads.

As she pulled the rounded ballooning hood on my head, rows of stitched-down pleats made it fit close to the head. Black chicken feathers framed my face, almost down to my eyes. Between the appliqués of feathers were strung tiny bones which gently touched my cheeks. The bones came from the sparrows which the cats had killed out in the garden, she reassured me. She then suggested that I walk around the room so that she could get a good look at me.

As I moved, the cat's paws rubbed against my hands and the bones of the sparrows bounced like what I imagined snowflakes would feel like on my face. Then she put a necklace over my head which reached to my waist. It too was made of bones of sparrows strung on the finest glittering black thread, with little cascabeles inserted here and there. I raised my arms and danced around the room, and the little bells sounded sweet and clear in the silence. As I glided about the room I noticed in the mirror that Librada was sitting in the next room, laughing under her breath. Without thinking I walked up to her and asked what she thought of my cape.

"Hijita, pareces algo del otro mundo. Mira que hasta me acabo de persignar. Me da miedo nomás en pensar del montón que te vas a llevar contigo al infierno. ¡Qué Dios nos libre!"

As I looked at Librada for the first time, I felt that the room was not big enough to hold all the emotion inside of me. So I put my arms around Amanda and kissed her two, three, four times, then dramatically announced that I was going to show this most beautiful of all creations to my mother. I rushed outside hoping not to see anyone in the street and since luck was to be my companion for a brief while, I made it home without encountering a soul. Pausing outside the door of the kitchen where

I could hear voices I took a deep breath, knocked as loudly as I could and in one simultaneous swoop, opened the door and stood inside, arms outstretched as feathers, bones and cascabeles fluttered in unison with my heart.

After the initial silence my sisters started to cry almost hysterically, and while my father turned to comfort them, my mother came towards me with a face that I had never seen on her before. She took a deep breath and quietly said that I must never wear that outfit again. Since her expression frightened me somewhat, I took off the cape, mumbling under my breath over and over how certain people couldn't see special powers no matter how much they might be staring them in the face.

I held the bruja cape in my hands, looking at the tiny holes pieced through the bones of the sparrows, then felt the points of the nails on the cat's paws. As I fingered the beads under the heart I knew that on that very special night when the green lights of the linternas were flickering much brighter than usual, on that calm transparent night of nights I would sleep in my wondrous witch's daughter's cape.

Sometime after the Júdases were all aflame and spirals of light were flying everywhere I slowly opened my eyes on a full moon shining on my face. Instinctively my hand reached to my neck and I rubbed the back of my fingers gently against the cat's fur. I should go outside I thought. Then I slipped off the bed and tipped-toed to the back door in search of that which was not inside.

For a long time I sat on a lawn chair, rocking myself against its back, all the while gazing at the moon and at the familiar surroundings which glowed so luminously within the vast universe, while out there in the darkness the constant chirping of the crickets and the chicharras reiterated the reassuring permanence of everything around me. None of us is allowed to relish in powers like that for long though, and the vision of transcendence exploded in a scream as two hands grabbed me at the shoulders, then shook me back and forth. "What are you doing out here? Didn't I tell you to take off that awful thing?"

Once again I looked at my mother in defiance but immediately sensed that she was apprehensive rather than angry and I knew that it was hopeless to argue with her. Carefully I undid the tiny rounded black buttons from the soft braided loops and took off the cape for what I felt would be the last time.

Years passed, much faster than before, and I had little time left for dark brown-lavender puddles and white lechuzas in the night. Nor did I see my cape after that lovely-but-so-sad, once-in-a-lifetime experience of perfection in the universe. In fact, I often wondered if I had not invented that episode as I invented many others in those endless days of exciting and unrestrained possibilities.

Actually the memory of the cape was something I tried to flick away on those occasions when the past assumed the unpleasantness of an uninvited but persistent guest; yet, no matter how much I tried, the intrusions continued. They were especially bothersome one rainy Sunday afternoon when all the clocks had stopped working one after another as though they too had wanted to participate in the tedium of the moment. So as not to remain still I mustered all the energy that I could and decided to pass the hours by poking around in the boxes and old trunks in the storeroom.

Nothing of interest seemed to be the order of the afternoon when suddenly I came upon something wrapped in yellowed tissue paper. As I unwrapped the package I uttered a sigh of surprise on discovering that inside was the source of the disturbances I had been trying to avoid. I cried as I fingered all the details on the little cape, for it was as precious as it had been on the one day I had worn it many years ago. Only the fur had stiffened somewhat from the dryness in the trunk.

Once again I marvelled at Amanda's gifts. The little black cape was so obviously an expression of genuine love that it seemed a shame it had been hidden for all those years. I carefully lifted the cape out of the trunk wondering why my mother had not burned it as she had threatened, yet knowing full well why she had not.

From then on I placed the little cape among my collection of few but very special possessions which accompanied me everywhere I went. I even had a stuffed dummy made upon which I would arrange the cape in a central spot in every home I made. Over the years the still-crisp little cape ripened in meaning, for I could not imagine anyone ever again taking the time to create anything as personal for me as Amanda had done when our worlds had coincided for a brief and joyous period in those splendid days of luscious white gardenias.

When the end came I could hardly bear it. It happened many years ago when the suitcase containing the little cape got lost en route on my first trip west. No one could understand why the loss of something as quaint as a black cape with chicken feathers, bones of sparrows and cat's paws could cause anyone to carry on in such a manner. Their lack of sympathy only increased my own awareness of what was gone, and for months after I first came to these foggy coastal shores I would wake up to lentejuelas de conchanacar whirling about in the darkness, just as they had done so long ago in that magical room in Amanda's house.

Back home Amanda will soon be eighty, and although I haven't seen her in years, lately I have been dreaming once again about the enchantment which her hands gave to everything they touched, especially when I was very tiny and to celebrate our birthdays, my father, she and I had a joint birthday party lasting three consecutive days, during which he would make a skeletal frame for a kite out of bamboo sticks to which Amanda would attach very thin layers of marquisette with angel cords which my father would then hold on to, while I floated about on the kite above the shrubs and bushes and it was all such fun. I cannot recall the exact year when those celebrations stopped, nor what we did with all those talismanic presents but I must remember to sort through all the trunks and boxes in my mother's storeroom the next time that I am home.

Part Five

COMPLEX COMMUNICATIONS
Beliefs, Perspectives, Prejudices

BORDER CROSSINGS

A group of travelers—an elegant, educated city man, a crude parvenu and his pretty, frustrated wife, a herdsman from the countryside seeking revenge upon a brutal profiteer, a wry driver—pass the time of their journey talking about a madwoman. From behind their exchanges, their glances, their intolerances, the madness in their own lives seeps into the open, unrecognizable to them. The servants in a household feel their accustomed world of unquestioning submission disturbed. Something is out of kilter, something closes in, something threatens violence. When the master and the mistress of the house were white people, secure in their sense of superiority, their racism, their boy did not feel like he was being buried alive. But the master and the masterful mistress, now, are black people, and a web of madness has descended on the world. An explorer in darkest Africa makes a startling discovery—the world's smallest woman. People all over the world read about it in their newspapers. Everyone is, each in his or her own way, touched, disturbed, excited, awed, repelled. A certain madness seeps out over the world. Only the still center of this storm, the little woman herself, is imperturbable, content, happy to be alive; only she is sane in her self-enclosure.

In Global Cultures, you can find, in a myriad of guises, a keen appreciation for how narrow—how invisible—is the border between sanity and madness. With the merest accident or shift of perspective or wind of change, the border can be crossed. This was clear to **ABD AL-SALAM AL-UJAYLI**, born in Raqquah, Syria, in 1918, a doctor who constructed intricate narrative circles within circles, mirrors in mirrors, in his story "Madness," to present his diagnosis—a social psychology in miniature—of how class differences, sexism, family loyalties and disloyalties play into the crossing of the line. Abd al-Salam al-Ujayli is one of Syria's most prolific producers of novels, short stories, plays, poetry, and essays, and is well known for incorporating in his work traditional Arabic literary devices, such as the Scheherazade-like narrator or the story-telling within story-telling, as in "Madness."

LEONARD KIBERA's "The Spider's Web" is also intricately constructed, involving dream and fantasy sequences, almost hallucinatory moments, abrupt changes of tone, place, time—a picture of madness. He was raised in Kenya, where an entire generation was traumatized by a violent revolt (1952–1956) against British rule led by Kikuyu tribespeople and aimed, in part, at restoring Kenya to its pre-European way of life. During the so-called Mau-Mau Emergency, many blacks—like the woman named Lois in Kibera's story—participated in demonstrations to throw British teachers out of schools. After Kenya's independence was achieved in 1963, many Europeans and Asians left the country, and, sadly, a decade of interethnic or tribal violence followed. It is this decade and its madness in which Kibera's story is set.

In South American literature, there is an abiding fascination with "The Dark Continent," from which so many South Americans' black ancestors came as slaves. At the beginning of Gabriel Garcia Marquez's great novel, A Hundred Years of Solitude, for example, schoolboys learn from their teacher that "in the southern extremes of Africa there were men so intelligent and peaceful that their only pastime was to sit and think." No image like this one—so appropriate to pre-colonial southern Africa—has ever been taught to the French explorer or the worldwide newspaper readers who discover the existence of the smallest woman in the world in Clarice Lispector's story. They cannot imagine that the pygmy woman is human, much less that she has lived quite beyond their madness of preconceptions, their crazy need for categories, their anger, their false romanticism and delusions about love. CLARICE LISPECTOR was born in 1925 in the Ukraine but was raised by her Russian-speaking Jewish parents in Recife, Brazil, where her father was a laborer, the family quite poor. She eventually took a law degree, but writing was what she did constantly, including the years when she was a diplomat's wife, a mother of two sons, and living in Italy, Switzerland, England, and the United States. She spent the last years of her life—she died of cancer in 1977—in Rio de Janeiro. Since then, her reputation has grown enormously in Global Cultures: she is "the premier Latin American woman prose writer of this century," a reviewer proclaimed in The New York Times.

Madness

Abd al-Salam al-Ujayli

I

THE SEASON was summer, the time was midday, and the road between Humaymah and Jubb al-Safa, on the way to Aleppo, was empty of
cars and people.

The car sped along the asphalt road, but its speed was not enough to
cool the hot fiery air which blew against the faces of the car's five occupants. Suddenly the passengers were shot forward in their seats as the car
slowed down without warning. The husband, sitting in the rear seat, cried
out to his wife: "That's her!"

The driver joined in: "Yes, that's her. That's why I braked. She doesn't
usually step off the curb and walk in the middle of the road. I almost ran
over her once because I forgot she was mad."

As he said this the car drew level with the subject of their exchange,
then quickly left her behind. Everyone except the driver craned around to
peer at her. She was wearing a striped dress with a ragged belt. A dark-
colored head scarf with a spotted pattern was wound around her head.
From under it her hair appeared short, like a man's.

The wife was nearest to her as they passed, and she was able to see
clearly her wrinkled, burned, coppery face, with its traces of tatooing. It
was a foolish face, the face of a madwoman. All of them observed her
peculiar gait. She walked stooping forward, without ever glancing aside to
notice what was going on around her, and she walked quickly, as though
she were pressing on toward some goal from which neither searing sun
nor scorching simoom could deflect her.

The judge, who was occupying the front seat next to the driver, said:
"How is it that they let her go around like this? Why don't they tell the
police about her so that they can put her into custody?"

No one answered his question. This was the first time he had opened
his mouth since he had gotten into the car at Raqqah. This morning he
had reserved both seats next to the driver, so that he would not have to
share the front seat with anyone else. Then he had started on his court
work quickly and finished it in the late morning. Ensconced in the front
seat, he said nothing. He only stirred from time to time to light a cigarette,
staring ahead fixedly as though he were listening to a boring submission from some obstinate defense counsel. The silence lasted long enough

for the driver to begin to feel embarrassment at no one's answering the judge's question. It was really up to the husband sitting in the back seat to answer, as it was he who had started talking about the madwoman, but he said nothing. The driver said: "But what could the police do with her, Bey? She's been going on like this for twenty years and has never harmed anyone."

The wife joined in: "For twenty years or twenty-five years? You said for twenty-five years, Ahmad."

Her husband returned: "What's the difference? She is mad and that's all there is to it. I've been along this road a thousand times between Aleppo and Raqqah, and I've seen her a thousand times between these two villages, Humaymah and Jubb al-Safa, walking along like this, summer and winter, rain and shine."

In saying this the husband was addressing his wife, but he raised his voice so that the judge should hear. From the start he had been irritated by the haughtiness of the latter. The judge's disdaining to take part in conversation with the other passengers annoyed him, and he had therefore pointedly refrained from answering his question. But he felt the desire for talk coming over him, and he said to himself: "Well, he is a judge after all, always laying down the law in court—he has a right to be a bit distant and proud of himself."

Meanwhile the judge had raised his head and was pretending to puff the smoke from his cigarette into the air. In reality however he was bending his head a little in order to be able to see, in the small mirror in front of the driver, the eyes of the wife, which were looking at him in the same mirror. Two beautiful wide eyes beneath finely arched eyebrows—and the bridge of a delicate nose and two rosy cheeks—were reflected in the mirror.

She was a young woman, and beautiful. She did not seem a fit match for her talkative, paunchy, middle-aged husband, whose clothes bespoke wealth unaccompanied by good taste, and good living unaccompanied by enjoyment.

The fourth passenger spoke. He was a bedouin, who was cloaked in a withdrawal that lay somewhere between pride and uninterest in what was going on. From his appearance he seemed better off than his fellows. He said: "I've been along this road many times, and never seen this poor creature. Or perhaps I have seen her, and no one has been good enough to point out to me that she is out of her mind."

The husband retorted: "It's as I told you. She takes this road every day. She covers the length of it twice between morning and sunset—once going and once returning."

His wife inquired "Why?" without showing much interest, as she was looking into the mirror at the eyes of the youthful judge beneath their thick eyebrows, obscured now and again by ascending puffs of smoke from his cigarette. In the intervals between the puffs she could see the eyes gazing at her in the mirror. They were just the eyes of a man, with nothing remarkable about them. But she noted his youthfulness and elegance later, when the car stopped in front of the law courts and the judge went inside.

Her husband went on: "There are a thousand stories about her. Once, when I was a lorry driver, I gave a lift to a man who lived around here, and he told me the truth of it."

At this point the judge abandoned his air of superiority, and replied to the husband—the eyes of his wife attracted him, and her persistence in looking at him in the mirror gratified him—asking in an ingratiating tone: "And what was the story exactly?"

2

The husband replied: "It happened when this woman was young. She came from a village near Humaymah. A pretty girl. Twenty-five years ago—and if my wife doesn't like me saying twenty-five years I will say thirty—private cars were few and far between. Only the rich could afford them. One such was the landowner of this village. He was well known for his affairs with women. He caught sight of her on a public holiday, standing with her father on the main road, where they were waiting for a car to take them to her mother's relatives in Jubb al-Safa near Nahr al-Dhahab; and so he gave them a lift in his car.

"He sat them next to the driver, while he sat in the back seat. Her father was one of his tenant-farmers—that's why he gave them a lift."

The wife, with a pertness she had never before shown—at least in public—said: "You said that she was a young girl, Ahmad, and that the Bey was known for his affairs with women. Isn't it more likely he gave them a lift because of her good looks?"

The husband snapped: "Lower your voice, woman! It's true that he had his fair share of entanglements with women, women from all over the place. But not with peasant girls like this one. All the same, I expect you're right. Anyway, the Bey sat in the back and she sat with her father in the front. He kept looking in the mirror—the mirror placed in front of the driver to allow him to see behind—and saw nothing but her eyes in it. You all know how attractive the eyes of some of these peasant girls are. The longer the Bey looked at her the more attractive she seemed. And the wretched girl kept looking—in the mirror—into his eyes."

At this point the eyes of the young wife flickered in the mirror, and the judge noticed she was smiling. His eyes flickered as well—he smiled—while the husband continued his story:

"Since the peasant girl seemed so attractive to the Bey he started a conversation. He asked Abu Abdullah, the girl's father, whether he would be marrying off his son Abdullah soon. The man replied: 'Yes, we are arranging an exchange: I am giving my daughter Khalisah to Husayn, son of Abu Husayn, and I shall take Nu'aymah, daughter of Abu Husayn, for my son Abdullah.' You know the custom of 'exchange marriages' among the country people and the bedouins, and how if one of the two 'exchangees' quarrels with his wife, so that she cannot stand him, or he drives her out, then the other drives out his wife, the sister of the first man—even if there is no reason why she should be driven out. The customs of these people are barbaric."

The voice of the fourth passenger was raised in protest: "And why are our customs barbaric, effendi? You speak as though you townspeople have no objectionable customs whatsoever. Shall I mention a few?"

Making a tactical withdrawal, the husband interrupted him: "I was only speaking about the peasantry. Are you a peasant? You are surely a bedouin of shaykhly family . . . you surely are an Arab shaykh . . ."

The fourth passenger replied: "I'm neither a shaykh nor an agha.[1] I am like other people, a son of my tribe and my country. Every place has its customs, and people should look at those customs with the eyes of the local people, before saying they are barbarous or quaint. But you townsfolk take no account of people with rough hands. Anyone who works with his hands is not worth twopence as far as you are concerned."

The husband rejoined: "You seem to have taken me seriously, my dear fellow. All of us work with our hands. I used to be a lorry driver on wages. I was a manual worker and slept rough, in the open. God helped me and I bought my own lorry. Eventually I gained control of a fleet of lorries and tanking facilities. As soon as I'd become a successful man no one in town looked down on me any more. This girl's people took her from school and married her to me. The great thing is for your pockets to be full—then you will get the prettiest girls of all classes eating out of your hand."

His wife inquired coquettishly: "Whatever do you mean by that, Ahmad?"

Her husband paid no attention to her, but added: "Never mind. Don't take it to heart. Let me finish the story of the madwoman. Now where was I?"

The youthful judge, smiling appreciatively at the tart exchange between the bedouin and the ex-lorry driver—and also at the smiling face of the

---

1. Originally a chief officer, military or civil, in the Ottoman Empire; also a title conferred to denote personal distinction.

young woman looking at him in the mirror—responded: "We had reached the discussion of the marriage arrangements between Husayn's father and Abdullah's father."

The husband exclaimed: "Ah yes; well, the Bey asked the father of Abdullah: 'Is this the girl Khalisah you intend to exchange for a wife for your son?' The farmer replied: 'No, this is Jamilah. She is my third daughter.' The Bey then said: 'Why not allow me to give her in marriage?' Abu Abdullah said: 'To whom?' The Bey answered: 'To this chauffeur of mine, sitting beside you—Ishaq. Don't you like the looks of him?' So Abu Abdullah peered at Ishaq, and so did the girl. According to the man who told me the story, this Ishaq was a good-looking chap, with fair hair and blue eyes, and Jamilah liked the looks of him. She stopped staring at the Bey, even in the driving mirror. I know these sheep farmers' girls. I know them well enough, as God is my witness. Before marriage they have the roving eye, but as soon as the question of marriage comes into the picture, or the girl actually gets married, she quiets down."

At this point the fourth passenger broke in maliciously: "Town girls of course are just the opposite: your town girl is quiet and steady-going until she gets a husband—then she gets the roving eye!"

The judge laughed loudly at the fourth passenger's sally, and his laughter was followed by the laughter of the wife, musical and attractive. Her husband chided: "Be quiet, woman! What are you laughing for?"

She returned: "I was laughing because you seem to know the story down to the last detail. You know all about Abu Husayn and Abu Abdullah and Nu'aymah and Khalisah and Jamilah. How can you remember all those names, Ahmad?"

He answered: "Shut up and listen! The girl, as I said, looked at Ishaq and Ishaq looked at her. He pleased her, and probably she pleased him. Who knows? We passed through Nahr al-Dhahab a few moments ago, and here is the village of Jubb al-Safa, the village of Jamilah's uncles. We are just getting to it. It's around fifteen or twenty kilometers between this place and Humaymah, and the madwoman covers them in four or five hours. She wanders on and on and then goes back to her family's village near Humaymah, getting there before sunset. She sleeps in the village, and then as soon as the sun rises she is on her way again, back on the road once more. Look, everybody! Here's the road which turns off to Jubb al-Safa . . ." And as though staring at the madwoman the passengers all craned to the left side of the road, trying to descry the village which the husband had indicated. Then they resumed looking straight ahead, as the car sped on its way to Aleppo. The eyes of the judge began to peer again into the eyes of the wife in the mirror, and her eyes looked out at him.

3

The judge said to himself: "It's now twelve-thirty. Let's say we'll reach Aleppo by one and be home by one-fifteen. That should be about right. I shall have enough time to ring up Samiyah before her husband gets back from work . . . this young woman in the back seat with the middle-aged windbag of a husband—her eyes are beautiful, very beautiful. They remind me of Samiyah's eyes . . ."

For the last two or three or even four years this had been the youthful judge's routine. Every Thursday he conveniently calculated his arrival in Aleppo before the government offices had closed their doors and the civil servants had left to go home, so that he could telephone Samiyah. This had been simple when his court was at Idlib—it was only a short distance away, and most of the civil servants (many of whose families lived in Aleppo) had come to a mutual understanding to knock off work on Thursdays by as much as an hour before the official end of office hours. But it was more difficult in his new post. He had to travel two hundred kilometers to reach Aleppo. Certainly this distance did not seem so much, when he imagined himself listening to Samiyah's voice and talking to her, and her talking to him, and the idea that he might see her on the road, or might visit her at her home, or perhaps . . . perhaps she might meet him at the other house. When he imagined all this any distance dwindled and disappeared. But work . . . it was very difficult to abandon litigants and adjourn cases in order to get from his office in Raqqah to his house in Aleppo, before the civil servants there had traveled from their offices to their homes.

Nevertheless he had managed to do this on frequent Thursdays since his transfer—as on this Thursday. He had traveled the road every day, back and forth, between Humaymah and Jubb al-Safa. He traversed it just as she did, though for a different purpose . . . for a purpose which usually demands a great deal of traveling and rushing from pillar to post . . . and what purpose could compare with Samiyah's eyes?

How strange is life, how short are distances, how peculiar are human desires! When he was studying law in Damascus he was attracted to this girl Samiyah, but never dared to speak to her. He used to see her at the students' club, and he would look at her and she would look at him. He would say to himself: "A lot of men have their eyes on her, but does she give any of them a second glance?"

He convinced himself that she looked at no one but himself—or at least that she looked at others but not in the same way as she looked at him. It was pure imagination and self-deception. But he derived satisfaction from such thoughts and beguiled himself with them. Then their ways parted.

They no longer came across each other in the students' club, the footpaths of the university garden or the colonnades of the Faculty of Law. Then one day he met her by chance in his home town of Aleppo.

By this time he had already become a probationary judge, and she was now married and had come with her husband to the city. She gave a shout when she saw him. He felt his heart jump violently, and then beat rapidly, turning his face scarlet and reddening his ears. They shook hands and chatted and he told her what had transpired since he left the university. She told him where she lived, and gave him her telephone number. All this was the result of one chance meeting in the covered Arcade of Awqaf, in front of the shoemaker's shop at the corner.

In the days that followed the judge discovered, during the long moments that the two of them spent on the telephone, that he loved Samiyah. And as they conversed with each other, that discovery became more and more firmly rooted in his mind. And Samiyah? She told him that he had often attracted her attention. True, she had not been thinking of love, but if her heart had desired anyone at that time it would have been him. But however that might have been, she had never loved anyone since. Her marriage was a marriage of convenience; or, to put it differently, they were meant for each other, as people say.

Now what were they to do since discovering from one meeting and numerous telephone calls that they were in love—that each loved the other? She had become a wife with two small children, while he had remained single and had never thought about marriage, until now. If only he had summoned up enough courage to speak to her during their time at the university . . . if he had spoken they would have dated each other; if they had dated they would have become engaged; if they had become engaged they would have married. If . . . but what use was there in "if"?

He met her again. Talks over the telephone were followed by meetings—in the street, the park, and once in a car which one of his friends lent him. He took her for a tour around the city after dark. They had stopped at a certain spot on the road and looked down at Aleppo beneath them, and she gazed on the lights of the city gathered into clusters, or set out in strings like the beads of a rosary, all twinkling like stars on a moonlit night.

She said: "Look at the lights in the windows of the houses and the buildings. They belong to people just like us—but they are able to love each other in the light—you and I can only love in the darkness!"

Her hand had been in his as she said these words. He had drawn her toward him and wrapped his arm around her shoulders. Then he let it fall to her waist, and he kissed her for the first time.

And after that? After that he had paid her fleeting visits on many occasions during the day and she had given him coffee. After that she had called on him one evening, at the house of a bachelor friend which was in a quarter of Aleppo known as al-Sabil, on a dark back street. What an evening that had been! He still remembered its happiness—and its torment. Samiyah, a married woman who had two children by a husband with whom she still lived, even though she did not love him; and he, a judge, a supporter of the sword of justice, who must come down firmly on those who transgress the law, and stray from the path of morality . . .

She and he had come together that evening: two people who knew quite well what they should do and should not do, yet who had come together as lovers, alone in a small house all to themselves. In a corner of the room there had been a record player and some classical records, and in another a bar furnished with a variety of drinks. In another room was a cozy bed, on one side of which stood a bronze statuette. Below it they read the name of the sculpture: "Eternal Spring," by Rodin. It was of a naked girl and a youth. Their lips were united in a passionate kiss, while their bodies were suffused with eager desire. And here they were, the two of them, alone in that house after months and years of waiting and dreaming of a love that was forbidden . . .

From that evening onward the young judge had lived in both heaven and hell at the same time: the heaven of mutual love and the hell of illicit courtship. Ever since, wherever he was, he had been in a hurry to be on his way to Aleppo, to reach her before the master of the house returned, to pour out his passion; eager to arrange a meeting in the park, or on the street, or under the eye of "Eternal Spring." And here he was today traveling in this car with these fellow passengers for this very purpose. Was it a purpose? Here was this man's wife sitting behind him, eyeing him enticingly—yet she did nothing but remind him of Samiyah. It was true that she had attracted his attention just as that peasant girl had attracted the attention of the Bey, but what possible connection could he ever have with this traveling beauty with her husband sitting beside her? He did not know what the Bey had done with the peasant girl, but he knew that no woman could take Samiyah's place in his heart, or arouse his emotions as she did. Wherever his official post took him, wherever circumstances took him, he would return to the place where Samiyah was. He would travel the roads back and forth, just as that mad peasant girl traveled the roads in pursuit of . . . in pursuit of what?

He had better listen to the end of that story about the madwoman, from the lips of the talkative, portly husband . . .

4

After the car had passed the turn-off to Jubb al-Safa the husband re-sumed his story: "I told you that the girl Jamilah was attracted to the Bey's chauffeur; and the idea of marriage entered her head. And it was more firmly fixed there when the Bey returned with his car by the same road three or four days later, and found the girl in front of her uncle's house waiting for someone to take her back to her village. Who can say? She may have been waiting there all that time for the Bey's black car and his chauffeur Ishaq, with his fair hair. Anyway, the Bey recognized her and offered her a lift, inviting her to sit beside the chauffeur. On this occasion she was by herself, and the Bey started talking about marriage again. Like any modest girl, Jamilah made no answer. But imagine what might stir in the mind of a girl when the local squire talked about marrying her to a fair-haired, fresh-faced young man like Ishaq, who wore a smart suit and turned the driving wheel as though he had been born with it between his hands!

"Jamilah was dazzled by this talk, and replied with a blush and a flutter of her eyelashes. Ishaq smiled at his master's remarks, and at the naiveté of the girl sitting beside him, averting her glance at one moment and steal-ing a look at his face the next. Some say that Ishaq's smile was a smile of approval, not of mockery, and that he had told the Bey that he would have wished to marry Jamilah, were he not aware that the bridal money of girls in these villages was more than he could afford from his modest wages.

"They say that the Bey undertook to pay Jamilah's nuptial gift himself, and that he stopped the car and put the girl's hand in Ishaq's, and prom-ised that he would come around at 'Id al-Fitr and ask for her hand from Abu Abdullah. Some people say this, and that a good many other things happened in the Bey's car between the two villages that day.

"Perhaps the whole business was a joke for the Bey to amuse himself with while touring around his estates in that area. But what happened afterwards was not amusing: everybody has heard of the disaster which overtook the Bey's car on the road to Beirut, just outside Tripoli. There is a dangerous curve there which overlooks the sea as you approach the tunnel. The car skidded and toppled over the edge. Not a trace of the car or its owner or the chauffeur remained."

The wife exclaimed: "Oh my God! Did they fall into the sea?"

Her husband returned: "Yes, and they have never been recovered. The story of the accident was the main topic of conversation for a long time in those parts, and especially in the villages owned by the Bey, particularly in the village of Abu Abdullah, the father of the girl Jamilah. People were upset by this accident which had killed the Bey, and they said prayers for his soul, remembering his good qualities and disregarding his bad ones. He had been a rich man, with a knack for getting his own way; at times a warm-hearted man, at others a harsh man; but now he had passed on to a higher judgment, as everyone said, privately and publicly—except Jamilah.

"Jamilah would not believe that the Bey was dead, or that the car and her Ishaq who had been driving it had plunged into the sea on the Tripoli road and never been seen again. She believed that the Bey would not lie, in spite of all the disparaging things that the village people might say about him. He had promised her he would come and arrange the engagement with her father . . . therefore he must be coming, must be coming in his black car, sitting in the back seat, allowing her to sit beside Ishaq."

The wife broke in: "The poor soul! How could she believe a man!"

The judge, apparently finding an opportunity to address the wife directly, asked: "Don't you believe men then?"

The wife laughed briskly and prepared to argue with the youthful judge, but her husband cut her off, resuming the story: "A slow-witted peasant girl. In her eyes the Bey was a man who could not be defeated by anything, even death."

Here the fourth passenger cleared his throat, and the husband, guessing he was about to protest this description, forestalled him by elaborating on his portrayal: "The poor girl knew nothing of worldly affairs. She had little experience. The point is that she did not believe the Bey and his chauffeur were dead. Secretly she went on waiting for the car and the chauffeur and the Bey, at first at home and later in the street. She would tell her family that she intended to visit her mother's brothers in Jubb al-Safa, and if they suggested she should take a hire-car going along the main road in the direction of her uncles' village, she always refused, remaining in the road, whatever the weather. She would stand for hours and hours, and would only return home after the cajolings and sometimes threats of her family.

"Gradually the secret of Abu Abdullah's daughter Jamilah came out: she was waiting for the Bey's black car driven by the fair-haired Ishaq to drive her to her uncles' village and then bring her back again. Jamilah began after a time to walk along the main road, in the direction of Jubb al-Safa . . . she hailed every black car, coming or going, and if the car stopped she would peer at the people inside. Then she would trudge on her way. At first she would walk on only a little way, then some hundreds of meters, then for some kilometers, then the whole distance to Jubb al-Safa and back . . ."

The husband said no more, regaining his breath after his lengthy account. The fourth passenger spoke up: "She was a poor soul right enough!

But her family—what did they do about it? How could they allow their daughter to wander alone along lonely roads?"

With genuine concern the wife exclaimed: "How weak we women are! Who would have thought that a few words spoken in jest would have brought all this on the girl?"

The judge delivered his opinion: "She cannot have lost her reason simply because of the promise of marriage, a promise which had not been confirmed. The family should have conducted a closer investigation of what happened on the road between the girl on the one hand and the Bey and his chauffeur on the other."

The fourth passenger answered him: "You are quite right, your honor. God forbid that we should think the worst. But this matter was no trifling affair. People are tough. They do not lose their minds for trifles."

At this point the driver broke in: "The human mind is like hard crystal. It can scratch even steel, but it can be smashed by simply dropping it on the ground. Do you honestly think that the people you see all around are sound in their heads? There are an awful lot of unsuspected madmen in the streets. This girl's madness just happened to make her stand out from the rest . . ."

The fourth passenger assented: "Perfectly true, cousin[2]—but I tell you . . ."

5

The fourth passenger fell silent before he had finished his sentence. He had had it in mind to say something, but he was afraid it might slight the judge. He had intended to say something insulting about townsfolk in general, but the judge was one of them; so he said nothing. He had been on the verge of saying that the girl had not lost her reason because she was involved with a young man whom she had lost, since being crazed by love was unknown to country people. It was a sickness of young men and girls of the towns, with their weak minds and silly emotions. In the countryside and villages love may be the reason for murder, but never for madness . . .

The truth was that the fourth passenger, in saying this—if he had said it—would have had only one object in mind: to pick a quarrel with this town-dweller who was telling the story of the mad Jamilah. Had he been quite fair, he would have acknowledged that the Sultan of Love lends his ear to everyone, and extends his favor to countryfolk and townsfolk alike,

2. A form of address in Arabic implying intimacy or sympathy, without necessarily indicating any relationship.

bestowing sometimes happiness and sometimes misery, and in sundry places bringing men finally to madness.

But perhaps the truth was that the fourth passenger had reached an age and a condition in which he regarded the emotion which bound a youth to a maid as being too trifling to cause either to lose their reason.

If it were not for his having taken this car, which had forced on him this company and this conversation to which he had been unable to close his ears, listening to the babble of the townsman would have been the last thing he would have endured, for all the man's elegant tone. Nor would he have endured the laughter of his wife, a brazen hussy for all her beautiful features. This was because the thoughts of the fourth passenger were preoccupied with worries of his own; they did not have room for this babble, and this shamelessness . . .

Ever since this passenger had taken his seat in the car, he had been asking himself: would he be able to catch up with the man who, he had been told, knew the haunts of Mashhur al-Dalman? He had learned the man had been in Aleppo for some days, and that he frequented a stall at the entrance of Suq al-Zarb in the city market. He was known by the name of his place of work, and was a dealer in hides, ropes, and fencing materials. He bought these on behalf of Mashhur al-Dalman, who lived somewhere in the country between Najd and Jordan, or between Najd and Iraq, or somewhere in the Badiyat al-Sham. Thus there was nothing between the fourth passenger and finding Mashhur except an interview with this man; and then the worries of years, the fires of hatred, and the numerous long journeys would have an end.

The fourth passenger would not have recognized Mashhur al-Dalman even if he had seen him. He had only been a child when Mashhur al-Dalman had attacked his tribe; and that was the only thing that had saved him from the fate of all his elder tribesmen: death.

Now conditions had changed, and time had moved on. No one carries out armed raids on peaceful bedouin encampments any longer, or carries off sheep and camels, or slaughters innocent people wholesale. However, a chance dispute between two women had roused memories of the old days of lawless raiding, and had stirred up old emotions. One of these women was the wife of the fourth passenger. He had heard the other woman saying to his wife: "You keep telling us about your husband and his wealth. If you had a real man for a husband, he would not have spent all his time enlarging his herds and selling lard and wool, while the man who murdered his father and uncle and brother lived only a stone's throw away— Mashhur al-Dalman!"

But the truth was that Mashhur al-Dalman was not living a stone's throw away; he was nowhere to be found, and was in fact not in the country at all. But the rebuke had been uttered and the fourth passenger could no longer sleep at night. It had made his life, which had to this point been happy, intolerable. He had now become the eternal wanderer in search of vengeance; he had no fixed abode.

Where would this implacable avenger track down Mashhur al-Dalman? Everyone knew the usual encampments of Mashhur's tribe; but the passenger could not be satisfied with merely harming the tribe—he wanted Mashhur himself, and Mashhur had not been in this country for years. Lean years and seasons of drought would bring him to the borders of the irrigated lands on the plains of al-Jazirah and the Euphrates; at other times he would range across remote deserts as far as the Empty Quarter of Arabia. Mashhur had ceased to camp in this country ever since laws and regulations had been imposed upon it; it was now under the control of a police force and Desert Guards mounted on armored cars using wireless communications. This may have been partly due to fear of the consequences of deeds he had perpetrated in the past; but principally it was a result of the rebellious spirit of al-Dalman and his ilk, which shunned restraint and authority.

On one occasion the fourth passenger had heard that his enemy had settled in a certain locality in the wilderness, a featureless site on the desert frontier, where he smuggled prohibited goods, tobacco, weapons, drugs, tires, and sugar to and from Kuwait, Aqabah, Saudi Arabia, and Iraq.

It was reported to him that a trap was going to be set by government forces against one of the smuggling caravans which al-Dalman protected in person. Accordingly the fourth passenger accompanied the expedition and was involved in an armed clash in which he had shown himself more daring than the government troops. The caravan had stumbled into the ambush, and three of its men had been wounded, but al-Dalman had vanished after shooting two customs officers.

The fourth passenger had escaped unharmed from a shot which tore his clothes but failed to graze his body. He had almost been killed in his unfulfilled quest; and once more he resumed his chase down every path that might lead him to his prey. That had been but one occasion; there had been many others.

He would continue to gather news of Mashhur al-Dalman and pursue him, while the latter avoided his net like a drop of quicksilver. He was aware that al-Dalman had no fear of a fight, but the malefactor still evaded the avenger's wrath. How long would this evasion succeed? One day they would meet face to face, and in expectation of this encounter the fourth passenger imprinted the days with his steps, tracing and retracing.

Compared with this quest, of what importance could the madwoman's trudging back and forth on the highway be, in pursuit of her fatuous, imaginary aim?

"Fatuous, imaginary aim, what else?" said the fourth passenger to himself. As for *his* aim . . .

6

The fourth passenger was of the opinion that it was impossible for the village girl to have lost her reason merely on account of the chauffeur to whom the Bey had promised to marry her. The judge had agreed with his expression of doubt, or rather he had agreed with the judge. The husband, who had told the story, insisted on holding to his view of the matter. "She was only a simple girl, as I told you: she didn't have much experience or knowledge of the world . . . she was not very intelligent: clutched at a straw . . . I know women."

Having delivered himself of these sentiments he subsided. He certainly was acquainted with women, for he had six daughters, the eldest of whom was the same age as the wife beside him. He was still married to his first wife, but he had deserted her in despair of her ever bearing him a male child. Or was this merely an excuse for deserting the poor creature and running after a girl who, although he had made her his wife, was no older than his daughter?

Indeed, he was still chasing his wife, because she constantly slipped away from him. On one pretext or another she was forever going off visiting, or traveling, or sulking, or pretending to be ill. On this trip he was bringing her back from her sister's house. She had gone there on a week's visit, and the week had lengthened to almost a month. If he had not gone to fetch her in person her visit would certainly have been prolonged indefinitely.

When he got into the car at Aleppo to bring her back he kept asking himself what his wife had found at her sister's to make her so extend her visit. Her sister's husband was a minor civil servant in Raqqah. In his house were neither the space nor the gracious accommodations which she could enjoy in her own husband's house. He had denied her nothing; he had installed her in different quarters so that she would not be living with his first wife and their daughters; he had bought her new furniture when she had refused what she described as throw-aways from the old house; he had bought her the television set for which his daughters had long begged, and which he had long refused on the grounds that times were bad and he could not afford it.

In spite of all this, Nazmiyyah, this new wife of his, would not settle in this house which he had equipped with everything she could ever desire. Every time he returned from one of his trips he found her at her family's home in the Banqusa quarter, or with one of her married sisters in the eastern part of town; or he would not find her in Aleppo at all. Her family would tell him that she was paying a visit miles away—today it was Raqqah, a couple of months ago it was with her aunt in Hims.

When her people had told him that day that she was in Hims, and that her cousin, a driver employed by one of his rivals, had taken her there in his car, he lost his head in blind fury—the fury of jealousy. He had not forgotten that Nazmiyyah had been engaged to her cousin before he came along and snatched her away with his money to become his wife. How on earth could her family agree to let her accompany her cousin all the way to Hims, to stay with her aunt and the family of her former betrothed? How on earth could she go? That night he had almost lost his mind. However, he had found comfort by telling himself that her cousin was no more than a brother to her in view of her marriage to him. He was sure that Nazmiyyah was innocent of the behavior of which he had at first been suspicious. In spite of her flirtatious manner, her beckoning eyes and sly smile and the way she had of slowly cracking mastic with her teeth, she was still only a child no older than his eldest daughter. She would not behave as more mature women might behave when smitten by desire for a man. She was his wife . . . he was on intimate terms with her. He knew how shy and inexperienced and ignorant she was in these matters.

Nazmiyyah had returned with him from Hims on that occasion without protest. She had displayed no opposition to returning, and her husband's suspicions were thus banished all the more quickly. But she was soon slipping away again. She tired him out. If only a baby boy would arrive and relieve him of the need to chase after this girl, with her constant attempts to fly off. He wondered whether she would even settle when she had a baby. He wondered whether he would ever be able to rest from this tiresome business. It was as though he were a Jamilah, forever running toward a goal and returning every day empty-handed and frustrated, and then resuming the chase the following day.

He sighed as this passed through his mind, and then, emerging from his silence, he addressed the judge: "Yes, I know all about women . . . and I don't believe what a certain person once told me—someone else, not our fellow passenger here—the man who gave me the first account of the story."

His wife broke in: "What did a certain person tell you, Ahmad?"

In an exasperated tone, as though his brooding on her going off with her cousin had hardened him toward her, he snapped at her: "You be quiet. I am telling the story to the gentleman. No, I didn't believe this other fellow when he said that the peasant girl did not return to her village on the same day that the Bey and the chauffeur took her. At that time cars were rarities and communications were not very good. How could Jamilah's family know whether their daughter had left her uncles' place that day or the day before? That's what this chap said. May God judge between us if the girl did not return to the village—which is near Humaymah—a whole day after leaving Jubb al-Safa, and passed a whole night and part of the next day in the company of the Bey and his chauffeur Ishaq. Where might that have been? The Bey had a house on its own grounds in one of his villages, miles away from the main road. He used to go there with his foreign acquaintances and his actress friends, and there was a cottage for the chauffeur there as well. Did the girl spend the night in the house or the cottage? No one knows. This fellow said that the girl never spoke a word when she went back home. When the news spread three days later that the Bey's car had been lost in the sea near Tripoli with him and the chauffeur in it, she ran the whole way from Humaymah to Jubb al-Safa and spent the night at her uncles'. The next day she ran back the whole way from Jubb al-Safa to Humaymah. He said that the secret of her madness lies in what happened that night. Just imagine: a girl of seventeen, a great big house and a cottage, with a lady-killing lord and a strapping young man with blue eyes, of whose real character nobody knows a thing . . ."

7

After saying this, the husband fell silent again, and no one ventured to comment on the narrative of the "other" narrator. Although he had not gone into much detail about what had taken place, or about what the man thought had taken place, the manner of the husband's alluding to the conversation strongly suggested what in all probability *had* taken place.

The fourth passenger said to himself: "Confound these townspeople! If this business really happened then the whole thing is disgusting. If it didn't happen then the suggestiveness of these people is revolting. They've no shame and no fear of God!"

The judge's mind was agitated by the thought of the apparent violation of a gullible girl by two unscrupulous men whom she trusted. But his imagining an empty house with a girl all alone recalled an empty house with a woman all alone—a woman to whom he had given the key so that she could let herself in while she waited for him. The resemblance was uncomfortably close between this house and the other, between the girl and the woman, between the girl's circumstances and the woman's; but the youthful judge's thoughts evoked other connections whose nature he did not fully grasp. Then the agitation within him calmed down, and became a feeling of impatience which would not be stilled by feelings of guilt, nor deadened by a premonition of impending danger.

The young wife, Nazmiyyah, looked at her husband after he had finished retelling the "other man's" story, with wide eyes which had a strange look in them. Her husband said that he didn't believe the story, yet he obviously relished telling it. Here he was, casting suspicion on the Bey, but she was quite certain in her own mind that what had happened—if anything had happened—had nothing to do with the Bey. She imagined that it was something between Jamilah and Ishaq. Something between a strong, handsome young man and a beautiful girl. She turned away from her husband and threw her head back with her eyes closed. Normally she thought little, and had a dull imagination. But her husband's story had agitated a strange feeling, stirred up by the images which filled her mind. She thought that the madwoman was not Jamilah, the peasant girl, but herself, Nazmiyyah. It was she who was running along the road in vain, seeking something she had lost. Now she was able to recognize what she had lost, and until now had not been able to secure. It was her cousin, or her love for her cousin.

When he had accompanied her on that journey to Hims, the car had been empty but for her. He took no passengers with him, even though he had paid the car's owner the fares of five passengers out of his own pocket. During the early part of the journey, between Aleppo and Hims, the two of them had talked a great deal. They had talked innocuously about their childhood and about his brothers and sisters and their mothers, and she had talked about her husband. Then they both fell silent.

After they had passed through Ma'arrah they reached a winding road which wound around a small hurst, and he leaned against her as he turned the car to follow the road. When the road straightened out again she leaned against him, and he embraced her with such force that the car almost leaped across the shoulder at the edge of the roadway. She had not resisted the embrace, but had yielded to it, and as a result the journey took longer—but seemed to be over more quickly.

Now, traveling beside her husband, she thought of that day and that embrace. Did not Jamilah have every cause to lose her reason in her search for Ishaq? Here she was, Nazmiyyah, almost going out of her mind, almost going crazy in her desire for her cousin—even in just thinking about him. She was returning unsuccessfully to Aleppo like the mad Jamilah going back to Humaymah . . . going back to her husband! How could she share the bed of this corpulent man with his malodorous breath and heavy snoring? She had begun to hate men the first time she got into his bed: all men, when she felt him lay his hand on her and draw her toward him, naked, calling to her with shameless words and vile gestures.

But when her cousin had put his arm around her in the car as they raced along, and when he had stopped the car and touched her, running his hand over her breasts and thighs, and when her eager body had nestled against his sturdy form, she loved manhood and men and felt a great joy at being a woman, feminine . . .

Yes, she was crazy, like Jamilah, and would remain so.

The silence of the passengers in the car lengthened, until they were soon nearing Aleppo. The driver announced: "We're here. I expect you'll be going home or going on to your business engagements. I'll be going back again. I shall have a bit of a rest and then return by the same route—like Jamilah! I travel to and fro just like her, but my errand has less significance. She's looking for someone she loves that she's lost, but what am I looking for?"

The judge remarked drily: "You're earning your family's daily bread."

The driver sighed, and then in the tone of one whose patience is exhausted, replied: "Earning my family's daily bread or money to pay for my girlfriend at the pub, what's the difference? I beg your pardon, lady, for my manner of speaking. But whatever it is I'm looking for I come back empty-handed. Night and day I'm tearing around between one town and another after dirty bits of colored paper. And every time I think I've got my hands on them they just evaporate and slip away like water between my fingers. I'm more mad than she is, that Jamilah. Journeys, journeys, journeys, there and back again the whole time."

The judge replied: "If it's a question of journeying, we are all on a journey. All our life is taken up coming and going—the outbound journey and the homecoming."

The driver returned: "My dear Bey, when you travel you enjoy respect and prestige, and by traveling you expect to gain more respect and prestige. Soon I expect you will be made president of the court of cassation—then perhaps a minister. But the likes of me do nothing but run after illusions, like Jamilah. If I let my attention wander from the road for just a moment the same thing would happen to me as almost happened to her once, when I nearly ran her over."

The judge raised his eyes to the mirror, where they once more met the eyes of the young wife—she had roused herself from her dejected pose with her head on the headrest—but her eyes were wide open, with no trace of flirtatiousness. Perhaps, like him, she was absorbed in her thoughts.

He was pondering over the driver's delusions—his saying that he, the judge, traveled to increase his respect and prestige. What respect, what prestige? He was traveling to find Samiyah, to seek Samiyah's love. He had to roam streets in which hidden hazards lurked. If he stepped falsely, a disaster might overwhelm him and rob him of his position or even of his life. He might be killed by a bullet from a jealous husband; there might be a scandal, which would just as surely destroy his career; or on the other hand Samiyah's leaving him, or the withering of his love for her, might finish him off. Despite it all he was just like the driver, like Jamilah, continually running after something that was of the world of illusions . . . illusions based on the fantasies of the vanished past, or of vanished pleasures, which he fondly imagined could continue into the present, or last into the future . . .

The fourth passenger spoke: "Are we going to stop at the City Market near Suq al-Zarb?"

The driver laughed. "Surely you know Aleppo! Suq al-Zarb is right off our track. I've got to stop at the garage to book my arrival time. The City Market is not far to walk from there, especially if you're used to walking across deserts. Just imagine yourself like Jamilah, walking between Humaymah and Jubb al-Safa twice a day."

The fourth passenger was not amused by the driver's pleasantry. "What has that crazy woman got to do with it? God ordained she should be so. Who knows? Her fate may be easier than ours. We are all wayfarers on one road . . . people on the road to Jubb al-Safa, to al-Dayr, to Ma'arrah . . ."

At the mention of the road to Ma'arrah the young wife felt a longing that caused her to melt inwardly. If only that road, the road to Ma'arrah, had been blocked at that turn-off! If only her cousin had dragged her to that hut which was at the side of the road! Then she would have spent a night in the hut, like the night Jamilah spent with Ishaq, and her madness would have some precious, significant experience as its origin. Her present madness was spawned only from deprivation.

Her husband spoke up: "Before you get to the garage take us past the quarter around Baghdad Station—our house is not far off your route."

The driver replied: "As you please. We owe you something for your amusing story about the madwoman. It seems to me I'm just like her. As our friend here says, there are many mad people on the roads, but the roads vary."

The husband returned: "May God keep you in your right mind. I used to be a driver, the same as you—only a lorry driver, which is a good deal tougher. I traveled many routes, longer than yours. And have I gone mad? The man who has money, my dear chap, does not go mad, and if he does go crazy for money—well, the more crazy for money, the more sense he's got."

The driver laughed as the car plunged into the crowded streets of Aleppo, and, adroitly turning the wheel to avoid a fast-moving lorry, said: "Please yourself. I'll pray to the good Lord to increase your wealth—I mean to increase your madness."

All joined in the driver's laughter. Nazmiyyah laughed loudly and hysterically, but artificially and without amusement. The judge gave a short mirthless laugh. Even the fourth passenger cleared his throat loudly to mask a malicious guffaw. Then the laughter quickly died away into the din of the city and the heat of midday. The people in the streets jostled and pushed amid uproar and clamor, as though all of them were mad.

The Spider's Web

Leonard Kibera

I N S I D E T H E coffin, his body had become rigid. He tried to turn and only felt the prick of the nail. It had been hammered carelessly through the lid, just falling short of his shoulder. There was no pain but he felt irretrievable and alone, hemmed within the mean, stuffy box, knowing that outside was air. *As dust to dust* . . . the pious preacher intoned out there, not without an edge of triumph. *This suicide, brethren . . . !* They had no right, these people had no right at all. They sang so mournfully over him, almost as if it would disappoint them to see him come back. But he would jump out yet, he would send the rusty nails flying back at them and teach that cheap-jack of an undertaker how to convert old trunks. He was not a third-class citizen. *Let me out!* But he could not find the energy to cry out or even turn a little from the nail on his shoulder, as the people out there hastened to cash in another tune, for the padre might at any moment cry *Amen!* and commit the flesh deep into the belly of the earth whence it came. Somebody was weeping righteously in between the pauses. He thought it was Mrs. Njogu. Then in the dead silence that followed he was being posted into the hole and felt himself burning up already as his mean little trunk creaked at the joints and nudged its darkness in on him like a load of sins. *Careful, careful, he is not a heap of rubbish* . . . That was Mr. Njogu. Down, slowly down, the careless rope issues in snappy mean measures like a spider's web and knocked his little trunk against the sides to warn the loud gates that he was coming to whoever would receive him. It caved in slowly, the earth, he could feel, and for the first time he felt important. He seemed to matter now, as all eyes no doubt narrowed into the dark hole at this moment, with everybody hissing *poor soul; gently,*

gently. Then *snap!* The rope gave way—one portion of the dangling thing preferring to recoil into the tight-fisted hands out there—and he felt shot toward the bottom head-downward, exploding into the gates of hell with a loud, unceremonious *bang!*

Ngotho woke up with a jump. He mopped the sweat on the tail of his sheet. This kind of thing would bring him no good. Before, he had been dreaming of beer parties or women or fights with bees as he tried to smoke them out for honey. Now, lately, it seemed that when he wasn't being smoked out of this city where he so very much belonged and yet never belonged, he was either pleading his case at the White Gates or being condemned to hell in cheap coffins. *This kind of thing just isn't healthy . . .*

But he was in top form. He flung the blanket away. He bent his arms at the elbow for exercise. He shot them up and held them there like a surrender. *No that will not do.* He bent them again and pressed his fingers on his shoulders. They gathered strength, knitting into a ball so that his knuckles sharpened. Then he shot a dangerous fist to the left and held it there, tightly, not yielding a step, until he felt all stiff and blood pumped at his forehead. Dizziness overpowered him and his hand fell dead on the bed. Then a spasm uncoiled his right fist which came heavily on the wall and, pained, cowered. Was he still a stranger to the small dimensions of his only room even after eight years?

But it wasn't the first time anyhow. So, undaunted, he sprang twice on the bed for more exercise. Avoiding the spring that had fetched his thigh yesterday morning between the bulges in the old mattress, he hummed "Africa Nchi Yetu" and shot his leg down the bed. Swa———ah! That would be three shillings for another sheet through the back doors of the Koya Mosque, Ngotho dragged himself out of bed.

It was a beautiful Sunday morning. He had nothing to worry about so long as he did not make the mistake of going to church. Churches depressed him. But that dream still bothered him. (*At least they could have used a less precipitate rope.*) And those nails, didn't he have enough things pricking him since Mrs. Knight gave him a five-pound handshake saying "Meet you in England" and Mrs. Njogu came buzzing in as his new memsahib borrowing two shillings from him?

Ngotho folded his arms at his chest and yawned. He took his mustache thoughtfully between his fingers and curled it sharp like horns. At least she could have returned it. It was not as if the cost of living had risen the way employers took things for granted these days. He stood at the door of the two-room house which he shared with the other servant who, unlike him, didn't cook for memsahib. Instead, Kago went on errands, trimmed the grass and swept the compound, taking care to trace well the dog's mess for the night. Already Ngotho could see the early riser as good as sniffing and scanning the compound after the erratic manner of Wambui last night. (Wambui was the brown Alsatian dragged from the village and surprised into civilization, a dog collar and tinned bones by Mrs. Njogu. A friend of hers, Elsie Bloom, kept one and they took their bitches for a walk together.) Ngotho cleared his throat.

"Hey, Kago!"

Kago who was getting frostbite rubbed his thumb between the toes and turned round.

"How is the dog's breakfast?"

"Nyukwa!"

Ngotho laughed.

"You don't have to insult my mother," he said. "Tinned bones for Wambui and cornflakes for memsahib are the same thing. We both hang if we don't get them."

Kago leaned on his broom, scratched the top of his head dull-wittedly, and at last saw that Ngotho had a point there.

He was a good soul, Kago was, and subservient as a child. There was no doubt about his ready aggressiveness where men of his class were concerned it was true, but when it came to Mrs. Njogu he wound tail between his legs and stammered. This morning he was feeling at peace with the world.

"Perhaps you are right," he said, to Ngotho. Then diving his thumb between the toes he asked if there was a small thing going on that afternoon—like a beer party.

"The Queen!"

At the mention of the name, Kago forgot everything about drinking, swerved round and felt a thousand confused things beat into his head simultaneously. Should he go on sweeping and sniffing or should he get the Bob's Tinned? Should he untin the Bob's Tinned or should he run for the Sunday paper? Mrs. Njogu, alias queen, wasn't she more likely to want Wambui brushed behind the ear? Or was she now coming to ask him why the rope lay at the door while Wambui ran about untied?

With his bottom toward memsahib's door, Kago assumed a busy pose and peeped through his legs. But memsahib wasn't bothered about him. At least not yet. She stood at the door legs askew and admonished Ngotho about the cornflakes.

Kago breathed a sigh of relief and took a wild sweep at the broom. He saw Ngotho back against the wall of their servants' quarters and suppressed a laugh. After taking a torrent of English words, Ngotho seemed to tread carefully the fifty violent paces between the two doors, the irreconcilable gap between the classes. As he approached Mrs. Njogu, he seemed to sweep a tactful curve off the path, as if to move up the wall first and then try to back in slowly toward the master's door and hope memsahib would make way. For her part, the queen flapped her wings and spread herself luxuriously, as good as saying, You will have to kneel and dive in through my legs. Then she stuck out her tongue twice, heaved her breasts, spat milk and honey onto the path, and disappeared into the hive. Ngotho followed her.

Kago scratched his big toe and sat down to laugh.

Breakfast for memsahib was over. Ngotho came out of the house to cut out the painful corn in his toe with the kitchen knife. He could take the risk and it pleased him. But he had to move to the other end of the wall. Mr. Njogu was flushing the toilet and he might chance to open the small blurred window and see the otherwise clean kitchen knife glittering in the sun on dirty toe nails.

Breakfast. Couldn't memsahib trust him with the sugar or milk even after four years? Must she buzz around him as he measured breakfast for two? He had nothing against cornflakes. In fact ever since she became suspicious, he had found himself eating more of her meals whenever she was not in sight, also taking some sugar in his breast pocket. But he had come to hate himself for it and felt it was a coward's way out. Still, what was he to do? Mrs. Njogu had become more and more of a stranger and he had even caught himself looking at her from an angle where formerly he had stared her straight in the face. He had wanted to talk to her, to assure her that he was still her trusted servant, but everything had become more entangled and sensitive. She would only say he was criticizing, and if he wasn't happy what was he waiting for? But if he left, where was he to go? Unemployment had turned loose upon the country as it had never done before. Housewives around would receive the news of his impertinence blown high and wide over Mrs. Njogu's telephone before he approached them for a job, and set their dogs on him.

Ngotho scratched at his gray hair and knew that respect for age had completely bereft his people. Was this the girl he once knew as Lois back in his home village? She had even been friends with his own daughter. A shy, young thing with pimples and thin legs. Lois had taught at the village school and was everybody's good example. She preferred to wear cheap skirts than see her aging parents starve for lack of money.

"Be like Lois," mothers warned their daughters and even spanked them to press the point. What they meant in fact was that their daughters should, like Lois, stay unmarried longer and not simply run off with some young man in a neat tie who refused to pay the dowry. Matters soon became worse for such girls when suddenly Lois became heroine of the village. She went to jail.

It was a general knowledge class. Lois put the problem word squarely on the blackboard. The lady supervisor who went round the schools stood squarely at the other end, looking down the class. Lois swung her stick up and down the class and said,

"What is the commonwealth, children? Don't be shy, what does this word mean?"

The girls chewed their thumbs.

"Come on! All right. We shall start from the *beginning*. Who rules England?"

Slowly, the girls turned their heads round and faced the white supervisor. Elizabeth, they knew they should say. But how could Lois bring them to this? England sounded venerable enough. Must they go further now and let the white lady there at the back hear the queen of England mispronounced, or even uttered by these tender things with the stain of last night's onions in their breath? Who would be the first? They knit their knuckles under the desks, looked into their exercise books, and one by one said they didn't know. One or two brave ones threw their heads back again, met with a strange look in the white queen's eye which spelled disaster, immediately swung their eyes onto the blackboard, and catching sight of Lois's stick, began to cry.

"It is as if you have never heard of it." Lois was losing patience. "All right, I'll give you another start. Last start. What is our country?"

Simultaneously, a flash of hands shot up from under the desks and thirty-four breaths of maize and onions clamored.

"A colony!"

Slowly, the lady supervisor measured out light taps down the class and having eleminated the gap that came between master and servant, stood face to face with Lois.

The children chewed at their erasers.

Then the white queen slapped Lois across the mouth and started for the door. But Lois caught her by the hair, slapped her back once, twice, and spat into her face. Then she gave her a football kick and swept her out with a right.

When at last Lois looked back into the class, she only saw torn exercise books flung on the floor. Thirty-four pairs of legs had fled home through the window, partly to be comforted from the queen's government which was certain to come, and partly to spread the formidable news of their new queen and heroine.

Queen, she certainly was, Ngotho thought as he sat by the wall and backed against it. Cornflakes in bed; expensive skirts; cigarettes. Was this her? Mr. Njogu had come straight from the University College in time to secure a shining job occupied for years by a Mzungu. Then a neat car was seen to park by Lois's house. In due course these visits became more frequent and alarming, but no villager was surprised when eventually Njogu succeeded in dragging Lois away from decent society. He said paying the dowry was for people in the mountains.

As luck would have it for Ngotho, Mr. and Mrs. Knight left and Mr. and Mrs. Njogu came to occupy the house. He was glad to cook and wash a black man's towels for a change. And, for a short time at any rate, he was indeed happy. Everybody had sworn that they were going to build something together, something challenging and responsibile, something that would make a black man respectable in his own country. He had been willing to serve, to keep up the fire that had eventually smoked out the white man. From now on there would be no more revenge, and no more exploitation. Beyond this, he didn't expect much for himself; he knew that there would always be masters and servants.

Ngotho scratched himself between the legs and sunk against the wall. He stared at the spider that slowly built its web meticulously under the veranda roof. He threw a light stone at it and only alerted the spider.

Had his heart not throbbed with thousands of others that day as each time he closed his eyes he saw a vision of something exciting, a legacy of responsibilities that demanded a warrior's spirit? Had he not prayed for oneness deep from the heart? But it seemed to him now that a common goal had been lost sight of and he lamented it. He could not help but feel that the warriors had laid down their arrows and had parted different ways to fend for themselves. And as he thought of their households, he saw only the image of Lois whom he dared call nothing but memsahib now. She swam big and muscular in his mind.

Ngotho wondered whether this was the compound he used to know. Was this part connecting master and servant the one that had been so straight during Mrs. Knight?

Certainly he would never want her back. He had been kicked several times by Mr. Knight and had felt what it was like to be hit with a frying pan by Mrs. Knight as she reminded him to be grateful. But it had all been so direct, no ceremonies; they didn't like his broad nose. They said so. They thought there were rats under his bed. There were. They teased that he hated everything white and yet his hair was going white on his head like snow, a cool white protector while below the black animal simmered and plotted: Wouldn't he want it cut? No, he wouldn't. Occasionally, they would be impressed by a well-turned turkey or chicken and say so over talk of the white man's responsibility in Africa. If they were not in the mood they just dismissed him and told him not to forget the coffee. Ngotho knew that all this was because they were becoming uneasy and frightened, and that perhaps they had to point the gun at all black men now at a time when even the church had taken sides. But whatever the situation in the house, there was nevertheless a frankness about the black-and-white relationship where no ceremonies or apologies were necessary in a world of mutual distrust and hate. And if Mrs. Knight scolded him all over the house, it was Mr. Knight who eventually seemed to lock the bedroom door and come heavily on top of her and everybody else although, Ngotho thought, they were all ruled by a woman in England.

Ngotho walked heavily to the young tree planted three years ago by Mrs. Njogu and wondered why he should have swept a curve off the path that morning, as memsahib filled the door. He knew it wasn't the first time he had done that. Everything had become crooked, subtle, and he had to watch his step. His monthly vernacular paper said so. He felt cornered. He gripped the young tree by the scruff of the neck and shook it furiously. What the hell was wrong with some men anyway? Had Mr. Njogu become a male weakling in a fat queen bee's hive, slowly being milked dry and sapless, dying? Where was the old warrior who at the end of the battle would go home to his wife and make her moan under his heavy sweat? All he could see now as he shook the tree was a line of neat houses. There, the warriors had come to their battle's end and parted, to forget other warriors and to be mothered to sleep without even known it, meeting only occasionally to drink beer and sing traditional songs. And where previously the bow and arrow lay by the bedpost, Ngotho now only saw a conspiracy of round tablets while a *Handbook of Novel Techniques* lay by the pillow.

He had tried to understand. But as he looked at their pregnant wives he could foresee nothing but a new generation of innocent snobs, who would be chauffeured off to school in neat caps hooded over their eyes so as to obstruct vision. There they would learn that the other side of the city was dirty. Ngotho spat right under the tree. Once or twice he would have liked to kick Mr. Njogu. He looked all so sensibly handsome and clean as he buzzed after his wife on a broken wing and—a spot of jam on his tie—said he wanted the key to the car.

He had also become very sensitive and self-conscious. Ngotho couldn't complain a little or even make a joke about the taxes without somebody detecting a subtler intention behind the smile, where the servant was supposed to be on a full-scale plotting. And there was behind the master and the queen now a bigger design, a kind of pattern meticulously fenced above the hive; a subtle web, at the center of which lurked the spider which protected, watched and jailed. Ngotho knew only too well that the web had been slowly, quietly in the making and a pebble thrown at it would at best alert and fall back impotent on the ground.

He took a look at the other end of the compound. Kago had fallen asleep, while Wambui ran about untied, the rope still lying at the door.

Kago wore an indifferent grin. Ngotho felt overpowered, trapped, alone. He spat in Kago's direction and plucked a twig off one of the branches on the tree. The tree began to bleed. He tightened his grip and shed the reluctant leaves down. Just what had gone wrong with God?

The old one had faithfully done his job when the fig tree near Ngotho's village withered away as predicted by the tribal seer. It had been the local news and lately, it was rumored, some businessman would honor the old god by erecting a hotel on the spot. Ngotho hardly believed in any god at all. The one lived in corrupted blood, the other in pulpits of hypocrisy. But at least while they kept neat themselves they could have honored the old in a cleaner way. How could this new savior part the warriors different ways into isolated compartments, to flush their uneasy hotel toilets all over the old one?

Ngotho passed a reverent hand over his wrinkled forehead and up his white hair. He plucked another twig off the dangerous tree. Something was droning above his ear.

"What are you doing to my tree?"

The buzzing had turned into a scream.

"I——I want to pick my teeth." Ngotho unwrapped a row of defiant molars.

The queen flapped her wings and landed squarely on the ground. Then she was heaving heavily, staring at him out of small eyes. He tried to back away from her eyes. Beyond her, in the background, he caught sight of Mr. Njogu through the bedroom window polishing his spectacles on his pajama sleeve, trying desperately to focus—clearly—on the situation outside. A flap of the wind and Ngotho felt hit right across the mouth, by the hand that had once hit the white lady. Then the queen wobbled in midflight, settled at the door, and screamed at Mr. Njogu to come out and prove he was a man.

Mr. Njogu didn't like what he saw. He threw his glasses away and preferred to see things blurred.

"These women," he muttered, and waved them away with a neat pajama sleeve. Then he buried his head under the blanket and snored. It was ten o'clock.

Ngotho stood paralyzed. He had never been hit by a woman before, outside of his mother's hut. Involuntarily, he felt his eyes snap shut and his eyelids burn red, violently, in the sun. Then out of the spider's web in his mind, policemen, magistrates and the third class undertakers flew in profusion. He opened up, sweating, and the kitchen knife in his hand fell down, stabbing the base of the tree where it vibrated once, twice, and fell flat on its side, dead.

Then with a cry, he grabbed it and rushed into the house. But Mr. Njogu saw him coming as the knife glittered nearer and clearer in his direction, and leapt out of bed.

Suddenly the horror of what he had done caught Ngotho. He could hear the queen at least crying hysterically into the telephone, while Mr. Njogu locked himself in the toilet and began weeping. Ngotho looked at the kitchen knife in his hand. He had only succeeded in stabbing Mr. Njogu in the thigh, and the knife had now turned red on him. Soon the sticky web would stretch a thread. And he would be caught as he never thought he would when first he felt glad to work for Lois.

He saw Wambui's rope still lying in a noose. Then he went into his room and locked the door.

The Smallest Woman in the World

Clarice Lispector

I N T H E depths of Equatorial Africa the French explorer, Marcel Pretre, hunter and man of the world, came across a tribe of surprisingly small pygmies. Therefore he was even more surprised when he was informed that a still smaller people existed, beyond forests and distances. So he plunged farther on.

In the Eastern Congo, near Lake Kivu, he really did discover the smallest pygmies in the world. And—like a box within a box within a box— obedient, perhaps, to the necessity nature sometimes feels of outdoing herself—among the smallest pygmies in the world there was the smallest of the smallest pygmies in the world.

Among mosquitoes and lukewarm trees, among leaves of the most rich and lazy green, Marcel Pretre found himself facing a woman seventeen and three-quarter inches high, full-grown, black, silent—"Black as a monkey," he informed the press—who lived in a treetop with her little spouse. In the tepid miasma of the jungle, that swells the fruits so early and gives them an almost intolerable sweetness, she was pregnant.

So there she stood, the smallest woman in the world. For an instant, in the buzzing heat, it seemed as if the Frenchman had unexpectedly reached his final destination. Probably only because he was not insane, his soul neither wavered nor broke its bounds. Feeling an immediate necessity for order and for giving names to what exists, he called her Little Flower. And in order to be able to classify her among the recognizable realities, he immediately began to collect facts about her.

Her race will soon be exterminated. Few examples are left of this species, which, if it were not for the sly dangers of Africa, might have multiplied. Besides disease, the deadly effluvium of the water, insufficient food, and ranging beasts, the great threat to the Likoualas are the savage Bahundes, a threat that surrounds them in the silent air, like the dawn of battle. The Bahundes hunt them with nets, like monkeys. And eat them. Like that: they catch them in nets and *eat* them. The tiny race, retreating, always retreating, has finished hiding away in the heart of Africa, where the lucky explorer discovered it. For strategic defense, they live in the highest trees. The women descend to grind and cook corn and to gather greens; the men, to hunt. When a child is born, it is left free almost immediately. It is true that, what with the beasts, the child frequently cannot enjoy this freedom for very long. But then it is true that it cannot be lamented that for such a short life there had been any long, hard work. And even the language that the child learns is short and simple, merely the essentials. The Likoualas use few names; they name things by gestures and animal noises. As for things of the spirit, they have a drum. While they dance to the sound of the drum, a little male stands guard against the Bahundes, who come from no one knows where.

That was the way, then, that the explorer discovered, standing at his very feet, the smallest existing human thing. His heart beat, because no emerald in the world is so rare. The teachings of the wise men of India are not so rare. The richest man in the world has never set eyes on such strange grace. Right there was a woman that the greed of the most exquisite dream could never have imagined. It was then that the explorer said timidly, and with a delicacy of feeling of which his wife would never have thought him capable: "You are Little Flower."

At that moment, Little Flower scratched herself where no one scratches. The explorer—as if he were receiving the highest prize for chastity to which an idealistic man dares aspire—the explorer, experienced as he was, looked the other way.

A photograph of Little Flower was published in the colored supplement of the Sunday papers, life-size. She was wrapped in a cloth, her belly already very big. The flat nose, the black face, the splay feet. She looked like a dog.

On that Sunday, in an apartment, a woman seeing the picture of Little Flower in the paper didn't want to look a second time because "It gives me the creeps."

In another apartment, a lady felt such perverse tenderness for the smallest of the African women that—an ounce of prevention being worth a pound of cure—Little Flower could never be left alone to the tenderness of that lady. Who knows to what murkiness of love tenderness can lead? The woman was upset all day, almost as if she were missing something. Besides, it was spring and there was a dangerous leniency in the air.

In another house, a little girl of five, seeing the picture and hearing the comments, was extremely surprised. In a houseful of adults, this little girl had been the smallest human being up until now. And, if this was the source of all caresses, it was also the source of the first fear of the tyranny of love. The existence of Little Flower made the little girl feel—with a deep uneasiness that only years and years later, and for very different reasons, would turn into thought—made her feel, in her first wisdom, that "sorrow is endless."

In another house, in the consecration of spring, a girl about to be married felt an ecstasy of pity: "Mama, look at her little picture, poor little thing! Just look how sad she is!"

"But," said the mother, hard and defeated and proud, "it's the sadness of an animal. It isn't human sadness."

"Oh. Mama!" said the girl, discouraged.

In another house, a clever little boy had a clever idea: "Mummy, if I could put this little woman from Africa in little Paul's bed when he's asleep? When he woke up wouldn't he be frightened? Wouldn't he howl? When he saw her sitting on his bed? And then we'd play with her! She would be our toy!"

His mother was setting her hair in front of the bathroom mirror at the moment, and she remembered what a cook had told her about life in an orphanage. The orphans had no dolls, and, with terrible maternity already throbbing in their hearts, the little girls had hidden the death of one of the children from the nun. They kept the body in a cupboard and when the nun went out they played with the dead child, giving her baths and things to eat, punishing her only to be able to kiss and console her. In the bathroom, the mother remembered this, and let fall her thoughtful hands, full of curlers. She considered the cruel necessity of loving. And she considered the malignity of our desire for happiness. She considered how ferociously we need to play. How many times we will kill for love. Then she looked at her clever child as if she were looking at a dangerous stranger. And she had a horror of her own soul that, more than her body, had engendered that being, adept at life and happiness. She looked at him attentively and with uncomfortable pride, that child who had already lost two front teeth, evolution evolving itself, teeth falling out to give place to those that could bite better. "I'm going to buy him a new suit," she decided, looking at him, absorbed. Obstinately, she adorned her gap-toothed son with fine clothes; obstinately, she wanted him very clean, as if his cleanliness could emphasize a soothing superficiality, obstinately perfecting the polite side of beauty. Obstinately drawing away from, and drawing him away from, something that ought to be "black as a monkey." Then, looking in the bathroom mirror, the mother gave a deliberately refined and social smile, placing a distance of insuperable millenniums between the abstract lines of her features and the crude face of Little Flower. But, with years of practice, she knew that this was going to be a Sunday on which she would have to hide from herself anxiety, dreams, and lost millenniums.

In another house, they gave themselves up to the enthralling task of measuring the seventeen and three-quarter inches of Little Flower against the wall. And, really, it was a delightful surprise: she was even smaller than the sharpest imagination could have pictured. In the heart of each member of the family was born, nostalgic, the desire to have that tiny and indomitable thing for itself, that thing spared having been eaten, that permanent source of charity. The avid family soul wanted to devote itself. To tell the truth, who hasn't wanted to own a human being just for himself? Which, it is true, wouldn't always be convenient; there are times when one doesn't want to have feelings.

"I bet if she lived here it would end in a fight," said the father, sitting in the armchair and definitely turning the page of the newspaper. "In this house everything ends in a fight."

"Oh, you, José—always a pessimist," said the mother.

"But, Mama, have you thought of the size her baby's going to be?" said the oldest little girl, aged thirteen, eagerly.

The father stirred uneasily behind his paper.

"It should be the smallest black baby in the world," the mother answered, melting with pleasure. "Imagine her serving our table, with her big little belly!"

"That's enough!" growled father.

"But you have to admit," said the mother, unexpectedly offended, "that it is something very rare. You're the insensitive one."

And the rare thing itself?

In the meanwhile, in Africa, the rare thing herself, in her heart—and who knows if the heart wasn't black, too, since once nature has erred she can no longer be trusted—the rare thing herself had something even rarer in her heart, like the secret of her own secret: a minimal child. Methodically, the explorer studied the little belly of the smallest mature human being. It was at this moment that the explorer, for the first time since he had known her, instead of feeling curiosity, or exhaltation, or victory, or the scientific spirit, felt sick.

The smallest woman in the world was laughing.

She was laughing, warm, warm—Little Flower was enjoying life. The rare thing herself was experiencing the ineffable sensation of not having been eaten yet. Not having been eaten yet was something that at any other time would have given her the agile impulse to jump from branch to branch. But, in this moment of tranquility, amid the thick leaves of the Eastern Congo, she was not putting this impulse into action—it was entirely concentrated in the smallness of the rare thing itself. So she was laughing. It was a laugh such as only one who does not speak laughs. It was a laugh that the explorer, constrained, couldn't classify. And she kept on enjoying her own soft laugh, she who wasn't being devoured. Not to be devoured is the most perfect feeling. Not to be devoured is the secret goal of a whole life. While she was not being eaten, her bestial laughter was as delicate as joy is delicate. The explorer was baffled.

In the second place, if the rare thing herself was laughing, it was because, within her smallness, a great darkness had begun to move.

The rare thing herself felt in her breast a warmth that might be called love. She loved that sallow explorer. If she could have talked and had told him that she loved him, he would have been puffed up with vanity. Vanity that would have collapsed when she added that she also loved the explorer's ring very much, and the explorer's boots. And when that collapse had taken place, Little Flower would not have understood why. Because her love for the explorer—one might even say "profound love," since, having no other resources, she was reduced to profundity—her profound love for the explorer would not have been at all diminished by the fact that she also loved his boots. There is an old misunderstanding about the word love, and, if many children are born from this misunderstanding, many others have lost the unique chance of being born, only because of a susceptibility that demands that it be me! me! that is loved, and not my money. But in the humidity of the forest these cruel refinements do not exist, and love is not to be eaten, love is to find a boot pretty, love is to like the strange color of a man who isn't black, love is to laugh for love of a shiny ring. Little Flower blinked with love, and laughed warmly, small, gravid, warm.

The explorer tried to smile back, without knowing exactly to what abyss his smile responded, and then he was embarrassed as only a very big man can be embarrassed. He pretended to adjust his explorer's hat better; he colored, prudishly. He turned a lovely color, a greenish-pink, like a lime at sunrise. He was undoubtedly sour.

Perhaps adjusting the symbolic helmet helped the explorer to get control of himself, severely recapture the discipline of his work, and go on with his note-taking. He had learned how to understand some of the tribe's few articulate words, and to interpret their signs. By now, he could ask questions.

Little Flower answered, "Yes." That it was very nice to have a tree of her own to live in. Because—she didn't say this but her eyes became so dark that they said it—because it is good to own, good to own, good to own. The explorer winked several times.

Marcel Pretre had some difficult moments with himself. But at least he kept busy taking notes. Those who didn't take notes had to manage as best they could:

"Well," suddenly declared one old lady, folding up the newspaper decisively, "well, as I always say: God knows what He's doing."

Translated by Elizabeth Bishop

CONFLICTING WORLDS

In *The Collector of Treasures and Other Botswana Village Tales*, **BESSIE HEAD** (see biographical note in Part IV) worked many variations on the theme of traditional village customs and religious practices conflicting with Christian missionary culture. "Heaven Is Not Closed" is one of these. Khama III or Khama the Great, Botswana's leader during the time it was set up as a British Protectorate (1895) and unified as Bechuanaland, did a great deal to preserve his people's land ownership, but he also allowed the Protectorate to be religiously ruled by Christian missionaries. Bessie Head felt that this policy resulted in the "complete breakdown of family life," [1] and, as this story shows, it meant that old customs were so nearly forgotten that Galethebege's grandchildren had no idea she had ever been anything but a Christian.

The Vietnamese priest **THICH NHAT HANH** became known in America when he was chairman of the Vietnamese Buddhist Peace delegation during the Vietnam War, for which Martin Luther King, Jr., nominated him for the Nobel Peace Prize. He has lived much of his life in exile in France, working with refugees and writing many volumes about Vietnam and about Buddhism. His short stories are available in English through White Pine Press, this one in a collection entitled *The Pine Gate* (1987). The two worlds in conflict in this story are the one of Buddhist enlightenment—the mountaintop monastery—and the material world below where pain and evil flourish and where self-knowledge is unknown.

Spiritual and material realms conflict in **XAVIER HERBERT**'s "Kaijek the Songman," as well, but very differently. Herbert, who was born in 1901 in western Australia, worked for a time as superintendent of the aborigines in the city of Darwin, and on the basis of his experience produced a novel, *Capricornia* (1938), focused on the aborigines. Later, he returned to the people in his autobiography

---

1. Bessie Head, *Serowe: Village of the Rain Wind* (London: Heinemann, 1981), p. xv.

and in a collection of stories, *Larger than Life* (1963), where the often anthologized "Kaijek" first appeared. The story is an allegory for the difficulties faced by a people whose nonmaterialistic, nomadic culture—represented in the story by Kaijek's song and the celebration he is preparing it for—must literally feed off the crass pioneer capitalist world of the gold prospector and his drug, tobacco. The white Australian prospector displays the usual racism of his kind toward the black Kaijek and his wife, until they show him a gold nugget they have found—then they become golden "tools." They do triumph over the white man, and Kaijek does complete his song, but the story conveys the precariousness of the aborigine life, a precariousness that continues even though preservation of aboriginal culture has become an official Australian policy.

Heaven Is Not Closed

Bessie Head

A L L H E R life Galethebege earnestly believed that her whole heart ought to be devoted to God, although one catastrophe after another occurred to deflect her from this path. It was only in the last five years of her life, after her husband, Ralokae, had died, that she was able to devote her whole mind to her calling. Then, all her pent-up and suppressed love for God burst forth and she talked only of Him, day and night—so her grandchildren, solemnly and with deep awe, informed the mourners at her funeral. All the mourners present at her hour of passing were utterly convinced that they had watched a profound and holy event. They talked about it for days afterwards.

Galethebege was well over ninety when she died and not at all afflicted by crippling ailments like most of the aged. In fact, only two days before her death had she complained to her grandchildren of a sudden fever and a lameness in her legs, and she had remained in bed. A quiet, thoughtful mood fell upon her. On the morning of the second day she had abruptly demanded that all the relatives be summoned.

"My hour has come," she said, with lofty dignity.

No one quite believed it, because that whole morning she had sat bolt upright in bed and talked to all who had gathered, about God—whom she loved with her whole heart. Then, exactly at noon, she announced once more that her hour had indeed come and lay down peacefully like one about to take a short nap. Her last words were:

"I shall rest now because I believe in God."

Then, a terrible silence filled the hut and seemed to paralyse the mourners for they all remained immobile for some time; each person present cried quietly because not one of them had ever witnessed such a magnificent death before. They only stirred when the old man, Modise, suddenly observed, with great practicality that Galethebege was not in the correct position for death. She lay on her side with her right arm thrust out above her head. She ought to be turned over on her back, with her hands crossed over her chest, he said. A smile flickered over the old man's face as he said this, as though it was just like Galethebege to make such a miscalculation. Why, she knew the hour of her death and everything, then at the last minute forgot the correct sleeping posture for the coffin. Later that evening, as he sat with his children near the outdoor fire for the evening meal, a smile again flickered over his face.

"I am of a mind to think that Galethebege was praying for forgiveness for her sins this morning," he said slowly. "It must have been a sin to her to marry Ralokae. He was an unbeliever to the day of his death . . ."

A gust of astonished laughter shook his family out of the solemn mood of mourning that had fallen upon them and they all turned eagerly towards their grandfather, sensing that he had a story to tell.

"As you all know," the old man said wisely, "Ralokae was my brother. But none of you present knows the story of Galethebege's life, but I know it . . ."

As the flickering firelight lit up their faces, he told the following story: "I was never like Ralokae, an unbeliever. But that man, my brother, draws out my heart. He liked to say that we as a tribe would fall into great difficulties if we forget our own customs and laws. Today, his words seem true. There is thieving and adultery going on such as was not possible under Setswana law."

In the days when they were young, said the old man, Modise, it had become the fashion for all black people to embrace the Gospel. For some, it was the mark of whether they were "civilised" or not. For some, like Galethebege, it was their whole life. Anyone with eyes to see would have known that Galethebege had been born good; under any custom, whether Setswana custom or Christian custom, she would still have been good. It was this natural goodness of heart that made her so eagerly pursue the word of the Gospel. There was a look on her face, absent, abstracted, as though she needed to share the final secret of life with God who could understand all things. So she was always on her way to church, and in her hours of leisure at home she could be found with her head buried in the Bible. And so her life would have gone on in this quiet and worshipful way, had not a sudden catastrophe occurred in the yard of Ralokae.

Ralokae had been married for nearly a year when his young wife died in childbirth. She died when the crops of the season were being harvested, and for a year Ralokae imposed on himself the traditional restraints and disciplines of boswagadi or mourning for the deceased. A year later, again at the harvest time, he underwent the cleansing ceremony demanded by custom and could once more resume the normal life of a man. It was the unexpectedness of the tragic event and the discipline it imposed on him, that made Ralokae take note of the life of Galethebege. She lived just three yards away from his own yard, and formerly he had barely taken note of her existence; it was too quiet and orderly. But during the year of mourning, it delighted him to hear that gentle and earnest voice of Galethebege informing him that such tragedies "were the will of God." As soon as he could, he began courting her. He was young and impatient to be married again and no one could bring back the dead. So a few days after the cleansing ceremony, he made his intentions very clear to her.

"Let us two get together," he said. "I am pleased by all your ways."

Galethebege was all at the same time startled, pleased, and hesitant. She was hesitant because it was well known that Ralokae was an unbeliever; he had not once set foot in church. So she looked at him, begging an apology, and mentioned the matter which was foremost in her mind.

"Ralokae" she said, uncertainly. "I have set God always before me," implying by that statement that perhaps he too was seeking a Christian life, like her own. But he only looked at her in a strange way, and said nothing. This matter was to stand like a fearful sword between them but he had set his mind on winning Galethebege as his wife. That was all he was certain of. He turned up in her yard day after day.

"Hullo girlfriend," he would greet her, enchantingly.

He always wore a black beret perched at a jaunty angle on his head. His walk and manner were gay and jaunty too. He was so exciting as a man that he threw her whole life into turmoil. It was the first time love had come her way and it made the blood pound fiercely through her whole body till she could feel its very throbbing at the tips of her fingers. It turned her thoughts from God a bit, to this new magic life was offering her. The day she agreed to be his wife, that sword quivered like a fearful thing between them. Ralokae said very quietly and firmly: "I took my first wife according to the old customs. I am going to take my second wife according to the old customs too."

He could see the protest on her face. She wanted to be married in church according to Christian custom. However, he had his own protest

to make. The God might be all right, he explained, but there was something wrong with the people who had brought the word of the Gospel to
the land. Their love was enslaving black people and he could not stand it.
That was why he was without belief. It was the people he did not trust.
They were full of tricks. They were a people who, at the sight of a black
man, pointed a finger in the air, looked away into the distance and said
impatiently: "Boy! Will you carry this! Boy! Will you fetch this!" They
had brought a new order of things into the land and they made the people
cry for love. One never had to cry for love in the customary way of life.
Respect was just there for people all the time. That was why he rejected
all things foreign.

What could a woman do with a man like that who knew his own mind?
She either loved him or she was mad. From that day on, Galethebege knew
what she would do. She would do all that Ralokae commanded as a good
wife should. But her former life was like a drug. Her footsteps were too
accustomed to wearing down the footpath to the church, and there they
carried her to the missionary's house which stood just under the shadow
of the church.

The missionary was a short, anonymous-looking man who wore glasses.
He had been the resident missionary for some time, and like all his fellows he did not particularly like the people. He always complained to his
own kind that they were terrible beggars and rather stupid. So when he
opened the door and saw Galethebege there his expression, with its raised
eyebrows said: "Well, what do you want now?"

"I am to be married, sir," Galethebege said politely, after the exchange
of greetings.

The missionary smiled: "Well come in my dear. Let us talk about the
arrangements," he said pleasantly.

He stared at her with polite, professional interest. She was a complete
nonentity, a part of the vague black blur which was his congregation—oh,
they noticed chiefs and people like that, but not the silent mass of humble
and lowly who had an almost weird capacity to creep quietly through life.
Her next words brought her sharply into focus.

"The man I am to marry, sir, does not wish to be married in the Christian way. He will only marry under Setswana custom," she said softly.

They always knew the superficial stories about "heathen customs" and
an expression of disgust crept into his face—sexual malpractices were
associated with the traditional marriage ceremony (and shudder!), they
draped the stinking intestinal bag of the ox around their necks.

"That we cannot allow!" he said sharply. "Tell him to come and marry
in the Christian way."

Galethebege started trembling all over. She looked at the missionary in alarm. Ralokae would never agree to this. Her intention in approaching the missionary was to acquire his blessing for the marriage, as though a compromise of tenderness could be made between two traditions opposed to each other. She trembled because it was beyond her station in life to be involved in controversy and protest. The missionary noted the trembling and alarm and his tone softened a bit, but his next words were devastating.

"My dear," he said persuasively, "heaven is closed to the unbeliever . . ."

Galethebege stumbled home on shaking legs. It never occurred to her to question such a miserable religion which terrified people with the fate of eternal damnation in hell-fire if they were "heathens" or sinners. Only Ralokae seemed quite unperturbed by the fate that awaited him. He smiled when Galethebege relayed the words of the missionary to him.

"Girlfriend," he said, carelessly, "you can choose what you like, Setswana custom or Christian custom. I have chosen to live my life by Setswana custom."

Not once in her life had Galethebege's integrity been called into question. She wanted to make the point clear.

"What you mean, Ralokae," she said firmly, "is that I must choose you over my life with the church. I have a great love in my heart for you so I choose you. I shall tell the priest about this matter because his command is that I marry in church."

Even Galethebege was astounded by the harshness of the missionary's attitude. The catastrophe she did not anticipate, was that he abruptly excommunicated her from the Church. She could no longer enter the village church if she married under Setswana custom. It was beyond her to reason that the missionary was the representative of both God and something evil, the mark of "civilisation." It was unthinkable that an illiterate and ignorant man could display such contempt for the missionary's civilisation. His rage and hatred were directed at Ralokae, and the only way in which he could inflict punishment was to banish Galethebege from the Church. If it hurt anyone at all, it was only Galethebege. The austere rituals of the Church, the mass, the sermons, the intimate communication in prayer with God—all this had thrilled her heart deeply. But Ralokae also was representative of an ancient stream of holiness that people had lived with before any white man had set foot in the land, and it only needed a small protest to stir up loyalty for the old customs.

The old man, Modise, paused at this point in the telling of his tale but his young listeners remained breathless and silent, eager for the conclusion.

"Today," he continued, "it is not a matter of debate because the young care neither way about religion. But in that day, the expulsion of Galethebege from the Church was a matter of debate. It made the people of our village ward think. There was great indignation because both Galethebege and Ralokae were much respected in the community. People then wanted to know how it was that Ralokae, who was an unbeliever, could have heaven closed to him? A number of people, including all the relatives who officiated at the wedding ceremony, then decided that if heaven was closed to Galethebege and Ralokae it might as well be closed to them too, so they all no longer attended church. On the day of their wedding, we had all our own things. Everyone knows the extent to which the cow was a part of the people's life and customs. We took our clothes from the cow and our food from the cow and it was the symbol of our wealth. So the cow was a holy thing in our lives. The elders then cut the intestinal bag of the cow in two and one portion was placed around the neck of Galethebege and one portion around the neck of Ralokae to indicate the wealth and good luck they would find together in married life. Then the porridge and meat were dished up in our mogopo bowls which we had used from old times. There was much capering and ululating that day because Ralokae had honoured the old customs . . ."

A tender smile once more flickered over the old man's face.

"Galethebege could never forsake the custom in which she had been brought up. All through her married life she would find a corner in which to pray. Sometimes Ralokae would find her so and ask: 'What are you doing, Mother?' And she would reply: 'I am praying to God.' Ralokae would only smile. He did not even know how to pray to the Christian God."

The old man leaned forward and stirred the dying fire with a partially burnt-out log of wood. His listeners sighed the way people do when they have heard a particularly good story. As they stared at the fire they found themselves debating the matter in their minds, as their elders had done some forty or fifty years ago. Was heaven really closed to the unbeliever, Ralokae? Or had Christian custom been so intolerant of Setswana custom that it could not hear the holiness of Setswana custom? Wasn't there a place in heaven too for Setswana custom? Then the gust of astonished laughter shook them again. Galethebege had been very well-known in the village ward over the past five years for the supreme authority with which she had talked about God. Perhaps her simple and good heart had been terrified that the doors of heaven were indeed closed on Ralokae and she had been trying to open them.

The Pine Gate

Thich Nhat Hanh

I T W A S a cool, almost chilly, autumn evening, and the moon had just risen, when the young swordsman arrived at the foot of the mountain. The wilderness was bathed in the light of the full moon glimmering playfully on branches and leaves. It seemed to him that during the seven years he was away, nothing in the surroundings had changed. Nothing had changed, and yet nothing seemed to be greeting him with any warmth—he who had once lived there for years, and who was now returning from afar.

The swordsman paused at the foot of the mountain and looked up. Above him, the narrow path was barred by a pine gate which was tightly shut. He pushed at the gate's sturdy doors, but these remained immovable under his powerful hands.

He was puzzled. Never, as far back as he could remember, had his Master had the gate closed and locked like this. Since this was the only way up the mountain, he had no choice. Slapping the handle of his sword, he rose swiftly from the ground. But that was all. A strange force gripped his whole body and pushed it back down; he could not jump over the low gate. In a moment, he had unsheathed his long sword, but the sharp blade bounced back from the soft pine wood as if the latter were steel. The impact was so powerful it sent a shock through his hand and wrist. He raised his sword and examined its gleaming edge under the moonlight. The gate was indeed too hard; most certainly his Master had endowed it with the strength of his own spirit. It was closed, and no one was to pass. That was the way his Master wanted it. The swordsman sighed deeply. He returned his sword to its sheath, and sat down on a big rock outside the gate.

Seven years earlier on the day he was to leave the mountain, his Master looked at him for a long moment without speaking. There was a kind expression in his eyes and something else, too, something that resmebled pity. He could only bow his head in silence when his eyes encountered the compassionate and tolerant eyes of his Master. A while later, the old man said to him, "I cannot keep you at my side forever. Sooner or later, you must go down the mountain and into the world where you will have many opportunities in which to carry out the Way and to help people. I thought that perhaps I could keep you here with me a little longer, but if it's your will to go, my child, then go in peace. There is only this: Remember, always, what I have taught you and given to you, always. Down in the world below this mountain, you will need all of it."

Then his Master went over briefly again what he was to avoid, seek, leave alone, and change. Finally, he put a gentle hand on his shoulder: "Those are the yardsticks for your actions. Never do anything that could cause suffering either to yourself or to others, in the present or in the future. And go without fear on the road which you believe will lead you and others to total enlightenment. Remember, always, the standards by which happiness and suffering, illusion and liberation must be measured. Without them, you would betray the Way itself, let alone help the world!

"I have already given you my precious sword. Use it to subdue monsters and devils. But I want you to look upon it more like a sharp blade that comes from your own heart with which you will subjugate your own ambitions and desires. Now, I have this for you, too, and this will make your task easier." Then his Master pulled out of his wide sleeve a small viewing glass, and handed it to him.

"This is the Me Ngo glass," he said. It will help you to determine good and evil, to separate the virtuous from the wicked. It is also called the Demon Viewer, for looking through it, you will see the true forms of demons, evil spirits, and the like . . ."

He received the fabulous viewing glass from his Master's hand, but he was so grateful and so deeply moved he could not say one word. The following day, at the break of dawn, he went up to the central hall to take leave of his old Master. The old man walked down the mountain with him, all the way to Tiger Brook, and there, in the murmuring of a mountain stream, master and disciple bade farewell. His Master again put a hand on his shoulder and looked into his eyes. He went on looking as the young man started walking away. Once more, he called after his disciple, "Remember, my child, poverty cannot weaken you, wealth cannot seduce you, power cannot vanquish you. I will be here for the day you come back, your vows fulfilled!"

He recalled the first days of his journey vividly. Then, months, and years went through his mind. How humanity had revealed itself to him under different guises! And how helpful the sword and the Me Ngo viewing glass had been to him! Once, he met a priest whose appearance instantly inspired reverence, who—such an honor for the young swordsman—invited him back to his retreat where they would, in the words of the old sage, "discuss how best to join their efforts for the purpose of helping their fellow human beings." At first, the young man listened with rapture, but then, something odd about the priest struck him. He whipped out the Me Ngo and looked through it. In front of him, there was a gigantic demon! Its blue eyes sent forth crackling sparks, a horn stood out from its forehead, and its fangs were as long as his own arms! In one jump, the young man backed away, drew his sword, and furiously attacked it. The demon fought back but, of course, had no chance. It prostrated itself at the young man's foot, begging for mercy. The swordsman then demanded that it swear, under oath, it would return where it had come from, to study the Way, pray that one day it would be permitted to come back into the world of men as a true human being, and refrain from ever disguising itself again as a priest to bewitch and devour the innocent. Another time, he met a mandarin, an old man with a long white beard. It was a happy encounter between a young hero out to save the world and a high official, a "father and mother to the people," bent on finding better and better ways to govern and benefit the masses. Again, the young man's instinct was aroused: under the Me Ngo, the handsome, awe-inspiring old official turned out to be an enormous hog whose eyes literally dripped with greed. In one instant, the sword flew out of its sheath. The hog tried to flee, but the swordsman, in one jump, overtook it. Standing astride the main threshold of the mandarin's mansion, he barred the only escape route. The beast took on its true form and cried out loudly for mercy. Again, the young man did not leave the monster without extracting from it the solemn oath that it would follow the Way, that it would never again take the form of a mandarin so that it could gnaw the flesh and suck the blood of the people.

And there was that time, walking by a marketplace, when he saw a crowd surrounding a bookstall. The picture-and-book seller was a very beautiful young woman whose smile was like an opening flower. Seated nearby was another young woman, also of stunning beauty, who was singing softly some melodious tunes while plucking the strings of a lute. The beauty of the girls and the grace of the songs so captivated everyone present that no one left the stall once they had stopped, and all anyone could do was stand and listen, enraptured, and buy the pictures and books. The young man himself was attracted by the scene. He finally approached and held up one of the pictures. The elegance of the design and vividness of the colors overwhelmed him. Yet, an uneasiness rose within him. He reached for his Me Ngo. The two beautiful girls were actually two enormous snakes whose tongues darted forth and back like knife blades. The swordsman swept everyone aside in one movement of his arms, and with his sword pointing at the monsters, he shouted like thunder, "Demons! Back to your evil nature!"

The crowd scattered in fright. The big snakes swung at the young man, but no sooner did the fabulous sword draw a few flashing circles around their bodies than the reptiles coiled at his feet in submission. He forced their jaws open and carved out their venom-filled fangs with his sword. Then he put the bookstall to the torch and sent the monsters back to their lairs with the solemn promise, against certain total destruction, that they would never come back to bewitch the village people.

So, the young swordsman went on from village to village, and from town to town, on a mission he had set for himself, using the weapon and the viewing glass his Master had given him, along with priceless counsels. He threw himself into his task. For a time now he had come to think of himself as The Indispensable Swordsman. The world could not do without his presence. He had come down from the mountain into the world, and he participated fully in the life down here. Facing the world where treachery and cunning reigned he had to learn flexibility and patience, and at times he had to bend with the tide because his goal was to vanquish and to persuade. He experienced great pleasure in his actions for the good. He went so far as to reach the point where he forgot to eat and sleep. And he did more, much more, because of the joy and satisfaction he derived from the pursuit of his goal—helping the people—rather than because of this goal itself. He served because that fulfilled him, not necessarily because the people needed him.

And so, seven years passed. One day, as he was resting on the bank of a river, watching the water flow by quietly, he suddenly realized that for some time now he had not used the Me Ngo viewing glass. He had not used it, he was now aware, not because he had forgotten that he had it, but because he had not felt like using it. Then, he remembered that there had been times when he did use the glass, but only very reluctantly. Those days when he first came down from the mountain, he fought to the death every time he saw, through the Me Ngo, the true natures of whatever evil faced him. He recalled his great happiness each time, through the glass, he saw the image of a virtuous man or a true sage. But, obviously, something odd had happened to him recently, and he did not know what. It seemed to him he began to feel no great joy when he saw wisemen in his viewing glass, just as he felt no great fury when he saw in it the images of monsters and devils. When monsters appeared in his miraculous glass, the young swordsman couldn't help noticing that there happened to be a certain familiarity even in their horrifying inhuman features.

The Me Ngo remained safely in his pocket, even though it had not been used for a long time. Then the young swordsman thought he would return some day to the mountain to ask his Master's advice: why did he have such reluctance to use what obviously had been such a great help to him? But only on the twelfth day of the eighth month, while he was crossing a forest of white plum trees and was struck by the snow-white blossoms gleaming under the autumn moon, did he suddenly yearn for the days when he studied as a young man under his old Master, whose cottage stood at the border of just such an old plum forest. Only then did he decide to return. In his wish to see his Master, the journey back seemed interminable: seven days and seven nights of climbing hills and crossing streams. But as he reached the foot of the high mountain where he would begin the ascent to his Master's abode, darkness descended. The rising moon showed the two leaves of the heavy pine gate shut tightly, preventing him from going any further up the mountain.

There was nothing he could do but wait. At dawn, he thought, one of his "brothers" would certainly come down to fetch water from the stream and could open the gate for him. By now, the moon had risen past its zenith. The entire mountain and forest were bathed in its cool light. As the night wore on, the air became chillier. He pulled out his sword and watched the moon gleam on its cold, sharp edge. Then he sheathed it again and stood up. The moon seemed extraordinarily bright. The mountain, the forest, everywhere—all was still, and quiet, as if the world was oblivious to his presence. Feeling dejected, he dropped down onto another rock. Again, the seven years of his recent life passed before him. Slowly, ever slowly, the moon edged towards the distant summit of a far mountain. In the sky, the stars shone brightly but then they, too, began to recede, becoming paler and paler. There was already the hint of a glow in the east. The outlines of the mountain became suddenly sharper against the pale sky. Dawn was about to break.

There was rustling of dry leaves. The swordsman looked up and saw the vague form of someone walking down the mountain. He thought it must be one of his younger "brothers," though it was not light enough and the figure was too distant for him to make out the latter's features. It must be a "brother" because the person was carrying something like a large pitcher. Whoever it was came closer and closer, and the swordsman heard him exclaim happily:

—Elder Brother!

—Younger Brother!

—When did you arrive? Just now?

—No! As a matter of fact, I arrived here when the moon was just coming up! I've waited all night down here. Why, in Heaven's name, did anyone lock up the gate like this? Was it the Master's order?

The younger disciple, smiling, raised his hand and pulled, ever so lightly, at the heavy gate. It swung open with ease. He stepped outside it, and, grasping the swordsman's hands in his own, looked at his senior:

—You must be chilled to the bones staying down here all night. You're covered with dew! Well, I used to come down here all day, picking herbs and watching the gate, you know . . . If I thought someone deserved an audience with the Master, I'd bring him up, and if I didn't, I'd just make myself invisible! I'd just stay behind the bushes, and they'd just give up!

You know that our Master doesn't want to see anyone unless he has a true determination to learn. Lately, the Master has allowed me to move on to further studies, and as I stay most of the time up at the retreat he told me to close the gate. He told me it would open itself for virtuous people but would stay shut and bar the way for those too heavy with the dust of the world! There is no way anyone could ever climb it or jump over it. Especially someone burdened with the spirits of demons and the like! The swordsman knitted his brows:

—Would you say I am such a person? Would you? Why did the gate stay shut for me?

The younger man laughed heartily:

—But of course not! How could you be such a person? Anyway, we can go up now, you see that the way is clear. But just a moment, Elder Brother! I must fetch some water first. Come with me. Smile, Brother, smile! Who are you angry at?

Both men laughed. They made their way down to the stream. The sun was not yet up, but the east already glowed brightly. The two disciples could now see clearly each line on the other's face. The water was tinted a pale rose by the dawn. There, they could see their reflections next to one another. The swordsman was bold and strong in his knight's suit; a long sword slung diagonally over his back. The younger disciple's figure was gentler in his flowing page's robe, a pitcher in his hands. Without speaking, both looked at their own reflections, and smiled to one another. A water-spider sprung up suddenly and caused the rose-tinted surface to ripple, sending the images into thousands of undulating patterns.

—How beautiful! I would certainly destroy our reflections for good if I dipped the pitcher in now. By the way, do you still have the Me Ngo viewing glass with you? Master gave it to you when you came down the mountains years ago!

The swordsman realized that it was true, that all these years he had used it only to look at others, but never once had he looked at his own image. He took the glass out, wiped it on his sleeve, then pointed it at the water's surface. The two heads came close to look through the small glass together.

A loud scream escaped from the throat of the two young men. It reverberated through the forest. The swordsman fell forward and collapsed on the bank of the stream. A deer, drinking water further upstream, looked up in fright.

The younger disciple could not believe what he had seen in the glass; there he was in his flowing robe, a pitcher in hand, standing next to a towering demon with eyes deep and dark like waterwells and long fangs curving down around its square jaw. Yes, he saw the color of the demon's face. It was a bluish gray, the shade of ashes and death. The young man shuddered, and rubbing his eyes, looked again at his senior who was now lying unconscious on the blue stones of the bank. The older man's face still expressed shock and horror; suffering had been etched upon this man who, for seven years, had ceaselessly braved the rough and cruel world down below their mountain retreat.

The young disciple rushed down to the stream to fetch water and to douse his elder's face with it. Moments later, the swordsman came to. His face was ravaged with despair. His true image had appeared in the Me Ngo so unexpectedly, bringing self-knowledge to him in such a swift, brutal fashion that he could do nothing but collapse under this blow. All his energy seemed to have left him. He tried to stand up, but there was no strength in his legs and arms.

—It's all right, it's all right, my brother! We'll go up now.

To the swordsman's ears, his brother's voice was like an imperceptible movement of the breeze, a faint murmur from afar. He shook his head. His world had collapsed, and he wanted to live no longer. He felt as if his body and soul had been in the path of a hurricane. He could not possibly entertain the idea, the affront, of bringing himself, ever, into his beloved Master's presence.

The younger man brushed some sand off his brother's shoulder:

—No, you shouldn't worry about it. You know that the Master had nothing but compassion for you. Let's go up now. We'll again live and work and study together . . .

Up the steep, rock-strewn path snaking up the mountain, the two figures made their way slowly. It was not, as yet, day; the silhouettes imprinted themselves on the thin veil of dew stretching over trees and rocks. The first sun rays finally reached the two men and heightened the contrast: the swordsman only seemed more broken in both body and spirit, walking next to the younger disciple whose steps were firm and whose mien gentle.

And over the mountain top, far away, the sun rose.

Kaijek the Songman

Xavier Herbert

KAIJEK THE Songman and his lubra, Ninyul, came up the river, picking their way through wind-stricken cane-grass and palm-leaves and splintered limbs and boughs that littered the pad they were following. It was a still and misty morning, after a night of one of those violent southeast blows which clean up the wet monsoon. Mist hid the tops of the tall river timber and completely hid the swirling yellow stream. The day had dawned clear and cool; but now it was warming up again.

Sweat was trickling down Kaijek's broad gaunt face and through his curly raven beard, and down his long thin naked body from his armpits. He wore nothing but a loin-clout, a strip of dirty calico torn from a flour-bag and rigged on a waist-belt of woven hair. On his right shoulder he carried three spears and a woomera; and from his left hung a long bag of banyan-cord containing his big painted dijeridoo and music-sticks. Fat little Ninyul, puffing at his heels, bore the bulk of their belongings—swag balanced on her curly head, big grass dillybag hanging from a brow-strap down her back, tommy-axe and yam-sticks in a sugar-bag slung on her left shoulder, and fire-stick and billy in her right hand. She wore a sarong made from an ancient blue silk dress.

Ninyul sniffed at the strong effluvium of her man. Not that she objected to it. Indeed, she was as proud of it as of his talent, of which she considered it an expression. As her wide fleshy nostrils dilated, she thought of how lesser songmen always came to him during corroborees to have him rub them with his sweat. And she glowed in recollection of the great success he had made at the last gathering they had attended—amongst the Marrawudda people on the coast—with his latest song, "The Pine Creek Races." Apart from the classics, corroboree-crowds liked nothing better than a good skit in song on the ways of the white man. But this pleasant recollection lasted only for a moment. Ninyul became aware again of her man's dropped shoulders and his frenzied gait; and her anxiety for him in his struggle with his muse returned. At full moon they were due to attend a great initiation gathering amongst the Marratheil of the Paperbarks. The moon was nearly full already; and they were getting further from the Paperbarks every day; and still Kaijek had not composed the song that would be expected of him.

Kaijek was the most famous songman in the land. His songs were known from the red mountains of the Kimberley to the salt arms of the

Gulf. Wherever they went, Kaijek and Ninyul, who was always with him, were warmly welcomed; for, though Kaijek's songs always travelled ahead of him, he never failed to come to a gathering with a new one. Not that Kaijek found composing easy. Far from it! Often his muse would elude him for moons. And so wretched would he become in his impotence, and so ashamed, that—pursued by Ninyul—he would fly from the faces of his fellows, to range the wilderness like one of those solitary ramping devil-doctors called the Moombas.

He was in the throes of that impotence now, while he went crashing up the river through the tangle of wrecked grass and trees. So he and Ninyul went on and on, travelling at great speed, but heading nowhere. Wallabies heard them coming and fled crashing and thudding from them. White cockatoos in the river timber dropped down to pry at them, and wheeled back shrieking into the mist. And on and on—till suddenly they were stopped in their tracks by a burst of uproarious dog-barking in the mist ahead.

Kaijek, staring ahead, heard the click of Ninyul's tongue, and turned to her. She gave the sign "white man," then pointed with her lips to the left. Kaijek looked and saw the stumps of a couple of saplings of size such as no blackfellow ever would fell to make a camp. Ninyul was already aware of the likelihood of a white man's presence in the neighbourhood, because some little distance back she had observed fresh prints of shod horses, and just before the dog barked had fancied she heard a horse-bell. Kaijek had seen and heard nothing consciously for miles. He turned and looked ahead again.

Then the dog appeared, a little red kelpie. When he saw them he yelped, turned tail and disappeared, yapping shrilly. They heard a white man yell at him. Still he yapped. They judged the distance. For a moment they stood. Ninyul glanced into the mist to the left, thinking of wheeling round that way to avoid what lay ahead. Then Kaijek turned to her again and hissed, "Inta jah—tobacca!"

She nodded. They had been without tobacco for a long while. Kaijek had often moaned in his despair that if he had only a finger of tobacco he might find his song.

They went ahead cautiously. A score of places brought them into dim view of a camp. There was a tent, a bark-roofed skillion, a bark-covered fireplace, a springcart, and pieces of mining gear. Kaijek and Ninyul knew what the gear was for, because they had often worked for prospectors. There was only one white man, and no sign of blacks. The white man was sitting on a box in the skillion, kneading a damper in a prospecting-dish between his feet, and looking into the mist in their direction. His dog was crouched before him, silent now, but tense.

Kaijek gave his spears and bag to Ninyul, but retained the woomera. Ninyul slipped behind a tree. Kaijek went on slowly. The white man soon saw him, stared hard at him with bulging blue eyes that bade him anything but welcome. Kaijek stopped at the fireplace. He knew the man slightly. He had seen him working a tin show in the Kingarri country, and had heard blacks describe him as a moody and often violent fellow. He was Andy Gant, a man of fifty or so, stout and stocky, with a big red bristly face and sandy greying hair and a long gingery unkempt moustache.

Andy Gant was in a particularly bad mood just then. The heavy humidity had upset his liver and brought out his prickly heat; which was why he was doing camp chores at that time of day, instead of digging gravel from the bench behind the camp and lumping it down to the sluice-box. To slave at digging that hard-packed gravel and washing out the lousy bit of gold it yielded was heart-breaking at any time, and too much to bear with a lumpy liver and fiery itch. He had slaved at that mean bench-placer throughout the wet, and had not won enough gold from it to pay for tucker, although the indications were that there was rich gold thereabouts. And most of the time he had been alone, deserted by the couple of blacks he had brought with him. He was just about ready now to shoot any nigger on sight.

Kaijek spat in the fire to show his friendliness, then grinned and said, "Goottay, boss!" And he stroked his beard and lifted his right foot and placed it against his left thigh just above the knee, and propped himself up with the woomera.

For answer Andy raised a broken lip and showed big yellow teeth. Then he gave attention to his damper.

Kaijek coughed, spat again, then said, "Eh, boss—me wuk longa you, eh?"

Andy's face darkened. He kneaded vigorously.

A pause, during which Kaijek coveted the pipe and plug of tobacco on the sapling-legged table at Andy's back. Then Kaijek said, "Me prop'ly goot wukker, boss. Get up be-fore deelight, wuk like plutty-ell . . ."

Andy could contain himself no longer. With eyes ablaze he leapt to his feet and roared, "Git to jiggery out of it, you stinkin' rottin' black sumpen, before I put a bullet through you."

And his dog joined in with him, yapping furiously and dancing about.

"Wha' nim?" cried Kaijek, dropping his leg.

Andy grabbed a pick-handle with a doughy hand, and shouted, "I'll show you what name, you beggin' son of a sheeter—I'll show you what name—the ghost I will!" And he rushed.

"Eh, look out!" yelled Kaijek, and turned and fled back to Ninyul with the dog snapping at his heels. Ninyul bowled the dog over with a stick.

Then together they snatched up their belongings and bolted back along the track.

They stopped at the sapling stumps, "Marjidi naijil!" grunted Kaijek, and spat over his shoulder to show his contempt. Then he pointed with lips to the left, and set off in that direction. But though they were not seen as they skirted the camp, and though they went warily, their going was followed every step of the way in imagination by Andy's dog yapping at his master's side.

They had gone no more than fifty paces past the camp, and were still at the foot of the flood-bench, when they came upon a river-gum that had been uprooted in the night. Kaijek paused to look among the broken roots for bardies, and saw gold gleaming in a lump of quartzy gravel. He knew gold well, but had no more idea of its value than any average bush black-fellow. He gave his spears to Ninyul, and fished out the lump of gravel and freed the gold. It was a nugget of about two ounces on a piece of quartz. Kaijek picked it clean, spat on it, rubbed it on his thigh, weighed it, then looked at Ninyul and said with a grin, "Kudjing-gah—tobacca!"

They turned back, heading straight for the camp. The dog knew they were coming, and barked blue murder. Andy, now at the fireplace setting his damper in the camp-oven, rose up and peered into the mist again; and when Kaijek appeared he let out a stream of invective and grabbed up the pick-handle and rushed.

"No more—no more!" yelled Kaijek, and held out the nugget in his palm.

Andy had the handle raised to hurl it at him. He saw the gold. But his dog was flying at Kaijek.

"Goold—goold!" yelled Kaijek, and flung it at Andy's feet, and made a swing at the dog with his woomera.

Andy snatched up the nugget, goggled at it, then looked up at Kaijek fighting with the dog, and rushed in with the handle to put the dog to flight. "Where—where'd you find it?" he gasped.

Kaijek pointed with his lips and replied, "Close-up behind."

"Then show me," gasped Andy. "Show me!" And his voice rose shrill. "Quick—where is it? Show me!"

Kaijek knew the symptoms of the fever. He turned and led the way with a rush.

Andy fairly flung himself at the roots. In a moment he had another nugget of an ounce or more, and then found one as big as a goose-egg. He turned his jerking face to Kaijek and cried, "Go longa camp. Gettim pick an' shovel. An' the axe. Quick, quick!"

Kaijek moved to obey, then turned and said, "Me hungry longa to-bacca, boss."

"Tobacca there longa camp."

"No-more gottim pipe, boss."

"Pipe there, too," yelled Andy. "Take it. Take anything you like. But be quick!"

Kaijek flew. Ninyul, in the background, set down the belongings and followed him. It was she who took the things to Andy. Kaijek stopped in the camp to chop up tobacco and fill Andy's pipe; and when he went to the fireplace to light the pipe he swigged a quart of cold stewed tea he found there. Then he strolled back to the tree, puffing luxuriously.

Andy now had a good dozen ounces of gold on a rock beside him, and was chopping off roots with the energy of a raving madman. And it was the eyes of a madman he turned on Kaijek when at length he paused for breath. He lowered the axe, and stepped up to Kaijek, and laid a great wet hairy hand on his slim black shoulder, and gurgled lovingly in his face, "Thank you, brother, thank you! It's what I've been lookin' for all me flamin' life. An' I owe it all to you. Yes, to you who I nearly druv away." He shook Kaijek till he rocked. "I won't forget it," he went on; and now he was near to tears. "My oath I won't! I'll look after you, brother, don't you worry. I'll pay you the biggest wages a nigger ever got. I'll pay you bigger'n white man's wages. Oh, ghost, I love you! I'll buy you everything you ever want. Gawd bless you!" And with that he flung himself back at the roots.

For a while Kaijek watched him. Then he said, "Eh, boss, me two-fella lubra hungry longa tucker."

Andy stopped chopping and gasped at him, "Plenty tucker longa camp. Take the lot. Take the rintin' jiggerin' lot! And when you're comin' back bring another pick an' shovel, an' a dish. There's damper in the oven. Eat it! Eat anything you flamin' well want to, brother. Everything I got is yours!"

Kaijek turned away, and signed to Ninyul, who picked up the belongings and followed him to the camp.

They sat by the fireplace, gorging bully-beef and hot damper and treacle, and swilling syrupy tea, while the racket of Andy's joyous labouring went on in the distance. Then they sat taking turn about with the pipe. Twice Andy yelled to them to come see fresh treasures he had unearthed. The first call Kaijek answered. Ninyul answered the second, because Kaijek, the artist, staring fixedly at the fire and humming to himself, did not hear it. Then suddenly Kaijek leapt up and smacked his rump and danced a few steps and began to sing:

O munnijurra karjin jai, ee minni kinni goold,
Wah narra akinyinya koori, mungawaddi yu . . .

He swung on Ninyul, whose eyes were shining and lips aquiver. For a moment he stared at her. Then he began to clap his hands and stamp a foot.

Kaijek stopped, turned panting to Ninyul. She leapt and cried joyously, "Yakkarai!"

Then Andy's voice rang out through the thinning mist, "Eh, brother— come here! Come quick! Come quick an' see what the angels've planted for you an' me. O Gawd!" He ended with a sob.

Kaijek looked towards him for a while. Then he turned back to Ninyul and made a sign. She went to their belongings. He followed her, and gathered up his stuff and shouldered it, then led the way down the river again, heading full speed for the gathering in the Paperbarks.

SPIRIT JOURNEYS

In Global Cultures, many stories deal with emigration to other lands and migrations within one land, but there are also stories that deal with the spirit journeys and transmigrations of souls that are expected in so many of the world's religions. In "Last Night I Dreamt of You," a book of Sufi mysticism circulates among three Egyptian professionals, alienated men living as foreigners in Europe, shunned—because of racism—by the people they meet on the streets and in the laundromats. Two of them embrace this philosophical religion, which originated among the Shiite Muslims of Persia as a complex blend—a syncretism—of Neo-Platonic, Buddhist, and Christian elements but which eventually congregated around the idea that an individual's soul can be in immediate union with God by traveling out of the body and that, after death, it migrates to a new body. For the office manager Fahti, Sufism means that he can cultivate peacefulness in his heart, a fruitful garden in his chest as he calls it. The banker Kamal is completely alienated from his Muslim heritage because he violates the Koran by practicing money-lending and because he has married a European woman. He feels Sufism might save him from unsettling dreams in which he blurs Muslim history or fails at learning to play a Western instrument, dreams of total disorientation. But the central character rejects Sufism. He wanders about in his alienation—thinking of *Hamlet*, seeing *La Traviata* at the cinema, intellectually Westernized, fatalistic, depressed. Then he stumbles into the life of a European woman who is just as unhappy about the state of the world and the people in it. Her father, now dead, once traveled to Egypt and was—so an old photograph reveals—guided by an Egyptian who looks like the central character's father. Somehow, their lives have touched previously and in ways they cannot fathom—they lack the book of these mysteries. And, the author implies, people who have no cultural resources, who drift through urban European wastelands, do not have any insight or any way to help themselves or each other. BAHA' TAHIR, born in 1935, has written novels and plays as well as short stories and, as an employee of the United Nations, has much experience with peoples' lives in cultures other than their own. He attended Cairo University, where he received a degree unusual for a writer—a diploma of higher studies in mass communications.

Mrs. Ba, the old Vietnamese lady in UYEN LOEWALD's very simply constructed story, is also concerned with journeys of the soul. She believes that her ancestors' souls may not be able to find their way to the family's new home, Los Angeles, when she calls to them. She needs to learn English, she thinks, so that she can find her way back to Vietnam after her death and then guide them to the new land. She is also afraid that her grandchildren will call to her soul in this language, English, and she must be able to respond to them. Her two sons, already Americanized and successful, stand on the edge of their mother's world, understanding her concerns but not really sharing them. Uyen Loewald, who now lives and writes in Australia, was a student of literature and mathematics when she was imprisoned in 1962 by the Diem regime in South Vietnam. She was born in North Vietnam, near Hanoi, in 1940, but her characters in the ironically titled "Integration" are South Vietnamese, nonpolitical people who have simply been caught in the wave of the North Vietnamese Tet Offensive of 1968, one of the most destructive events of the Vietnam War.

Last Night I Dreamt of You

Baha' Tahir

I

I GO to work in the morning and return home in the evening.

This happens five days a week. It happens in a foreign city in the North. When I go out in the morning I frequently find a blonde girl at the bus stop with a beauty-spot on her cheek. When she sees me coming in the distance she immediately turns her face away. She never looks me in the eye, no matter how long we have to stand there.

When I get home after work I turn on the television, and turn it off. I turn on the radio, and turn it off. I walk around the empty apartment. I rearrange the pictures on the wall and the books on the shelves. I wash the dishes. I talk to myself in the mirror. Night falls.

Most nights my friend Kamal, who lives in another city, calls me on the telephone. He usually asks me if there is any news, and I tell him there's none. He complains a little about the way things are going for him, and I complain a little about the way things are for me. Finally he sighs and says, "Perhaps I'll call you tomorrow."

After a while I go to sleep. Most often that happens while I am reading.

This week Fathi, my colleague at work, gave me a book on Sufi mysticism. There are a few of us Arabs who work in an Arab-owned firm in this city, but the boss and most of the employees are foreigners. In these surroundings Fathi developed a love for Sufism. I began to read the book that evening as I was going home on the bus. I got to the part where the author says that sometimes the spirit leaves the body and goes on excursions. That happens at night when one sleeps, although sleep is not a necessary precondition. A person's spirit occasionally encounters other spirits, good as well as evil, and sometimes a link is formed between them.

I felt afraid, and closed the book. The man sitting next to me on the bus asked me what language the book was in. I knew he was a foreigner like me, because the people in this country do not speak to strangers. When I said Arabic, he said it was a fascinating language because most of its letters fell under the line. I told him I didn't understand. He took the book and pointed out some Arabic letters that start on the line and extend below it, and some letters at the end of syllables that have a flourish below the line. Triumphantly I pointed to several other letters which stand on or above the line. He insisted that when you looked at the page, you noticed most of them were under the line. I asked him what his point was, and he seemed embarrassed.

That night Kamal called me earlier than usual. He wanted to know if there was any news. I told him that the spirit takes excursions and that most Arabic letters fall below the line. He was silent for a while. Then he asked if it was cold where I was. I said yes. He said, "It's snowing here." Then he said abruptly, "How does the spirit take an excursion? Where does it go?" I said, "I don't know. I probably won't read the book." "Could you mail it to me then?" he asked. I promised him I would.

The next morning, I left for work. I walked fast and vigorously because it was cold. The blonde girl was at the bus stop and, as usual, she averted her face. I could not understand why her behavior should bother me at all. "Damn her," I said to myself.

I had Fathi's book about spirits with me so I could mail it to Kamal. There was nothing extraordinary about it, I told myself as I boarded the bus. Perhaps I ought to read a page or two more in order to learn how the spirit makes its excursions and what it does. But I resisted the temptation. While I was on the bus it began to snow. At first it fell like scraps of white paper flying about in the gloomy sky. Then it became heavy and thick. It covered the world outside the bus like an endless, rippling white blanket. I decided to get off at the post office despite the weather. I put the book inside my overcoat so it would not get wet. I ran quickly but cautiously to avoid slipping in the soft snow. As I stopped to shake the snow from my hair and coat before I went in, someone bumped into me from behind. I turned. It was the girl from the bus stop. Our eyes met for a few seconds. We stammered an excuse at the same time. Then she stepped around me and hurried inside.

I joined a short line in front of the window for registered mail. It had not yet opened. When it did, I saw her sitting inside. She had taken off her wool coat. Her blonde hair was cut shoulder-length and parted in the center. The bangs across her forehead and the beauty-spot on her cheek gave her pretty, round face a childish look. When my turn came I handed her the book. For a few seconds she looked in surprise at its cover with the gold decorations, and then her features once more assumed the rigid look customary with the people of this country when they are working. She placed the book on the scales and told me the cost. She did not look at my face.

The snow was still falling heavily when I left. It had already carpeted the pavements. The roofs of the slow-moving automobiles were now cloaked in white. They were indistinguishable from one another in their delicate wrappers. I did not have my umbrella with me. I stood sheltering myself at the entrance of the post office. I began to worry I might be late getting to work, but there was nothing I could do about it in this weather. A man ran across the street and stood beside me. He was panting as he shook the snow off his clothes. When he finished, he put his hands in the pockets of his overcoat. The air which puffed from his mouth and nostrils turned to steam in the cold. Cars passed slowly in front of us. Their tires carved a black line into the snow on the road. The man darted out and tried to thumb a ride with a number of cars, but no one paid any attention to him. He returned. New snow had accumulated on him. He turned to me, somewhat angrily, and said, "You're a foreigner, aren't you?" I nodded my head. "Do you have scoundrels like these who won't stop for you even with snow like this?" I told him that we had only sunshine. He asked what had brought me here. I pointed to the heavens. He laughed.

At the office my foreign boss waved his hands and said to me, "Shu-wayya, shuwayya." He thought that meant "You're late." In fact it is Arabic for "Just a little." I told him there were mitigating circumstances. In any case, he was happy he had spoken Arabic and that I had understood. He asked me how I was feeling. I said fine.

When I met Fathi, he asked me if I had read any of the book. I said no. He shook his head. "That's a pity," he observed sadly. "Your spirit is diaphanous." Then he poked a finger in my chest and said, "You have a heart which can bring forth fruit." I told him my heart was heavy enough already. He said, "In my chest, there's an orchard growing." I poked my finger in his chest and said, "One orchard in the office is enough." I left him.

I went home that evening.

The snow was piled high on the sidewalks. It was spread out like a soft, gleaming carpet on either side of the black street, which had been cleaned off. The snow had turned the branches of the leafless trees into white, twisting snakes. It had daubed luminous flowers on the few evergreens. It was warmer; the way it gets after the snow has stopped and the winds have died down. Once home, I did not turn on the television. I looked out of the window. There was snow everywhere. The cars parked along the curb were dome-shaped mounds with no identifying features. It was quiet and sad. I sat down and thought about my situation.

When Kamal called me I told him it had snowed. He told me he had just about had it with the snow. I asked him why. He said he'd realized he'd been working for banks there for ten years. He had married a native of the country who was kind and beautiful. He had obtained citizenship. People envied him, but all the same, he was miserable. Again I asked why. He said, "Isn't banking a form of usury? I have a troubled conscience." I told him not to worry about it and that I had mailed him the book. I added that if he had a diaphanous spirit he could grow an orchard in his chest. He laughed and said, "My temperature's up because I've been out in the cold. I ate some garlic butter, too, so I think my spirit is heavy." I told him to take an aspirin and go to bed.

In the morning I did not go to work. It was Saturday, but I woke up at the same time as on working days. While I was still in bed I thought about the things I would do. I would buy food to last me the rest of the week and take my clothes to the cleaners. In the evening I would go to the cinema. When I had that all worked out, I got out of bed.

I looked out of the window. The snow was just the same, but it had lost its luster. In the center of the sidewalk a muddy track had been carved by footprints breaking through the crusty snow. By the curb, there were muddy piles of snow created by the plows clearing the road during the night. I gathered from the way the few people passing by were dressed and from the way they were walking with their heads bowed and their hands in the pockets of their overcoats that it was bitterly cold.

I bundled up as carefully as I could before I went out, but I knew there was nothing to be done for those critical areas: the nose and the ears.

Sometimes I raised my scarf till it covered my nose, but I felt smothered, and it was cold around my neck. In ordinary circumstances it helped to walk fast or run, but this was impossible when there was snow on the pavements. All the same, I had to go out. I entrusted myself to God's care. Just to be on the safe side, I put on two pairs of thick socks. I decided to start with the laundromat. I went outside carrying my clothes in a bag.

The laundromat was a self-service shop with about ten machines. There was one woman there to supervise things and sell soap in small quantities to people who did not bring any. When I went in, all the washers were busy. An old woman, a native of the country, was sitting in a chair, waiting, with her bag of laundry beside her. I too, sat down in an empty chair to wait, but a vicious draft was coming in through a small gap between the two panels of the glass door. I got up and began to prowl among the washing machines. I watched the round, glass eyes, trying to guess from the way the clothes were moving and the cycle which of the machines was almost finished. I heard the old woman say in a sharp voice, "I'll take the first washer to finish." I did not look at her and continued my tour, trying to keep warm.

A gust of cold air entered bringing with it two African men. One of them carried a bag of clothes. The other had an empty one. They were speaking in their language and laughing. They headed for one of the washers which had indeed just stopped. One of them set it to spin dry the clothes. They stood there watching.

Once again, the old woman said in her sharp, loud voice, "I'll take the first washer to finish." She was thin, with a long neck. Her eyes were pale. They had round grey pupils with a small chestnut circle in the center of them. Her face was sweaty and glistened as if coated with oil.

The man with the full bag turned and said to her gently, "I came here with my friend before you, Madam. I made an agreement with the young woman to use the washer when he finished." He pointed to the young woman sitting at a small table. She nodded her head in agreement.

The older woman stood up and moved toward her, her eyes open wide and her face flushed. "What's this?" she demanded. "I wait all this time, then someone comes in and takes my turn? And a black, too?"

The African's eyes flashed. He took a step toward her and said in a low voice, "What do you mean by that?"

She backed away and said, "In this country we respect the system. We're not like countries which . . ."

He cut her off, moving closer. "I don't care about your system or your country. What do you think of that?"

She backed away further. "What did I say? Aren't you a black?"

Standing face to face with her, he said, "Yes, and I'm proud of it. So what do you mean? The young woman told you I came before you. What does my being black have to do with that? Tell me what you mean?"

All at once she sat down in her place, and said in a scarcely audible voice, "Nothing."

He leaned back and laughed loudly. "Then you lack not just manners but courage too," he said. "Manners and courage . . ."

His friend took his hand and pulled him away. He was still laughing loudly. They started talking and laughing together again.

Addressing no one in particular the old woman burst out, "In any case, I'd just as soon not use that washer."

The man who was getting his clothes out of the washer and putting them into his bag feigned distress. "Oh, what a pity! I'll be really sad about that."

She looked at the young woman who was sitting behind the table. "Did you hear that?" she said.

Looking at the ceiling, the young woman replied, "It's none of my business."

The old woman looked around for someone else to talk to, but all she found was me. So she turned her face toward the glass door, muttering and shaking her head: "What's become of this country? What's come over it?"

When I'd finished washing my clothes, I headed out to the store to buy my provisions for the week. My face was hot when I left the laundromat. I walked some distance until I felt the cold and had to wrap the scarf over my nose.

At the store, while I was buying some cans of tomato sauce, tea, and sugar, I saw the young woman from the post office. She was pushing a shopping cart in front of her. It had a bouquet of roses, some soap, and some vegetables in it. Our eyes met. There was a hesitant smile on her lips. I turned my face away.

When I got home I telephoned Kamal. I asked him how he was. He said his fever had gone down, but that he still felt dizzy. I asked him if the book had arrived. He said it had, and that he would return it when he finished with it. I told him I did not need the book, or good or evil spirits. Evil people were quite enough for me. I told him what had happened at the laundromat. I grew a little emotional, but he replied quietly, "What's the big deal? I've lived here for years. I know what the people here think about foreigners. But I don't pay any attention to it. I see myself as someone living in a desert. My apartment is my tent. When I set off for work I don't have anything to do with anyone else. I don't acknowledge that there are people there. That's the best way to deal with them. That isn't the problem."

"What is the problem then?" I asked.

"We are. The problem is inside us, but I don't know what it is. I've been searching a long time, but I don't know. Can you interpret dreams?"

"I'll give it a try," I said.

"Last night I dreamt I met Muawiya ibn Abi Sufyan.[1] I was mediating a truce with him on behalf of our Lord al-Husayn.[2] Muawiya got angry and said, 'Put him in prison with Taha Husayn.'[3] But I was able to get away. I caught a taxi and found myself in Ataba Square in Cairo."

I told Kamal that al-Husayn's conflict was with Yazid,[4] not Muawiya.

"Is it a dream or a history lesson?" he replied impatiently. "What do you make of it?"

I thought about it but could not come up with anything. "What did you do before you went to bed?" I asked him.

"I was practicing typing on a Western typewriter."

"Is that necessary for your work?" I asked.

"No, but it's useful."

"I can't interpret your dream."

"It doesn't matter," he said. "Do you have any news?"

"No."

That evening I went to the cinema. The film was *La Traviata*. I stood at the entrance waiting for the early show to let out. I tried to keep warm by crowding together with the other people. I was looking at pictures from the film to see how the director had portrayed the heroine. She was just the way I had imagined: thin, beautiful, with large, black eyes. I heard a voice behind me: "Would you be so kind . . ." I turned and there she was again with the beauty-spot on her cheek. She was holding a cigarette near her mouth.

"Would you be so kind as to light my cigarette?" She was wearing a white turtleneck sweater and pants. She had no powder on her face. She was blushing and embarrassed, and looked more like a child than ever before. She looked strange holding a cigarette. I smiled at her and took out my lighter.

"It seems we meet everywhere," she said.

"It's a small city," I said.

"My name's Anne-Marie."

I told her my name. She smiled as she moved the cigarette about in her fingers quickly.

"I decided to confront you," she said.

1. Arab Muslim caliph, seventh century A.D.
2. Beloved grandson of the Prophet Muhammad.
3. Influential twentieth-century Egyptian author.
4. Muslim caliph and son of Muawiya.

"Are we at war?" I asked her in astonishment.

"No," she said. "Don't be alarmed. Are you going to the film?"

"Yes," I said.

"Do you like *La Traviata*?"

"I've heard it a number of times at the Cairo Opera," I replied.

"Is there an opera house in Cairo?" she asked.

I said there was. She continued to fiddle with her cigarette nervously. Then she asked, "Would you mind if we talked a little after the film?"

I told her I'd meet her there.

After the film, the music of Verdi was still haunting me with the same delicate sorrow I had experienced when I first read *La Dame aux Camélias*. It comes back to me every time I see *La Traviata*. When Anne-Marie came out of the film she was with a friend. She introduced me to her. The other girl looked at me inquisitively. Then she shook hands with me and went off. We walked down the cold street which was almost empty after the people leaving the film had dispersed. *La Traviata* was still on my mind.

"You seem sad," she said.

"Yes."

Then she said, "Me too." She remembered a line that Hamlet recites about the actor weeping over the tragedy in which he has starred: What was she to him or he to her that he should weep for her? She shook her head. "What's the heroine to us, or we to her, that we should weep for her?"

"It's more real than real people," I replied.

The cold was piercing. I asked her, "Are you heading anywhere in particular?"

"No," she said.

So we found a place to sit down in the nearest café. We were sitting opposite each other at a small table. We each had a glass of tea in front of us. I said to her with a smile, "Here you are confronting me, so what's it all about?"

She smiled too. "It just required some courage, that's all. I'm not used to talking to strangers." Then she added quickly, "I mean people I don't know."

I laughed and said, "I'm not ashamed of being a foreigner."

She leaned over her glass of tea, blushing. "Naturally. Naturally, why should you be ashamed?" Then she raised her head and looked at me. Her face grew even redder as she said, "Please don't get me wrong. My father was a Protestant minister. He taught us to love Christ and to love all people through Christ. I . . . I'm not like the others."

I said, "That's clear, but aren't you a little concerned to have these other patrons see you sitting with a foreigner—someone with a swarthy complexion at that?"

Her blue eyes were still fixed on my face. "Not at all." Then she added in a low voice. "That isn't what's upsetting me."

"What is?"

"Something is happening. I can't describe it. Perhaps you can help me."

I kept still and sipped my tea, expecting her to say something more. But she, too, fell silent and began to drink her tea. She stared at the table between us.

Suddenly in a soft voice and as though it took a lot of effort to speak she said, "I would like to ask you, if you will, to tell me about yourself. Who are you? Where do you come from? I, as you can see, am from this country. I work at the post office. My father died and I live with my mother. I love films and music and reading. So who are you? What do you do here?"

I told her my name and my profession.

"What about the book you mailed from my window, the one with the decorated cover—what was it?"

"A book of Islamic mysticism, Sufism. It's hard for me to explain it to you. Some people believe the heart understands, not the intellect. They train their spirits so their hearts will be pure."

"Like monks?"

"Not exactly, but actually, I can't explain. I haven't read their books. I don't understand them very well."

"What do you believe then?"

I kept silent.

"At one time I wanted to convert to Roman Catholicism and become a nun," she said. "I was in love with Saint Francis of Assisi because he loved the poor and the sick. In fact, I keep his picture in my room, although my mother doesn't like it." She changed the subject abruptly. "This world makes me sick. It's no use. Many people have tried, but it's no use. The same stupidity in every age. The same hatred, lying, misery. I've thought about going to Africa; perhaps I could help, even if it's just one person. I've thought . . ."

She stopped talking suddenly. Beads of perspiration appeared on her forehead. She wiped them off with her hand which she then put over her eyes. With her eyes closed, she said, "I'm sorry. I feel I've imposed on you. I saw your expression change when I asked you what you believe. Please forgive me. I didn't mean to pry."

"That doesn't matter," I said. "What's happened is that I've been told the beliefs of Anne-Marie while all I've told her is my name."

She smiled and twirled a cigarette in her fingers. "I decided to be blunt with you."

"In the past I had ideas, but today I've forgotten them," I told her. "In my country no one needed them or me, so I decided to forget them. I've forgotten a lot of things. But you said I might be able to help you. How can I help you? You said there's something about me that disturbs you. What is it?"

She took her hand away from her eyes. She looked at me for a time. Her eyelashes were trembling. Then she said in a matter-of-fact tone, "It's just that I see you so often, almost every day, once or twice."

"What's strange about that? What's so strange since we live in the same neighborhood and take the same bus at the same time?"

"Nothing," she replied in the same tone. "Nothing except that I see you even when I'm not seeing you. I feel you're there before I meet you. I look up and there you are. Sometimes I imagine this and that's all. You're not there, but I can almost touch you."

Trying to smile I said, "Perhaps you're in love with me?"

She replied without smiling, "No." She averted her eyes and said, "Excuse me: the fact is I hate you."

Then she looked at me. Her face was flushed. Her eyes were red. Every trace of beauty had vanished from her features.

I stared at her eyes. She really did hate me.

2

The following week, as usual, I went to work and returned home. New snow fell and it got colder.

Once I went to Fathi in his office and told him, "This life troubles me. Please teach me something."

"How can I teach you something I don't know? Do what I do: let your spirit unfold. One day you and I will both discover behind this desert the flowers of limitless beauty which are promised us."

I told him, "That frightens me; it doesn't console me. I want to know something specific: how have you reached this state of equilibrium and peace?"

"I have annulled my own will and made it subservient to the Lord's will."

It was not possible for us to continue the conversation.

Kamal spoke to me on the telephone a number of times. He did not mention anything about the book, but he told me that he had decided to resign from the bank. During this period, Kamal said, he'd been having a lot of dreams. One element recurred frequently in his dreams: he was learning to play the violin. In one dream he lost his bow and was forced to use a ruler to continue his performance. In another, a jury was going to judge his performance, but the bottle of medicine which he used to help him play the violin broke. All the pharmacies were closed. He wanted to ask the jury's permission not to perform, but he could not find his shoes. They made him go to the theater without any shoes. And so on.

That weekend Anne-Marie invited me to her house, to return my hospitality, as she put it. We had met in the morning a number of times at the bus stop and talked some. She had asked me to pardon her for being so frank that day. She wanted me to understand that she was having a personal crisis which was totally unrelated to me. The fact was that she had been in love with a compatriot, who had left her a few months before. He went overseas after they agreed to get married. From over there, he sent her his apologies. She said he might just as well never have promised to marry her, for she was in love with him and would have stayed with him, marriage or no marriage. What really upset her was that he should have made a promise without any pressure from anyone and then have broken it. She was almost glad that she had been separated in time from a person who could act like that. Then she talked about me. She said she was trying to study the matter with the utmost objectivity, as though she were not talking about me or her but about other people. She asked me to forgive her. Did she hate me because of the circumstances under which she saw me? Did I remind her of that other person she was now growing to hate? Why? Was there some resemblance? What? Was it, for example, because he had travelled abroad? She knew the question was complicated. She would understand completely if I refused to assist her. Indeed, she would apologize to me and thank me for agreeing to listen to her. If I was willing to help her, that would be exceedingly generous of me, and she would be very grateful for this favor.

That weekend we met at the bus stop. Dark clouds covered the sky and made the day gloomy. Snow blanketed the sidewalks and the balconies of the houses. Anne-Marie arrived at the appointed time. She was wearing pants, as usual, and a white, wool jacket. She had her hands in her pockets. There was a scarf tied around her neck. I never saw her wear an overcoat or dress. As she approached me with her hesitant step she appeared thin and fragile. I felt strangely sympathetic towards her.

She led me to her house. She lived in an old building with bowed balconies of wrought iron. I had frequently walked past it in the summer and stopped to admire the delicate balconies decorated with green plants and large red flowers. Now they were bare. Snow had accumulated on their protruding bars.

We said nothing until we reached her apartment, except that she mumbled an apology as we were climbing the stairs. There was no elevator and she lived on the third floor. She unlocked the door. At the entrance of the apartment there was a white curtain. We went through it to the sitting-room where there were small tables with dolls and small wooden statues set on dazzlingly white, embroidered cloths. The tables were placed at regular intervals between vigorous, carefully-tended plants, large white, red, and pink carnations. On either side of the room was a wooden cabi-net full of books, with glass doors covered by lace curtains. Exactly in the middle, between the cabinets, was a long, wooden table where a lady with braided white hair was sitting. She was wearing glasses with thick lenses and reading a magazine.

"This is my mother," said Anne-Marie. She went and kissed her on the forehead, saying in a loud voice, "Here he is."

The woman nodded her head and smiled. "Good morning, sir."

"Good morning."

"Speak louder," said Anne-Marie, "She can't hear very well."

I took a chair beside her and kept still. With her head bowed, she smiled and looked at me through the clear blue eyes which Anne-Marie had in-herited. She looked at me for a long time through her thick glasses, which were slipping down her nose.

"From Africa?" she said.

I nodded. She pointed to a pair of black masks hanging on the wall on either side of a wooden cross. She said, "I like African carving." She clasped her white, wrinkled fingers together and waved her hands, saying, "It's strong." Then she opened her fists and moved a hand in a wave-like gesture. "It's also elegant and smooth. Where in Africa are you from?"

"I'm from Egypt," I said in a loud voice.

She raised her eyebrows in mild astonishment. "Egypt? I've always wanted to visit it. My husband went to Egypt in the year . . . the year . . . I don't remember. We weren't married then, but I still have the pictures. She supported herself with a hand on the table and started to rise, then stopped for a moment. "I remember my husband told me they're very good at magic in Egypt."

"Magic?" I asked, amazed.

She nodded her head. Trying to make a joke of it, I said, "Perhaps that was in the days of Moses."

She was still leaning on the table. "My husband saw things."

"Perhaps," I said.

She rose with difficulty from her chair, just as Anne-Marie returned carrying three glasses of tea on a tray. "That's enough, Mother," she said loudly.

"But I want this gentleman to see the pictures," she protested. Slowly, with her back bent, she went to one of the cabinets and opened it.

Anne-Marie apologized as she placed the glasses of tea on the table. "She doesn't go out much. When she sees someone, she doesn't stop talking."

"It doesn't bother me."

Her mother was talking to herself, saying, "Where did it go? Where can it have got to? It was always here."

Anne-Marie picked up her glass of tea in its metal holder and said, "Come. Let's go to my room." I brought my glass and followed her.

Her room was small and neat. The furniture was new and, unlike that of the parlor, simple. One wall was taken up with shelves filled with books. In the center of one of the shelves stood a tall crystal vase with a single, large, white flower in it. On another wall were pictures of Saint Francis with his shaven head. The color white was everywhere: in the table runners, the bedspread, and the lace window curtains. When she opened the curtain at the window, I noticed a large cedar tree outside. Its broad, green boughs, like outspread hands, were heaped with snow. Other trees stood around it, their branches intertwined and glazed with ice. Anne-Marie sat down in a small chair beside the window. She put her hands on her knees, which were pressed together. She stared out the window.

I was still standing by the door holding my glass of tea.

"The view from your window is pretty."

She looked at me with a smile and said, "Thanks. Why don't you sit down?" She pointed to a round stool in front of a small mirror. I sat down, my knees practically colliding with hers. We gazed out the window and sipped our tea.

Without looking at my face she said, "Last night I dreamt of you."

"I'm sorry," I said, and laughed.

She looked at me steadily. "Why are you sorry and why does it make you laugh?"

"What can I say when you tell me in such a sad tone that you dreamt about me yesterday?

She shook her head. "The night before last I dreamt of you too. I dreamt that a large hawk was knocking at my window with its wings and staring at me angrily. It was beating against the glass, trying to get through. Then you came and the hawk enfolded you in its wings. I woke up and found I was crying."

I did not laugh, but bowed my head.

"What do you do to make this happen?" she asked, calmly.

I raised my head in astonishment as I repeated her question. "What do I do to make this happen?"

"Yes."

"Are you serious? Do you believe it's possible for me to do something to make you dream about me?"

She laughed nervously, then stretched out her hand to take my empty tea glass. She rose and went out.

Outside the window a crow landed on the cedar.

It hopped clumsily from branch to branch, searching for one not buried in snow. When it found one it stretched out its sad, black wings and shook them. Then it closed them.

Anne-Marie returned and closed the door. She stood beside me.

"What are you thinking about?"

"If I told you, you'd laugh," I said.

"In that case please tell me. I'd like to laugh."

"Why is the crow on that tree so miserable? Why do people all over the world hate crows, even though nobody's ever been hurt by one?"

"You feel sorry for crows and for the heroine of La Traviata. Why don't you take an interest in the affairs of real people?"

"I gave that up a long time ago."

"I find it sad that in this world delicacy and sensitivity are defeated and evil triumphs. I grieve when the heroine dies, because she fell in love and sacrificed herself; but I also grieve that in this world there are hungry people who can't find anything to eat. There are poor people who are sick and can't find medicine or if they get some they die anyway. Death makes me sad."

"All that, and a lot more, used to make me sad once."

"When did you stop?" she asked.

"I don't remember exactly. Perhaps it's since I came here. Perhaps before that, when I decided to come here."

"So what do you believe in now—emptiness, nonexistence?"

"Not even those."

She stared out the window in silence for a time. Then pointing at the cedar tree she said in a different tone, "I think you've got this tree in your country."

"No, but it grows in the region."

"If you don't mind," she said, "I prefer electric light to this dim daylight which feels like night."

She closed the curtains. The room was rather dark, but she remained standing beside me with her face towards the window. In a faint voice she asked, "Are you sure you can't help me?"

I stretched out my hand and took hers which was beside me. It was cold as ice. I held it between my palms. She knelt down, facing me.

"Who are you?" she asked in a low voice. "What do these dreams mean? Why do they haunt me?"

"Who are you? Why have you appeared in my life?" I said. "What do you want from me?"

She crept closer to me on her knees and kissed my forehead. Her lips were icy. I put my arms around her shoulders. "I wish I could help you," I said. "I wish I could help myself."

All of a sudden, with a swift movement, she slipped off her sweater and bra. She pressed against my chest. Her arms encircling me quivered. She said, "Let's go. If this is what you want, here's the bed."

I tore myself from her arms. In a choked voice I said, "No, this isn't what I want. You're probably beautiful. In fact you are beautiful, but I've never seen you as anything but a child."

I rose, picked up her sweater from where it had fallen on the floor, and handed it to her.

She took it from me and sat on the edge of the bed. She wadded it up and buried her face in it. She began to weep violently. Her whole body was shaking as she repeated, "Then tell me, tell me, please, what do you want? What do you want?"

"What I want is impossible."

"What is it?"

"For the world to be different. For people to be different. I told you I don't have any ideas, but I do have impossible dreams."

"How do I fit into that? Why should I suffer?"

"How am I to know? What can I do? Tell me and I'll do it. Do you want me to leave this neighborhood? This country?"

"Would that help me?"

"How do I know? If I don't know how to help myself, how am I to know how to help you?"

She searched for the sleeves of her sweater, then put it on slowly. For some time she sat silently on the edge of the bed with her shoulders drooping. In a low voice she said, "Now I understand everything. Yes, now I see everything, but how sad it all is."

"What have you understood?"

"That's my secret," she said in the same low voice.

She stretched out her hand without moving from where she sat and pressed a button beside the bed. A light suddenly came on in the room.

She looked at me and said, "Please forgive me." She tried to smile. "Every time I meet you, I'm forced to apologize to you. But I promise it won't happen again."

Her eyes were red, and her face very pale.

When we left the room her mother was sitting in her place at the table. She was leafing through the pages of a thick album. When she saw me, she said impatiently, "Come here, sir. I've found the pictures."

I went over to her. The pictures were old, those old sepia prints in which dark areas look brown and light ones grey. They were of the Temple of

Karnak, Dayr al-Bahri, and the pyramids. She pointed to one in which a man sat on a camel that was kneeling on the ground in front of one of the pyramids. The man had a round, smiling face. He was wearing a dark jacket and a white collar. In front of him, holding the camel's rope, stood a man wearing Egyptian clothing. A thin arm stuck out of the wide sleeve of his shirt. I looked at his broad mouth topped by a moustache, and his sad, frowning face. He looked like my father.

I said to the old woman, "Should I take this picture?"

She raised her head to look directly at my face. She said without smiling, "I understand you perfectly."

Suddenly she closed the album and said, "Sorry. You can't take this picture."

Anne-Marie was standing there, lost in her own thoughts. She was resting her arm on the table.

3

The third week the snow melted, although some piles of it remained like sand beside the curb. The sky was still cloudy, and the daylight weak.

Fathi told me anxiously that I was getting thinner day by day and ought to see a doctor. I told him he could help me better than any doctor if he would explain to me how to understand the world.

"You are your own doctor," he said. "Just don't fight it." I told him talk like that would not help me. He shook his head sadly.

My boss called me in too and told me the same thing. Trying to use Arabic he said that my health was *basita tamam*—"totally basic"—and that although he was against giving vacations at this time because of the pressure of work, he would not refuse my request, because he didn't want to work me to death. I thanked him and told him I did not need a vacation.

Kamal got in touch with me during the middle of the week. He said he had tried to call me many times without success. Where was I evenings?

"I go out and walk," I said.

"In this cold?"

"Yes."

Anne-Marie did not appear at the bus stop. Once I went to the post office on my way to work, but she wasn't there either.

I dreamt of her one night. In the dream she had long hair and was running on the beach. She was afraid. Something was chasing her. When I woke up I was covered with sweat. I felt uneasy.

Towards the end of the week, Kamal phoned me. He was excited. He said he had done it. He had finally done it and felt better. He said he used to believe that all his afflictions—headache, insomnia, nightmares, bouts of weeping—were caused by waves of electricity, but he had been wrong.

"What sort of electricity?" I asked him.

"Don't you know that in this country they have electrical storms that affect the brain?" he said. I told him I had never heard of that.

"It's a well-known fact. Don't you see how strangely all these people behave?"

"I'm astonished," I said, "because they still seem to handle their affairs intelligently. They are successful in their business, prosperous, in excellent health. Does this electricity affect certain portions of the brain and not others? Does it afflict only some people?"

Still quite excited, Kamal continued, "You look at things superficially. All these things are just paper cutouts—the tall buildings, the huge factories, the fast airplanes, and the cemeteries with statues and flowers—all these are just toys made from cardboard which deceive nobody but children. Look inside and you'll find only ruins. Look at the people talking to themselves in the streets, at people in the cafés staring with eyes like dead fish. Look at the loneliness, the insanity, the hatred. What forces us to be this way? Existence is vast and glorious, but we bury ourselves in our skins. We blind our eyes to true happiness and real joy." Why didn't I open my eyes? Why didn't I follow his example? Why didn't I read the book?

I asked him what he was going to do now. He said he had resigned from the bank and was planning to return to Egypt. He advised me to return with him. We would build a house somewhere in the desert. Behind us would be a vast emptiness, in front of us the sea, and above us the sky. We would live far from competition, struggle, overcrowding, and the quarrels of adults who act like spoiled children. We would live out the remainder of our lives in the true happiness of that heavenly bliss.

I thanked him. I wished him the happiness he desired and said I would think about it.

I did not sleep well that night. I thought a lot about Anne-Marie.

The next morning, I left home early, before it was time to go to work, and headed for her house. It was already morning, but the roads were dark. The street lights were still on.

I worked out how I would apologize for calling at such an early hour: I had inquired unsuccessfully at the post office and had been unable to find their telephone number in the directory. So I had come just to reassure myself about her. I did not know whether or not conduct like this would be considered improper by the people of this country.

I rang the bell once. No one answered.

Was it possible that she had already gone out at this early hour? What could have happened?

A man carrying a briefcase came out of a neighboring apartment. He looked at me curiously. He locked his apartment door and went towards the stairs. When he saw me press the doorbell again, however, he turned around and came back towards me.

"I doubt that anyone will answer the door. The young woman is dead and the mother is sick."

"The young woman? Who? How?"

The man said, "Don't you know? Perhaps I shouldn't tell you, but since you are going to meet the mother I guess it's best."

I asked again, "Anne-Marie? How?"

"The young lady took her own life," he remarked sadly, "from the balcony of the apartment . . . in the middle of the night. We were . . ."

But at that moment the door opened. The old woman held it open. She was wearing a nightgown. Her white hair stood out wildly around her head. There was a black shawl around her bent shoulders.

When she saw me, she screamed once and backed away.

"Have you come for me now, sir? Is it my turn?"

Clutching at the doorknob, she collapsed to the floor. The man dropped his briefcase and rushed to her. I ran too. I ran to the staircase. I ran to the street. I ran through the city.

I did not go home. I did not go to work. I did not go anywhere. But that evening I was in bed.

Was I asleep or awake when those wings began to flap about in the room? Was it a hawk or an apparition which I saw? I stretched out my hand. I heard a rustling and stretched out my hand. There was a burst of lights and colors more beautiful than anything I had ever seen before. Wings were rustling around me. I stretched out my hand. I was weeping without any sound or tears, but I stretched out my hand.

Integration

Uyen Loewald

SUSAN, a teacher of immigrants, has a special regard for her Vietnamese refugee students; they have hardly recovered from the shock of leaving their homeland and being robbed at sea, but already they've become achievers. It is difficult for her not to feel they're special. Unlike the Mexicans who live next door to the United States, or many native Americans, the Vietnamese take advantage of every free service; community colleges are full of Vietnamese students. The number of Vietnamese seeking welfare keeps dropping daily. Maybe it is their culture; maybe it is their natural industry. Whatever motivates them, Susan would like to know about it. She wants to know why old Vietnamese women who can no longer enter the work force, who have children to interpret for them, keep coming to school night after night to learn English.

The Vietnamese surprised many people by not wanting to do physical work and being keen on intellectual challenges; they have won prizes in several fields. Electronics firms in San Jose are full of them. Susan can understand that: they know they cannot compete against American six-footers so they turn to areas where they have special skills.

If Susan could discover what makes women like Mrs. Ba persist in learning English, she would be able to help other minorities who are still reluctant to integrate. Vietnamese people do not form ghettos. That surely must help them progress.

Mrs. Ba does not need to learn English; she lives with two well-educated sons: an engineer and a doctor; both are devoted to her. They speak English without any trace of an accent. The engineer is exceptionally brilliant; he has become an architect since he arrived and has won a national prize.

Maybe deprivation sharpens keenness. Mrs. Ba told her, in her broken English, that she had never gone to school before she left Vietnam. Maybe if state governments forbid minorities from attending schools, the way they forbid drugs, it would spur them to learn. Americans take too much for granted, the Vietnamese have often told her that.

Susan is excited about having dinner at Mrs. Ba's house; she worked hard for the invitation. But she thinks she'll tell the sixty-five year old woman not to come to class any more. There are such things as failing teachers and hindering age. Mrs. Ba could catch pneumonia one day; she is not used to cold weather. And her persistence has been sapping Susan's patience.

There is so much Susan wants to know about Confucian society and about extended families. She can ask Mrs. Ba's sons everything; then she won't see Mrs. Ba's contortions as she curls her tongue trying to pronounce the "w" and "th" sounds; it always pains her to see Mrs. Ba's distorted face. Susan has often wanted to comfort Mrs. Ba, to pat her hand and tell her not to come to class; her sons can interpret for her. There is no need for her to go out, particularly on windy and rainy days, when her already pale face turns bloodless and her teeth chatter. But body contact is forbidden in the East. Or do Vietnamese conventions and habits give way in integration? Mrs. Ba looked lost that time when she tried to shake hands with Susan. Her hands looked as if they had suddenly become detached from her body.

Susan briefly saw the inside of Mrs. Ba's home only once, on a rainy day, when Mrs. Ba had a fever and could not go home by bus. Shyly, Mrs. Ba had accepted Susan's offer of a ride home. It had been interesting to see how Mrs. Ba sat at the edge of the car seat, her face turned away, her body drawn tight to avoid Susan's dog, who tried to lick her.

It took Susan a while to understand that teachers command absolute respect in Confucian societies, just as parents do. That's why Mrs. Ba hadn't asked Susan to visit her at home, although she never failed to bring her presents for Christmas, her birthday, and the Vietnamese New Year. The ability to progress while retaining their own culture is their key to successful integration. It is an outstanding Vietnamese quality.

As she parks her car in front of Mrs. Ba's home, behind two new Honda Preludes next to their neat lawn, Susan realizes she's hungry. There is no indication that the occupants of the house are relatively recent arrivals in the country. Only the smell of incense as the door opens and Mrs. Ba's dark silk *ao-dai* make the house different.

"Miss Susan, please come in," Mrs. Ba joins her hands and smiles as she leads Susan to the living room. Long stemmed red roses are arranged beautifully in a crystal vase in the middle of a large glass-top coffee table. A modern sofa and four chairs match the color and design of the Danish dining set in front of the wide glass sliding door leading to the courtyard which has orchids in full bloom growing on all sides. A chest against the wall facing the sun is the altar, displaying a round tray of steaming food, a vase of white lilies, miniature glasses half-filled with rice wine, an open decanter, a tray of paper money, rice cake, fancy French assorted biscuits and tropical fruit. The incense is burning.

Susan shyly hands her gift to Mrs. Ba. "I hope I didn't do the wrong thing," she says.

Mrs. Ba chooses to relax instead of practicing English. Her handsome son, who looks like a well-behaved teen-ager, says, "You have done the right thing by bringing a present; our New Year is like Christmas; people exchange gifts. But you should know that most Vietnamese don't like chocolate or cheese. But we are learning." His smile feels like a caress; it makes her self-conscious.

She sees there are four places set at the table. Mrs. Ba's children must be single.

"This house is too big for three people. My sons have to find wives as soon as possible." Mrs. Ba looks proud after her long sentence.

Susan blushes. Could it be an invitation? They are integrated.

"My mother told us to get married as soon as we arrived here. We did not marry in Vietnam because we did not want our children to be victims of the war. My mother has been reminding us ever since." The doctor laughs. "She doesn't want us to be lonely; she wants grandchildren."

The architect says something in Vietnamese. Mrs. Ba springs up, goes to the altar, bends to make four deep bows, then three light ones. She says something in Vietnamese. Her sons remove the food from the altar.

"Now you can see how we Vietnamese blend culture with technology; we heat shark fin and fish bladder soup in the microwave oven." The doctor holds the tray as his brother loads the large microwave oven in the corner near the dining table and under the shelf displaying Vietnamese artifacts.

Susan notices the landscape paintings on the walls. She admires the lacquerware panels inlaid with mother-of-pearl; they are skillfully carved into the gentle shapes of autumn leaves and spring flowers.

"These are the scenery of four seasons," the architect says, looking at his mother. "I was too young when we left the North, so I only know one season. In Saigon, it's hot all year round. In Vietnam, only rich people can afford those things. We were too poor."

Susan likes his honesty, but she feels uncomfortable when he looks so intently at her. She moves to the picture on the altar. She can see the resemblance between the handsome man in that picture and Mrs. Ba's children.

"This is my husband." Mrs. Ba frowns. She must have been a beautiful woman once, when her teeth were intact. She wipes her eyes. "The Communists killed him. He never did anything to them. He did nothing harmful to anyone. They killed my daughter and son-in-law, too. He was an American." Mrs. Ba weeps.

The architect says something in Vietnamese to his mother, then turns to Susan. "According to Vietnamese custom, we must not think of anything sad today because whatever we do on the first day of the year will happen during the rest of the year. My father was killed in 1968, during the Tet offensive. You must have read about it."

The doctor adds, "The Vietcong almost took over Saigon, Hue and many other cities."

The microwave oven bell breaks the awkward silence. Mrs. Ba leads Susan to the dining table as her sons serve. She pulls her *ao-dai* to place its back panel on her lap, but she stands up again to take over the cutting of the rice cake with red chopsticks. They help Susan with soup and pork pâté. Mrs. Ba says something in Vietnamese, then the doctor explains: "Red is lucky; yellow is royal, used to be anyway, used to be forbidden too, when we still had an emperor. Chinese people wrap money in red paper, to give to children during the New Year. That's why we use red chopsticks. During the rest of the year, we just use ordinary bamboo or plastic ones." He removes the bowls which were used for soup, then distributes clean ones as Mrs. Ba puts pieces of pork pâté and cinnamon pork into her bowl.

Susan asks: "How long did it take you to prepare all this?"

Mrs. Ba smiles and the architect answers. "My mother did everything yesterday. In Vietnam, Tet is celebrated for at least a week. Special kinds of foods are prepared so that during that period people don't have to work. Rice cake keeps for two weeks. When you feel hungry, you just cut a piece and eat. Fish stewed in tea also keeps well. It is made of the cheapest kind of fish and when all its flesh has been eaten, its bones and spices are stewed with pickled cabbage. People eat the lot. Pork pâté and pork cinnamon are prepared in the same way. The paste used to take a strong man hours to make. But the food processor has simplified everything. My mother made this in a matter of minutes." He offers her jellyfish salad. "This dish used to take women all day to make: carrots, cucumbers, everything had to be shredded by hand as thin as possible, the thinner they are, the better the chance for the maiden to get married. It's part of the *Four Virtues*. Japanese invention has simplified the maidens' tasks. Even I can make it in half an hour. But the maidens need not worry; there is a shortage of Vietnamese women among refugees."

His eyes make Susan feel self-conscious again. But his gestures remove her disgust from eating jellyfish. It tastes like a delicious crisp salad with a rich yet delicate flavor. Its color is superb: red, green, yellow, white, all mingled together.

Mrs. Ba eats like a sparrow. To Susan she says, "Please, have some more," and she loads her bowl again. There is something about Mrs. Ba which makes Susan feel protected, nurtured.

Now Susan feels sufficiently comfortable to say: "Please tell me why Vietnamese people are so keen to learn English. Why you are so keen when you don't really need to learn? You are the most studious person in my class."

"Learning is difficult for me." Tears return to Mrs. Ba's eyes.

The doctor gives her a box of tissues as he says: "My mother is worried that my father's and our ancestors' souls can't find their way here; they may be wandering, homeless, and hungry. That's why she goes to school every day by bus to learn English. She wants to know the map of the city and speak English well, so when she dies, her soul can go back to Vietnam and bring theirs here with her. Knowing English will also help her understand her grandchildren when they call her soul back on her death anniversary. She has known many Vietnamese children who cannot speak Vietnamese. And she is not sure that we are going to marry Vietnamese wives!"

DO YOU
UNDERSTAND?

It is not an easy matter to explain to a child why a group of boys would attack someone—a boy by himself—and beat him up because of the color of his skin. It is not an easy matter to explain at all, much less to a child. And how can two newly married young people, one of whom had never before left their village in the mountains, understand what they see and experience in the city? A group of fair-skinned lowland people, painted and costumed to look like black-skinned village people, march by in a parade, a kind of Mardi Gras, for the amusement of other city people. Then, another group of these fair-skinned lowland people chase them, rob them, because of the color of their skin. If you are of a people who, because of the color of your skin, are reviled and attacked, how do you understand? or learn to defend yourself?

In "A Way of Talking," **PATRICIA GRACE**'s answer to the last question is certainly graceful: You talk smart, you stick up for yourself and get your group behind you. This personal and local answer goes along with the "marches and demonstrations" happening offstage in Auckland, New Zealand's capital city. These political actions were part of the 1970s Maori bid to win for themselves equal rights in a country where they, the original inhabitants—migrants from Polynesia—had been displaced by white colonialists from Europe and from neighboring Australia, the "pakehas." In New Zealand, the cultural result of the political agitation has been the emergence of a brilliant young generation of Maori writers. Like Patricia Grace, who was born in 1937, these writers use English in a kind of Maori dialect, or with Maori speech patterns, to preserve their culture and advance their people's political cause. Her stories in *Waiariki* (1975) and *The Dream Sleepers* (1980) and her novel *Mutuwhenua* (1978) are "a way of talking."

But the father in **JOSE EMILIO PACHECO**'s story has no way of talking to his little girl about the beating they have just witnessed. He knows that he is only telling her the kind of thing he himself was told as a child, and he knows it is hopelessly inadequate. Pacheco, a Mexican poet born in 1939, was a relentlessly realist writer, a literary opponent of the "magical realism" so commonly practiced in his generation, and many of the stories in his collection *Battles in the Desert* (New Direction, 1987) have a stark, unredeemed quality about them. Julio Ortega, the Peruvian writer and critic (see his story in Part I), has predicted that Pacheco "will be considered the best Latin American poet of this decade," the 1990s.[1]

With childlike eyes, the two Ati-Atihan villagers in **LEONCIO P. DERIADA**'s story approach the city, with its traffic and noise, its bustling markets, and its parade. Just as the couple realizes that there is something ominous in this minstrel show, that the players are not in any way kindred or even desirous of being kindred, they are set upon by a pack of racists. Their purchase from the market, a yellow ready-made dress for the wife, is ripped to shreds—they cannot wear the costumes of the city world while that world mocks and derides them as primitives. Leoncio P. Deriada, the southern Philippine writer whose story "Daba-Daba" appears previously in this volume, chose not to explore how the young Ati-Atihan villagers understand what has happened to them—they simply set out to make the long walk home. But their silence is eloquent.

A Way of Talking

Patricia Grace

ROSE CAME back yesterday; we went down to the bus to meet her. She's just the same as ever Rose. Talks all the time flat out and makes us laugh with her way of talking. On the way home we kept saying, "E Rohe, you're just the same as ever." It's good having my sister back and knowing she hasn't changed. Rose is the hard-case one in the family, the kamakama one, and the one with the brains.

Last night we stayed up talking till all hours, even Dad and Nanny who usually go to bed after tea. Rose made us laugh telling about the people she knows, and taking off professor this and professor that from varsity. Nanny, Mum, and I had tears running down from laughing; e ta Rose we laughed all night.

At last Nanny got out of her chair and said, "Time for sleeping. The mouths steal the time of the eyes." That's the lovely way she has of talking,

1. Julio Ortega, "Latin America's Literary Line-up," *World Press Review* 38:51 (June 1991).

Nanny, when she speaks in English. So we went to bed and Rose and I kept our mouths going for another hour or so before falling asleep.

This morning I said to Rose that we'd better go and get her measured for the dress up at Mrs Frazer's. Rose wanted to wait a day or two but I reminded her the wedding was only two weeks away and that Mrs Frazer had three frocks to finish.

"Who's Mrs Frazer anyway," she asked. Then I remembered Rose hadn't met these neighbours though they'd been in the district a few years. Rose had been away at school.

"She's a dressmaker," I looked for words. "She's nice."

"What sort of nice?" asked Rose.

"Rose, don't you say anything funny when we go up there," I said. I know Rose, she's smart. "Don't you get smart." I'm older than Rose but she's the one that speaks out when something doesn't please her. Mum used to say, Rohe you've got the brains but you look to your sister for the sense. I started to feel funny about taking Rose up to Jane Frazer's because Jane often says the wrong thing without knowing.

We got our work done, had a bath and changed, and when Dad came back from the shed we took the station-wagon to drive over to Jane's. Before we left we called out to Mum, "Don't forget to make us a Maori bread for when we get back."

"What's wrong with your own hands," Mum said, but she was only joking. Always when one of us comes home one of the first things she does is make a big Maori bread.

Rose made a good impression with her kamakama ways, and Jane's two nuisance kids took a liking to her straight away. They kept jumping up and down on the sofa to get Rose's attention and I kept thinking what a waste of a good sofa it was, what a waste of a good house for those two nuisance things. I hope when I have kids they won't be so hoha.

I was pleased about Jane and Rose. Jane was asking Rose all sorts of questions about her life in Auckland. About varsity and did Rose join in the marches and demonstrations. Then they went on to talking about fashions and social life in the city, and Jane seemed deeply interested. Almost as though she was jealous of Rose and the way she lived, as though she felt Rose had something better than a lovely house and clothes and everything she needed to make life good for her. I was pleased to see that Jane liked my sister so much, and proud of my sister and her entertaining and friendly ways.

Jane made a cup of coffee when she'd finished measuring Rose for the frock, then packed the two kids outside with a piece of chocolate cake each. We were sitting having coffee when we heard a truck turn in at the bottom of Frazers' drive.

Jane said, "That's Alan. He's been down the road getting the Maoris for scrub cutting."

I felt my face get hot. I was angry. At the same time I was hoping Rose would let the remark pass. I tried hard to think of something to say to cover Jane's words though I'd hardly said a thing all morning. But my tongue seemed to thicken and all I could think of was Rohe don't.

Rose was calm. Not all red and flustered like me. She took a big pull on the cigarette she had lit, squinted her eyes up and blew the smoke out gently. I knew something was coming.

"Don't they have names?"

"What. Who?" Jane was surprised and her face was getting pink.

"The people from down the road whom your husband is employing to cut scrub." Rose the stink thing, she was talking all Pakehafied.

"I don't know any of their names."

I was glaring at Rose because I wanted her to stop but she was avoiding my looks and pretending to concentrate on her cigarette.

"Do they know yours?"

"Mine?"

"Your name."

"Well . . . Yes."

"Yet you have never bothered to find out their names or to wonder whether or not they have any."

The silence seemed to bang around in my head for ages and ages. Then I think Jane muttered something about difficulty, but that touchy sister of mine stood up and said, "Come on Hera." And I with my red face and shut mouth followed her out to the station wagon without a goodbye or anything.

I was so wild with Rose. I was wild. I was determined to blow her up about what she had done, I was determined. But now that we were alone together I couldn't think what to say. Instead I felt an awful big sulk coming on. It has always been my trouble, sulking. Whenever I don't feel sure about something I go into a big fat sulk. We had a teacher at school who used to say to some of us girls, "Speak, don't sulk." She'd say, "You only sulk because you haven't learned how and when to say your minds."

She was right that teacher, yet here I am a young woman about to be married and haven't learned yet how to get the words out. Dad used to say to me, "Look out girlie, you'll stand on your lip."

At last I said, "Rose, you're a stink thing." Tears were on the way. "Gee Rohe, you made me embarrassed." Then Rose said, "Don't worry Honey she's got a thick hide."

These words of Rose's took me by surprise and I realised something about Rose then. What she said made all my anger go away and I felt very sad because it's not our way of talking to each other. Usually we'd say, "Never mind Sis," if we wanted something to be forgotten. But when Rose said, "Don't worry Honey she's got a thick hide," it made her seem a lot older than me, and tougher, and as though she knew much more than me about the world. It made me realise too that underneath her jolly and forthright ways Rose is very hurt. I remembered back to when we were both little and Rose used to play up at school if she didn't like the teacher. She'd get smart and I used to be ashamed and tell Mum on her when we got home, because although she had the brains I was always the well behaved one.

Rose was speaking to me in a new way now. It made me feel sorry for her and for myself. All my life I had been sitting back and letting her do the objecting. Not only me, but Mum and Dad and the rest of the family too. All of us too scared to make known when we had been hurt or slighted. And how can the likes of Jane know when we go round pretending all is well. How can Jane know us?

But then I tried to put another thought into words. I said to Rose, "We do it too. We say, 'the Pakeha doctor,' or 'the Pakeha at the post office,' and sometimes we mean it in a bad way."

"Except that we talk like this to each other only. It's not so much what is said, but when and where and in whose presence. Besides, you and I don't speak in this way now, not since we were little. It's the older ones: Mum, Dad, Nanny who have this habit."

Then Rose said something else. "Jane Frazer will still want to be your friend and mine in spite of my embarrassing her today; we're in the fashion."

"What do you mean?"

"It's fashionable for a Pakeha to have a Maori for a friend." Suddenly Rose grinned. Then I heard Jane's voice coming out of that Rohe's mouth and felt a grin of my own coming. "I have friends who are Maoris. They're lovely people. The eldest girl was married recently and I did the frocks. The other girl is at varsity. They're all so *friendly* and so *natural* and their house is absolutely *spotless*."

I stopped the wagon in the drive and when we'd got out Rose started strutting up the path. I saw Jane's way of walking and felt a giggle coming on. Rose walked up Mum's scrubbed steps, "Absolutely spotless." She left her shoes in the porch and bounced into the kitchen. "What did I tell you? Absolutely spotless. And a friendly natural woman taking new bread from the oven."

Mum looked at Rose then at me. "What have you two been up to?

Rohe I hope you behaved yourself at that Pakeha place?" But Rose was setting the table. At the sight of Mum's bread she'd forgotten all about Jane and the events of the morning.

When Dad, Heke, and Matiu came in for lunch, Rose, Mum, Nanny and I were already into the bread and the big bowl of hot corn.

"E ta," Dad said. "Let your hardworking father and your two hard-working brothers starve. Eat up."

"The bread's terrible. You men better go down to the shop and get you a shop bread," said Rose.

"Be the day," said Heke.

"Come on my fat Rohe. Move over and make room for your Daddy. Come on my baby shift over."

Dad squeezed himself round behind the table next to Rose. He picked up the bread Rose had buttered for herself and started eating. "The bread's terrible all right," he said. Then Mat and Heke started going on about how awful the corn was and who cooked it and who grew it, who watered it all summer and who pulled out the weeds.

So I joined in the carryings on and forgot about Rose and Jane for the meantime. But I'm not leaving it at that. I'll find some way of letting Rose know I understand and I know it will be difficult for me because I'm not clever the way she is. I can't say things the same and I've never learnt to stick up for myself.

But my sister won't have to be alone again. I'll let her know that.

You Wouldn't Understand

Jose Emilio Pacheco

SHE TOOK my hand as we crossed the street, and I felt the dampness of her palm.

"I want to play in the park for a while."

"No. It's too late. We have to get home; your mother is waiting for us. Look, there's nobody else around. All the little children are home in bed."

The streetlight changed. The cars moved forward. We ran across the street. The smell of exhaust dissolved into the freshness of grass and foliage. The last remnants of rain evaporated or were absorbed by the sprouts, leaves, roots, nervations.

"Are there going to be any mushrooms?"

"Yes, I guess so."

"When?"

"Well, I guess by tomorrow there should be some."

"Will you bring me here to see them?"

"Yes, but you'll have to go to bed right away so you can get up early."

I walked too quickly, and the child had to hurry to keep up with me. She stopped, lifted her eyes, looked at me to gain courage, and asked, slightly embarrassed, "Daddy, do dwarfs really exist?"

"Well, they do in stories."

"And witches?"

"Yes, but also just in stories."

"That's not true."

"Why?"

"I've seen witches on TV, and they scare me a lot."

"They shouldn't. Everything you see on television is also stories—with witches—made up to entertain children, not scare them."

"Oh, so everything they show on TV is just stories?"

"No, not everything. I mean . . . how can I explain it to you? You wouldn't understand."

Night fell. A livid firmament fluted with grayish clouds. In the garbage cans, Sunday's refuse began to decay: newspapers, beer cans, sandwich wrappers. Beyond the distant drone of traffic, raindrops could be heard falling from the leaves and tree trunks onto the grass. The path wound through a clearing between two groves of trees. At that moment, the shouts reached my ears: ten or twelve boys had surrounded another. With his back against the tree, he looked at them with fear but did not scream for help or mercy.

My daughter grabbed my hand again.

"What are they doing?"

"I don't know. Fighting. Let's go. Come on, hurry up."

The fragile pressure of her fingers was like a reproach. She had figured it out: I was accountable to her. At the same time, my daughter represented an alibi, a defense against fear and excessive guilt.

We stood absolutely still. I managed to see the face—the dark skin reddened by white hands—of the boy who was being festively beaten by the others. I shouted at them to stop. Only one of them turned around to look at me, and he made a threatening, scornful gesture. The girl watched all of this without blinking. The boy fell, and they kicked him on the ground.

Someone picked him up, and the others kept slugging him. I did not dare move. I wanted to believe that if I did not intervene, it was to protect my daughter, because I knew there was nothing I could do against all twelve of them.

"Daddy, tell them to stop. Scold them."

"Don't move. Wait here for me."

Before I finished speaking, they were already running quickly away, dispersing in all directions. I felt obscenely liberated. I cherished the cowardly hope that my daughter would think they had run away from me. We approached. The boy rose with difficulty. He was bleeding from his nose and mouth.

"Let me help you. I'll take you . . ."

He looked at me without answering. He wiped the blood off with the cuffs of his checkered shirt. I offered him a handkerchief. Not even a no: disgust in his eyes. Something—an undefinable horror—in the girl's expression. Both of their faces were an aura of deceit, a pain of betrayal.

He turned his back on us. He walked away dragging his feet. For a moment I thought he would collapse. He continued until he disappeared among the trees. Silence.

"Let's go. Let's get out of here."

"Why did they do that to him if he wasn't doing anything to them?"

"I guess because they were fighting."

"But there were lots of them."

"I know. I know."

"They're bad because they hit him, right?"

"Of course. That's the wrong thing to do."

The park seemed to go on forever. We would never reach the bus. We would never return home. She would never stop asking me questions nor I giving her the same answers they undoubtedly gave me at her age.

"So, that means he's good?"

"Who?"

"The boy the others made bleed?"

"Yes, I mean, I don't know."

"Or is he bad too?"

"No, no. The others are the bad ones because of what they did."

Finally we found a policeman. I described to him what I had just witnessed.

"There's nothing to be done. It happens every night. You did the right thing by not interfering. They are always armed and can be dangerous. They claim the park is only for whites and that any dirty nigger who steps foot in here will suffer the consequences."

"But they don't have the right, they can't do that."

"What are you talking about? That's what the people in the neighborhood say. But when it comes down to it, they won't let blacks come to their houses or sit in their bars."

He gave the child an affectionate pat and continued on his way. I understood that clichés like "the world's indifference" were not totally meaningless. Three human beings—the victim, my daughter, myself—had just been dramatically affected by something about which nobody else seemed to care.

I was cold, tired, and felt like closing my eyes. We reached the edge of the park. Three black boys crossed the street with us. No one had ever looked at me like that. I saw their switchblades and thought they were going to attack us. But they kept going and disappeared into the grove.

"Daddy, what are they going to do?"

"Not let happen to them what happened to the other one."

"But why do they always have to fight?"

"I can't explain it to you, it's too difficult, you wouldn't understand."

I knelt down to button up her coat. I hugged her gently, with tenderness and fear. The dampness of the trees encircled us. The park was advancing upon the city and again—or overtly—everything would be jungle.

Ati-Atihan

Leoncio P. Deriada

THE SUN had not yet risen, but Sibukaw felt warm. He turned to his wife behind him. Kainyaman looked at her husband with anticipation, her face damp with sweat. Sibukaw did not say anything. Instead, he walked faster.

They had been walking since the second cock crow. In their home at the foot of the mountain, the whole world was awake before the sun. This time of the year, the mornings were unusually cold, and before they left for this morning's trip, Kainyaman had to wear a dress under her *patadiong*. Now, both of them felt warm. The long walk had quickened their pulses and their blood and, presently, they felt the need to jump into a pond or a lake or a river.

Sibukaw and Kainyaman were newly married. They lived at the foot of the mountain far into the hinterland where no roads ever brought to their Ati tribe the sound of trucks and the smell of gasoline. Most of the older men had been to town at least once in their lifetime. Sibukaw had been there only twice. The first was when he was a boy of ten *kaingin* seasons. The second was only a month ago, the week before he took Kainyaman as his wife.

Kainyaman had never been to town. She had never gone there to sell medicinal roots and leaves. Neither had she joined any Ati group trudge the mountain path to the national highway before sunrise for the yearly custom of asking for salt and rice from the lowlanders. Going to town had remained only a dream. She wondered how it was to ride on a bus. When Sibukaw told her that he was bringing her to town, she was so excited that she could not eat that night's supper of boiled roots.

Now they were on their way to the national road where they would wait for a bus from the north. They were barefooted.

Suddenly, the sun rose and the east blossomed into a brighter riot of colors. The fog slowly dissolved in the grass and the trees and the hills.

At the foot of the last hill was a brook. There was no need to hurry, Sibukaw thought. The road was only a shout away. There was much time even for a leisurely swim.

Sibukaw stripped and jumped into the brook. The pleasant coolness of the water blended with the heat in his body and he felt rested. The water was not deep, but then Sibukaw, like any other Ati brave, was very much shorter than the ordinary lowlander. The shallow water was well above his waist.

Kainyaman stood on the bank of the brook. Sibukaw watched her undress. Now completely naked, her body shone in the early morning sun. Standing there, among the grass that still glittered with dew, Kainyaman's body was firm and full and fertile like an anthill.

With a little shriek, she jumped into the brook. Sibukaw caught her, and like little children, they cavorted in the foam. They splashed water on each other. Their black bodies shone in the sun.

Soon they felt cold. They jumped out of the brook and shook their bodies to dry. Their hair, deep black and kinky, looked like crows' nests on their heads.

Sibukaw put on again his green shirt and a pair of stained khaki pants. His clothes smelled of sweat and decayed leaves. He wore these only when he went to the lowlands.

Kainyaman put on her clothes fast. She was slightly shivering. The dress under her patadiong had a deep pocket where she kept some coins she had been saving for years. The coins were wrapped tightly in a red handkerchief. On top of the handkerchief was a roll of *buyo* leaves.

They sat on a big stone beside the brook. Kainyaman opened a little *banban* basket that contained boiled camote and pieces of roasted dried monkey meat. They ate breakfast silently.

After the simple breakfast, they waded in the brook and scooped water with their bare hands. They drank deeply.

Kainyaman put back into the basket what was left of the camote and the meat. The meager food would be their lunch wherever they would be at noontime.

They were ready for the rest of the mountain path to the highway. Sibukaw walked with a newer strength in his legs. He carried a bundle of medicinal roots and leaves and dried innards of strange reptiles and birds. The money from the sale of these forest products would be more than enough to pay for their fare going back home in the afternoon. Maybe he could buy a little salt, a little sugar, and some dried fish. Maybe he could even buy Kainyaman a blouse printed with flowers.

They sat on a dead tree trunk by the road and waited for the bus. The sun was now high above the trees on the crest of the eastern hills. It was beginning to be warm.

At last the bus came, roaring in the distance in a cloud of morning dust. Kainyaman stared at this magnificent thing. She clung to her husband's arm as they squeezed themselves into the vehicle, careful not to step on the various objects other passengers had laid on the aisle. Most of the passengers eyed them indifferently. A few were dozing. They must have come from as far as Cuartero or Dumarao and like Sibukaw and Kainyaman, had left their homes at the second cock crow.

The bus started before they could be seated. The sudden movement of the vehicle jolted them and Kainyaman, unprepared, teetered sideward and almost fell into the lap of a fat woman eating a boiled egg. With a little shriek, she dropped the banban basket on the aisle. Sibukaw steadied her as she dizzily picked up the little basket. Kainyaman caught the fat woman's sharp glance as she raised her eyes, which were now enrapt in a sight that momentarily dislocated her sense of direction. In a swirl of speed and sound, she saw the trees and the hills and the sky race away from where she was, and for a few giddy moments, she thought she was flying backwards, hurtling into some immeasurable depth. She was afraid.

They found a place in the last row, among sacks of palay, crates of vegetables, and bundles of firewood. Some chickens struggled under the wooden seat. They sat down, Kainyaman by the window. Sibukaw could feel her anxiety, and he pressed close to her. The wind rushed in violently, but their crown of hair was thick and defiant like a wild mass of fine, curly wires.

Soon the bus was packed with passengers. Some of them stood on the aisle. There were no other Ati passengers and Sibukaw felt a little uncomfortable especially now that four other men had occupied the available space in the last row. Sibukaw and Kainyaman held on to their seats as if that bit of space by the bus window were a precious piece of their mountain territory. Sibukaw remembered stories about the bus conductor who would tell an Ati passenger to stand up and give his seat to a lowlander.

No one disturbed them. Sibukaw inched closer to his wife and he knew she was no longer afraid. Kainyaman looked at the wide, flat world outside, awed by the big, beautiful houses beside the road and the seemingly endless expanse of rice paddies and cane fields beyond. She was deep in thought, wondering about these new sights until Sibukaw shook her gently . . .

The conductor was asking for their money in exchange for two little pieces of paper punched with tiny holes. Kainyaman dug into the depths of the pocket of the dress under her patadiong. Her hand fumbled among the buyo leaves, now loosened from their neat roll, and deep into the bottom where the coins settled tightly in the womb of the red handkerchief.

Sibukaw counted the coins carefully. The conductor did not say anything but stood patiently, his dirty pockets bulging with coins and paper bills. He must be the richest man in the lowlands, Kainyaman thought. She had never seen so much money before.

The bus was entering the town. First there was a bridge. Then the road was no longer rough and the bus glided slowly. It was one of the various vehicles that crowded the town's main street.

Kainyaman gaped at objects she had never seen before. Sibukaw pointed out to her cars and pedicabs and bicycles and jeepneys and cargo trucks. Like strange, hallowed animals that stalked the well-ordered jungle of streets and stores and fair-skinned, tall people, these sights filled her with reverence, anticipation, and a hint of fear.

The bus terminal was near the market. Sibukaw and Kainyaman remained seated until the bus had disgorged the other passengers. Tired but noisy, the men and women and children got off fast. They spoke in Kinaray-a, so Sibukaw understood what the excitement was all about. It was the town fiesta.

What beautiful luck, Sibukaw thought as he held Kainyaman's hand. He had heard stories about how the town would look during the fiesta. Old man Salinggapa, who had been to the fiesta three times, spoke of strange sights and sounds and smells of food and drink a poor Ati of the mountain would remember forever.

Gently dragging Kainyaman behind him, Sibukaw jumped off the bus. The conductor eyed them silently as they hurried towards the makeshift stalls in front of the public market.

Never before had Kainyaman seen so many people. Their voices and the sound from motor vehicles and strange instruments and big boxes scared her. In a sudden, she longed for the silence of the forests and the hillsides. But it was only for a moment. Soon her ears got used to those alien sounds, and her eyes, distracted by new sights, searched for newer adventures.

They joined the people milling around the crowded confines of the market. Kainyaman felt the urge to touch, to fondle a head of the whitest cabbage, the petals of a bunch of plastic flowers, a roll of smooth, yellow cloth. She stopped in front of a store and stared at dresses and bags and shoes. Yes, shoes. She looked at those fantastic objects behind the glass and then at her black, dirty feet. She moved her toes and they spread wider. She wondered how it was to walk in heels.

There was much to explore before it was time to go home. Kainyaman cast a last glance at a plastic woman wearing an exquisite drape of transparent cloth. For a while she thought it was a real woman—tall and pale and beautiful in her cage of glass.

Sharper than their sense of sight and hearing was their sense of smell. Wafted from the open stalls was the odor of assorted food. The spicy aroma left a tang in the palate, stirring a hunger keener than the hunger sharpened by a roasted wild boar or bird. Sibukaw and Kainyaman sniffed the delicious air and decided it must be high noon. They were hungry. They could not see the sun but they were sure it was there above the buildings, its fiery ball directly above their heads.

So this was the abundance of the fiesta, Sibukaw thought. So these were the things lowlanders ate, Kainyaman thought as she hungrily looked at the display of chicken and pork and beef and fish cooked in various ways and placed in plates as colorful as the viands themselves. There was a whole pig, its skin glossy brown and deliciously cracked in places, crouching on a spread of banana leaves on a counter that also held trays and baskets of fruit. There were entire chickens resting on their backs in nests of halved tomatoes and diced onions—their clawless legs pointing to the roof. Pieces of fish, or the whole fish themselves, swam in thick sauces strewn with bright bits of vegetables.

Kainyaman felt the coins under her patadiong, wondering how many of them could buy a chicken or a slice of fish. She did not tell her husband how much she wanted to taste any of those delicacies. Instead, she opened the banban basket and took a piece of camote. She was about to peel it with her fingers when Sibukaw noticed her. Wordlessly, he took it from her and returned it to the little container. Then he held Kainyaman's hand and hurriedly led her to the other side of the market.

An old woman in a grey patadiong and a grey kimona sat on a stool behind a makeshift table laden with roots and herbs. Among the leaves and roots and twigs were bottles of different shapes and sizes. Each bottle contained roots, leaves, seeds, bits of plant bark and other unidentifiable objects packed inside, their oily preservative making grotesque patterns in the inner wall of the bottle.

The old woman, her thin face emphasized by streaks of white hair gathered into a severe coil, looked up from a soiled copy of *Almanake Panayanhon* opened on her lap. She remembered Ati Sibukaw and his promise to bring her medicine for various maladies like headaches and stomachaches and backaches and asthma and consumption and insomnia and diarrhea and goiter and pimples.

She grinned in greeting. Her teeth, stained by a lifetime of buyo-chewing, were black stumps sticking out of her gums. Kainyaman looked at her in repulsion. With a jerky movement of her clawlike hands, the old woman cleared a space on the table.

Sibukaw laid his little bundle on the table. He spread open the dark piece of cloth and revealed the precious medicinal treasures of the forest. Expertly, he sorted them out into little piles, each kind—leaf, root, twig, bark or dried animal part—in its own group.

The exchange was fast. The old woman drew out from her breast a grimy purse made of cloth and placed on the table a crumpled twenty-peso bill. Then she added an assortment of coins. Sibukaw counted the metal pieces carefully and gave all the money to his wife.

They went to a corner *carinderia*. They sat on the shellacked stools timidly, aware of the stares of well-dressed people feasting on piles of food in front of them. Sibukaw asked for rice and pointed to a bowl of noodle soup and a plate of fried fish. He was too shy to ask the aproned girl for something else. He did not know how to name any of these delicacies.

Kainyaman waited for her husband to begin eating. She did not know how to eat except with her fingers. She watched Sibukaw clumsily hold the spoon and the fork. Sibukaw urged her to eat. With difficulty, she scooped a spoonful of rice and speared a piece of fish. What a terrible way to eat, she thought, as morsels of rice fell from the spoon. Her hunger was unbearable. She looked around. Nobody was watching. She put the spoon and the fork down and with both hands, lifted the bowl of noodles to her mouth . . .

The next hour found them in various parts of the market. With newer vigor in their bodies, they explored shops and groceries and the open stalls they had seen earlier. They bought a little sugar and a little salt and some pieces of dried fish. Sibukaw wrapped them all together in the dark cloth he had used to wrap the roots and leaves from the mountain.

They stood longer in front of a counter. Kainyaman gaped at the riot-ous piles of clothing in a profusion of colors and designs. Shirts, dresses, blouses, trousers and many other types of wear for men, women, and children spilled out of their boxes onto the long counter.

Kainyaman picked a yellow cotton dress with huge prints of red flowers and green leaves. She held it high and the dress bloomed in magnificence. She did not let it go until Sibukaw counted a total of four big coins and five tiny coins to pay for it.

The salesgirl wrapped the dress in a piece of brown paper. Without smiling, she placed the little bundle on the counter. Kainyaman grabbed it, her heart throbbing with excitement. No woman living at the foot of the mountain had a dress as beautiful as this one in her hand.

They left the market for the main street of the town. The sun was now on the other side of the shining rooftops. The air had become thicker with the heat and the dust and the noise, but Sibukaw and Kainyaman walked the hot pavement, seeking further adventures. A little breeze flut-tered the paper streamers strung over the main street. Sibukaw thought of the knotty vines that extended from tree to tree in the familiar forest, their matted growth spreading a canopy of green and yellow leaves over the mosses and the ferns below.

They walked on the sidewalk and peered into the colorful depths of textile and shoe stores. They passed the crowded front of a strange build-ing and, in fear, wondered what was going on inside. They heard screams and explosions and loud voices speaking a strange language.

Soon both sides of the street were full of people. They stood there, apparently waiting for some important happening that would suddenly emerge from the southern end of the street. Most of them craned their necks towards that direction.

Sibukaw and Kainyaman found themselves standing behind people who positioned themselves close to the street. Wondering what they were wait-ing for, Sibukaw and Kainyaman looked for a place where they could stand unobstructed by taller backs and heads.

They found a place under an electric post that stood like a tall tree over the spot where a side street crossed the main. The place was exposed to the slanting sun, so no fair lowlander occupied that little bit of ground. The post cast a long shadow but this slender piece of shade was enough for the Ati couple.

Suddenly, the street was cleared of traffic. Like wild beasts, the jeepneys and cars and pedicabs fled to unknown lairs. The asphalt lay smooth and naked, in some places mottled with buried bottle caps and fragments of torn paper streamers.

Then a motorcycle came roaring from the southern end of the street.

His helmet reflecting the sun, the policeman on the motorcycle slowly zig-zagged by, his gloved hand signalling children and adults not to cross the street and the others to step back from the asphalt.

The fiesta parade was coming.

The people applauded. First came a trio of motorcycles mounted by three severe-looking policemen. Just behind them was a brass band led by a tall, bare-legged girl holding a stick. She was lean and extremely beautiful, and she looked taller in her high boots, flowing cape of shiny cloth, and a white cap topped with red tassels.

Sibukaw and Kainyaman stood unmoving until the band had passed them. Then the people applauded again. Some men whistled. The most beautiful part of the parade was coming.

It was the vehicle bearing the fiesta queen. She was the most beautiful woman Kainyaman had ever seen. Seated on her throne, she smiled, her teeth white and even and sparkling like the countless jewels on her crown. Her dress was long and beaded with glinting stones. A handsome man in fine, almost transparent shirt, was beside her. He must be her husband, Kainyaman thought.

Other decorated vehicles passed by, but the girls on them were not so beautiful as the queen.

The parade was quite long. Some participants were not interesting at all. There was a line of young men in khaki uniforms, each one carrying a wooden gun. There was a group of boys also in khaki uniforms, but they wore short trousers. They were followed by girls in green dresses.

The most awaited group came at the rear of the parade.

The Ati-Atihan!

The people clapped their hands. They were excited. They stretched out their necks towards the line of black faces that brought the fiesta parade into a frenzied finale.

"*Hala bira!*" the people chorused, anticipating the ritualistic chant.

Announced by the muffled beating of drums, the Ati-Atihan group passed by. Puzzled by the spectacle, Sibukaw and Kainyaman stared at the strange black people parading in front of them. Definitely, these men and women did not belong to the Ati tribes that inhabited the mountains and the hills. They were tall. Their hair was straight. Their facial features, in spite of the blackness, were clean-cut and handsome. They did not have the facial flatness of Ati men and women.

Sibukaw and Kainyaman watched in wonder. There was an old man seated on a rattan hammock carried by four muscular warriors. He must be the king for he sat stiff and regal, his head crowned with a *salakot* painted gold. Behind him must be his queen. Also seated on a hammock carried by four warriors, she held her head high, unsmiling but beautiful.

She had no crown but she displayed a long necklace of sea shells studded with golden stones. Their retinue was composed of spear-wielding men and women holding an assortment of objects like stalks of ripe palay, ears of corn, twigs of *lomboy* and *bugnay* trees, and bundles of *alibhon* leaves. Four men marked time by pounding drums. Directly behind the drummers were four boys beating hollow bamboo tubes.

"*Hala bira!*" they chanted and the black men and women gyrated and skipped and minced their feet in the maddening tempo of a primitive dance.

The Ati couple stood. The drums and the bamboo tubes created a low, muffled sound. Their music was urgent, overpowering. It thickened the blood and conjured images of rituals celebrated around anthills in seasons when the moon was full and the *manaol* birds whistled on the top of *kalumpang* trees.

Sibukaw and Kainyaman watched. Then suddenly they knew: these men and women parading in front of them were not mountain people at all. They were lowlanders blackened into the color of charred tree stumps in a kaingin. Their skimpy but stylized loin cloths and patadiongs betrayed bits of fair skin in their thighs. Their bare feet were smooth, unused to the roughness of the earth. Their headgear and spears and shields were things only lowlanders could invent. Some of them wore masks with devil eyes and fangs.

Sibukaw and Kainyaman were amused now. They had forgotten the motorcycles and the brass band and the fiesta queen. For now they had found a remote kinship with these lowlanders made up to look and act like them—the poor simple Ati folk of the mountain. Yet there was something repulsive in this show. They were vaguely aware of a certain threat, and in an instant, they felt a strangeness they had not felt before.

The drums and the bamboo instruments now beat in a manic pace, maintaining a low, primeval groan such as the moan of the wind caught in a cave or the surge of the flood in the beginning of the world . . .

The parade was ending. The people dispersed and filled the street. Children followed the Ati-Atihan. They chanted and danced, parodying the movements of the blackened men and women.

Then a group of young people noticed Sibukaw and Kainyaman.

Ati, Ati sa bukid!" they chorused.

"Negritoes of the mountain!"

"*Itum ila tinai!*"

"What kind of food do you eat?"

"*Ano inyo kalan-on?*"

"Rice."

"*Indi!*"

"*Mais?*"

"*Indi!*"

"Negritoes of the mountain!"

"*Ati, Ati sa bukid!*"

"*Ano inyo kalan-on?*"

"What kind of food do you eat?"

"*Balinghoy!*"

"*Kamote!*"

"*Banayan!*"

"*Ati, Ati sa bukid!*"

"What kind of food do you eat?"

"*Halo!*"

"*Ibid!*"

"*Bao!*"

They danced around Sibukaw and Kainyaman. They closed in around them.

"*Hala bira!*" they chanted.

Cowering in fright, Kainyaman pressed into her husband's side. These young lowlanders scared her as would a pack of wild boars. In an instinctive gesture of protection, Sibukaw put his hand on her shoulder.

"*Ati, Ati sa bukid!*"

"*Ano inyo kalan-on?*"

Kainyaman dropped her *banban* basket. It opened and the pieces of camote rolled out into the dust.

"What kind of food do you eat?"

"*Kamote!*"

"*Kamote!*"

"*Kamote!*"

They shouted in derisive exultation as Sibukaw bent low and picked up the pieces of their former breakfast, his eyes wild with fear and confusion.

And tightly holding his wife's wrist, he broke the line of the cruel revelers and ran madly towards the left side street.

Shrieking in perverse delight, the young men ran after them.

The narrow street was deserted. All the people here must have gone to watch the parade. Sibukaw and Kainyaman ran as fast as they could, their hearts throbbing wildly inside them, their minds gripped by a horror more terrible than any cast by lightning and wind, by rain and flood.

The young men were close behind them.

"*Ati, Ati sa bukid!*"

Kainyaman dropped her little bundle wrapped in brown paper. It was the dress.

She stopped to retrieve it but Sibukaw dragged her.

The young men picked up the little bundle. They tore the brown paper. One of them waved the dress high like a multicolored flag. The others frantically reached for it. And in one insane shout, they tore the dress to pieces.

Kainyaman looked back and saw a flash of yellow cloth rent into bits of red flowers and green leaves.

"Aieee!" she screamed in utter sorrow and burst into tears.

Sibukaw led her to an alley that snaked into the backyards of little nipa houses. They were now at the edge of the town. The young men did not pursue them anymore.

Soon they were on the bridge. Kainyaman was still crying. Sibukaw put his arm around her and, together, they looked at the outline of the distant mountains.

The sun was now low in the west. They had all the night to walk home.

INDEX OF AUTHORS
AND TITLES

AUTHORS

Different cultures use different systems for ordering surnames. If you have any question about how a name might be alphabetized, check under several possibilities.

TITLES

ELISABETH YOUNG-BRUEHL is Professor of General Programs at Haverford College and editor of *Freud on Women: A Reader* (1990). Her books include *Creative Characters* (1991), *Mind and the Body Politic* (1989), *Anna Freud: A Biography* (1988), and the prizewinning *Hannah Arendt: For the Love of the World* (1982).

Library of Congress Cataloging-in-Publication Data
Global cultures : a transnational short fiction reader / edited and
    with an introduction by Elisabeth Young-Bruehl.
        p.   cm.
    ISBN 0–8195–5278–X. — ISBN 0–8195–6282–3 (pbk.)
    1. Short stories.   I. Young-Bruehl, Elisabeth.
PN6120.2.G58   1994
808.83′1—dc20   94–15402
∞